TREE ISLAND

*A novel
for the new millennium*

by
LINDA GROVER

FRIENDS OF TREE ISLAND, INC., PUBLISHERS

A NOTE FROM THE AUTHOR

Tree Island is an imaginary place. Though it's set just off Squaw Point in the real Upper Klamath Lake in the real state of Oregon, North America, the island itself is make-believe, as are the events and the people–except for public figures–that are described in the story.

That being said, there are some significant things about this novel that *are* real–for example, the magical area that lies between Mt. Shasta and Crater Lake, its wildlife and natural beauty, its ancient human habitation. The animal characters in the book, Blackdog, Sillvester, and Shalise are real, as is the delightful town of Klamath Falls, the algae in the lake, and the *August Celebration.*

The trials of learning the sport of windsurfing are quite painfully real; the author will attest to that. However, the rewards are sheer ecstasy.

It's known that 7,700 years ago when our story begins, the people in this region of the Cascade Range lived in small family groups rather than tribes and, like many, or even most, societies around the world at that time, were essentially peaceful. Females and males were still equals and, for the most part, happily joined.

It is true that the Mount Mazama volcano erupted with a force forty-two times greater than Mount St. Helens, and that because of the wind direction, a person thirty-five miles to the south *could* have survived. It is also true that a surprisingly detailed–and accurate–eyewitness account of the series of explosions that took place has somehow been passed on intact by the indigenous people for more than *four hundred* generations.

Hanowas, or *henwas,* ancient male and female carved stone figurines found near Klamath Lake, and similar to European artifacts of the same period, do exist. According to local legend, they possess the ability to travel together from place to place. That these partnership symbols, or the concept they represent, might have been carried across the land bridge from Asia is pure conjecture, but if it is true, it would suggest that a message of love once circled the globe.

Last, the barriers to our happiness and threats to our world that are described in the story are all too frighteningly real. However, as our heroine archaeologist LeeAnn Spencer and her friends point out, our potential for mitigating these dangers is equally real.

I'm happy to say that the book's "fictional" character Martyn

Williams is real, as is his planned **Pole to Pole 2000** expedition. And since I started writing this book, the fictional **22ⁿᵈ Century Group** has also become real, as readers of an early draft have begun turning fiction to reality.

Tree Island is about people who are finding a way. It is an invitation to adventure, to optimism, and to the healing that can come from simply *celebrating* together.

You'll find a sealed envelope in the back of the book. Please don't open it till you've read the story.

Linda Grover
November 10, 1997
(Day 782 of CountUP 2000)
Klamath Falls, Oregon

ACKNOWLEDGMENTS

The experience of writing *Tree Island* and trying to manifest its heroine's vision at the same time has taught me a great deal about the power of partnership. Many people have helped; warm thanks to all.

At William Morris, to my first and forever agent, Owen Laster, and Debra Goldstein, a new and wise friend. To my editors, Upton Brady, who helped me put *Tree Island* together; Gene Young, who always thought I could do a novel; and Diane Reverend, who showed me keys to clearer writing. In television, to Marian Rees and Mary Ellis Bunim, who taught me much about story.

In the windsurfing world, to Barry Spanier, designer of Neil Pryde Sails. To John Chao, publisher of *American Windsurfer*, whose criticisms were severe but helpful; Bjorn Dunderbeck, who taught me how to play cards; Scott See, American Windsurf Industry Association; Terry Tico and Carl Stepath, Save Our Seas; Will and Liz Brady, Floras Lake resort; and the entire Schweitzer family, inventors of the sport. Also Brett Percival, whose CatSurfer enables even the disabled to sail. To Pete Phillips of Hood River. And Bernard Dunayevich of Flying Stamina, who organized the Golden Gate Bridge event. To the hundreds of sailors at a dozen sites from New Caledonia to Texas who followed LeeAnn's dream by marking the 1,000-day CountUP on April 6 with a tiny but vivid statement about the need for global unity.

In the *August Celebration* world, to Katharine Clark, who hosted the first ever 22nd Century Group event, in Atlanta. To Tony Kent who read the first draft under *extreme* conditions, and to Cindy Bertrand and Loren Spector who encouraged me when I needed it on Kauai. To Harriet Fels, whose generous surprise contribution made the formation of the 22nd Century Group possible. To Chitra Turner for her belief early on, to Richard France, and to Rich Hosking and Donia Alawi for their wise counsel and friendship. To Russell and Megan, Michael and Carla, with love. To Kate and Bill, who helped me through wintry first draft loneliness at the Rivers of Light ranch. To Gilles, for his vision and heart, and John and Wendy Justice for their nurturing care. To June Johns for words I will never forget; to Beth and Sherri; to Kare and Haris; and to Charlotte and all the women of the Women's Retreat, who lent me courage for more than one kind of fire-walk. To Gary Pool for his bumper stickers. And Eddie Knickman for his spontaneous Amtrak pilgrimage. To Jan Smith, a terrific networker. To Bernard Voyer for his inspiration, and to Martyn Williams for telling me about his dream. To Daryl Kollman, who taught me much about celebration, and Marta Kollman, who gathered, nurtured, and gave to me seeds of the thousand-year-old story tree.

In Klamath Falls, thanks to City Manager Jim Keller and members of the City Council for their support. To Gordon Bettles, Cultural Heritage Specialist of the Klamath Tribes, and Elder Andrew Ortis, Chair of the Cultural Heritage Committee. To archaeologists Dorothy Fleming and Bill Yehle; the accurate details are theirs, any errors are mine. To Oregon Institute of Technology geologist and friend Dr. John Lund, to Sergeant Glen Smith, Oregon State Police, retired. To Laura Olsen, Checks and Balances. To Julianne Murray of OIT, and Tezea and Ron Collins for the loan of Blackdog, and the gift of Shalise.

In the big arena of global networking, my thanks to Robert Muller for the most treasured letter I have ever received, and to Barbara Gaughen-Muller, his bride. To Bob Silverstein for his hospitality and for persuading twenty governors to sign a proclamation for the thousand-day CountUP! To Maurice Rosenblatt, to Cory Flintoff for his excellent critique, and Matty and Jean Forbes. To Dan Keeney, Molly Sherden, and Liz Hasse. To Craig Ricketts at Morganics for the world-changing work he is doing.

For helping in the task of endlessly arranging and rearranging 200,000 words–and who knows *how* many commas–and for having the patience to put up with me, my thanks especially to Tracy Marcynzsyn in Kauai, Kim Cooper and Janet Dean in New Hampshire, Tawny Blinn, Nancy Good (and Roberta Great), Pat Hedelman, Deanna Scott, Sky Shiviah, Andrea Walker, Cat, the late Betty Mason, Linda Speers, Luana Silverthorne, Susan O'Connell, Susan Richards, Mary Eichstadt, Ellen Burton, and more.

For research help, the Klamath County Library, and in New Hampshire, Ann Whytemare and Peg Patrisso. To Fern Edison for the idea of *AM (Authors for the Millennium)* and Bob Silverstein for refining it to *AM/PM (Artists and Media for a Partnership Millennium)*. Now we just need to get people to join.

To Tom Daugherty, for sharing ten years of his life and opening new worlds to me. To Adam for more recent inspiration. And to all the other men in the world. Men are great.

To Vincent Bode, Arthur Graphics, Jill Law at Graphic Press, and Steve and Megan at Middle Kingdom. To Agnes Furler and Mary Hyde Martin for their help in designing the Earthflower. And to designer Donna Temple for finishing the job yesterday, from the hospital, *after* she went into labor with her first child. (Natalie Marie, six pounds, seven ounces.)

Last, my thanks to family who helped. To my mother Muff, to my poet-aunt Amy, a beautiful energy at 87, and to my supportive cousin/accountant, Joan Arloro. To my children: Jamie for being there through it all, for his ideas, his wisdom, and his tenderness; to Steven for his help in clarifying my goals, my direction and my designs; to Cindy, a stalwart helper and an awesomely good actress whose work has helped to inspire my own. Finally, thanks to Riane and David, and the John Robbins family, who got me started on this whole path in the first place.

CONTENTS

PART ONE

Ancestral Memories

In the beginning, religion was love and love was religion.

PROLOGUE

The place was Klamath Lake. The time 7,700 years ago . . .

There were two mountain spirits in her world, one huge white-capped figure standing quietly in the north, one in the south. The one to the north, the nearer one, was rounder than the other. Between lay the vast inland sea that was their lake. Their land of peace.

It was a warm day in early spring, the wind was blowing from the south. She stood at the shore of the lake, looking toward the mountain from which he would return. They had come back from the Celebration two days before and then he had gone to seek his vision. She remembered their calling to each other one last time as he headed away on the path to the north.

She remembered the last touch of his body on hers . . . as his fingers traced a living fire on her skin. The touch, just the touch heating her, his hands starting on her belly, cupping her naked breasts that were so round. He traced her face, and love was in his touch. Then he traced her neck and her arms. He ran his fingers through her hair and at last he held her hands. It was their *Ceremony of Good-bye.*

There was a starlight rain that night and it fell down upon them. Their bodies became wet and the light from above made their skin glow and glisten. Again he stroked her body, touching every part of her, that his love would cloak and protect her the while that he was gone. For what he worshiped was her being, as she worshiped his.

She in her turn touched his body, for she did not know if she would touch him again. It was the ceremony they always shared before either would go to their separate visions, because the future could not be known.

She went to her knees. She stroked his skin in holy silence. *Oh this body that I adore.* His feet, his fine ankles, his long straight legs, the deep scar on his knee.

After her hands had moved everywhere, caressing, she gave the final worship with her mouth. Then she knelt astride him, reaching her hands up to the sky under the starlight rain and rejoicing, holding her arms high and wide as she had done so many times before in the exalting triumph of love.

She felt the force of the current joining them then, felt it as it gathered from the earth, from him, ecstasy pushing straight through her body and up into the sky. Then she was connected to the heavens and to the earth and to him.

There could be no more joy; there could be no more to want on the earth than this. She was *One* with another being, and for that she would give thanks all her life, every day of her life. For her the joining was life. For her their joining was *All*.

On the night of their parting, the sacred ceremony lasted from sunset to the dawn, when first light broke from the east on the opposite shore. They stood in silence and in thanks for their lake, and they knew it was time for him to go. Then he left, their golden dog following him, and she went about her work.

He will return on the sixth or seventh day, she thought. And when he did, she would go on her own quest, to the hot waters to purify and then two days' journey to the mountain. Two days to return.

She looked down into the clear water of the lake, where schools of bright fish swam. Soon they would come in infinite profusion. Summer was on the way.

That afternoon, she sat mending a net to receive the fish, as the sound of dripping water from a tree marked the passing of time.

When the net was finished, she took up work again on the water basket she was making from the reeds that grew in abundance at the side of the lake. It was woven strong and tight, for it had to be trusted with their lives when they traveled across dry land. A good water basket was much revered by the People, and she enjoyed the task of making them.

Picking up a pair of reeds, she began twisting them together for strength before adding them to the body of the basket. Like the reeds, she thought, she and her mate were strong together, their lives pleasantly entwined from first waking to end of day. They were seldom hungry, and they laughed often, playing as they worked. Grandfather once told her that *work* and *play* used to be the same word.

As most of their people did, she and her mate lived to themselves and were content to themselves. Yet always their greater family encircled them, as a basket encircles its reeds, and each season the people gathered at the solstice to reweave their love. They were one people, the

People of the Island of the Trees.

It was not so elsewhere. From her earliest years the woman had heard stories of a land beyond the mountains where the raw strength of man over-lorded woman and the sacredness of the partners was not honored. Where a child watching his father hurt his mother was taught it was the right thing to do. *A crazy, angry world*, her grandfather had called it, *a place where women were owned by men. And children killed babies.*

Again she picked up a pair of reeds, twisted them tightly together and began to add them to the basket. Then some small sound or movement caught her attention. The surface of the lake went suddenly brilliant silver and she looked up just as a blinding brightness half the size of the sky flashed from the side of the mountain to the north. She saw it and then it was gone. For one instant her world was the same, before clouds of smoke and steam came racing from the erupting volcano to fill the sky, and the sound and motion reached her.

A horrible shaking began and the world went wild in grief. The trees, the water, the wind. She fell prostrate as a wall of water from the lake struck her body. Then somehow she scrambled to her feet on the convulsing earth to flee the crashing waves that were engulfing her camp. Again she fell and clung to the ground, clung to the mother, to the bleeding earth that seemed for an almost impossible length of time to be trying to shake her from it.

Where is he? It was all she could think of. All she wanted was to be transported north in the sky to wherever he was, in smoke, in fire, or in death. Or in the clear, past the fire, and safe. Which was it?

After that there was no day and no night, for how long she did not know. The only light by which she worked and tended her injuries, found food, and restored their camp was from the fires to the north. The moonless, sunless sky was filled with ashes and the scent of burning stone; still, the terrible shaking returned and returned. Sometimes she felt she could not breathe; the hot, acrid smoke assailed her lungs until she thought she was burning up inside. That she would be consumed from within, and burst into flames. Sometimes she saw his body burning in her mind, and she cried out.

At last, after how many weeks, the sun returned dimly to the sky, revealing the devastation. Her eyes strayed always to the path to the north. Would he come around that turn in the trail soon? Was he safe?

Had he been caught in the fires or merely behind them, well and eager to find his way back to her?

Gradually, a few more of the People who had survived passed by, heading south, stopping to speak to her about conditions in the north and to offer her comfort. All travelers came from the north, none from the south. Of course no one would approach the great destruction, which was becoming greater all the time.

Still, she stayed. He had always thought her stubborn. Well she was. Fearful, and stubborn, too. The People understood that she needed to stay behind; they had respect for others' wishes. If she left and traveled across the land to the east where the rest had fled, she knew she would not find him again.

How many times did she look up quickly at the trail as some slight noise reached her ear? Or as a splashing ripple in the lake sounded like a canoe paddle moving softly. How many times did she imagine his look, and the feel of him? How his hands had traced her body in worship of her mortal form.

At the end of her work each day, she would sit at the point of land looking out toward the Island of the Trees, watching the lake and its mood. She was tired. She watched the wind dance across the water, remembering how, as a child, she had played in it and felt its force as it pushed her canoe across the lake. Dressed in her winter skins, standing and holding her arms out, she would let the wind send her tiny boat skimming across the water. And would laugh with the joy of it. The sound of laughter echoed still.

One afternoon she walked out to the end of the point and looked across at the island. A grove of ancient trees crowned a hilltop on its nearest shore, and there was a pair of massive boulders that could be seen from a long distance away, marking the place where the spirits lived. She saw that one of the boulders had fallen during the eruption.

About halfway between the place where she stood and the island, she noticed an object floating down the lake. Light in color, bobbing on the waves, about the size of an otter, it looked like gray ice to her. But it could not be ice, for it was late summer now.

She swam out to it and found it was a piece of light *sky-rock*, the stone-that-floats. Surprised, she pushed it to shore ahead of her, where she inspected it curiously. Sky-rock had always before been brought from somewhere far away. She had never seen it in the lake and had never seen a piece so big. She carried it to her camp and continued to study it, turning it over in her hands.

As a child, she'd been fascinated by the different kinds of rock. This kind, that would float on the water, light, with tiny holes in it, and scratchy to the touch, was for smoothing things, for polishing. The other, used to make tools that would cut and scrape, was heavy and shiny, glossy black or sometimes almost clear, with swirls beneath its surface showing it had once flowed as water. And so in her child way, her parents told her, she had called that kind *water-rock*. This kind she called *sky-rock* because she knew it came from the sky.

She put the piece of sky-rock away. Then in her loneliness she sat at the shore and looked into the water again. She would often stare into its depths and try to see things. Wondering. Her bleeding had come, bringing sadness there would be no child, and she had wept. Then, on the second day, the bleeding ceased.

When the summer was well advanced, she decided to go north to search for him. The first night at the hot water place, she bathed, scenting herself with a fragrant burning plant, preparing herself for the trip. If he came to the camp while she was away, she thought, he would see the signs that she had recently been there and would wait.

Next day she began her journey into the land of no life. The bleak, white powdery ash was everywhere. Hot rivers of mud flowed, and sulfurous smoke from dying fires rose in the distance. As far as she could see were blackened sticks of trees, twisted and shrunken, rising raggedly from the ash, covered up to half their depth in swirling drifts. For several days she traveled around that desolate land to a place farther than she had ever been before. Then at the top of a hill she stopped and stood in awe.

Below her a vast river of gleaming water-rock seemed to flow without motion. It was a river hard as life. Still as death. She walked toward it and climbed its frozen waves and ripples, imagining its heat when it had flowed from the mountain. She could see her reflection in its surface.

Her grandfather had taught her to look into water for its wisdom. So perhaps water-rock, too, would hold wisdom for her. She looked down through it at herself, staring into the reflection of her own eyes in the silent river depths, till suddenly she could see *his* eyes in death.

At that moment she knew. She saw him and knew that he was gone.

All that had existed in him existed somewhere still, but she would not meet him again in this life. She would never touch him again, never touch his blessed body. *Can such a thing that has been, not be?* Her mind cried the question, and her tears fell for a long time, joining the solid river of rock that flowed without motion. But then they dried, as all human tears do, in the wind and the sun.

She stood. Walking back along a path where piles of water-rock lay in sharply curling shards, broken in the curved way that water-rock does, she stooped to pick up a small piece that lay at her feet. It was roughly oblong with two rounded fractures that made a narrow place near the middle. Like a woman's waist.

She tied it into her clothing, a skin that she wore, and began to return to the lake. The winds grew cold, and by the time she ended her journey, early snow had begun to fall. Heavy, deep, and crusted, it covered the land, holding the powdery ash in its frigid grip. The air cleared and the Peoples' two sentinel mountains were revealed once more.

It was late to go south for the winter. A second bleeding had not come, so perhaps a child was growing. If it were, she might stay the winter, living on the dried fish and other stores of food that she had prepared. Before long, she was certain of her child, for she felt, like the flutter of a feather, its gentle kicking in her belly. The kicking reminded her of the child they had lost at birth last summer. She must stay, she decided. She would not travel again until spring. As the weather continued to worsen, she gathered a great quantity of wood and dried reeds for burning.

When all was prepared at her camp, she began to work on the rock she had brought back from the river of glass, first striking it to make other small fractures around the middle that would help to form the shape she desired. Then she began to mold its form, grinding it gently with her hammer-stone. And her tears fell upon it. Hundreds of hours of love, mourning, and remembrance went into her work. It must have the beauty she had seen reflected in his eyes when he looked at her form. It must be smooth like the softness of her skin, pleasing to the touch.

She worked on the figure slowly, for it was very fragile, fashioning it as a gift of her femaleness to his spirit. The dark, shiny rock was nearly transparent in some places, clear, with a red line running through it and gray streaks. A red line like blood. Black was the death and clear was the light. All of her energy went into the water-rock figure, for it was to be her final tribute to their love.

Throughout the days of autumn as her body changed, the anger of the mountain to the north continued. The snow on the summit melted away and its top turned black. She could see that the very shape of the mountain was changing, as a woman with child changes. It had begun to bulge on the side where the fire had come out. Still, she stayed.

By now most of the animals had left, except for a black dog, father of their golden one, who came one day and sat at the edge of her camp. He would not move closer, but his presence comforted her as he watched with calm loving eyes from a distance. They were so alone, and the quiet of death was all around. He stayed for several days.

Before she could finish her work on the water-rock figure, there was another terrible explosion, more cataclysmic than the first. Fire belched from the north with rolling, rising clouds of smoke and steam and sound. But her camp was well prepared and she was able to survive.

Then the ash storms began again, and the stone-that-floats, the sky-rock, now pushed in great pieces, some as large as her canoe, down the length of the lake. It was as though the grieving mountain were pushing everything away from it. Pushing *her* away, with its ever more violent eruptions of ash and fire and smoke. It was clear that overwhelming destructive powers were at hand.

Now the sky-rock powder blew constantly with the wind. When she touched her face, blood came away on her hand. Although it was almost not possible to travel, she had to leave now; there was no choice. She would go by lake as far as possible. Then across the great cold desert to the mountains in the east where she had never been.

Raising the canoe that she had sunk in the marsh for the winter, she began to load it for her journey, with food, with skins. And she tied the new water basket at her waist.

The lake had a raging current now, like a swift and passioned river, and there was a punishing ash-filled rain. Nevertheless, she took the unfinished figure she had carved and, paddling against both wind and current, made her way across to the island where for many ages the spirits had dwelled. There, in the place of sacred celebration, she had decided she would place her gift. There she would leave for him the person he had loved, the body he had worshiped, the spirit of herself.

Steering her canoe into a tiny, sheltered cove, she stepped out onto the surface of a large, flat boulder and followed the ancient path worn into it by passing feet. Then she climbed a steep and rocky path to the top of the hill. Kneeling on the wet ground, she held for the last time the figure that fit so familiarly into the palm of her hand, and turned it about.

The front, the breasts, the belly, and the legs, were polished, shining, and alive. But the back and buttocks, still rough to the touch, gave her pain because she had not finished. And incompleteness hurts. It was imperfect, and she had so wanted her love to be perfect. *Oh, how I shall miss you. How I want to lie in your arms and be yours.*

She laid her gift in the earth, joining him there as best she could. The air was thick with ash and she shielded her face to keep from breathing it. As she covered the figure with dirt and stones, she felt a deep sadness for all those gone before who had suffered in separation, and all those who would suffer.

As the wind buffeted her, she stood and headed down the hill to a place between the two great boulders on the southern shore.

Passing through a narrow entrance in the earth below the two massive rocks, she entered a small cavern fashioned by her ancestors. There a male and a female figurine carved in stone were propped together on a boulder, surrounded by gifts. It was evident they had once been one, standing side by side, arms about one another. But worn edges where they had fit together showed they had long been broken apart.

She cupped the figures with her hands, touching them lovingly, but did not disturb their placement. Then, turning away, she climbed out of the shelter and walked down to the water's edge. Stepping into her canoe and pushing off, she left a last imprint of her sandal in the muddy earth.

The wind had become so powerful by now she found she could no longer return to shore for the rest of her provisions. Feeling alone now in every way, she set off down the churning, roiling dark waters of the lake. The sky flashed with lightning and the sharp ash blew against her skin and eyes until her vision was almost gone.

In pitch darkness, the storm pushed her boat into the reeds. They whipped against her body and held her boat fast; she could not get free. And so she waited. At the edge of the marsh on the eastern shore of the lake, she stared out at the dark water and thought about the elemental Force.

Toward dawn the wind abated. As she traveled further to the south, there was more destruction, with fireballs from the mother mountain flaming into the sky and raining down. The earth rumbled loudly, whole sections of it around her lifting up, then collapsing again.

Her canoe was carried swiftly down the lake. Then toward evening, as darkness grew, there was one more climactic explosion, a fearful, deafening, roaring detonation. The enormous waves that followed overturned her craft and she was plunged into frigid water. Coughing and choking, she tried to resurface, but was caught by her clothing underneath the canoe.

She knew if she could not take a breath, her child could not. So as her canoe continued to be swept south, she struggled with strength she had never had, and somehow, just before her lungs burst, she pulled herself free.

As she came back up into the fiery night she saw an immense piece of sky-rock floating beside her. She climbed up onto it and lay on its rough surface, shivering in chilled exhaustion as it drifted in the current. Except for the water basket tied to her waist, all her belongings were lost. Colder and colder, she curled herself into a ball so that the last of the heat within her would go to her baby. Sleep stole over her.

A long time passed, and then a gentle bump, bump, bump, brought her to consciousness again, as when she was a child sleeping in her parents' canoe and they had reached the shore. She heard voices. Hands reached to lift her.

Then she was lying by a campfire, looking into the flames. She slept for a long time, then she woke to see faces of several people looking at her. She became aware of the heat from the fire and then of the four men and the woman who watched her. None was known to her.

The look of one of the men was threatening; his eyes lingered on her. Then he came toward her. When she tried to pull away, he held a sharp rock at her belly, showing with his terrible eyes that he would cut her child if she did not submit. So she ceased her struggling as her clothes were torn from her and her body taken in violence in a way she had never known.

When he, and then another man had finished with her at last, they left her on the ground. Naked, bruised, and sickened, she crawled away into the desert. There, bleeding from her birth opening, cold and alone, hugging her belly, she tried to will her child life. In the night she nearly died from the cold, and in the day the desert sun beat down, increasing her thirst.

At evening, the baby was still moving within her, so she returned to her captors' camp to drink water from her basket. She knew now that, for her child's sake, it would not be wise to try to escape.

Traveling with the others in a life that was harsh and full of pain, she made her way to the east. One day she thought she saw the black dog again, following in the distance. That night an animal came and sat at the edge of their camp, eyes gleaming in the firelight. Was he the same? Was it the father of their golden dog? In the gloom and darkness of the ash-filled air, she could not be sure.

Next morning the wind was too strong to move on, so they stayed at their camp for several days. And in that time, in peaceful effort, her child was born. She called the infant Starlight Rain. In the days that followed, as she walked on the trail, her child securely swaddled on her back, tears of bitter stubborn joy streaked her face, banishing for now her tears of grief.

Slowly they approached the dry mountains to the east. Once, in a high wind, the skies cleared briefly and the woman saw that the mother mountain, the People's companion and eternal protector, had fallen in upon itself. A piece of the blue sky that used to be obscured could be seen now, but a boundary of her world was gone. Where the mountain used to rise, there was only a jagged line across the horizon. The People's sanctuary from the outside world was no more.

The group was halfway up the first range of low mountains to the east when the path led at last around to the back. There the woman dared to stop and stand for a moment, to look once more back at the lake, to memorize their land of peace.

She remembered the last blessed touch of his hands. She thought of his eyes as they gazed upon her body, holding it in reverence. She would always be held in reverence by that memory.

Then she recalled her fears, the ground shaking, the peak of the mountain turning black. She would think about that blackened vanished mountaintop at night. Dream of it, and of the way of life that was lost. It was as if she knew that times would be terrible for all her people, long into the future. She must teach her children to endure. And to remember.

PART TWO

Present Lives

". . . a new global compact for sustainability can only be built upon a new era of partnership at the individual, community, and institutional levels. . . . Experience and knowledge must be shared among scientists, non-governmental organizations, communities, and individuals. In the end, it will depend upon the emergence of a global citizenry that sees itself bonded by a common goal, the achievement of an equitable, sustainable world."

Union of Concerned Scientists Briefing Paper, May 1994

CHAPTER ONE

22nd Century Yearnings

It had all begun one hot night the previous summer when both LeeAnn and her brother Peter were home in New York for a visit over the Fourth. Her friend Audrey was there too. They were all up at their friend Jeffrey's old apartment near 105th and Broadway about 10 p.m., which was when Jeffrey's day just started cranking. LeeAnn was tired, having flown in from Oregon earlier in the day. The four of them had been talking with the same intensity that they used to at Joan of Arc Junior High–and about the same cheery subjects, like species extinction and nuclear Armageddon–while they waited for their two large veggie pizzas to arrive. Audrey always took charge when it came to ordering food and always ordered plenty.

Jeff had been filling them in on rain forest viruses run amok–he was an epidemiologist who had a dull job, but kept up on the hot stuff–and Audrey had been talking about the dying reef in Florida that she studied as a biologist. According to her, in ten years max there wouldn't be any living reef there at all. Both of them were playing the "Ain't it awful" game, it seemed to LeeAnn, whose own field was archaeology. Still, it was comforting in a way; they'd always talked like that.

The way they got onto the subject that led eventually to LeeAnn's wacky idea was when Jeffrey, who thought about the future a lot, suggested the four of them ought to celebrate the millennium together, and LeeAnn and Audrey remembered they already had a date to meet. They'd made it when they were eleven years old.

"Three o'clock in front of the left-hand lion at the Fifth Avenue library, wasn't it?" Audrey said.

"Wasn't that always the place?" LeeAnn didn't think people ever really met in front of those lions; they just planned to, some day way off in the future. Of course, the other standard meeting place, the clock at Grand Central, was different. People actually did get together there; you saw it all the time.

"But is your date on December of 1999 or 2000?" Jeff asked. "We don't *start* the new millennium till we've *finished* the year 2000, you know." Audrey looked puzzled.

"You don't finish two thousand of something *till you finish the whole two thousand*. We don't start the third thousand years till 2001."

"That's right," said Peter.

Both women were momentarily slowed. "But going from 1999 to 2000 sounds more exciting," LeeAnn said. "More like watching an odometer. Plus, we'll be too excited to wait."

"And that way," Audrey rationalized, "we get to celebrate twice, at both ends of the year."

"I can do that," said Jeffrey, grinning.

"It's a *celebration sandwich!*" exclaimed Audrey.

LeeAnn laughed. Then, looking at Audrey, "So, December 31, 1999. Three o'clock."

"Right. You could come too," Audrey added magnanimously to Peter and Jeff.

"With whoever our various mates are at the time?" from Jeffrey. He would want to bring Kevin; they'd been together ten years.

"Sure. Okay," Audrey answered.

"*You* only get to bring one," LeeAnn said, pointing at Audrey, who kept quite a collection of males around. Peter, LeeAnn's hunk of a brother, with his sky-blue eyes and long, thick blond hair of a shade Clairol would pay big money for, would have some woman to bring. He was into serial monogamy. And of course at that point, back last summer, LeeAnn had thought for sure David would want to be with her. He was the artist LeeAnn had lived with these past five happy years out in Oregon. "I'll bring David," she said.

So it was settled, and they fell into a discussion of what the new century might be like. "It could be the last for humanity, you know," Peter said in his dry way. "Or at least the last one we want to celebrate."

"We might just make it through okay," said Jeff. "Look at the mine-fields we've negotiated in the 20th . . ."

"Yeah, but don't forget there's going to be ten billion people on the planet by 2050." And they went on as it evolved into a somewhat heat-ed discussion about which unsustainable trends would have to be reversed, how soon, in order to ensure a happy 22nd century for humankind.

As the others talked, LeeAnn let herself slip into reverie; she had a habit of doing that. Her dad used to kid her, called her the *Reverie Girl,* because she was always sitting around dreaming up things. She'd tilt her head to one side and gaze at everything from a slight angle, her lovely face alert, but her mind clearly somewhere else. She was doing that now, staring idly out of the window, listening to the traffic sounds and wondering why they sound different at night. Her fingers uncon-sciously scissored long straight hair the color of clover honey, and so thick it swung as though weighted at the ends when she turned her head, as she did now to try to tune back in to the conversation.

Lounging barefoot on an old brown bouclé couch, LeeAnn wore cutoffs and a faded blue tank top that showed off her shoulders. It was a sweltering night, but there was a little breeze on the seventh floor so she was feeling pretty comfortable, except that all the little loops in the rough upholstery fabric were scratching the back of her thighs. *Nobody should ever make sofas out of bouclé,* she thought, rolling her ankles in small circles and looking down at her newly polished toenails.

Five foot seven with a long-waisted, wonderfully proportioned body, LeeAnn Spencer had high, full breasts just the right distance apart, and long, tanned, smooth legs. She was only one-sixteenth Native American, so puny a percentage she was almost embarrassed to claim it. But it was the part of herself that she identified with most, and it was the part of her that nature seemed to have favored as well.

Her features were inarguably classic, with a high-cheeked face so close to flawless that it might have conveyed the hauteur of a high-fash-ion model. Except for a couple of things. Her small, well-shaped nose was just marginally off center, casualty of a junior high basketball game; she never could see the sense in getting it fixed. And she had dis-tracting hazel eyes, too distracting for a model's face, with equal amounts of joy and pain in them, plenty of both. She was thirty-six.

"You know, it's absolutely amazing to me," Audrey was saying, "these days, how the whole infrastructure seems to be falling apart at once. Have you noticed . . ."

"Right," said Jeff, cutting her off. "Hey, did you guys know," he said, leaping into one of his frequent tangential asides, "that the word *infrastructure* wasn't even in the dictionary in 1971?"

"I *thought* so," said LeeAnn. "It's so overused, one of those *in* words people seem to have to keep proving they know."

"We apparently didn't need a word for it till it all started crumbling," Jeff said.

"Infrastructure," LeeAnn repeated aloud, "*the systems of support that we base our lives on.*"

"It means underpinnings," said Jeff. "But underpinnings is also another name for women's underwear." He *would* say that; he had a dictionary on a stand right out there in the living room and he consulted it constantly.

"Actually," LeeAnn mused, "I guess it isn't the *word* I object to as much as the gargle-y self-important way people have of saying it. As if just saying it is going to fix things."

"In-fra-struc-ture," Jeff intoned in one of his quirky professorial voices. "And it's not just crumbling, it's downright collapsing, if you think about it. I mean *parenting's* gone, subcontracted out to fast-food restaurants and day care centers. Government? Ha!"

"Ha!" Peter echoed.

"And religion isn't getting its message across," Jeff went on. "Just look at almost any headline."

Audrey nodded. "Did you see where twelve percent of high school students have already been shot at, for godsakes?" she added, in her gravelly little voice.

"Twelve percent? Where'd you see that?" LeeAnn asked.

"*The Times.*"

"Yeah," Jeff said, "*Thou shalt not kill.*" He shook his head. "That seems a pretty plain instruction. Why do people choose the dark side, I wonder."

"Because we're all a mixture," LeeAnn said. "We've all got some partnership and some dominator in us, probably about 49% partnership, 51% dominator. It's just that the dominator side by its very nature tends to dominate. All we've got to do is change that 2% in all of us and we've got it made. Change our attitude and we change the world. The whole new paradigm idea."

"And the easiest time to transform something is when it's in a state of total disequilibrium, like now."

"No doubt," said Peter, nodding.

"When it's completely screwed up." Jeff nodded his agreement with himself as he said that. He was lying on the floor, his head resting against a bright mustard-colored vinyl beanbag chair. A cloud of softly curling dark hair and beard outlined his so-white ascetic face, with the yellow of the beanbag around that like a double aura. "There just needs to be a force that will make that start to happen," he said.

Medium tall, with thin, expressive shoulders, he was LeeAnn's brother's best friend from music school, Jeffrey Long-Hair Levine, as opposed to Jeffrey Short-Hair Malloy, who went into podiatry. Jeff and LeeAnn's brother Peter had built a house together upstate on spec after high school, which was how Peter had gotten interested in being an architect.

"So forget for a moment family, government, and religion; that leaves business as the only successful institution around," Audrey declared.

"I would dispute that," Peter challenged. "Define success. What's successful about an infrastructure that's sucking all of its content right up to the top? It's going to collapse of its own weight. We've already got half the wealth of the world in the hands of fewer than one percent of the people and it's getting worse . . ."

"At the speed of light," Audrey finished for him.

"Which is precisely why there's almost nothing left for roads or education . . ."

"Or high-speed rail," LeeAnn contributed; she loved trains.

"Soon the *one-percenters* will have it all. It's plain as the nose on your face," Audrey said. It was a phrase Audrey's mother used to use, LeeAnn realized. She never thought she'd hear her friend say it.

"So when the whole money system fails, where will business be *then*?" said Peter.

"You guys have got to stop dooming and glooming. Why don't you talk about some of the good stuff?" But of course they didn't. LeeAnn felt herself beginning to space out. She never liked to acknowledge jet lag, but tonight that's what it felt like. Plus she'd forgotten to eat her algae.

"The biggest threats to our society at the moment, in my opinion," Audrey was saying a few minutes later, "are bad diet, bad sex, and stress . . ."

"Yeah, and what causes stress? Lack of money . . ."

". . . and in the U.S. the unequal distribution of wealth is particularly exaggerated." Jeff was rolling on relentlessly, as a night subway train rattled underneath the building, "The money is way, *way* more evenly divided in Britain, even with all the inherited wealth, and . . . Well, let me get you the article," he said, getting up off the floor just as the loud buzzer of the building intercom sounded out in the kitchen. "That would be the pizza. I'll get it," he said, and he started out, his slim shoulders held slightly forward as he left the room. Jeff was on a mission.

It was always kind of a jolt to be back home in New York, LeeAnn thought, looking around; what with the relative grime, gloom, and crowded feeling of even her more successful friends' apartments, she sometimes felt sorry for them. This huge old place that Jeffrey had shared with six roommates for the past ten years was an excellent case in point—with its slightly murky decor contrived out of mismatched furniture along with ungainly plants resurrected from dumpsters, brown at the edges and clearly angry about being brought back from the brink. Towery, spindly, rubbery things, most of them, reaching for a sun they couldn't find. Nestled among them LeeAnn saw an abstract iron sculpture, a newcomer to the scene that in her opinion would have done better to continue rusting on a trash heap. Peter, however, she saw, was eyeing it with some grudging admiration.

Growing up in Manhattan, Jeffrey and Peter had become inveterate dumpster divers early on; with Peter reaching his pinnacle at Stanford the night after his graduation, sifting through spoils abandoned by the well-heeled heedless among the new alumni. One girl in his dorm, he said, left thirty pairs of shoes behind.

Living in Berkeley now, he was carrying on in the dumpster tradition on an even grander scale, his architectural studio crammed with impressive discards from the warehouse area where he lived. Recycling had become so ingrained in both Peter and Jeff, LeeAnn thought, they were probably incapable of not using both sides of a piece of paper.

Of course, it was natural that the boys would become conservation nuts. After all, Maggie, LeeAnn and Peter's mother, had taken the boys to the first Earth Day in Central Park. And, being the kind of purists and idealists both of them were at nine, standing up there on that big, flat plateau of rock right by Central Park South, pledging to the planet, how could they help but become compulsive recyclers?

Perhaps because she and Audrey had ventured out of academia, or because they were more worldly to begin with, neither woman suffered greatly from the affliction. LeeAnn operated on the theory that over a lifetime perhaps the writing she did on the subject of archaeology would be worth the sacrifice of a couple of trees. And Audrey used enough nail polish alone to threaten the biosphere. *Of course, these guys are doing the right thing,* LeeAnn acknowledged to herself, looking around the apartment. *Out in the hinterlands we waste more, probably because there's the illusion we have more to waste.*

Jeff came back with his article and began reading aloud to them. That was the thing about Jeffrey; he'd read out loud whether you wanted him to or not. After a while Peter looked at his watch. "Where is that pizza guy anyhow?"

"Or woman," Audrey admonished.

"It was a *guy* on the intercom that I buzzed in," Jeff said.

"Well I wish he'd get here."

"Hungry, Peter?" Audrey teased; LeeAnn's brother was always hungry. Audrey's seductive tone made LeeAnn wonder briefly if she and Peter had ever made it together. Probably they had, though neither had ever mentioned it. And she'd never asked.

Audrey, in a hot pink silk jumpsuit, sat across the room, curled up in an overstuffed velveteen chair from the seventies that was done in a harsh shade of royal blue bordering on purple. Tiny little Audrey Garcia always chose the biggest chair and then looked lost in it, reminding LeeAnn of a Superball; all that contained energy.

Just now, Blackdog, a saint of a dog who belonged to Jeff's partner Kevin, was sitting leaning up against Audrey, radiating love. He had a way of tilting about ten degrees off, in bliss. In trance, against a person's legs. Going through a karmic experience with them. It was powerful. Blackdog was a powerful being. LeeAnn watched as Audrey bent to pet him.

Audrey's father was Puerto Rican, her mother Lebanese, so she was definitely ethnic. She had a perfect little body, dark short ringlets that she sometimes hennaed, a large mouth and olive complexion, minute wrinkles by her nose when she laughed, which was often, and the slightly pinched look about her face that the children of alcoholics sometimes have. Audrey had an immoderate interest in clothing, makeup, and fashion jewelry.

She and LeeAnn had been inseparable since the day they started kindergarten together at PS84. Once, holding hands, crossing Central Park with their first-grade class, they had almost been hit by a number ten bus because they were dawdling. And later, LeeAnn was always having to haul Audrey out of fights. In combined third/fourth grade, back when open classrooms and open thinking were rampant, they had been among the very youngest of the *"Clean for Gene"* McCarthy-for-president cadre.

Later, they'd also gotten to go and interview the gorgeous new mayor of New York, John Lindsay. He had jogged past them one Sunday morning in June in Central Park, with an aide on a bicycle next to him, and both girls had fallen in love right there on the bridle path. Except for his teeth, which you could see when he smiled were a little crooked, the man was god-like. The blond, wavy hair. Those blue eyes. That heavenly body in gray sweatpants, and a pale yellow T-shirt which was quite tattered for a mayor to wear. As he passed, he smiled as though he recognized them, and then said, "Good morning," in that rich, familiar voice of his.

Afterward, still in shock, the two little girls had started walking down the slightly serpentine pathway that leads ultimately to the drinking fountain at 96th Street. For some reason, it was the path LeeAnn always pictured when she thought of the yellow brick road, though it bore little resemblance. Stunned by the encounter, LeeAnn and Audrey walked slowly with their heads down, replaying the scene in their minds. "I betcha he'd come to our class," LeeAnn said at last.

Audrey agreed instantly. "Yup, I betcha he would." It was just *how to accomplish it.*

When they got back to LeeAnn's building, they sat chewing on ice cubes and plotting in the tiny maid's room that Maggie and Cliff had done up for their daughter in lavender and dotted Swiss, with a home-made canopy bed. Audrey spent a lot of time at the Spencers' since her mother was dead and her father was a drunk.

"I wonder," Audrey said at last, picking up a cube of ice that dripped on the bedspread and carefully sprinkling salt on it from a battered silver salt shaker before popping it in her mouth–apparently the salt pitted the ice in a way that pleased her tongue. "What if we did it for our summer project?" Everyone in PS84 had to do a summer project.

"Right on!" LeeAnn replied. Two birds with one stone. The girls high-five'd each other and then set to work. They giggled a lot as they filled in their flowchart, something they had just learned about in class, and began to contrive a step-by-step plan of action to ensnare the mayor.

First, LeeAnn wrote a long letter of invitation on her lined notebook paper, sending copies to the borough president and their assemblyman and the district leader, and anybody else they thought might help. Then Audrey, who even in those days gave great phone, began her relentless telephone campaign. Slowly and stubbornly, they worked their way toward a dream that they quickly learned was shared by a majority of prepubescent girls in New York City.

Battling the fiercest of odds and employing total teamwork, they finally landed an interview with the mayor for September, though at his place rather than theirs. And of course it ended up they had to share the experience with all the other students, *plus* both teachers.

So they were doers. But then that was natural. Cliff and Maggie Spencer, LeeAnn's parents, were political. All their teachers were political. The whole Upper West Side was political back in the late sixties and early seventies when they were growing up. The neighborhood then was about a third black, a third Puerto Rican, mostly poor, like Audrey, and a third Central Park West Caucasian. Barbara Streisand lived across the street from the Spencers, Sybil Burton a block farther down, so both were included in the school candy sale runs. All of which made for a wildly diverse multicultural situation that seemed to be actually working. A *hothouse of hope*, as it were.

In seventh grade, Jeffrey Longhair, a child actor who went to music school with Peter, joined the group at Joan of Arc Junior High—a New York City public school that by some mysterious miracle had been named for a Catholic saint. (Probably only because Joan of Arc was a woman, LeeAnn used to think as she wrote the heading in her notebook every day. "I mean, after all, there aren't that many to choose from," she'd complained to Audrey once. "Clara Barton? Helen Keller? *Ladybird Johnson* for godsakes?")

Jeff had gotten into show business only because he'd happened to go along one day when a friend auditioned for a Pepsi commercial and landed the part himself. After that, he specialized in off-camera work so they wouldn't make him cut his hair, eventually earning enough money lip-synching cartoon rabbits and ghosts and scarecrows to put himself through Johns Hopkins, and buy the land in the Catskills that he and Peter had built that house on.

The four of them had hung out together till ninth grade when Audrey opted for an hour and three-quarter subway ride out to Far Rockaway every day to attend the High School for Marine Sciences. Audrey always went after what she wanted, and usually got it. She presently worked in conservation bio, measuring how much coral was dying from salinity and general human abuse.

Jeff looked at his watch. It had been a good ten minutes now since the pizza guy had been buzzed in. Lost, perhaps. LeeAnn thought it was becoming critical for her hungry brother, who was starting to look stricken.

"We've been having trouble with the elevator lately," Jeff said, and was about to go on a search, when there came at last the sudden horrid ring of the front doorbell. It was a rude, penetrating New York sound, way up there in decibels like a school bell at the end of a period.

"Finally." Audrey, in that clinging silk jumpsuit with matching, exquisitely tailored toenails (LeeAnn's feet had *never* looked that good), climbed out of her chair and went to the door, Blackdog padding after her. You could hear her bantering with the deliveryman in the entry in a mixture of English and Spanish. Clearly the guy was hot for her. "Well, be careful," Audrey said at length. "I really think you'd do better to take the stairs this time."

"I take my chances. Later!" they heard the cheerful Latin-accented male voice say as the elevator door clanged.

"Cuidado!" Audrey called after him and listened to the heavy electrical click as the motor engaged, followed by an *arumph* as the car started up again, then the sound of three deadbolts being flipped as Audrey relocked the apartment door.

Through the living room she came then, carrying the two boxes, as the scent of cheese, oregano, and garlic wafted through on the sooty summer nights' breeze. Blackdog didn't follow her into the kitchen but instead came over to LeeAnn to bestow his blessing, sitting quietly in front of her and gazing *through* her with such a noble look of love, it felt as if it penetrated her soul. Blackdog reached up then and put his paw on the back of LeeAnn's hand. He kept it there, holding it there, holding her hand down.

22nd century yearnings

Half border collie, half golden retriever, Blackdog was all black, as one would imagine from the name, except for a white star on his chest. A small purple plastic heart on his collar lay right in the middle of that star when he sat and gazed at you. He had the faintest trace of white, like eyeliner, around his caramel eyes, highly intelligent eyebrows, and a wonderfully shaped head that you *had* to touch. The only demand Blackdog ever made was to push your hand up with his cold nose when he hoped for acknowledgment.

Audrey came back in now with plates and napkins and the pizza on a platter in all its dripping, gooey, cheesy glory, with plenty of tomato sauce for a change, LeeAnn saw. *West Coast pizza will never satisfy a true New Yorker.* They all dug in, stringing temporary cheese lines from plate to mouth with abandon. But Blackdog paid no mind. In fact, LeeAnn noticed, he made a point of staying busy while they ate, lying on his back, holding his beloved stuffed bunny up between his paws and tossing it around, so you wouldn't even *think* he was interested. So you wouldn't have an uncomfortable moment. Not the flicker of a nostril betrayed any desire, though LeeAnn happened to know for a fact that Blackdog adored pizza.

Peter was getting ready to say something, LeeAnn saw, noting the almost imperceptible lifting of her brother's head that signaled data spooling to his printer. So she waited to hear what it would be. Since Peter tended to be sparing with both words and dollars, splurging only on software and gifts for his girlfriend, and speaking only when he had something to say, people tended to pay attention. Peter Spencer was the most honest person LeeAnn knew and, in her estimation, everything a brother could be. He forced people to look at themselves, for one thing; that was the greatest gift he gave. He demanded logic, order, and organization, all things often in short supply in her own life.

A specialist in quantifying things and finding lowest common denominators, Peter tended to be quite solemn and intense except when he was silly, which was actually quite often, and quite outrageous; like LeeAnn and their mother Maggie, he had his ups *and* his downs.

"You know," Peter said now, "it's really *all one deal*; there's only one thing the matter with anything in the world, and you can say it in two words."

"Which are," Jeff prompted.

"*Human behavior.* It's obvious isn't it? Change that and everything

35

will be fine–I mean there's nothing wrong with *animal* behavior that we haven't messed with already, is there? There's nothing else to cause us pain and suffering."

"Except bad health, which is mostly our fault. And natural disasters," Jeffrey said.

"Yeah, and most of those aren't so natural any more," from Audrey. "We've had a part in them. Or we live somewhere we shouldn't, like on a floodplain."

"In fact, there aren't even a whole lot of natural predators for man," Jeff said. "The viruses would prefer to avoid us if we'd just stay out of their territory. And stay healthy. *Eden exists.*"

"If we'd just behave ourselves." That was Audrey, as she finished her pizza, gathering the last crumbs from the plate on her fingers, and licking them.

"Take Blackdog for instance," said Jeffrey, warming to his subject. Jeffrey was into metaphors, and here, after all, was an actual, tangible metaphor, with four paws and a tail. "Look at him. He doesn't hassle anyone so he doesn't get into any trouble. Instead of yapping and peeing and chewing furniture, bumping up against people and sniffing crotches, he's just a total saint. So everyone adores him and his life is a breeze. It's wonderful. Because he attracts good energy."

LeeAnn, who was given to strong visual images, began picturing the world as a giant kennel filled with yapping dogs, big and little, black and white, brown and yellow, every color, barking and leaping and nipping at one another. Then the image was gone. "If we'd all just quit biting each other on the rear end . . . ," she said. *And killing each other over the kibbles*, she was tempted to add, but didn't. This save-the-world talk tended to embarrass her; she never knew if you were supposed to joke or be serious. "The whole kennel just needs to quiet down," she said finally. "I mean it isn't like what we want is so complicated. Staying alive, finding love, continuing life . . ."

"Continuing the continuum," Peter said. "Or making sure it's continued by someone else." Peter wasn't planning on having kids. "In the final analysis, it's continuity that's important," he declared.

"Connection," LeeAnn corrected him. "Connection is the greatest human need. Connection *ensures* continuity. If we could just all connect again, we'd be okay. Starting one on one." Then she stifled a yawn; she was having a hard time staying awake. That came from hanging out with her nocturnal brother, who, like Jeffrey, probably stayed up to avoid the sense of crowding that daytime in the city represented. Understanding his habit didn't make it any easier to deal with, however.

"It's like they say, 'the one have become the many,'" Jeffrey said, quoting Yogananda. "And now the many need to become the one again." They were getting into philosophy now, politics to philosophy, then probably to silly; it usually went that way. "And with the amount of knowledge that we can expect to acquire in the next fifty years, we'll probably have all the answers we'll ever need."

"Including what life's all about?" LeeAnn asked.

"Maybe. Meanwhile, more of us have to start paying attention. It's like Krishnamurti says," Jeff was into Indian mystics tonight, "'The minute you acknowledge a problem, it's already on the way to solution.' More people need to know what the critical areas are, and specifically what we need to achieve in each decade so we can *have* a 22nd century."

"More people," Audrey interjected loudly, "need to realize we're whizzing along in a goddamn spaceship at about a zillion miles an hour with nobody at the controls!" Her little burst of energy seemed to fall short, however. Nobody reacted.

Peter was looking thoughtful again. "It could be reduced to about twenty numbers," he said, "in the areas where human behavior has to change."

"Which are?" said Audrey. "Would you quit making us wait for your pronouncements?"

He paused. Peter always considered his words carefully. "There's actually four of them," he said finally. "Our bodies, our *health*," he said, "that's one. Our habitat–the *environment*–is the second. Our *relationships*, one-on-one and a billion-on-a-billion, number three. And our *commerce*, what we do with the bounty of the earth, how we divide everything up; that's four. Is that all?" He looked around the room for confirmation.

"I think that covers it," says Jeff.

"Health, environment, relationships, and commerce. Fix the way we deal with those four things and we'd all be okay."

"It would be possible to monitor each of those areas," Peter said, "and publish the scores regularly–like five figures for each. Are we making it or not making it in that realm? Simple."

"Remember that fifty-ways-to-save-the-planet book?" said LeeAnn. "That succeeded because it was so simple."

Peter nodded. "Keep it simple," he said.

"We can change things just the minute enough of us realize we want to," LeeAnn said. "We *are* pivotal. Our generation is pivotal. What we have now is chaos. Almost no connection." Then they were quiet. You could almost feel the mood in the room drop. Nobody had anything to say.

Finally Audrey spoke up. "You know," she began, "I think what *pisses me off* the most is people like us sitting around agreeing with each other, getting off on it, and then getting almost nothing done. *We're the ones who are failing to connect with the rest of us!*" She stared at each of them in turn. "Blathering on about new *paradigms*, which most people could care less about, let alone spell. When what we need to do is to dream up something that's going to attract the attention of the K-Mart shopper. Get everybody involved in this thing."

"Define K-Mart shopper," said Peter.

"The family that's trying to work three jobs and hasn't got time to figure out what's happening," LeeAnn contributed.

"You know what you could do," Audrey said. "You could run those scores you were talking about on the bottom of people's television screens, like they run the sports scores on CNN."

"You'd never get them to do that."

"Why *not?*" Audrey sounded indignant, like it was Jeff's fault.

"Very few people care," Jeff said, leaning up against his beanbag and looking up at the ceiling. "Or very few people know enough to care."

"It's ridiculous," Audrey swept on. The evening may have been winding down but Audrey was just getting fired up. "You've got all those scenes of destruction and tragedy on the news and then you have these silly ball scores running along the bottom of the screen. You see *Maryland* or *Alabama,* and you think that's where the event is happening. I think it sucks."

"That's only because you don't like sports," Jeff commented and Audrey threw him a look. It was true, she loathed sports, probably because her drunken father always had his games blasting on TV in the project where they lived on Amsterdam Avenue.

"It's not because I don't like sports," she declared. "It's because those figures are not relevant to my life. Nor are the goddamn stock market figures. Put the daily ozone score, the carbon dioxide rate, the violence rate. Number of days without a major genocidal event. Twenty-one? Hey, let's celebrate! How about the daily distribution of wealth rate–how much more of our money got sucked upstairs today? Instead of the stupid ball scores." Both Audrey and LeeAnn used the word stupid too much. "Put something relevant on instead."

"How about *in addition to?*" Jeff said pointedly, as he sat up some, looking a little threatened. As a serious cyclist, he had some investment in sport.

"Fine!" Audrey retorted.

Jeff nodded and sat up some more, till he was completely upright, sitting cross-legged like Ghandi, but a moment later he uncrossed his legs again and hugged his knees to his chest. Jeff tended to restlessness during strenuous conversation, and he was still getting back on track after Audrey's intrusions. "Health, habitat, the human violence quotient . . . I suppose we could put together numbers nobody could argue with. Passing score, failing score. Get people as familiar with the overview as . . ."

"Hey, base a lottery on it if you have to," Peter threw in. "Bet on your future! Win a billion dollars betting right on humanity's fate."

"That's not a bad idea, to be honest with you," Audrey said. "Die rich."

"Then, by the time we hit the millennium, we'll all understand exactly what we have to do to create a 22nd century."

"If there is one," Audrey retorted. "If we could talk some sense into CNN," she huffed. Jeff clasped his hands behind his head now and flopped back against the vinyl beanbag, which was getting more flattened as the evening wore on.

"You know," Peter said, as he reached for his fourth piece of pizza, "people *are* aware, and they *are* trying, in their own way. The whole Internet, the whole talk radio thing, it's *all* based on an urge to join . . ."

"An urgent urge . . . ," Audrey interjected. "I think we all really know what's going on, we're all trying to reach out and find some way to link up before it's too late. Form a safety net around the earth before it all goes boom."

As Audrey spoke, LeeAnn pictured in her mind the world covered with the kind of steel mesh they put over explosion sites to keep things from going every which way. Then the image changed to the plastic mesh bags they put grapefruit and oranges in. She pictured the earth as a navel orange with that plastic mesh around it, only the mesh was made up of people holding hands. The image was a strong one, in color, the blue sky behind as backdrop. Then it was gone.

"I think we're trying to switch a vertical system over to a horizontal one before it all topples," Jeff was saying. "Trying to find some way to link up that's not based on the old stuff. You know, in their own way, even those people starting militias–I think that's what they're trying to do, too. When it comes down to it, most people are more afraid than they are hostile."

"When people are afraid, you have to get them to think logically," Peter said.

"Like I said before, there has to be some new catalyst," Jeff went on, "to bring us together, other than government or religion, other than the dissolving patriarchal family . . ."

"Or the patriarchal megacorp . . . ," from Audrey.

"It's kind of . . . like the Wave at a football game," Jeff said, getting excited. "Take the Wave as a metaphor for what we're all trying to do . . . for the instinctive urge we feel to be acting together. I mean, there's a situation, the Wave, where *everybody* has to cooperate for it to work, and you get *absolutely nothing* out of it except you feel good. Yet everybody does it, just for fun. The motivating force is the fun of it. Just having a good time with other people. Celebrating."

That got LeeAnn thinking about a friend of hers who was always saying that celebrating is all you ever really have to do and the rest takes care of itself. *That celebration leads to joy, and hope, and inspiration, which leads to planning and action and accomplishment and then to more celebration, which starts the cycle all over again.* And if that works for individuals, she thought, then why not for the whole planet together?

She let her mind travel a few more moments. Still picturing the orange and the earth, and the mesh of people holding hands. Then she saw the orange as though it were being peeled along the lines of the segments that divide it in the way a globe is divided by longitudinal lines. *Time zones.* As she watched, the orange transformed itself into a flower with the segments spread out as petals, joined in the center where the blossom would be. Wow, it was beautiful.

Time zones, that was it! That was when her mind first grabbed onto the concept for their new Summer Project. *How could we all celebrate in a way that would be best for the world,* she wondered. And then she saw the whole answer in a visual flash, millions of people in each of the time zones, crowds all around the earth. She drew in a quick breath and tried to concentrate.

In its creative mode, LeeAnn Spencer's mind worked like a series of sunbursts, each idea leading not to just another, but to about six more and then each of those threatening to become a dozen. Just now, she sat very still so as to let all the spokes of the sunburst ignite, and the synapses connect. And as they did, she tried to follow all lines of reasoning at once, but it was hard. Even harder was trying to capture the whole concept in her memory for future reference.

As suddenly as it began, the miniature fireworks display in her head was over. In the space of probably a tenth of a second, LeeAnn had seen how one idea, the central one she'd had, the image of the orange and the net of people and the *time lines* that divided them, could affect so much. She saw all that it could ultimately create, *if she could just communicate it intact to others.*

She broke in. "I've got a thought," she began. She must have said it in a funny tone of voice because everybody, including Blackdog, turned to look at her.

And then Audrey announced, "All right, everybody be quiet. LeeAnn has a thought."

CHAPTER TWO

The Year in Parentheses

"So what's your idea?" Jeffrey asked.

"A party. A twenty-four-hour party!" LeeAnn said.

"What are you talking about?"

"Okay, you know what you were saying about the Wave? Well, this would be like a wave around the world. For the millennium. One *simultaneous* global event."

"You mean," said Audrey, "like we all lean out the window at the same time and yell, 'I'm mad as hell and I'm not going to take it any more?'"

LeeAnn ignored her. "It's like Peter said, what are people doing? They're doing Internet; they're doing talk radio. They *want* to link together. People seem to be aching for a global moment. So what about one global party for the millennium?"

They all looked at one another as if what she was saying was nothing. "There's going to be *a lot* of parties, LeeAnn," Peter said. "That's obvious."

"I *know* that, but I don't trust any of it. It's all going to be corporate or political or religious or something that will end up dividing us even more."

"Lee-*Ann*," Jeffrey remonstrated, "the date is *based* on a religion."

"That's beside the point—pretty much everybody acknowledges the Roman calendar." She shifted on the uncomfortable scratchy sofa. "The point is, nobody's talking about *one party*," she said, pushing her fingers through that dark-honey-colored hair. "*Are* they?"

Okay, they gave her that. A slight nod from Jeff. "Celebration is so important. The *way* we celebrate is important. If we celebrate separate-the year in parentheses

ly, it's just going to screw up the 21st century. You know it will. Anybody see that? Because we can't be separate any more. But do *the right kind of celebration* and the world will never be the same." LeeAnn sighed. She was afraid they wouldn't understand.

"And what's the right kind? Do you have any idea all the stuff that's being planned–all the different things?" said Jeff.

"Exactly. What we're looking at right now is about a million different parties, a million different news stories that are just going to compete and do us no good at all. When the more we can experience the same thing, the better off we're going to be in the 21st century. We all need to have the same focus." LeeAnn sighed; she was still getting blank looks.

"You know, when people lived in small settlements," she said, trying a different tack, "–and this is one of the first things you see when you start to study archaeology–everybody would gather periodically for some kind of festival. Every solstice, every season, every full moon, whatever. All the people in the known world in many cases. And that's what sustained them and renewed them and kept them together– Ceremony, *Celebration*.

"Then when other people came along that they didn't *celebrate* with, they'd fight with them. *People who don't share ritual don't trust one another.*"

Audrey nodded. "So they fight it out till they agree on one ritual and then they share that."

"Right. And guess what most of our wars have been about the last ten thousand years. Okay, so now our world's gotten smaller, and there's all these separate groups that we're really just becoming aware of, most of which have different rituals than we do. *Which automatically makes them suspect.* But now we have to be in close contact and it's only going to get closer when we have ten billion people in the year 2050. We need to have some shared rituals so we can get along.

"Up till now, and I mean just the last few years, we didn't have the ability–we didn't have the electronic global hearth that would enable us *all* to get together. But now we can. Plus the millennium gives us the best excuse we'll have for a party for another thousand years. But unless we do something quickly, we'll blow it on what's probably going to turn out to be the biggest beer bust in history." LeeAnn looked around at each of them. "Which means we start the 21st century with a global hangover." Jeff was nodding slightly.

"If we're going to do any good with our celebration, we need to orchestrate it a little. We've got to start planning and not just let it happen helter-skelter." Peter got up and started walking around, which meant he was either listening intently or not listening at all. "Celebration is key. Quality celebration. Meaningful celebration. You know, we have only three basic human drives, and one of them is the need to celebrate."

Peter turned to look at his sister.

"We need to survive, reproduce, and celebrate–some people call it worship. In that order. And that's *all* we need. A pretty neat package, actually." She couldn't tell what they all were thinking, but she felt so strongly about what she was trying to get across. "You know, people in India, even desperately poor people who live in the street in Calcutta, they have their celebration clothes that may be almost their only possessions . . ."

"Exactly what did you have in mind, LeeAnn?" Audrey wanted to know.

"Okay. Think about the world as an orange," she began.

"An orange?" asked Audrey, her eyes widening slightly.

"I *like* thinking about it as an orange, okay?"

"Ooooo-kay." Peter seemed to be headed for the kitchen.

"Peter?" she called.

"I'm going to get some beer."

"Then I won't start till you get back," his sister told him, and they all waited in uncomfortable silence. Presently he came in with four frosted cans of Coors and handed them around.

LeeAnn held the can in front of her and watched as a droplet of cold water condensed on its side and fell onto her thigh. She wiped it off as everybody popped their tops, the sounds coming one after another around the room. Peter took a long gulp, set the can down beside the contorted iron sculpture in the bay window, and stood behind Audrey's chair, kneading her shoulders.

At last all attention was on LeeAnn and her idea. "You know the segments inside an orange?" she said, trying to speak slowly. "Pretend there's twenty-four of them."

"Wait a minute." Jeff started to get up.

"Where are you going?"

"To get an orange."

"Jeff, forget it, will you?" She sighed and started again. "Twenty-four segments, twenty-four time zones."

"There aren't twenty-four time zones, you know," Jeff started.

"Yeah, but those are people's time zones. I'm talking *logical* time zones, if we just divide the globe up into twenty-four equal parts the way the sun hits them. Okay? Along the meridian lines. Each of those twenty-four segments will be entering the millennium at a different time. So if the people in each segment could start to identify with one another now, if they could start to feel like a group, then when their time comes, we could all pay them special attention. And they could feel like they're important, like they're the adventurers that are going into the new age together." Audrey was frowning slightly.

"The rest of us celebrate with them, we connect with each segment of the earth in turn, devote all of our attention and thoughts to them for that hour." She couldn't tell what anyone was thinking. "And then we do that for the next one. Focus on the segment that's having its millennium that hour–its moment in the sun. And we find some simple ritual . . ."

"It's going to be midnight, L.A.," from Peter.

"All right, midnight. The moon, we celebrate with that. You think it might be a full moon that night? Both nights? New Year's Eve 1999 and 2000?"

"I'll go look it up." Jeff headed for his room with that mission walk of his, returning a few moments later with an almanac in his hand.

"Why segments?" Peter asked his sister at last. "A new way of looking at division?"

"Yeah, and the best way. No race, sex, nationality; it just wipes all of that out. Every segment contains Arctic and Antarctic, the prosperous northern hemisphere and the poorer southern. It cuts through political and cultural and economic lines, so in the celebration there'd be *only time lines to divide us. We'll be separated only by time.* Which is the only way people should ever be separated."

"And even through time we're linked," said Audrey.

L.A. nodded. "If we can just be sensitive to that. If we could all listen to the past. Like David does. Listen to our DNA."

"But why do you need *any* groups, *any* divisions?" Peter wanted to know.

"Because we're not ready to be totally one world yet, Peter. We still have a need to hang onto a them-and-us mindset. That's just the way we are. We seem to need the team feeling. That we're Segment 17, or 22, or whatever."

She took a breath. "So that's my idea about the segment of the orange thing. We could all feel connected to our own group, like we belong to something. And all of us in the world could identify with all of the rest of us at the same time, minus most of the usual prejudices. Everybody could still have the parties they're already planning, just let the rest of the world in. Just start to *think bigger*."

Now Peter nodded slightly.

"Like Jeff was saying, the many become the one again."

"Yogananda said it, actually," Jeff demurred modestly.

"If the media were to start a series of programs, educating us about our segment of the earth . . ."

"Right. Let the media do something *good* for a change," said Audrey.

"Media's just a show." Peter said. "Nowadays so much of the news is staged . . . like the Gulf War, for instance."

"Of *course* it is. But that's the whole point. Because what's staged by media, *and perceived by enough of us to be reality*, *becomes* reality. We have to accept that's the way the world works now."

"And learn how to use it," Jeff said.

"And maybe it's the best way, because it means we can make things happen. Media becomes a power to create our future. We create the world we want. If the media were to pick up on the idea of *one* Global Celebration while there's still time to plan, it *can happen*," LeeAnn said. "We can all gather around the communal hearth, like four or five billion of us, on those two nights and do something that will really bring us back together again."

"I don't know. It seems like you'd just create chaos, trying to plan for everybody to do the same thing at the same time," said Peter.

"It'll be chaos if we *don't* try to plan," argued his sister. "And it's what people want. They can handle it. Remember the Bicentennial, the Tall Ships? New York was *totally* peaceful. It behaved perfectly. And remember the closing of the Olympics in '84, in Los Angeles—how much that affected everybody who saw it? It seems like we're all looking for a global joining, trying to have one. And the millennium is it!

It's the natural one."

"One global birthday party, huh?" from Audrey, looking pleased with the idea. Audrey liked birthday parties.

"Not so much a birthday party as a prom," LeeAnn replied, and Audrey looked even more pleased. "Time to grow up. Graduate into a New Age."

"*Commencement* is probably a better word than prom," said Peter.

"Probably."

"And *human family reunion* is better than that."

"There you go," said Jeff, and everybody nodded; they seemed to really like that.

"Then after twenty-four hours of celebrating together and truly paying attention to one another, we'd be a lot better motivated to spend the millennial year learning to deal with our human behavior problems in a whole new way."

"Start some *genuine* planning for that population of ten billion," Jeff said.

LeeAnn's brother was still looking dubious, she saw. "One party's not an impractical idea, Peter. I mean they shut whole countries down for a one-day strike. Look at France. And whole big parts of Japan close down at once for a fire drill for godsakes."

"Are you saying everybody stay up for twenty-four hours?" Audrey asked. She was yawning.

"So how would you handle all the people who can't gather, villages that don't have television and electricity?" Peter wanted to know.

"Satellite. Generators. You could build some kind of shelter in places where they were needed so people could gather–you remember, Peter, you were talking about inflatable molds–that would hold them all, let them watch together."

"It could be done," said Jeff.

"It's no biggie. And make sure everybody has enough to eat for a change. Hey, you know when we start a war, all *kinds* of logistical miracles become instantly possible–unbelievable stuff. All we need to do is put the same kind of energy into starting a peace. It could be a form of celebration just getting ready for it. It could be fun. Do you realize we've never shut the business of the world down? Not even for a day. We've never given the whole world a day off to just hang out together!"

Audrey considered that. "LeeAnn," she said then, "Just exactly *who* are you thinking would organize this party?"

"I don't know." LeeAnn shrugged, trying to look innocent, playing casually with the flip-top on her beer can. "What we could do, I guess," she said, "is kind of write the idea up and then turn it over . . ."

"Oh come *on!*" Peter, who was taking a sip of his Coors, sputtered and put the can down. "You're talking about getting your idea together and then *handing it over to other people*? And you, *Lee-Ann Spencer*, Miss Cause Organizer of PS84, actually expect us to believe that?"

"Maybe we could start a group or something," Audrey started. "Call it the . . ."

"The U.M.," said Jeff. "*The Unified Millennium.*" Everybody laughed.

"Naw," said Peter, "that sounds funny. How about ..."

And then LeeAnn and Audrey broke in and said it at almost the same time, "*The 22nd Century Group!* That's it!!" they all shouted, as they high-fived each other.

"It would take a couple of years . . ."

"And millions of people working on it."

"Create a lot of jobs."

"What do you think the chances are of actually pulling it off?"

"About a billion to one," Peter said.

"I don't know, it has a certain P.R. appeal," from Audrey. "The *celebration aspect.*" You could tell she liked the phrase. "And a lot of people would get into it because they'd figure they could make a lot of money."

"So what's wrong with that?"

"We wouldn't promote it through the usual power structures. This would be a whole new way of networking."

"Do you mean us? *Us* give the party?" Peter broke in. He seemed to be just catching on.

"That's *exactly* what we're talking about, dear Peter," Audrey said in a mock-syrupy tone. "Listen up."

So they went on for awhile, discussing all the pros and cons, the fascinating logistical puzzles that would be involved in staging something as gigantic as a global commencement. Jeff went off to check the web for the phases of the moon on the two New Year's Eves but instead came back with all sorts of pertinent information on time zones, informing his less erudite companions that Russia was represented in no fewer than eleven. "Of course, some of the zones have been heavily gerry-mandered," he said. "There's even a couple of places, like in Australia, where adjacent time zones are only a half hour apart."

"How do they manage that?" Peter wanted to know.

"Who *cares*?" said Audrey. "Would you guys quit with the minutiae already? Try to stay with the bigger picture."

But the evening seemed headed downhill.

"Do we all get to have paper hats and party favors?" Jeff asked a few minutes later. In response, Audrey uncurled herself from the blue velveteen chair, stood up, stretched and said, "Well I don't know about the rest of you guys, but I need to get some sleep."

"We all do," LeeAnn snapped. "I need sleep, *too*, you know." She was quite aware that she sounded whiny and argumentative, but it pissed her off–here was Audrey, the first one to show interest, and already she was bored. Now it seemed suddenly to LeeAnn, who'd been so hopeful a few minutes before, that this would be like most of their projects back in the smoke-filled seventies and just waft off into the ether of eternity.

Then Peter, who'd been quiet for awhile, suddenly cut in. "If you're serious about this, then be *serious*," he said. LeeAnn saw his resolve instantly. Her brother had genuinely adopted her idea–and Peter was always the quickest to pooh-pooh something, particularly if it cost money. "You're still going to be here tomorrow, aren't you, Aud?" he said. "You don't leave till Tuesday?" Audrey nodded.

"Then let's think about it," he said, "and get together again tomorrow night."

They had said they'd meet at 9:30, but it was nearly 10 p.m. when LeeAnn hurried into the musty lobby, rode the clanking elevator, and knocked on 7G. She'd been reeling with ideas all night and had hardly slept at all, waking Maggie and talking to her about it till the wee hours.

"I'm afraid we're going to be in the kitchen tonight," were the words Jeffrey greeted her with, after opening each of the three dead-bolts to let her in.

"That's okay. Sorry I'm late." She stepped into the apartment and watched as Jeffrey refastened the locks, recalling the parable about the

Harlem woman so plagued by thieves she eventually had seven locks on her door, and they still broke in. Until she got clever enough to lock only *three*, randomly, so that as the thieves were trying to let themselves *in* they were also locking themselves *out*.

"Rebecca has people coming over later," Jeffrey explained, "or else we could have the living room." Rebecca was one of Jeff and Kevin's housemates, a peculiar, bulky young woman who was studying cubism. LeeAnn suspected it was she who had sponsored adoption of that bizarre iron sculpture in the living room.

"So, I'm sorry," said Jeffrey, leading the way through the tangle of parked bikes in the skinny hall.

"No problem." Actually LeeAnn was relieved. One more evening of having to confront the dusty rubber plants that longed for release would do her in, she thought. Blackdog, who had come to greet LeeAnn, his nose nuzzled in her hand, took up the rear as they headed through the apartment.

"Well, I've been thinking about the Global Celebration," Jeffrey began. Jeff and Kevin had talked about it all night.

"Did you find out about the moon?"

"Moon over Millennium," he sang. "Yeah, I checked the web and then I talked to the planetarium, and this is what's really neat." He stopped to explain, so concentrated on his idea he seemed unable to walk and talk at the same time. "The astronomer told me that on December 31, '99, it's going to be a crescent moon, 29%, positioned like the letter C." He gestured in the air with a cupped hand. "And on December 31, 2000, it'll also be a crescent, 28%, but a *backward*-C, curving to the right." He held the other hand up, engulfing the air between them. "So it's like a celestial parentheses . . ."

"The Year in Parentheses!" LeeAnn exclaimed triumphantly. *"A year set aside to turn our world around.* That's fantastic!"

"Plus, it'll be a leap year, so we'll have more time to do it," Jeff concluded, as he set off again. "And I'm looking up some stuff that I want to show you if I can find it." LeeAnn followed as he marched happily through the living room toward the kitchen. Jeff's way of walking was so full of eagerness and belief it almost hurt LeeAnn's heart to see it. Knowledge excited him; ideas captured him.

"So how's Kevin?" she asked.

"Great. He's working tonight," he said. Jeff's partner was a long distance runner, very tall, with sandy hair and an impossible Boston accent. He wrote encrypting programs for some Wall Street firm while he was getting his doctorate. And he worked a lot of hours; he and Jeff were saving to buy a brownstone together.

"Well, where are they?" LeeAnn demanded as they approached the kitchen and she realized she didn't hear any voices. She knew Peter and Audrey had planned to "converge," as Audrey put it, at 9:00 at the Seventy-Second Street IRT; she'd heard them make the plan. Smart people didn't do subways alone at night anymore. "Where's my brother? Where's Audrey?"

"Worrywart," Jeff teased, looking back at her. "Do you worry all year when you're not with Peter or Audrey?"

Well she did, but she didn't want to admit it, so she said nothing. The kitchen, fairly large by New York standards, had been enlarged more when somebody had chopped out the maid's room some years back, probably in the fifties, judging from the cabinets; the flooring still didn't match.

An old Grand Rapids mahogany dining room table was plunked in the middle of the room, with six wildly assorted chairs grouped around it. Various eclectic reading material was stacked haphazardly at one end. This apartment's residents appeared to be big on magazines like *Atlantic Monthly*, the *New York Review of Books,* and *Chemistry Today.*

Jeffrey had sat down and was thumbing through a stack of *Futurist* magazines that did seem to be in some sort of order. "Have a seat," he said.

LeeAnn chose a chair that had a missing rung in the back but a mashed cushion in the seat to compensate. Jars and glasses and mugs they'd used the night before for their tea were washed and in the drainer by the sink, next to Jeff's faithful juicer and Vita-mix. But the two pizza boxes still sat out on the counter, reminding LeeAnn of the night's indulgence. *"You're going to have roaches,"* was right on the tip of her tongue, but she held it.

Jeffrey by now was intent on the magazines and was quiet for quite some time. "I'm looking for an article," he said finally.

"Yes," LeeAnn replied dryly. "That's what it *looks* like you're looking for." Several more minutes went by but Jeff said nothing further. LeeAnn concentrated on the old school clock mounted on the kitchen wall as the big hand visibly inched its way along. *Hurry up and wait.* "Where are they?" she muttered.

"This piece I'm looking for is . . . okay . . . anyway . . . it's about what we ought to *call* the years after the turn of the century."

"And you've spent fifteen minutes looking for *that*?!"

"No, it's important. Now tell me, which one do you like? Two-thousand-and-one, twenty-ought-one, twenty-*oh*-one, or two-*oh-oh* one?"

LeeAnn laughed. "That last one sounds like an orgasm."

"Hmm," said Jeff, thinking. Some new tangent, no doubt. "I wonder," he began, "if anybody's ever correlated frequency of orgasm with general health, . . ." but just then the kitchen buzzer rang and LeeAnn jumped.

Jeff leaned back in his chair and punched the intercom button on the wall behind him. "Who is it?" he asked over his shoulder.

LeeAnn was relieved to hear Peter and Audrey's voices as they answered, "It's us!" in unison over the intercom; their voices bubbling over each other's. They were in a good mood. And they were safe. *God, cities. You worry so much,* she thought.

Jeffrey buzzed them in and then loped out toward the dead-bolted door to collect them. LeeAnn picked a *Futurist* off the top of the stack and began leafing through. A piece on future buildings that built themselves stopped her. Biomorphic was the word, meaning it would grow itself. Preprogrammed to become some fanciful shape, it would replicate its own molecules.

She stared at a drawing of a biomorphic skyscraper shaped like a giant seashell with room in it for seven hundred thousand people. *Neato.* It reminded her of those science project capsules Peter used to send away for. Just add water, stand back, and watch them grow. It took hours–or was it days–for them to finish growing; she couldn't remember which. Her architect brother would undoubtedly love to *grow* buildings, new kinds of spaces for togetherness of the human race.

Jeff wasn't back yet. Peter and Audrey were probably stuck downstairs, the elevator out again. At last she heard the front door of the apartment bang shut, the three locks click, and a regular happy buzz of chatter as the trio approached. "You're going to have roaches," was the first thing Audrey said as she spied the pizza boxes. So the evening got off to a good start.

Half an hour later they were well into it, Peter in his intensity declaring that, "You're not going to motivate people by saying, 'Let's have a party!' For a pitch, you have to use fear, because it's the only thing anybody understands. A stick. Carrots don't work anymore."

"People aren't going to come to a party just for the *fun* of it?" LeeAnn asked.

"Of course not."

"Why not?"

"Because we feel too guilty about fun."

"Well, that's a point," Audrey conceded. "It's about the only thing that's going to stop us. Guilt. Isn't that weird? Guilt about sex and guilt about having fun. No guilt at all about murder and mayhem. They'll say a party is frivolous."

"But it's not. We *need* a party."

Peter looked at his watch. "Shouldn't we order some food?"

"Later," said Audrey.

"What we could do is we could prepare a mailing piece," Jeff said, "send out like ten thousand invitations and explain why it will be important to celebrate together."

"Do you have any idea what that would *cost?*" said Peter.

"So, five thousand," he looked at Peter for approval, "and tell the recipients to send it out to everybody *they* know. They say we're only six people away from knowing everyone in the world."

"What does *that* mean?" Audrey asked.

"That everybody knows so many people, who know so many people, and so forth," Jeff replied.

"Oh."

"We put out a trial balloon and see what happens. See if it spreads. It might cost us a grand each to do it."

Everybody was quiet. "That wouldn't be so bad," said Audrey. "I could do that." She paused. "So if we did decide to try this thing, when would we do it?"

"Well, not before Christmas, I'm gonna be gone . . . let me see . . ."

Whipping out their calendars, they all began talking like yuppies about the complications in their lives. They decided nobody could really do anything till next summer when all of them except Peter thought they could get a month free. "But that's still plenty of time to get something going before the millennium."

"Maybe you could all come out to Oregon," LeeAnn suggested.

"We could prepare the mailing from there, write news releases, stuff the envelopes, design the invitation . . ."

"With an RSVP?"

"Right. Send it out and then still be together to deal with the response, if there is any. It'd be a lot cheaper. And I could maybe promote a free office. I bet I could. The town is like empty these days."

Her real reason, of course, for wanting to meet in Oregon was she didn't want to be away from David that long. Saving the world was one thing. Being away from David longer than she needed to be, another. "You could have the attic, Audrey; there's a whole apartment up there. The cabin will probably be rented, but there's the summerhouse, Jeff. It's just a shed, but we could run a power line."

"That would work," Jeff said. "I have my cellular, and I could run off batteries."

Funny, LeeAnn thought, *how people these days have merged their identity with their electronics.* "So you could both stay at our place. You'd finally get to meet David."

"How do you think he'd feel about all this?" Jeff asked.

"Oh, David would be thrilled." She hoped he would but of course she couldn't be sure. "And I'll finally be back from the Russian dig, for good." For the past three summers, LeeAnn had been traveling to the arctic to work on an Upper Paleolithic excavation there. "We could work out of Klamath and go to Peter's, too. It's only a five-hour drive." *Six, actually.* But why discourage them. A lot of people in Klamath preferred to maintain that it was only five hours to San Francisco. "Or Peter could come up on the weekends."

Audrey nodded. "Rendezvous for August and kick ass, huh? It would be fun." Then she started restlessly leafing through a *Village Voice.* "So." Nobody said anything.

"That's what we would do if we were to do it, huh?" said Jeff. The conditional tense was starting to be contagious. Silence, except for the old school clock on the wall, ticking. LeeAnn felt transfixed by the big hand as it moved visibly but jerkily along, pulling back slightly before each little leap forward. *Which is kind of the way life seems to go,* LeeAnn thought. The old clocks seemed to treat time with more dignity. Everyone was thinking.

"So," Peter said, "the proposition is to organize a global celebration, the first human family reunion in a couple million years, with the

simple goal of changing the behavior of six billion people. Is that it?"
More silence. More clock ticking.

Then Audrey broke the spell, scraping her chair back abruptly and
heading for the phone. "Well, I don't know about the rest of you," she
said, "but I think it's going to be a blast." She turned around to stare
them all down. "We *are* going to do it, you know."

Both Jeff and Peter nodded then. LeeAnn knew they meant it. That
even though it was a year away, they'd stick to their pledge. She felt
pride in her heart and her throat that her friends were ready to try out
the farthest fantasy she'd ever had in her life. For a moment, LeeAnn
Spencer felt entirely *connected.*

Just then Blackdog, who'd been leaving them alone while they
talked, came into the kitchen, went over to his water bowl, and began
to drink, the little purple plastic heart on his chest ringing like a
Buddhist temple bell against the steel bowl in rhythm with his tongue,
intoning the importance of the occasion.

"So," said Audrey, "riffling through a stack of well-worn menus by
the phone. "Moroccan, Argentine? Somebody say." Of course, nobody
did because they knew she'd decide for them anyway.

At that point Peter started taking over and assigning homework for
the year while they waited for the food to arrive. It turned out that vegetarian Chinese was the only place that would deliver that late.

"You know that remark of Jeffrey's last night, about could we all
wear paper hats?" LeeAnn said. "I was thinking this morning how cool
it would be if everyone *could* have *one thing* the same. And the one
thing that basically everybody in the world has access to is a newspaper. We could all make newspaper hats, like we used to in school. We
could color them or bead them, or . . . some people could work on them
for a year . . ."

"Oh, good idea!" said Jeff. He grabbed the Business Today section
of the *Times* and started folding, but to no avail. After that, L.A. and
Audrey gave it a go.

Finally, Audrey sighed. "I just can't remember how," she said, giving up finally on the paper hats.

"Isn't it funny," LeeAnn said. "None of us can. We'll have to call
Mrs. Jackson." Mrs. Jackson had been their sixth-grade teacher. "And
when it's all over, we could gather them up–like six billion newspaper
hats–and put them in a museum."

"It would make a lot more sense to recycle them," Peter suggested. "That's a lot of trees."

"Fine, Peter," said Audrey, rolling her eyes. Peter looked satisfied.

"Or I'll tell you what people could do," said LeeAnn, who was having another one of her visions. "How about if everybody gave one other person a favorite stone. Almost everybody can get a stone–even in the poorest village in Africa. Call it a *connecting stone.* Connecting back to the earth and to each other."

"That's a much better idea," said Audrey. "Quit it, Jeff." And she took the newspaper he was still fussing with away from him.

"A connecting stone would get across the idea to share the earth more," LeeAnn said. "You could give stones from your garden, or diamonds, whatever."

"The jewelry stores would make out like bandits," said Audrey. LeeAnn thought of the beautiful obsidian rock that she and David dug out of the Warner Mountains for his artwork. That's what she'd give the people she loved for a connecting stone.

Somewhat later, sitting around with a table littered with aborted paper hats, plus the empty containers from six entrees–plus fake pork potstickers that were really pretty good; *it's actually mostly the texture of meat that we miss,* LeeAnn thought–they continued to make their plans.

"So, let's see what the mailer could look like," Peter said.

"Call it an invitation," LeeAnn urged.

He took a piece of paper from a legal pad that was sandwiched in among the magazines, folded it in half and then half again and then opened it out again so there were four panels.

"It's an *or-i-ga-mi* party!" Audrey remarked, as she got up, swept all the folded newspapers together, and deposited them on the counter.

Peter picked up a pencil. "You want something that's easy for people to copy, or translate. Good, simple graphics."

"Oh, I know," said LeeAnn. "The way I was picturing it, you take the twenty-four segments and you connect them at the top, where the stem of the orange would be, and then you open it out, so all of them connect at the north pole, so it looks like a flower. And you get the idea of connection that way, how we're all connected at the poles." Peter started to sketch. "Each petal is a map of that segment."

"Then you'd have to do another one," said Audrey, "connecting at the South Pole," so there wouldn't be any favoritism–I always hate how so many times they show the earth with North America right in the middle."

"Anyway," said Peter, as he completed a rough drawing of the twenty-four-petal flower that was our earth. "Is that your idea?"

"That's exactly it."

"We're going to need to make this invitation as attractive as possible," he said, looking troubled. "I'm afraid it's going to cost some bucks."

"Oh, it has to be primo," said Audrey. "Especially the envelope. Packaging is *sooo* important."

"We'll probably each have to put up a couple of grand," LeeAnn figured. The ante was going up already. She knew that with all of them still struggling to pay off student loans, it would take some sacrifices.

"I can do that," Jeff said finally, "if I just put off getting a new bike, which I don't need anyway. It's worth it, just to see what happens."

"Yeah, it is," Peter agreed. "The other thing is, between now and next year, we each have to come up with the names of the people we think would be most likely to carry this thing forward. Get our list really honed of who we're going to send it to."

"I can do that, too," said Jeff.

"Ask all the people we send to, to be co-sponsors of the party."

"What's the first name you think of?" asked LeeAnn.

"The Dalai Lama," said Jeff.

"Deepak Chopra," said Audrey. "Who do you think of, L.A.?"

"Pat Schroeder was the first name that popped into my head. And Hillary, of course."

"Pat Schroeder?"

"I was hoping she'd be the first woman president."

"How about Oprah Winfrey?"

"How about the pope?"

"How about my mother?"

There were so many names that sprang to mind, so many people to think about. "And how can any of them possibly refuse?" As Audrey put it, "They're going to be against togetherness? They're going to say, 'Sorry, but I'm planning to be off-planet that day'? Nope, they're all going to tumble. Every last one." LeeAnn wasn't so sure.

"Okay," Peter said, as he picked up the piece of lined legal paper. "This'll be the family reunion side, all the persuasive stuff for that. The invitation to the party, the when, where, how, what . . ."

"The where is pretty clear," said Jeff. "Planet Earth."

"The positive stuff–the carrot. Now on this side," he turned the paper over, "this side is the stick. This is the Year-in-Parentheses side. We'll show them where we are now in all the critical areas and where we need to be to make it through to the 22nd century. How we need to use the Year In Parentheses to start making improvements in the four areas of human behavior. Like maybe we could concentrate on each of them for a quarter of the year."

He began creating blocks at the top of the four panels he'd created. "HEALTH" he wrote in the first. "That's you, Jeff, the epidemiologist. You're going to be in charge of researching all behavior related to the human body, figuring out what needs to change by when."

Then he wrote "ENVIRONMENT" on the second panel. "You're in charge of all environmental problems," he said, looking at Audrey, the reef biologist.

"RELATIONSHIPS," he inscribed on the third panel.

"That's me, I guess," LeeAnn said. It's what she'd been studying her whole life, how humans had related since the beginning of time.

"COMMERCE," he wrote on the fourth.

"And commerce is you?"

Peter nodded. Which made sense, since he dealt with the goods of the earth. Habitat.

"You know what's pretty amazing," said Audrey, "is that one of us works in each of the four fields? Is that wild? Synchronicity."

"What a *coincidence*," LeeAnn remarked, in order to prompt Audrey's predictable retort. Audrey was always talking about *The Celestine Prophesy.*

"There are no coincidences," said Audrey.

LeeAnn laughed. "How did I know you'd say that?"

Audrey smirked at her.

"All right," Peter went on, "each of us comes up with the five critical stats in our area to demonstrate whether we're making it or not. Five attention-getting trends, not just figures on where we are now, but the speed with which we got there. And taking the same examples, we project where we need to be by the end of the first decade of the 21st century, and the second, and so on, if we're going to make it to the 22nd. Okay, you have this amount of space to explain it on," Peter said, pointing to one of the panels.

Jeff frowned; it would be tough to get all that he wanted to impart into such a small area.

"But here's the fun part. At the bottom of the panel, you each get to give one piece of advice in your field. Just one."

"Like a set of guiding principles?" LeeAnn asked.

"Yeah. Words that people can use to measure any action they're taking, in *health, commerce, environment,* or *relationships.* Like a verbal yardstick. Make it so they can measure every decision by that guiding principle."

"Like, is it a partnership act or a dominator act when you throw a beer can out the window?" Jeff said.

Peter nodded. "Am I clear? And keep it short."

"You mean like twenty-five words or less?" LeeAnn said.

"Oh, hell no." Peter chortled rudely. "People don't have any attention span. How about twenty-five *letters*?"

"Oh come on. Pet-er . . ." They all looked at Peter like he was bananas.

"Twenty, then," he said.

And so to stop him from reducing it further, they had to quickly agree, though Jeff continued to complain, in one of his cartoon bunny voices. "What about *one syllable?* Da. Ug. Ooh."

"And the person who gets the shortest one wins."

"Peter?" LeeAnn had her planner open and was starting to write in it.

"What?"

"Do spaces count?"

"Do spaces count with Macintosh or IBM? Of course spaces count," he answered in a tone of pleasant ridicule. And so it went.

Eventually they all helped Jeff clean up a bit. Then Audrey gathered up the kitchen trash in a tall white wastebasket and LeeAnn followed her with the pizza boxes, out the apartment door and down the hall to what used to be the incinerator chute but what was now cleverly divided into a recycling thing, with different holes for cans and bottles.

"Exciting, huh? A Summer Project again," Audrey said as she fed cans into the chutes and they clattered toward the basement. "And I'm stoked about coming out to volcano country." Audrey had always been fascinated by volcanoes. "Right on the Pacific Rim. The Ring of Fire, such a beautiful name."

"They're going to put geothermal sidewalks in town," LeeAnn told her, as she stacked their incomplete newspaper hats on the newspaper shelf and put the pizza boxes into the recycled cardboard container.

"No, really, you're kidding! Then I've got to come. Be great to be close to that kind of power. Plus I'm dying to see the lake where the algae comes from." LeeAnn and her mother had introduced Audrey to eating algae several years before.

"So, you don't think David's going to mind having a bunch of crazy New Yorkers descend?"

"No, why should he? You know, we've been meaning to learn to windsurf—you guys could come with us. We'll have a ball."

"Why do you want to windsurf? That's a terribly tough sport, isn't it?"

"Because . . . I don't know why. I just need to. Of course, David will get ahead of me immediately. I'm such a klutz; I think I just need to find something I can be good at."

"So you pick the hardest. I don't know, Girlfriend."

Trailing back down the hall with the empty wastebasket, LeeAnn wondered why it was that one piece of paper always got stuck to the damp bottom and you don't notice till it's too late. "So did you ever make it with my brother?" she asked Audrey then.

"Actually, no," Audrey said without missing a beat. "We had a sibling thing. What did you think? That we did?"

"I wasn't sure," said LeeAnn. "I was just curious. So how *are* things of late? How wild were you in the balmy Bahamas?" That was where Audrey had just come back from. They stopped then in the hallway while Audrey took time to tell LeeAnn about the beautiful man named Byron she'd just spent two weeks with who was a taxi driver on Eleuthera.

"He had this really fastidiously kept little house and he always cooked with a lot of pepper."

"I'll bet you loved that."

"He'd come home on his break," Audrey told her, "to make love." Then she described how he had carried her down the beach one night in her white gauze dress, running as fast as he could, "with the moonlight and the whole thing."

"Geez. It sounds like he was quite something," LeeAnn said, wastebasket in hand.

"He wanted me to get nipple rings," Audrey added.

"Gawd." They started walking again.

"Would you ever do a thing like that?" LeeAnn asked.

"Well, no, I'd never do anything just to please a man. On principle. It doesn't help in the relationship. It never does."

She was probably right. "Will you ever see him again?"

Audrey shrugged, and then smiled. "I don't know. Maybe. He's pretty sweet."

LeeAnn worried about her friend. "You're doing safe sex?"

"Oh, for sure." They reached the apartment door now, and started inside. "You know what I'm starting to wish, though?" Audrey said then. "That I could have a *baby*."

"You?" She never thought she'd hear Audrey say that.

A little later, as they all prepared to leave, there was a moment, waiting for the elevator that had apparently got stuck on three, that felt awkward, embarrassing almost. Why was it that even having an idea this positive seemed wrong somehow? Let alone trying to *do* something about it, like making it *happen*.

As Jeff went out the stairwell door on his way down to three to clear the elevator, he broke the silence. "Well, like they say, '*The winds of grace are always blowing, . . .*'"

Audrey completed it—"'*but you've got to raise the sail.*'"

"'*Absolutl.*'" That from Peter, but he looked faintly embarrassed, too. He was quoting from *The Power of One.*

"Be interesting to hear what people are going to think of to be against it," Peter remarked.

"Oh, they'll think of something. It'll be un-American, or irreligious, or uneconomic, or just plain hokey."

"Yeah, hope is not chic," LeeAnn said.

Audrey shrugged, "So, we just state our case. If people pick up on it, fine. Probably most people will think we're batshit."

LeeAnn laughed. "Maybe people will be afraid that while we're all celebrating, the aliens will attack," she said as the old-fashioned indicator on Jeffrey's elevator finally started to move.

"More likely the aliens will cheer us on," Audrey was starting to say as the elevator arrived.

CHAPTER THREE

Airplane

The 737 pulled away from the terminal and began to taxi toward the runway. *Finally.* The flight from San Francisco to Portland had been delayed almost two hours–with the past ninety minutes spent sitting on the ground. LeeAnn was on the last leg of her journey home from the Russian arctic. It was August of the following year and time had come to begin the Summer Project.

LeeAnn had got back to the U.S. yesterday, and then sat up last night with Peter in his studio in Berkeley thinking up copy for buttons and bumper stickers. Some of the slogans for the Year in Parentheses were a little labored, she thought, as she looked down the list she'd scribbled in her planner, like **Y.I.P.ee!** *It's a Celestial Coincidence!* But the idea was to get a great quantity stockpiled for the Peter and LeeAnn Spencer team, which would be going up against Jeff and Audrey in this particular contest.

Some of the others weren't so bad. Like:

Once in a Thousand Years . . .
Celebration Helps the World, Ask Me How
Celebrate, Connect, Cooperate
Practice Random Acts of Celebration
And finally, at the bottom of the list:
Will You Party for the Planet? Which was their favorite so far.

Could this whole crazy scheme work, LeeAnn wondered, as her eyes moved down the list. When they dreamed it up last summer, they all thought it just might. *But then I always believe I can do anything when I start out.* Right this minute however, since they were actually on the verge of attempting it, LeeAnn could also imagine the whole thing fizzling from the get-go. No response, no interest, just that brick wall of apathy you so often ran into these days.

Quit it, she told herself. *No negative scenarios, LeeAnn. It will happen if you just visualize it. If you believe it, you'll see it. Wayne Dyer said that. Visualizations do work, Martyn Williams told me so. And the man ought to know.* LeeAnn still couldn't get over having run into him. Vladivostok. Of all the places on earth to meet and all the people to meet there. *That has to tell me something. It tells me that this thing is going to work, that it's supposed to. We'll get the invitations out in the next two weeks and people will start to say yes right away. CNN will come running and then all the other networks too. We'll at least get the concept off the ground.*

And, she concluded, *even if all else fails, it will be good having Jeff and Audrey around for awhile. I'll have my own friends, my own activities, and David will just naturally become a part of all that. It can actually help our situation to have them there,* she told herself, though she didn't really believe it.

She looked down at the planner in her lap again. This idea of making everything a contest bothered her just a bit. Even though the others had agreed to do the project with her, they seemed to need to keep it a game, with limits, while a part of LeeAnn wanted to go for it without limits.

The plane gunned its engines, raced down the runway and lifted off, rising steeply over the concrete, over the buildings, and up into a clear, blue, windy August sky. The pollution seemed to be all but gone today; the thick brown layer of air that usually shrouded the earth had blown out to sea and disappeared. *Maybe it's a sign,* LeeAnn thought before experiencing that little burst of scared adrenaline she always felt when she contemplated the month ahead.

The flight pattern took them almost immediately out over the waters of San Francisco Bay, where tiny sailboats and one even tinier windsurfer (the sail was orange and magenta, it *had* to be a windsurfer) zipped around down below. Every time she thought about windsurfing LeeAnn could feel the sensation, leaning back on her board and flying across the water–although it had been only once, back in the spring on Klamath Lake, that she'd ever really felt the thrill people kept telling her was in store. For a few minutes, probably two at most, she was *finally* actually planing, leaning way, way out and even starting to look around. She began to imagine herself in an old Wide World of Sports shot and then of course, KER-SPLAT!

But it was enough to have firmly, completely, deeply, and utterly addicted her. Now it was important, actually it was urgent, to become better at the sport quickly, particularly in view of the plans she and David had made to sail the whole length of the lake later this summer. They'd promised each other that no matter what happened in their relationship, they would do that all-day trip down the lake together. "My *wind-sister*," he'd said one night right after he moved out to the cabin. He'd called her his wind-sister and then they'd both wept.

She shook her head. That crazy night, that crazy fight. *Who would have dreamed last summer when we set out to promote partnership that my own would be in such trouble now?* She wondered if David had moved back into the house since she'd been gone, or if it was all over. Of course he would wait till she got home to break the news. *He's much too nice to tell me on e-mail. He wouldn't leave me weeping in Siberia.*

All these thoughts went through her head in the few moments it took before the wing of the plane had obscured that lone windsurfer who was booking it on the bay. Then they were headed straight toward Berkeley; she could see the city laid out like a relief map, sloping up toward campus. Below them was the waterfront, and then the freeway, and there was the old ketchup factory where Peter had his studio, and where she'd just spent the night. Looking down now from probably ten thousand feet, LeeAnn thought she could almost make out the little footpaths leading from the Marina Marriott across the freeway from Peter's to a point of land bright with California poppies that she'd explored on her run this morning.

After Berkeley, right over the bell tower, the scenery dulled out into vast tracts of urbia and exurbia. Hills began poking up, and houses built everywhere they shouldn't be, despoiling the land. *Too many people.* David was always saying that.

She wondered if he'd be at the gate to meet her when they landed in Portland just a little over an hour from now, or at Baggage Claim. They'd been communicating mostly by e-mail lately and hadn't settled it. But it was important–there's such an immense difference between the two. Between the gate, where there's this wonderful coming together as the voyager steps off the gangway from adventure into the arms of the waiting one, and Baggage, where you're already hypnotized by the carousel, planning your move, and hoping your laptop won't get grabbed while you reach for your bag.

And then somehow people *look* different in Baggage Claim when you finally spot them or they spot you. Time seems awkwardly out of joint and you're stumbling toward each other with luggage underfoot as you try to embrace, murmuring banalities about parking in the white zone. It's a whole different kind of energy–upstairs, people's souls being reunited, downstairs, their bodies being shoved back together–along with all life's baggage.

However, LeeAnn thought, as she worked on resigning herself, *that's probably how it will be. Baggage Claim. A meeting on the lower level, the mundane level, will be the way we start out again, just when there's so much at stake.* Of course, she was always doing that, she knew, it was always "everything at stake." And life isn't like that. *But it is,* the other little voice inside insisted. *When you go to the grocery store, whether you turn down one street or the next can change your whole life. Everybody knows that. Or the way you start a conversation. It* is *all at stake. All the time.*

She let herself imagine David waiting at the gate as he usually was when she came back from somewhere. How many times? The gray ponytail, the strong, gentle, patient face. David, so tall. Holding her tight and swinging her around. The whooshing, wonderful, wild feeling of being up against him. All those pheromones, his scent. They say that familiar smells are what astronauts miss most up in space. So they packaged up little sniffers of Joy for them. Joy perfume or detergent, she couldn't remember which.

I love the way he smells, she thought. *Like I used to love to smell the top of my baby's head. Breathing it in, like breathing in love. The feeling that sweeps over you like ether. It changes you that much. Puts you in a different state. You're floating.*

The plane's engines, her surroundings, the seatback in front of her, all spun back into view. She started to pull out the in-flight magazine. Tight elastic, though, it seemed to want to stay in there. She stretched her cramped legs as best she could, resettling herself in her seat. On her lap, LeeAnn held a Sue Grafton mystery novel along with her brown leather planner that was about the same size as the paperback. She fidgeted with them now, planning, worrying, once again lost in thought.

During her eight long weeks in the Russian arctic, living in a tent and scraping endlessly at the permafrost on a project that was under-funded, over-ambitious, and not very fruitful, LeeAnn had soaked up too much sun to be in style. Her burnished bronze skin, stretched tight over those cheekbones, contrasted with the pale, worn texture of what she called her MASH outfit, her usual summer airplane garb.

She wore a faded-green denim miniskirt that fit splendidly, an olive sleeveless T-shirt with "Vallarta" printed neatly over one breast, and a medium-weight gold chain that disappeared under the T-shirt; whatever was on it was hidden from view. One black satin bra strap peeked out slightly at the shoulder of her T-shirt. Seven-year-old brown leather sandals from Crete and a tan canvas waist pack completed the pragmatic and nearly indestructible outfit.

LeeAnn had great affection for her clothes, which she kept forever. Like her friends, clothing generally had to have accumulated some longevity and familiarity to be of any real value to her. Her seatmate this morning, however, seemed like she might be an exception to that rule. LeeAnn had liked Pamela the minute she'd stowed her blue-and-green cross-training bag and sat down, providing that sense of relief the traveler always feels with the discovery that an assigned seat companion looks like an actual human being.

The two women had had more than an hour on the ground to get acquainted while some engine part—*LeeAnn didn't want to even think about which one*—was being checked. So they'd talked quite a bit, jumping into instant camaraderie with total comfort and abandon, like jumping into a warm pond in summer. Though now that it was over, she had the feeling she might have said too much, both about David, and about the Summer Project.

LeeAnn glanced over. At the moment, her new friend was hunched over a small pocket mirror as only contact wearers can hunch, probing with a tastefully manicured finger, intent on a problem in her left eye. In her late forties, Pamela had expensive platinum streaks in wavy ash-blonde hair, top-of-the-line athletic shoes, four kids, a personal trainer, and what seemed a totally non-nourishing relationship with her husband. "Nothing. Zero, zip, nada. Beyond a good spirit of cooperation. We live our own lives, though most of mine revolves around supporting his," Pamela had revealed during that long wait on the ground.

"And that's okay for you?" LeeAnn asked.

"It's *Oh-Kay*," Pamela answered, careful to accent both syllables evenly before going on to talk about her four teenage boys. She seemed to have a good attitude, LeeAnn observed, despite the affluence that she felt so often ruined people. (Affluence was not one of LeeAnn's current problems; she was still up to her knees in student debt six years after getting her masters in archaeology, an occupation that was notoriously underpaid anyhow.)

Pamela was currently wrestling with the rigors of her husband's high-echelon corporate transfer from Atlanta to the Portland-Beaverton area, so she had talked about architects and private schools. Then they'd talked about the dig LeeAnn had just come from, and about New York where they'd both grown up, before finally getting onto the subject of the Summer Project. Pamela was only the second person LeeAnn had talked to about the project, besides her family, since Peter had insisted they keep it quiet till they were ready to do it. As he said, "In this throw-away world, there's nothing deader than last week's idea." So she'd been resisting the urge to talk about it.

But then when she heard herself trying to describe it, the whole concept had seemed kind of absurd; she noticed Pamela looking more than a little incredulous. But once started, LeeAnn felt she had no choice but to keep rattling on, on the lookout for glazed eyes and a repeat of the *Airplane* movie scenario, till an especially noisy takeoff had interrupted her ordeal. Pamela still hadn't told her what she thought of it, which was kind of a letdown.

LeeAnn's seatmate was still fussing with her eye. "How are you doing with that?" LeeAnn asked. Pamela folded the mirror, put it away in her Gucci purse, and twisted around to assess the line in front of the restrooms. "Still bothering you?"

"Damn contacts." Pamela let out a little sigh. "I guess I better go deal with them; that line's not getting any shorter." She unbuckled and stood up. She wore spiffy custom stonewashed jeans and a hand-done pale-blue decorative sweatshirt that was not ostentatious–no kittens in sequins or anything like that. She seemed about LeeAnn's size.

"Be back in a minute." Then she disappeared down the aisle, leaving LeeAnn to wonder if the woman thought she was a total nutcase. LeeAnn sighed. The only other person she'd broken Peter's rule with was Martyn Williams the day before yesterday, and that was just an entirely different experience. Looking back on it now, it seemed almost unreal. Storybook stuff.

It was her last day in Vladivostok, pouring down rain outside; LeeAnn had stopped at the desk of the fairly crummy hotel where she was staying to try to find out where she could get some laundry done in a hurry. It seemed pretty clear that's what he was trying to find out too– he was standing there with a laundry bag in his hand. They waited till the clerk got off the phone, but the answer, delivered in some detail, was complicated and less than encouraging. LeeAnn decided to give up on the laundry, but in the process she and Martyn got to talking. It turned out he was Canadian, and an expedition guide. He had just come back from a whitewater trip down an unexplored river in China and was attending a conference of explorers.

"And that's how you make your living?"

He nodded. "Most of my life. About twenty-five years." He was fifty, he said. "Then recently I got involved in something else."

"Which is?"

"It's . . . I'm a distributor of blue-green algae."

LeeAnn was astonished. *"You have to be kidding!!* That's what my mother does. The algae from Klamath Lake?"

"That's right."

"That's where I live!"

And, of course, the coincidence meant they had to sit down and get acquainted. Soft-spoken, very gentle in his manner, about six feet tall, Martyn had reddish-blond hair that was thinning, unassuming hazel eyes, and a face more weathered than David's. He didn't volunteer much about his own experiences, but when she'd looked at a brochure he showed her, she found out he was the first human ever to lead successful expeditions to three extremes of our earth–the North Pole, the South Pole, and Mount Everest.

"I'm in awe," she said, and they immediately got into a discussion about fear. LeeAnn figured if this was her one chance in her lifetime to talk to someone like this, she wanted to learn as much as she could about the unwelcome phenomenon of fear that had haunted, taunted, and crippled her so often in her life. *Fear.* Clearly, he must know it well.

Indeed he did. But he told her how he coped. "In our business," he told her later on that long rainy afternoon, as they drank glasses of

Russian tea that scalded their lips, "we *know* that visualizations work. We know the power that they have. That helps a lot."

LeeAnn believed him. She tried to imagine the number of times, in some unbelievably awful situation at 80° below, that he had had to call on that power to keep himself and the people in his expedition alive. She hoped she would remember what he said the next time she began to lose it. *Just visualize success. Write down what you want to have happen. Read it over every day. Think about it. Repeat it to yourself.* LeeAnn promised herself she would.

After they talked about fear, they got onto family. After being single for many years, Martyn had finally gotten married about four years ago to a woman he clearly adored, who had two boys. And then they'd had another son. He showed her some pictures.

"That's Eolo, which means Greek god of the wind. He's the oldest. And there's Tavi. He's our middle child. His name is Hopi for watersong. And Teja means rainbow." His wife was beautiful. The children were beautiful, and so, obviously, were his feelings about them.

"Since Teja was born, I haven't been doing so many trips. I've been staying at home and my desire to do any big expeditions has just dropped away." His focus lately, Martyn told her, had been on being with his family and trying to help make the world better for his kids. Recently, he'd come up with a plan. "Hey, so did I," LeeAnn exclaimed.

"Or maybe the plan came up with me. I had this dream, . . ."

"Tell me about it."

"Basically what happened is just before my fiftieth birthday, I dreamed that I was on a train with my family and it was being attacked by four hundred soldiers. I remember the number four hundred. It's kind of hard to picture just where the scene was. Maybe in Afghanistan or someplace like that. The soldiers were pretty rough looking, not all that well dressed.

"I expected it to go into a chase scene, but instead I found myself getting off the train and somehow approaching them. And I said to them, 'This isn't how it has to be. You know, you don't have to be controlled like this. There are other opportunities.' And so I got their attention somehow. Then I ended up helping them make the transition from being soldiers to being self-sufficient farmers. Not controlled by anybody."

"That's a partnership dream, do you know that?" LeeAnn said excitely. "It's about turning dominators into partnership people. Have you ever read *The Chalice and the Blade* by Riane Eisler?"

"No. I don't think…"

"I'm sorry. I interrupted you. Go on."

"Well, the next morning I told my wife about my dream, and we talked about it, and that day the idea came to me." What he was planning to do, Martyn told her, was to organize what he called the Pole to Pole 2000 expedition. Twelve young people, 20 to 25, selected from many different cultures, would leave the North Pole early in 1999. They'd travel in teams by different routes, stopping in sixty cities along the way, participating in youth events and collecting people's new millennial resolutions–their visions of how the world should be, and their vows to help make it so. Then the teams would rejoin at the South Pole and place the collected vows there at the dawn of the year 2000.

"This is *exactly* the focus that the world needs!" she said excitedly. "It's perfect. It's wonderful. Think of the drama, that everyone in the world could follow. They'd get to know all the personalities, they'd learn about geography." He showed her a pledge he'd been writing that people could repeat every day. It ended with, "My words will be frozen in time, my actions will impact generations for the next thousand years."

"It's wonderful," she said. When LeeAnn told him about the Summer Project, her ideas about the time zones and one global celebration, and he seemed to think that was an awfully good idea too.

"Those twelve people that you pick to make the trip," she said. "You're going to need twelve alternates, too, aren't you?" He nodded. "So, in a way, you'll have twenty-four participants."

"That's right."

"Do you think there's any chance you might be able to pick one finalist from each time zone?"

"It might be possible." Then they began to consider the zones that had almost no population, so it might not be feasible. Probably wouldn't be. Oh, well. She showed him Peter's drawing of the *earthflower*, which was what they'd decided to call it, with the twenty-four zones connecting at the poles, arranged like the petals on a blossom. "See how beautiful it is," LeeAnn said, "each one so unique, each one containing every element of society and climate and ocean."

"I wonder," he began, and then stopped.

"Go ahead."

"I wonder if in the invitation to your celebration you might ask people to send their promises to be included in the microchips that we take to the pole."

"Of course," she said. "Of course we'll do it. I don't even have to ask the others. Because this is exactly what we've been dreaming about–something that would provide a totally global focus–a global moment–for almost everyone. Talk about metaphor. Exploring our earth and the depths of our courage at the same time. Our ability to grow."

Then she spent some time imagining aloud how their two projects might tie in together, and he took some time to tell her how things were shaping up for his. He already had some Canadian newspapers interested, some funds raised, even some hopes of reaching someone at the White House. "That's through another algae distributor my wife knows who allegedly sings in a choir with someone who works there."

"Networking," LeeAnn said, and Martyn smiled.

LeeAnn wondered why she'd never heard about Martyn before, and he replied that he'd never wanted to be in the news, but now he was willing to be. However, he confessed he was more fearful of that than of any expedition.

Then he had a plane to catch. And just then, LeeAnn had begun feeling a little hesitant. He was already much farther advanced in his plan than they were with the 22nd Century Group, and she didn't want to seem to be piggybacking on his trip. Also, his plan contemplated brave acts, while hers only involved sending party invitations. "Well, think about it," she told him after she gave him her e-mail address. "I'll wait to hear from you."

They said goodbye then.

"Don't you want this back?" she asked, holding up the copy of his brochure.

"No, you keep it," he said. Then he got in the clanky elevator and went back to his room to pack.

One good thing about the encounter with Martyn, LeeAnn thought now, as she looked down at the scenery of Northern California, *whether anything ever comes of it or not, is if through sheer chance I met him, then there have to be lots of other people out there quietly planning their own transformative activity for the millennium. We just need all of us to get together and link, and we can do* wonderful *things.*

Martyn had said he'd be in touch as soon as he got through white-water rafting down some wild river in the Yukon on his way home. She just hoped he'd take care of himself and be safe.

Pamela came back just then and sat down. LeeAnn hadn't mentioned meeting Martyn to Pam; there was no point blabbing and bragging about him until something actually came of it.

"Better?" LeeAnn asked.

"Better." Pamela's eye looked slightly irritated. "I was wondering," she said, "if you don't mind my asking."

"No, of course not."

" How much is that project of yours going to cost?"

"Including the envelopes, postage, the news releases, RSVPs and everything, not counting the labor, of course, about ten thousand dollars."

"And how are you going to fund it?"

"We're each contributing twenty-five hundred."

"Of your own money?"

"We'd like to do more, of course, but twenty-five hundred seemed about right. My friend Jeffrey said if he just didn't buy a new bicycle this year he could afford it." Pamela didn't say anything right away; she was just kind of shaking her head. "And then we each get to pick two hundred and fifty names and organizations."

"Out of the whole planet?"

"Mmhmmm. The people we think would be the least likely to let us down."

Pamela was quiet for a moment. Then she said, "Well, it's certainly a novel idea. *Save the world on your summer vacation,*" she added in a slightly acerbic tone and LeeAnn felt like she'd been hit in the teeth.

"Not that I don't wish you well," Pamela added quickly, maybe realizing that she'd hurt LeeAnn's feelings. "I do."

LeeAnn was sorry now she'd ever started telling her about it. If this was the kind of reaction they were going to start getting from people . . . But she laughed as though she didn't mind. "I know it's kind of bizarre."

Pamela's smile and the silence that followed signaled they were both through with that subject for a while. "That trip of yours must have been really something," Pamela said, "Mucking around in the tundra, living in a tent . . ."

"I remember thinking," LeeAnn said, grateful for the change in subject, "that if you could have taken all the bugs in, say, one cubic yard of air and squooshed them all together, you'd still have had something about the size of a meatball."

"God. You couldn't pay me."

"The abundance of life up there is amazing."

Pamela was still shaking her head and saying, "Uh-*uh*. Not me."

"But look at it this way. I also got to study a ten-thousand-year-old house made entirely out of mammoth bone–two hundred and some in all."

"You're kidding."

"These huge bones fitted together so intricately and artistically . . ." (It was hard to describe, impossible, really.) ". . . in a dome-shaped structure. With painted musical instruments that they found inside."

"Think of the acoustics," Pamela commented. "What a treasure."

LeeAnn nodded. She felt more at home talking about the past than the future. "That area of the arctic is one of the most pristine in terms of archaeology. Of course, it's also sitting on some of the greatest oil and gas reserves in the world, and you know who's going to win *that* fight."

"I'm sure."

"It's kind of the Holy Grail of archaeology to connect the cultures of the world via the arctic." LeeAnn said.

"So did they hunt all those animals, I wonder?" Pamela asked after a moment.

"I wondered that too. Apparently not. Apparently most of them had been recycled from bones of various ages that were lying around. Just good use of a natural resource. Very little evidence of hunting. *Lots* of evidence of good taste."

"You wouldn't have imagined that about people that long ago, would you?"

"Oh yes you would. People used to be lots more civilized early on. We know that."

Pamela looked at her quizzically. "Just *how* do we know that?"

"Well, for one thing, most people settled in places which couldn't possibly be defended–places chosen just for their beauty. We've got lots better ways of dating things now. We know that ten thousand years ago people didn't fight as much. Men and women did the same kind of work, and they lived in communities where most of the dwellings were more or less equal. And they spent a lot more time creating art than they did making weapons."

"You're saying Eden existed."

"Without the gender bias, of course it did. Here," she said, reaching for the chain around her neck, thinking, *Here I go with my show and tell*, "This is the kind of thing we're finding. All over the world. By the thousands." She pulled out a small, graceful figure, a female torso carved in bone that looked very old and yellowed.

"That's beautiful! Wow."

"It's a replica, of course. David made it for me. The original's been dated at twenty-five thousand years."

"You're *kid*-ding," said Pamela.

"I found it in what used to be Yugoslavia." LeeAnn held it out away from her chest and Pamela reached to take the figure in her hand. Grasping it by the waist, rubbing her thumb on the smooth but deeply pitted surface of it, she took her time examining the carving, giving LeeAnn time to remember the moment of discovery in a valley east of Zagreb, almost fifteen years ago now. The grid she was kneeling in, the brush in her hand, the sun on her back. Then just the torso, carved in fragile bone, lying in the dry powdery earth. It all came back, almost every time.

"Wow," said Pamela again. "It's spec-*tac*-ular. It's *won-der*-ful." A lot of what Pamela said was in the way she emphasized syllables. "Your boyfriend made this copy, hmm? He does gorgeous work."

"He certainly does; he's a sculptor," LeeAnn added, unnecessarily. "I mean most of what he does is *big*," and she gestured, holding her hands wide apart to demonstrate. It was awkward though; Pamela was still holding the chain that was around LeeAnn's neck; LeeAnn thought it probably looked like she was about to clap her on the ears.

So she put her hands down, remembering as she did, David at his workbench carving away with a photo of her find pinned up in front of him. "You know it's always *your* body I'm sculpting," he said. "It's always your body I'm thinking of." After that, when he touched her, LeeAnn always felt like a work of art as it was being formed. And she learned to celebrate him in the same way, so they both felt the force that flowed from the figure she had found and he had recreated.

"And this is the kind of thing," Pamela asked thoughtfully, as she let go of the figure at last, "that you were looking for in Russia?"

LeeAnn noticed the lunch cart approaching; she realized she was hungry. "I work at some of the upper Paleolithic sites in northern Europe and Asia where a lot of the artifacts are being found. The erotic figures are only part of it, but it's my particular area. I don't advertise what I do because a lot of people get the wrong idea."

"Like what?"

"They think we're out to prove the world used to worship a female god."

"Aren't you?*"*

"Of course not. That has nothing to do with it. It's what the culture was like that's important. It only makes sense that because new life comes from the female body, people used to assume that's where the magic was coming from. Then they got it right later, and started adding the male. Have you ever read *The Chalice and the Blade?* By Riane Eisler?"

"No."

"You know what it's about?"

"Uh-uh."

"It came out in about '87, and someone, I forgot who, Ashley Montagu I think, said it's the most important book since *On the Origin of Species*. I met her once. Anyway, it's about the difference between the partnership and dominator ways of living. All of our actions are either one or the other, and we all have both qualities. Right now we're living in a society that's still mainly dominator-run. But we used to have a mainly partnership society. Linking rather than ranking. Horizontal rather than vertical.

Then for some reason, about ten thousand years ago, there was a split between male and female–personally, I've always thought the quarrel in the Garden of Eden was probably over the sex of god. Which is pretty silly when you consider that nobody's ever seen God, dressed or undressed, so who really knows for sure?"

Pamela laughed.

"Anyway, something happened to unbalance the partnership model–nobody really knows what. Women began to be thought of as property. Men started to use their physical strength to dominate them, fight over them, compete to acquire more of them and more wealth to adorn them. And the whole dumb false value system got started." LeeAnn was launched on her favorite topic now. There was no stopping her.

"Children watching their mothers getting beat up on, or being beaten themselves, started thinking it was okay to abuse anybody or anything smaller and weaker than themselves. Other people, other races, other creatures."

"That makes sense," said Pamela. "The whole hierarchical thing."

"And that started the endless cycle of repression and war that we're still caught in today. It's basically an anti-pleasure, anti-life system that I don't think either sex wants. Back when we were equal everything was better. The thing I think a lot of men forget is that they were once part of a free-will society that chose to honor both sexes. It was not imposed on them, nor do women want to take over the world now. In fact, in the dominator mode, I think men have had it a whole lot worse than we have."

"How so?"

"Sorry. I do tend to run at the mouth."

"You sound like you know a lot about the subject."

"I'm doing my dissertation on partnership societies."

Flight attendants were uncovering trays for the people in the row ahead. "So, no wonder things are all screwed up," Pamela said. "That's why the world doesn't work."

"Hey, when the most fundamental link between us–the one between woman and man–is also our *weakest* link, how can we expect anything *else* to work right? So that's the first thing we need to fix."

Pamela's eyes sparkled. She had a nice, crinkly smile. "Are you saying that if we made love more, the world might be a better place?"

"Abso-frigging-lutely!" They both cracked up. "But, unfortunately these days, not enough love gets made."

Pamela was nodding her agreement. "Which is kind of ironic when you consider that's the one commodity we're so desperately short of."

"Instead, we get unhappy, obese, hostile, and morose. Which is so sad when the magic that makes everything work is right there for us to use. It's approved, heaven-sent if you will." LeeAnn paused. "Which brings us back to the fact that it's really just the system to blame. I firmly believe . . ."

"Chicken cordon bleu or baked sole here?" the young Asian stewardess inquired.

"I have *found*," Pamela said, looking up with a wicked smile, "that it's normally the *kiss of death* when cordon bleu is offered on any menu."

The stewardess laughed to indicate she knew what she was serving. Pamela finally elected to take the cordon bleu anyway. LeeAnn, who was on a slow path to becoming vegetarian, accepted a miserly briquette of fish covered with library paste, surrounded by small dabs of unidentified matter.

Pamela sat contemplating the unveiled tray before her for some time before finally lowering her fork into it. Then she smiled. "I've got one for you," she said. "Someone asked me this the other day. What if . . . ," and she had a look of fun about her as she started. "What if, instead of being in pairs, people were in threesomes? What if you had to choose between being one woman with two husbands for your life partners or two women with one man?"

"Having two men or being one of two women? That's a good one. Well first of all, I'd rather not, but if I had to . . ."

"It's just the three of you," Pamela went on. "Desert island. And you can have sex with whoever you want to. Whomever. Or not. That's up to you."

"Wow. Well . . ." LeeAnn laughed.

"I'll take two guys, any time," said the stewardess who was busy serving the overstuffed businessman across the aisle.

Pamela grinned. "At the same time?" she whispered to LeeAnn, and they both laughed.

"Me, too, I think," LeeAnn said with uncertainty. "Two men. But then, of course, you'd miss the whole woman thing. It's great to be with other women. Tough choice."

LeeAnn's mind went back to her own choices, that really weren't so different. And the night she'd thought about all summer, when she and David had sat up till dawn talking. "I'm so sorry," he said. "I've been thinking about it so long," he said. "and I just can't hide my feelings any more. I don't know if I can go through the rest of my life this way."

She had started to cry and then tears rolled down his cheeks as well. "Oh, honey," he'd said then, reaching out to take her in his arms. "I don't want to hurt you." *Dear, honest David.* Even in their distance they were close.

LeeAnn looked at her watch, and then out the window again. She would be seeing him in less than an hour. She wondered if she would want to stay in Oregon if they weren't together.

"So how did you ever get out to Oregon?" Pamela asked then, as though she'd heard LeeAnn's thought.

"Oh? Oh, after my mother's divorce, she got so enamored of the idea that her grandmother had been a Klamath Indian–everybody was very big on origins then–that she pulled us out of school early my sophomore year and loaded us in the station wagon . . ."

"What kind?" Pamela interrupted.

"Of station wagon? Oh. '71 Ambassador with fake-wood trim. Blue."

Pamela nodded as though that were okay.

"Complete with our school transcripts. So we headed out to make a new life, straight through Kansas and all. She and I would be singing, *California Here We Come.* At that point we thought we were going to Klamath, California, where the Klamath river empties into the ocean, but it turned out she lived in Oregon–and my mother would be keeping time, banging on the steering wheel. And the whole time my brother–he's a year younger–is sitting in the back seat, glum; he didn't want to come."

"Oh."

"Maggie couldn't handle it though, once we got out there, so we ended up back in New York in the fall."

"Too country?"

LeeAnn nodded. "Too many of the guys who asked her out had that little, round worn place on the back pocket of their jeans."

"Chewing tobacco."

"Or snuff. Whatever you call it. She couldn't hack that. Maggie's a city girl. Plus my brother got into Music and Art High School, he plays violin and viola–so we had to go back. Right back through Kansas . . ."

"Singing what this time?"

"American Pie, mostly." The song echoed softly in her head. "Peter had met the producer in Central Park and he gave him a tape, which my brother finally *deigned* to share with us on the way back." Here she was, accenting syllables like Pamela.

"But how'd you finally get to *live* in Oregon?" Pamela persisted.

"Oh. I met David when I was out on vacation and just basically never went back."

"How long ago was that?"

"Six years. We bought the house two years ago." *And he moved out in May.* LeeAnn was quiet for a minute, letting the years play, the good parts anyway, then changed the subject in her head–switched tracks. "I think the best way to illustrate Maggie–my favorite memory of my mother is the time she got caught on the top of the Central Park reservoir fence . . ."

Pamela laughed. "Oh, no."

"Actually, there were several fence stories involving my mother."

Pamela shook her head. "I don't think our childhoods could have been more different. Great Neck was pretty tame. Which is probably what's the matter with me. And, of course, it was earlier; ten years makes a big difference. Plus, having a mother like yours."

"Maggie's–mercurial. A cause lady. Very affected by matters of the heart. Very passionate about what she believes in. Whatever is her idea of the moment, or whoever she loves at the moment, boy does she love them."

"You don't take after her, of course."

LeeAnn acknowledged with a quick grin but went on. "She's always one extreme or the other, as far as hope goes. Which is I guess what I do."

Pamela laughed. "So you admit it."

"From the ultimate high to the ultimate low. I'm always diving into the unattainable and then imagining the worst possible scenarios right after committing myself to the best."

"I don't tend to do that," Pamela said. "I guess what I do is just set myself a norm, kind of set parameters for my life and plan neither to exceed nor fall below some kind of standard of happiness."

Parameters, LeeAnn thought. Another buzzword for our times. Dusted off and brought to popularity out of need, *perimeters* no longer being strong enough. Two quite different words, the one having to do with borders and the other regulating a whole function. Much more intrusive.

"I just don't let myself explore those frontiers," Pamela said. "Too afraid of getting hurt, I guess."

"I would probably try to do that too if I knew how," LeeAnn said. "I would like to live without major hurt. But somehow I end up giving myself over to things. Utterly and entirely. I'm kind of like a one-speed hair dryer, I guess. That's what David says. Either I'm on or I'm off."

Pamela laughed with her and then regarded her thoughtfully for a moment. "We'll have to trade notes, you know? Sometime. Say a month from now. And see where our differing ways have brought us. See what our quality of life and love has been."

"Good idea." LeeAnn had forgiven her for the earlier remark about saving the world on her summer vacation. You couldn't really blame her since that's exactly what they *were* trying to do.

Pamela pulled a card out of her Gucci bag and LeeAnn dug around in her waist pack till she came up with a fairly crumpled one, which she handed to Pamela. "Sorry. Oops. I think it's got something written on it."

"Do you need it?"

LeeAnn looked.

"No, that's okay."

"A one-speed hair dryer," Pamela repeated. It tickled her.

"And as unpredictable, David also tells me," (LeeAnn's mind was still on appliances) "as a vibrator in a backpack."

Pamela stared at LeeAnn for a moment.

"Oh yes," LeeAnn confirmed.

And then Pamela absolutely lost it. The florid fellow across the aisle looked over, but clearly didn't know what they were laughing about. "That didn't actually *happen* to you," Pamela said when she recovered.

"He'll never let me forget it," LeeAnn laughed. "Right at the check-in counter at Klamath Falls International, when he was putting me on a plane to Bulgaria. Battery-operated."

Pamela was continuing to crack up. "Wow."

"I take the batteries out now."

"I guess!"

"Can I get those out of your way?" The older attendant was back to collect their trays. A senior stewardess, dyed red hair and probably thirty-five years in the air. She eyed the tray in front of L.A.

LeeAnn had cut her fish briquette exactly in half and then forced herself to eat the right side. Plus, she'd consumed half of a sliced canned peach drenched in syrup and sitting on a pale lettuce leaf. The small turd of a candy bar she had spurned, but watched now, a little regretfully, as the stewardess took it away.

"So will your boyfriend be meeting you at the gate?" Pamela asked.

"Do I get to meet him?"

"I'm not sure . . ." *Bad luck to declare he would be there.* "I hope he will be." *Okay to express a preference.*

"Then you'll go straight home from there?"

"No, we'll be hanging around Portland a couple days because my friend Audrey is flying in from New York on Thursday to start our project. We thought we might use the time while we're waiting to drive over to the Gorge. Maybe sail a little and look for some used equipment. Till now, we've been taking turns on a big old relic that a friend of ours left when he went into the Peace Corps. An original Windsurfer, probably twenty years old."

"Oh, really?" They chatted on then in a desultory sort of way for a few more minutes. About windsurfing, the Peace Corps, and other things, but by the time the plane got about even with Salem, conversation slowed as the women began the separation process so familiar to talkative travelers everywhere.

LeeAnn supposed they might get in touch. More likely they wouldn't; still, they'd both benefited, she thought. For wasn't one of the best perks of travel just connecting with another humanoid without all the usual complications? *Funny how your life sounds when you're telling it to someone else.*

"Well, I hope all goes well this summer for you," Pamela said at last, in a kind of formal closure statement. "You seem to have a lot riding on it."

"I do."

And that was kind of *it*, those last words between them signaling as clear an ending as when it says on your computer, "Are you sure you want to sign off? Enter Y for Yes." *Yes.*

A few minutes later, LeeAnn realized she'd been staring out the window for quite a while without really seeing. All those trees. It seemed crazy there weren't enough.

Then suddenly the plane began slanting down fairly steeply, as if the pilot had forgotten to start descending earlier. The seatbelt sign flashed urgently and then his dulcet voice came on to announce smoothly that they'd be on the ground in Portland in five minutes and everyone ought to start gathering their personal items. LeeAnn was instantly soothed. Voice training, she reflected, was probably an important part of pilot school, that rich mellow tone so vital in convincing us everything is okay.

Looking out, she saw the Willamette River ahead. So they *were* close. Dutifully following the instructions to break camp, LeeAnn zipped up her planner and put it away safely in her waist pack. Trees and cars and houses below were getting closer.

Do I have everything? she wondered, then thought about the Sue Grafton paperback she'd taken out when she first came aboard. Before she started talking to Pamela. She always carried a book in her pack in case she got bored, though fiction reading was legal really only at bedtime.

She felt under her seat, then put her head down to look. Then, thinking it might have slid forward when they started down, she tried uselessly to lift up and look ahead as if it might be floating in the air or something. Eventually she had to tap the woman ahead of her on the shoulder and ask her to check. Then the couple behind got interested. By the time detective Kinsey Millhone's adventure story had been located two seats ahead and the red beefy man across the aisle had illegally undone his belt to bring it back triumphantly, LeeAnn felt a complete fool. She hated losing things. It always cost her her confidence.

CHAPTER FOUR

Hood River

LeeAnn closed the door of the room at the Best Western very gently, and made her way to the end of the corridor where double doors led out onto a grassy slope that beckoned her down to the water's edge. The wind was up, a breeze blowing the white shirt she wore over a gray silk bikini that modeled her breasts in silver. She carried her waist pack and a towel from the hotel in one hand, the new binoculars in the other.

Standing as close to the riverbank as she could get, she raised the glasses to her eyes and took in the scene. It was spectacular, with brightly colored sails like butterflies all up and down the wide sparkling river. The thing that made the Columbia Gorge spectacular for world-class windsurfing, LeeAnn had learned, was that the really powerful current of the river goes one way, downstream of course, while the strong winds, funneling through the deep canyon, come upstream straight off the ocean, teasing and tossing the water into magnificent turmoil. It was the most alive inland body of water she'd ever seen.

To her right, sheltered by an island, a beginner class from the windsurf school flopped and flailed about in the area that had been roped off for them. Wearing life vests, and color-coded T-shirts that marked them as rank amateurs to be watched, herded, and retrieved as necessary, the newest flock of recruits was tooling about on great big boards with little bitty sails, so happy to be finally up and moving that even inevitable collision with another sailor would not deter them from their appointed course.

LeeAnn laughed as a triple pile-up occurred, then turned the glasses to focus on the bridge to the left where a steady stream of cars and trucks and camper vans, mostly with Gorge racks, board after board on top, streamed across from Vancouver on the Washington side. These were the board-heads who pursued an endless round from one wind-site to another, following every rumor and report to catch that elusive air. LeeAnn watched a guy in his truck and imagined she could lip-read what he was saying to the others on his CB.

Turning the Nikons to the right again, scanning upstream, way off in the distance, she could spot the expert sailors, plying their way between the riverbanks, nimbly avoiding the barges and other commercial traffic that passed up and down before them. Having one of those humongous things coming at you could make a windsurfer feel like the tiniest butterfly on earth. But one that couldn't fly to get out of the way. *These glasses are great*, LeeAnn thought, as she sat down on the grass to look some more. Still, it was curious the way David had presented them to her; it was a gesture so unlike him.

He had *not* been at the gate to greet her when she and Pamela got off the plane, and that had almost caused her heart failure. She was already feeling rattled about the scene with the lost book. Then they'd come down in a kind of B-minus landing, scuffing the wheels several times as they hit. And then it had seemed to take *forever* to get out of the plane.

So her heart was palpitating as she finally reached that critical turn in the passageway where you can see if anybody's there to meet you. Her eyes searched the skyline of the small, anxious group standing behind the ropes, looking for that familiar silhouette of David that usually rose above the rest. But it wasn't there, and suddenly all seemed lost. She felt Pamela see the change in her expression, like it went *ker-clunk*. As though it were almost audible.

"Maybe he's a little late," Pamela said, as they paused uncertainly at the gate.

"Never. David's incapable of being late." They stood for a moment, watching other people embrace, and LeeAnn was conscious of the awkwardness of it all. "I know he wouldn't just desert me in Portland," she said, trying to keep it light. She hadn't thought to listen to the announcement that had just come over the P.A.–it could have been for her. "Do you have a bag to get?"

"No, this is it," Pamela said. LeeAnn had mountains of gear.

"You were going to go find a rental car, as I remember." She felt numb.

"Yeah, I forgot to reserve one."

"Then I'll walk you as far as Hertz." They started off. "So call me," LeeAnn said. "Or if you're ever home in Great Neck, and you're going to be in the city, call my mom."

"I'd like to do that."

"Actually, that's her new number on the back of my card. I think you'd enjoy her."

"Well, that's an understatement. I know I would." Pamela laughed. "Your mother sounds like a real trip. How come you had her number written down? She just move?"

"No. She was getting crank calls."

"Sign of our times."

"Isn't it something?" *Where was David?*

LeeAnn and Pamela looked good together, striding along, no doubt about it. LeeAnn in her MASH outfit, at about the perfect peak in her womanhood, Pamela with her muted pastel sweatshirt and tailored jeans, a decade or so older, but giving promise that the aging process would be so gradual as to be almost imperceptible. A few more lines, that was all.

"So what does your mother do?" Pamela asked.

"Well, she was going to go to med school at one point a few years ago. Now she's becoming a massage therapist, and blue green algae distributor, the algae from Klamath Lake."

"What's it for?"

"It's a food. It's a natural food."

"I hadn't heard about that."

"Call my mom. I'm sure she'd be glad to tell you."

"Thanks. Maybe I will," Pamela said and then was quiet. LeeAnn wondered if that last remark had sounded pushy, like she was trying to sell algae. She was about to start chattering about rental cars, preparing a monologue to fill the silence when, a long way off, as far away as you could see in that long corridor, she spotted him, broken field running, carrying a small bag that bumped against his knee as he came toward her, dodging luggage carts and old ladies. LeeAnn's heart hit her throat and then began bouncing around in her chest.

He was wearing his tan Sportif shorts and an old khaki short-sleeved shirt from when he'd been a cop. It was taking a while for him to get to her, so LeeAnn had time to watch him without his watching her, which was kind of like seeing him for the first time. His age, forty-five, was definitely there in the lines on his face and the graying hair, but his were the rugged, craggy kind of good looks teenage girls go wild for. And his body had become young again since she'd known him and gotten him running and lifting. He still hadn't seen her.

LeeAnn wondered about the bag he carried. It was plastic, green-and-white striped, with the kind of fancy self-handle that upper crust stores affected. Not a gift, surely. David seldom gave gifts. He also almost never carried anything–he'd make a detour at the mall to put even the smallest item in the van. And he was definitely never late. But here he came barreling along, nimbly avoiding a suitcase on wheels, headed to meet her at last.

It felt like a film slowing down at the end. Or a commercial where people are running toward one another in slow motion, and the slower the "mo," the more significant the drama, until in final freeze frame it's frigging profound.

At last he glanced up and saw her. A current passed between them and that's when her meltdown started.

David had been excruciatingly embarrassed about being late. After they'd finished hugging and shmushing and introducing Pamela, who seemed suitably impressed, and seeing her to her car rental, he'd explained what happened. When he knew LeeAnn's plane would be delayed by almost two hours, he'd wandered around, got ensnared by the fancy gadgets in an airport shop and then hopelessly hooked on some high-powered waterproof binoculars.

"I must have gone back by there three or four times trying to decide," he said, "but I felt guilty about the price, so at the last minute I got the van out of short-term parking and raced over to the mall to get a better deal." For one of the first times since she'd known him, David seemed aware he sometimes spent money foolishly.

"But I did think they'd be nice to have for our trip down the lake," he repeated, as he opened the green-striped bag right on the spot and handed them to her.

So the windsurfing trip meant something to him, too, LeeAnn thought, surveying the compact, costly instrument he had placed in her hand. And she'd thought he wasn't at the gate because he didn't love her anymore. Shades of *Gift of the Magi*. Maybe he did love her after all. Did it mean anything to their future that he'd chosen something as *farseeing* as a reunion gift? Something that could gaze into other orbits?

Of course that could work two ways.
Stop it! she told herself. *Stop analyzing, stop symbolizing. Just live in the moment.* Which should not be that difficult today. For these were all delicious moments. The last time they made love had been fun and bawdy. Then in the midst of the giggles and rolling around and play-acting, all of a sudden that holy connection. Suddenly that deep, serious look flowed from his eyes into her mind as he began the journey into outer space that she accompanied him on, sometimes as passenger, sometimes as co-pilot, and sometimes as one being. The magic was still intact. There was still an entity extant on the planet called David/LeeAnn that was whole and perfect unto itself. What a relief. What a joy.

Now David was conked out. The night before, he'd had an order of twelve knives to finish, plus work on the obsidian bust he was hoping to show a dealer in Portland, so he hadn't had any sleep at all. And what energy he'd had left, he'd definitely bequeathed to her. And then some– she felt intensely energized. How wonderful it is to wear a man out, she thought, to help take away all those tensions that if they didn't get released would make him surly. What could be more fun? Making love and making peace.

Smiling to herself, she picked up the binoculars again to look at the sails upstream. One was down. Then up. Another one down. Then, moments later, reborn. A real butterfly wouldn't be able to do that.

Suddenly LeeAnn wanted to sail. Today. This afternoon. Right now. They hadn't planned to do it till tomorrow, but why not? *It's either that or sit around the room, catching up on my e-mail and watching David sleep.* He said he just wanted to close his eyes for a minute, but if she let him, he'd be out for hours; the man knew how to sleep. And he needed his sleep. She looked at her watch and the idea took hold. *This is a perfect place to practice, and after all, we can't go on the trip till I get my water-start.*

It was true. In light winds, you could do what they call up-haul. You stand on your board, pull the sail up by a rope that's attached to it, grab the boom, and take off. That's what the people playing bumper cars in the kindergarten class next door were doing. But out there in the mid-dle, with the wind ripping and the waves rolling, there was no way you could do that. The only way to get up when you fall out there was to sit in the water, put your foot up on your board, lift the sail just enough to catch the wind and let it pull you up instead of the other way around. Simple enough in theory, but it was a maneuver fraught with difficulty and almost impossible to learn. The process of learning to waterstart was often referred to as slow drowning–for months. Ninety percent of the time you spent in the water, choking on the waves, banging your shins, wrestling a rig with about ten times the wind resistance you have. LeeAnn knew all about it; she'd been working on it for some time without success. But it was important beyond belief. For though she knew there was no logic to it, she still harbored the hope that windsurfing down Klamath Lake with David would prove to be the re-bonding experience they needed, that the lake would somehow work its magic on them.

She stood up, collecting the towel and the binoculars. Then, dangling her waist pack by its strap, she tried to decide what to do with it. She didn't want to put it on under her shirt because it would make a peculiar bulge. And she couldn't wear it outside the shirt because that would really look dumb. Audrey was always bugging her about how the little leather pack wrecked everything LeeAnn wore, and she was finally sensitive to that, yet knew from bitter experience that anything not attached to her would get lost. Finally, she fastened it around her waist with the pack in front and let the shirt flap open over it.

A guy with a black dog on a bright blue leash was coming across the grass. Like most of the people she'd seen in Hood River so far, he looked like a typical board-head. Tan, long sun-bleached hair, twenties. Probably the kind that did triple loops. As he approached, she noted that he seemed to be relatively unscarred and to have all his teeth. For all the thrills it offered, windsurfing was reputed to be a very low injury sport. "Do you know if I can rent a board down there?" LeeAnn asked, indicating the roped off area to the right.

"No, that's just beginners." He must have assumed she was beyond that, which was good. "You need to go on down to Rhonda's other place. That way." He pointed down the asphalt path that led along the riverbank, where a small gaggle of Canadian geese was marching along like pedestrians.

"How far? I'm walking."

"Just a little ways. You go under the bridge, it dead-ends there, you walk into a boatyard. There's a gravel area. You'll see the Gorge Café and the windsurf school's right there."

LeeAnn liked to go under bridges. She thanked him and set out, walking slowly so she could keep an eye on the river and make sure that the sails she was watching and the people in their charge made it successfully from one bank to the other and back again. She was currently keeping track of a pink one, a green, a clear, and a purple one.

Imagine, she thought, *if I could go back to the hotel and tell David that I had water-started.* She started to plan in delicious detail just how she would wake him up to tell him, then realized she was smiling one of those private little smiles to herself just as she passed a couple with a stroller. The woman read her smile in its entirety and they exchanged a grin.

Isn't it funny, LeeAnn mused, *when you've just made love of truly magical quality, how everybody and everything seems to notice.* The first time she and her ex-husband Bo ever did it, she'd walked out of his brownstone onto West Seventy-Fourth Street and a tree had talked to her. Today felt kind of like that.

Lost in thought and in keeping track of those four sails, she passed under the bridge, barely aware of it; usually she looked up from below and studied bridges. Then there was Rhonda Smith's Windsurf School up ahead and the Gorge Café, where a few people lazed in the sun over lunch. *Good idea,* she thought as she walked up the steps into the shop. *He's out cold, I'm out sailing. This is fun.* She told the guy behind the counter what she wanted and he led her back to the rental boards.

"Well, let's see what we've got. Do you water-start?"

She smiled. "I'm trying."

He headed for the longer boards.

"Are you into your harness yet?" He was referring to the body harness with a hook or pulley at belly button level that you attach to the boom to take the strain off your arms.

"Ahhh, no, actually, not yet." LeeAnn didn't do that either. In her mind, there were two dangers attached to wearing a harness. The first, well chronicled in the oral tradition of the sport, was that if a sudden gust came while you were hooked to your sail and you weren't ready for it, you would get "launched," an initially out-of-body experience in which you get snatched up by the wind–hauled up by *God*–flung over your own bow and smashed down again on the water, or worse, the board. Brought back to earth in a hurry. It was why some people wore helmets. Getting launched was an experience that was unknowable unless you actually had it. LeeAnn hadn't. And she wasn't at all sure she was ready for it.

There was a second drawback as well, less feared by most, apparently, but high on LeeAnn's list. This was the *claustrophobia factor*. Just the idea of being under water and still hooked to something was mildly terrifying for someone who tended to panic just getting out of a sweater with a tight neck. For these reasons, LeeAnn had been putting off getting into her harness. Meanwhile the procrastination had done marvelous things for her upper arms.

"You can pick one out over there if you want." He pointed to a pile of harnesses.

"I'll pass."

"You're going to have to commit to it eventually, you know."

"I know." People always used the word *commit* when they spoke about harnesses. *Next time*, LeeAnn told herself. Right now it was just a matter of selecting a board and a sail and getting out on the water. Eventually she settled on a 10-foot Mistral even though she knew she ought to have taken a bigger one. Pride, however, always has some part in these decisions. Small boards are cool; big boards are not.

There was a little more latitude in picking out sail sizes and still maintaining self-respect. You weren't necessarily un-cool if you picked a small sail–in this case, smaller was wimpy and bigger was brave. You could always claim you were expecting stronger winds to come up. *Man, I thought it would be shredding out there. I didn't want to be overpowered.*

"So, you can go with the five-oh," the clerk, whose name was Phil, was saying. "Or a five-five." The number referred to the sail area, five and a half meters in this case. "Not much wind out there today."

Not much wind! She looked at him. "Let's go with the five-oh."

"Okay."

"Looks like it might get windy out there later."

"Uh-huh." He knew exactly what she was doing. Wimping out. He pulled a rigged sail out of its rack. "There's a trailer back there where you can change but . . . I guess you don't need to go change," he said, looking only at her eyes, but letting her know that he was intensely aware of the rest of her.

"I don't suppose you could keep these for me." She held out the towel, the waist pack, and the binoculars. "I won't be very long."

"Well . . . sure." He probably wasn't supposed to. She handed him all her stuff. Phil started to put it away under the counter, then pointed to her gold chain with the Venus figurine from Yugoslavia on it. "How about that? Do you want to put that in here?"

"Oh, yes, thanks," she said, hastily undoing the clasp and taking it off. He returned her pack; she stuffed the necklace inside, zipped it up, and handed it back.

Then she helped him carry the board and sail outside and down some steps made of railroad tie–the last one was a doozie–there evidently had been a washout. He snapped the rig together and set it in the water. She put on a lifejacket and then over it the ubiquitous T-shirt that identified the class of fool they were dealing with. Hers was yellow.

There was a guy headed out right now to make a jet-ski rescue, she noticed. Behind her, about a half dozen sailors were working on various skills in a little harbor by the seawall. Others, more advanced, were zipping back and forth across the river.

The four sails she had watched earlier, purple, green, clear, and pink were all coming toward her at once. Like the chorus line on some watery stage, they approached, curtsying, it seemed to LeeAnn, as they turned almost in unison, cutting almost simultaneous carving jibes and racing away toward the opposite shore. It looked so wonderful.

Then she was standing knee deep in water, ready to go, but feeling uncertain. "It drops off pretty fast," said Phil, "so you may want to uphaul. There's not enough wind here to beach-start." A beach-start is when you stand on the beach, pick the sail up till it catches the wind, then jump on the board as it starts to take off. A simple maneuver when you make it, and a hilarious way to entertain your friends when you don't. LeeAnn was glad she didn't have to try.

"So, you got everything?"

"I think I do. Thanks, Phil." But he didn't go away, just folded his arms over his chest and stood watching as she climbed onto her board, stood up, awkwardly, and raised the sail. *I will not fall, I will not disgrace myself.* It had been almost three months since she'd sailed. She hesitated for a moment, and it felt like she was starting to lose her balance. To forestall disaster, she quickly reached around, grabbed the boom, and sailed away.

"Just don't get out beyond the wind line," Phil called after her, but she was so busy being self-conscious she didn't really hear, just stored the words away in her memory to call up later.

To her amazement, almost immediately LeeAnn's board was planing. *Bump-bump-bump-bump,* she could hear it. *Omigosh, I'm doing it.* Just like last spring. She leaned back further and further. Pulling against the wind. Feeling like part of the rig. *Soooo happy. How can I be so lucky?* she thought, listening to that satisfying staccato as the board raced over the chop.

It was the sound that till now she'd heard only from sailors speeding either toward her or away, zipping as she slogged. All summer she'd thought about that sound and the slight vibration that came with it that felt so good. It was like being the soundboard on a piano that makes wonderful music. You felt it all through your body. You're part of it. The energy flows through you.

This is the essence of celebration, she thought, *I'm here, right now,* she thought. And for a moment or two she was. Before she began putting together an idea about getting windsurfers around the world to sail on the same day to herald the advent of the millennial season. *Like on day 500 before the Year In Parentheses starts, maybe.*

In her mind's-eye, LeeAnn saw windsurfers in the North Sea, and in Bali, and at the Golden Gate Bridge, and everywhere else in the world, flying global unity banners from their masts. *What a great idea. Windsurfers are so visible. A global festival for windsurfers.*

Then she saw the windsurf industry organizing all the other sports for another celebration as the year 2000 got closer. *Maybe on day 400 people in all the water sports could get out there to celebrate the oceans and rivers and lakes. Popularize their own sport and promote global celebration at the same time.* She saw people everywhere rowing, paddling, swimming, diving, sailing, snorkeling, ice skating. Her mind was moving rapidly. On day 300, the way she would plan it, people in all the land sports from the top sports heroes on down, hiking, running, climbing, biking, skiing, sledding, tobogganing... No reason they wouldn't all want to do that. And then day 200, . . .

Suddenly LeeAnn realized she was *more* than far enough out in the river. This was suddenly big boy territory. The real wind surfers were out here. *Time to turn around.* LeeAnn spilled some wind out of her sail so she could slow down and assess the situation.

It might be best, she thought, to just accept the inevitable, drop into the water, swim the rig around, and then get up again. But it was pretty windy out here. It wouldn't be easy to up-haul. And if she went down, which way would she drift? Probably right into the barge lane. *Well, let's give it a try.* She stepped back on the board, released the rest of the wind from her sail, and came to a kind of bobbing halt on the water. Grabbing the mast and then teetering, holding her breath, inching around, LeeAnn proceeded to execute the slowest , bumpiest turn in windsurf history. But she did it. It was probably the first time ever, she realized, that she had started back to shore *still dry. Yay!*

On the way back in, she let herself look around. Out here among the advanced sailors the colored sails were starting to become individuals. The purple one, the really *radical* sailor, turned out to be an old guy, probably in his sixties, freckles, reddish hair, a real potbelly and bandy legs. But so good at what he did, so graceful. The green was a gray-haired woman who looked like a banker. The pink was a hotshot kid who was currently doing tricks, sailing backwards, sailing with his board upside down.

Near the shore LeeAnn made another turn, just barely. Again she went out into the river a little farther than she meant to, then failed to make her turn and fell in. By now her arms were aching from taking all the strain from the boom in this strong, gusty wind, and she found she couldn't get up. The fatigue, the choppy waves, the wind, plus the fact she hadn't sailed in months all combined to defeat her efforts. She had just failed for the third or fourth time when the old guy with the purple sail came whizzing past, acknowledging her with a kindly smile. She smiled back gamely.

The wind was much stronger now. *Oh. So this is what Phil meant by wind line.* She decided to attempt a water-start, because it was about all she *could* do. Yet something that up until now she'd never done. Because everything had to be perfect. You had to be facing exactly the right way, put your foot on the board in exactly the right place, then arrange your body weight just so, scrunching yourself up into a ball. You had to read the surface of the water for coming gusts, sheet in with your back hand just enough to give yourself power to get up (the back hand being your throttle hand) but then remember to throttle back as soon as you're up . . .

She was doing it all just so, but before she was ready, the wind snatched the sail out of her hands and flung it over to the other side where it promptly sank. LeeAnn climbed back on her board, stood up, and pulled on her up-haul as hard as she could till the sail finally popped up, tipping her backwards into the water. She came up sputtering.

Once again, of course, the sail was on the opposite side of where it ought to be. She would have to swim the board around, or . . . Right now she was confused about *what* she needed to do. The whole rig seemed a hopeless tangle. All the circuit breakers in her brain seemed to have flipped off; she couldn't remember which way anything was supposed to go. And it was blowing harder all the time.

"You all right?" It was the man with the purple sail in the water behind her; he must have stopped to check on her.

She nodded breathlessly. "Oh, I'm fine." *Why did I say that?* He was up again and gone. For him it took only an instant. In no more than the blink of an eye, he was up on his board and off, potbelly, bandy legs, and all.

Off in the distance, LeeAnn noticed an ocean-going barge had appeared. Clearly it was coming in this direction, but she still had some time. She began to alternate between trying to water-start and trying to up-haul; there was a nice rhythm to it, though neither seemed even remotely possible to accomplish any more. Each time she pushed the board around, her sail seemed to seek the bottom of the river. Or else it would flap madly in the wind, which seemed to be shifting around to the south. If that was the south over there still. She was beginning to attract attention on shore, she saw.

LeeAnn finally got everything into position one last time. Here came a gust. Pissed with herself, she plunked both feet on the board (which you're not supposed to do), then clung to the boom for dear life as it suddenly pulled her *up!* She was so astonished she just hung on as she felt herself continuing to go *up, up, up* in an arc over . . . and . . . DOWN! Knocking the breath out of her.

In the long moments it took to come up to the surface and catch her breath, LeeAnn saw in her mind a toy she and Peter used to have when they were small–a loose-jointed figure that would go up and over a bar and down again for as long as you'd turn the handle. She saw herself doing it, a rag doll in the air. It shook her brain up; she almost felt renewed.

A whole bunch of people were watching her now. Some were pointing. They must have seen what happened. And there was a guy on a jet-ski, who looked like he might be getting ready to head her way.

She was drifting further out into the river, and that barge kept on coming. *Get yourself up now, honey,* she told herself–*or take a failing grade–get yourself rescued. And humiliated.* And so she really hunkered down this time and tried to get all her muscles to think alike. Ready, set . . . then suddenly she was up and in shock, riding her board! *I don't believe this. I water-started. I did it I did it I did it!!!!* She screeched with joy. As she rocketed back toward the Rhonda Smith Windsurf School, she imagined herself swooping in for a landing, jumping off her board in knee-deep water. But of course she miscalculated and got herself too far downwind in the lee of the island where she stalled out completely. Twenty minutes later, she pulled her board up on the beach, detached the sail, and took it and then the board back up to Phil.

"How was it?"

"It was fine. I did it, did you see?"

"Looked like you were having a little trouble."

"But I got back. I did it."

"Yeah, you did. Good for you."

"I actually *did* water-start once," she told him again one more time, just in case he didn't understand.

"Hey. *Congratulations.*" And he sounded like he meant it.

It felt like a really indolent afternoon, sitting at the Gorge Café a little later, luxuriating in a feeling of tired muscles and accomplishment. She was out on the deck, wearing her sunglasses, David's shirt over her shoulders, her silver bikini and her sandals from Crete. She wriggled her toes, looking down at the sandals with satisfaction. Seven years. Resoled twice. She wore them all summer, every summer.

Oh, yes. This day is good. In the end she'd had to drag and walk and swim her board quite a ways, but it was good exercise. That was the thing about windsurfing. LeeAnn found she was often perfectly content when she was pulling her board back home. Marching through knee-deep or chest-deep water, or sometimes just barely getting a purchase with her toes on the bottom and pushing off like a moon-walker–it was all good. It all made her feel more alive than usual. *Even getting launched is okay, I can now officially testify,* she thought.

The waitress with a blonde ponytail and a great body brought her iced tea with lemon. LeeAnn retrieved the lemon slice and squeezed it, watching the tiny bursts of essence from the rind sparkle in the sunlight. Then she sipped deeply, emptying the glass instantly and barely escaping the temptation to keep sucking on the straw the way she and Audrey did when they were eight.

Leaning back, relaxed, she stared out at the water. *If I'm lucky enough to be savoring my favorite memories when I die,* she thought, *they will be three; making love, giving birth, and skimming over the water, free as a bird. Sailing on the wind. Dancing on a blue-green planet. Living like this.*

Earlier in the summer when she'd been up in the arctic, wondering what she'd do if she and David did break up, she'd consoled herself by building a scenario that involved a station wagon–a silver Subaru, she thought–with a golden retriever in the back and a sailboard on top. She would take her laptop and work on the road, she'd decided. Follow the wind. Corpus Christi in the spring, maybe the Chesapeake sometime, or Baja. She'd get one of those new pop-up tents she'd seen advertised; as soon as you take it out of the bag, you throw it in the air and it springs into shape, so you don't have to fumble around in the dark at the KOA campgrounds.

Now she added David to the meandering daydream. They could *both* go. How lovely it would be to make camp with him every night . . .

"More iced tea?" the girl asked her, pitcher in hand.

"No thanks."

"So you did okay out there today, did you?"

"Haven't got bit by a barge yet!" LeeAnn grinned. She paid for the tea, gathered up her things and started back to the hotel, studying the island ahead as she walked. Happy. She'd had her rag doll adventure. Christened at the Gorge.

Maybe the whole summer would go like this. Maybe there was still a way to get free of all the hassles. Send out the invitations to the global party, get the Summer Project off the ground, with a whole lot of people helping so it wouldn't eat up her whole life. Maybe a whole lot of windsurfers. Get the report on her Arctic trip written. Get her relationship back together. Then maybe they actually could go on the road in the van for a little while. David could sell his artwork, she could start studying northwest sites. . . . Again she saw the tent in her mind. The Subaru, with *two* boards on top.

She thought about all the people she'd seen since she'd been in

Hood River down by the shore, rigging and de-rigging those itsy bitsy boards. License plates from all over. Some of those people had been sailing ten or fifteen years and never got tired of it. She doubted that she ever would either.

As she approached the double doors of the hotel, LeeAnn let herself fantasize about David again. The scent of him, the feel of him. She speeded up, hurried down the corridor, slid her key into the lock very, very slowly and opened the door quietly. There he was, sprawled on his back in the bed with the afternoon sun on his body. He was lying almost precisely the way she'd left him, one arm behind his head, the tan Sportif shorts provocatively unzipped. So beautiful.

She set the waist pack and the binoculars down. And the hotel towel. Then she went to stand beside the bed, looking at his body, the long brown legs, the sinewy forearms. You could just stare at an arm like that for hours and wait for it to move, knowing each time it did, new beauty would be created.

Her eyes moved to his legs now, so tan, so perfect, with a deep scar on one knee that only made them more perfect.

Once again, LeeAnn realized she was a limb lady. With David, of course, it was the right leg and arm she was best acquainted with, because it was David who always drove. So she had hours and hours to watch that strong right thigh and feel the muscle under her hand as his foot moved from accelerator to brake and back again.

That just a few hours before he had had those arms and legs wrapped tightly around her was sheer bliss to remember. To have had him moving inside her with such sureness and love, sheer ecstasy. Every fantasy she'd had during a long, cold, lonely, and celibate summer tramping around in eastern Siberia had come true then, in such great yowling joy that he'd had to put his hand over her mouth to muffle the sound. "You're going to have the cops up here," he said.

A spasm of remembrance hit her now, as it often did hours after lovemaking. David must have heard her quick intake of breath, for he smiled in sleepy self-congratulation and then opened his eyes. She kissed his forehead.

"Fribben," he said, a word from his private language which, roughly translated, meant "All's well with the world."

"Fribben," she replied, looking deep into his eyes. They still hadn't really talked, so she had no idea what she might find there. Till last spring, she'd thought she could read him. And right now it felt like that too, so much love seemed to be radiating from him. He gazed at her, that delicious lower lip of his seeming to tease and tremble ever so slightly.

"You know," he said, stretching languorously, "I've noticed you have entirely too many clothes on."

"I do?" she answered, delighted, promptly ripping off the damp shirt and flinging it in the corner.

He looked up and down her body, clad in his favorite swim suit. "My," he said.

She knelt up on the bed and he moved over slightly to accommodate her. She bent to kiss him on the mouth, lingering a while, then bestowed a tender artichoke bite on each earlobe. It was fun to breathe into his ear, just the slightest bit, and watch the hair stand up on his arms as she did.

Her fingertips caressed his chest lightly and she bent to rub her cheek against it. She touched his shoulders, then ran her hands down his arms. It had long been LeeAnn's opinion that no man can resist tensing when his biceps are stroked, though in David's case it genuinely was not necessary. Once more she tested her theory, and once again he confirmed it.

"Why don't you roll over," she said, and he complied. Straddling him in her damp bikini, she took off the bra and flung it on the pillow beside him. Then she bent to rub just her nipples on his back. He moaned.

She loosened his ponytail then. Taking the band off and spreading the graying hair out, she ran her fingers through it. It wasn't that thick, but it was long and silky and wonderful. She buried her face in it, nipping at his neck. "Oh yes. Oh yes." David said. Then she slowed her motion and stopped. Her hands were on his temples and forehead now, wishing them into relaxation.

"Recess," she said. Taking a deep breath herself, she held his rib cage for a moment, signaling him to breathe, and he did, taking a very long breath and then letting it out. She kissed his back all the way down to the shorts, then over the shorts and down his legs, playing at the inside of his thighs with her tongue for a moment, as he groaned. She grinned, then ran her hands up *under* the shorts to knead and tease the soft white flesh of his beautiful butt.

"LeeAnn. This is getting very hard to lie on. May I turn over?"

"Not yet." She reached up between his legs to adjust his problem. "Is that better?"

"Only marginally."

"Well, I guess we're going to have to take those shorts off." He picked his head up off the pillow where it had been happily buried for the past several minutes and gave her a look. "Fine by me, lady. Be my guest."

So she pulled his shorts down now, kissing the little dimple at his coccyx. Gradually she worked them down to his feet, with considerable cooperation on David's part, then pulled them off, stopping to bite his right foot as she did. He promptly raised the other one for equal treatment.

"Oh, so *that's* what you want." She moved down to the foot of the bed, where she massaged each foot in turn, dug her knuckles into the soles of his feet, and scratched them with her fingernails so that they curled involuntarily. She imagined she could feel in her own body exactly what she was doing to his. Judging from the sound, David was in a state of rapture. He moaned and groaned and sighed with pleasure.

By now it had been at least ten minutes since she started, and she wasn't up to his knees yet on her return trip. But it was time. Definitely time. So she left off nibbling on his Achilles and traced a path with her tongue straight up the back of his calves, as though she were painting a stocking seam on his hairy legs. Then she stopped and grasped his leg with one hand just above, the other just below the back of his knee; it was one of his special spots.

"LeeAnn, you're not planning to . . . "

"Oh yes I am."

"Oh no. No," he said in mock protest, as she bent to trace a slow circle with her tongue on that exquisitely vulnerable place, first clockwise, then counter clockwise. Then she moved to place one tiny dot of wet in the middle. "Stop it. Don't stop it."

"I won't. But don't squirm, not even a little bit." She moved to the other leg, repeating the circle and the dot. She blew on it, then suddenly plunged her whole mouth into the back of his knee, deeply, wetly teasing with her tongue and her teeth, as David bucked and howled. A man maddened by desire, he rolled over without warning and reached for her, cradling her safely in his arms as they tumbled off onto the floor. Now the silver bikini bottom was removed as rapidly as possible by both of them working together. In the next instant he entered her and it was LeeAnn's turn to howl, rather loudly. "Shh," said David. "You're going to have the cops up here." His words failed to stop her, however.

CHAPTER FIVE

David and LeeAnn

Afterwards, she rolled over and sat up, feeling pleased with herself and with him, and with the watery world outside. It was like sitting over a champagne glass, the river radiating its sparkling energy up toward their room. It was a wonderful room, and only a ten dollar upgrade from a view of the parking lot. There was a separate sitting area with a loveseat and a coffee table, and best of all, the television was discreetly tucked away in an armoire.

Now that, to LeeAnn's mind, was the dividing line between just a room and a classy room. If the television's right out there, its unblinking eye staring at you, it can destroy your sense of peace. But here it was shut away, so it was just she and her love and a much-rumpled bed, water and wind outside. She was starting to wonder whether the parking-lot-view rooms had their televisions tucked away when David pulled her back down beside him and hugged her.

For a while they just lay there on their backs, holding hands and staring up at the ceiling. Then they got going again, a little, on the rough carpet, but it was mainly just to tease and roll around. There is a limit, after all, no matter how horny you've been for how long. When she was little, LeeAnn had thought she could take all her baths for the whole year at once and get it over with. "It doesn't work that way, Honey," Maggie had explained. So LeeAnn and David would have to catch up gradually. She sighed.

"Hungry?" David asked her.

"Getting there."

"I suppose we better get our ass in gear then," he said as he propelled himself up from the floor and headed for the bathroom. She wondered if he knew his butt jiggled just slightly as he walked.

When David came out of the shower and stood wet on the bathmat, she knelt and carefully nuzzled the part of him she loved best. His balls so tight as the water cooled on his skin. Laughing, he had to stop patting himself dry with a towel as she explored, burrowing into the place between his legs where she could take a deep breath of wonder, a breath that smelled like the sea. She could scent the semen through his skin, even with the shower water on it. It went to her soul.

She kissed him, then went to stand in front of the mirror, trying to decide between the hot pink cotton mini and an ivory off-the-shoulder crocheted top. David was down on one knee at his backpack, unfolding dress jeans that already had his brown leather belt threaded through the loops. He pulled them on and zipped them up. Why is it so sexy when a man buckles his belt? *God.*

"So, which one would you like me to wear?" she asked, standing there in her underpants, holding first the dress up and then the top. "This one with jeans," she explained.

"Mmmm. Let me see the dress again. Wear the jeans," he said. He almost always said wear the jeans. So she pulled the crocheted top over her head, thinking about her mother as she always did when she wore it. They'd bought two of them many years ago, at Bullock's in L.A., when they'd both happened to be out there–not so they could match but because they'd both liked them so much. Both wore them for at least ten years, then when LeeAnn wrecked hers by putting it in the wash, Maggie gave her hers. *Bless you, Maggie.*

She pulled it down over her shoulders then and tied the sash as David, wearing his cream-colored Baja shirt, came to stand behind her. "You look wonderful," he said. He grasped her shoulders, "Take a look at yourself." Then looking down, "Where's your necklace?"

Hot, cold. The sudden shock hit LeeAnn as she stared in the mirror at her bare neck and thought of the figurine tumbling in the Columbia river, lost under tons of sand and headed for the ocean. Almost instantly she remembered, but the next rush of adrenaline had already been ordered up and so it hit anyway.

"Oh, my god you scared me. I took it off at the rental shop." She unzipped her pack and took it out, seeing again how precious it was. She began to undo the clasp but he took it from her, unclasped it, and fastened it around her neck. Then they both looked in the mirror to gauge the effect.

"You scared me for a moment. I don't ever want to lose that." She put her hands over his larger ones, which were resting on her shoulders, and squeezed them. "And I don't ever want to lose you."

There was just the tiniest flicker in his eyes, reflected by the mirror, of a person trapped. *I am going to lose him, I know I am*, a voice inside said, but she tried to ignore it.

Automatically she put on her jeans and her sandals from Crete, and they went out the door. But she was still thinking about it.

They ate dinner at an unremarkable place nearby and then started to wander, going from arms around to holding hands to arms around again, always touching as they walked. Surely that proved something. Eventually they found their way under the whizzing roadway that separated the waterfront from the old town beyond. Apparently almost no one ever walked to town; it wasn't arranged for walking, so they had to stop in at a gas station and wrest directions from an unwilling attendant.

Once downtown, they cased all the by-now closed windsurfing shops, looking for used boards, putting their hands up against the glass to shield the light from outside, and trying to peer around corners. "See? There. Over there. *See?* There's a couple of boards that look beat-up."

"Yup."

"Those aren't new, so there's definitely a consignment section here." A car went by and LeeAnn imagined what she and David looked like from the back, holding hands, peering in. *How long will this last?* LeeAnn wondered, then tried to put the worry out of her head.

By the time they got back to the Best Western and undressed, it was 11:52, according to the digital alarm beside the bed. LeeAnn lay there with her Sue Grafton paperback, beside David, who had abandoned his Ann Siddons novel in favor of the *Windsurfing* magazine LeeAnn had bought him. They'd been back together only a few hours, she thought, but had already fallen into that addictive joining of bodies and thoughts and chores that had always comprised their union.

It was this moment of the day that provides the ultimate good feeling, lying in bed with your partner, LeeAnn thought. *You're both reading, maybe reading something aloud to each other once in awhile, and you stop to look around and feel lucky. This was what it was all about. Cocooning.* It's what LeeAnn and David had been about since the very beginning.

They had met in the spring six years before when she was on vacation from New York in Klamath Falls. Wandering into a gem and mineral show at the fairgrounds her first day in town, she'd been immediately captured by a display of primitive tools, mostly obsidian knives with antler handles. She'd stood at the case, admiring the work, which had a feeling of authenticity to it, as though whoever made it really understood the spirit of the ancients.

Wishing she had a chance to tell that to the artist, she became conscious that someone had stepped up behind her. Through a trick of light as a door was opened or shut, she saw his face reflected for a moment in the glass and became aware of the presence of someone clean and tall and strong. She turned to see warm friendly eyes of brown and a healthy grin. Nice profile. Strong chin.

She looked back at the case, where there was an article about the artist, and a photo. She turned to compare. Same face. "*You* did these," she said and he nodded. Then they'd talked a few minutes and it came out that she was an archaeologist.

"*Are* you? That's pretty impressive."

"I have to tell you," she said, "that your detail is absolutely superb. It's as though you're inside the mind of an ancient flint-knapper when you work these pieces."

"Why not?" He grinned at her.

"Are you Native American?" If he were, she might tell him about her one-sixteenth.

"No, I'm not, but aren't we all just a few generations removed from a Stone Age toolmaker?"

"I guess you're right."

"We just have to reach back into our memories."

"Is that what you do?"

He nodded.

"*Really?*" She was fascinated.

"The first time I ever made a stone tool," he said, "I had the realization I'd done it before in the past."

"I know the feeling." And she did. *The first time I ever made love,* she thought, *I had that feeling of, Oh yes, I've done this before. I remember.* He looked down at her as though he had just read her thought and it didn't embarrass her at all. His lower lip seemed to tease. "Genetic memory," she said.

"Or *ancestral* memory."

"Are you saying we can remember things our ancestors have done?"

"It makes sense, doesn't it," David said. That our DNA is encoded with all the wisdom we've acquired over time. If we're afraid of something, then there's probably a reason in our past. I believe there's millions of years of memory, guiding memory I like to call it, built into our brain, of all the significant things that have happened to all our ancestors. And it's available to us if we listen. It's what we're doing, I think, when we stare into the fire."

"Connecting with our memories?"

He nodded.

"So if I have some unnatural fear or strange premonition . . . , LeeAnn started.

"You pay attention. You listen carefully. You try to tap into it."

"Why do you suppose it's difficult to do that?"

"I have no idea."

"But it's not difficult for you?"

"Not really."

LeeAnn thought about it for a moment. "I've read that there's a special part of the brain that records only the very significant events." She thought some more. "So you're saying that when you have *déjà vu* it may be something that happened to somebody in your family way back when."

"Something like that."

"I think you may be right," she said. Then somehow, she didn't know quite how it happened, they were sitting in a coffee shop across the street and there were yellow roses outside. Old wild rose bushes with little yellow roses in full bloom. He was saying he'd grown up in Florida till he was nine. "Both my folks worked for Disney."

"Did you ever get to go in those underground tunnels and stuff that I read about?"

"Yeah, once." Then he proceeded to tell her about it. *I'm mad for this man*, she thought, watching as much as listening while he told the rest of his story. After his parents' divorce–apparently these days everyone's parents divorced–he got sent to his grandmother, who lived in the high desert country of eastern Oregon. "It was supposed to be temporary, but I never got to go back. Neither one of my parents ever had time or space for me, and my grandmother did. She was pretty good to me, but I was always kind of a loner," he said.

Then David began telling her how he became interested in primitive things. "In Florida everything was wet and green and plants grew overnight, so I never got a sense of time, because new life was constantly replacing the old. But in the desert . . . it all grows slowly; there's more space for the old life to hang around. Everything is so weathered and beaten by the harsh elements. The environment out here in Oregon was much more conducive to the thought processes that take you back to the past. Or at least that's the way it seemed to me. I'd find arrowheads, and could just imagine the people who used them being right around me. So of course I grew up just *knowing* instead of learning."

"Mmmm." *Wow,* LeeAnn thought, *anybody this open, this clear about himself, who looks like this* . . . She wanted to jump his frame right there and then. Roll in the yellow roses. Astound the coffee shop customers. She'd ordered tea and now she dabbled the teabag up and down, watching it release more color into the white porcelain mug. This man was real, he was sensitive and artistic. He was refreshingly wonderful.

"Would you like to get something to eat later?" he asked her eventually. *Silly question.* They agreed to meet in an hour. So she walked across to her motel–it was too nice to drive–showered and got all dressed up.

But then when he picked her up, he took her to a fast food fried chicken place, which after her initial astonishment seemed kind of campy. Was it his sense of humor? Was he poor? Or was it just because there weren't any better restaurants around? She didn't particularly care.

At dinner she'd learned more. He was essentially fresh out of a nineteen-year marriage that had produced one child, a daughter, and very little else. His wife was a small-town girl bonded to her mother. He fished twenty hours a week, at least. And they grew apart.

In her little black recycled Donna Karan and heels, in this fried chicken shack with this beautiful man who wore khaki chinos and a pale yellow golf shirt that was tight around his tan biceps, LeeAnn found herself wanting David to the point where she couldn't think straight. She was pulsing. That he wanted her too had already passed between them in a number of looks that had taken just a fraction too long. At least she thought it had.

The sheer magnetic pull as they were having dinner–extra crispy with white dinner rolls, coleslaw, combat zone mashed potatoes and gravy–became unbearable as they took in a movie later that she never saw. The need to be touching his body overwhelmed everything else. It didn't happen that often, but when LeeAnn got taken over by desire, there was no hope for her.

Halfway through the movie he still hadn't touched her, she remembered. Shifting around, feeling hot and squiggly, she wondered what he was thinking. Could he possibly not notice? *Please, hold my hand. Pat me on the head. Let your knee touch mine just for a moment. Grab me. Seize me in those remarkable arms. Do something.*

But he didn't. Afterwards, she squirmed around on the seat of his white Dodge van. By the time they got back to the fairground where she'd left her car, she'd just about given up. She opened the passenger door and was about to say good night. *I'm going to go die in private . . .*

"LeeAnn?" he said then.

"Mmm?

A very serious, very sweet look passed over his face. He said, "If it's okay with you, I'd like to follow you back to your motel and make mad, wild love to you."

"Fine by me," she said. One of those spasms went through her then, *kerklunk.* He watched her face carefully as it did. It was an anticipatory spasm instead of the aftershock kind. *But the phenomena are really quite similar*, she thought, *so maybe time is just a concept. Maybe I'm remembering all the other times–all the other millions of times in other lives that he and I have met and made love.*

Then his hand touched her for the very first time, at the nape of her neck, right where he would bite her so often in the years to come, his fingers running through her hair. He touched her shoulders that had been so tense all evening and then her face, brushing her chin and cheeks, then bent to kiss her, in the white Dodge van in the parking lot at the fairgrounds in Klamath Falls, Oregon.

They spent the whole week together, rarely out of bed except for long walks–one of them almost twenty miles–and swims and talks. Not so much talking, though, as observing together and feeling. She felt that hum about him–*there was always a kind of silent, humming sound when you were with David, coming from his energy. He was so organized and contained, connected with the earth, self-sufficient and steady.* Before she left at the end of the week, he had become her connection to the earth as well, her ground.

LeeAnn came back to Oregon as soon as she could–two months later–and they took a backpacking trip together, her first, in the Trinity Alps in California. Five days out without seeing another soul. And at that point she never *did* want to see anyone else. There's got to be nothing more perfect than a six-foot-three frame when you're a five-foot-seven female and your breasts touch on just the right part of his chest and your arms go just the right amount around his neck, and his lips are in exactly the right place.

She gave up everything else that was going on in her life and took a job for peanuts, editing a series of college texts written by one of her more prolific professors from Columbia, Dr. Driscoll. She could fix Ruth Driscoll's books from anywhere–and work for her summers on European or Arctic digs. Then she moved out to be with David in his apartment on the hill, in a building occupied mainly by college students.

And that's what they felt like the first four years. They were like kids, with their little altar to nature in the tiny living room, displaying treasures they'd found on their hikes. It was framed by their cross-country skis and poles, and a Mexican bird tapestry in bright colors that they loved. Everything was un-serious and un-subtle; it was a life in primary colors.

In their bedroom they slept on a mattress on the floor with sheets that they tie-dyed themselves. The second bedroom was her little office where she toiled on the dull manuscripts for as many hours as she could bear not to be with him. Listening to the lovely chink, chink, chink of his flint-knapping as he sat at the dinette table (they'd drilled a hole in its leaf so he could mount his vice) making tools of the ancient vanished people. She also heard the occasional chink, chink, *chunk!* when the blade in progress broke, followed by his soft, "Damn."

The obsidian knives with antler handles went for fifty, eighty, and a hundred dollars, according to size, and they sold to shops all over the U.S., and even in Japan. Each was unique. On some, the blades were black and shiny, some nearly clear, with streaks of gray, or red. And some looked like a rainbow when you held them up to the light. Every antler handle was different, too.

When he ran short on money, David supplemented their income with temporary jobs waiting tables and selling cars. It went on like that for four simple, beautiful years, until LeeAnn had almost forgotten about the past, about the east, about her life with Bo, and the death from leukemia of their daughter Florence, at the age of three. The death that had shattered her for years. Leukemia was an environmental disease, the doctors told her, and that had made her acceptance all the more difficult. She was bitter that their child had become a victim to humans' pollution of the planet.

LeeAnn went back East now only about once a year to visit her family. And Peter came up from Berkeley once in a while. Her brother and David hit it off pretty well.

When LeeAnn wasn't working, or fussing over her long-overdue doctoral dissertation, she and David spent their time backpacking, cross-country skiing, and running, choosing different six-mile squares in the country. There were lots of those; the land had been divided up in cross-hatched miles all across the west. Urban running–running in Manhattan–couldn't compare. The cattle, the coyotes, the thousands of geese that rose up in the wildlife refuge when they passed a certain point on their run, it was all exquisitely exciting to her.

At sunset from their balcony, they watched the big sky, and it was like watching movies. A million moods, a million shows, a million different skies. And the same bird that, David had noticed, flew to its roost at the same time almost every night, every year. They began to feel like it was a friend of theirs. LeeAnn loved living in Oregon.

Evenings they sat in front of the television, David's right leg and her left touching, thigh to ankle, their feet rubbing fondly as they watched McNeil-Lehrer, and the Discovery channel, and flew around an electronic world together. David always pointed out so much more in the shows they watched than she would have noticed herself, just as he did on their hikes and their runs. He was her nature tutor, the best she'd ever had, she the New Yorker who'd never slowed down enough to see much more than the grass growing up between cracks in the roadway.

There wasn't much downside to their life together (except that money was always tight and LeeAnn tended to worry about that). The lifestyle they'd chosen took care of most of her favorite things to do. And the other thing . . . well, she didn't let her desire for another child overtake her, though she always felt like she was just barely outrunning it. One of these days it was going to catch up and snag her. For time was ticking away. The years between thirty and thirty-six had been tough years not to have a child if she was ever going to have one again, but life with David was too close to perfect, and his feelings on the subject too clear for her to press the issue. It was a compromise with life she made willingly, however reluctantly. It was a trade-off.

As she got to know him better, LeeAnn came to realize that David was immensely deep in some areas and immensely non-deep in others–an emotional virgin in one sense, yet very evolved in the sense that he accepted everything as natural. No struggle, no angst; you love, you live, you die–while LeeAnn struggled every step of the way. The way he put it, she was too worried, too busy and yet always taking on another cause. She couldn't argue with that.

Exploring their ideas together, LeeAnn found that they agreed on a lot. Except David felt there was no sense trying to save humanity, that it was just naturally going to self-destruct and justifiably so. David was not wrestling with great questions–or looking for answers. Though he liked to think he was open to all input, in some ways she found him almost closed. So she was always trying to reach into his soul and pull it forth. She'd succeeded to some extent, she thought. He was communicating a whole lot better with other people than when she'd met him. He enjoyed talking to people more. That's what she'd done for him. That and introducing him to the world of books and politics. Over the past five years, starting with *Serpentine,* then working his way through Steinbeck to Rosamunde Pilcher, David Jamison had become a reader.

Some nights they'd lie together for hours, reading. Or they'd go for walks late in the evening and observe the people who lived in real houses; they'd look at the lighted windows–and the darkened ones–and speculate on the lives going on inside. Then in the fourth year that they were together, a big old house on the hill came up for sale at an absurdly low price. All that land, almost half an acre, including a guest cabin and a dilapidated summerhouse for under sixty thousand dollars. Right downtown. It was unbeautiful from the outside but you could walk anywhere, and it had a fairly decent view of two mountain ranges.

They knew they'd have to stretch to afford it. But about that time LeeAnn received some royalties on Dr. Driscoll's new textbook series, which made it all seem providential. With what David was making, there was enough for a down payment, with a little left over for the endless work that fixing up an old house would entail. So they did it, they went for it.

And it was great. When they'd first moved into the house and it was still empty, David had chased her one morning, and when he finally caught her, they lay on the living room floor on the round blue Chinese butterfly rug–which was considered major furniture at the time–panting and laughing. Then suddenly they were wonderfully joined. Celebrating LeeAnn with immense abandon, David whispered in her ear, "Aren't we lucky nobody's noticed we're living here unsupervised?"

Then over time, it began to change. LeeAnn reflected now, looking around the river-view room, that probably it was *things* that were doing them in. Things, and debts. Maybe a guy with all that territory to snow-blow, and all that grass to cut, and all the fixer-up jobs inside, and all those bills to pay, just naturally began to pull away. Maybe you couldn't properly care for your soul, or your soul mate, when you were involved in the maintenance of a bunch of shit. *Maybe that's what the ancient people knew that we've forgotten.* Back when they lived in the apartment, LeeAnn thought, he couldn't have moved out to the cabin. The biggest gesture you could make was to sleep on the sofa, and neither of them had ever done it.

"You about ready?" from David, who was putting down his windsurfing magazine and ritually plumping up his pillow, as he did every night of his life.

"Just about."

"Then I'm going to call it a day. You take your time, though," he added, as he always did. He reached for her, his mouth pursing perfunctorily. She kissed him. He took an extra moment with the kiss, making some kind of a statement, it seemed to her. Then he put his light out. She lay there staring at page 142, of *A Is For Alibi*. She had wanted to talk tonight, she wanted to know everything was all right again. Or was it? What had gone wrong? How could it all be that good and then not? Or maybe it was like yogurt. Maybe there was a date stamp on relationships these days and they were only good for a certain length of time.

What was it going to be like when they got home and David figured out–as he probably already had–that she was about to be busier and more worried than she ever had been in her life. Saving the world, for god's sake. Maybe that's why he gave her the binoculars. *Here, take these glasses and watch me leave.* She switched out her light and lay in the dark for awhile. *I know I'm losing him. I saw it in his eyes and I should have talked to him then. No.* David hated talking about anything like that. And she could just hear herself starting in. "David, don't you think we need to talk?" She sighed. Now there was a real loser for an opening remark.

CHAPTER SIX

Hooking In

Seven forty-five the next morning found them parked outside the likeliest of the windsurfing shops in the old white Dodge van they'd named Vanna, practically leaning forward in their seats, waiting for the store to open.

"On their answering machine it said they opened at eight," LeeAnn repeated; she'd already told David that at least once.

Then I'm sure they'll be here soon."

"Or do you want to go for breakfast first?" he asked her. He'd already said that once, too.

"Are you kidding? I'm staying right here." LeeAnn thought back to the phone call. "They had a recorded wind report."

"What did it say?"

"Ten to twenty for most of the places. I didn't hear what Hood River was," LeeAnn added, and then they fell silent again. "What do you suppose all that milk is for?" she asked a couple of minutes later, pointing to two crates of gallon jugs standing outside the windsurf store.

David smiled, took her hand in his and arranged her index finger so it was pointing up to the sign above the shop where it announced in small letters that espresso was served inside.

She laughed. "Oh my god, well of course. Latté-land."

Soon, somebody fairly official-looking was walking around inside. Then arms reached outside the door to gather the milk crates in. LeeAnn opened the van door.

"Whoa, let's not rush them," David cautioned as she started to get out. "Give them a chance to get started." So she pulled the door shut again. "Do no harm," was David's chief motto in life.

"I'm going to get my water-start, you know," LeeAnn said as she waited, her hand on the door handle. "If I did it once . . ."

"Oh, I know you are. And you're going to need to get a harness."

At last the garage door started to roll. "Curtain going up," she declared. David grinned at her and they got out of the van.

Once inside the store, LeeAnn found herself pulled like an iron filing to a magnet toward the used-sails department. There she stood in an aisle between the racks where hundreds of sails of orange and green and blue and purple and yellow hung on huge racks like sixteen-foot dresses. She and David wandered among them and asked questions. Or rather LeeAnn asked questions; David just looked and learned. He seldom asked direct questions of anyone; he learned by looking.

There were racing sails and slalom sails and performance sails (whatever that meant; she didn't see any *non* performance sails). Also wave sails and combination wave-slalom sails, and that was just the beginning. The next few hours were an exercise in bewilderment as they started getting multiple divergent opinions and admonitions as to what they should buy, with their fellow shoppers every bit as vocal as the salesclerks. Maybe more so. The trouble was, everyone's theories made sense, everyone was super-nice, and everyone was trying to help.

There were all these complicated reasons why you needed this and you needed that, and over and over, compelling rationales as to why quality counts. "It's the only way to go," seemed to be the phrase of the day. And not just quality, but quantity. To hear board sailors talk, you needed whole quivers of expensive sails and a flock of different boards for different conditions.

David started to sort through a rack of harnesses but since he already had one, it was probably for her. She managed to steer him away. Yesterday's memory of what it was like to be launched *without* a harness was still too fresh. It could only feel worse to be attached.

At last, having tramped up and down the streets and exhausted all possible sources for secondhand rigs that they could find, as well as any possible combinations that they might put together–the mast from this store and the board from that–David and LeeAnn sat in a Mexican restaurant devouring a second bowl of chips. They'd put off ordering, as they sometimes did in iffy places, until they could see what food brought to an adjoining table looked like.

"So what are there?" David summed up, sipping his Bud with lime, "maybe four used longboards in the whole town?"

"In the wind capital of the world?"

"Yeah, well, that's why. There's always wind here. Short boards are all you ever need." The short boards were called sinkers, because they wouldn't hold you up unless you were going fast enough.

"But don't they imagine people might want to take something home?" LeeAnn asked. "To their ordinary lakes and ordinary winds?"

"I guess not."

She went back to the job she'd assigned herself of leafing through the pile of freebie literature she'd scooped up in every store they passed. "Look at this," she said to David, showing him an ad. "You just zip off part of the sail to make it smaller or bigger, and then you don't need as many. Maybe we should get that." He shrugged.

She opened a copy of *American Windsurfer*, a beautiful, coffee-table-sized magazine, leafed through, admiring the spectacular photography and layout, then stopped at a two-page spread that showed a group of children posed with a Sunboard in front of the Eiffel Tower. It was a message about windsurfing and world peace. Omigosh. Just exactly what she'd been thinking about yesterday when she was out sailing–*that the windsurf industry could become a leader for peace. This is wonderful*, she thought.

"To the leaders of all nations," the ad read. "The world is full of innocent humans giving love, faith, and hope. We are trying to create human kindness so earth can be enjoyed. The world is also full of evil. Racism and pure hatred, pointing fingers in religious conflict. . . ." It went on to talk about how leaders could help to promote peace if they only would.

This was meant to be, LeeAnn told herself. *Maybe there are no coincidences. Maybe I was meant to rally the windsurf industry. These are the perfect people to bring awareness about what we can do; it's such an international sport. Plus windsurfers have such a conscious-ness about the earth, and our human spirit and courage and all that, because how could they help but have? Out there alone in settings that other people only dream of seeing? It's a sport that demands you work with the forces of nature, not against them. And it calls on all the inner strength we can possibly muster. I know that already, and I've barely begun.*

And in what other sport could you possibly see more or be more aware of the fragile beauty that is everywhere? And what sport could possibly be more wonderfully visual, more perfectly symbolic for other people to watch? Dancing on a blue-green planet... A wind-powered sport . . . and a brand new sport. Only thirty years old. A perfect sport to help usher in the 21st century.

She turned the magazine around and showed it to David. "Here, read this." He did.

"Hmmm," was all he said when he finished.

"You know, I was thinking, we could probably get windsurfers to help get the word out about the global celebration. If just a few of them were to go out and sail in all the different time zones, all twenty-four, on a particular day, I'll bet you the media . . ."

"Hey, we're on vacation. Okay?" He turned the magazine back around toward her.

Oh, boy. David wasn't even slightly open to it. At least right now he wasn't. So she went back to reading through all the equipment ads, searching for any solution to their basic challenge, which was to put a decent rig together for five or six hundred dollars.

Cannily, she had saved till last the small town *Advertiser* that she'd scooped up along with everything else. And sure enough, "Ooh, ooh, listen to this. 'Fanatic Viper with mast, 6.2 sail and Chinook, $375. Good condition.' We could both use it, couldn't we? Isn't it the right size? Should we call?"

David seemed to think about it for a moment, then looked at his watch. "We can call when we get back to the motel."

Pfft, LeeAnn thought. *Never happen.* When David was through for the day, he was through. *Of course*, she thought quietly, *I could go and call right now.* So she took the ad with her when she went to the ladies room, hoping there'd be a phone nearby. But there wasn't one, so she had to sail right past David without saying a word, out the door and up the street till she found a telephone.

Heading back into the restaurant five giddy minutes later, she marshaled her arguments for canceling this chip-and-salsa fest and chasing down what sounded like the bargain of the year. She told David all about what the man had said.

"So where is it?"

"A little town just across the bridge."

"Over in *Washington*?"

"Right. Washington state. But not very far. And the guy sounded intelligent."

"*How* far?"

It turned out it was fifty miles, but David wanted a board as much as she did. He even stopped at an ATM en route in case they happened to have a sudden need for $375.

They crossed at the next bridge upstream and drove on into a tree-less moonscape in the barren part of the state. She was remembering the full moon when they met. That first night at the Cimarron. Or the *Simmer On*, as he had called it. They had celebrated just about every full moon since.

Then she remembered the night last summer Jeffrey had stopped in his tracks on the way into his kitchen to describe the crescent moons that would bracket the millennial year.

"You know, it's really incredible," she said to David, "the way the two moons are going to match on New Year's Eve 1999 and 2000." David nodded. "Like a set of celestial parentheses. It's just inviting us to spend the year usefully." He seemed like he was a little more open to hearing her–he usually was when he was driving. So she went on.

"I haven't told you this but the last night I was in Vladivostok, I met a guy who really . . . "

"Turned you on?"

"No, of course not. He was married, and he was fifty years old for godsakes." She couldn't resist ribbing him; David was so sensitive about being forty-five. "The important thing was–David, listen to me, will you. He's an explorer, Canadian, been to the South Pole and the North Pole and Everest and everywhere else–and I was fascinated to meet him. Somebody with all that courage.

"We'd both stopped at the desk of this crummy little place I was staying–we were both trying to find a place to do some laundry–any-how, we decided to give up and have tea in the lobby there. And got to talking. He's got this idea about putting together an expedition for the start of the millennial year where twelve young people would start from the North Pole, and travel in teams, stopping at about sixty cities along the way and doing events with youth and all, and then ending up at the South Pole in time to catch the first light of the millennial year. They're going to gather and carry the new millennium resolutions of hopefully millions of people with them.

hooking in

"And so I told him about the Summer Project, and he thought maybe what he could do is get them to carry all the messages we get back from people about celebration and what they want for the world. And it was absolutely sheer chance that I ran into him. In his brochure, it says, our words will be frozen in time, but our actions will affect generations to come for a thousand years. Or something like that. His name is Martyn Williams. I can't tell you what it meant to me to meet someone like that. To know that there's other people out there trying to do things, too. You know?"

"Mmmhmm," said David noncommittally. "Yeah, he sounds like an interesting guy."

"One thing he said, and it keeps coming back to me–he's been an expedition leader for years, and he said in our business, we know that visualizations work. We know that if you pledge to do something, and you imagine it being done, and you repeat that pledge every day . . . "

"We're going to be coming up to that intersection in a minute," David interrupted. "Which way are we supposed to go?"

I won't let myself feel hurt, I just won't. Not today. "Well, let's see." Once again, LeeAnn tried to decipher the directions she'd scribbled in her planner, but it was difficult. "I think we take a left."

She was wrong, but David, who seemed to have a Loran installed in his head, managed to find the address they were looking for with no problem, at the end of a long gravel road. "Nice house," LeeAnn said as they started up the walk.

Wonder of wonders, the board was exactly as advertised. The moment they laid eyes on it in the guy's spotlessly perfect garage packed with a plethora of perfectly spotless toys, they knew. Both of them managed to keep their mouths shut as they went through a charade of careful inspection, trying not to do anything that would blow the deal. *Are you sure you don't mean* eight *hundred seventy-five dollars?* LeeAnn wanted to ask him.

The guy, a forest ranger who had a couple of kids and a fat dog that were peering around the corner, insisted on laying out everything on the floor and showing them exactly how it all worked. David handed over the money still warm from the ATM, after which the two men climbed up and strapped the prize onto the sagging ski rack David had brought along. Then just like regular board-heads, LeeAnn and David drove off to join the endless parade of wind seekers circling between the two states.

119

"All *right!*" David shouted. He put the van into a delicious spin as soon as they were back out on the gravel road again, screeching to a halt to high-five her. David almost never played with a vehicle, but his skills were amazing the few times he did. All that defensive driving training he had as a cop. And that hundred-miles-an-hour chase that he told her about when his patrol car had come to rest just teetering off a bridge.

"This is great," David said, as he started off again.

"And we can both use it. But it's really *your* board," she said. "I'll try it, but it's a better size for you. I'll hold out. I can use the barge till we find something. I really think a three-ten would be plenty big, don't you?" There she was, already up on the nomenclature. It had to do with liters, she thought. Or meters.

"But I'll tell you this," David said as they headed back over the bald hills of moonscape country, "one thing we can buy you while we're here, is your harness."

That got her attention. "I don't know that I'm ready yet."

"No, I want you to have it. I'm sure I can sell something at that gallery tomorrow. It'll be a present."

LeeAnn remained highly doubtful. To be truthful, she was scared shitless. She pictured in her mind the rigid, phallic-looking gismo wind-surfers strap onto themselves. Wearing this contraption, you reach out with your pelvis and hook into the boom strap, a typical mating movement, only this time you're the guy, hooking into the loop and going for a ride. Hooking in tight, like dogs mating, so you might not be able to get loose if you wanted to.

"LeeAnn, you can't possibly support yourself with just your arms in high winds. You've got to hook in!"

"I know."

"You have to *commit* to it."

"I know," she nodded.

But the claustrophobia was terrible to think about. Getting caught under water, with her sail still attached. LeeAnn's nightmares, which had plagued her throughout her childhood, were always about darkness and suffocation. She took a deep breath.

Forty-five minutes later they pulled up in front of the jazziest equipment store in Hood River. The high-class joint was arranged like a car dealership, with New Age music playing and the latest models of boards and sails spaced out on the showroom floor so you could walk around them and murmur and point in tones of awe. They'd done that earlier in the day.

LeeAnn immediately started pawing through a table of used harnesses that seemed to have been placed there as a courtesy to the locals, but David said, "No way." He enlisted help from a startlingly handsome blond clerk with a dark beard, and the two men consulted on brands, sizes, and designs, eyeing LeeAnn's frame from time to time. Then they brought one over that had a blue-and-white checkerboard pattern on the butt. *Checkmate,* she thought. *No getting out of it now.*

David held out the leg straps and said, "Step into this," putting her hand on his shoulder just as the clerk reached out to balance her. She stepped into the black nylon loops. David pulled the contraption up around her waist and snapped small buckles in place, one around the waist, the other at the hip. Then the two of them got busy with all the straps and adjustments and whatever.

LeeAnn relaxed and let herself concentrate on the sensation of being dressed by two men. She decided this felt for all the world like she was being buckled into a chastity belt before the knights who knelt before her now went off to war. Or maybe they were buckling on her cock so she could go with them. Whichever it was, she liked the way they were tugging at the straps, trying to get it fitted on her. It was kind of sexy.

The tag on his shirt said his name was Adam and he was quite a hunk. Perfect features, perfect teeth, perfect body, great buns. Undoubtedly a magnificent windsurfer as well. Adorable was the word she would have used to describe him to another woman.

"How's that feel? You want it snug now," Adam said, raising himself up so he had one knee and one foot on the floor, and was ready to stand. Or equally ready to kneel back down and help her some more if that's what she wanted. Actually, she noticed, David was kneeling in exactly the same position on the other side.

She looked at the image of herself in the full-length mirror, with this *thing* sticking out on the front of her, the two men kneeling at her feet. LeeAnn was careful to avoid Adam's eyes. It was disturbing to her that she could be attracted to someone else.

"Here's your quick release here," Adam said, tapping her on her right hip buckle.

You mean my dick release, she thought and smiled.

"You've got one on both sides," he added, guiding her hand to it. "These are safety releases. They're there just in case."

She looked at him. "In case of what?" She did not want to hear it, and yet she did.

"In case you should get caught underwater," he said, "and you can't get loose. Very unlikely to happen," he added, his forehead wrinkling sweetly as he gazed earnestly up at her. But she remained unconvinced and he could see it.

"You'd have to get flipped over on your board, and then get twisted somehow on the way down," Adam gestured with his hand the way people demonstrate airplane stunts, Immelmanns, and such, "so that you do a 360, and then come up under your sail." His hand stopped in midair right after that elaborate maneuver. "It almost never happens."

Maybe. LeeAnn had already come up under her sail a couple of times, coughing and choking, and as a result had decided she would buy a very clear sail. That way she could see while she was drowning.

"Let me ask you this," she said to Adam. "Does anybody ever *die* that way?" She saw David wince as she asked the question. He got up from his one-knee position and walked around in a circle.

"Not around here, nobody does," Adam said. "I've never heard of it."

No, LeeAnn thought. *Around here they get hit by barges.*

"These buckles feel hard to flip," she persisted. They were the kind you wear on a weight belt, scuba diving, which was another tough learning experience she'd had because of a man. (Her ex-husband Bo had been a commercial diver, so it would have been impossible for her not to learn how.)

David gave her a look that told her not to say another thing about drowning, so she picked up one knee and then the other to see how the harness fit. It was binding a little on her left thigh so they adjusted some straps.

"There. That's better, I guess." Both men were staring at her crotch.

"Okay?" asked David.

"Okay."

David turned LeeAnn around one more time and then approved the fit.

She looked at herself in the mirror again. "So," she said, feeling a little better now. "I get to walk around in this thing," and she strutted back and forth. "Kind of like being an honorary male," she said.

"With a permanent woody," David added. Both men laughed and she joined them. Adam's smile was wonderful; he seemed warm, genuinely interested to help. Or maybe interested in a little more than that. She realized that when they walked in she had felt that jolt you get just a few times in your life when you first look at a perfect stranger. She'd felt it and then repressed it. Or was she just imagining this attraction because of feeling insecure about David? Was this a rehearsal for going back out there? *Dismiss this man from your mind,* she told herself. She was ashamed she'd even thought about it.

"Okay," she said at last. She took off the harness, like you'd take off a pair of shorts, and handed it to David to take up to the register. Eighty bucks–a hundred including the fancy reactor bar instead of a hook. Another gift from David.

They looked briefly at a rainbow array of shiny helmets while they waited for VISA approval, but LeeAnn was firm. "We've spent enough money for one day. And we can probably get them cheaper by mail order." She was eager to get out of the store.

"Don't worry," David said, putting his hand over hers on the counter as the charge slip was printing out, "I know you're feeling like you're not ready. So, just take your time. Wear it. Get used to it. Okay?"

She nodded. "And thank you for buying it for me." Like most couples they played that game, even though it was both of their money.

"You're welcome."

Well, it'll be good to have when we get home to Klamath, she thought, walking out of the store without a backward glance. *Good training for courage, in all departments.* But she felt more than a little bit of dread.

Next morning, after gathering up all the free shampoo and checking out of the Best Western, they stopped at a new art gallery on their way to the airport. Since Audrey's plane wasn't due in till 9:30, David had called and persuaded the owner to meet him before regular hours so he could show him his work.

LeeAnn sat outside in the van in the parking lot of the upscale mini-mall where the gallery was located, watching David, who was engaged in animated conversation with the owner and his assistant, the curator.

He'd been in there thirty minutes according to LeeAnn's watch, but it was still more than an hour before Audrey was scheduled to arrive. No hurry. She looked around for a phone, thinking about calling home to see how Jeffrey was doing all by himself with the cat at their house in Klamath. She hoped he was happy in the new environment. He'd be missing Kevin; the two men were probably the closest partners she'd ever seen. She had been hoping Jeff and David would become friends. When she'd asked David how they were getting along, he said fine, but didn't elaborate.

Were they making departure gestures yet? David always unconsciously signaled by moving from one foot to the other that he was about to wrap things up. She'd gotten pretty good at reading his body language. Back when they went on a lot of road trips and she'd first started waiting out in front of stores that David sold to, they'd been mostly gift-shoppey-type places that featured Kermit the Frogs and pet rocks. And paintings on velvet in the window. Nowadays he was marketing full-scale sculpture to chic galleries, working in stone, moose, and deer antler, crafting animals and ancient people whose faces and musculature were so real, someone had recently said his work belonged in the Louvre.

Spotting a phone down at the end of a group of stores, she got out of the van and walked over toward it. She dialed home and got the machine. "Hi, Jeffrey, I don't know if you'll hear this. I hope you're okay and that David and Sillvester have been taking good care of you. We're on our way to get Aud-ball now; her flight will be here in about an hour. So we should be home by . . . " She looked at her watch. "Maybe eight. See you then."

Because she didn't have anything else to do, she called her voice mail and listened back through all the messages she'd already heard, then hit delete, delete, delete. Then she walked back to the van. She realized she was feeling more than a little antsy about Jeff and David and Audrey and the whole happening that was about to descend, as the 22nd Century Group began its pursuit of her ridiculously ambitious idea. *Yet if we don't do anything . . . We have to do something. We have to get everybody together who's trying to do something.*

Her mind went into a fantasy of introducing the explorer, Martyn Williams, to the sailboard manufacturer who had the ad in the magazine. And Riane Eisler, who wrote *The Chalice and the Blade*, and who'd called LeeAnn after she'd written her a letter once and they'd arranged to meet. And to Robert Muller, the former assistant Secretary-General of the U.N. who had great visions of how the world should be, and wrote such neat poems. . .

hooking in

LeeAnn's latest reverie was interrupted when the back door of the van opened. She turned to watch as David put his artwork in its boxes back inside, stacking them meticulously as he always did. He smiled enigmatically at her. Then he closed the door, came around and climbed into the driver's seat. He started up the engine and was out of the parking lot and almost back up on the highway again before he reached into his shirt pocket and handed over a check for one thousand eight hundred and fifty dollars.

"David!" He always did that, never letting her know right away if he'd made a sale. The tradition had started back when he worked in the car lot. They were on the ragged edge financially and he hadn't wanted to ruin her day by telling her about the sixteen "be-backs" who hadn't. Then to make sure she didn't guess from his silence that it was a bad day, he had started hiding the good news as well, making her wait at least half an hour before announcing it.

They were passing a Burger King. The entrance to the interstate was just a few blocks ahead. LeeAnn's hand rested on David's right leg, feeling his muscles as he moved his foot from brake to accelerator, and she relaxed into letting him guide them along. She'd gotten so she didn't drive at all when they were together. She patted his knee and then rubbed it, reflecting that it was strange both sides of him still matched, one got so much more attention than the other.

Soon they were swinging up onto the highway. LeeAnn felt the centrifugal force as they drove up the curving ramp. That was probably what a jibe felt like. As they headed west toward the airport, they could still see the Columbia River, but it was getting more business-like. There was more shipping here and the windsurfing was becoming lost to commerce. It was still forty-five minutes before Audrey's flight was scheduled to land.

CHAPTER SEVEN

People of the Lake

They waited at the United gate–naturally they'd meet Audrey at the gate. There was no way LeeAnn would think of doing the Baggage Claim/White-Zone number. The flight had landed; LeeAnn stood beside David, watching attentively as the passengers began to disembark.

"She's a trip," she said to David, as other people's loved ones paraded out of the plane. Someone in the arrival area held up a hand-lettered sign for the stranger he was seeking in this human meeting ground.

Audrey came into view then, with her short, dark ringlets and her glossy nails, a little shrimp of a thing, bouncing along, so delightfully, annoyingly New York. Wearing a bright print mini-dress–which in her case was more like micro–and with her hair freshly hennaed, she was looking excited and expectant, darker than usual from an adventure on the Big Island in Hawaii. Audrey always arranged her life for fun, and it looked like nothing had changed in that regard.

When she saw them, she stopped about twelve feet away to make a dramatic moment of it, so the people behind her had to go around. "My *God, look* at you," she said in tongue-in-cheek imitation of a Jewish mother. LeeAnn looked quickly at David to see what he thought. His face exhibited surprise more than anything. Surprise about what? She would have to ask him.

LeeAnn had wondered if David would be put off by her forcefulness, her bossiness, but he didn't seem to be at all. Just surprised. Maybe he didn't expect her to be so little–he had to bend way over to hug her, like you would a child, when they were introduced.

They retrieved her bag and walked across to short-term parking as David related how he'd raced through here the other day when he was late. He was pulling Audrey's enormous suitcase-on-wheels like a large blocky dog behind him. It was a bag that held, no doubt, a complete collection of accoutrements for grooming. By the time they got to the van, he seemed completely at ease, and of course you never had to urge Audrey out of shyness; she was talking a blue streak and so was David, as they all piled into the van. LeeAnn climbed in back to give Audrey the comfortable seat.

A few minutes later they were stalled in a construction jam. "Are you starving?" LeeAnn asked Audrey. I am. We haven't had breakfast yet."

"I had something on the plane but I'm not sure what it was."

"We'll stop as soon as we get out of this mess," David announced as a huge yellow Caterpillar lumbered by on the shoulder. He gave it a wide berth. Then he added, "You know those things scare the shit out of me."

"How come?" Audrey asked.

"Something happened when I was a cop."

"Oh come on, you weren't a cop," Audrey said. "For real?"

"Oh yes he was," LeeAnn said from the back of the van. "But the nice kind. What was it, seven years you did that? Deputy sheriff out in eastern Oregon. Seven years, and he was just started on his second ticket book."

"I wasn't on highway patrol . . . ," he interjected.

"That's the kind of cop I like."

"I tried not to bust anybody for something that I might have done."

"I should get so lucky. I accumulate speeding tickets like junk mail."

David just smiled. He disapproved of fast driving; he'd cleaned up too many messes on the highway, but didn't say anything now. He was still looking at the Caterpillar and Audrey was looking at him expectantly for the story.

"What happened was–I was still a rookie–I went by a construction site at night once and noticed one of the Cats still had its engine running, so I climbed up and tried to turn it off, but the thing lurched and threw me. I came within a heartbeat of running myself over."

"And getting mashed," Audrey said, looking at the big machine. "Applesauce. Scary." David shuddered in remembrance.

Traffic was just inching along. It was a hot August day in Portland, and the air conditioning had been out in the van since heaven knew when. Since two summers ago, LeeAnn thought, but it was the compressor, and for fifteen hundred bucks you could sweat a little. "Sorry about the A.C.," she said to Audrey.

"No problem. At least I'm not as hot as *she* is." A harassed-looking flagger, saddlebags on her hips, love handles bulging over her jeans, was sweating rivers. Her orange vest looked miserably hot in the blazing sun.

LeeAnn, lying on the air mattress in the back of the van, her head up close between David and Audrey, could smell the familiar melange of Audrey's scented makeup, her lipstick, her musky perfume. Audrey looked perfect and smelled that way, too.

Along the side of the highway, a new complex of storage units was going up. "You know," LeeAnn said, "I've always imagined myself hiding away in one of those. If things ever got rough, I could go store myself. 'Hello, I've come to turn myself in for self-storage.'"

"Home shopping and self-storage," David said. "Too many people and too much shit."

"It's plain as day," Audrey said.

"Hey, don't get David started. Overpopulation is his thing."

"Too many people," he repeated.

Finally the cars ahead started to move. By fits and starts they were approaching what looked to be a genuine greasy spoon about a quarter of a mile down.

"That looks like the kind of place," LeeAnn said, "where David always says people are killing themselves with a fork."

"Shall we stop?" David asked.

In a fit of madcap irresponsibility, they decided to do it up right. "Let's all order the worst thing we possibly can. Like pancakes and syrup."

"With a side of sausage gravy," LeeAnn added as they walked through the smoking section where all the good seats were. She watched the cigarette smoke as it curled quickly and discreetly up into the super-suck vent system that this caring fork-killing restaurant provided for its customers' comfortable demise as they ingested their daily infusion of grease.

"And an extra order of that yummy sausage gravy," Audrey told the waitress. "Ah, good," she murmured appreciatively when the plate of poison arrived and was set down before her. She was about to dig in when there was the sudden, fairly loud sound of a cricket nearby.

"Chirp, chirp."

Audrey looked around.

"Chirp, chirp, chirp."

She looked around again.

David knew how to make a noise that sounded exactly like a cricket. He'd perfected it during all those years that he was married and fishing. He would practice when he was out alone at night. It was the sound he used to locate LeeAnn in the supermarket when they got separated; he was doing it now to fool the waitress and Audrey, who was scared of bugs. Entomology was the only part of her biology studies that bothered her, and she had never gotten over it. It may have had to do with cockroaches in her crib in the project on Amsterdam Avenue where she grew up.

Finally, when it was clear Audrey was getting genuinely freaked, David picked up a piece of parsley on her plate and peered under it as he chirped one more time.

"It's you!" She punched him lightly on the biceps and he looked pleased as they began to eat. It was his customary way of breaking the ice with new acquaintances.

"Fribben," he said quietly to LeeAnn when he got up to let her out of the booth so she and Audrey could go to the restroom. Everything seemed to be going okay.

L.A. and Audrey bonded some in the ladies room, which was a pretty grungy place. There were little dribbles of gray enamel over the Revlon-pink paint that were evidently meant to disguise the bumpy walls.

LeeAnn hit the *Flush Here* button, and went out to where Audrey was beginning to wield her lip brush before the mirror. LeeAnn washed her hands slowly, taking her time with the lathering like she had when she was a little girl. "Oh, by the way," she said. "Good news. I got us that free office."

"You did? That's terrific."

"Right in downtown Klamath Falls. Wait till you see it. It's only about a mile from the house." LeeAnn rinsed the lather off.

"So what is this shit about you two not living together?" Audrey asked her then. "Or are you?"

"Who knows? I don't know," LeeAnn answered, unfolding one of the brown paper towels, and watching it darken with the water from her hands. "We haven't been home yet. Right before I left, he'd moved his things to the cabin, which simply turned out to mean we'd sleep out there some nights and in the house other nights. So your guess is as good as mine. The homecoming was yummy though."

"Men are from Mars, you know." Audrey leaned forward and did that fishy sucking thing to spread the lipstick around on sexy lips that had looked since kindergarten like she'd had collagen added.

"So, what do you think of him?" LeeAnn had taken her brush out of her purse and was now yanking it through her windblown hair.

"David? I'm impressed." Now Audrey was busy with her midnight-blue eyeliner. "The way you always described him I didn't know if you'd be good together. But it seems like you are. The vibes I'm getting anyway. You're purring."

LeeAnn laughed.

"I suspect your troubles are over."

"What do you mean, you thought we wouldn't be good together?"

"He always sounded like such a silent loner. So I decided it must be that the sex was great."

"It is."

"But he's really bright as well." Apparently satisfied with her handiwork, Audrey put the eyeliner away.

"I told you."

"Yeah but I didn't believe you. You always think if they can talk and chew gum at the same time, they're brilliant."

Audrey was right. She did. "Well, you do, too."

Audrey shrugged. "We have these little failings." She leaned forward, leaning close to the mirror so she could get her blush on just right. "So why did he move out?"

"Because I reacted badly to the open-relationship idea."

She stopped. "I see. And when did *that* come up?"

"Gradually. It was probably over a period of like a year–I just kept hearing this new word in his vocabulary. *Polyfidelity.*" Audrey turned to stare at her. "It just kept coming up in conversation.

"So I finally just called him on it, and he was excruciatingly honest. He said he'd been thinking about it for a long time, that he wanted other women. He said he needed to find out about more women before he died. I guess I can't blame him. He got married at eighteen–and then we got together almost right after they broke up. So he never really had a chance."

"So has he . . ." Audrey wanted to know.

"Oh, no."

"Are you sure?"

"David would never . . . without telling me. He would never put me at *risk*." Audrey nodded. "I'm sure. That night, when he first told me what he wanted, we sat around and talked about it till God knows when, and really, rationally, I could understand what he felt. He'd been having to bury his feelings for so long. We both cried. And right then I felt like maybe I could deal with it. But then by the next morning, I just lost it, cried myself into anoxia."

Audrey shook her head.

"The kind of crying where you're sob, sob, sob, and then you're gasping for breath, *aaarggh*." She demonstrated and Audrey laughed.

"So he moved out. I'm such a mess where he's concerned," LeeAnn said, shaking her head. "I think I would have moved out too, the way I was acting. So leave it to David to find a pragmatic solution. We're still on the same property, but . . ."

Audrey interrupted. "You should have just *decked* him."

"I couldn't. I just become this wimpy little thing when I'm around him. I can't help it. Pawing and clinging."

"*Co-dependent.*"

"You always have these buzzwords."

"They're true."

"Oh, Audrey, he's my candy store, I'm hooked on him and I know it. It's partly why I took the job away this summer."

"Weren't you afraid you would lose him by going away?"

"I *know* I'll lose him if I cling."

"Could be." Audrey snapped her makeup case shut and regarded the finished product in the cloudy mirror of the fork-killing restaurant.

Outside in the sunshine, David had an Oregon road map spread out on a picnic table. Later, LeeAnn would remember being very aware of herself and Audrey walking toward David, his eyes fixed on the two women. Life was a series of snapshots, just that. And the rest gone. Like of the eight years she'd been with Bo, four of them married to him, how much of it could she remember? Very little.

"So, what'll it be? Straight down or over to the coast? Here's Klamath down here." He showed Audrey on the map.

"It's not near anything," she said.

"Not if you're talking about cities," David said. Klamath was five long hours from the Bay Area, five hours from Reno, five hours from Portland."

"Hmmm." Audrey studied the map.

"Ashland's only an hour and a half. Where the Shakespeare Festival is. We could stop in Ashland for lunch if you want," David said. "Or we could go to Crater Lake."

"Crater Lake! *Got* to see it," Audrey said. "Is it far out of the way? I've *always* wanted to see Crater Lake."

LeeAnn hoped aloud it would still be light when they got home. "So you can see our lake, too."

"We'll make it," David assured her as he folded the map neatly and put it in the glove compartment. "It's not out of our way really. We can do it."

"You're going to like Klamath Falls," LeeAnn said. "Very quiet, now with most of the logging gone. But it used to have the highest homicide rate in the U.S."

"They don't shoot New Yorkers, do they?"

"I would hope not."

"You want to drive?" David asked LeeAnn. "That way you two can talk."

She almost took him up on it. But much as LeeAnn hated back seats, David's silent backseat driving was worse. And she *certainly* didn't want Audrey to drive. So David opened the back and LeeAnn climbed in on the air mattress again. He patted her butt as she wiggled her way forward past the boxes of artwork, then closed the doors on her.

Audrey climbed up onto the passenger seat, shutting the door with a bang that would have rattled David if LeeAnn had done it. They were on their way as Audrey chattered on about the whales off Maui, her helicopter flight over the live volcano on the Big Island, about the guys she'd met over there and the uncertain status of her job back in Florida. What she was hoping to do someday, she said, was work with marine mammals, and given that she usually got what she wanted, she probably would.

"So, what do you think of Girlfriend's grand plan?" she finally asked David.

David hesitated.

"No, go ahead, tell her what you think," LeeAnn urged him. "You won't tell *me*."

"If you want the truth, I think it's a pretty crazy idea."

132

"Why do you think that?" Audrey wanted to know.

"Because it's getting involved, like LeeAnn always does, in trying to change the entire world." He stopped then. David was seldom that direct; apparently Audrey being there must be giving him courage. "I don't care what you imagine you can do, you're not going to change people," he said glancing at LeeAnn then. "I hate to say this but you're just not. People are not going to celebrate the millennium the way you want them . . ."

"Do you have any idea, David," Audrey broke in, "what happened the *last* time we had a millennium? People went nuts! Everybody thought the world was coming to an end. Total chaos. You don't want to let *that* happen again, do you? Somebody's got to see that we can *celebrate constructively* for a change. Capiche?"

And David shut up. Immediately. He didn't even look bothered, just shrugged and kept on driving. She kept at him.

"So. I don't want to hear any more complaints, all right? At least we're not just sitting around bitching. We're doing something." Thank god for Audrey, LeeAnn thought, staring up at the ceiling of the van as they hurtled down the interstate. It was always so comforting to have her around. She'd almost forgotten how close they were.

When they got to Crater Lake, the wind was blowing hard. They stood behind the glass barrier, looking out at the storm-tossed water. It was the first time LeeAnn had seen the lake that way; she was used to cross-country skiing or biking around it with no barriers in between. But the spirituality and magic came right through the glass. Audrey was enchanted, and suitably silent.

Later, back in the van, traveling through alpine forest, past Fish Lake and Lake of the Woods, Audrey was reading aloud from the books she'd picked up at the Crater Lake bookstore.

"Wow, this is great. These legends, this is real feminist stuff. Listen to what it says here. They're talking about when Mount Mazama went off and the people were trying to decide whether or not to offer a sacrifice. It says, 'but the elders wouldn't allow a maiden to be taken. So they threw themselves in instead.'"

"In the volcano?" David asked.

"Uh-huh."

"That's a switch."

"Then there's this story about this woman, how she dresses up like a brave and becomes fleet of foot and skillful and leads the people."

"We're in partnership country," LeeAnn said. "Do you know the Klamath tribe never used to have chiefs until the white man came along and said, 'Hey you got to have somebody to sign these papers.'"

"So if they didn't have any chiefs, who was in charge?"

"Whoever happened to be good at something, one of the tribal members told me."

They were about to come over the crest of the hill where Klamath Lake would be spread out below them. David had gone out of the way to take the most scenic approach, so LeeAnn was hoping Audrey wouldn't be looking down at her book at the wrong time; she wanted her to fully appreciate that first stunning view. "In just a minute," LeeAnn warned, "you'll be able to see it. Right over this rise. Riiiiiiight....... now!"

Speechless for a moment, Audrey reacted with proper awe at the panoramic view of the vast inland sea that was Upper Klamath Lake, with forested hills and white-capped mountains in the background. "So that's it," she said. "So that's where the algae comes from."

"Yup."

"It's got islands in it."

"Mmmhmmm."

They started down. Lying on her stomach on the inflatable air mattress with the tie-dyed sheets on it was like riding on a sled down the long hill toward the lake. LeeAnn imagined herself sailing down from the sky toward the lake and the village on the other side where her Klamath Indian great-grandmother had lived, seeing it the way it must have been back then. The only thing LeeAnn had to remember her by was an old-fashioned picnic basket fitted with all the silverware and everything that had allegedly belonged to her at one time. Which didn't tell her much about her great grandmother, except that perhaps she had a romantic streak. Maybe she liked picnics as much as LeeAnn did.

As they got down toward the bottom of the hill, LeeAnn exited her reverie and directed Audrey's view to the north. "That's the caldera of Mount Mazama, where we just came from. Crater Lake's two thousand feet deep, so it goes down below Klamath Lake. Like a tall glass of water next to a saucer-full."

"How deep is Klamath Lake?

"Ten to twenty feet, most of it," David told her. "Some places are deeper."

"But it's *huge*."

"It's the biggest natural lake west of the Rockies, I think. Bigger than Tahoe, bigger than San Francisco Bay."

Audrey took it all in. "So where does the tribe live?"

"The Klamath Tribe. Over on the other side of the lake," LeeAnn told her. "The main part of the tribe is still in Chiloquin mostly. But people have been living all over this area for at least ten thousand years–and they've uncovered settlements older than that just north of here."

"I can believe it," Audrey said. "If I were coming through twenty or thirty thousand years ago, I think I'd be ready to stop here. It's spectacular." She gazed admiringly at the scene. "And imagine what it looked like with mammoths and camels running around."

"They just recently spotted a Siberian swan on the lake," David said.

"You're kidding."

"First time ever."

"So. A new immigrant. I wonder if he's starting something."

"The lake's way down this time of year," David said, as they started to ride along the shore. "See all that?" He pointed to an expanse of mudflats. "All that should be lake. The problem is California keeps getting our water. There's lots of controversy about water rights around here just now. The tribe is hurting, and so are the ranchers."

"It all comes down to water, doesn't it? It always does." Water was Audrey's field, and one of David's favorite subjects too. Right after population control.

It was a beautiful day to be driving along the lake. There was a strong wind from the north and the resultant updrafts were amazing. It looked as though invisible helicopters were hovering here and there, driving the water away in all directions simultaneously. It occurred to LeeAnn that if you were windsurfing, getting hit by something like that would be like getting hit by a freight train . . . or a barge. "Can we stop for a minute?" LeeAnn asked David. Obligingly, he pulled into the next overlook, which was a little bit before Squaw Point.

The wind whipped at their clothing as they got out of the van, so LeeAnn grabbed an old windbreaker of David's out of the back and handed it to Audrey. "Here, you little tropical wimp, put this on."

Audrey had to turn her back to the wind to get the jacket zipped. It came to her knees. She turned around and stood there, looking at the lake. "What's the name of the island?" she asked.

"That one's called Tree Island," David said. "There's Buck Island. And the one down there's called Bare Island."

"It's got bears on it?" Audrey wanted to know.

"No. Bare Island. B-a-r-e. Nothing on it. Which is probably why they named the other one Tree Island, because it has a tree on it."

"Oh." Audrey turned her attention back to Tree Island. It was pretty big, about a quarter or a half mile out, with dry grass of a beautiful golden color, and one permanently windblown tree on the top, silhouetted against a ragged horizon in the east.

"What kind of tree is that?"

"It's a juniper," LeeAnn told Audrey. "And it's about a thousand years old. From up there," LeeAnn said, pointing to the tree, "you can probably see Mount Shasta to the south and Mazama to the north."

David had walked down to look into the water at the shoreline the way he always did; now he beckoned Audrey and LeeAnn to join him. "Would you like to see the algae?"

"Ooh, yeah." Audrey and LeeAnn joined him, kneeling down on the bank to peer down at tiny strands of what looked like cut grass suspended in the crystal water. It was the super food the lake was known for. There was enough of it that bloomed each summer to help substantially in feeding the planet. By some estimates, Klamath Lake could provide many hundreds of millions of people with their daily protein plus their B vitamins, carotenes, and about forty minerals.

"That's exactly how it looks in the pictures," Audrey said at last. "But I had to check it out for myself. In its native setting." She looked up at the mountains and the sky. "This place is pretty damn spiritual, you know."

"Yeah, it is. The way I think about it is the two mountains are male and the lake is female. The water is the mother spirit, the birthplace of the algae. So the male essence is fertilizing the life-giving water with the mineral ash."

Audrey liked that. She nodded. "And the algae is like the phoenix rising from the ashes."

"You could look at it that way," LeeAnn said.

"The total life cycle. Seven thousand, almost eight thousand years after the eruption."

"That's a pretty neat thought, actually." They were quiet for a minute.

"Those gusts are amazing." David had pulled out the new binoculars and was looking through them at the embryonic water spouts out on the lake.

"Do they remind you of dust devils, David?" LeeAnn teased.

"Same thing really, only over water," David said.

"David is overly fascinated with dust devils," LeeAnn whispered sotto voce. "I'm always accusing him of being in love with them."

"From living out in the desert, I guess. It's all I had to love."

LeeAnn looked at David's grin under the binoculars–his lips were sexy. "But you like water spouts, too," she laughed. "There's one for you," LeeAnn pointed. "She's a beauty. Look at her dance." They watched the graceful column of water bending and twisting its way across the lake. "Wow."

"You know," she said, as they turned to get back in the van, "there were three things about this that impressed me when I first came to Klamath, three numbers. The first one was three hundred days of sunshine."

"That's enough right there," said Audrey, the eternal sunseeker. Little Miss Coppertone.

"And forty-two hundred feet, which is the ideal training altitude for athletes. Best place to run. Absolutely ideal conditions for the human body to thrive. And for the algae, too, apparently." It was the only still clean lake in the world where this particular strain of algae was flourishing.

"And the other thing?"

LeeAnn was busy climbing into her niche in the back of the van, making her way past the boxes of David's artwork that were stacked on the right; even bigger sculptures meant even bigger boxes. "Give me a minute." It was a tight fit, any tighter and she would have begun to feel claustrophobic. When she'd gotten herself settled and Audrey had slammed the door loudly again, LeeAnn continued.

"The other figure that fascinates me is that it was seventy-seven hundred years ago when Mount Mazama erupted. They say the ash from it, up in the stratosphere, went all around the world, and that it would have created these amazing blood-red sunsets . . ."

"Like Pinatubo."

"Only much, much more."

"And that it would have been unnaturally dark thousands and thousands of miles away. The Celts in Ireland would have wondered what was happening–can you imagine?"

"And the people in China."

"The funny thing to me–total coincidence, of course–is that right about eight thousand years ago, when the eruption took place, was when the partnership era was really starting to be on its way out all over the world. So, sunset on partnership, too."

"Like the earth was mourning," Audrey murmured. "How very Celestine."

"There's no connection of course."

"Don't be so sure."

As David started the van again and they took off, Audrey went on about *The Celestine Prophesy* for several minutes. "So you see, there *are* no coincidences," she concluded.

"Maybe you're right," LeeAnn said. "But maybe you're not. Maybe it's just what we *invest* these 'coincidences' with that's important. It strikes me that we need myth to live by."

"Joseph Campbell said that," said Audrey.

"We need magic in our lives. Or most of us do," she said, looking at David, who seemed to do just fine on a diet of reality.

"So you're going to read it, okay? '*The Celestine Prophecy.*' " She'd been on LeeAnn for a year to read the book.

"Yes, Audrey, I'll read it."

"While I'm here."

"While you're here."

They were headed past Moore Park now and Audrey looked back up toward the northern part of the lake. "You're planning to windsurf this entire distance?"

"Why? You want to go with us?" David asked as LeeAnn's heart dropped down into her gut. Surely he didn't mean that.

"Uh-uh, no way," Audrey replied, with a quick look back at LeeAnn. She winked.

"You could learn."

"No, no, no. I'd break my nails."

David smiled happily. Usually long fingernails and bossy women bothered him.

CHAPTER EIGHT

Coming Home

The van went bump, bumpety-bump up into the driveway. There was a specific rhythm, a certain bumpety-bump pattern that LeeAnn realized she would remember until the day she died. It was in her bones. She'd been all the way around the world and now she was back in her own driveway. A safely completed trip was always a small miracle to her.

There was Sillvester, the cat yelling at the gate. Everything was the same, back to the way it had been. Except for herself and David. And perhaps that would be too, as soon as Audrey had him properly brainwashed.

"Nice house," Audrey said. The old, square, squat home that greeted them was charcoal gray, with turquoise and white trim. It looked a lot better since David had painted over the incomprehensible apple green, but its basic lines were still somewhat lacking in grace. A sturdy, pragmatic house, it sat on its haunches on the hill without preening, and that suited LeeAnn just fine.

David came around to let her out of the van. She went straight over to pick up Sillvester, who, as usual, was fluffy and beautiful, a study in black and white *catapuss*, as David called him. "But not very lovable," she told Audrey. She carried him over for an introduction. "Sillvester, this is Audrey. Audrey, this is Sillvester. We call him Silly. Born out here, but he has a New York attitude."

"Strong personality, huh?" asked Audrey, cautiously petting Sillvester on the top of the head with one finger. He narrowed his eyes.

"Just yells all the time," LeeAnn said fondly, "but he doesn't purr."

"He doesn't purr?" And if you insist on picking him up, he won't *do* anything, but it's about as much fun as picking up frozen road kill." Sillvester obliged them with a demonstration. LeeAnn set him down

139

and he walked along beside them, complaining loudly about LeeAnn's months away as David started hauling luggage out of the van.

"Here, I can get my own bag for godsakes." Audrey began trailing her fancy suitcase on the gravel and dried mud that constituted their driveway. And of course it tipped over and of course David sprang ahead to right it.

As they walked in the back door, past the weight machine, Audrey noticed the swing. "Oooh, a swing," she said with a big smile, kidding LeeAnn with her look. *Yes*, they had a swing in the weight room, and *yes*, they sometimes made love in it. But then they'd also hike its chain up a few notches and use it as a chinning bar. It was a multipurpose swing. Maggie always believed that any building that housed primates ought to have monkey bars–and it had become a Spencer tradition. Peter had a great Tarzan rope in his studio, with its twenty-foot ceilings.

There was a large stack of papers on the kitchen table. LeeAnn saw her mail was laid out in police-academy precision, along with several issues of the *New York Times* that had arrived in the spring before she'd remembered to cancel. Talk about *old* news. And a short stack of the local paper.

They got Audrey settled in the attic apartment, an attic, LeeAnn pointed out, built especially for Lilliputians. David was always hunched up and forever banging his head when he went up there. But for Audrey it was great. Tiny little tub under the eaves, with ball and claws taken off, little tiny kitchen area. Audrey seemed happy as a clam. She zipped open her bag immediately in order to reconnect with her grooming instruments, and LeeAnn could see it was replete with all sorts of lovely lingerie.

"We'll let you get unpacked," LeeAnn said, and went with David back downstairs and through the kitchen, where they picked up LeeAnn's bags, and headed on through the spacious old dining room and sunny living room. LeeAnn took in the familiar objects, all in their place, all of them having behaved perfectly while she was gone.

Well, now we'll see, she thought, as she turned into the hall that led to their room. *Maybe he's moved everything back in. Maybe we can go back to where we left off.* But when they got to the bedroom and David set her bags down, LeeAnn saw his tall, skinny dresser was still nowhere in sight, leaving hers without a mate. The space that had held the maple chiffonier was empty. David of course caught her dismal glance in that direction.

"Would you want me to move my stuff back in?" he asked, sounding half-hearted about it. "I will."

"That's up to you, David. Not if you don't want to." He'd asked her that several times before she left and she'd always said no, or no, not yet. Maybe being in the cabin for awhile would be enough for him. *If I don't push this issue.* She couldn't let herself be needy. It was bizarre living in separate quarters, she thought, but heck, some couples had separate bedrooms their whole married life and claimed it was sexier that way.

Turned away from David, LeeAnn started opening up a bag and taking things out. Only there was nothing filmy or lacy or satiny inside. Mostly long johns, none too clean, balled up in the corners of her bag. She'd flown straight out of Vladivostok and hadn't had another chance to get her laundry done.

She opened her middle dresser drawer, saw it was just as messy as when she'd left, then started for the closet where the laundry hamper would be. David had been standing there watching her. Now he went ahead and opened the door. "Surprise," he said.

Peering around him, LeeAnn saw that some of the closet floorboards had been taken up and there was a new wooden ladder that he'd evidently built, going down into the basement where his studio was. Before, they'd always had to go outdoors and around to get to it.

"Neat," she said, bewildered. Obediently she climbed down and then back up again, admiring his handiwork. "Well, it'll be handy, especially in the winter," she remarked, for lack of anything better to say. *Does this mean that we connect through this hole in the floor now that I'm home? A ladder for conjugal visits? Do I let him have as much or as little of me as he chooses? What's he telling me? I wish I knew how to deal with this.*

Of course, they had to take Audrey on "the tour." It started in the living room with the old sea chest from Maggie's family. It had been a toy chest when they were all little. "Oh, I remember that," Audrey exclaimed as she saw it. "I helped beat that thing up. Remember when we put Peter inside and broke the hinge?"

Next Audrey looked at the old wooden figure of a couple in embrace on the mantel. Nineteenth century lovers, carved, probably with a penknife, in cherry wood, and picked up in a secondhand store somewhere. LeeAnn had always loved how the woman's long skirt, blowing in the wind, wrapped around to enclose the man's trousered legs too. She had always thought of the pair as Cliff and Maggie, her mother and father, till they divorced when she was thirteen.

They showed Audrey the small, round, blue Chinese rug they'd had in the apartment, their first piece of furniture. And the massive dining room chairs they'd found in an antique store that were so comfortable it was impossible to get people to leave after dinner. The lace curtains LeeAnn had made, eight pairs of them, so that wonderful Klamath sunlight could pour through the windows all day long. And there was the huge old hutch filled with David's magnificent work that Audrey stood in front of and drooled over for quite some time.

"Your work's gotten really good," she said (LeeAnn had sent Audrey an arrowhead from David's work the year she moved out west). There was a raven in the case carved in obsidian and a woman done in deer antler, kneeling, weaving a water-basket. Both were graceful and splendidly done. David claimed they came to him in a dream after he started eating algae from the lake. LeeAnn could believe it; her dreams had become vivid too. She could see so many beautiful objects in her mind's eye; she just couldn't create them.

Moving on, Audrey admired the wood moldings that David had sanded, and the arch he and LeeAnn had refinished with steel wool and varnish remover, when the place was empty–before LeeAnn's furniture had arrived from New York and started to weigh the relationship down.

Things had gotten way too domestic, that was what was the matter, LeeAnn thought. Nonetheless, home felt good on the soles of her bare feet as they walked out onto the old-fashioned front porch that was partly enclosed, and showed Audrey how you could see mountains in California from here.

"So when was this place built?" Audrey asked as they went back inside.

"In 1917. Used to be a foster home, store, and even a church at one time." These were parts of the spiel, LeeAnn realized as she spoke, "We found a cheap ring in a box up in the rafters. We've always wondered who put it there and whether it was or it wasn't given to the intended recipient." These were fairly standard lines in David and LeeAnn's spiel when they did their house tour–the song and dance about their home.

"So, there's ghosts in the house?"

"Lots of them," LeeAnn said. "Native people have lived on this plot for probably thousands of years." Ancestors of her great-grandmother most likely, LeeAnn always thought. "We've found some of their tools in the garden."

"You really have?"

"Since it's right above the river, it would have been a pretty popular spot. Come on." They went out the back door, in the waning light toward the summerhouse, past the garden where corn, peas, beans, tomatoes, pumpkins, peppers, and cucumbers grew in great profusion in neat, orderly rows that David tended with seemingly no effort at all.

There were tree stumps all around the garden where he had set the obsidian scrapers and cutting tools that he dug up when he was plowing or weeding, along with broken bits of crockery and a rusted tin soldier from the early part of the century. He would always place them carefully, as though the owner might come by and pick them up again at any moment.

"What's this, David?" Audrey asked, as she explored a strange-looking object on one of the tree trunks.

"Oh, that? I was fooling around trying to make a rabbit trap like the Modoc used to make." David and Audrey examined the wood and sinew contraption. It looked authentically old.

"Nice."

Next, Audrey dutifully admired the beets and the arugula, and the algae-fertilized soil that was dark and rich, with a pungent fragrance. Then they all peeked their heads in at the window of the summerhouse to see Jeff conked out on his cot, his Mac and his cellular phone nearby. Jeff's phone was never far from him. When he was traveling, he and Kevin talked or e-mailed several times a day.

LeeAnn decided the temporary transplant of Jeffrey Long-hair Levine to the wild west had been successful for the most part; he looked comfortable. His ever-present super-high-powered Vita-mix sat on a table next to a five-gallon jug of water that David had set out there for him, and his helmet was hanging on the wall next to his two-year-old two-thousand-dollar bike. LeeAnn could never see the point in spending that much to make pedaling easy when the whole idea was to expend effort.

"Let's not disturb him," David said.

On the way back to the house, LeeAnn pointed out the hot tub to Audrey. "It's made out of a fish cooler," LeeAnn said. "Insulated fiberglass; they ship fish in it."

"A *cooler* hot tub," Audrey said. "How clever."

"Peter brought it up on top of his station wagon. He found it on a beach somewhere."

"Naturally."

"He and David put it together, but the plumbing's never worked quite right."

"I gotta get Stan over to look at it," David said, as they stood before the dysfunctional toy. "Sorry. Just haven't been able to get it together."

Why? LeeAnn was disappointed. *What have you been doing? Stop it, LeeAnn.* She was looking down into the few inches of scummy water at the bottom of the tub.

"So, would you like to take a look at my shop?" David asked, and Audrey agreed enthusiastically. She was a very good tour guest.

"Yeah, let's see what you've been up to all summer," LeeAnn added, feeling almost left out but not quite.

So, followed by Sillvester, they all trooped around the house to the outside basement entrance. When David opened the door, the cat slipped in, got admonished, and retreated defiantly, stamping his feet as best he could. "He's always trying to get in here," LeeAnn said.

"There are mice in the furnace room," David explained, as he closed the door behind them. Then they walked on into the cool belly of the house that was always at a perfect temperature. There was a pine-paneled four-room apartment down there from the last Klamath boom in the forties or fifties.

"Neat." Audrey said as they entered the living room. "This place has *got* to have a pool table. It just cries out for it."

"That's just what I was thinking," David exclaimed. "We'll have to get one. And this is what we call our toy room." He gestured toward an alcove on the right where skis and tents and frisbees and boogie boards and windsurfing gear and camping stuff all vied for the limited space.

The rest of the basement held an orderly collection of the things of David's world–garden tools, bundles of herbs drying, and mason jars of dehydrated vegetables. Windsurfing posters and a couple of plants. A small aquarium with a colorful community of happy fish. It was a peaceful, practical place. Just like David's being, his workspace hummed. The star attraction on the tour, his studio at the far end of the basement apartment, would be last. David was not overly modest, but for best effect, he always arranged the tour that way.

He looked tense as he showed Audrey into the rock room, which was the next to last stop on the tour. It was a narrow little closet of a place about four feet wide by twelve feet long with shelves on all four sides. Every available surface on every shelf was covered with chunks of shiny volcanic glass, all shapes and sizes, and all the different types, mahogany and rainbow and ribbon and snowflake–although snowflake wasn't good for chipping, LeeAnn told Audrey. There didn't appear to be any order in the arrangement but David knew each rock personally, and constantly sorted them according to the figures that their shapes suggested.

"We dug up every one of these ourselves," LeeAnn said, "over in eastern Oregon. We camped on top of a hill, and the coyotes howled at each other every night from the tops of all the other hills around us."

"I'm sure you howled back," Audrey commented in an arch tone.

"Of course." LeeAnn went on. "The way you find the rock," she said, demonstrating as she spoke, "is you kick a piece that's sticking out of the ground with the heel of your boot. If it doesn't move, that means it's big enough to be worth digging for. We were going to call his business *Kicking Rock Studios.*"

"Good idea." Audrey took a big chunk of obsidian off the shelf to inspect it.

"Be careful," David told her. "It can cut you badly. They use obsidian sometimes for brain surgery," he added. "Sharper than surgical steel. Wherever you find it, all you gotta do is knock off a spall and you've got yourself a blade, or instant tool."

"And it's all from a volcano. Isn't it marvelous?" Audrey said. "A hardware store for the ancients."

"That's iron oxide running through there," LeeAnn said, pointing out red streaks in the gray-striped rock Audrey was holding.

"And this they call rainbow," said David, picking up another rock, holding it up to the light. "Come here, look at the pinks and the blues." He took the piece over to the window to show Audrey. "See." Then he turned it slowly. "There. There's green."

"And purple! I see purple." Audrey was indeed mesmerized. She went back to get another rock and spent the next five minutes oohing and ahing as she turned rocks to catch the light. "Look L.A., look at the blue."

"You could keep that piece if you want," said David about

Audrey's favorite.

"David, thank you."

"So . . . ," David said in an offhand way when he felt the time was right, "would you like to see what I'm carving right now?"

"What a dumb question," Audrey replied.

Again, he looked nervous as they made their way toward the last room. It was soon clear why. When LeeAnn and Audrey caught sight of the figure on his workbench, both of them stopped dead in their tracks. LeeAnn gasped. Then the two women looked at each other for just an instant.

It was the bust of a woman, and it was absolutely stunning. Just the head and shoulders, carved in mahogany obsidian. Part of the rock was black, and part was dark red. The sharp and exotic features of her face were dark, but red flames flowed upward where her hair would have been. Audrey was the first one to speak. "It's Pele. The fire goddess."

"You know, people keep telling me that's who it is," David said as he went over to rotate the stand so they could see it from all angles. "But I don't know. I just do it. It keeps coming. I don't know *who* it is."

LeeAnn did. She was still struck dumb. For she saw not one fire goddess but two. One small, ethnic volcano goddess in flesh and blood staring at an image of herself carved in stone.

"She looks just like you, Audrey," LeeAnn said at last.

"So she does," David remarked brightly, as Audrey's words, *There are no coincidences,* flashed through LeeAnn's mind. She knew the same thought was flashing through Audrey's head too. Her best friend from kindergarten. *A fire goddess,* LeeAnn thought, avoiding David's eyes. *She is the fire I have to go through. So what do I do now? What do I say?*

"She'd make a great model for you," LeeAnn heard herself remarking then. *Shuddup.*

"You know, actually," David said nervously, "it would help me with the face if I had some *snapshots.*" He was making it clear he didn't intend for Audrey to come down and sit for him.

"There's always my driver's license," Audrey responded, trying to avoid LeeAnn's eyes as she carefully made the same point. Everyone avoiding everyone else's eyes. But at that moment, as they protested, LeeAnn could practically *see* the current arc between them, and she could certainly feel it. Snap, crackle, pop, as the electricity ricocheted around the room now.

Glancing out of the high window above David's work-bench, LeeAnn saw that the barn-like door to the summerhouse was open. "It looks like Jeff's up," she said. "I think I'll go see him and take him some algae. He's never had any." These two didn't need her right now. Or at least she didn't need to be with them. She couldn't stand it actually. The vibes were much too strong for comfort. "See you in a bit." LeeAnn hurried out past the rock room, out the basement door and up the steps, around the house and into the kitchen. *Mazel tov, LeeAnn. Now you've done it. You brought her here,* she thought as she grabbed a bottle of algae capsules, pushed the screen door open and reeled out into the yard. There were tears in her eyes as she hurried past the place where they'd been planning to add a greenhouse someday. She and David had stood out in the yard with a neighbor and his dog one day last summer, earnestly considering what the roof pitch should be on the dormer they planned to build. Then they had driven all over Pacific Terrace and Moyina Heights, picking out likely designs. *Hah!*

The thing LeeAnn decided she felt worst about as she made her way past the woodpile and out into the yard, was the Summer Project, which now seemed entirely unattainable. No way can I concentrate on it–there's no way any of us can function with all this happening. *But nothing's really happened,* the little voice inside of her said. *Yeah,* she answered herself, *but it's going to. I can tell.*

Inside the summerhouse, wearing a pair of baggy shorts, Jeff was sitting at his computer.

"Hey! L.A!" He got up to hug her. Bony knees, oversize bermudas, his chest white, forearms brown, and the raccoon eyes of a cyclist's tan. They hadn't seen each other since last summer at his place.

"You look fantastic," she said.

"Mmmm." He took time to study her face. "And you look troubled."

"Here," she said, going over to the water jug and pouring a glass for him. "Eat this. It might help you stay awake more of the daylight hours."

"Wonderful," he said, making a face. "Goldfish food. Pond scum."

"Shuddup. Think of it as–it's like seaweed, seaweed is algae. You eat nori all the time. And kelp."

So he obediently swallowed a capsule. But he was looking at her face the whole time.

"You may not notice anything right away; sometimes it happens with the very first capsule, and sometimes you have to eat it for months before . . ."

Jeff stopped her. "Hey baby, why you cry?"

"Me? No reason."

"Bullshit," he said equably.

She shrugged and sat down on the edge of the cot. He'd get it out of her. "Just my whole life blown apart, that's all."

"David?"

She nodded.

"What is this thing with you and him anyway? Him out in the cabin . . ."

"God, are you going to get on our case too? Maybe some people *like* to live that way." But then she spilled out the whole story, repeating more or less what she'd told Audrey and ending with what she'd just seen. "So now I've positively blown it by bringing my best friend aboard. My almost-best friend," smiling through new tears at Jeffrey.

He smiled back. Some things she'd always been able to share better with Jeff than with Audrey. In certain ways she felt closer to him. "The worst thing is I know how strong the sex drive is in both of them. And if it's there for them like I think it is, there's no way they're going to be able to ignore it. How can anyone concentrate on the work? Jeffrey, it's absolutely spooky how much that bust looks like her. Do you believe in..." she trailed off, as the lump in her throat got worse.

Jeff just continued to look at her, so she tried to regroup. "You know, I saw him do a double take at the airport, but I thought maybe he just didn't expect her to be so little. But he must have seen the resemblance then. There's no way he could've missed it. I mean, he carved the thing. Presumably he knows what it looks like."

"LeeAnn," Jeff said firmly, "Audrey would not go after David, you know that."

"Right, I know. But that only takes care of *one* of them," then she sighed. "How is the Summer Project going to fit into all this. We're just starting. How are we going to . . . I just feel like it's all going to fall apart. Everything!! Everything in my life."

Then she broke down and cried. "My partnership is falling apart, she sobbed. To her, that word was everything, her comfort, her belief system, her love. Jeffrey handed her a tissue, and then another.

She wiped her eyes. "I don't know, relationships these days . . .

What about you and Kevin? How do you guys manage to keep it together?"

"We're lucky. Our world is a little more dangerous these days than yours; there's more incentive to stay together. We also work at the relationship. You get so you care about it more because you've spent all that time polishing it." LeeAnn nodded. *She thought about Maggie's silver, that she polished for years and years.* The two old friends were quiet for a few moments. "I'll come inside with you," Jeff said then, getting up.

A little later, Audrey, Jeff, and LeeAnn were in the kitchen rustling up something to eat. Engaged at the moment in ransacking cabinets, Audrey was standing on LeeAnn's formica counter in her bare feet looking up into the top shelves. "Where's the tamari, where's the Braggs? What is this supermarket soy sauce doing here, didn't I teach you better?" She jumped down, the offending bottle in hand, and opened the fridge. "I thought we'd do the broccoli with a peanut sauce."

"Whatever you want," LeeAnn said.

Jeff was busy dicing up green onion and scrambled egg for the fried rice, and David, who'd just come in from the garden with vegetables, was standing around looking a little put out. He was used to being in charge in the kitchen, and Jeff, in creative mode, was making a spectacular mess.

LeeAnn walked out through the living room to the front porch, took the elastic band off of tonight's *Herald and News*, and, heading back to the kitchen, automatically stuck it over the doorknob like her grandmother used to do.

She opened up the paper and glanced at the headline. "Oh, no!!" She sank down into a chair. "Shit!"

"What's the matter?" asked Jeff, turning to her from a wok that billowed steam.

"Look at this." She turned the paper around.

"BILLION-DOLLAR TREE ISLAND DEVELOPMENT IS APPROVED," the banner headline proclaimed. "Area Economic Woes Ended," the subhead read.

Below the two headlines was an architect's rendering, done in pale pastels, of Klamath Lake's Tree Island with a huge futuristic spaceship-looking thing perched on it. A cylindrical black glass structure ten stories tall and seemingly about as wide, with fountains and parks and private helipads and all kinds of fancy "improvements."

"Why?" she said to David, looking up at him plaintively. "Why? When there's only one lake in the world like this one, do they have to mess it up just to make money?"

The look that he gave her conveyed that he understood. David loved the lake too, but he was a fatalist, a pragmatist. "Jobs," he said. "Simple."

"Which is nothing but a euphemism for profits," LeeAnn said. "When a new industry is announced, do they ever say, 'Think of the huge profits,' no, they just say, 'Think of all the *jobs*.' Oh god, I hate to see it happen. That beautiful island. That beautiful lake with enough food in it to cure half the world's malnutrition. And they're going to put a billionaire's playground there instead?"

Audrey left her peanut-sauce-in-progress to come over and look at the newspaper, which LeeAnn had spread out on the dinette table. "Pretty fan-cy," Audrey observed. "Mmm, the company's headquartered in Singapore, it says. 'The sixth in a series of ultra-luxury eco-resorts.'"

"More like eco-*pirates*," LeeAnn muttered.

"'... the others in Sri Lanka, Brazil ...'" Audrey scanned the article. "'Klamath Lake has been chosen as the newest location, says CEO Ernst Vanderveer, because of its numerous attractive assets ... the fly fishing ...'"

"Jimmy Carter comes here to fly fish," David contributed.

"'... the skiing, U.S. ski team trains at Mr. Bachelor,' it says."

"Is that right?" Jeff asked.

"They've got *great* skiing around here," said LeeAnn.

"The wildlife, the airport with a two-mile runway." Audrey was continuing to read. "It says it was once designated as alternate landing site for the space shuttle..."

"I didn't know that," Jeff said as he tossed diced veggies into the wok and they sizzled impressively. "Two miles is a pretty long runway."

"It says they're going to ferry the guests in on giant luxury jets," Audrey went on, "fitted with private staterooms. ... Well, I could deal with that. Better than the red-eye any day. 'The resort will have office facilities in each suite, and servants' quarters. There will be one suite with thirty rooms;' that's gotta be for a Saudi prince. Imagine how much they charge for something like that?"

"Just one more citadel of the super-rich," said LeeAnn disgustedly. She had never been fond of the rich.

Audrey picked up on the tone of LeeAnn's voice with its implicit criticism of her for admiring the luxury. "Look, I agree with you it's too bad. It's a shame, but the lake's already being used commercially and it says here that studies by the EPA . . ."

"What does the friggin EPA know? Come *on*, Aud, I'm not in the mood!"

"*Chill out*," Jeff was silently mouthing the words at LeeAnn from the stove.

"I'd be pissed even if it weren't for the algae," LeeAnn went on, oblivious, "but if it's the one lake that still has any harvestable quantity in it, then there's got to be a delicate balance. And you know with all this development, all these helicopters and hydrofoils, something's likely to tip that balance."

"Yeah, but it's a done deal," said David, the pragmatist.

"I *know* it is!" she snapped at them. "That's what makes it so terrible."

"So don't angst over it," he told her. Easy for him. David went over to the kitchen window then, rang the "shoulders-down" chime, and gave LeeAnn a significant look. It was a finger-cymbal they'd found up in the attic; LeeAnn used to imagine it belonged to the same person who hid the ring box up in the rafters. David had polished it up and hung it over the kitchen sink on a leather thong. Every evening when they quit work and popped their nightly Bud-with-lime, he would hit the tiny cymbal with a chopstick so it chimed through the house. "Shoulders down," he'd tell LeeAnn and its pure, clear sound almost *made* her relax. Tonight, however, it would take the Liberty bell to get those shoulders down.

Audrey was still reading. "This says the resort is expected to attract some of the wealthiest people in the world. So can that be all bad? Progress." She was trying to keep LeeAnn from being upset. "At least it's not a factory belching smoke. You can't keep Oregon empty, you know. With all the teeming hordes . . ."

"Hardly teeming hordes, Audrey. You're talking about the one percent in the world who already own more than half of everything."

"It'll make your property worth more."

"*So what?*" Now she was practically livid. What the hell difference was it going to make?

David had come over to look at the paper, too. He and Audrey standing side by side, both dark-haired and olive-skinned. Looking good together, LeeAnn thought. Almost like sister and brother. "It says they'll hire a thousand people initially," he said. "Do you know what that's going to do to this town?"

"Yeah, we'll just be a little feudal village outside the one-per-centers' castle." LeeAnn looked down at the picture of the transformed island again. The pale colors annoyed her. Happy pastels just as if it were a happy story. Poor Tree Island. Just one more heartbreak.

Of course, it had been quite a day. Had this morning really started in their river-view room at the Best Western with wake-up love and a shared shower? And now was ending with a wrecked life and a Club Med for the Donald Trumps of the world right here in this sacred place? *And this is only my first night home,* she thought. *What else is in store?* Suddenly all of LeeAnn's enmity gathered in one place; everything bad that had happened all day she now blamed on these eco-pirates.

"Is it ten, yet?" It was, just. She jumped up and headed for the television. "It'll be on the news." As she walked past Jeffrey, he gave her another warning look, but she paid no mind. She turned the television on with a vicious snap. "It's nothing but greed. I hate greed!"

"LeeAnn, you're ranting. We're all on your side, you know," Jeff said.

Clearly, David didn't care for the vibes. "I'm going out to the cabin," he said then. "It's been a long day," as he headed for the door.

"It certainly has," LeeAnn muttered.

"And a long drive." Pointing out he'd done all the driving. He opened the door.

"Aren't you going to at least eat with us?" she called after him, as panic took hold.

"I don't think so. I've got some stuff out there. You coming out later?"

"Maybe. I don't know yet."

And then he was gone.

The screen on the kitchen TV always took a long time to light up–it was the little set they'd had back in the apartment–but then it did, just in time to catch a wholesome looking heavyset girl with marble-sized pearls around her neck, doing her promo for the stories that would follow.

"*Major* news tonight. We all know Klamath is a 'heavenly' place. Well, now the rich and famous will know it as well . . . as our lake becomes their second home! Stay tuned for coverage of the arrival today of top executives from VHRI, Vacation Heaven Resorts International."

"Eww, yuck, barf. What a *no-class* name," Audrey said, as the announcer's face was replaced by a wide-angle view of a jumbo jet in rainbow colors taxiing at Klamath International. It was followed by a quick shot of a strikingly handsome man, probably in his late thirties, blond and tanned, coming off the plane in a five-thousand-dollar suit. He was followed by some other people who were clearly his lackeys.

"Oh my gosh, will you look at that," said Audrey. "The guy looks like Mayor Lindsay, doesn't he, L.A.?" She was right but LeeAnn didn't answer.

The newscaster's voice, higher pitched than usual, continued against a backdrop of the town's official greeters, shaking hands with the arriving delegation. "We'll be chatting with CEO and Chairman of the Board, Ernst Vanderveer, of the Singapore-based company that's about to lend a *giant*-sized boost to our sagging economy.

"VHRI is a subsidiary of one of the world's largest international corporations, with food divisions, pharmaceuticals, chemicals, plastics, and electronics. . . ." And her voice went on. "There were the Ambassadors, a whole crew of folks in their red Chamber of Commerce blazers. The mayor, and the woman who owned the television station, and the state legislator who'd taken a seminar from LeeAnn once at the college, along with other civic types LeeAnn knew from back when she was trying to help promote the Winter Olympics for Klamath. *This little town sure knows how to put its act together*, LeeAnn thought. *I'll give it that.*

"That guy is yummy," Audrey said. "Isn't he? So what kind of bod do you think he's got, L.A.? Can't tell much under that suit." Almost certainly Audrey was feigning more interest in Mr. Megabucks than she actually felt, wanting to cheer LeeAnn up, or send the message she wasn't going to seriously chase David.

LeeAnn decided to take her up on the offer of rapprochement. She studied the man on the screen as he gracefully shrugged off his suit jacket, then hooked it on his middle finger and held it over his left shoulder, like a G.Q. ad. "Looks like a swimmer's body to me," she told Audrey after careful assessment. "Long muscles. Not the kind I like, especially. Though you can't be sure."

"What do *you* think, Jeff?" Audrey said. "Hard body or soft?"

"I'd say hard. The rice is ready by the way."

"Look how he's doing the mingle-with-the-folks bit, like he's running for president." Audrey remarked, carefully deprecating him just a bit to please LeeAnn. "What's the suit, silk?"

"Probably from pedigreed silkworms. Who cares? Imagine the tailors they have in Singapore. That's where he's from, isn't it?"

There was a quick shot of Vanderveer shaking hands with the news anchor, which made LeeAnn feel good. At least for once the poor woman wasn't lugging her own camera around. "Perhaps you'd like to take your viewers on a tour of our new airplane that we've just named *The Klamath Traveler*," Vanderveer said. He had a faint Dutch accent that was quite charming.

"I'm sure our viewers would love that," Klamath's news anchor replied, looking into the camera at her audience. "I know you'll want to stay tuned." Then they went to a Pizza Hut commercial.

"I bet they make us wait till after the weather before they come back to him," Jeff said.

"Probably. It's the station's best chance for ratings in years. Or ever."

The three of them waited through a feature about the potato harvest being late or early this year. Then they watched a report on the girls from Henley High, who were great athletes, in a sneak preview of the upcoming basketball season. The girls were willowy and tall and most of them had blonde ponytails. Healthy.

Back to the news story at last. Klamath's news anchor was being led up the ramp by Vanderveer, who towered over her. He was pointing out lettering up by the cockpit that did indeed read "The Klamath Traveler." *There's probably five other airplanes just like this one,* LeeAnn thought, *one named for each resort, at how many hundred million bucks a shot? I wonder how many staterooms there are? It's like the world belongs to these people. They just hop around it, using it as they will.*

There were several quick cuts–a formal dining room, an unbelievably cushy suite, and spacious lounge areas–you would never imagine all of this on an airplane; it put *Air Force One* to shame. Then the picture switched to executive offices and a three-shot of Vanderveer and the news anchor, Kathy, seated at a monster coffee table with a fiftyish brunette woman he was introducing as the Klamath Project Chief. A maid was serving what looked like Turkish coffee and baklava.

"Oh, my, my," said Audrey, as they went to a close-up of Ernst with his ready smile and wavy hair in a natural pompadour.

"A girl-catcher they used to call that years ago," Jeff said. "His pompadour." Vanderveer was devastatingly good-looking, in a ruthless kind of way, LeeAnn decided.

The newscaster began, "Welcome to Klamath Falls."

"He's going to say, 'Thanks, Kathy,'" LeeAnn said.

"Thanks, Kathy," Vanderveer said.

"Ha!"

"Klamath Falls is a wonderful town . . ."

"I hope you think so, you just *bought* it," muttered LeeAnn.

"I understand your family's been in business in the Far East for four hundred years. That they started the Dutch East Indies Company."

Vanderveer shrugged modestly.

"A veritable prince of commerce," Jeff commented, catching LeeAnn's critical spirit. The three of them were like sharks circling now. It felt good.

"I wonder if he's married?" Audrey asked.

"I wonder if his wife can stand him?" said LeeAnn.

"And I'm told you're a polo player . . . ," Kathy was saying, having clearly done her homework on his bio.

"*Polo-player* muscles, Aud! What are they like?" Jeff teased. "You ought to know."

"I'm not sure I remember," said Audrey. LeeAnn couldn't hear what Kathy was saying.

"Have to consult your files?" he smirked.

"Well, there was this Argentinian dude . . ."

"Hey, Shhhhh, you guys," LeeAnn interrupted. "Be quiet. I want to hear."

". . . and our offices will of course be open to the entire community," the woman sitting next to Ernst was saying. "Please feel welcome to come in and visit, or phone us with any questions." She, as well, had a slight accent, but LeeAnn couldn't place it.

"Where's she from?"

"Middle East is my guess," said Audrey. "Probably some cousin of mine."

"Well here's a question for you," said Kathy. "The Tree Island tree, of course, is a local landmark said to be a thousand years old. Our viewers will want to know if you're going to be able to preserve it."

"You can depend on it," the woman answered. She spoke very softly and very quietly in English that was almost too impeccably perfect. "We will take very good care of that marvelous old juniper." *Sure, protect the tree, screw the lake. Smart.*

With her sleek cap of perfectly coiffed black hair clipped short, the project chief wore huge, gold button earrings and a simple collar-less black linen suit. Very French. Very chic. Just the right sort of woman to send to a place like Klamath, LeeAnn thought. Where it was still good-old-boy territory. A woman who seemed soft and submissive. "They'll eat her up, they'll love her here," commented LeeAnn.

"Actually I suspect she'll have them for breakfast," said Jeff.

"Pretty gutsy not to wear a collar at her age." Audrey was being bitchy. Then the woman's name came on screen. Sonja Al Amin. "See, I told you. Arab. But *Sonja*? And one of those too-cool types who speaks just below audible so you have to listen up. I thought about trying to talk that way once."

"You? Pffff!" said Jeff

"She's already had at least one lift," Audrey observed.

Jeff scolded Audrey then. "Audrey, quit it! The woman looks good. Just admit it."

LeeAnn's thoughts were quite separate from their chatter as the camera went back to Vanderveer, who was talking about putting the unemployed to work. He smiled, but his expression seemed cold. Some of the top football coaches have that look, LeeAnn thought. And something about his eyes was different; she couldn't quite tell what it was. *So what really goes on inside heads like his? The people with all the power and money?* LeeAnn wondered. *It's strange the way it works. We can at least try to know them, and in fact come to believe that we do. But they can't know us. So much of our contact these days is that way. One-sided. It's like the luminaries of the world exist and we don't.*

She began twisting her hair around her finger, as she often did when she was thinking hard. *They're so busy playing their Monopoly game, carving up the world and chasing the dollar, they hardly pay any attention to the rest of us. Except for making public appearances from time to time and doing their 'I'm just regular folks' act. What if I'd sat beside him on an airplane and told him about the 22nd Century Group? Are people like him going to pay any attention to the Global Celebration idea? I doubt it. And if these guys don't want it to happen, we won't get it. Because they run the world.* Unconsciously, she put a strand of hair in her mouth and began to chew on it, something she hadn't done since grade school.

"Stop it," said Audrey, softly.

And she stopped.

Then Kathy was back out on the tarmac; the interview was over. But the reception was still going on outside the terminal building as executive types from the VHRI group wandered about, gobbling home-made goodies from long tables with tablecloths and flowers. The town had definitely pulled out all the stops. No high school band, but almost.

Two automobiles appeared now on the runway; LeeAnn noticed a white Mercedes and a maroon Jag, nice-looking cars but not too high-profile for Klamath consumption. Vanderveer and his lady executive were chatting with a little coterie of starstruck locals. As LeeAnn watched, the Mercedes pulled up close to the group. A man of medium height, about thirty, with a stocky, no-ass body, new jeans, slicked-back hair, and a distinct military bearing, got out of the car and came around to Ernst and Sonja, shook hands with Ernst and kind of nodded his head at Sonja. Didn't touch her.

"Look at them being chummy with their chauffeur for the camera," said Audrey.

"Bodyguard, probably," said LeeAnn.

"Her pet pit bull, more likely." Jeff said. "The guy looks mean." They watched as he bundled the project chief into the back seat of the Mercedes, got in front, and drove her away.

"Pretty slick," said Audrey. "Having them leave in different cars to make it clear they're not together."

"They wouldn't be. She's twenty years older."

"So?"

Another man, an extremely burly Polynesian fellow who was quite *obviously* a bodyguard, performed the same basic drill with Ernst, shaking his hand and then escorting him over to the Jag. Ernst hopped in, in the manner of someone accustomed to publicly climbing in and out of chauffeured vehicles. The driver shut the door and they sped away, just as the closing commercial came on. LeeAnn got up to switch off the television.

"Why are you turning it off? How do you *know* I don't want to buy a John Deere?" Jeff complained.

"Because I don't want to hear any more." She snapped the set off.

"About anything." And she didn't. Not about Tree Island or *fire goddesses* or one-percenters, or Vacation Heaven Resorts International or *anything* that wasn't related to the Summer Project. *Tomorrow, come hell or high water, we start convincing the world it needs a human family reunion. And,* she promised herself, *I absolutely refuse to let anything or anyone get in the way of that. Including David?* a small voice inside her asked. *Including David.*

CHAPTER NINE

The Medical-Dental Building

The old office building out of the thirties from which the invitations to the Global Celebration would be sent was called the Medical-Dental Building by most people in town, though its official name was still the Oregon Bank Building. The bank was no longer there, having departed some decades before; its dramatically high-ceilinged ground-floor space was now occupied by the gallery that David and twenty-two other local artists were partners in. And it was not really the Medical-Dental Building any longer either, most of the doctors and dentists having begun to meander slowly a few years before, as medicine had become big business, to the spread-out complex on the hill below the college and hospital, where some had whole buildings devoted to themselves and their paperwork.

Nowadays, the solid six-story structure, having survived the recent Klamath 5.7 earthquake with only a few face bricks missing, was about half occupied. There was a masseuse, a teen pregnancy center, a part-time family therapist, a bookkeeping service called Checks and Balances, and a judo academy with small, neat kids in white outfits scampering in and out of their classes.

There was a commodious conference room on the second floor and a lunchroom on the third, with wonderful art-deco design throughout the building. And LeeAnn's favorite–an operator-attended elevator, the last in the state of Oregon, which added immeasurably to the building's charm. Two women of impressive years took turns running it, the pale redhead in the morning and the salt-and-pepper brunette in the afternoon. Both were hale and friendly, warm and thoughtful, both vociferous readers and more or less constant babysitters–or at least attractors of children. There was almost always at least one small child standing in the back of the wood-paneled elevator, well out of the way, talking to and having fun with the morning or afternoon operator, riding up and down endlessly. Well-behaved, curious, often playing with some simple toy, like a top.

It made LeeAnn think she'd stepped into a time warp when she walked into that magical elevator; she always expected a Brigadoon fog would begin to waft up around them. There was a small electric heater in there at the operator's feet, some plastic flowers, a stand with knick-knacks on it, a phone book, an old radio. It was a tableau out of the fifties, or maybe the forties.

Up on the top floor of the tallest building in town and down at the end of the hall was the plain, square room with two large casement windows that was serving as temporary headquarters.

The "22nd Century Group, *Making sure we get there*," it said on a paper sign on the door. One window framed a vista of downtown, with a magnetizing view of Mount Shasta some sixty miles to the south, guarding the town. The other window featured a view to the west of the original subdivision where LeeAnn and David lived, up near the top of the hill, in their 1917 house.

LeeAnn liked the office a lot; everything was so simple. Four desks, four light strings hanging down from the four old-fashioned ceiling globes that lit the room, a fifth in the tiny pantry featuring hot and cold running water that adjoined it. The space, along with the furniture and office equipment, was the temporary legacy of a woman LeeAnn had met when she'd worked on the Winter Olympics bid.

Several years back, a group of local citizens had tried hard to get the 1998 Winter Games for southern Oregon, and LeeAnn had jumped right in to help. They got the whole town going, with yellow ribbons tied on all the plum trees downtown when the site selection team came to visit. It turned out that Klamath had matchless natural venues, according to the committee from Colorado Springs, but insufficient infrastructure. *That word again.* LeeAnn had pointed out that Klamath had a heck of a lot more infrastructure than Lillehammer, Norway, where she'd spent a summer once, which had already been awarded the '94 Games. But to no avail. *Another pie-in-the-sky idea I got myself into.*

In any event, she knew that an elderly colleague from those days, the sharp-as-nails Harriet Duvall, who was descended from one of the original settlers, had lots of empty office space around town. She was holding it against the inevitable boom Klamathites had been expecting momentarily for the past twenty years. When LeeAnn wrote to her from Russia, she replied that she wouldn't mind letting her group use a small space on the top floor of the Medical-Dental Building for a month or so. This particular office said Property Management on the frosted glass door. "Hey, how apt," Jeffrey had remarked when LeeAnn took him down to see the office for the first time. "Only it's property management of the planet we're talking about." Then he promptly hung the four newspaper hats he'd finally managed to make for them on the wall for decoration.

Generally, Jeff, L.A., and Audrey worked down at the office during the day, composing news releases, getting a database up, and entering the names of the one thousand people they were in the process of choosing to receive an invitation. In the evenings, they sat around David and LeeAnn's dining room table with their mastermind Peter on speakerphone–Jeff called it the Voice of Oz–hashing things out in great long discussions.

The first thing they had to agree on was the rules. The way it ended up, there were basically three.

First, they would stay at or under budget. "We agreed each of us could scrape up twenty-five hundred bucks. But that's it, okay? No matter what. No martyrs. And no fund raising at this point. It would only corrupt or distract us. It's *our* idea; we run with it." He was right about that too, LeeAnn thought. Fund-raising nearly always corrupts.

Second, it had to stay fun. "If we're not having fun, then people aren't going to want to join us." Audrey approved of that.

Third, they would consult with one another liberally, but in the end, each would be responsible for picking one quarter of the invitees; it would be their return address on the envelope. "And the person who gets the most acceptances wins something." They hadn't agreed yet on what the prize would be. Peter was something of a tightwad; his initial suggestion was a six-pack of Coors.

All of them came to pretty quick agreement that the best way to get their message across was not by harping on dire facts and prognoses but by showing visually what people could do during the Year in Parentheses to get everybody on the same page. So they'd come up with a calendar for the year 2000, which would be printed on the reverse of the invitation. Being mainly pictorial, and practical, a calendar would cut across language barriers. "And later we can make them into big, colored posters and sell them."

At the top, it said 2000 and below that was the logo of the earthflower framed by the two facing moons of the Year in Parentheses. "A year set aside to turn our world around."

Then across the page, over the four quarters, it said:

JAN-MAR Health
We all think about our bodies, how we use them, what we put into them, who else we let use them and how. (We make sure that everyone has enough to eat, for a change, because you can't feel better when you don't have food.)

APR-JUN Environment
We take a good look at all the miracles around us and start figuring out how we can stop destroying them.

JUL-SEP Relationships
We examine our human relationships, from one-on-one to a billion-on-a-billion, seeking to end wars between peoples and the ancient war between the sexes as well.

OCT-DEC Commerce
Feeling better about our health, our housekeeping, and our love for others, we begin to think more about sharing.

DEC 31
Everyone takes time to ring a bell, as the people of each time zone cross the bridge into the 21st century.

THE 22nd CENTURY GROUP, *planning, decade by decade, for a future world of partnership between women and men, humans and nature, groups and nations.*

I don't know, LeeAnn thought, putting it down and sighing. *I hope it expresses the plan we're trying to get across. Start by fixing our bodies, then fix our planetary home and our relationships, then fix our fairness.* She hoped it would at least get people to thinking.

In its first week of operation, the only major problem the 22nd Century Group had encountered–apart from the agony of trying to express themselves on one small card–was money. They had already spent–or allocated $9,416.98 of their $10,000.00 budget. That included printing the four-color invitations and the reply cards, buying the envelopes, mailing in the U.S., with the LOVE stamp, of course, and foreign postage. Then there was the cost of Jeff and Audrey's travel to Oregon, which Peter insisted they factor in, and phone bills from all the time they'd been talking about it. So they were still under budget, but just barely. Barring unexpected calamity, Peter thought they could squeeze by.

They'd originally hoped to be able to send out several thousand invitations, but gave that idea up as soon as they realized that bulk mail would have to be involved. "Ewww, ugh, I hate bulk mail," said Audrey, and that put an end to that. And faxing or e-mailing wouldn't do. To have the best chance for success, they all agreed, you had to put a tangible invitation in somebody's hand. "And we only have one shot at getting their attention, so it better be gorgeous." Whether it was going to Bill Gates or a peasant in Bangladesh, it would have to *feel* like an invitation to a party. "Celebration is the idea. Let's not be dreary." And so they weren't.

The envelopes, which had been delivered the day before, and represented 20% of their budget, were gorgeous . . . so bumpy with their luscious handmade-looking texture that they were almost hard to write on. The paper, made by a Lebanese friend of Audrey's, looked as though somebody had mashed a bunch of wood pulp like you'd roll out pie dough, then tinted it the color of straw in autumn sunshine. Even Peter agreed it had been worthwhile to splurge on envelopes. Each would be hand-addressed, using a good fountain pen, with a return address of L.A. Spencer, P. Spencer, A. Garcia, or J.L.H. Levine, with a P.O. box–they were trying to get 2200–Klamath Falls, OR 97601.

Now the big question–who to send to? Who on the planet was most likely to commit to this idea right away and then act on it? Who would rush right out and copy it or translate it and then send the invitation off to all their friends, who would immediately do the same thing? They'd tossed around ideas and theories for months, ad nauseam. Should we send to all clergy? All business people? All heads of state? Who's got the clout? Who's got the connections? Who's got the imagination? "How about if we started with just teachers?"

"Film stars. They have the most global recognition, hence, the most power," said Audrey.

"Larry King," said Jeff. "That's all you'd need is Larry King."

"What about car salesmen?" David contributed from the kitchen and everyone laughed. It wasn't a bad idea. They were probably the most persuasive people on the planet.

"How about first ladies? First spouse, from every country. No, I'm serious. First spouse. They're usually bright and lots of them don't have enough to do."

"Or choose someone who's skilled in networking in each time zone and get them to organize their zone."

"The whole principle is picking people who won't drop the ball," said LeeAnn.

"Suppose we have a 50% return . . . ," Jeff began. "That's 500 . . ."

"You'd never get that," said Audrey.

"How do you know we won't? If we pick carefully and make our case well. Nobody's ever got this kind of invitation before. So how do you know?"

Audrey had no answer.

"We need to pick people with a diverse field of acquaintances," LeeAnn mused.

"Scattered around the world," Audrey added. "We can't make this just a United States kind of thing."

"No, but it's the base we know best; it's where we need to start. The postage is less. Just be sure the people you pick know people in other countries."

Then they started talking about whether they could invite organizations. "We'd be stupid not to utilize *infrastructure* that's already there," Audrey said.

But Jeffrey was of the opposite opinion. "Yeah but you lose the purity of going just people-to-people, one-on-one, as soon as you get into bureaucracy of any kind."

"We *have* to invite organizations to join. Do you know what we'd get in one fell swoop if the pope called up and said, 'Okay, we're there.' Or the AARP for godsakes. Do you know how many members *they* have?"

They finally decided that organizations could be invited as such if it was understood they leave all their special interests behind. "Groups exist only in our own minds, after all," LeeAnn said "except for family and that's biological. All other groups are made up."

"They're useful but we shouldn't take them too seriously." That was Peter's pronouncement. "Work with them and through them but don't let them take us over."

"And let's not *exclude* people just because they're famous. We can't get into that kind of inverse snobbery."

"Ross Perot?" Peter wanted to know. "Are you going to put him on the list?"

"Give me one good reason why *not* Ross Perot? He's been a major wake-up call. He gives good media."

"The thing about media," LeeAnn tended to harp on the subject, "is that it's still anybody's power. If you've got a good enough news story, you've got their attention."

"Even with only ten thousand dollars," said Audrey.

Jeff nodded in agreement. "It's probably the last surviving forum for democracy since we gave up on participatory government–and now have rule by instant popular opinion."

"*Uninformed* instant popular opinion," added Audrey.

"Media *is* the world's leader," said LeeAnn. "It's really the only power . . ."

"Could we stay on the subject, please?" said Peter from the speakerphone.

So they started making their lists. Though all four 22nd Century Group founders tended toward shameless liberalism in their own politics, they were resolute about including a fair representation of conservatives among their invitees. Rush Limbaugh, Pat Robertson, Newt Gingrich, Susan Molinari. Israeli Prime Minister Netanyahu. LeeAnn, who was toying with the idea of sending an invitation to every head of state in the world, wanted to know how far out in the political fringes they should go. Milosovic? Castro?"

"Hey, everybody's got a partnership side. Appeal to that."

"Invite 'em all!" said Jeff. "Invite the bankers, the Illuminati, the Tri-Lateral Commission, the KGB, the CIA, the Council on Foreign Relations . . ."

"And E.T.," said Audrey.

" . . . and our friends from other constellations and planets, the Pleiades, from Cyrius, from Orion, from Mars . . ." Jeff was on a roll.

"Okay, Jeff. Let's move along," said Peter, who was not much into UFO's.

Then they started kicking around the names of public personalities.

Some of them, of course, were shoe-ins.

"Robert Redford."

"Got him."

"Robert Fulghum," said Audrey. "You've got to include Robert Fulghum and the rest of the Unitarians. *Everything I Need to Know I Learned in Kindergarten.*"

"I already did."

"And Wayne Dyer."

"Check. I like him."

"Authors! Boy is that going to be a toughie."

"How many authors did we say, max?" Audrey was counting names on her list.

"Fifty."

"No, a hundred, remember we upped it because we said writers have enough imagination to picture what the world can do. Let's pick two future-positive writers from every time zone." So they ended up inundating themselves with ideas and possibilities, rules and criteria. LeeAnn guessed the reason they were becoming obsessive was that they were so afraid what they would think about humanity if everybody they sent to *did* let them down.

David, who was out in the kitchen loading the dishwasher, said, "You ought to send to Soros."

"Who's Soros?"

He came to the doorway. "George Soros. A Hungarian refugee who made good and has given about a billion dollars to struggling countries. They did a thing on him on 'Biography' the other night."

"Okay, Soros. You got it." So David was helping in a way, though he continued to maintain that everything they were doing was a useless exercise.

For her own group of invitees, LeeAnn tried to focus on people who'd already been proved to be especially skilled at linking. She hunted down an acquaintance who'd been a leader in *Hands Across America*, and somebody else who'd helped to foster the idea of sister cities. She researched organizations like the *International Rescue Committee, Union of Concerned Scientists, Physicians for Social Responsibility,* and *Earthwatch.* She also included, as they all did, a few personal friends who just seemed to have the right spirit. "So even if no celebrity, or world leader, or rocket scientist . . ."

"Or sports hero . . . ," said Jeff.

" . . . gets the ball rolling, we'll still have a chance of building grass roots support . . ." LeeAnn thought about the image of the orange again, and the mesh around it, people holding hands. "Till we get to the critical mass . . ."

"The hundredth monkey. . . . And we all decide the smartest thing we can do is party together."

Everybody decided it would be a good idea to include in the total list a hundred names picked at random out of phone books from around the world. "But that's not totally random," Jeff argued. "Did you know half the people in the world have never made a phone call?" So they added an equal number not in phone books–either in a third-world country, or homeless, or just plain poor. So in one way or another, every kind of person in the world would be represented.

"Suppose we get half," Jeff was always calculating possible responses," and each of them sends it to ten more, and half of those come through; that's . . ."

"We can do the arithmetic," said Peter.

"No, stay with me, this is fun . . . let me finish," Jeff said. And he did, working it out so that if they picked the right people, within six steps everybody in the world would have an invitation to the Global Celebration in their hand. Within sixty days, theoretically.

"But *half* have to do it."

"And if people keep sending them, pretty soon everybody will have two. So they'll *know* they are welcome."

"But if nothing's happening in thirty days," Peter said, "we give up. No martyrs. If people are of the same mind that we are, they'll pick up on it. If not, we'll just put our feet up and join in the general decline."

"Unless some new idea strikes LeeAnn."

"Forget it," she said.

"You know a couple of months ago," Audrey said, "I got a letter about dishtowels," she said. "I did. You send off six dishtowels and one day in the future you will receive bezillions. Enough to dry dishes stacked from here to Mars."

"Did you do it?"

"Yeah, I wanted to see what would happen."

"Anything happen?"

"No, but presumably this cause is a bit more compelling."

tree island

The Plan was that as soon as the invitations were printed in Oakland, Peter was going to drive them up to Klamath for an envelope stuffing-and-stamping party that would last all weekend. A celebration. Then they'd send out their news releases, sit back, and wait to see who would respond. They hoped they'd have answers back from a few hundred people within a week. And maybe bags of mail pouring in right after that. People volunteering their time, sending money, ideas, mailing lists. Teachers taking the invitation to their classes, kids sending in drawings.

In a couple of weeks, maybe they wouldn't need just this office, they'd need the whole Medical-Dental Building and then some. Banks of 800-number operators. And mainframe computers to hold the names and addresses of the first few million charter members of the 22nd Century Group, headquartered in downtown Klamath Falls, Oregon.

"Or, who knows? What if nobody at all answers? LeeAnn said. What if we sit here and we don't get one single RSVP?"

"Time will tell," said Peter.

"Negativity attracts," said Audrey.

On this seventh day of operation, Jeff was at home working by modem with Peter to fix some last-minute glitches in the graphics before the disk went to the printer. There was evidently a problem with the way the cities showed up on the petals of the earth-flower. The two men had been going all night with all kinds of crises and crunches and crashes that LeeAnn tried not to know too much about. Computer problems tended to send her into a state of panic. Apparently, everything had finally come out all right.

Downtown in the Medical-Dental Building, Audrey was on the telephone as usual, broadcasting enormous energy, enviable chutzpah, and immutable logic as she dickered with the printer in Oakland. "Yeah, but if this thing goes, Hal," she was saying from the big executive chair that she'd commandeered from the start, "we'll be getting reprints of the calendar by the *bezillion* . . . we really do need to own all the artwork . . ."

LeeAnn, on this late Wednesday morning in early August, was on her hands and knees, starting to probe the innards of the huge copy machine and getting ink all over her hands. *It's always the little things that get to you*, she reflected. *I think I could handle it all, anything in the world–including maybe even the thing with David and Audrey–if this machine would just behave.*

From the very beginning, they'd been battling mechanical problems–the aging fax that would send only the messages it particularly liked and this copier that was positively bulimic. It suffered a growing internal disorder that caused it to eat paper, mangle and mash it, swiping great streaks of black across its surface.

They'd tried to coax it through its various crises, but it had finally demonstrated its acute distress by shredding every single piece of paper fed to it. Now *no* amount of stroking helped. You had to open it up, reach into its gut, and forcibly remove the poor hostage, then try again with about a one-in-ten chance of success. It was as if all the machines were telling them they were trying to accomplish the impossible. And they hadn't even started to get *human* reaction yet.

Extracting the latest mess with a sigh, LeeAnn carefully shut the machine and stood up. "Okay, you win," she told it, patting it on the lid. They'd have to go to PIP Printing today to make copies of a technical report they were preparing, and she would also have to call Harriet, her Winter Olympics friend, to see about fixing the machine. When they'd talked about LeeAnn taking the place, it hadn't been that clear about who was going to pay for repairs, so it very well could become sticky. LeeAnn was intensely aware that one hefty service call could blow the rest of their budget.

She eyed the telephone briefly. She had already put in one call the other day but Harriet hadn't called her back, and she didn't look forward to bugging her again. She thought again about quietly paying for it herself, but it was against the rules. "No martyrs, please," Peter had said. Peter had always demonstrated enormous discipline about spending; his sister often made the claim that he still had his first allowance.

LeeAnn went back to her task of hand-addressing a list of small-town civic leaders, two from each state. She'd picked the people out from news stories about their unusual effectiveness, or their innovative ideas. She tried to think about sending energy to each person in turn as she wrote their name. Finishing that list, flexing her wrist, trying to shake out the writer's cramp, she reached for another batch of envelopes and tore the white paper wrap that was binding them, enjoying the newness of each one as they spilled their straw sunshine out onto her desk.

Observing Rule 2, that this was all supposed to be fun, LeeAnn was addressing her envelopes in the order she felt like. What did she feel like now? Sports heroes, multinational corporations, third-world farmers? *I think I feel like doing powerful women today.* One Hundred Women On Top, Audrey had labeled the file.

She went down the list, picking out the names she wanted to start with. Jeanne Kirkpatrick, Fianna Fail, Madeleine Albright, Barbara Walters, Tipper Gore . . . and the list of notables went on. *At least it was no longer just Clara Barton and Lady Bird Johnson, for godsakes; there were some pretty impressive women making it in the world these days.* But how great was the chance this envelope would actually land on these women's desks? *It's such a shame the celebrity cult has to exist,* LeeAnn thought, *a group that's kept apart from the rest of us, and maybe not really by their own choice.* "If you have a hero, you have diminished yourself," read a poster on Maggie's bedroom wall. *And you've probably diminished them, as well.* Maggie always said that having a plethora of superheroes was a sure sign of a society in decline. LeeAnn earnestly hoped that she herself would never become famous.

"Ms. Jane Fonda," she wrote boldly on an envelope. It actually looked very good, for being left-handed.

Then LeeAnn remembered the fax she'd been trying to send all morning still hadn't gone through–the automatic redial wasn't working again. So she went over and punched the number in one more time; it played Kevin and Jeff's number in New York, a now-familiar doot-dooti-ly-doot musical pattern. Kevin was helping her get statistics on children who kill, for the news release on relationships that she was writing.

She prayed, hit SEND, and listened, hoping for that great howly mating cry you hear when two fax machines recognize each other and start warbling the excitement of connection. David always laughed that she got such a kick out of the sound. "They're doing it, they're doing it," she'd say. But instead of putting out that nice yowly sound, the old fax machine mocked her with the irritating *ehh-ehh-ehh* of its malfunction signal. So she went back and sat down.

Audrey was still gabbing on the phone. Though Peter had made a rule about soliciting donations right now, she was taking the opportunity to soften up a few of her best contacts for a frontal assault later. "I don't think I need to make a case for relevance here, Phil," That was probably Phil Wilson from college, who was a big deal in some oil company. "We've got six times the degenerative disease we had fifty years ago. We've had eight hundred wars in this century alone. Three hundred thousand kids in this country carry guns to school every day. We've lost

25% of our ozone, and amphibians are dying right and left. It's a curve that's not sustainable . . ." She listened impatiently for a few moments. "Phil, let me ask you this. What is it exactly that you're waiting for before you sit up and start noticing how related it all is?" Deep sigh. "I'm not *asking* for anything right now, and I'm *sure* you have a lot on your plate." She rolled her eyes at LeeAnn; the phrase bugged her. Half the people Audrey called claimed they had too much on their plate. And it was probably true. "But just think how you'd feel if you suddenly discovered that *it's all one problem*. Only one, think about it. One cause and one action that could start fixing it all. And a fun action at that, really fun. Change our attitude and we change the world . . . No, I *won't* say anymore. I'm sending something in the mail; you should get it by the fifteenth. Get back to me, Phil baby." She hung up. "What a ding-dong."

"Dominator tactics don't make for a partnership world," LeeAnn said sweetly.

"No, but sometimes they help." Audrey picked up the phone and started dialing again.

Unable to crowd the subject of Audrey and David from her mind for another instant, LeeAnn stopped writing. And all the feelings she'd been keeping at bay flooded over her as she gazed out at Mount Shasta, so cold, so mystical, so pure. *"Lonely as God and white as a winter moon,"* she remembered the Joaquin Miller quote. She sighed.

In the seven days Audrey had been staying at the house, it had become undeniably clear she and David were both wildly attracted to each other and trying resolutely to ignore that attraction. But the electric arc between them hummed loudly every time they were in the same room together; it was like living next door to a major power line.

They all worked long hours, but at home in the evenings it was kind of a "Big Chill" scene as, together and separately, they found various activities to entertain themselves. David had put up a badminton set in the back yard and they all took turns whacking away at the poor little birdie. The hot tub was still broken, so that wasn't available to them, but LeeAnn thought it was probably just as well, what with the intimacy sitting in hot water tends to promote.

The foursome cooked meals together, which generally turned out to be something of a production–as Jeff made a mess of the kitchen–Jeff and David still didn't seem to be getting along great in that department. Most nights after their speakerphone meetings with Peter, they sat around in the living room, with David contributing to the conversation in an unusually voluble way. He was always wanting everyone to go windsurfing.

Once in a while in a relaxed moment, LeeAnn would catch David or Audrey looking at the other momentarily. That wasn't the worst, though; it was catching them looking quickly away again that caused LeeAnn the most pain. They would often grin in the same way when something funny happened, keeping their eyes off of each other, LeeAnn making the link for them as she looked first at one then the other. It was tough knowing that, to at least some extent, she could feel what was going on inside both of them. She could; she knew them both so well.

LeeAnn and David had never had a great deal of intellectual discussion with each other; instead they just *sensed* things together. Now she saw Audrey was doing that with him too. Decorously, Audrey watched David as he'd go out to feed his birds each morning; LeeAnn could sense how much her best friend wanted to devour him. And vice versa.

But then just as often, David would look into LeeAnn's eyes and the same electricity was still miraculously there. His fax machine would locate hers, and they'd warble off together in the most delightful way, then soon excuse themselves and go out to the cabin. Their sex this past week had been of unparalleled quality. In the years they'd been together, they'd unfailingly made love about every day or day and a half. Now it was more like twice a day that she found herself out in the cabin banging away. Knowing it was Audrey he was pouring it into. Or both of them.

So they were all living strenuously. No longer was David an emotional virgin; she could see it was all very trying for him, as well as exhilarating. *Midlife crisis,* she told herself. That's what Jeff said it was. "David will get over it," he assured her. But would he?

Go for it, she almost wanted to say to the two of them. *Just do it and get it over with.* Affairs never lasted with Audrey. Though somehow LeeAnn thought this one might be a longer fling if it were allowed to happen, she being the allower or disallower, an unattractive role at best. LeeAnn sighed, looked over at Audrey, then reached for yet another stack of envelopes.

And there was always that remark Audrey had made last year about wanting a baby. David had never liked long fingernails or bossy women, but now both seemed to thrill him, so pretty soon he might start wanting to expand the earth's population by one, as well. *Which would make me a godmother. When all I ever wanted to be was a mom.* LeeAnn wanted to cry.

So far, she and Audrey hadn't talked about it at all, and neither had she and David. Of course, David was downstairs in his gallery in the Medical-Dental Building right now, she remembered, just an elevator ride away. He was working a lot of shifts to make up for time he'd taken for the trip to Portland. Maybe they should go have lunch. No, it didn't feel like a good time to talk. David didn't like to talk in public places. He didn't like to talk, period.

When she finished addressing the powerful women list, LeeAnn picked up the color printout of the invitation Jeff had downloaded for her this morning. Then, as she had done several times already today, she folded it, put it in the yummy envelope with the reply card, and set it down. Then she picked it up, opened it, and read it as though she were just getting it in the mail. She tried to imagine what it would be like to receive the invitation if she were this or that kind of person. What her reaction would be. *This time I'll be a mother of six from Toledo,* she decided. *Toledo, Spain.*

But, once again, she couldn't seem to think about the woman from Toledo. Instead, she kept wondering what *Ernst Vanderveer's* reaction to this invitation might be. Her interest was acute; in fact it gnawed at her. The quintessential one-percenter was close at hand, right here in Klamath Falls; she longed to know how he would react. Perhaps she should take a copy of it out to him at VHRI headquarters. Or try to bump into him somewhere else; she knew what his car looked like. She just felt that he was the perfect laboratory animal. If the one-percenters went for this idea, then it was almost a sure thing that the whole world would, because the one-percenters had that kind of power.

It wasn't as though she could get away from her speculation about the Singapore tycoon. In the evenings while they fixed dinner, they watched the local news and read the paper. Because Vanderveer was constantly being photographed or interviewed on his daily site visits, she really couldn't get him out of her mind. *I know I can't do anything about Tree Island, but maybe I can persuade him that the larger Tree Island, our earth, needs his money, time, and talents a lot more than this bezillionaire's playground.* He needs to know that partnership power could be a lot more fun than the kind he's wielding.

If we wait to send Vanderveer's invitation with the rest of them, he'll probably be back in Singapore before he gets it. *So I'm going to do it. I'm going to send Ernst-baby an early invitation,* she decided. *I won't go see him. I don't want to do the sexual attraction number, which is almost undoubtedly what it would end up being. If we met in person, I probably wouldn't be able to resist trying to make points that way, and that would make me feel cheap.*

She went to the copier to make a black-and-white copy of Jeff's color proof of the invitation. She hit START, and by golly it did. When the copy emerged from the massive machine, she picked it up and examined it carefully. It didn't look too bad; there were fewer smudges than usual. It was just a little dreary in black and white.

She took a manila envelope down from the shelf. Then, before folding the invitation one last time and putting it in the envelope, she looked at the four maxims for change that Peter had made them come up within twenty characters or less. They'd all done pretty well, she thought.

Initially, Jeff had gone back and forth between two different phrases for HEALTH. *Respect your self,* with eighteen characters, was his original choice, but then he finally settled on *Honor your body,* which was only sixteen and made him the winner.

For ENVIRONMENT, Audrey maxed out with *Partner with nature.* Twenty characters.

LeeAnn privately thought her own motto for RELATIONSHIPS was best because it really applied to all four areas of behavior. *Link with others.* Her original idea was *Link don't rank,* but everybody said that wasn't clear. Linking, of course, didn't mean you don't have leaders, but they should be leaders that were freely chosen and freely followed.

Share the abundance, was the nineteen-character credo Peter had finally settled on in the area of COMMERCE. Because, he said, like warm fuzzies, abundance not shared is no longer abundance.

So a total of twelve words cover it all. A pledge of allegiance to the planet, to oneself, and to one another. *I promise to honor my body, partner with nature, link with others, and share the abundance.*

"And don't overpopulate," David had wanted them to add.

"Don't need it. Overpopulation is a symptom, not a cause," Audrey pointed out.

"Population," David reiterated. "It's going to get solved one way or the other, you know. Either we solve it or Mother Nature does." He still wanted them to add that.

So maybe what they'd come up with wasn't perfect, but the words seemed to work. LeeAnn couldn't help but think of one of the four whenever she was about to do something. The *Link with others* should have helped her with David, but she was still putting him up there on a pedestal. Of course, nobody could possibly do it right all the time. So *Forgive yourself* should probably be the unspoken fifth. LeeAnn wondered what Blackdog kept in his head for guidelines.

She addressed the envelope to Ernst Vanderveer, with the address out by the college where VHRI had their headquarters. For a moment she thought about adding a personal note, her own plea, but then changed her mind. She would just send the standard RSVP postcard that Audrey had designed. It reminded her of the warranty card you send back when you buy a new appliance. A harmless little questionnaire with lots of little boxes that were so tempting to mark with an X. Like the questionnaires in women's magazines. "Does he usually bring you to orgasm? Sometimes? Often? Never?"

The boxes for the Global Celebration response card read:

❏ **YES**, if I'm on planet earth, I will help to host the Human Family Reunion. During the *Year in Parentheses*, I pledge that I will learn more about my cousins from other cultures or countries as well as my neighbors next door. I promise we'll take time to have more fun together.

  ❏ I'm copying and sending this invitation along to:
    ❏ ten friends
    ❏ a hundred
    ❏ a thousand
    ❏ bezillions

  ❏ I'm sending you lots of money and a list; you take care of it.

  ❏ I'll bring a hot dish.

❏ **NO**, thanks. I don't think it will work because _____

That last was Peter's suggestion. "Let the naysayers have their say," he said. LeeAnn placed the reply card in the envelope to Vanderveer, along with the copy of the invitation. On the spur of the moment, she added some material she'd been collecting about the algae as a global food resource and the fragility of the ecosystem of Klamath Lake. She was about to seal the outer envelope and put a stamp on it, but then she hesitated. That smudged invitation just wouldn't do. "It looks *so* much better in color," she said out loud. "Might as well go for it."

She pulled out the smudged black-and-white copy, put the colored original Jeff had given her in it, sealed the envelope, and carried it over to the mail basket by the door. She hadn't shared with Audrey that she was going to send Vanderveer an invitation, but she didn't hide the envelope. Just set it in the basket with the rest of the outgoing mail.

There. Perhaps that would take care of it. Ernst Vanderveer had been in her thoughts much too much. What was it she felt about him, besides her basic rage and suspicion? Attraction to his power? She hoped that wasn't so. Well. It was done. She could not imagine the man would respond positively, but at least she'd tried.

"So. Lunch?" Audrey put down the phone, swung her legs off the desk, and stood up, stretching that perfect little body and interrupting LeeAnn's thoughts in the process. She was alternately lovable and annoying these days. Just now she seemed to be both, as she stood there in her little flowered minidress and heels–in Klamath Falls.

High heels weren't to David's taste, but this morning when she'd made her daily entrance from her attic abode all dolled up, you could see him wanting to whisk her off her feet and carry her, like that guy in the Bahamas had done, so she wouldn't have to walk on those little stick heels. Men always wanted to carry Audrey, and they always wanted to give her gifts. Like nipple rings. David had already presented her with a pendant made from the rainbow obsidian she picked out, although that wasn't wrong in itself; he often gave bits of his work to visitors who toured his studio. She was wearing it today. LeeAnn wanted to snatch it off of her neck.

"So? Are you ready?"

"I guess. I've got to do something about this damn copier before we go," LeeAnn said. "I need to call Harriet."

"So call her." Audrey opened the desk drawer to get her purse. "She told you, 'Anything I can do.' I heard her say it. The woman has bucks."

LeeAnn flashed a memory of Harriet's ring, an umpteen-carat diamond, as she had rested its weight on the copier and said something about either having or not having a maintenance contract on the office equipment. It often bothered LeeAnn to deal with people who had money; they were usually so careful with it. She was always afraid they were going to think she was sucking up to them for the favors they could do for one of her causes, which of course in a way she was.

Audrey seemed to be waiting around for LeeAnn to make the call.

"I think she said they didn't keep a contract on it," LeeAnn said.

"They're her machines and the stuff was wrong with them when we got them," Audrey said firmly. "She knows we're a good cause." She hefted her bag onto her shoulder. "Call her and tell her we need the help." Audrey opened the door to the hall. "There's no money left, you know that. And you know the rules." She started out. "I'm going to go fix my face."

LeeAnn could hear Audrey's heels clicking down the hall. She almost never went without some kind of heel or wedgies to compensate for her height. *Of course, we all compensate.*

Audrey was a tough little girl who had been molested by her dad from infancy on and she compensated by needing to attract all men. That perfect presentation of hers was probably part of the function of covering up. It was quite impressive; people stared at Audrey as if she were a movie star when she walked down the street in Klamath.

LeeAnn in her own perverse way compensated for the attention she tended to attract by not dressing sexy. She subdued her beauty around town. Today she was wearing jeans and a reasonably conservative tank top.

Of course, ruminating about Audrey's childhood trauma or her own–though she didn't really think she had any–wasn't going to get the job done. Reluctantly, LeeAnn picked up the receiver and began to dial. She'd have to handle this carefully. When they'd talked earlier, Harriet said she knew people who would possibly be willing to donate a thousand acres of Oregon forest for a center for Partnership Solutions if the party idea took off, so it was important not to bug her. Maybe she'd be at lunch.

Unfortunately, their benefactor answered the telephone herself. "Mountain View Properties."

"Harriet, it's LeeAnn Spencer. You mentioned the trouble with the copy machine. I just wanted to let you know it's worse."

"Oh?" Harriet murmured politely. LeeAnn went on to describe in some detail the maladies of both copier and fax, structuring her story to stress that both were pre-existing conditions. Harriet seemed sympathetic but detached.

"So, what I was wondering," LeeAnn finished, "was who I should call." *There, that was pretty good.*

"I think L & P fixed it the first time. Though you may want to call Goebel's, too. Check their prices. I know you're on a budget."

Silence. "Well, thanks."

"Both would do a good job."

"Okay then, I'll give them a call. Thanks so much," she said again, redundantly. *Shit, shit, shit.* She hung up. *God, I hate it when I blow a phone call.*

She dialed the two office supply stores, but the ailments she described were deemed too severe for local treatment. It became clear that somebody would have to come over the hill from Medford town. LeeAnn sighed, opened the Medford phone book to Office Machines, Repair and Service, picked up the telephone again, unzipped her planner, pulled out her VISA card, and dialed the place with the biggest ad. Then she waited, with that combination feeling of power and fear that anybody who's ever abused a credit card feels.

"Tomorrow after ten?" the man was asking her.

"That'll work."

"And how did you want to take care of that?" The dreaded phrase. A euphemism for pay up. As she recited her VISA number, LeeAnn heard the click-clack of Audrey's heels on the polished marble of the hall floor. She hadn't quite gotten through the part about, "and the expiration date is . . ." when her personal policeman walked back in the office.

Audrey looked at LeeAnn's VISA, then at her. "So, you handled it, huh! You know what Peter said," she scolded. "No martyrs!" She said loudly.

"Shhh." She got off the phone. "It can't be more than a couple hundred bucks and I've got that in a money market." LeeAnn had exactly five hundred dollars in a Klamath First Federal account that she'd established when she first got to town. It wasn't David's money, she rationalized; she had it before they met. So it was *her* business if she spent it. Forget Peter's rules.

"You know," Audrey said, plopping herself down on LeeAnn's

desk, "I've been meaning to tell you this. You gotta have more guts."

"I know."

"You're just making things harder for yourself in the long run. For instance," and she looked at LeeAnn as if she was going to say something really painful, "you don't even have the courage to bring up this business about David and me."

LeeAnn looked away, and then back at her friend. "You're right," she said after a minute. "Why don't I?"

"Why don't you?" Audrey repeated. "It's the most important thing going on in your life, isn't it? Except for the Summer Project, maybe."

LeeAnn thought about it. Ultimately, it was her life with David that mattered to her. *All my altruism aside, I'm probably only into saving the world if it doesn't mess up the rest of my life. Is that bad? Are most people like that, I wonder? I bet they are.*

"If you don't show courage *now*, you're going to need more eventually."

"That goes for the world, too."

"Forget about the world for a minute, will you, L.A. You've got to face your own fears and your own life, not just other people's."

"Sometimes I can't." Her eyes strayed back to Mount Shasta, cold and truthful; it didn't pretend life was easy.

"People who look at you from the outside see you as very confident, you know." Audrey went on. "Only a few of us realize it takes you more courage to function because you're afraid of more things."

She's right, LeeAnn thought. *Fear has dominated my existence from the first days of my memory. I don't know why. Mostly fear of not pleasing someone.*

"I mean, like this David thing." Audrey was relentless. "Let's talk about it. Right now."

"Right now?"

"You probably want to know what I'm feeling for David, and what I plan to do about it. Well, don't you?"

"Yes."

"So *ask* me."

LeeAnn sighed. She felt like a little child being told to "repeat after me." "You're attracted to David. I know that," she finally got out. "How much?"

"I'm attracted to most beautiful men."

"David more than any other?"

"At the moment, yes. But that's okay. I go away, it goes away."

"Maybe not for David."

"No, maybe not."

"Well, what do we do?"

"Like I said, I can leave town."

"Not till the Summer Project's done."

"I can decide not to wash my hair," said Audrey. "Heck, for you, I could stop wearing makeup. Then for sure he'll go away."

"I'm not so sure."

"Well what are *you* going to do about it? It's your life. What . . ."

"I *don't know!*" For once LeeAnn was getting snappish. "Sorry."

"No, that was good. Displaying a little anger once in a while might save you a lot of grief."

"Audrey, could we talk about this later? Please?"

"We can talk about it at *lunch*," Audrey announced decisively. "Okay?"

One more sigh. "Okay." Grimly, LeeAnn grabbed her pack. They locked up the office and headed down the hall to finally talk it out. Though there was no acceptable resolution that LeeAnn could see; these were just three decent people caught in a terrible quandary.

CHAPTER TEN

Lunch With Stan

LeeAnn could tell they were late going to lunch because the afternoon elevator operator was already on, reading a paperback and grumbling about it.

"How's the book?"

"Just more shoot-em-ups. I swear there's nothing else to read anymore."

"You're right," said LeeAnn.

"So where is it going to be today?" Gladys asked, as she pulled the accordion metal door shut and started to work the hemispheric throttle that looked like something off the bridge of a ship.

"Klamath Grill, I think." They'd been to different restaurants each day, LeeAnn trying to demonstrate to Audrey the entire repertoire of culinary delights in a town not noted for its adventures in eating.

Gladys nodded approvingly. "They do a good salad." The elevator started down.

"So, Klamath Grill it is," LeeAnn said. "See you later, Gladys." They left the building and turned right. As they marched on past the gallery David belonged to, both women involuntarily glanced inside. As usual, its window was filled with mostly pottery; David was too nice to insist on getting his pieces in prominent display. Today only a spear and the bust of a Native American in moose antler represented him.

He was busy with customers in the back, LeeAnn saw, but his eyes were on the two women. He was looking at them the same way he had that day outside the fork-killing restaurant on the way down from Portland. Some days he would come to stick his head out the door and say, "All *right!*" as they walked past. David was on duty now almost every morning and today would be a double shift. He didn't like doubles; he liked to take life easy.

They walked on down the sidewalk that was about to be replaced by geothermal. Audrey often remarked on what a neat idea it was. *A fire goddess* would *be fascinated by that,* LeeAnn thought. *Of course, a fire goddess is more interesting than a wind-sister. A weak sister.* Audrey, beautiful Audrey, with the fire of Pele and the style of Fifth Avenue, except for her speech which betrayed her beginnings. With a New York accent, you can hear the difference of just a few blocks.

"Oh, look, a new window." They paused at the Humane Society Thrift Store, which featured seasonal-theme windows that LeeAnn had come to look forward to as she used to the windows at Saks, or F.A.O. Schwartz. This was a back-to-school display, a splendid demonstration of the recycling of book bags, muffin tins, lunch boxes, and little dresses and jackets. "How Klamathy," Audrey said, one of her new words. "How nice."

As they walked on toward the Grill, a small breeze stirred, blowing Audrey's skirt Marilyn Monroe style, and causing two teenage boys to have an epiphany. LeeAnn barely noticed. She was rehearsing what she'd say at lunch. At the moment she considered beginning the conversation with, *Do you think monogamy is natural?* Of course she knew what Audrey would say. "Three percent of mammals are monogamous, I already told you, and some of those will fool around if they think they can get away with it."

Another opening remark might be, *So why don't the three of us just move in together?* How would that be for getting it all over with in a hurry? They passed a newspaper vending machine; the *Herald and News* had another article about business trends in the Basin. Last week, all of Klamath had been inundated with crowds of blue-green-algae people who were in town for their "August Celebration" of the harvest. Several thousand mostly vegetarian, highly energetic folks from all over North America had lit up the town. They were gone now and the streets seemed deserted by comparison.

The two women crossed Seventh Street, walking past Beach's Jewelry Store where they'd replaced LeeAnn's watch battery for free last time because they thought they might have sold her a bad one. "I don't think we did, but you never know."

"Ha! Will you look at the bumper sticker?" Audrey pointed to a beat-up blue Ford pickup that said, "My boss is a Jewish carpenter," on the back of it and had an overweight white terrier running around in the back barking its head off.

"How are *you*, Melanie?" LeeAnn called. They approached the truck, where LeeAnn went into a whole disgusting coo-coo, goo-goo ritual of greeting with the small, portly animal, who looked like she was ready to burst, shaking her whole body in excitement at LeeAnn's approach.

"This is Melanie, Audrey. She owns Stan." Melanie stood up on her hind legs to be petted, a major balancing feat considering her girth. "You've got to meet Stan. He's the guy who's going to fix the hot tub. Genuine local color. An authentic good old boy."

"Oh?"

"Just don't get into an argument with him, okay? I need to get him to come fix it before Peter gets here." LeeAnn didn't want her brother spending precious time fiddling with plumbing pipes instead of celebrating the stuffed and stamped invitations.

"So how do you know this employee of a Jewish carpenter?" Audrey said, as they walked toward the entrance. Her harsh pronunciation of the word "carpenter" made LeeAnn homesick.

"He fixed our retaining wall when we moved in. It was about to fall down."

Audrey was peering through the restaurant window. "Is that the guy over there?"

"We need to have lunch with him," LeeAnn nodded.

Audrey stopped still and gave LeeAnn a long, long look that said she understood *exactly* what she was doing.

"Oh, Audrey," LeeAnn groaned, "can't you leave me alone?"

"Going into avoidance mode, huh?"

"Just not *today*, okay? I don't want to think about it today."

Audrey shrugged. "It's your *kuleana*." LeeAnn gathered that *"kuleana"* must be Hawaiian for "business," or "responsibility." Audrey didn't bother to translate. "Looks like he's all wrapped up in that book. Are you sure?"

"He's always wrapped up in a book, usually about fishing or God, but he likes people, too. Get him started talking, he's a trip." Audrey shrugged and for once, let LeeAnn lead the way.

"Promise me you'll be nice?" she said as they walked in the front door. "The guy is your quintessential conservative."

"Oh!"

"He doesn't proselytize, though."

"Don't worry, I'd out-talk him if he did."

She opened the door. Before entering the smoking section, LeeAnn took a breath, as she usually did, and held it till they'd passed through into the back room.

Stan leapt out of his chair as soon as he saw the two women, his good-old-boy belly rising like an eight-month pregnancy. Usually big bellies bothered LeeAnn, but she made an exception for Stan. He was big and hearty, grey-haired and red-faced, with features that were a caricature of Saint Nicholas. Of course, there's something about extravagant mustaches that fosters that look; Stan's was an authentic cookie duster.

"This is Audrey," LeeAnn said as she gave Stan a quick hug that made him look embarrassed. "We went to kindergarten together."

"You must have made quite a pair," Stan said as his small blue eyes darted from one to the other and back again.

"And still do," said Audrey.

"Well, sit down, have a french fry."

Audrey snatched several off of a plate that held a half-eaten Reuben sandwich. Then she reached and took some more.

"You know," Stan said, addressing Audrey and gesturing with his head toward LeeAnn. "She's from New York and yet they call her L.A. That's the part that seems funny to me."

"It's these sneaky big-city liberals, always trying to confuse the opposition," LeeAnn said.

One of the waitresses came over then with a hamburger patty in a styrofoam container. Stan inspected it and then closed the cover again. "Melanie's lunch," LeeAnn explained to Audrey.

"Well, what'll it be?" the waitress asked.

"You take care of these friends of mine then, Angie, you hear?" Angie was one of the three Klamath Grill waitresses, all skinny, all fast, who automatically knew that LeeAnn wanted the tomato stuffed with tuna fish, garlic bread, and iced tea.

"What are you going to have?" Audrey asked LeeAnn.

"She already knows," said LeeAnn.

"Oh. I'll have the same."

"Your friend here got me out to the college once for some talk she gave on this whole theory of partnership," Stan informed Audrey.

"So she's got you going on it, too, huh? What did you think?"

"Well, I don't know . . ."

"How's the work going?" LeeAnn asked, deliberately giving Stan license to ramble on one of his favorite subjects, *rocks*, and how to work with them. A safe subject. She and Audrey listened politely till at last, he ran out of breath.

"One reason I was asking about your work," LeeAnn said, "was because David was wondering if you could stop by and look at the hot tub."

That of course got Stan into a lengthy description, for Audrey's benefit, of the jury-rigged contraption that LeeAnn's brother had put together, along with some of his views on why it wasn't working.

"Can't David fix it?" Audrey asked.

"David doesn't think he ought to mess with it himself, since it involves plumbing," LeeAnn told her. "He's pretty strict about doing everything to code." She turned back to Stan. "So if you think you could come by . . ."

"Sure, most any time. Except tomorrow. I'm bidding a job out to Tree Island tomorrow."

LeeAnn looked at him. "You're not bidding the masonry for the resort?"

"Oh no, no, no, that's *way* out my league. They're bringing in a San Francisco outfit. They want to restore the old stone house at the dock and put a big glass and steel frame over it. Fix it up as a greeting area for the guests when they get there," he said. "I guess they called me 'cause there's not many can do that kind of stonework any more."

"Stan's a real artist," LeeAnn said. "He rebuilt our wall down in front of the house."

"Oh, I saw it," Audrey said. "Beautiful work."

Stan shrugged modestly. Tenting his work-worn fingers, Stan looked down at the roughened skin and thick calluses. It was clear that he'd picked up thousands of rocks in his time. "Main thing is I'll finally get to see Tree Island. All those years growing up on the lake and it's the one island I never got to go on." Angie brought the two tuna-stuffed tomatoes then and they began to eat.

"So how come you never got to Tree Island?" Audrey asked, and LeeAnn couldn't stifle a small sigh; Tree Island was a painful topic for her, and it was constantly on the news; she couldn't get away from it.

"Because of the geezers . . .," Stan said. He looked at LeeAnn expectantly. "Well, I'll tell you, if you really want to know." She nodded reluctantly. "Interesting thing about how the VHRI got the place," he said. "See, it was owned by these two old guys, the geezers–Carleton brothers, and their family since way back . . ."

"How far back?"

"Oh, turn of the century, before that sometime. Of course when we were kids," he wasn't about to be derailed by a question, "they were geezers to us, so that's all we ever called them. The geezers. They looked kind of goofy, too, scraggly eyebrows, something a little off about them. You'd see one of them in town, couldn't tell which one it was, unless they were together. But usually one stayed home . . ."

LeeAnn started to drift away.

"Anywho . . .,"Stan was saying a few minutes later, " . . . we always had a blast riding around the lake. Had this little fourteen-foot runabout."

"What was its name?"

"*The Pink Lady.*"

"Was she pink?" Audrey demanded to know.

"Oh yeah. Hot pink with a 35 Evinrude on it. So we knew the lake like the back of our hand. Except Tree Island, because the geezers kept everybody off with a shotgun." He chuckled. "Of course you know when you can't have something you want it even more."

"I know about that!" Audrey agreed, chuckling with him. LeeAnn knew *exactly* what she meant. She was staring out the window just as the broker who'd sold them their house walked into the Grill with her oldest daughter, who was one of her star agents. They had clients with them so they just waved. LeeAnn waved back, while her mind went straight to the image of a Coldwell Banker sign in the front yard.

She sighed. She and Audrey could have been talking right now, getting it over with. Instead, she was listening to stories about Tree Island residents who sounded as greedy as Ernst Vanderveer.

By now, Audrey and Stan were talking about snakes, how many there were back then and whether there might still be any on the island. Then they were talking about the old homestead. "House is all tore up. Bad concrete. Course there's a problem with all the early concrete work around here. Just falls apart."

"Why? What causes that?" Audrey asked as if she really cared.

186

"It's because there's too much mineral in the water, or in the aggregate. This is a very mineral-rich area, you know."

"Oh, I know. From the volcano."

"You might've noticed the sidewalks at your friends' house here," he began, indicating LeeAnn. "Hers are real bad."

Yeah, and they may not be my problem much longer, LeeAnn thought, sinking deeper into her worse-case scenario.

Having finally polished off his Reuben sandwich, Stan leaned back in his chair, obviously pleased with Audrey's attentiveness. He had those same stiff, painted-on rosy cheeks Peter had had as a little boy, only his were the old-man kind.

"So, back to my story. We used to find a lot of mortars and pestles out around the lake. That was before it was illegal to pick anything up." He glanced at LeeAnn out of the corner of his eye. "We had quite a hoard–used to just about sink the *Pink Lady* taking the stuff back." The archaeologist in LeeAnn cringed. "You know kids," he said in an aside to her, then turned back to Audrey.

"I saw some of those mortars in one of the windows we go by on the way to lunch," Audrey said. She liked to stop and look at them. LeeAnn had told her that when a woman who had spent her whole life working with one died, "her family would break out the bottom to let her spirit free."

Audrey's eyes had widened. "That's heavy."

"You should see my collection of arrowheads," Stan said then.

"Oh, I'd like to," she said. Audrey was being very good indeed.

"Some of them eight thousand years old. David's made me a couple of really nice fluted ones, too. I really prize them." said Stan.

"Yeah, they sent me one, too, a few Christmases ago."

"Anyhow, getting back to the story," Stan went on "there were always artifacts you could see lying around on Tree Island, right on the shore, on the beach there. But we left 'em alone because you never knew when those guys might blow you out of the water just for coming ashore."

"Can I get that out of your way, Stan?" Another of the fast waitresses was hovering like a hummingbird over Stan's nearly empty plate.

"Mary, darn it, it's my food, I'm paying for it, and I'm going to keep it!" He swatted at her and she darted away, laughing. "They guarded that place pretty fierce. You could always hear guns going off."

"What'd they shoot? Snakes?"

"Well, target practice I guess." LeeAnn tried to zone out again by concentrating on her stuffed tomato and hard-boiled egg. She always tried to eat all of the lettuce on her plate, unless it was too pale.

". . . so now it's the only building left on the island. That and the trailer. One of the geezers lived in it up on the hill. Pulled a trailer way up there on the top. Don't know how they did it. It's still up there. And the other one lived in the house. I understand they didn't get along too well. And they had this running feud with the county commissioners about property taxes. Sent letters to the paper that could've burned up the editorial page."

Audrey was nodding, evidently following every word.

"Anyhow, to make a long story short, the county finally put a lien on the island and they had to pay up–it was a pretty hefty assessment for those days. But . . . ," and he waggled his finger at Audrey, "the geezers got the last laugh." He laughed a little himself in anticipation of telling her about it. "Heh, heh."

"How?"

"When they croaked, they left the whole island to the Feds. Heh, heh. The BLM. The Bureau of Land Management. Took it right off the county tax rolls. Heh, heh, heh."

Stan was the only person LeeAnn knew who laughed so you could spell it. *"Heh, heh, heh."*

"Of course, the BLM wasn't so interested in owning that island in a lake as they were in picking up agricultural property to turn back into wetland. They've been doing a lot of trading lately, all kinds of land deals. So they made a trade with VHRI for a ranch down in California. And that's how VHRI got to come to town."

Why is this bothering me so much? LeeAnn wondered. *Is it because of my great-grandmother? Because it's ancestral land? Do I believe in that kind of déjà vu? Is that why I'm so invested in Tree Island?*

"I didn't know the government could make trades like that."

"Sure they can." Stan loved telling somebody something they didn't already know.

"Weird."

"I guess it works for them. And it *is* helping to restore the wetlands."

"So," LeeAnn said, joining the conversation at last, "you'll finally get to see the place. Hope you get the job." And she did. Stan never had money, not because he wasn't good at his work–he was superb–but because he always undercharged people. Setting a price was painfully difficult for him. "No, that's okay, you don't owe me nothing," he had said more than once to LeeAnn and David, till LeeAnn told him that was not an acceptable response. He was a widower with nobody to take care of but himself and Melanie he was always saying. But everybody's got to live. David would usually have to force money on Stan.

After they took their leave, LeeAnn and Audrey walked back down Main Street in the gusty wind, past the jewelry store, the thrift shop, and the store with the old mortars in the window. Audrey had to stop to see if any of them had the bottom broken out. There was one. Both women stood looking at it. LeeAnn was thinking about the hours every day for a lifetime that a woman would have spent with her mortar. No wonder her spirit would need to be released.

She thought about a time when she had first moved out to be with David, and an archaeologist with the BLM that they met at a Unitarian Fellowship potluck had taken them out for a hike that Sunday afternoon. And how they had stumbled on a vision quest site. So timeless a place that she imagined the people who had built the stone cairns were right beside her.

In these tribes all the people had done vision quests. The pile of rock the left was large sometimes in the case of men, medium for the women, and tiny for the children. Next to the cairn sometimes there were tiny mortars, several in a row, that had been carved in a boulder, to hold small offerings. The archaeologist had poured water from the canteen into each of the small mortars as a mark of respect, and LeeAnn had thought that was nice. It felt good to live in Klamath. "Well," she said to Audrey, "we better get back."

As they crossed Ninth Street, LeeAnn's eyes went to the gallery again, but David wasn't there any more. Where was he? Funny how different the place looked when he was absent. *Much* less interesting.

When they got upstairs and unlocked the office door, Audrey stooped to pick up the mail. The message machine was blinking. "What's this?" she said, as she tore open an expensive-looking square powder blue envelope. "It's a check! Hallelujah, it's money? Made out to the 22nd Century Group."

LeeAnn was shocked. "How much?"

"Two hundred and twenty dollars"

"From who?"

"Carlisle, who's Carlisle?" asked Audrey.

LeeAnn snatched it out of Audrey's hand. "Pamela Carlisle. That's the woman I met on the plane." She pulled a Tiffany formal note card out of the envelope. "For the coffers of the 22nd Century Group," she read. "Good luck to you, LeeAnn. The world does need saving. And good luck with everything else too." She meant David.

"Audrey, do you believe this? Two hundred twenty bucks. I never asked her for any money. That's going to be enough to fix the copier *and* buy toner."

"Hey, didn't I say it's going to work? Now let's see who called. Probably the AARP. Or the pope." She hit the Play Messages button as LeeAnn continued to stare at the check.

The first call was from Peter, sounding uncharacteristically excited. "*The deed is done!*" he said. "I delivered the disk to Hal's office about twenty minutes ago. We're finally *at the printers!* Talk to you later."

"Yahooo!" Audrey and LeeAnn high-fived and bumped their hips together like they used to when they were teenagers. "Done!"

"Do you realize Pamela is almost the only person I've talked to about the project so far? Except for Martyn Williams." LeeAnn hadn't heard from the explorer yet, but she was hoping; to, any day now. He was probably still on his Yukon trip. "All I did was tell her what we were doing. And then we get an unsolicited check in the mail like this? I thought she thought I was batshit!" LeeAnn couldn't get over it. She went straight over to her desk to get a deposit slip while Audrey hit the message button again.

Message number two. It was David's voice, with that wonderful timbre in it. "Wind's up," he said. "It's cooking. I found somebody to switch with me at the gallery so if you want to meet me at Harbor Isles as soon as you get this, come on down. I'll have your rig ready and in the water by three." *He wants to be with me; maybe we don't have to sell the house after all.*

"Go," Audrey said. "There's nothing to do here that won't wait till tomorrow." So LeeAnn raced home, put on her bathing suit and shorts, then decided to take her bike so she could ride home with David. Besides, the exercise might get rid of some of her excess energy. How quickly things change. Right now she was feeling on top of the world.

CHAPTER ELEVEN

Water-Starting

LeeAnn pedaled against the strong wind all the way over to the lake. *He's going to make me do my harness today, I know he is,* she thought, as she pumped up the little rise to where she could see David out on that lush green lawn, unrolling her new pink-and-green sail. She could also see the whitecaps as the lake came into view, and her heart sank. It was definitely blowing up a storm, but there was no putting it off any longer.

LeeAnn had tried wearing the harness and even hooking in a couple of days ago when there was almost no wind–just testing, like trying intercourse for the first time. In for just a little bit, then out for a little bit, gingerly hooking and unhooking. It had been an entirely uneventful experience. Today, she suspected, would be different.

David whistled at her appreciatively as she approached. "Hey, your timing's perfect," he said. "Just in time to rig your new sail." She threw the bike down on the grass and went over to kiss him hello and admire the sail, which had arrived by UPS the day before, to go with the secondhand board LeeAnn had just picked up–an old ten-foot-eight "F2" for $150. LeeAnn planned to call her new board Eff-tu, or Effie.

Trying not to look at the waves out on the lake, LeeAnn dutifully threaded the sail onto her mast and attached the boom. She tightened her down-haul some and then started on the out-haul. "You want to be sure you don't leave any wrinkles," David, who was sitting on his haunches, watching, reminded her. "Here, use your rigging tool."

After LeeAnn finished to David's satisfaction, they stood the rig up to check it in the wind. The single cam flipped immediately, with a satisfying snap.

"Okay, that's good." David then began reviewing what he had been telling her last night about the balance point she was supposed to achieve hanging in a harness. "You're holding on but your hands are limp; they're just guiding the boom. Your full body weight's balanced against the wind and you're moving upwind at a little bit of an angle . . ."

David had it all picture perfect in his mind. When he explained how to do something, LeeAnn could usually imagine herself doing it. She thought about how much of the physical world she'd experienced the past five years through David's observation and interpretation of it.

"Oh! David, look," she said then. Two dragonflies, joined in iridescent flight, landed on her sail briefly, then took off again to hover in the sunshine, floating in the breeze, seeing the world together, locked as one. Tantric togetherness. She pointed the pair out to David, and he seemed to understand completely. They watched together for a few moments. "Want to try that?" he asked with a grin. "On a windsurfer? You and me?"

"Tandem windsurfing? Hmmmm . . ."

"I wonder if anybody has?"

"You know somebody has. A lot of people, probably."

"I could stand behind you."

"Well, you'd have to, ding-ding. How else would we do it?" She put her harness on then and started pulling the waist and pelvic straps tight as David watched.

"Come here," he said and he adjusted it for her, though it didn't really need adjusting. Then he held her orange life jacket out for her like she was a little kid, she put her arms in and he zipped it up. "Okay," he said, smacking her on the butt like he was a little league coach. "Get on out there. I want to see you hanging on that boom all afternoon."

"We'll see." She picked up her board.

"And sitting on the mast tonight," he added with a leer, which she returned in kind after the moment it took her to get it. "*That* for *sure*." Then she carried her board down to the water.

David picked up the sail, with the mast leading into the wind, so it wouldn't buffet him about, and it didn't. The way he carried it, the wind did all the work. Whenever LeeAnn picked up her sail in the wind, it would either try to bash her in the face or take off down the beach. But it was no problem for David. He laid LeeAnn's sail down next to her board and snapped it into place. Then he checked the length of her harness lines. "You're all set."

"Okay, David, but first I want to just get used to it." LeeAnn climbed aboard, up-hauled with some difficulty, and was on her way across the lake as David went back for his rig. *Good Lord, this wind is strong.* The first time across, she didn't hook in. *Still getting used to the board, and the wind, and the sail,* she told herself, no point in adding something new right away. She started a second run without hooking in, hoping David wouldn't notice, but of course he did. You can tell from way far off if somebody's using a harness or not.

He was standing on the shore when she got back, almost ready to sail. "You didn't get hooked in that time."

"It was too late."

"LeeAnn, *you have to commit to it!*"

"I am."

"Hook in the minute you get up; otherwise in this wind it's going to be too late." There was repressed irritation in his voice.

So she *had* to do it. No way out. She up-hauled, hooked in like he said, and was immediately launched forward onto her sail. In the twink of an eye. That fast. Nice soft landing though. *This isn't so bad, when you fall on your sail. You hardly even get wet,* LeeAnn thought, climbing off of it into the water. *Try again.*

"You have to *lean back,*" David was hollering at her as she stumbled over a submerged rock on the slippery bottom, scraping her shin, "or you're going to get launched every time."

"I know that." She was beginning to feel uncomfortably self-conscious; this was like taking driving lessons from your father.

"You have to *sit down.* Do you want to try doing a beach-start?"

"No, one thing at a time." She felt rattled that he was standing there, watching her every move, as she climbed on her board. "Okay, I can do it. I'll do something. It's oh-*kay*," she said.

"Fine, I'll go work on my jibe then," said David, hearing the note of dismissal in her voice. He expertly guided his rig out into knee-deep water, stepped aboard effortlessly and was gone.

It took more strength just to up-haul her sail in this god-awful gale than LeeAnn had ever imagined she possessed, but she finally managed it. And she tried to remember about sitting down the second she hooked in. But apparently she didn't, because just then this Primal Force simply swept her off her feet, spun her around at rocket speed, and hurled her smack down onto her board, knocking the breath out of her and implanting the quick release buckle into her right hip before depositing her in the water, under the sail, still hooked in. The pain was *awful.*

Fortunately, the water was only a couple of feet deep, so she was able to sit on the bottom and push the sail up so she could breathe. For a couple of minutes she just sat there. Granted, it was a small injury, but wildly excruciating for the moment. When the worst of it had passed, she began to work on detaching herself. She found that the plastic harness line was so tightly twisted around the bar on her harness it took almost a minute to get it free. And that was sitting where she could see it and where she could breathe. *How long would this take underwater, in a panic? And* **this**, *she thought, is what he and that adorable Adam say almost never happens. Ha. I won't tell David though. He probably wouldn't believe me.*

Next time up, LeeAnn leaned back too soon, too far and immediately went in under the sail, choking, hyperventilating, coughing, waves sweeping over her and her nose and mouth full of water as she struggled to unhook herself. David sailed by just then, checking on her.

"You okay?"

"I think I'm going to try practicing my water-start," LeeAnn said. "I think there's too much wind today for my harness."

"Whatever." Which meant that he was giving up on her.

"I have to do this myself, David."

"Okay by me." He took off again. The rig was a mess. "Swim the board around first," it said on the video, "point the nose toward where you want to go. Scissor the mast toward the tail of the board, then flip it over."

But every single time, as soon as she started to get up, the board would round up or the sail would get away from her and flap over with an annoying whack, forcing her to start all over. It seemed hopeless. While of course a hundred yards away, David was whizzing back and forth, efficiently teaching himself to jibe. Usually she noticed, he'd get about halfway around, then stall and slip under the water. But you could see he was making progress. His was an orderly, productive learning process.

All right, LeeAnn finally told herself, *just up-haul and go for a ride.* Plan C. But then she couldn't seem to do even *that.* She would stand on the board, feeling uncommonly clumsy, start to pull the sail up, and then a wave would come to unbalance her and tip her back into the water. Down, up, down. Marx brothers stuff. Up again. Down again. David, noticing her obvious distress, gave up on his jibe and came back to lend her courage. Or witness her defeat. *One of the two.*

"Anything I can help with?" His sweet patience was driving her crazy.

"I can't do it, David." It was evident she was near tears. "I did all right at the Gorge when I was alone."

"Let's go home."

"I did *fine* then." Utter humiliation. *This is total regression,* LeeAnn thought, *like back to babyhood, and I'm about to suck my thumb. I can't even get up on the damn board any more; Audrey with her fingernails would have done better. And here I was starting to call myself a windsurfer.* Instead, *wimp, failure, quitter* were the words that sprang to mind.

David, just as patiently as he'd helped her rig, began derigging her board. She didn't dare help. When he finished loading their gear, he put her bike in the back of the van. *Which is just as well; I probably can't even ride a bike any more,* she thought. She climbed in front, buckled her belt, and sat staring out the window, sulking.

David continued to be maddeningly helpful on the way home. "I'll show you some stuff tonight–rig up something in the cabin and give you a harness lesson." She was silent.

Bump, bumpety-bump up over the driveway. David turned off the engine, kept his hand resting on the key in the ignition and, looked over toward the cabin like he was waiting to be released to it. But then he said something that surprised her. "Come over and I'll cook you dinner. I've got some scallops and crab and calamari."

There was a lump in her throat. *It's just charity; he's just trying to get through till our trip and then it's splitsky.* But being fed dinner in the cabin might be more enjoyable than sitting home feeling sorry for herself. "Okay." *Who did he buy all that seafood for anyway?*

"See you in a bit," David said, climbing out of the van and looking after her as she headed toward the back door. She went straight into the bath off of her bedroom, turned the shower on as hard as it would go, then stripped and stood under it, trying to blast her fear and discouragement away. She started to scrub, then, "Ouch!" She had inadvertently hit the spot on her hip where the quick-release buckle had nailed her; a giant bruise was starting to develop.

The phone was ringing as she turned off the shower and got out of the tub; she ran for it, getting water all over the floor as she grabbed a towel from under the sink.

It was Maggie, so LeeAnn forced her voice into cheerful gear. But of course a parent can tell; parents have a built-in voice index that measures even the most minute gradations.

"How are you feeling?" Maggie asked.

"You tell me."

"On a scale of one to ten, I'd say about a two."

"That's about right. For one thing, my windsurfing is in the cellar. David says he's going to show me some more tonight, but what's ridiculous is I got him into this sport and then he immediately gets better than me. He's *pro*-gressing, I'm *re*-gressing."

"That tends to happen when it comes to sports and men. I know it's not fair." Maggie had the same kind of hole in her head that LeeAnn did when it came to simple physical actions.

"Well, I finally got myself a board anyway, secondhand," LeeAnn said. "It's got this funny little scallop in the end just like David's. Which means they can mate, I guess. Produce a line of short boards."

"Hey, there you go."

Who started, "Hey, there you go," LeeAnn wondered. It seemed to be the catch phrase of the year. Maybe it was something on television. She was walking around her room naked, talking on the portable phone, trying to decide what to wear. Twisting around, she once again inspected her bruise. It looked pretty bad, that really dark purple kind. She couldn't find any clean underwear in her drawer, so she pulled on a bathing suit bottom and a wrinkled T-shirt.

"Well, at least you got the invitations off to the printer," Maggie was saying. "That's good." Take one thing at a time was always Maggie's way of cheering people up. Measure your progress, not your failures.

"Oh, and we got a check in the mail from a woman named Pamela I met on the plane. Do you believe it? I didn't even ask for money–I just told her about the project and she said after she got home she decided she really liked the idea . . ."

As she dressed, holding the receiver up to her ear, LeeAnn could see David through the window. Sitting at the picnic table in front of the cabin, he was cracking crab for their dinner on spread-out newspapers. He was barefoot, in shorts and a torn T-shirt with the sleeves cut out for running, and an arrowhead on a thong around his neck. It was so evident looking at him how much his body had changed with the windsurfing. His muscles seemed to ripple even when he wasn't moving.

Sillvester was sitting companionably beside him, but the cat's interest in the crabmeat seemed only academic. David had evidently had the forethought to stuff him first.

God, I love that man, she thought. *Good, old, calm, patient David who does everything so logically.* Except she'd noticed his fingers were worn down to the nubs from chewing at his nails. She'd seen that when she came back from Russia, so the stress was definitely there. Probably from thinking up *"fifty ways to leave your lover."* LeeAnn talked to her mother then about Audrey and David, and what was either happening or not happening there.

"As I reflect on your relationship with Audrey," Maggie said, "it's brought a lot of grief over the years."

"I know. It isn't her fault. I don't think volcanoes *mean* to be destructive."

"Of course not."

"And the thing is, when David and I are together, he seems just as devoted as ever, but I know there's this underlying excitement for Audrey and it just breaks my heart."

"Are you sure you aren't trying to do too much?" LeeAnn's mother knew *it* was in her nature to be in turmoil. "Save your relationship, water-start, do the Summer Project."

"I suppose. Oh, I know I am." It helped just to be talking about it all with Maggie. LeeAnn pictured her mother sitting at her desk or lying on her bed in that neat studio apartment of hers on Sixtieth overlooking the Hudson. L.A.'s mom, who favored worn blue jeans on her long-legged frame, and who wore her curly blonde hair at varying lengths over the years, adopting each new vogue just as soon as it was safely passé, was a lithe and kooky sort of parent, giggling with her children in the kitchen with hot cookies at midnight, running in the spring rain through the park to the Plaza and back, wearing a trash bag to stay dry. LeeAnn and her mother were close again these days; they hadn't always been.

LeeAnn was also close to her dad, but in a different way. Cliff had married a younger woman and had become totally absorbed in a new set of children. LeeAnn didn't like to trouble him with the problems of his still-not-grown thirty-six-year-old adolescent. So she only told him about the good things.

"I think what you really need to do is sit down and talk to both of them–Audrey *and* David–separately, of course."

"I know. I just haven't done it." LeeAnn went to get a glass from the kitchen cabinet for some water. "Oh look, here's a note. Jeff and Audrey went to the movies. They're giving us our space."

"So you go have fun tonight with David. Maybe this is all just a wake-up call for your relationship. But don't try to define it. Sometimes you can destroy things by analyzing them. Just go have your evening."

"Thanks, Mom." LeeAnn hung up, put on some eyeliner, threw on a little shadow, dabbed musk on her throat and her thighs, and walked across the yard in her bathing suit bottom and wrinkled T-shirt to the cabin, where she knocked on the door. "Is it soup yet?" she asked as David let her in.

"Almost." He was busy draining pasta and sautéing seafood. LeeAnn sat down. The cabin always had an off-duty feeling about it, and despite all the other ramifications on the evening, it felt good to be here. All the bills were in the house, all the adult responsibility, too. *I need to just have fun tonight. I need to get into my never-mind mode.* The year she'd been a sophomore in high school, the Spencers had rented a house on Fire Island called "Never Mind," and that was how the summer felt. Everything in life had seemed so simple then.

LeeAnn looked around the cabin some more, absorbing the surroundings into her being, or trying to. Windsurf booties on the floor, life jacket, mast protector, a cooler on top of the fridge. A couch that had been given to them, their old coffee table from the apartment, and a TV-VCR; David loved to watch old movies. When LeeAnn was with him, she did, too. A dozen books, all the books David needed to own, were propped up on a shelf with two chunks of obsidian as bookends. And there were his ribbons on the wall from the cross-country ski races they'd done together. *I left adult life once for you. Now I'm ready to escape again, if you'll take me with you.* But he probably wouldn't.

There was the infamous skinny dresser David had carried out the night she cried herself into anoxia. She imagined him carrying that skinny little dresser through his whole life, strapped onto his back, in and out of relationships with other women.

She looked at the pass-through to the kitchen, a slightly uneven arch he'd cut by hand in the drywall. They'd redone the guest cabin for guests, but now it was his house. *Am I a guest here? If so, I might as well enjoy it.*

Dinner was exquisite. David was even thoughtful enough to break out a bottle of merlot he'd been saving forever. After they'd polished off the wine and most of the seafood, LeeAnn went into the tiny bathroom and sat down to pee, watching through the crack in the folding door as David started to gather materials to construct a makeshift windsurf trainer. Some rope, her boom, a new shovel handle. She had no idea how he was going to do it, but evidently he had a plan. It looked like he was going to tie his contraption off on the ladder to the loft.

She stood up, flushed the toilet, and stared at herself in the mirror as she slowly washed her hands and then her face. She looked kind of scruffy. Her hair was getting longer and blonder. Despite the sunscreen that she halfheartedly applied, her skin was getting darker, especially over those prominent cheekbones. *I've been bronzed*, she thought.

She hadn't brought a comb, so she borrowed one of David's. Then she wished she had lipstick with her. She looked in his medicine cabinet but there wasn't any in there. Not that she thought there would be.

When she came out of the bathroom, David was tying white nylon line onto her boom. "You're going to have to trust this apparatus," he said, as he tied a knot. Then something seemed to occur to him quite suddenly and said, "Oh!" in a pleased sort of voice, as though he had just been touched by divine inspiration. "I've got a much better idea. Come with me."

"Where are we going?" She picked up her harness.

"You'll see."

"Do I need my boom?"

"Nope, already got one." David went back, picked up a short piece of clothesline, grabbed LeeAnn's hand, and headed out the door. The sharp gravel hurt her feet as he led her along the driveway and into the house.

"It's perfect. A perfect trainer," he said, surveying the weight machine in the back room with satisfaction. Then he quickly tied the clothesline in two places to the pull-down bar. "There. That'll be your harness line; this is your boom." He set three weights. "We can put as much wind on this baby as we want. Let's start with about ten knots. That should be about twenty pounds. Now put your harness on."

She did, slipping it over her bikini bottom and buckling the straps; then she stood in position in front of the weight machine.

"Okay, hook in. Hook out." She did. It was great–she could really lean back.

"This feels like I'm actually on a board."

"Now, down! Sit. When you feel that gust, just sit down on it. Balance your weight against the weight of the wind."

"Hey, I like this feeling," LeeAnn said, "I think I'm starting to get it. *Finally.*" She realized that till now, her board had always been in control of her instead of the other way around. She hooked in, hooked out, sat down, stood up, over and over again, counter-balancing against the weights, feeling more confident all the time.

"Okay, come on back to neutral." He put on another ten pounds and she tried it again. "All right," David said, finally, standing behind her, and taking hold of the boom. "Let's say now you want to go upwind, tilt your boom back." He did it with her. "Now forward." They did that for a while. "Feel that, see that? Find that sweet spot."

"Good girl," he kissed her neck. "*Now*," David whispered in her ear a few minutes later, "let's try sailing *together.*" He bit her neck softly.

Ooooh, she was very willing. The closeness of him, spooning behind her felt outrageously good, as did the stiffness that soon was poking up against her back. Then his hand was guiding him past her bikini bottom and the harness straps, and they were joined. In tandem trip, just like the dragonflies.

David caressed her breasts and her belly and her legs. And he kissed her shoulders. *I will never windsurf again in my life without thinking about this,* LeeAnn realized. He was just once again starting to nuzzle that oh-so-sensitive place on the back of her neck that gave her goose-flesh, when they heard Audrey's rental car pull up in the driveway.

She started to pull away. "No, don't," said David. "Wait. We've got time." He thrusted quickly then, and then more quickly, and then the soles of her feet were tingling. The tingling spread through her whole body, like champagne in her veins. And then it was over. Bump, bump, bump, bump went her heart. She lay back against the ten-knot weights with her eyes closed as David reluctantly withdrew.

They heard the crunch of gravel from Jeff and Audrey's footsteps on the drive. *"Ha-kun-a ma-ta-ta,"* they were singing, loudly.

LeeAnn had barely got the flowered bathing suit bottom back in place before Jeff and Audrey burst in the door, like a chorus line, and skittered across the floor. The whole room was steaming with sex but they seemed oblivious. And then they immediately started in with a blow-by-blow replay of *The Lion King*, with Jeff demonstrating his roar. "You really missed something."

Oh, no, we didn't, LeeAnn was thinking. Audrey went for the teakettle and started boiling water for tea. "Orange spice, black raspberry, red zinger . . . You know, L.A., you really need to get a new teakettle."

"Whatever." LeeAnn was feeling blissful; at the moment nothing could bother her. It was a *Never Mind* summer evening all over again. They got their tea and then all went in and draped themselves around the living room. They started talking about making a movie, a kids' movie about the *Year in Parentheses*. "Animation is the very best way these days to recruit people, and inform them, and amuse them," Audrey summed up, and they all agreed. "Jeff, you can do the voices," LeeAnn said. Then they started working on the plot.

The next couple of days were good ones. LeeAnn and Audrey would head down to the office early, stopping at Ted Swan's Bakery to pick up latte and pastries. Then while Audrey worked the phones, LeeAnn edited the news releases. There was not a whole lot more to do. Around 3:00 in the afternoon, they'd knock off, and LeeAnn would head for the lake to meet David and practice sailing techniques; she was improving every day.

Each evening, after the speakerphone meeting with Peter, she'd sit glued in front of the television, watching windsurf videos and trying to learn her water-starts by osmosis. The next afternoon she'd try out what she'd learned.

On the third day, she finally started getting it down. The first time she water-started, she shrieked with delight and was halfway across the lake before she could stop reliving that exquisite moment of being lifted out of the water by the sail. It gave her a whole different feeling, at least momentarily, about herself and life. About working *with* the forces of nature instead of against them. Then the next time she tried it, miracle of miracles, she did it again. And again.

Of course, you had to learn to do it going both directions, under any conditions, coming and going, right-footed and left-footed. But it wasn't too tough. At least she had the idea; she knew what it felt like. And everything else was going pretty well. Peter was coming up on the weekend for the invitation stuffing and stamping party, and she was somehow keeping the David/Audrey thing at bay. So, life was looking up.

Late on that third afternoon, LeeAnn was practicing her new skills about a hundred yards from shore. She got up, hooked in, let herself back down in the water, and was flipping her sail, getting ready to crouch under it and get up going the opposite way, when she noticed a figure on the shore waving frantically. It was Audrey; she recognized the rental car. LeeAnn jumped onto her board and started to sail in. Without even noticing, she'd water-started automatically.

She could begin to hear Audrey shouting. "Car . . . missing . . ."

"Whaaatt?"

"Peter . . . car . . ."

No, no. No, not Peter. Not an accident. Oh my God. She didn't dare fall. When she finally got close enough, LeeAnn jumped off and started to run toward shore, abandoning her rig.

"Peter!? Tell me! What happened? Is he . . . ?"

"His car got stolen."

"Is he all right?! Tell me my brother's okay!"

"He's fine, LeeAnn."

"Ohhhh." LeeAnn felt dizzy.

Audrey was coming toward her now. Realizing what she'd done, she waded out into the water, fully dressed in her fancy lavender culottes, and started helping LeeAnn drag the board out.

"Damn it, Audrey, why do you have to scare me like that?" LeeAnn snapped.

"The invitations, they were in the car."

"Oh no." LeeAnn stopped dead in the water, staring at Audrey. "No. You're kidding?"

"They're gone. All of them. But they may be in some dumpster. We're going to go down there and look."

"You're going to go *what* . . . ?"

"Peter's a mess. You can imagine how he feels. If we find them, maybe he'll feel better. Jeff and I are going to drive down right now."

"How did it happen?" They were back on shore now.

"Let's go. He wants to tell you about it himself."

"Okay." LeeAnn was reluctant to wait, but she understood. She spotted David, who was still creating a hole in the water with his incomplete jibe. As she watched, he disappeared into it one more time. When he came up, she pantomimed going with Audrey in the car. He held his arms up in question, didn't understand.

She went back through the pantomime again. Leaving her board. *Going* in the car. Then she waved. *Good-bye.*

He gestured with a *whatever* motion, then went back to what he was doing.

"So when did he call?" They were in Audrey's rental now, red of course. The kind of car where seat belts move over automatically to pin you down when you shut the door.

"About ten minutes ago," Audrey said, slamming hers.

"Who would want Peter's station wagon? It looks like a piece of junk." Peter loved that car; he'd had it ten years.

"Some kids probably."

Audrey obviously didn't want to talk any more. She started up the car and barreled out of there as LeeAnn's mind flashed back on a time when Peter was about six and she was eight and the family had just finished wrapping all the homemade Christmas presents for relatives near and far. Thirteen packages in all. Brown paper and string and labels. The Spencers always did something homemade. Jelly and marmalade and apple butter in little baby-food-jar gift sets. Caramels one Christmas, homemade perfume the next. That particular year it had been sand candles made from sand they'd lugged back from Jones Beach (and that the cats had subsequently gotten into), and little bean-pots of fragrant chutney that had been bubbling on the stove for days.

They had carried the packages down in the elevator and loaded them into the '71 Ambassador station wagon to take them to the post office. Then, because Peter announced he was hungry, they went back upstairs to grab some lunch or something, which only took a few minutes, but by the time they got back, the car window was smashed, the fruits of their Christmas labors had vanished, and some poor thieves were undoubtedly sitting around in Central Park wondering what to do with badly made sand candles and little pots of mango chutney. She wondered what a similar group would make of a thousand invitations to the Global Party.

Then she came back to the moment and found she'd been staring at Audrey's hands on the steering wheel. Her fingernails had those little glittery ornaments embedded in the fresh lavender polish; she'd found somebody in Klamath Falls who could do the fancy stuff.

"So where did it happen?" LeeAnn asked.

"Somewhere near Whole Earth Access, in Berkeley. He parked across the street and ran in for a minute to pick something up."

At the house, they dialed a disconsolate Peter, and LeeAnn and Audrey each got on an extension. He felt *so* bad. LeeAnn could hear it in his voice clearly; it made her feel like a parent. He was at about a *minus*-two.

"The file with the original artwork's gone too, L.A," he said in a dull, hollow voice.

"It is? The disk was in there. You have it on the hard drive."

"No, remember? It crashed right after I made the disk."

"Did you pay Hal yet?"

"Yeah, of course I paid him."

"The whole thing?"

"He did the job. They looked great."

"Hey, we may find them," Audrey interjected. "Stranger things have happened. Peter knows every dumpster in Berkeley."

"Does the box they were in have your address on it?"

"I don't know. The RSVP does. It has the P.O. box . . . and my credit card receipt is in there. Oh, *shit*," Peter said.

"What?"

"I need to cancel my credit card. I better get off the phone."

"Wait a minute. If it was just a joyride," Audrey observed, "your car will turn up with the boxes inside. I'll bet on it. We would never have messed with stuff like that."

"Audrey, you heisted a car?" LeeAnn asked her.

"A couple of times."

"A couple?"

"A few."

"I didn't put the Club on it," Peter said. "Just that one time."

"Well, people shouldn't have to disable their car every time they get out of it, for crying out loud," Audrey was trying to be comforting.

"How do you steal a car in broad daylight?" LeeAnn wanted to know.

"Easy. Who's going to stop and ask you, 'Excuse me, but is that your car?'"

LeeAnn felt like she was just getting pushed along by events, life out of control. All that work, all that money and as far as LeeAnn knew, only one invitation had actually gone out, to Ernst Vanderveer.

"What do you think they're going to do with them?" LeeAnn wondered.

"Maybe they'll read them," Peter said.

"They *can't read!*" Audrey snapped. "They'll probably piss on them." There was a long silence.

"What's it going to cost us to reprint? This throws the whole schedule off."

"Another couple of thousand, I don't know."

"Look, we can handle $750 apiece."

"No." said Peter, "I'm taking care of the whole thing. It was my fault. And I'm the treasurer so I get to make the rules."

"Do we even want to do it again?" from Audrey.

"I don't know." And they ended the call on that note.

Jeff came back from getting gas in Audrey's car, and LeeAnn saw them off a few minutes later. Audrey was trying to joke about hanging upside down in dumpsters for the next twenty-four hours. Then she drove off down the street. LeeAnn stood watching till the car disappeared over the hill, then she started back toward the house as David drove up behind her in Vanna.

"Where were *they* going in such a hurry?" he asked as he got out.

LeeAnn told him what had happened while she helped him rinse off the windsurfing gear and put it away. Then she followed him out into the back yard so they could keep talking while he watered the garden.

"Peter said he'd make up the money we lost."

"Like I say, just one more example," David remarked as he started hauling hoses around, turning on valves, "it's society stabbing itself in the gut. It's a sign. Live your own life. They don't want help and *they don't want hope.*" He started squirting water on the tomato plants, LeeAnn watched the ground grow muddy. "Besides, you've already put in enough effort. More than enough. You can't *kill* yourself over it."

LeeAnn was staring at a growing puddle in the algae-fertilized black earth. "Maybe it's a test," she murmured. "Maybe the universe is trying to see if we mean business."

"Do you really *believe* that?"

"'*There are no coincidences*,'" LeeAnn said, and of course could see David recognized it as Audrey's line.

"So," he said with a small smile to acknowledge the reference to his favorite houseguest, "one thing we can do while they're gone, let's take our trip."

She looked at David, "Do you mean it? Our windsurfing trip?"

"I think you're ready. You're doing great."

"When, then?"

"Tomorrow. They're forecasting fifteen to twenty. "

"Tomorrow? Our helmets aren't here yet."

"LeeAnn, it's not going to matter this one time."

"We were going to have our helmets," she repeated. But she was happy about the prospect of the trip. And the more she thought about it, the more all the other problems receded from her thoughts. It looked like saving the world could very quickly take second place to being with David. *At least I'm learning what my value system is. Maybe, after all, the best thing to do is just live in the moment, like David does.*

A couple of hours later LeeAnn stood in the Safeway, trying to figure how romantic she could get with the picnic lunch without being too obvious. Too bad she couldn't use her great-grandmother's picnic basket, but it was hardly something you could carry on a windsurfer. Picnics were important to LeeAnn; to her, they were the part of an outing that proved you were having fun. She was considering Carr's Water Crackers and a container of caviar, the black kind in a thick little jar that surprisingly was only $4.95. She debated with herself, then decided to settle for tuna salad with celery and whole wheat bread. David would feel more comfortable with that.

She looked at her list, hard-boiled eggs and carrot sticks, throwaway camera. She'd pick up the camera on the way out, so she could record the magic moments if there were any. She thought about buying a couple of beers for David, but remembered alcohol would be dehydrating and picked up a plastic bottle of mineral water with lemon instead. That would taste good on a hot day.

She stood in line behind a couple of ragged-looking men with food stamps. Klamath was a way station for railroad vagabonds, and this particular no-frills Safeway seemed to be where they felt most comfortable. LeeAnn could understand; she felt comfortable here, too. She said hello to the checker, paid her, and carried the groceries out to the jeep. Like a lot of New Yorkers, LeeAnn never used a cart to wheel groceries. In Manhattan, wheeling a shopping cart outside a store is an invitation to arrest or worse, and she'd never quite gotten over the feeling.

It wasn't until she got in the jeep and was headed down Pine Street toward Third that LeeAnn realized she'd forgotten to buy the camera. Oh well, maybe they could get it in the morning. She began to wonder how she would do on her trip tomorrow; she was trying hard not to think of it as her final exam when she heard a loud beep right behind her. Startled, she glanced guiltily into the rearview mirror, which was something she almost never remembered to do. *Wake up, L.A.* She was not the most conscious driver in the world.

It was Stan in his blue Ford pickup. She pulled over and he double-parked beside her, leaning past Melanie to roll the window down. Both man and dog stuck their heads out. "Sorry I couldn't get by there yet," Stan said.

"Well, my brother can't make it anyhow. We've had a little complication." A bloody catastrophe is what they'd had, but of course she wouldn't say that to Stan.

Other traffic, she saw, was making its way around them with no problem. This was a typical Klamath Falls two-vehicle chat, left over from the days of horse and buggies, no doubt.

"So when's Peter coming up?"

"I'm not sure. Next week. Not before next week anyway."

"I'll try to get your tub fixed before that." Then he added with a little pride in his voice, "Starting next week, I'll be working out on Tree Island."

"So . . . you got the job." *Tree Island again.* But it was good that he had the work.

"I finally got to see the island." He looked pleased.

"How was it?"

"I'll tell you, LeeAnn." He looked both ways up and down the street. "I found something you might be interested in." He stopped, waiting for her go-ahead signal.

She looked around too, wishing she had an excuse to move on. Somehow she felt this wasn't something she wanted to hear, but there wasn't an impending traffic jam in sight. "Tell me about it," she said finally and turned off the engine. This might be a long one, considering.

"Well, the guy who's going to be taking care of the place during construction took me out there, guy by the name of Paul something or another. Can't say I cared for him too much. The trouble with a guy like that . . ."

"What did you find?" She would have to try to keep him on track.

"Well. I was checking out the south wall of the house," he paused for effect. "There's a *petroglyph* in one of the stones in the wall."

"Is there?" LeeAnn tried to sound interested, but was only mildly so. Petroglyphs were very common in these parts. "On a rock about so big." He indicated something about the size of your basic breadbox. "I almost asked the guy if I could have it. I'll have to take the stone out anyway when I repair the wall. I was going to bring it back here and give it to you. "

"Well, thanks. Best probably to leave it where it is." *Will people ever catch on that you don't move artifacts around?* "Stan, just let it be. It'll be a nice authentic touch for the house when it's restored." She looked up at Stan, who was really only trying to be helpful. "What did it look like?" she asked him. "What was on it?"

"A couple spirals, lines, I don't know, a marking like . . . ," and he drew on the little clipboard that he kept in the car, then turned it around to show her a sketch that looked somewhat like the McDonald's arches. "Something like this."

"Painted on?"

"No, this was carved right into the rock. Did a pretty good job."

"If it's carved, it's probably pretty old."

"It looked old. I seem to remember from your class that you can date things from lichen growth. It had a lot of lichen on it."

Now LeeAnn was interested. "A *lot?*"

He considered. "Quite a bit."

"Did you show it to the guy, Stan?"

"No, you know, I figured he'd probably take it home himself if I did. He seemed like that kind." Stan went on into an examination of the man's personality. "Very unpleasant if you ask me," he summed up. LeeAnn wasn't asking him. She was starting to think about that petroglyph.

"LeeAnn, I'd like to have you come out and take a look at that rock."

"Well, we're going on a trip down the lake tomorrow on our boards," she said, indicating the groceries beside her on the seat. "Maybe we could stop by and take a look and I could do a rubbing. That way I'd have it for my records and it wouldn't have to be moved."

"Oh, good idea." Stan seemed cheered by that. "Well, I'm glad I ran into you. Let me know what you think of it." He rolled up his window and drove off.

The prospect of discovering a very old petroglyph, even one that had been built into the old geezer's stone house, grew on LeeAnn as she drove the rest of the way home. But she waited until she thought David was in a compliant mood before broaching the subject.

"You know, a stop on Tree Island is going to make for a lot of complications, L.A."

"We have to eat our lunch somewhere."

"Let's keep it simple, okay? You're always getting too much on your plate. This is just a trip. And we can't necessarily count on the wind, you know. You can go out to Tree Island some other day, by boat," though she knew she wouldn't. And right now, she felt as though she'd *always* wanted to go out there. It was becoming very important.

The phone rang then, and David picked it up. It was Audrey calling to report they'd arrived safely at Peter's studio. LeeAnn noticed David's voice changed as soon as he heard who it was. It seemed to go down into a slightly lower register. "She wants to talk to you," he told her, handing the phone to LeeAnn.

As soon as she got on, Audrey said, "They found the car."

"Who?"

"The police."

"And . . ."

"Nothing."

"Oh. Where was it?"

"Not too far from here, on a street off Ashby. But we've got some flashlights and Jeff and Peter have ridden around and marked down all the dumpsters, and so now we're headed out to check them. Wish us luck." LeeAnn did, but she didn't have much hope as she hung up. It felt to her that unless by some miracle they found the invitations, the whole project would start to unravel. They'd all be back at their jobs before the new ones could be printed, which could seriously damage their follow-up efforts. *Well, at least we got the bad news tonight. Maybe by morning,* LeeAnn thought, *I'll be adjusted to it.* The phone rang again just after they turned the light out that night in the cabin. LeeAnn climbed down the ladder from the loft and answered it. It was Audrey. "Well, we found a hundred of them," she said, sounding pretty proud. "The rest of them are pretty bad, but a hundred we can use."

"Wonderful. I'll talk to you tomorrow." LeeAnn was glad for them; it just wasn't something she wanted to think about right now. "We'll see you tomorrow night," and she got off the phone as soon as she could.

She climbed back up into the loft and tried to go to sleep. No good. She tried to let the space she was in help her–the loft that always made her think about her childhood heroine, Heidi, who slept on a bed of hay under a round window that looked out at the Alps. Heidi's grandfather, she remembered, had only two bowls and two spoons that they ate with; their life was that simple. Maybe not easy, but simple.

Lying in the little cabin in the moonlight beside a gently snoring David, LeeAnn gazed out toward the Mountain Lakes wilderness that rose above Upper Klamath Lake and wondered about the ways in which she might be tested tomorrow.

CHAPTER TWELVE

The Tree Island Trip

When LeeAnn woke, it was still dark and David was missing from the bed. She could smell coffee, so she leaned down from the loft to look. He was pouring a fresh pot into the thermos. Probably the aroma had awakened her, for he was being very quiet.

Still in bed, because there was no room in the loft to stand up, she wriggled into her blue-flowered bikini and a pair of shorts, then donned her new "To Air is Human" T-shirt that showed a windsurfer leaping recklessly out of the water. They'd bought it at the Gorge but it was fraudulent of her to wear it; the only air she ever caught was when she was totally separate from her board and headed for a face-plant.

David's mood was ebullient this morning. He picked her off the ladder as she climbed down and hugged her. "Are you ready for this, Babe?"

"I am." They were smooching as the alarm clock rang and she had to climb back up to turn it off and then down again. "What time did you get up?" she asked him, yawning.

"Before dawn."

"It's still before dawn."

David put their booties, life jackets, and harnesses into the purple nylon gear bag she'd made for them on the ancient sewing machine Maggie had sent her when they got the house. Then he headed out to the van with a load of stuff as LeeAnn started putting their lunch together. Sillvester was already yelling vociferously outside the door, so she rewarded him with some of the tuna she was piling onto the whole wheat bread.

By the time David had gotten everything stacked inside the van and tied down on top, and she'd packed the sandwiches, the carrot sticks, the mineral water, the raisins-and-raw-almonds mix in sandwich baggies, and the requisite hard-boiled eggs–in LeeAnn's mind there was no such thing as a picnic without hard-boiled eggs–by the time she'd secured the lunches in their waterproof containers and they'd locked the door, started out the driveway, forgotten her sunglasses, and then gotten them, by the time they'd locked the door again, then actually got on the road, LeeAnn in the jeep and David behind her in the van, she realized she had forgotten to bring pencil and tracing paper for rubbings. By then, they were thirty minutes behind schedule, which was about par for the course.

They left the jeep outside the chain-link fence at the local yacht club, which they hoped would be the endpoint of the journey on their boards, "If we make it this far."

"Do you want to stop at Safeway for one of those throwaway cameras?" she asked hopefully as she climbed into the van. "I forgot to pick one up last night."

"I don't think we'll need it. We've got the binoculars." But it wasn't the same for LeeAnn; binoculars are only for living in the moment. She wished she'd remembered. Or at least remembered the tracing paper, just in case.

They headed north along the west side of the lake where ripples on the water showed evidence of early morning wind. It augured well for the day. Most of the time the ordinary workings of the solar system went almost unnoticed by LeeAnn, but today was different. She was grateful for the light, and for the lake. *Morning has bro-ken,* she thought, like the song. "Did you call the weather?"

"Still fifteen to twenty with gusts is what they said. But the winds are fickle, as we know."

By the time they passed Tree Island off Squaw Point, a gorgeous sun had begun to poke up on the other side of the lake, silhouetting that stalwart juniper high up on the ridge. "Remember the PBS show we watched," she said to David, "where the Native American woman said her mother had taught her the spirits will watch over you if you get up early in the morning? That you're supposed to get up early because that's when they're present? I see what she means."

David smiled a little and kept his eyes on the road. By the time they got to Rocky Point and parked Vanna, there was a pretty healthy breeze blowing.

"Grab that end, will you?" LeeAnn helped David carry the boards, masts, and sail-bags down to the shore, conscious of the touch of wind on her skin. *Probably*, she thought, *every time for the rest of my life when I feel a breeze stirring, it'll get me like this. That little bit of adrenaline will kick in.* She pulled her pink-and-green Multi-Sail out of the bag–it was zipped down to its 4.8 size–rolled it onto the grass, and started threading it onto her nice secondhand carbon mast.

"So, what do you think, David? Should I rig bigger?"

"Yeah, put the extra piece on," he advised. "You can always take it off if we get a gale." He was *almost* convinced that her convertible sail was a good idea. "Right now you should use all the sail you can get."

LeeAnn zipped the addition onto her sail and attached the boom. David helped her with the out-haul, and then he knelt down to attach her fin to the board with the fin screw that he carried in his shirt pocket. He was getting good at taking it on and off quickly. They always had to take the fin off her board to transport it so the two could nest together on top of the van.

She stripped off her shorts and T-shirt, strapped on her harness, and slipped her arms into her bright-orange life vest, which, once again, he zipped up for her. Then they slathered sunscreen on each other's faces, arms, and legs and were about ready. They each carried their own lunch and water (David carried the new binoculars) in the waterproof packs they strapped around their waists. He locked up the van and put the key in the velcro pocket of his life jacket.

They put on their booties, slid their boards into the cool water, attached the sails, and stood there together, looking down the long, narrow Rocky Point inlet. By now a very satisfying wave pattern was spreading evenly across the surface of the water. Consistency of the wind was important.

"Ready to go exploring?"

"Born ready," LeeAnn said.

"Columbus, Magellan, who else comes to mind?" David asked as he made a last-minute adjustment to his boom strap.

"How about good old Vitus Bering?" Bering was the Russian sea captain that the Bering Straits were named for. Beringia–LeeAnn's personal Atlantis–was the Arctic subcontinent that vanished beneath the sea eight thousand years ago.

LeeAnn centered her boom over the back of her board just as David was doing. She told herself it didn't matter to the quality of the day if she screwed up her first beach-start and took an ignominious spill. It was important to get past the idea that the way something starts is how it will continue. *It's how we do every step of the way that counts.* As it happened, she got a thrilling start, stepping up onto the board as if she'd jumped onto a Number 10 bus.

"Way to go!" David yelled. She looked back. He was right behind her. "All right, Vitus, lead on."

LeeAnn hooked into her harness and hunkered down, moving quickly with an audible chop-chop-chop over the small waves, cutting in close to the marsh and hoping she wouldn't get caught in the reeds. She didn't.

She did come upon a pair of nesting grebes with their babies, and wanted to show David, but he was already way over on the other side. It was amazing how far apart they could get so quickly. The babies were riding on top of their mother's back, clinging tightly and looking astonished as the largest pink-and-green bird they'd seen all day swooped past.

Soon David and LeeAnn came out of Pelican Bay and into the main body of the lake. Though their destination was straight down the length of it, they were zigging and zagging in huge tacks to take best advantage of the wind. *When you go across the wind rather than straight downwind, you can go faster than the wind; a lot of people don't know that,* LeeAnn thought to herself.

The expanse of water seemed nearly endless, an enormous playground that was entirely theirs. No boats, no other people. They would pass close by each other, then LeeAnn would head for the eastern shore and David for the west. In just a few minutes she could barely see him, his purple sail just a tiny triangle on the horizon. Approaching shore, LeeAnn would do one of her slow but increasingly smooth downwind turns to head back out and join David in the middle so that their paths entwined like laced shoestrings down the sparkling, windswept lake.

That first hour and a half out, LeeAnn knew she could never forget. She was building lifelong banks of technicolor memory in her mind. The marsh, the snow-capped mountains, the sky, the utter freedom–it was about the most exhilarating experience she'd ever had. Self-affirming too–because in all these miles, she hadn't yet crashed and burned.

"Take a little rest?" David suggested a few minutes later, as they approached each other one more time.

"I thought you'd never ask." For in spite of the continuing glory of the experience, the muscles in her arms and legs were beginning to cramp, and the sun was hot. He led the way like a mother duck toward a small cove on the eastern shore where, with a magnificent splash, LeeAnn let herself fall backward into water that was deliciously cool and green, with new-blooming algae suspended in it.

"Oh, ah, ooooh. So good." They dove and swam and played for a few minutes. It all smelled so sweet with life force. When LeeAnn surfaced, she was covered with the algae.

"Green goddess," laughed David, treading water.

"Green god," she returned, smiling as she regarded her equally colorful partner.

"Although actually," David teased, "I think I prefer thousand island."

She shoved him underwater, shouting, "David salad!" They began wrestling in love play but both were wearing too much paraphernalia to make much progress. LeeAnn pulled herself back up on her board and tried to lie on her stomach, but was impeded by the roller bar that stuck out like a phallus. "Silly thing." She flipped over onto her back so that it pointed straight up in the air. "It's not easy to lie on a hard-on," she remarked.

"Now you know why it's so urgent that we get rid of them," David said, climbing back up on his board, lying down and reaching for her hand to raft up with her. They settled down for awhile and just looked up at the sky.

"Did you see those eagles above me?" David asked.

"Yes, two of them."

"I couldn't tell if they were leading or following me."

"Probably a little of both."

"Were they bald eagles?"

"Uh-huh." The area was home to bald eagles by the hundreds. "You know what I saw? I saw a whole bunch of pelicans swimming in a circle, closer and closer together . . ."

"And then they all went bottoms-up."

"How did you know?"

"Team fishing. They herd the fish together that way and have a banquet."

"Great." LeeAnn sat up and looked around. From her vantage point, straddling her gently bobbing board, she could see Eagle Point on the opposite shore. "Remember when we went up there?"

"Mmmhmm."

"And all the stuff we found?" The spa at Eagle Point had flourished back in the twenties before the hot springs–which were probably thousands of years old–finally went dry. LeeAnn and David had discovered a part of an old brass bedstead there. They imagined the guests arriving by old-fashioned motor launch, swimming in their full-length bathing suits and shtupping on the old brass bed.

That was the thing about this lake, you could imagine layers and layers of people, going back thousands of years. And now here *they* were, living in what was surely one of the most confusing times ever. So many things were *so* absurd. LeeAnn had the sudden vision of gang members standing on street corners in front of dumpsters handing out invitations to the Global Party. *What if they actually did? And what if people took them?* She allowed the daydream to carry her forward to a triumphant conclusion.

"Do you realize it's only nine o'clock in the morning?" she said then to David, sculling the water with her feet.

"We've made good time." She offered to get her homemade trail mix out of its waterproof pack but David declined. "We should get going–we've got miles to go before we sleep." He looked at his watch. "If we're lucky, we can make Tree Island by eleven."

"That sounds good," she said, trying not to sound too eager. He *did* realize how much she wanted to go there to see that petroglyph before it was too late.

Two hours later, LeeAnn had begun to realize they still had a long way to go. The wind had diminished, making it harder to stay balanced. You had to torque your body more; and LeeAnn's back ached from the effort. Also, she was beginning to fall. A lot.

So after a half-hour more of inglorious wipeouts, the final approach to Tree Island looked pretty sweet. The legendary tree seemed to beckon them, its upper branches moving slightly in the light wind.

On the island's north shore, there was a beach about a hundred yards long, mostly pebbles and rocks. They started for it. David motioned toward a boulder poking its head just barely out of the water and she nodded, correcting her course to avoid snapping off a fin.

Above the beach the land rose sharply up toward the cliffs on the south side. Dry grass of a gorgeous golden color no metal could ever match covered much of the hundred and fifty or so acres that comprised the island. For the first time that day, LeeAnn thought about Ernst Vanderveer and the monstrosity the one-percenters were planning to build here. Even the thought of it was obscene, especially on a day like this.

As they got closer to shore, the tree for which the island was named was slowly obscured by the brow of the hill, till they could see just its top branches. Around on the west side, out of sight, was the stone house that contained the petroglyph.

When she noticed the lake bottom was coming up fast, LeeAnn kicked back her daggerboard and jumped off, promptly sinking into the soft spongy sediment up past her knees. It felt good on her tired legs, though. David, of course, timed his landing perfectly, barely getting wet. They flipped their boards over and parked them, fin side up, half in the water and half out. Then they staggered to the beach and collapsed with perfect satisfaction on the shore. LeeAnn hauled out the bottle of mineral water with lemon, twisted off the top and offered it to David.

"You first." She took a swig and handed it to him. It tasted wonderful. They'd half-emptied the bottle and David was blowing across the top of it to make a sound like a train whistle when he stopped and pointed toward something in the shallows. "Look at that. Is that what I think it is?" He screwed the cap back on the bottle, then got up to go see. LeeAnn followed him.

"Yup, just as I thought." A large stone mortar lay upside down, half-exposed among the pebbles. They looked carefully but didn't touch. "You can see the bottom's been broken out."

"So her spirit went free. That's good," said LeeAnn.

On the way back to the beach, she spotted a perfect arrowhead, a tiny bird-point sparkling in the sand, and they squatted down to look at it. "Are you sure you don't want it?" David asked.

LeeAnn shook her head. "Nope," she said, then looked up at him. "Remember the movie where Ruth Gordon flings a gift into the water . . ."

"'So I'll always know exactly where it is.'" He smiled quietly; it was a nice moment. "We're probably going to want some shade for lunch," David said, looking around.

"Yeah, but let's just sit for a minute first. I can hardly move."

"Me either." Once more they looked back over the distance they'd covered, and gloated briefly. Then they took off their life vests and harnesses and set them down in a pile. A moment later David retrieved his vest to sit on and LeeAnn followed suit. "I wish we had a towel," he said. "God will dry us." God always did. "Do you suppose the ancient people here sailed?" she asked after a moment. Then she went on to answer her own question. "They lived on a lake, so they had to know all about wind power; it only stands to reason they did. They had canoes and they had animal skins. If they just stood up in the canoe and held the skin up on a windy day, it would have been faster than paddling. And more fun. They had to have figured that out."

"So," David teased, "I suppose you're going to say next that they were windsurfers. Pretty soon you're going to start digging up universal joints along the beach."

"Somebody could have invented universal joints," she argued unseriously. "It's just like a bone socket." David leaned over then and kissed her on the mouth with great tenderness.

"You know, I can see the Klamath in you right now. You look like your ancestor."

She smiled. "Do I?" They sat quietly for a bit.

"Okay, maybe they rigged some kind of sail," he conceded then. "With all the wildlife and everything that grew around here to eat, they had plenty of time to fool around with inventing things. And play is natural. Animals play."

"I read once," LeeAnn said, digging in the pebbles with her toe, "and it really stuck with me, that play is our *natural state.*" She thought for a moment. "And I remember a story in *Reader's Digest* about a guy who was in the Iditarod. He got to a place to camp one night and saw there was already another dogsled there. The driver was lying at the edge of a cliff, looking over the side. It turns out there were a whole bunch of moose on a frozen lake down below. They were standing in line, like little kids, taking turns sliding across the ice and then coming back around and doing it again."

David laughed. "I've watched ravens catch the thermals," he said. "They circle up, way up in the air," he spiraled up with his hand, "then just throw their wings up over their heads, let their feet hang down and drop like dead weights, pulling out at the last minute. Then they go back up and do it again."

"There's a place in a cathedral in Europe somewhere, I don't remember where I saw it, where the crows have made a depression in the stained-glass window from hundreds of years of sliding down on their butts." She looked out at the water. "Isn't it funny how play so often has to do with moving fast? Fast motion is one of our most primary desires."

"Which is precisely why people need Ferraris and Porsches."

LeeAnn laughed. "I don't."

"Should we break out the food?" David said then, looking at his watch.

So they did. One of the sandwiches was a little soggy; both insisted on eating it. LeeAnn had packed little aluminum foil twists of salt and pepper for her hard-boiled egg like her grandmother used to make out of waxed paper. She sprinkled it carefully on the egg as she ate it. *Ah, bliss.* She found herself not thinking about anything, a very rare occurrence.

Of course, lunching on an island in paradise quite naturally led to the most magical thing about any adventure with David. Shielded from the heat of the midday sun and from the open water by an obliging shrub, they began to make love on that beautiful beach.

David lay LeeAnn down tenderly, paying careful attention to every inch of her body. He pulled down the wet bottom of her suit and she kicked it off. Then he entered her from above and his moving silhouette created a strobe effect against the bright sunlight, even through her closed eyelids.

As the heat of their bodies built, she began to feel disoriented, as though she were becoming lost in time, lost in all the hundreds of generations that had been locked in love. Then she had a most extraordinary feeling. It was as though the earth's magnetic force was pulsing through her, inducing her orgasm, making it impossible to stop. Again and again, the surge rolled through them both as through a great wave, as if they were being pulled toward the earth and released, and pulled toward it again, and let go. Both cried out. At last, exhausted, they trembled together and held each other, and the ancient tree looked down at them from above, seeing the sweetness of it.

All they could hear in the silence that followed was the sound of gulls in the distance and the gentle whisper of the pebbles shifting companionably against one another in the small waves that lapped the shore. LeeAnn wept for joy. And David nearly fell asleep.

Gradually LeeAnn began to be conscious of the fact that she was lying in a bed of sharp pebbles. She sat up carefully, feeling all the little indentations on her back as she did. David lay still, his eyes closed. Then, from his somnolent state, with only his lips moving, "Did you say something about a petroglyph?"

"Mmmmhmmm."

He opened his eyes then and roused himself. "Are you ready to go look?"

"I am."

David thought they ought not to leave their boards out in plain sight, so instead of climbing over the hill, he decided they should sail around to the little harbor on the inner side of the island. LeeAnn was disappointed they weren't going to hike to the other side; she'd hoped for a chance to see something of the island before Ernst Vanderveer and his crew got hold of it and desecrated it. Still, LeeAnn didn't say anything; David had been nice enough to plan things so they could stop here, and that was enough.

They waded back out, turned their boards over, up-hauled, and headed into the passage between Tree Island and the western shore of the lake, where they suddenly got caught up in what was almost a wind-tunnel effect as the wind necked down to go through the narrow space. It gave them both quite a kick. "That was a rush," David said, as they sailed into the tiny harbor and the lighter winds there. "It took us no time at all."

The old stone house sat blank-eyed, its windows long gone, and its south wall crumbling, but placed perfectly, LeeAnn had to admit, to serve as a picturesque welcome center to an antsy-fancy resort–particularly with the glass tower that would enclose it, and gardens inside. It would become a giant tropical greenhouse, not perhaps appropriate to the island, but attractive nonetheless.

There was a rotted wooden dock out front where LeeAnn wanted to leave their boards. "Shall we tie them here?" But David spied a better spot behind some rocks where they couldn't be seen from out on the water. He pulled the rigs up on shore, then took great pains to hide them. She felt impatient.

Finally, David was satisfied and they headed toward the house. "Hey, looky there," he said, pointing to an old jeep that was parked on the far side of the house. "That's World War II vintage–probably belonged to the geezers." LeeAnn had told him about Stan's story. They walked over to investigate. "There's some recent tire tracks, so it must still run. I wonder who's been driving it?" David seemed enthralled, sniffing excitedly around it like a puppy. "They probably drove this across the ice in the winter to get their supplies."

Meanwhile, LeeAnn spied a pile of old wooden boxes, the kind you always want to take home when you see one abandoned somewhere. "There's something so pleasing about wooden boxes, don't you think so?" she said.

"Those are shotgun shell boxes." Suddenly she was less pleased. Piles and piles of them.

"The geezers, no doubt," said LeeAnn. "And all their shooting."

The house smelled of cool, damp stone as they entered the section of it that until a couple of years ago had been occupied by one of the brothers. They took a quick look around and moved on. It was dank and kind of dark, with old rotted rags and assorted debris in a corner of what must have been the living room.

They made their way through to the area of the house that was so tumbled down it was now effectively a courtyard. "It should be right around here." LeeAnn said, recalling Stan's instructions. "He said it was on the outside wall." Then they walked through a doorway. "Fifth rock in, two up from the bottom." And there it was, plain as day, as Audrey would say.

The design wasn't just pecked in, but as Stan had said, it was incised deeply into the rock. A curious pattern, spirals in a meandering line that seemed to tell a story. LeeAnn saw that in a moment. But what her eyes fixed on was the lichen covering many of the markings, and the depth of its growth. It indicated to her that the petroglyph she was looking at may have been carved several thousand years ago. What a wonder that the lichen survived, even after the stone was moved, she thought. "It must have faced the same way, probably not far from here, in its original location," she said to David, as she crouched down and reached out to touch the stone with her fingers.

"What does it mean, I wonder?"

"Well, let's figure." They both sat cross-legged in the dirt to study it.

"They say spirals are life journeys, that's one meaning," LeeAnn said. "These," indicating other lines, "may represent the passage of time. I wonder if . . ." Then she looked at the M-shaped mark, quite large, that Stan had sketched. "It's so hard to interpret these hieroglyphics. Nobody really knows. I don't suppose there's any more inexact science–we could theorize endlessly."

"You know, this isn't the whole petroglyph," David said, "because the lines go right off the edge. See, look here. And over here."

"You're right." LeeAnn had noticed the same thing.

"So," he went on, "if this was native rock, then they must have blasted bigger rocks apart when the house was built. I wonder where this came from? When *was* it built, the house? Eighteen-eighties?"

"I don't know," LeeAnn looked at the ruin of the old house. "Stan didn't know either. I guess we could find out. It looks about a hundred years old." LeeAnn wondered why the settlers would have built on an island.

"The rock probably came right from here," David suggested after a moment or two. The island was full of boulders, big ones, all over the place. "But why, with all this other rock around, did they have to blast a *petroglyph* apart? Why?" Then he answered his own question. "Just basic contempt, I suppose. That attitude pisses me off," he said. "It really pisses me off." "Well you've got to remember how belligerent the geezers were," LeeAnn said. "Their ancestors probably weren't much different." David nodded. Some people around Klamath still referred to the Native Americans as "wagon burners."

David wasn't through with the subject. "You know, the thing I like most about working in stone is that there's a chance it may still be around in a few thousand years," he said, implying that perhaps this artist had hoped that too.

"I know," LeeAnn said. She could feel how much David identified with that person.

"I'll bet if we looked, there's more pieces of this rock around. We might be able to piece it together." He looked at her. "I mean where *else* would they be? The only problem would be to find them." LeeAnn's eyes strayed to a mountainous pile of rubble from the caved-in section of the house, then back to David.

"It shouldn't be too tough," he remarked cheerfully as he walked over to the pile and plowed in. He handed LeeAnn some rocks to inspect. And then she found herself starting to pick through the rubble as well.

And so the two began hefting rocks in the noonday sun. Half an hour later, their backs were aching, their hands were cut and scraped, they were filthy and dripping with sweat. But they'd found two small pieces of rock with markings similar to the petroglyph. Back to work. Another half-hour and they had collected five. Fifteen minutes more and there were seven. Of course, David had found almost all of them, just as he always found the four-leaf clovers.

"So," he said, carrying them back to the original petroglyph in the wall of the house, "what have we got?" They tried to fit the pieces together, but it was difficult. There were so many different possibilities and evidently there were still some pieces missing. The original petroglyph must have been carved into one very large boulder. Or else there were several petroglyphs. Still, the stones they'd found seemed to match, so they might all have been from the same rock.

LeeAnn looked at her watch. 12:33 p.m. Funny. It seemed later. Then when she looked at it again a couple of minutes later, it was still the same time. *Oh well. It must have stopped right after lunch. When we were rolling in the pebbles. No wonder—just the magnetic force alone could have stopped most any watch.* She didn't say anything to David about the time. He'd been so careful about maintaining their schedule, and now he'd forgotten all about it. That was okay with her.

Heaving and straining at a rock the size of a small radiator, David managed to roll it up on its end and was brushing off the back of it. Then he gasped, "Omigod! LeeAnn, come here. Look!" In her haste, she tripped over the rock she'd been moving and scraped her shin quite badly. But it didn't even hurt.

She squatted down beside David and they stared at the petroglyph on the underside of the rock together. "It's a man and a woman!" she exclaimed.

This couple from the far distant past was standing, side by side, arms around each other. Together they formed a kind of rounded letter M, vaguely the shape of the two-handed mano, the unique pestle the people in the area used to grind their grain. Or like the M-shape on the petroglyph in the wall. Separate but joined–partnership shape. There were marks for her breasts and belly and for his genitals. Small bits of lichen still clung to the figures incised in the rock.

"Oh look, she's smiling," LeeAnn observed. And it was true. The female had five little dots across her face, a great big brimming connect-the-dots smile–as well as an unabashed female triangle, entrance portal to the world for all humans. The male boasted a proud protuberance where his penis would be. Unselfconscious. Perfect design. Male, female together. Lovers. It made all the sense in the world. *I've seen this before, I know I have, and in this lifetime,* she thought, but at the moment she couldn't think where. "If this is part of *that* petroglyph," she pointed toward the wall, "this is a major, major find."

"How old do you think?"

"Thousands of years." They were both quiet. "I think we need to listen to what these two guys have to say to us," she said at last, feeling quite stilled, quite hushed by the discovery. David nodded, his hand resting lightly on her back. For awhile then, she wasn't sure how long it was, LeeAnn was conscious only of David's touch, her own breathing, and of this couple before them who seemed to speak across the centuries about the *wholesome power of love.* She knew that this discovery was why they'd come to the island today. Besides being an incredible discovery, this would be a re-bonding experience for herself and David; she was certain of it.

Only very gradually did her archaeologist's mind start coming back to consciousness. A *hanowas.* That's what it must be, she decided. She knew the Klamath people had stone figures, female and male.. Though not double ones. Not joined. At least not to her knowledge. And this didn't look Klamath. To tell the truth, this looked more Siberian, or even European. *Of course, that couldn't be.* And then she was off on a journey as her mind reeled back through time, trying to connect shapes and facts and feelings. All the years and all the artifacts. But it was no good.

"I wonder if this piece could possibly still exist somewhere around here?" she said to herself more than to David.

He looked at her. "It's right here. Of course it exists."

"Oh no, I mean the *figure* that it represents."

David looked puzzled. "It's a picture of a man and a woman," he said.

"No it's not, David. Not at all. It's a picture of a figurine. Don't you see?" She pointed. "If it were just showing a man and a woman they'd be stick figures, almost certainly. This is the *drawing* of an object that was either carved out of stone or made of clay. Although the Klamath didn't fire clay . . ." She trailed off. She had an idea, but it was just too huge to even think about, let alone share with David. She couldn't wait to get home to her reference materials. The lichen . . . "I'm wondering, what's the rainfall here David? Do you know?"

"It's about ten, eleven inches."

"That's what I thought. That would affect the lichen growth." It would be important to piece the petroglyph together and then study the lichen that remained on the other parts of the rock Stan had found, to determine the age of the piece. Amazing stuff, lichen, the product of a symbiotic union between fungus and algae. Amazing that it could last thousands of years, grow so slowly, and tell us so much. Enable us to date something thousands of years old. She was still staring at the figure carved in the rock. *It looks so much like something I've seen before.* But what? Her mind would not answer. Where?

"Let's suppose this does represent a figure that exists. And suppose the rest of this, the rest of these markings we found could tell us something about where..."

But David's attention was somewhere else. "It's gone," he said, abruptly looking around.

"What's gone?"

"The wind."

It was true. The day was growing increasingly hot. There wasn't a breath of wind and the lake was still. LeeAnn looked up; the sun was no longer directly overhead. "What time is it? My watch stopped."

"Twenty after two. I think we've done enough damage here." Several deep sighs emanated from his chest as he surveyed the decimated rock pile. His main rule was always *do no harm.* "We've got to put all this back where we found it." You could tell David was kicking himself that he'd let time get away from them. "We're in the doldrums now," he said. "May not get any more wind today. We might be stuck here." LeeAnn could think of worse fates.

They put the petroglyph fragments they'd found back in the rock pile, face down, then started moving as many of the rocks as they could back over it into some semblance of their original position. "Here, give me a hand." David was getting ready to lay the radiator-sized rock with the partnership pair back on its face.

"I wish we could at least have a sketch of it," LeeAnn said. "I forgot to bring paper to do a rubbing, and we don't even have a pencil with us."

"Well, this might work." David pulled the key to the van out of his life vest pocket and picked up a piece of slate. Then he started sketching a rough outline of the piece with the end of the key. She let him do it. He was a lot better at drawing than she was.

"Let's put the other designs on there too so we can figure out how they go together." She was going to explain to him what she hoped those marks might be able to tell her, but doubted that he'd be receptive just now.

When he finished, David tucked the slate into his pack; it would weigh him down quite a bit. Then they gently laid the partnership pair face down and covered it with rocks. "Sleep well," LeeAnn said, pledging to herself not to do any more speculating for the rest of the day. "This ought to do for tonight. In the morning we can see about getting a team in here."

"LeeAnn, you're going to get yourself in over your head again. Don't get too involved. Please? For your own sake?"

"I won't." She looked at the rock-pile longingly. "I just wish we could take it with us."

He laughed. "Can you imagine trying to get it back to town on a windsurfer? The *"bofe ob us"* would end up on the bottom."

"Bofe ob us," LeeAnn repeated in her mind. It was his Floridaese, a part of the private language they'd developed. Sometimes LeeAnn thought you could tell how close a couple was by how many words they'd invented together. "Why do you have to be so practical?" She kissed him. Then they waded into the water to wash off and tend the scrapes on their arms and legs and hands. "So, what do we do now?"

"Wait. Not much else to do," he said, looking out at the now-glassy surface of the lake. "If the wind doesn't pick up pretty soon, we may be here all night."

"There's certainly worse places we could be stuck."

"We don't have anything to eat."

"We still have trail mix. And an orange." LeeAnn decided that being marooned would be just fine. For one thing, they could guard the petroglyph, which increasingly she was beginning to feel could be a very significant find. And to spend a night under the stars in this powerful place with David could be incredible, given the extraordinary experience they'd had already on the pebble beach.

"As long as we're waiting," she said, "could we hike up to the tree? It would be a shame to visit Tree Island without paying our respects."

David surveyed the hill.

"*Could we?*" she asked and he smiled. It was another phrase in their private language–her mock-plaintive "*Could we?*"

"Oh, I think we could," he said at last. "It looks like that jeep road goes all the way up." So they set off, hand in hand, up the rough gravel road that spiraled to the top and the Tree Island tree. Like a life spiral.

"They say it's supposed to be more than a thousand years old. And of course *it* came from another tree that came from another tree, all the way back. Probably only about eight trees back to the time of the Mazama eruption." She turned to David. "Do you remember the bhoti tree that Buddha sat under?"

"I've heard about it."

"I've read there's a direct descendent of it that people can go and sit under. I think trees are a kind of metaphor for the way we're all connected."

David helped her up over a steep place where the road had washed out. "And the tree knows everything that all the former trees in its family have known."

Fifteen minutes later they reached the peak that comprised the southeast corner of Tree Island. There was a spectacular view in all directions. They walked over to the edge of the cliff and turned in a slow 360 to take it all in.

To the north and west lay the slightly lower hill that would be flattened and widened to create Vacation Heaven. This craggy peak and the tree would be spared. To the south, huge mudflats that were barely under water extended perhaps a half-mile out from the island before the cerulean blue of the lake began.

"The lake's really down this year," David said. Only an inch or two of water covered the mud, which LeeAnn knew was thirty feet deep in places, clean, spongy, loamy, mineral-rich, mud-bath mud. Glorious. She thought about what it would be like to walk out on the flat, rub mud over their bodies, then lie down and let it bake in the sun. This was the most sensuous place that she'd ever been.

For a moment it felt as if she understood it all–what it must have been like to be that sensible, happy male and female in the petroglyph as they bonded, thousands of years ago. Sailing on the lake and playing in the mud. *Happy them then, and happy us now*, she thought. *The basics don't change a whole heck of a lot*, she thought.

"Let's go meet the tree," she said, and so they did. Up close, the lone old juniper was bigger than LeeAnn had thought it would be, gnarled and twisted from the elements. The top of it leaned to the south, so it looked as though the wind was constantly blowing. *It leaned with its memory of the wind.*

They walked over to it and LeeAnn put her hand on the trunk to feel the life inside. They sat down in its shade, their backs up against it, so that the tree was joining them to each other and to all the faraway places that it could see. Down to Shasta and all the way up to the caldera of Mount Mazama, off toward the Warner Range to the east, to Mount McLaughlin in the west. David pointed and they both watched, as from the south, a large white egret, flying high, came in over the island, circled down, and landed on one of the highest branches of the tree.

LeeAnn thought of a song from the seventies about a white bird that had to fly or it would die. Then she saw herself and David under the tree, with the bird and the tree, on top of the world. It was Eden to her. No other words would do. She gazed at David, "Fribben," they said to each other almost simultaneously.

Lazing in the afternoon sun, LeeAnn imagined she could feel what the tree felt, sprouting from the earth, standing in the elements, dropping its seed under its branches, and sheltering its young. She thought about the custom of some ancient peoples who buried their dead standing straight up with an acorn in their mouth so their life force would become part of a new tree.

"Look," David was saying. "It's reproducing." He seemed to have heard her thoughts. He was pointing to several tiny juniper seedlings about eight inches tall just making their way out of the earth.

LeeAnn looked at the infant trees, and at the pebbles in the loose earth around them. Now one, shinier than the rest, caught her eye. Then another. They had a familiar look. "Olivella shells, David. Trade beads."

Or funeral beads, she thought. These did not seem to be charred from funeral fires, though maybe one of them might be, you couldn't tell really. "Somebody brought these all the way from the ocean. Imagine how long ago." She dug around halfheartedly looking for more. "I wonder what this island was used for? I wonder if it might've been a place where couples came to spend their first moon together?"

"Can't stop that mind from working, can you?"

"Nope." She put her head back against the tree, her face up to the sun, and closed her eyes, thinking of the ancient woman and man paddling their canoe, having babies, and raising them in Eden.

When she opened them again, David had taken out the binoculars and was scanning the surface of the water. Looking for wind. For a ripple anywhere.

"This place is so perfect," she said.

"Except for *that*." He pointed to an old derelict trailer that was parked in a hollow about fifty feet from the tree.

"I didn't even notice it." It was an ugly thing, up on blocks, its windows boarded up, and more of those ammo boxes piled up beside it. "That's the trailer Stan was telling me about, that one of the geezers used to live in. The other one lived down at the house."

"That wasn't their name, was it?"

"No, just a nickname Stan and his buddies gave them. Their name was Carleton. Want to check it out?"

David got up somewhat painfully. They were both starting to get stiff from their trip. They went over and tried the door, but it was locked. A second door in the back that looked like an add-on was fitted with a fairly new-looking padlock. The sheets of plywood over the windows also looked new. "Probably the BLM is responsible for this," David said.

"For what?"

"The plywood and the padlock. You know them. Those agencies are always being *responsible.*"

"This would have had a fantastic view of the lake," LeeAnn said. "That says something for the geezers. They couldn't have been all bad–if they hauled this thing all the way up here, they must have appreciated the view."

"Or maybe they just wanted to see what was coming at them–see if a flotilla was on its way from the county commissioners. So they could shoot at it."

"You're probably right."

There wasn't a whole lot more to see around the trailer so they went back to the tree. David sat down and scanned the lake again with the binoculars. "It looks like a little wind stirring from the south, which of course would mean tacking the rest of the way home," he said. "It might even be sailable the next half hour or so, you never know."

"No, you never know," she said as she slipped down to sit beside him. LeeAnn felt a little regret that their idyll here on this island might be over in a little while.

"What's that?" David said, focusing on a spot on the western shore of the lake, which was about a half mile away. "What's going on over there, I wonder?"

"Can I see?" He handed the binoculars to LeeAnn.

"There's a pickup truck over by the bushes there, by the landing," he said.

LeeAnn swiped the glasses around the shore for awhile as she always did when she was trying to home in on a target. She wasn't too good with binoculars. "One o'clock," David said. "Over," David said. "Down." Finally he took hold of the glasses and guided them for her.

"Oh, okay, I see it. It's blue," she added so he would know she really did. She adjusted the eyepiece till she could make out the figure of a man standing at the tailgate. "The guy's taking a box out of the truck," she told David. "He's carrying it down to the shore. Now he's putting it in a boat. This is kind of fun, being a voyeur."

"We have nothing better to do."

"You look," she said, handing the glasses back to David. "He's probably a fisherman."

"Maybe not," David said after he trained the glasses on him. "Those are several rifles he's transferring now." He kept the glasses. "Definitely not a fisherman," he said a minute later, sounding a little concerned. Finally the man got in the boat; they could hear the sound distinctly across the water as he tried to start the motor. *Vrrrrmmm.* It seemed very close. *Vrrrrmmm.* It stopped. Then *vrrrmmm* one more time and it caught.

"Where do you think he's going?"

"From the direction he's pointed, I think we can safely assume he's coming here," David said a little grimly. "Where else?" It was true, there was nothing else around; this was practically wilderness. So far, they hadn't seen another soul the whole trip.

The comfortable distance between the boat and them was being quickly eaten up. It looked like a Boston Whaler. As they watched, the boat continued to make a beeline for the island, slowing as it entered the little harbor, and then idled up to the dock that was almost directly below them, about two hundred and fifty feet down.

The man was wearing camouflage pants, a tight black T-shirt, and combat boots. He climbed out onto the dock and immediately began unloading, swearing as a rotted board gave way beneath him. The sound carried up to them. He hauled a cardboard carton into the section of the old stone house that was still intact.

"He's moving in."

"Shhh. Let's wait till he finishes. Maybe he'll leave." They exchanged a glance, both chagrined as they realized they'd already delayed too long without letting their presence be known. Now it was bound to be awkward. The man picked up two more gun cases from the back of the boat and carried them into the house.

"Should we yell down?"

"I'm not sure this is the kind of guy we want to know, LeeAnn," David said, his voice even grimmer than before. "That's a goddamn arsenal he's got there. You see those? Those are state-of-the-art scopes on those guns. The guy's got at least twenty grand in hardware right here."

It was as though the geezers were moving back, LeeAnn thought. *Oh, island, I'm sorry.*

She watched the man as he headed back to the dock for another load. She couldn't see his face clearly from this angle but he had powerful arms–a fitness freak obviously–and a tattoo she couldn't make out. Colorless skin and light brown hair in an odd cut. It was a surprisingly intimate view from their vantage point as the man hauled his belongings, neatly packed into liquor boxes.

The day's magic was gone; LeeAnn could see David regretting the whole adventure. He was back in his cop mode. "I don't see how we're going to get to our boards without his seeing us."

"Do you think he's a squatter?" LeeAnn whispered. Then as he approached the house again, it suddenly dawned on her. "No, I know who he is. I *recognize* him."

"You do?"

"I saw him on television that night. He's the guy who picked up the woman from VHRI at the airport. Her bodyguard, I thought. Or chauffeur. But it looks like he's moving in."

"I thought you said they hadn't taken title yet." There was an edge to David's voice.

"I don't think they have." The man had almost finished emptying the boat. He glanced briefly up at the sky, and then bent to re-tie the stern line. LeeAnn thought very likely he was the man named Paul that Stan hadn't liked, but it didn't seem like a good time to speculate aloud.

"Well, he's staying," David said. "So we have no choice. You ready for this?"

"Let's do it," she said.

Instead of going back down the jeep road for the inevitable confrontation, David elected to take a shortcut straight down the steep incline. Following him, LeeAnn found herself traveling more on her butt than her feet. David of course, like most men, never condescended to such tactics. Instead he hopped nimbly from one rock to another.

Then a stone that LeeAnn accidentally dislodged tumbled loudly all the way down the hill and the guy looked up.

"Hello," LeeAnn yelled, waving vigorously in what she hoped was a friendly manner. "We're up here."

Shading his eyes from the sun, the man spotted them. "What the hell you doing up there!" he shouted, and David hurried ahead to explain. When LeeAnn finally made it down to the bottom of the hill and approached the two men, she could see it wasn't going well.

The guy, who was about three inches shorter than David, was obviously feeling rattled about being intruded upon, and this was clearly not a person who enjoyed the feeling. You could almost hear the hiss of his rattle.

"I'm going to have to ask you to get the FUCK off this island," he was saying, clearly furious, and David immediately took offense, as though the obscenity had been hurled directly at LeeAnn.

"Watch your language, will you please?" he said in a cold, warning voice.

"You're on private property."

"As far as I'm concerned, this is BLM property."

"Well, it isn't any more. Title passed this afternoon."

"Okay, we didn't know that. There are no signs posted. Look, we were windsurfing down the lake. We'll be on our way just as soon as we get some wind." He was clearly embarrassed; the former cop caught trespassing.

"You got about five minutes to get off this island!" the guy said, deliberately moving into David's space.

LeeAnn felt herself starting to freeze. Like a scared rabbit, she was involuntarily slipping into the play-dead mode that was her normal defense against other people's anger. All capacity for speech or movement seemed to have left her. And all she could think was, David's going to hit this guy. Because she knew how David felt about his space;

she could get in it but most people couldn't.

David had gone completely rigid, too, she saw, but with anger, not fear. He's going to explode, I know it. He's going to punch this guy out and then we'll really have trouble. "LeeAnn," David was saying, "come on. We're going." He seemed to be speaking from a long distance away. "Like NOW!"

"But there's no wind . . ."

"I said NOW!"

She had never seen him like this. He marched over to where they'd stashed their boards and literally hurled them into the water. "Would you please hurry up and come?" he muttered through clenched teeth. Then without waiting for an answer, he stood up on his board, pulled his sail up and pushed his boom forward, taking a great angry bite out of the air with the sail and miraculously moving himself forward about a foot and a half. Then he did it again, moving another few feet.

LeeAnn forced herself into action. She waded into the water, climbed on her board, up-hauled and began to copy David. The man continued to stand there, glaring at their backs (LeeAnn sneaked a look). He was not the kind of person you wanted to turn your back on; she imagined him training one of those fancy rifles on them.

Awkwardly, they continued to propel themselves forward in a rowing motion that reminded LeeAnn of the *forward, back, forward back* motion of a railroad work car until at last they cleared the dock area and picked up the beginning of the afternoon wind. LeeAnn had the sudden sensation that they were actors in a Keystone Cops movie, and she fought back a desperate urge to laugh. It was a hot, giddy, excited, scared-as-hell feeling that was nearly irresistible.

She glanced over at David who was staying just ahead, undoubtedly to goad her into moving faster. She couldn't see his face, but the rage showed on his back. It was not going to be a fun trip home.

CHAPTER THIRTEEN

Ancient Lovers

LeeAnn's body was so exhausted and her mind so distracted that she found herself falling in almost every time she tacked. And then the wind died, so they ended up having to kneel on their boards and paddle the last quarter of a mile to the Yacht Club, practically in the dark, through clouds of midges and mosquitoes.

When they finally staggered to shore, their very bones aching, the ordeal was by no means over. They still had to de-rig, stash their boards temporarily, and then drive the Jeep some twenty miles back to Rocky Point to pick up the van. Not only was their fatigue overwhelming. David was also clearly angry at having gotten himself (or *LeeAnn* having gotten him) into a situation where he'd been caught not only trespassing but messing with private property.

"Moving their goddamn *real estate*," he had muttered darkly as he rolled up his sail and stuck it under their boards up against the clubhouse, where they hoped their pile of gear wouldn't be noticed.

It wasn't till they were in the Jeep on the way back up the lake that he finally blew up. "I'm sorry about what happened . . . ," LeeAnn began. And it was those words that triggered the fateful talk which ended in her surrender.

"We should *never* have gone to that island," said David, and we should *never, never* have moved any of their rocks, let alone a hundred and fifty of them!"

"Then nobody would have known about the *petroglyph*!" she shouted back, not at him, she told herself, but to be heard over the noise from the Jeep windows flapping because their zippers were broken. David and LeeAnn never yelled at each other, though they were doing a pret-

234

ty good imitation just now.

David fell silent, but LeeAnn could tell it still rankled. She looked out through the scratched, cloudy plastic into the gathering night and stared at a distorted image of the lake. She had a lump in her throat. "Do you think that creep's going to see what we've done? I just hope he doesn't start turning rocks over."

"Don't worry about it."

"Yeah, right." She was quiet for a while. Then she went back to talking about The Lovers, for she was profoundly stirred by their discovery, despite her weariness, despite David being pissed at her. But he was unmoved. "The proposition that it's a drawing of a statue I think is pushing it, LeeAnn. It's no more than *John loves Mary* on a tree, only in stone. And you don't know how old it is for sure."

"With *that* amount of lichen? Well, we'll see. As soon as I can get a team in there . . ."

"LeeAnn, watch your pronouns, will you! How about till *they* get a team in there! This VHRI is a *multinational* corporation, you know; they've got all the resources in the world to take good care of the petroglyph. And if it's as important as you think it is . . ."

"What makes you think they'd do it right?"

David sighed. "You're busy saving the world, remember?"

"But I have to stay with it long enough to see that . . ."

"You already have too much on your plate. Tree Island is not your problem, your 22nd Century Group–or your Summer Project, or whatever the hell you call it–is." It was the first time David had ever referred to the group by name.

"It's all the *same cause*, isn't it?" she snapped at him. "It's called, 'Let's not destroy our resources.' Including the wisdom our ancestors are trying to teach us."

"So are you going to let your friends down, while you go flying off on this new tangent?"

"They'll *understand!* There isn't really that much I can do right now anyway, till we get the invitations reprinted. That won't be till . . ."

"I thought you said it would all be over in a month."

"*I didn't make them steal Peter's car, David!* That had *nothing to do with me!*"

"It's always something."

"It isn't *my fault* . . ." Their voices were rising again.

"When you take on a project this ridiculously big, shit happens! Plan a party for the whole world and what can you expect? Just because you have some perfect *fantasy* of how things ought to be . . ."

"Please, David, please stop . . . PLEASE . . . STOP! I know you're about to say something awful."

"Maybe I have to say it, LeeAnn. And will you listen to me for a change. **You cannot save the entire world, single-handedly. If the world wants to be saved, it will help you!** You *have* to stop going off on these wild flights."

"But if I don't try . . ."

"LeeAnn, would you listen to me for a minute. You've got *too . . . much . . . going . . . on!!"* He banged on the steering wheel as he said it. Bang, bang, BANG! David had never done that; she was afraid for a minute, though he hadn't swerved or anything. "You're making life crazy," he said. Then he glared over at her just long enough to emphasize his point. Normally his eyes never left the road.

"You're making *our* life very difficult," he concluded, and it sounded like an ultimatum. She got the message. *I'm making your life difficult is what you mean.*

Then she was quiet for quite a long time. She'd come to a crossroads and she was all by herself there, the Jeep's engine her only company. *I have to choose. No one can have everything,* she thought. And I have too much. More than my share. I have to give some of it up.

And so, riding along beside the lake, she weighed the important things, the things that she cared about almost more than her own life. They were three.

First, her dream of the future. Her Aquarian dream of a future world people might actually want to live in. A world that was so achievable– if people would only relax and let themselves become a human family again. And love one another. If they would only understand that the best way to start is by celebrating. I know almost everybody in the world would go for this idea if we could just get the essence of it across to them. Make it one celebration.

Second, David, her love. The present time. This life with him, these six years, represented the first years in her own life in a way. The first fully realized years anyway. The first time she'd ever felt entirely alive. The rest of it had been just marking time–till she'd found her mate. It was a flawed relationship, no doubt, but how much better than most people have in a lifetime? Maybe a bunch of lifetimes. To have the experience of loving David made her the luckiest woman on earth. *What is that worth? What is it worth to me to be with David till I die?* She blinked back tears.

And then there was the past, the distant partnership past that she loved so much she often felt like she belonged there. She thought about the ancient icon of love that had just seared itself into her memory–and her heart–demanding to be protected, crying out to be interpreted. That was the third thing that meant the world to her. The penultimate experience in her chosen profession that might now lie before her. How could she possibly choose? Future, present, or past. *My dream, my partner, or my profession?*

Okay, let's be logical. Leave your heart out of it for a minute. Okay? Okay. Pursuing this find over the next few weeks would mean an immense amount of work, LeeAnn realized, with the amount of excavation and investigation that would be necessary. Particularly if it turned out to have the significance that she thought it might. And that's if VHRI was completely cooperative. And if they weren't? In any case, she wouldn't be able to do anything else. She'd have her hands full and then some.

But if she walked away from the Summer Project at this critical juncture, she knew in her heart it would not have the same push or drive. It was still LeeAnn's project that her friends were helping her with. It was still a game to them, a challenge to accomplish something they believed in but weren't ready to give up their life for. So if she quit now, even the infinitesimal chance that they might succeed in creating some public attention would likely be lost. For every opportunity that came up would have to be exploited relentlessly, every possible path that opened up as replies started coming in.

Then she almost laughed out loud. *How absurd, how crazy that I keep thinking what I do can actually influence anything. As if what I do is of some importance. Like I'm pivotal to the world. LeeAnn Spencer, get a grip, you're not even pivotal to your own partner.*

Can I give up David? she thought then, and keep the other two? In some ways I can see that if I can keep them both going they might possibly entwine someday. Prove our partnership past is real and that in itself can help prove a partnership future is possible. But start that by giving up on partnership present. She looked over at David. He was so silent. There was just the engine and the wind flapping the plastic windows. She could feel the tension, the coldness; the space between them in the Jeep in the cool night air seemed huge, the hostility palpable. *I've already lost his heart,* she thought. *Haven't I? Yet, today on that pebble beach, and then sitting under the tree on Tree Island, I knew for a certainty we were meant to be together always.* LeeAnn looked at the piece of slate on her lap that David had used to sketch the petroglyph. It was barely visible in the moonlight reflected off the lake. The moment of their discovery came back to her again. The love she had felt flow between the two them in those moments. No, she couldn't give up David.

But of course he was right; it wasn't as though she'd be effective at anything, spread as thin as she was at the moment. *Especially if he were gone.*

So, she told herself, let's think about turning the petroglyph over to someone else right away. That's the thing I probably need to give up. After all, there were plenty of competent people in her field; she knew dozens of them herself. Calling Vince Taurini, her own mentor, now at the Smithsonian, would be the best place to start if she wanted to find the right person. *Some specialist in Northwest cultures who doesn't mind going up against a multinational with a construction schedule. You're only going to be one of many people working on this project if you insist on staying involved,* she told herself, *so give it up now, LeeAnn. Otherwise you fail at everything. Otherwise you lose David for sure.*

On the other hand, said the little voice in her head, *look at what the man is asking of you. He wants an open relationship, but he still wants to control everything you do. And yet,* she thought, *do I have the strength to do anything but accept his conditions? I need him. I love him. At this moment I don't see how I could bear to be without him. If there's any chance at all to save what we have had. In the final analysis, it's my own partnership I have to look out for.*

So that was how she decided. It didn't make her feel good; for it was a decision that she already realized in some part of her mind was based more on selfishness than love. *David would do fine without me. In fact, he's signaling he's ready to move on. Yet I'm choosing him over the two things I could do that might actually help. That's what I'm doing.*

With great reluctance in her voice and shame at her weakness, she said, finally, "I'll tell you what. The very minute I'm sure that the petroglyph is in capable hands, I'll relinquish this find. I'll write it up, go out to the VHRI office tomorrow, and let them know what they've got. Then I'll call Vince Taurini and get him started on finding someone to take over. Okay?" As she said Vince's name, she was aware of the effect it would have on David.

David responded predictably by backing up a little. "Look, I'm not trying to be the bad guy. I'd like to know more about that petroglyph, too. But you've just got to keep things in perspective." That last sounded both patriarchal and condescending.

Oh boy, LeeAnn thought, *here we go, doing our old pattern. He challenges, knowing I want to please him; I acquiesce, and then he reassures me of the correctness of my submission. So maybe this is a more screwed-up relationship than I thought, but damn it, it's the only relationship I've got.*

The rest of the trip she worked on trying not to cry. *I'm doing the only thing I can,* she kept telling herself, but she wasn't sure she meant it. The radio in the Jeep didn't work, but the radio in her head seemed to have been turned on. She heard the plaintive tones of the country-western gospel, "*Stand by Your Man . . .*" When you don't have the guts to do anything else.

After collecting Vanna, and caravan-ing back to Klamath Falls– LeeAnn did let herself cry briefly when she was alone behind the wheel of Jeepers–they had finally bumpety-bumped up into the driveway about 10:00 p.m. to contemplate the unloading process.

Jeff and Audrey, thank god, were home and came out to help. They'd just returned from their dumpster-diving expedition in Berkeley and Oakland. "Jeff and Peter came up with some great finds, and I ruined my nails," Audrey said, holding them out for LeeAnn's inspection. The lavender polish was chipped, and some of the glittery ornaments had fallen off. She showed LeeAnn the hundred invitations which had survived in a trash bin just off Ashby. "Of course, now we have to start over and pick the *hundred* most likely people in the world to send to. Well, it can't be helped. Peter said to tell you he's still going to try to come up for the weekend."

Looking stiff-legged and awkward, David was trying to get out of the van with the least amount of pain, staggering slightly as his legs figured out how to walk again. "You guys are both walking funny, like you got shit in your shoes," Audrey observed.

"Thanks a lot," said David.

As they unloaded the gear and carried it into the cabin, LeeAnn told Audrey and Jeff about their day. David didn't say a whole lot. The two New Yorkers were quick to make the same leaps LeeAnn had in her mind about the potential importance of their find. And they were not nearly as trusting as David was about VHRI acting responsibly. "They won't do diddly squat unless you stay on them. You've got to go see the blond guy. You know, the hunk on TV?"

"I plan to. I'm going to call first thing tomorrow."

"And I'll call Kevin," Jeff offered, "get him to check up on the company. Poke around a little."

David turned around and eyeballed him.

"We need to know who we're dealing with," was Jeff's innocent response. "Especially if LeeAnn's going to turn it over to them."

"You guys aren't going to get her all fired up again, are you?" David said, as he hauled sail-bags out of the van. His question went unanswered. By the time they had the boards put to bed in the basement and were ready to go inside, it felt to LeeAnn as if they were in two separate camps, David versus the rest of them.

"David, clocks in archaeologists' offices measure years, not hours," Audrey told him–she seemed to be the only one who was able to oppose David with impunity. "The resort will be *built,* for godsakes before anybody gets around to investigating anything, unless LeeAnn gets on it. Plus she's the only one who's going to have that kind of energy."

"Well . . .," David was quiet. Then he stretched, trying to pop his back, "I'm going to go get horizontal; are you coming out, L.A.?" he asked, indicating the cabin.

"I don't think I'd be able to sleep," she said truthfully. "and I want to look some stuff up." She looked into his eyes, for what she didn't know. "So, goodnight." She kissed him lightly on the lips, then held his gaze. "We did it," she said softly.

"Yeah, we did." There was genuine warmth in his voice–and in his eyes. Then he took her in his arms and gently embraced her as if she were some precious, fragile thing. Afterward, he kissed her on the forehead. David then limped off to the cabin, and the other three went into the house.

Though she thought she wasn't hungry, LeeAnn made a beeline for the refrigerator, stuck her head in and resurfaced seconds later with stale, mangled pizza from Jeff and Audrey's road trip, along with a hunk of frozen Sara Lee cheesecake–both of which she wolfed down standing up. Then she fell into bed fully dressed, trying to let sleep take away the nightmare. It didn't.

A few hours later, LeeAnn was at the desk in her bedroom, her hair pinned up in disarray. It was hot, which was rare for Klamath, and it was still really early in the morning, though exactly what time she didn't know since her watch wasn't working. Sitting at her desk in her underpants and the most sunburn-friendly midriff top she could find, a pile of books around her, she was trying to call up text about Klamath *hanowas* on her computer and having her ritual battle with the maze of cyberspace that was the Internet.

Fighting her confusion and fatigue, she took a deep breath as she hit yet one more dead-end tangent and backed out of it. Jeffrey could have managed to find what she wanted in a New York minute, but she didn't want to wake him.

LeeAnn's mission this morning was to put together a couple of really professional pages on the implications of the discovery at Tree Island. And then hand over the most significant find of her career to other archaeologists. *I can't believe I'm giving this up before I even get started,* she thought. She put her hands on her lower back, pushing and rubbing as she tried unsuccessfully to straighten it. She'd been awake most all night, thinking and figuring, and in her mind walking over every inch of Tree Island.

Wondering how much longer it would be before she could reach someone at VHRI, she looked down at her dead watch one more time, then took it off. Now, of course, she would keep glancing at her naked wrist. LeeAnn had tried dialing Vanderveer's office last night as soon as she got home, to leave a message, but all she got was an announcement about office hours.

She tried again now but they still weren't answering, so she went back to punching keys on her computer. The little egg timer on her screen said to wait. Then it came up. *At last!* There was what she'd been looking for, from a book by Carrol Howe, a local Klamath author.

"The word *henwa*," she read, "derives from a word in the Klamath language that roughly translates into *rock standing upright*, a term that gives no clue to the purpose of these stone figures. Possibly shamans used these in their healing rites."

That makes sense, LeeAnn thought. *The healing of love.*

"According to legend," she read, "the figures, male and female, were once living beings but turned to stone when Crow laughed at them. However, as though still alive, *henwas* retained the ability to move of their own accord, to travel." So she was right; she thought she had remembered that.

She looked down the page. "Mrs. Lizzie Kirk, a Klamath, has said that her husband found two *henwas*, a male and female pair, side by side on the bank of the Williamson River. Afraid of them, the man threw the two into the water. The next day, however, when he passed by the spot, both *henwas* were back on the riverbank. *Henwas* are unique to Klamath County. Some male and female *henwas* have been found together, others found alone." There wasn't anything here about *double* figures.

She looked at the photo of male and female hanowas on the screen. They were crude, with very rough indications of belly, breasts, and genitals. She wondered vaguely if the myth that they could travel might have had its roots in a retold story of the originals having been brought from far away. She remembered the belief of some of the Russian arctic people that odd-shaped rocks were remnants of gods that had once protected them. *Put that together with the legend that these hanowas had the ability to travel . . . Maybe there was a highly developed partnership society that . . . Well, no sense speculating now.*

She hit PRINT, and, as the appropriate printer noises began, allowed herself to stretch her legs and her back–very slowly–because any abrupt movement would be instantly regretted. On this morning-after, incredible stiffness crippled every limb, which wasn't surprising after ten hours of standing on a lake hanging onto a huge flapping thing that's constantly trying to get away from you. Plus two hours of moving boulders around.

Her back was the worst, but her arms, her legs, her neck, her fingers, everything hurt. Her *hair* hurt. She felt barely able to move, and was sunburned to boot, with violently red places where her bathing suit had shifted. Not all the sunscreen in the world would have helped with the exposure they'd gotten.

For about the hundredth time since last night, LeeAnn looked at the piece of slate David had used to sketch the petroglyph with his car key, and then at the more careful drawing that she had made from it. It was so beautiful, so earthy, so *healthy*. And that connect-the-dots smile was the best! She was longing to see it again, touch it, feel it. Meantime her eyes caressed every detail of the drawings.

Then it suddenly connected with a blinding flash–the memory had been on the edge of her consciousness since the first moment she'd laid eyes on the petroglyph. What it looked like. Yes! Of course that's what it was. "Yes, yes, yes, yes, Yes!" she said out loud, as she hurried across the room to the bookshelf. *Why didn't I put this together before; I know that piece so well. I must have a blank spot in my head.* She felt a little dizzy and her heart started leaping around in her chest.

She pulled down her autographed copy *of Goddesses and Gods of Old Europe*, a Marija Gimbutas book, and immediately opened it to the right page; the photo of the *Gumelnita Lovers* smiled back at her. *No wonder I thought it looked familiar.* Dated seven thousand years ago, and discovered on an island in the Danube River, this *Sacred Marriage* figure of male and female was incredibly like the carving in the rock on Tree Island, half a world away. The same stance. The same connect-the-dots smile. Very similar markings and the same unmistakable pride in both sets of lovers. How could any two figures be so similar and yet unrelated? How? Yet how *could* they be related?

She took that and another Gimbutas book, went back to the desk, sat down, and began looking at photographs of European artifacts. There were so many, many ways to reverently express the magic of love and procreation, some of them so sophisticated and stylized that they appeared contemporary, or even futuristic. Several were abstract in a keenly intellectual way; they were all wonderful. Yet perhaps the warmest of all, the most normal, the most unabashedly happy and wholesome of all of the human figures pictured in the books were the Gumelnita Lovers. The most benevolent set of ancestors we could ever hope to have had. Ancestors who gave us permission to have pleasure.

LeeAnn always felt awe-struck by the work that her heroines, Marija Gimbutas and Riane Eisler, had done that was beginning to alter our perception of our past and ourselves so profoundly. Almost single-handedly they had sparked the first serious inquiry into the troubles of the human race that sprang from quarreling about the sex of God.

LeeAnn had had the chance to interview Gimbutas once. When she arrived at her Topanga Canyon home, Gimbutas was gravely ill, but still working with an assistant to finish a book. Sitting at her bedside, looking at the round Lithuanian face so bright with fever, LeeAnn had wondered if she could ever honor her work enough. Now, she realized, she might have that chance.

Once again LeeAnn sought out a passage of Gimbutas that she had read many times before. *" . . . this book explicitly seeks to identify the Old European patterns that crossed the boundaries of time and space. These systematic associations in the Near East, Southeastern Europe, the Mediterranean Area, and in central, western, and northern Europe, indicate the extension of the same . . . religion to all of these regions as a cohesive and persistent ideological system."*

And that's what this find could corroborate–*a cohesive and persistent ideological system.* Only all the way to the Americas, too. *At last, proof of the connection of the cultures all around the earth. The Holy Grail in the world of archaeology. Because how could this unique icon have simply been recreated, nearly perfectly duplicated, half a world away, by sheer chance?* Wasn't it more likely that the figure from the Danube and the drawing on the rock both came from the same incredibly ancient tradition–that had somehow spread and survived in separate corners of the world?

Or is there some way we don't understand that humans are able to communicate the essential thoughts to one another over space and time, mind to mind? The hundredth monkey. A way that makes actual travel unnecessary?

The enormity of the questions was thrilling, even without the answers. And she loved the symbolism of a curious, adventurous, and resourceful Adam and Eve, not stuck in a garden, but traveling or mind traveling around the world together.

What were the answers? *Which is the magic that is real?* For surely this "coincidence" showed that magic of some kind was operating. Was it genetic memory, ESP, or just the raw courage and faith of travelers across the land bridge? She tried to conceive what hundreds of generations would have had to endure to keep these figures they loved safe over thousands of years and thousands of miles, and hundreds of generations. The sheer persistence of the human spirit was mind-boggling.

And now, of course, I've promised David I won't pursue this project, she thought with a sinking heart. *How could I have done such a thing? And how can I ever keep that promise? If I'd known then what I just figured out now, I* never *would have done it. Her mind went back over last night one more time. The decision she'd made now seemed incomprehensible to her.*

She looked at her bare wrist one more time, to no avail. Well, whatever time it was here, it was surely late enough in D.C. to call Vince and start turning the whole thing over to him. LeeAnn took a tiny sip of the cold coffee she'd poured a couple of hours ago–yesterday's coffee, since she hadn't wanted to wake Audrey with the noise from the grinder. As she reached for the phone, she let herself think about Vince for moment, about what his life had done to hers and what hers might be about to do to his.

Vince Taurini had been an archaeology student working a site on her Uncle Theo's property on the island of Crete, where a golden goddess figure had been found, when LeeAnn was five and the Spencers were spending the summer there. She fell in love immediately, both with Vince and with the romantic science of archaeology, but waited till she was sixteen before choosing him, wisely, she thought, as her first lover. He was older, he was safe, and it solved the problem of her raging hormones. Maybe not an orthodox solution, but one that had worked well. She'd never had any hang-ups about love.

She picked up the phone and dialed Vince's number in McLean, Virginia, then waited through the predictable four rings before his answering machine clicked on.

It was that clear, intelligent, Ivy League voice of his, so intimately familiar. "Afraid you missed us," he said. "We're headed for our hideaway on the Eastern Shore for the month of August with, happily, noooo telephone!" He always did have to do his pilgrimage to the sea. "However, we'll be picking up messages periodically." *What does periodically mean?* she wondered. *Very occasionally, if I know him.* "If you'd like to leave a private message for Vince, press one, Sue, press two, Cody or Caitlin, press three."

LeeAnn pressed one. "Vince," (she didn't have to say who it was), "you're not going to believe this. Yesterday on an island in Upper Klamath Lake, I found a bas-relief representation of the Sacred Marriage figures that's so close to the Gumelnita Lovers, it's eerie. It's *old.* The lichen on another piece of the petroglyph would indicate several millennia, maybe more, and my thinking, as usual, is way out there."

Just then Audrey poked her head around the corner, tousled from sleep, looking adorable in a little white, shorty chenille robe. "I'm calling Vince," LeeAnn mouthed softly at her. Then into the phone, "Just open up your copy of *Gods and Goddesses of Old Europe* to page 229 and take a look. You'll see what I mean–I'll fax a drawing of the petroglyph we found to your office. Maybe they can get it to you."

She took a breath. "Okay, how could the figures be similar? I know it's mind-boggling, but what if . . . what if the tradition of these figures preceded the Danube River figure and eight thousand years ago had already spread halfway around the world . . . am I nuts?"

Audrey's eyes were getting bigger. LeeAnn pointed to the figure in the book and then to the drawing she'd made of the Tree Island petroglyph. Audrey gasped; she was having trouble keeping quiet. "And wouldn't you know, massive construction's about to begin on the site that will obliterate all possible clues. And in addition, for reasons I can't explain, I'm probably not going to be able to work the site myself. I need for you or somebody you assign to get on this and get out here fast.

"So help! Help, help, help! Call me. Any time of the day or night. God, you *would* be away. *Please* call in." Audrey gestured. "Audrey sends her love." She started to hang up, but couldn't quite. "Is it credible, Vince, is it even *remotely* conceivable that generations of people could have carried a figurine across the land bridge, the way the Hebrews carried the Ark? How else could it spontaneously turn up halfway around the world? Get back to me, I'm obviously losing it." She hung up.

"This is unbelievable, LeeAnn. Absolutely unbelievable," Audrey said.

"I know. It may be just a random similarity . . ."

There are no coincidences. "Uh-uh, no way. How many generations would it have taken for them to come across the land bridge, L.A.?" Audrey asked as she spun the globe on LeeAnn's file cabinet.

"It's supposed to have taken at least a thousand years. Fifty generations, following the herds of caribou, just to slowly migrate across. And not an easy life. Then there's the whole of Alaska, Canada, Washington, and Oregon."

"Yeah." Audrey was looking at the route.

"The people would have to have been carrying a lot of stuff, their kids, their fire, their food, and there would have been a lot of danger."

"But if they had something they believed in, something that symbolized their whole belief system, wouldn't they take special care of it?" asked Audrey. "Of all the things individuals might have brought, wouldn't this have had the best chance of making it here?"

"About a one in a *zillion* chance."

"Yeah, but like you said, if the Klamath people could keep a story going for hundreds of generations, then it's not inconceivable . . ."

"Audrey, what if the figure that this artist on Tree Island was copying–what if it still exists? And what if it could be proven where it came from? I know it sounds crazy but I just have the feeling . . ."

"Hey, don't apologize. Intuition is probably as important a part of your job, or mine, as anything else. You're always saying you get paid to speculate. So don't be ashamed of it. Right brain is okay. Right brain is good." Audrey sat down and studied the material on Klamath hanowas for a few minutes. "Look, L.A. Suppose you're wrong, suppose this isn't as old or as significant as you think it might be? What's the least old it could be? What's the worst case scenario?"

"Several thousand years."

"That means maybe older than the oldest Egyptian civilization."

"Oh, definitely."

"So it's still worth everything you can put into it. In our culture, we go bat-shit over something that's only hundreds of years old and here we're talking a few *thousand* at the least. You've *got* to stay involved."

"And then I lose David. I promised him . . ."

"Tell David to get a grip! I can't *believe* you could promise something like that."

"You had to have been there."

"LeeAnn, this is what you've been looking for forever, isn't it? Your whole partnership theory," she said. "We can handle the 22nd Century Group."

"You won't let it fall apart?"

"No way. And we can help you on this, too." She laid LeeAnn's papers back on the desk and stood up. "David doesn't run your life. I don't even think he *wants* to, if the truth were known. Have you been up all night?" she asked then, giving LeeAnn an appraising look.

"Just about."

"You look awful."

"Thanks."

"Well, I figured you'd be up all night and I figured you'd need some breakfast. After that miserable excuse for a meal last night. You want an omelet?"

"I don't know."

"You *need* an omelet. I just hope there's cheese," she said, heading back toward the kitchen. "And onions."

"Onions in the breadbox under the counter. Left of the fridge. Hold the cheese."

"Whatever you say," as Audrey vanished toward the kitchen. LeeAnn went back to her printout of the hanowas book. Then her eyes went to another picture on the page and the caption below it.

"Five *minutes*," Audrey called from the kitchen

"There are five examples of free-standing sculpture," LeeAnn read, "that are not classifiable as hanowas. Four appear to represent animals, one is a wind-rock . . ."

A wind-rock? She read on. "One of the few acts of outright magic among the Klamath relates to causing the wind to blow." *I love it,* she thought. *But why would they have wanted to control the wind?* LeeAnn asked herself. *For drying food, maybe. Winnowing grain. Probably a bunch of reasons, but I bet anything they sailed.* LeeAnn studied the photograph of a windrock; it was cube-shaped, and there was a circle with a dot in the middle incised on all four sides. They looked like pursed lips, blowing.

"Some wind-rocks were boulders," the printout said, "in specific locations, e.g., the Columbia River area. Others were portable; small enough to be carried around. The owner would hit the north side of the cube to cause a north wind to blow, the south for a south wind, etc. A blow to the top of the cube would calm the wind." Neat, this could come in handy for windsurfers.

"What time is it?" LeeAnn called to Audrey.

"Whaat?"

"What *time*!?"

"Ten after eight." She could hear Audrey banging around in the kitchen, probably down on her hands and knees looking for an omelet pan.

"I need to make a couple of calls, then I'll be right there." David should be getting up about now, she thought. He had to go to the gallery early today to redo his exhibit. She wondered if he'd stop in to say good morning. She thought about buzzing him in the cabin and decided against it.

As she picked up the slim Klamath Falls phone book to look for the number of the Klamath Tribes, LeeAnn was thinking that two hundred years ago they would have been the only listing. The original residents. She found the number. Maybe they could answer some of her questions.

"Good morning, Klamath Tribes." A young man's voice.

"Good morning, my name is LeeAnn Spencer. I'm an archaeologist. Could I talk to your . . . whoever handles cultural affairs?"

"That's Gordon."

"Oh, yes, of course." She'd heard him tell stories at a pow-wow.

"I'm sorry, he's out of town on vacation."

"Is there anybody else I could talk to about artifacts?"

"I could refer you to . . ."

August, LeeAnn thought. The month was so annoying–nobody was where they were supposed to be. She arranged an appointment to come up the next day. "Oh, and could you help with just one more thing? I work out of state and I wasn't sure which department of government regulates archaeological objects."

"Fish and Game," was the reply.

"With the state police?"

"Yes, ma'am."

"Thanks." LeeAnn hung up. Aromas from the kitchen were promising. Thinking she'd try to reach Ernst Vanderveer again right after breakfast, she picked up the listing from *Who's Who in Business* that Jeff had left on her desk before he went to bed. She figured she'd study Vanderveer and Sonja Al Amin's bios while she ate. She also brought along a 1930s book on Oregon petroglyphs that she'd found in a thrift store once.

Five minutes later she was working her way through the huge omelet, which was good, though she wished Audrey hadn't put salsa on it. Carefully ferrying forkfuls over an open page of the petroglyph book, she motioned Audrey to come and look. "See, this is what I mean," she pointed to a page of human figures. Some were dancing, some were running, and there was a whole row of people holding hands. "You notice all of these are rendered as stick figures. That's almost certainly what they would have drawn if they were just drawing people."

"Oh, look at this one," Audrey cooed, looking over her shoulder. "Look how the bottom of her ends in a little circle and the bottom of him in a little cross, that's so adorable!" She grabbed the book away from LeeAnn, pulled out a chair, sat down, and began turning pages. "You'll just get food on it anyway. Eat your breakfast." She read on. "Naw, I don't believe this. The old prude."

"What did you find?"

"Listen to this. He says the figures might be *intended* to be phallic design, but he thinks it's more likely that the artist didn't have the skill to control the lines he made. Pooh."

"Audrey, don't worry about it, just dumb academics."

Audrey read on. "Figures D and E, he thinks, may also be due to lack of skill on the part of the artist. Looks pretty skillful to me. *Numb-nut*. People! This is what's the matter with the world. We're fixated on sex, but ashamed of it at the same time. LeeAnn, this is a real book?" She looked at the cover. "This isn't a joke?" LeeAnn shook her head and Audrey went back to her reading, mumbling under her breath from time to time.

Sillvester, LeeAnn noticed, was watching the two of them through the window that separated his quarters from theirs. It was something that David had built for him, since he was allergic to cats. Sillvester came and went from it freely and even invited friends to share his comfortable carpeted space from time to time. Usually they were other cats; once it was a skunk.

LeeAnn slid the window open now and gave him the last bite of her omelet, then shut it again. Sillvester shook his head violently as he chomped down on the salsa and got the flavor in his mouth, swallowed, then glared briefly at LeeAnn. Sillvester's beef with the world, LeeAnn and David had figured, probably stemmed from the fact that he was fixed. And since humans had done the dirty deed, his bitterness was directed at them–he seemed to have no problem at all with other creatures. LeeAnn squinched her eyes to smile at Sillvester, who stared for a moment and then condescended to squinch back.

Audrey was chortling again. "This says that the two figures are joined ventrally. Hah! Well, that's a *delicate* way of putting it; we all know what 'joined ventrally' means, don't we? What *does* it mean?" And she grabbed Jeffrey's traveling dictionary still on the table from a heated debate about the buzzword "paradigm" a couple of evenings before.

"'Of or pertaining to the venter or belly; abdominal. Situated on or toward the *lower* abdominal plane of an animal's body, equivalent to the front in humans.'" LeeAnn thought of her harness, which attached *ventrally*.

The two figures are joined ventrally, Audrey repeated. "It says this might be a device to indicate that the two are joined in the one design. Or, it might have been an accident, the result of *carelessly applied paint*! Bullshit. *Patriarchal hogwash*. I'll bet this guy still thinks the stork brings babies."

Audrey got up, whisked LeeAnn's plate away, and went over to the sink to wash it. "Algae, you need algae. Lots of it." She brought over several bottles, plunked them down on the table, and started doling them out.

LeeAnn looked again at her left wrist. It was time to deal with Ernst Vanderveer. "I'd better get my ass in gear." She stood very slowly, trying once again to stretch; it was not smart to sit for very long. She limped over to the kitchen phone. "There's bound to be somebody there by now," she said as she started to pick up the phone.

"Want me to do it? Make the appointment? I'll be your secretary."

"Why not?" Audrey always gave great phone.

"Or, better idea. Do you want me to go with? We could double-team the Vanderveer hunk."

LeeAnn considered. "Well, we know *how*."

"Except I'm afraid it's going to take me awhile to get it together." Audrey looked at her ruined nails.

Forget it, LeeAnn thought, knowing it would take her two hours. "That's okay. I got to get moving."

"So I'll call for you. Is this what Jeffrey got you on VHRI?" Audrey picked up the two *Who's Who* bios, and scanned them. "It says Sonja Al Amin's father was some Middle Eastern oil baron. I wonder how she ever got the name Sonja? Hmmm."

Then she turned to the Vanderveer article and started scanning it. "Oh, how sweet. The Dutch East India Company. A nice mom-and-pop business. Four hundred years of exploiting Asians. He's the quintessential dominator, LeeAnn. Bred for it. He can't change, it's in his genes."

"But the whole premise of the 22nd Century Group is that these people *can* change. That we can all change."

"I doubt it." Audrey went on. "He's got too much to lose. It says divisions of the parent corp include chemical, pharmaceutical, petroleum, banking . . . with assets of twenty-eight *billion* dollars! How come I've never heard of this company?"

"There's a lot of companies that size you haven't heard of. Owned by the invisible one-percenters."

Audrey picked up the phone. "He's not going to want to hear about this, you know. There's no way that it's not going to slow down their construction schedule."

"Just don't tell them I'm an archaeologist till I get in there."

"Don't worry," said Audrey, dialing. "I'm not going to tell them diddly. Never tell *anybody* what you want to see them about when you call them, rule number one . . . It's ringing . . . Time enough to explain after we get you in. Plus we'll make you look so gorgeous the guy won't be able to think straight. You'll be like the proverbial carrot."

She spoke into the phone. "Ernst Vanderveer, please . . . Thank you. No I need to talk to Mr. Vanderveer please." She covered the receiver with her hand, and spoke to LeeAnn. "Not available, and his secretary's out." Then into the phone, "Are you sure? Mmmm. Oh, well then give me Ms. Al Amin's office."

LeeAnn was waving, *No, no, no.*

Audrey ignored her. "Yes, good morning, I'm calling from LeeAnn Spencer's office. She's just returned to the United States and needs to see Mr. Vanderveer." A beat. "Yes, I *understand*, but this is rather urgent." There was another pause. "Are you aware that in a recent television interview, Ms. Al Amin indicated that good community relations are *vital* to VHRI? Was that just for local consumption, I wonder? This *pertains* to community relations."

Perfect, LeeAnn signaled with a circled thumb and forefinger as she systematically swallowed capsules of algae from the huge pile Audrey had set out for her.

"Perhaps Ms. Spencer can explain that to Ms. Al Amin and then Ms. Al Amin can facilitate the meeting with Mr. Vanderveer." LeeAnn was shaking her head now, but Audrey waved her off. "Fine, 10:30 this morning. I'll tell her." She hung up.

"What'd you go and do that for? It's not her I want to see."

"He's in a meeting all morning, away from the office this afternoon, and going to San Francisco tonight, according to the   snippy guy I just talked to. What was I gonna do? And maybe this woman is the real boss anyway. Women usually are. They're the worst kind of dominators. When you get out there, just make sure you run into Vanderveer. Lurk until you do. Pace. Just make sure you run smack into him, LeeAnn."

"I'll do my best."

"All right now, go jump in the shower."

I couldn't jump if you paid me, LeeAnn thought as Audrey started herding her along toward the bedroom.

"We've got forty-five minutes for a complete makeover. Put some conditioner on that hair. God, your face–we'll have to cover up that sunburn somehow," she said. "And I have to find you something to wear." Audrey went to LeeAnn's closet and started ripping through a rack of clothes as though she were at Alexander's.

In the bathroom, LeeAnn stripped, pulled back the shower curtain and bent down slowly to lift out the little mat of hair that had dried over the drain. It was a cunning thing, made of David's darker hair entwined with her honey blonde, and it had the same little round holes in it as the drain. Detritus of a love affair; she could press it between the pages of a book, she thought. Instead she placed it delicately in the wastebasket.

Automatically, LeeAnn turned the shower on as hot as it would go; then, thinking about her sunburn, she adjusted it to somewhere between warm and cool, and was just about to step gingerly into the tub when there was a pounding on the door.

"I found you an outfit!" Audrey said, coming in without waiting for a reply. "I think this is going to work. It's the only thing you've got that *will* work." She held it up to LeeAnn's naked form. It was the beige power suit of heavy raw silk that she'd picked up at a posh resale shop on Madison Avenue years ago. It had been outrageously high-priced, even then, even secondhand, but well worth the money. And it still did the trick on the few occasions she needed to wear it, like getting the editing job that had allowed her to come out west and live with David. It was her outfit for negotiating with the dominator system. Audrey hung it on the outside of the shower curtain. "This has to steam," she said.

"It just came from the dry cleaner."

"Steam it anyway. Packaging, L.A. Packaging. You don't want wrinkles. You should see how you had it jammed in your closet." She hung it on the Christopher Robin hook on the inside of the bathroom door. LeeAnn reflected briefly that it was almost the same straw color and texture as the Global Party invitation envelopes. Packaging.

Audrey left and LeeAnn started shampooing her hair as her mind ranged back over all she'd learned in her studies these last few hours. She was still thinking about the wind-rock. *I should make one for David. Maybe he'd like that. I bet he'd carry it around with him.*

After rinsing and conditioning, LeeAnn conducted an inventory of her bruises, lathered up, shaved her legs, rinsed off, got out of the shower, and dripped on the floor while she looked for a towel. When she'd dried herself off and mopped up the floor, she hung her head upside down and turned on the hair dryer that she never used unless she was going somewhere. While her hair was still damp, she turned the ends under slightly and fluffed her bangs while Audrey rounded up underwear and accessories.

When she was finally dressed, made-up, and outfitted for her mission, both of them studied her in the full-length mirror. LeeAnn looked stunning; even she had to admit it. The suit still worked; it still made her look like an heiress in a novel who owned a perfume empire at least. Or an aerospace industry. The super-straight skirt was hard to walk in; you had to think about every step before you took it or you'd tip over. But there were epaulettes on the shoulder, which were great in a meeting when you were visible only from the waist up. In a roomful of males, it subtly declared rank.

"You look terrific."

"Thanks."

"Better than you have in years," Audrey declared. "You ought to have more clothes like that."

"I know." LeeAnn vaguely wished David could see her, but he'd already be down at the gallery. Maybe she could stroll by later. *Shuffle by,* she amended.

"Here, take my purse," said Audrey, holding it out to her. "You can't wear that ugly pack."

LeeAnn reached out to take the bag.

"What about those hands of yours?"

"I cleaned them up," LeeAnn said, hiding them. "That'll have to do." LeeAnn's fingernails were clean, but of somewhat varied lengths. "Audrey, men don't look at women's hands."

Audrey sighed, evidently giving up. "Okay, now, give me your model look. Suck your cheeks in. Drop your jaw just a smidge, stiff upper lip. Widen your eyes." LeeAnn tried to comply with all the orders at once. "All *right*, give me some snob, girl."

"I hate playing these games."

"Oh, it's fun, you know it is." Audrey looked at her watch. "Are you all set? You better get going."

"I'm going bananas without my watch," LeeAnn said. "I wish it worked."

"Take mine."

"No way." Audrey's watch, tiny and delicate, had diamonds for numerals, and it wasn't even *slightly* waterproof. Some rich Cuban guy had given it to her.

"Go ahead."

"No, first thing I'd do is get it wet, and then I'd probably lose it. Oh, wait a minute," LeeAnn started across the room, "I know what to do." She opened the top drawer of her dresser and pulled out the over-sized sports watch, still in its box, that David's grandmother had sent him for Christmas. She lived in a nursing home now and shopped by catalogue. Claiming it was too gadgety, David had abandoned it then and there under the tree, so LeeAnn had put it away, thinking they could give it to her brother some day. Peter liked gadgety watches.

She pulled the expansion bracelet off the dummy wrist in the box and looked at it. "It's still on standard time ."

"Give it here, I know how." Audrey took it and fiddled, punching buttons randomly. Little things lit up. Eventually she did manage to change the time. "Okay, that's fixed. Now don't let anybody see it. Here, shove it way up on your arm." It made a lump under the jacket, but Audrey pushed the sleeves up a bit, and that helped.

"Okay, stop already, Audrey! Quit fussing, I've still got to print my presentation out." Escaping Audrey's clutches, LeeAnn went back to her computer, made a few changes on her paper that she'd thought of when she was in the shower, then hit PRINT, praying the ink cartridge wouldn't go dry on her as it routinely did at critical moments. Then she proofread.

There were only two pages of text but she thought they were persuasive, plus three pages of references, and two graphics, one of David's sketch of the *Tree Island Lovers*, one a photo of the *Gumelnita Lovers* she'd copied from the book. Two good-looking couples. Pretty decent for a rush job.

She pilfered a folder from another report to put it in. Then she placed all of it in a slim leather portfolio along with her curriculum vitae and some news articles about her finds in Europe, in case she had to demonstrate her credentials. Funny, she wasn't feeling anything about David right now. Here she was, heading off on some new tangent, and it didn't seem right now like anything else mattered. That was the trouble with herself, she thought. She was so easily distracted and divided in her attention. *Everything is first priority.* The original ADD kid. LeeAnn had been reading about attention deficit disorder lately and decided she probably had it. *Oh, well.*

Audrey followed her to the back door. "That outfit is *bad*. You sure you don't want me to go with you?"

"No thanks."

"Promise you'll give me a call the minute you're out of there," Audrey said, finally waving her out the door. "They're going to love your bumper sticker."

"Partnership is Adam and Eve with a happy ending," were the words plastered on the back of the Jeep.

Negotiating the gravel driveway in the spike heels Audrey had insisted that she wear, LeeAnn looked despairingly up at the climb up into the Jeep that awaited her–it was basically a two-foot step in a one-foot skirt. She opened the door and considered her limited options. She could hitch her skirt to her hips, she could levitate, or she could (possibly) do a pull-up on the steering wheel.

Opting for the latter and flapping her legs in a dolphin kick, LeeAnn managed, painfully, to pull herself up into the seat. Then she started the engine, which was appallingly loud; the muffler had a small leak. Still, the Jeep had been freshly painted while she was away, a bright, happy fire-engine red, and the wrought-iron rack on the back and the wire wheels added a classy touch.

You certainly couldn't miss VHRI. The offices were prominently placed, suitably elegant, and already gloriously landscaped. The international megacorp was clearly intending to have a dominant influence on the town. *So the direction that Klamath Falls will take has finally been decided,* LeeAnn thought. At one point, after the Winter Olympics effort had failed, another group had tried to turn the town into another Branson, Missouri country music center, but that didn't seem to catch on.

There was also the growing, but still mostly ignored, agricultural business of harvesting the lake's unique algae that had the potential of

ancient lovers

becoming gigantic. But now it looked like the scale had finally been tipped toward high-end tourism instead. *Extremely* high-end. If Ernst Vanderveer had his way, the big mega-vacation group would decide the Klamath fate and control the Klamath future. It would become a support village for the global elite.

As LeeAnn pulled into the parking area, she saw Vanderveer's Jaguar. *Good, at least he's here,* she thought, and steered the loudly putt-putt-ing Jeepers into one of the slots marked "Courtesy Parking." The elaborate multicolored design on the curb looked vaguely ethnic. Hopi, or Southwestern anyway. Not at all like Northwestern art. She turned off the engine, looked down at her suit. She was already sweaty and had lap creases. LeeAnn knew there would never be creases across Audrey's lap, no matter what the fabric of her suit.

She opened the door with the broken window zipper and slid out as if she were going down a slide. Then she leaned against the Jeep to get her balance, pushed herself upright, and locked her knees.

When you're in this kind of condition, LeeAnn knew, it takes about ten steps before you can walk properly. Her legs were just beginning to function as she grasped the oversized brass doorknob and opened the oversized door to the VHRI Visitors' Center. These doublewide doors were at least twenty-five feet high, as though people might be carried in on a sedan chair into a lobby which she saw was big enough to hold a cricket match. *Enemy territory,* she thought.

Once inside, LeeAnn looked around. Everything about this place was rich and dulcet. The carpet, the lighting, the voices, all distinctly dulcet. It was a virtual reality rendition of weal-*thy*. There were plush sofa sets, marble coffee tables, and huge abstract oil paintings. And the whole thing was done in tones of yellowish beige, just like LeeAnn: straw-colored.

The receptionist sat at a blonde, kidney-shaped desk at the far end of the room. *Why doesn't anybody ever have a liver-shaped desk?* LeeAnn wondered. Trying to conceal her gimpy gait, LeeAnn managed to make it without ski poles across carpeting that you could sink into up to your ankles.

"Yes?" The brittle, auburn-haired young woman managed to take in LeeAnn's shoes, power suit, handbag, and hairdo in one continuous glance. Wondering if she passed, LeeAnn put on her best haughty-model look, just a flash of it. "I have an appointment with Sonja Al Amin."

257

"You wouldn't happen to have a cahhd?" the receptionist inquired, in what seemed to LeeAnn, an absurd and deliberately snobbish British accent.

"Oh, I think I just might," LeeAnn replied with a girlie-girlie giggle. "I just might." She rummaged in Audrey's bag that she had simply dumped the contents of her pack into. On her second time through, she located several at the bottom but they were bent. One was from her Museum of Natural History job with Ruth Driscoll. That wouldn't do. She handed the woman one of the 22nd Century Group cards that Jeff had made up, wondering as she did if Vanderveer had ever gotten the invitation she'd sent him.

Frowning, the receptionist inspected the crumpled card as though it was difficult to read, looked up at LeeAnn, then back at the card. She finally pushed a button on the phone, turning away as she did so. There was evidently no answer. She turned back. "It will be just a few minutes."

"Thank you."

"If you'll have a seat, please."

"No, thank you." LeeAnn had no intention of sitting down. *If I do,* she thought, *I'll never get up again.* She strolled, carefully examining each picture around the room, as she sometimes did in toney restaurants. It was a habit that tended to make maitre d's nervous.

At last the phone on the reception desk buzzed and the woman picked it up, once again turning her back as she did. She spoke softly. When she'd hung up, she called over to LeeAnn. "Won't you please take a seat?"

"No, thank you. I'm fine," LeeAnn said for the second time, waving her off cheerily. It was rather fun to defy her.

A couple of men in business suits, architect or high-class contractor types, speaking in dulcet tones that matched the decor, came out of an office near the reception desk. They glanced at L.A. several times as they walked past. Good clothes did make a difference; she had to admit that.

At the far end of the room, near another huge set of double doors behind which the men were just disappearing, LeeAnn noticed an alcove with a whole gallery of pictures memorializing VHRI magic moments. She strolled over to look. There were happy construction sites, with Vanderveer in a hard hat, looking virile. Dedication ceremonies, with Vanderveer cutting ribbons, looking benevolent and successful.

Then there were photos of Ernst Vanderveer entertaining celebrities, looking glamorous. One of his guests at VHRI Mexico, LeeAnn noticed, was a golfish-looking U.S. vice-president, along with heads of state of several other countries. And in another photo, at a polo match evidently somewhere in Asia, there was a man who looked like Prince Charles. It had to be Prince Charles, LeeAnn decided; there were just not *that* many people out there with ears like that.

Next, LeeAnn looked at architects' renderings of the six-and eight-bedroom suites with adjoining offices that would be featured at Tree Island. *Big enough for an entourage of sheiks, or Japanese magnates and their families. Or Trilateral Commission members,* LeeAnn thought, and then scolded herself for her suspicions.

A brochure for VHRI Klamath showed an elegant marble-and-black-glass restaurant with a six-story waterfall, and aquariums for fresh Dungeness crabs and lobsters and sea urchins. Elegant little private fishing huts, helicopter safaris to prime mountain-goat-hunting locations, and other assorted perks of the undeniably rich and famous. LeeAnn had to stop looking. It turned her stomach.

She'd just moved away from the photos and was starting to cross the room as another small crowd of executives erupted from behind closed doors and started across the lobby. LeeAnn was delighted to see Ernst Vanderveer leading the pack, a head above most of the others. There was a shock at her first sight of him in the flesh. Somehow he looked different from what she'd expected.

There was surprise on Vanderveer's face as he caught sight of her, then she saw his instant positive assessment. In one quick flash she saw mirrored in his expression the woman he saw: the long coltish legs, the classic bone structure, and the body-hugging beige suit that set off the summer highlights in her hair. From the angle he was seeing, her lap creases didn't show.

She started impulsively toward him. In one motion, her eyebrows and her hand went up, and she opened her mouth to speak. And in that instant, he gave her a *Yes-but-not-quite-yet* signal and squinched his eyes like Sillvester smiling. *I'll make time for you.* The look was mesmerizing. *I want to talk to you, I want to see you, I want to know you,* it said.

And then he and the power he exuded were gone; it had happened *so* fast. In locked step, he and the small squadron of his faithful had disappeared through the oversized double doors, presumably into the meeting that would occupy him for the entire morning. Well, all she had to do was wait. She had the hope that he would find a way to come out. He wouldn't keep her waiting too long; she knew he wouldn't. *Thank you, power suit,* she thought as she continued to wander.

What surprised LeeAnn most about Ernst Vanderveer was her own reaction to him. She didn't hate him on sight; on the contrary, she felt almost attracted. Maybe it was that he hadn't seemed to be wearing that dominator look his family had been practicing for so long you would have thought it was genetically ingrained. On the contrary, he had looked like a real human being.

A few minutes later, Sonja Al Amin, in another of her chic black outfits, entered the building and crossed the lobby without a glance in LeeAnn's direction. So she hadn't even been in when LeeAnn arrived. The heavy door shut behind her. LeeAnn pushed up her sleeve. It was already 11:10, the watch at her elbow said. Her appointment with the woman had been for 10:30. She wondered how long it would be before one of them would come out. *I wish I could lie down,* she thought. *But I better keep moving or rigor mortis will set in. I wish I had some aspirin.*

Twenty minutes went by. LeeAnn examined all the paintings on the walls again, trying to decide which one she would take if somebody offered her one; that took twenty minutes. *None of them.* One might be a Rothko, but it wasn't a good one. She began to check out the reading material spread out on the tables. She picked up a *Wall Street Journal.* She put it down.

Next she perused a copy of *U.S. News and World Report* with a cover story about economic opportunities in the new Russia. "Competing Western companies," it said, were hiring former KGB agents to perform corporate espionage. *Bunch of jackals,* she mused. *From cold war to corporate war. Doesn't anybody ever do anything out of caring? Suppose we'd opened up our hearts when the Iron Curtain came down and sent entrepreneurs by the thousands to teach? And suppose we'd offered a half million of the brightest young Soviets free college tuition in the U.S.? At a cost of a few billion dollars, maybe ten, we would have pumped new life into our struggling higher education system.* That was David's idea, and it was a good one.

Once again the door opened and L.A. heard the murmur of voices from the meeting. Then it shut like a vault, releasing a sharp-faced young paper pusher who disappeared into another office and appeared again a moment later with some rolled-up drawings. He re-entered the conference room. Again the distant burbling of voices, mostly male. And again the sound was cut off abruptly.

They've got to come out sometime, to go to the john if nothing else, she thought. Then she realized they probably had rest rooms off the conference rooms. *Maybe I shouldn't be just standing around,* she thought. *Kinsey Millhone would be checking, scoping the place out. Finding out where the plumbing is. Hanging out near the Men's Room. Come on, LeeAnn. What you don't want to do is get stuck with Al Amin if you can bypass her. Ernst is the ticket.*

LeeAnn went back to the reception desk. "I wonder if you could direct me to the Ladies' Room," she asked the aloof Brit, who was typing something on the computer. She didn't look up right away.

"Just ovah thay-ah," she said at last, pointing. "Threw those doors."

"Thank yew." LeeAnn made her way across the lobby. Following the path where the corporate types had marched, she turned the cantaloupe-sized doorknob and entered a broad corridor with several doors leading off it. The first entrance on the right, marked "CONFERENCE," had, naturally, more high double doors, so you could bring the sedan chairs all the way through.

LeeAnn couldn't hear a sound from where she stood with her ear pressed up against the crack between the doors. It must have been expertly soundproofed. Not wanting to get caught, she continued down the corridor till she got to the door marked "GENTLEMEN." But she didn't want to be caught lurking outside the Men's Room either. Conveniently, a pink-and-black-marble "LADIES" was right next door, so she loitered in there for awhile, listening for sounds of the conference room door opening again. But it didn't.

She peed, though she didn't really have to–she was still dehydrated from the day before–then washed her hands and checked herself in the mirror. Her personal makeup artist had done a masterful job; the sunburn was barely apparent. And though wrinkled, her suit still looked good. But the high heels Audrey had made her wear were killing her, and exhaustion was making her dizzy.

Back out in the lobby she continued to pace; the sofa she'd eyed earlier was calling to her quite loudly. Actually, every horizontal surface in the room was beckoning. "Sit down on me, lie down on me," they called. At that point even the glass coffee tables looked tempting.

Finally, succumbing to her fatigue, LeeAnn lowered herself into the downy depths of the beige sofa nearest the conference room doors, and the receptionist noted her surrender with satisfaction. *All right, I may have lost this battle*, LeeAnn conceded with a bold return gaze, *but don't think I'm going to give up.*

At last, Sonja Al Amin exited the meeting. She crossed to the reception desk for a hushed exchange with the redheaded Brit that culminated in a slow turn to inspect LeeAnn. As Sonja headed reluctantly toward her, LeeAnn wished she could make a point of noting the time, but the watch in question would definitely have blown her image. And, she thought, it's such a cowardly way to complain.

"I'm Sonja Al Amin," Sonja said, giving LeeAnn the kind of "genuine" eye contact that is so patently false. "It's so nice to have you here," as they shook hands. She had a soft grip. LeeAnn was about to rise when Sonja sat down. *So she's not going to invite me back to her office,* she noted. *Great, this way I get to catch Ernst as soon as he comes out.*

"I was interested to see that your name is spelled the Scandinavian way."

Another cool smile. "I'm afraid my mother was a fan of Sonja Henie." LeeAnn asked Sonja where she'd grown up. Feeling as if she was back interviewing for her college newspaper, she elicited the information that Sonja had started out in business as her father's interpreter. LeeAnn dragged that out as long as she could, then switched over to business, trying to compose the kind of questions that any self-respecting corporate booster is obliged to respond to at some length. But Sonja wasn't having any more.

"So," she said, "what brings you here today? Your secretary said it concerned community relations." She fingered the wrinkled card that the Brit had evidently given her.

Wondering just how much she should say, LeeAnn began. She tried not to make it sound like she and David had deliberately landed on the island to look for artifacts, which, of course, is what they had done. And she left Stan out of the recitation; no sense getting him involved. ". . . great antiquity . . ." "Upper Paleolithic . . ." "Possibly connected to figures from the Russian arctic and Europe . . ." She heard herself saying the phrases as she handed Sonja the presentation she'd prepared. Sonja barely looked at it. "I'll be glad to pass this along to our people."

". . . And in any event, it's clear that a very careful examination of the entire site is called for . . ."

"And you would like to have the assignment," Sonja said in a cutting tone. "Ms. Spencer, you've said that your field work has been primarily in Europe. Is that right?"

"Yes it is."

"Then it's quite understandable you're not familiar with procedures here in the U.S." She was doing that thing with her voice that she had done on TV–pitching it so low that she was almost inaudible. "The Bureau of Land Management is mandated to do a thorough archaeological search before title is passed on any property they own. And I assure you that all requirements have been met." She placed LeeAnn's report face down on the glass coffee table, with all the rejection the gesture implied.

"I *intend* to speak with Ernst Vanderveer about this," LeeAnn said forcefully.

"I think *you* ought to know that I am the Project Chief," Sonja said with a sweet smile. "Mr. Vanderveer can't concern himself with detail." Which freely translated, LeeAnn realized, meant, *Not on your life, fat chance, over my dead body will you see my boss.* "This is a large company." Sonja rose. "I appreciate your coming in." *But get your ass out of here right now or I'm calling Security*, her expensive smile seemed to say.

LeeAnn stayed put. "I think I'd better inform you that a copy of this report went to the Smithsonian this morning, along with a call to the head of . . ."

". . . And I'm sure the Smithsonian will corroborate what I have said. This is *not* an open question. A qualified archaeological team has already signed off on Tree Island. You have no recourse." LeeAnn could see why she was successful. Petite, efficient, and soft-spoken as a small-caliber weapon, she was the perfect corporate tool. *However,* LeeAnn vowed, *I will not let myself get booted by this woman.*

Just then both double doors to the inner sanctum opened. Ignoring Al Amin, LeeAnn kept her eye glued to the doorway as the architect and contractor types began filing out.

Then, taller than the rest, Vanderveer appeared. As he came

through the doorway, he looked immediately in LeeAnn's direction, seemed delighted she was still there and started walking toward her. She imagined he was formulating some witty phrase to introduce himself.

I need to be on my feet for this, she thought, starting to struggle up from the downy depths of the sofa, but Sonja, catching her look and turning to see her boss, was too fast for her. LeeAnn saw her shoot Ernst a high voltage look that froze him in place. Then with a fast, "Let me find out if he can see you now," the small and deadly Sonja crossed the floor, blocking Ernst's path, and LeeAnn saw instantly she'd lost this round. She could almost hear the bell ring.

Sonja spoke a few syllables to her boss, and his face changed. It went cold and expressionless as he turned and left. The man who had seemed so open had suddenly vanished, along with all of LeeAnn's illusions about him. *He's just another one of those powerful men who wear a mask born of boardroom greed and lies to their wives. Do something, LeeAnn,* she told herself. But she didn't.

I blew it, LeeAnn thought as Sonja came back to explain about Mr. Vanderveer's busy schedule. "He asked me to give you his apologies," she said sweetly. "I'm afraid I'm going to have to ask you to excuse us now." *Get out. Hit the bricks, bitch,* her eyes said. LeeAnn continued to look in the direction where Ernst had disappeared behind waist-high swinging doors and then through another door beyond. Presumably to his own inner sanctum.

"Well, thank you very much." *I should have sent Audrey,* LeeAnn told herself as she beat a humiliating retreat to the parking lot. *Audrey would have obliterated Sonja and had Ernst carrying her gallantly through those double doors. Damn.*

Outside in the hot sun, she used the steering-wheel trick again to hoist herself into the Jeep, then sat there staring at the fake Native American Vacation Heaven Courtesy Parking sign, feeling her resolve build and her anger grow. *I'm not giving up,* she swore. *There's no way in the world you're going to win this one, Sonja Al Amin.*

She started the engine, which sounded most uncultured and uncouth, and drove around to the exit of the parking lot. There she stopped again to compose herself. LeeAnn never drove angry, never slammed the door and screeched off like they did in the movies. When she was upset, she sat as she did now, waiting to calm down, taking deep breaths and hanging onto the steering wheel. She listened to the guttural roar of the engine and breathed in the exhaust fumes that seeped up from underneath. Finally, she had to get going so she wouldn't asphyxiate herself.

She pulled into the parking lot at the state police. She wanted to sit for awhile once again and collect herself, but a squad car pulled into the slot next to her with two troopers in it, and she felt self-conscious. Did she look suspicious? Did she and Jeepers look as though they were loitering? *I better go in.*

The two men watched as she slid out of the Jeep. LeeAnn's legs were elegant, and in Audrey's gossamer pantyhose, they were exquisite. Their appreciation was eloquent if unspoken as they got out of the car and started toward the building.

Following them, LeeAnn found herself staring at their holsters. *All that power, s*he thought. One of them held the door open for her, then followed her in. She was surrounded.

Inside, the office had a surprisingly friendly look. It was nothing like the coldly sumptuous VHRI interior. And you didn't expect to slip on a puddle of blood like you might have at the old 24th Precinct in New York. It all looked clean and cheerful. Out in the small, partitioned-off waiting area there was a writing desk, which was a nice gesture. So many visitors in places like this have forms to fill out, and usually have to write on their laps.

The only thing that puzzled her was that behind the counter were signs that said WHITE and COLORED. Wha-at? Then she saw the other sign. NEWSPRINT. *Oh,* she thought, r*ecycling bins.* There was also a twenty-four-hour clock on the wall, so the officers could write 19:24 on their reports instead of calculating 7 plus 12 as LeeAnn always had to do.

A pleasantly plump woman with blonde hair was talking on the phone, so LeeAnn took the time to review the photo display in this office as well. It consisted of strictly-business headshots of five sergeants, all male, with their names and titles written below. Criminal Supervisor. Game Supervisor. This one in charge of people, this one of animals.

"Sergeant Dominick Russo" was the name of the Game Supervisor. He had dark hair, a nice face, and large, expressive eyes that were certain to be brown. The picture allowed LeeAnn to ask for Sergeant Russo by name as soon as the woman had finished her call.

"He's not here right now." Another woman came in the front door then, evidently back from lunch, and the desk clerk asked her, "Do you know where Sarge is?"

"I think he was down to the courthouse."

How did that woman know which Sarge she wanted? There were five, after all. "Sergeant *Russo* is who I'd like to see," LeeAnn contributed.

They looked at her. "Right. Sarge. He'll probably be back soon." LeeAnn perched on the edge of a chair and waited. Ten minutes later, she went back up to the counter.

"Excuse me, is there a pay phone around here?"

"Local call?" the woman asked with a smile as she handed the phone to LeeAnn the way people almost always did in Klamath Falls. But she didn't expect that of the state police; didn't they have to keep their phones open in case the river flooded or the Martians landed?

"Thanks. I won't be a minute." LeeAnn dialed her number, then she leaned on the counter and waited. Three rings before she got Audrey.

"Hello?"

"It's me. I promised I'd call."

"How'd it go?"

"Not great," LeeAnn said softly. "I'm at the state police."

"*Willingly?*"

"Yes. They handle artifacts. I told you."

"What happened at VHRI, did you see Vanderveer?"

"Well, yes, but . . . ," LeeAnn paused. "I'll have to tell you about it later."

"I'm glad you called," Audrey said. Her voice was very loud. "Jeff wants to talk to you. He says Kevin's managed to *crack the VHRI computer system!* Jeff! Jeff-rey!" she yelled piercingly. "He doesn't seem to be here. Sorry. I don't know where he is, can't seem to find him."

"Audrey, I'll be there as soon as I can," LeeAnn said. Then she hung up hastily. "Thanks *so* much," she said to the woman.

"Oh, no problem."

LeeAnn was perusing a copy of *Police Officer* about five minutes later when the woman at the counter startled her by saying, "Excuse me?"

"Yes?"

"Telephone."

"For *me?* I'm sorry."

"That's quite all right." She handed LeeAnn the phone again.

"I found him; I found Jeff," Audrey said in that gratingly loud New York voice. "He was out in the summerhouse, but it's important. He's got some *dope* for you," she said.

Audrey! Please watch your nomenclature, she prayed silently.

Jeffrey got on the extension then; LeeAnn fancied the women could hear every word he and Audrey were blasting at her. "This outfit's not good news, L.A. A couple of their projects seem okay, but in Mexico they've been doing nothing but polluting and victimizing. They've got a tendency to go into pure places and defile them, L.A. This is the sixth project . . ."

"Wait a minute, Jeff," LeeAnn broke in. "I'm . . ."

". . . construction sites on sea turtle nests, destruction of rain forests." Jeff was just barreling right along. "Mexico put up with it, Costa Rica didn't."

"There was a big protest over water rights. And from what I've been able to figure, it may not be just vacation paradise they'll be offering in Klamath at umpteen thousand bucks a night. The high-tech communications equipment . . ." The woman behind the desk was writing something by hand so the office was dead quiet. LeeAnn jammed the receiver to her ear to muffle Audrey and Jeff's voices, wanting to tell them to shut up but not wanting to sound suspicious. "Jeff, I can't . . ."

The building door opened just then and a man in rumpled civilian clothing walked in. LeeAnn recognized him from his picture, though he had added about ten pounds and five years. He looked like a nice person.

Russo included LeeAnn in an observant glance around the room that seemed to take in everything in a split second. Including the fact that she was hanging on their counter, using their telephone.

"I gotta go." LeeAnn quickly got off the phone, walked over, stuck her hand out awkwardly, and smiled. The sergeant had an aura of tobacco around him, the fragrant kind from pipes. "My name's LeeAnn Spencer," she said. "I'm hoping you can help me."

CHAPTER FOURTEEN

The State Police and VHRI

LeeAnn handed Sarge her archaeology business card, which he looked at quickly and then slipped into his shirt pocket. "Let's go back to my office." On the way, three male troopers called to him with a, "Hi, Sarge," a, "Hey, Sarge," and a, "How's it going, Sarge?" LeeAnn got the distinct impression from the looks accompanying the remarks that though the man was surely popular, this sudden attention had more to do with her and her ridiculous power suit then it did with his return from the courthouse.

"I called the Klamath Tribes," LeeAnn said, catching up with him, "and they told me that in Oregon, artifacts are under Fish and Game."

"Fish and *Wildlife*," he corrected softly, and she instantly got the significance. *Wildlife has rights, game doesn't.* It was an enlightened change in bureaucratic labeling that must have happened since the Sergeants' mug shots were hung in the office.

They passed a conference table with a big tray of assorted home-made cookies. In an office this size, LeeAnn thought, there was probably always an occasion, somebody's birthday or whatever. One of the things she missed, working alone as she did so much of the time, was celebrations like these and the sense of community that accompanied them.

By the time they got back to the door of the sergeant's office, LeeAnn was feeling almost at ease in police territory. But not quite. She had her own and David's trespass on Tree Island to confess before she could ask for help. Sarge looked like a nice confessor, however.

He opened the door marked "Sergeant Russo," and LeeAnn was surprised by a space unlike anything she would have expected in a police station. Two enormous stuffed birds dominated the room. A bald eagle with a small duck in its claws occupied the place of honor; a golden eagle was perched beside it. "Wow. These are spectacular," she said, going over to inspect them. "Obviously a gifted taxidermist."

"This one's been here since before I was. The other one was killed on the road. Guy couldn't help it. It was feeding on a road-kill deer and there was a steep bank so it couldn't fly away from the oncoming car." He looked at the bird affectionately. "We got a permit to have it stuffed." There was a tag on its foot. "That's an evidence tag," he said, seeing her look at it. "That duck the eagle's got I shot myself."

"Oh," she said.

"That's the comfortable chair," Sarge said then, pointing.

She sat. So far she was being treated wonderfully. Pictures on the desk confirmed a smiling wife and four handsome, olive-skinned teenagers. She thought she recognized the background. "It looks like they're at the Bay of Naples," she said.

"Yeah, my wife was born there; I met her when I was stationed in Italy."

"That's a lovely family," she said.

"Thank you." There was a pause.

"So. What's it like to be called Sarge?" she began, in an attempt at an icebreaker. "Does everybody call you that?" Her second biographical interview of the day.

"Heck, even my wife does," Dominick grinned. "I think it's a function of having been a sergeant so long. Too long," he said, swinging his feet up on the desk. Black issue shoes, black socks. A man identified by rank instead of name. LeeAnn thought, though, it didn't seem to have hurt Sarge to be stuck in a slot that way. Of course, some are just so well-adjusted, they do okay even in a hierarchical structure. Like Blackdog.

Sarge sat back, ready to listen, as though he had all the time in the world. So LeeAnn began to tell her story about the windsurfing trip, the goal of going all the way down the lake, then the stop for lunch on Tree Island. "I don't know if we broke the law going on the island," she said, leaning forward anxiously. "We didn't realize the vacation company had already taken title."

Sarge nodded with seeming empathy. "Were there any signs up?"

"No."

"Then you weren't illegal. You have a right to go on private property if it's not posted. If the landowner asks you to leave, then you have to leave."

"And we did."

"Good."

"I've always been terrified of being arrested," she said.

"Me, too." They laughed.

"But that's not what I came to see you about. It's what we found when we were there." Wishing she had a copy of the presentation she'd given Sonja, she told Sarge about the petroglyph, leaning heavily on its possible antiquity and the fact that she'd gone by VHRI first thing this morning and had been stonewalled by Ms. Al Amin.

"How do you spell her first name?" he asked, writing something on a yellow pad. "I noticed the paper had it one way and the television the other."

"It's with a 'J,' like Sonja Henie. She told me that they'd complied with all the requirements, that I didn't know what I was talking about, and that I had no further recourse."

"Are you concerned about their acting responsibly?" Russo asked. It seemed to be a test question.

LeeAnn held his gaze. "I just found out a few minutes ago a little more about the company." But then as she glanced nervously around, she realized she was treading on dangerous ground; there were several Kiwanis plaques on the wall, and she suddenly recalled hearing that Ernst Vanderveer had spoken at Kiwanis last week. For a civic booster, there could be no better dream come true than VHRI jobs. "It seems they were involved in a situation in Mexico," she heard herself saying, "that wasn't . . . ," she continued, losing steam even as she spoke, " . . . aahh . . . There were some problems," she finished as his brown eyes narrowed. She should never have opened her mouth.

"Where did you get that information?" he asked.

But LeeAnn rushed on—maybe he wouldn't notice that she didn't answer. "I just wanted to know if there's anything I can still do."

He was silent. Like a good interviewer, he seemed to be giving her space to talk some more, so she did. About the significance of the discovery, its resemblance and remotely possible connection to the Danube River figure. "I can show you what The Lovers look like," she said, picking up a pencil. He opened to a fresh page in a yellow pad and turned it around for her. LeeAnn quickly sketched both figures.

"Well, I'll have to agree with you, what you've got does not look like a representation of a usual Klamath hanowas. Not from what I've seen, anyway. How old do you estimate it could be?"

"We believe people came across the land bridge possibly between twenty-two and twenty-nine thousand years ago," she said. "I think the petroglyph is a representation of something that might conceivably have originated in that period."

Sarge thought for a while. "Tell me this. This petroglyph," he pointed to the drawing, "or the figure that it represents, would you classify it as an object of worship?"

LeeAnn pondered. "I don't know if the figures were worshiped per se. I can't guarantee that."

"An object of cultural patrimony, then?"

"Definitely. No doubt about that." The term meant "something important to the culture."

"Well . . ." Sarge sat thinking for a few minutes, weighing something in his mind. "There's a law called Senate Bill 61," he said, tenting his fingers as Stan had done at the Klamath Grill. "And that law is very specific if human remains or sacred objects–or objects of cultural patrimony–are found."

He got up and started walking around the office, which was a good sign he was getting involved. LeeAnn had been wishing David were there. The two would get along and maybe his presence would add some credibility. Sarge stopped pacing for a minute. "Could Tree Island be a burial site, do you think?"

"I don't *know* that. It might be. The island is artifact-rich, but the only likely funerary objects I found are the two olivella shells I mentioned, and that's no proof of anything."

"A landowner or anybody who finds a grave or finds a sacred object is obligated to call the state police." Sarge sounded as if he were reciting the code.

"Do you have a copy of Senate Bill 61 that I could take with me?"

"I think I can find one." But he didn't make a note; she hoped she wouldn't have to remind him.

"And I wonder if you could tell me who conducted the survey for BLM? How do I get my hands on a copy of their report?"

"Shouldn't be a problem."

"What will happen to the petroglyph?"

"It will be sent off to be dated."

"No, I mean, who will eventually keep it? Who does it belong to?"

"Well, according to Oregon law, it will be returned to the tribe . . ."

"Unless it's deemed not to be a Klamath Tribe artifact." LeeAnn interjected.

"Then I guess it would depend ultimately on whose land it was found on. If it's federal land, then the federal agencies are probably going to claim it, put it in the Smithsonian."

Sarge thought some more as LeeAnn did her best to get her message across by mental telepathy. *Please think the way I want you to think.* "Let's do a little checking," he said finally. He reached for the phone, dialed a number, then sat tapping an old-fashioned #2 yellow pencil on his blotter. He asked for someone named Charlie, but Charlie turned out to be unavailable.

"Well if he gets back in the next ten or fifteen, have him give me a call."

I guess that means I've got that much more time, she thought. *Use it, L.A., use it well. But don't push. Quit chattering. Try listening for a change.*

As they waited, Sarge talked about some of the problems his office was having supervising an area the size of Connecticut with four men. The officer in Lakeview, a hundred miles away, all by himself in one of the most artifact-rich areas of the country, had to deal–in addition to regular police duties–with fish, wildlife, *and* artifacts.

"No way we can do a job protecting it all; we just can't. But here again, I understand the tribe's point of view to the nth degree. They won't tell us where their sensitive sites are, because for one reason or another–and they have a lot of just cause here–they don't trust us. They've been tricked and bamboozled time and time again by government officials, so they don't really trust law enforcement in general."

"I can understand why."

"Here's an example of the frustration we run up against," he said. Sarge seemed glad someone was listening. "I'm out in the boonies one day and here's this car parked in a kind of unusual place. A few days later I was out there again working with one of my troopers and here's this car again. We looked it over, ran the license plate, and lights came on all over the place. This guy was cited for numerous game violations and he's kind of a general no-good, been in trouble with other law enforcement. So we're thinking, 'What's he doing out here?' We look around, can't find him, but we don't stress it since it's kind of an unlikely place to hunt or poach.

"Then a few months later, we sit down with some forest service people and their archaeologist. Turns out that right down the hill from where that car was parked was a major camp. The guy was probably a hundred yards away, robbing a site we didn't know was there."

LeeAnn heard a siren start up. Looking out the window, she saw a squad car take off, tires squealing, lights flashing. She was glad David wasn't a cop anymore. "And then we had a case of someone working with a backhoe on a Sunday morning; they were burying drainage pipes. When all of a sudden, this guy says this round thing fell back into the hole he was digging. And he says to himself, 'Oh my gosh, it's a skull.' So he quit.

"They *did* the right thing, but they didn't know the law, so they delayed getting a hold of us. The word spread in the community that this grave had been found. Then Monday was a holiday and when he went to show his boss on Tuesday morning, it was gone. It'd been dug. Someone came in under cover of darkness and dug it."

"Did you find out who?"

"Well it turns out there's another guy in the community who's known as an artifact hunter/collector, who came onto the property without permission and dug the grave. His reasoning was he was afraid somebody else was going to go in there and destroy it. Well, he's not a trained archaeologist, so what the guy did, he cleaned the bones . . ."

"Erasing all sorts of evidence."

"Of course. He tried to glue the skull back together, built a little cedar box–obviously he knows some stuff about tribal culture–lined it with some juniper, put the bones in there, took a sweet-grass wand, wrapped it with red twine, laid it on the top, then took it over and put it on the front porch of a tribal member in the area. Left a little note."

"Like leaving a baby on somebody's doorstep."

"Then the tribal member in turn called us. It may have been the funerary objects the guy was after. They're worth money."

"What about the bones?" LeeAnn asked.

"A skull goes for around six hundred. Lot of skulls on the black market right now. The thing that made this case tough to take is the

273

bones came from *within* the pumice layer."

"Mount Mazama!" Almost eight thousand years ago.

He nodded. "So we'll never know the way the body was lying, the position of it. They figured the guy may have died in the eruption."

"It was a male?"

"They think it was a male. Anyhow, invaluable information's been lost."

LeeAnn nodded. "Location, location. They say that about real estate, but it's really archaeology it applies to. Move it and you've lost its value. At least a lot of it."

"We know he was a young man and had a broken kneecap once. An old injury, not sustained at his death. Though that same leg was shattered when they found it." LeeAnn pictured the skeleton, how it would have been lying, one knee raised, as though he had been running when he was caught by the hot ash raining down. The image was a strong one.

"So he probably did die in the eruption."

"Might have. It would tell us a lot about the eruption if we knew that." The phone rang then. Sarge rested his hand on the receiver for a long moment. then he picked it up. It was evidently not Charlie; she heard a woman's voice. And pretty soon he called her Adriana, so it must be his wife. "I shouldn't be too late," he was saying. LeeAnn wondered how many people were saying that to their mates at this very moment.

She thought again about the man found under the pumice. She imagined his feelings as he was caught, the last moments of struggle, trying to get away from the overwhelming force, trying to breathe. She thought about all that could be told about his life in the silence of death.

Off the phone, Sarge continued. "Then there was a case where somebody built a dam to create a marsh for a hunting club. Turned out it was a major encampment; they ended up with bones floating up all over the place. The whole thing's shut down right now."

"So what's going to happen?"

"We don't know."

"Could the project be stopped?"

"It's a possibility. Particularly if there was any concealment or fraud."

And that's when the whole delicious potential of what she was doing first tried to enter LeeAnn's mind. The possibility of stopping VHRI, stopping it cold. Or at least getting the resort moved to some part of the Klamath area that wouldn't be damaged as badly. She resolutely shut the idea out. It couldn't be done.

Sarge was talking about another case now, "The guy was taking soil with human remains in it, and he'd sieve the bones and teeth and stuff like that out of it and crush them up to put in his concrete mix. When we got to him, he said he'd stop after one more pickup load! But that's before we had the law to protect against that sort of thing." He sat there thinking for a minute, then seemed to come back to the present.

"Of course, BLM's got some pretty strict procedures they have to follow when they divest themselves of any land." The light on Sarge's phone was flashing again; she hoped he'd pick it up pretty soon. Finally . . . Sure enough, it was Charlie. "Hey, Charlie. I wanted to check on the archaeo survey for Tree Island . . . who did it, how long ago, what they found, that kind of thing. Yeah. I'll wait."

He picked up the yellow pencil again and began toying with it, then started to draw five-point stars on the yellow pad, moving his pencil up, down, over, over, down. He colored them in. Then Charlie evidently came back on the line, because Sarge started writing things down. "Hmmm. Okay, I think that does it. Either way. You could fax it or you could mail it. That'd be fine." He hung up. LeeAnn hoped Charlie would fax the report. Right now.

"It all seems to be in order; they had a team look over the land, check it out pretty thoroughly. Your petroglyph might have been an anomaly. Could conceivably have been from off-island."

"Wouldn't that be like carrying coals to Newcastle?"

Sarge shrugged. "At least that's the case they could make. What I'm saying to you is you probably won't be able to *prove* it's from Tree Island. There would be no reason to hold up construction if it likely came from somewhere else. And in their favor, I'm surprised other significant artifacts weren't found, considering the age and potential importance of the ones you say you turned up."

"Does the BLM conduct the surveys themselves–with their own staff?"

"Sometimes. In this case they used a contractor. Their own staff is limited." He looked down at the paper. "This was an outfit out of Idaho that they use quite a bit." He turned the pad around so she could copy it off, *Danielson & Harkins*. "I know something about that outfit. The tribes up there think quite a lot of them. It's a good bet they checked pretty thoroughly."

"So, what do we do?" She was laying it in his lap. "What do I do?"

"You say you saw Vanderveer at his office, but couldn't talk to him?"

"That's right."

Sarge put his hand back on the phone as if he were considering something. "Maybe we ought to give him a call." *Yes!* LeeAnn wanted to shout. He picked up the phone and dialed information. LeeAnn knew the VHRI number by heart, having dialed it a number of times this morning, but it would have seemed a little pushy to supply it. The two birds of prey seemed to be staring in her direction as Sarge got the number from information and dialed. "Mr. Vanderveer please, Sergeant Russo, State Police. Okay, sure, he can give me a call," and he gave the number. LeeAnn looked at Sarge as he hung up. "Site visit, they said. He just left."

"So he's on his way out to Tree Island." She looked at Sarge, hoped he was thinking the same thing. He was.

"You doing anything the next hour or so?" he asked.

"Uh-uh."

"Well, I'll tell you. I think this is worth what we call a *knock-and-talk*. There's something I want to check on down at the marina anyway, so we'll just buzz out to Tree Island and see what you're talking about. It won't hurt to check."

LeeAnn stood up. Having forgotten her infirmities in the excitement of the moment, she almost collapsed in a heap of bones on Sarge's floor. The birds of prey looked on with mild interest as she recovered herself.

It took a few minutes for Sarge to clear his calendar. They waited out in the lobby while one of the women made a couple of calls for him. He asked if a fax had come in from Charlie, but it hadn't yet. He did give LeeAnn a copy of Senate Bill 61.

LeeAnn followed Sarge in his truck with the *Fish and Wildlife* logo on the side of it, down Oregon Avenue and California to the Pelican Marina on Front Street. She waited while he went to conduct whatever business he had inside. Probably to do with fishing licenses, she imagined. Then they walked together out on the dock to a tethered jet-prop inboard. Sarge walked around the boat undoing the snaps and lifting the canvas cover off.

"Have you met Vanderveer?" LeeAnn asked him.

"Yeah, last week."

"At the Kiwanis lunch?"

"Uh-huh. Seems like a nice enough guy." Sarge folded the boat cover and stashed it in a compartment in the stern. "Small towns are very grateful to big companies that come in and bring jobs," he commented then. But it seemed obvious, from the way he said it, that he was a good cop, that if they were doing something wrong, he wouldn't cut them any slack. Temptations must be enormous for people in his position.

Sergeant Russo had put on sunglasses and a cap before he got in the boat; the additions gave him a sporty look. You could see he was in his best element–outdoors, in nature, on his way to take care of something. You could see why his wife loved him and would overlook the small paunch.

When he fired it up, the engine sounded just as LeeAnn had imagined it would, a deep bass baritone, impressively thrumpy. Sarge looked up at LeeAnn, who was standing on the dock, contemplating her skirt predicament. Reaching out, he lifted her carefully by the elbows and placed her on the deck. She sat down, he cast off, and they were underway. The thrumpy engine canceled out the chance for any more talk, so LeeAnn let her mind roam free.

She looked over the side of the boat as it skimmed along, eating up the miles that had cost her so dearly yesterday. She studied the algae, all those uncountable millions of little particles that were suspended in the water. How incredibly abundant it was, millions of tons of it, available to feed millions of people. Billions of years of knowledge coded in every strand of its DNA. *Food that can maybe help give us back our wisdom,* she thought to herself.

And it all probably got started after Mt. Mazama erupted, providing all that rich mineral ash for it to feed on. A phoenix risen from the ashes, indeed. And as much at risk from Vanderveer's project, she believed, as the other ancient treasure she was trying to protect. And all of this was connected to what she was trying to do with the 22nd Century Group; somehow today it seemed as if it were all one project. Maybe it was.

Sarge pulled back on the throttle. Just then LeeAnn saw, and Sarge did too, the helicopter that was landing in the field behind the stone house. Sarge put the boat into neutral, picked up his binoculars; "I think it's Vanderveer . . . you want to take a look?"

"Oh, sure." LeeAnn lifted the glasses to her eyes and started wildly swiping them around the horizon. "A little to your left, I think, no, to your right . . . there, you got it." Sarge was so understanding. She saw Ernst coming toward the shore, evidently having spotted the police boat. Four of his architects or contractors were with him, including one who looked rather like a balloon in a business suit. And another man who looked like–*yes*. It was the guy who'd thrown them off the island; he was wearing fatigues.

LeeAnn focused her glasses on a close-up of Vanderveer. *These police binoculars are even better than our Nikons, s*he thought. "He has four men with him. *Sonja must have told him what I found and he probably wants to see it.* There's Vanderveer," LeeAnn said, handing Sarge his binoculars, "One of the men with him is the caretaker who, ah . . ." (she was going to say accosted), *"challenged* us yesterday."

"That's good. Then we can talk to him as well. We'll just get permission to take a look at the petroglyph. I'm sure Vanderveer won't mind."

And there's not a thing he can do about it if he does, thought LeeAnn with some satisfaction. *Thank heaven for Sarge.* She had wanted to come back to Tree Island so badly and here she was, not twenty-four hours later, with official reinforcement. *With the law. And Vanderveer's party has just landed, so we're here in time.* LeeAnn wanted to get to the petroglyph before they mishandled it. She could imagine the man she had nicknamed Rambo treating it badly. Dropping it, breaking it, defacing it, stealing it..

As they idled in toward the dock, LeeAnn watched Ernst, the eco-pirate, against the background of the island, coming to greet them, looking proprietary, and pleased to have visitors on his island–clearly he thought of it as *his* island.

"State Police. Mind if we come ashore?" Sarge was following protocol.

"My pleasure."

Sarge then tossed a bowline to the Rambo creep, who looked wary of the invaders like the good watchdog he was. He quickly secured the boat. The thrump-thrump of the engine stopped abruptly, and there was silence for a moment as Ernst Vanderveer flashed another extraordinary smile.

"Welcome to Vacation Heaven," he said in a wry tone that indicated he appreciated the absurdity of the name. Perhaps it meant something else in Malay or whatever language it came from. He looked straight at LeeAnn as he spoke. The look said, *'Yes I saw you earlier, yes I admired you, yes I avoided you. But here you are now. So everything's fine and you're really quite beautiful.'* She swore she could almost hear the faint Dutch accent in his thoughts. The Dutch East Indies Company strikes again.

"I'm Ernst Vanderveer," he said to LeeAnn then, just as Mayor John Lindsay had said "I'm John Lindsay," when she and Audrey had finally met him. Completely unnecessary to explain. Taking in Ernest's features, LeeAnn saw what had struck her as strange about his blue eyes when they'd watched his arrival on television. There was a small segment missing from the bottom of his left iris, which gave the pupil an odd keyhole effect.

LeeAnn looked down and her eyes caught on his elegant eel-skin boots, then his brushed cotton pants and the blue polo shirt that said Princeville on the sleeve. He'd changed his clothes since she saw him at the office. He was younger than David; his body was younger. Muscles like steel cable, she saw. He seemed to wear a slightly amused look on his face; perhaps he always wore it. It gave her a funny feeling. The day was hot and she was sweating profusely.

LeeAnn stood to get out of the boat. Her sling-back heels made her unstable on the deck, and the tight silk suit felt rather like the wrapper around a piece of melting taffy. Being handed out of the boat was an ignominious experience, with both Ernst and Rambo reaching out to grab her, and the other men watching. She jumped with as much agility as she could muster under the circumstances, and landed on the rotting dock. Then she surveyed the slippery rock ahead, where there was no dock any more. She felt hobbled, as though she had bound feet.

Reluctantly, she took the arm of the man who had yesterday screamed at her to get the FUCK off Tree Island. As he helped her negotiate the rocks, it felt as though she were being ushered down a rocky aisle–a female sacrifice in a straw-colored power suit. LeeAnn was uncomfortably aware she was the only woman present. As she reached dry ground, LeeAnn said thank you and looked into Rambo's face long enough to see that he was steely cold, possibly quite clever. Definitely a nasty adversary.

Sarge stepped ahead of LeeAnn then and shook hands with Vanderveer. "Sergeant Dominick Russo, Fish and Wildlife." LeeAnn liked the word *wildlife,* he said it well.

"Glad to see you, Sergeant. This is our chief contractor, Douglas Santini," Ernst said, introducing the balloon.

"Call me Doug," he said. There was a ritualistic shaking of hands then, with a recitation of names that LeeAnn instantly forgot. "This is Ms. Spencer," Sarge said, indicating LeeAnn.

"Nice to meet you, little lady." Santini must be even older than LeeAnn had guessed, using phrases like *"little lady"*. He looked like New York but he said his offices were in San Francisco and Singapore. Santini had an important basso voice that resonated from a pouter-pigeon chest under the white starched shirt with the massive gold cuff links. Like a lot of very heavy people, he had great presence. Three underlings with rolled-up drawings under their arms stood behind him looking uncomfortably hot. There was not a breath of wind today.

"I'm sorry, I didn't get your name," LeeAnn said then directly to Rambo. She needed the name so she could get Kevin to investigate him. Of course, this maneuver meant she had to offer to shake his hand.

"Oh, didn't I introduce you? I'm sorry." Ernst said quickly. "I'm sorry. This is the man who's going to be caretaking the Tree Island site for us. Paul, um . . ." Ernst looked at Paul for help.

"Trautman," Paul supplied.

So he *was* the same man who'd brought Stan out here, the one Stan said he didn't like. This guy could win an unpopularity contest. "To what do we owe the honor of your visit, Sergeant?" asked Ernst.

Sarge explained their mission with a minimum of words.

"Well, now that's very interesting. Very goodt," he said, with just the faintest "t" sound at the end of "good."

"We'd like to take a look if you don't mind."

"No problem. I'll be anxious to see it myself. Why don't you lead the way," he said to LeeAnn. They started toward the rock pile, LeeAnn's high heels sinking into the dirt up to the hilt with every step.

"I suppose what's found belongs to Vacation Heaven, eh, Sergeant?" Ernst asked as they headed up the path.

"I guess that would depend," Sarge said, "on whether it turns out to be a sacred object."

"I see."

"Or an object of cultural patrimony."

LeeAnn noticed that the old World War II jeep had been moved; it was now parked directly in front of the house. "Say, does that jeep run?" asked Sarge. "It's quite a relic."

"Oh yes," said the architect. "Paul's been driving us around in it. He's been putting in his own time tinkering with it." Whereupon the men got into a brief discussion about the mystique of old vehicles that LeeAnn didn't bother to follow. Sarge and Vanderveer walked ahead of the others through the old stone house. The rags were gone from the corner; the room had been cleaned up and the floor swept. There was a cot and various belongings of Trautman's in the old living room. The whole group of them trooped out through the back to stand in front of the rock pile.

"LeeAnn, if I may call you that?"

"Of course."

"I will ask you to show us where the famous petroglyph is and we'll be happy to lift the rocks for you."

"Okay, we put them back as nearly where we found them as we could," LeeAnn said. She had to look carefully to be sure which one it was. She was beginning to perspire heavily.

"It should be under here," she said then. "Yes, right here," as she spotted the familiar shape of the square, radiator-sized rock near the bottom of the pile. Paul sprang forward and started moving the smaller rocks that were on top of it. Then one of the underlings started to help. "You want to be very careful as you lift those up." LeeAnn was uneasy about letting them handle the ancient relic, but she couldn't even think about bending over to help in that tight skirt.

"Okay, *that* one, you see right under there. Please, *please* be very careful not to break it." Her heart started to pound as she realized she was about to see the petroglyph again.

Another assistant jumped forward now. The three men laboriously pulled the rock over and laid it down carefully on the earth. It was *blank*. For a moment she couldn't comprehend it. Then she realized she must have the wrong one; it was the rock next to it. Several of the huge blocks had been about the same size and shape.

"I'm sorry. It must be that one. The one right next to the one I thought it was." Of course, getting to it involved moving more rock. One of them slipped and rolled. *"Don't touch that rock*! she wanted to shout at Paul; she hated the idea of his touching it. But then they turned it over and there was nothing on the face of *it*, either. LeeAnn caught a look from Sarge. *Have I lost him?* She was ready to kick off her shoes, pull her skirt up to her hips and wade in. Only she knew that would not help the situation.

Then suddenly there was an insistent chirping from somewhere. It sounded like David in the supermarket. Everyone looked at everyone else till LeeAnn realized it was coming from her. She had to pull her sleeve back and start pushing buttons till she finally silenced David's big watch. 1:23 p.m. "Sorry," she said, feeling humiliated. Everyone's eyes were on her.

"An appointment?" Ernst inquired, smiling. He glanced toward his helicopter and then back at her. "The person you are meeting is, I am afraid, quite out of luck." Now there was just a hint of a British accent overlaying the Dutch.

"No. No appointment." LeeAnn stared at the latest rock offered for her inspection. At the corner of it was a tiny fragment of the design, which was clear to her but might not be clear to anyone who wasn't trained. "This is part of it," she said. "When you see the whole design . . ." Then she realized they weren't *going* to see it; the petroglyph wasn't here any more. It was gone. The shock went through her body, hot and then cold. She looked at Ernst, and he stared back at her looking puzzled, that keyhole gaze directed solely at her. *Did he know? He had to. They had stolen it.* She looked at Sarge, then back at Vanderveer. "It was here yesterday." She spoke quietly, but the accusation was unmistakable.

"Would you like us to check over here?" Ernst said in a faintly patronizing tone, as though he thought her dotty.

"No, it wasn't over there." He was being so frigging helpful.

"Well, we'll just take a look anyhow." It was no good, of course. A dozen heavy rocks turned over; nothing. "I'll tell you what we'll do," Ernst said then. "We'll have the whole pile checked tomorrow. You were having a picnic, probably had a beer or two . . ."

"We didn't," she interjected.

"You were in a holiday mood and you're not sure where you left it. Perhaps you hid the pieces away somewhere else?"

So we could get to them again and take them away, is that what he was implying? "No, we didn't!" During this whole unrewarding treasure hunt, LeeAnn had sensed that Sarge's belief was being pulled back and forth. And now, snap, there it went like an errant garter; she could feel his opinion shift. LeeAnn Spencer had been thoroughly discredited by Ernst Vanderveer.

"I'm sure we can find it tomorrow," he said to Sarge then. "Meantime, perhaps before you go we'll be able to show you the rest of the island and what we have planned for it." It was a statement, not a question. "And ah, LeeAnn? Wouldn't you like to come with us?" As if she had a choice.

" . . . So he puts Sarge up front and squeezes me in back with the fat contractor and off we go on these dusty, bumpy roads . . ." LeeAnn had kicked the flimsy shoes off when she came into the house and was pacing up and down the living room in stocking feet with dried mud on them that was cracking and falling off onto the white Chinese rug that was normally her pride and joy. At the moment she didn't care.

Jeff and Audrey sat on the sofa, their eyes following her back and forth as though they were watching a tennis ball. "We had to go through this whole routine. He was being charming and I was seething because I had to be polite. I wanted to rip him up and down with my fingernails." *What fingernails?* she could hear Audrey thinking.

"Then we had to suffer through this grand tour, dust in our mouths and our eyes, the whole time having him go on and on about the gallons per hour for the stupid geothermal fountains they're going to build. They design it so people who have nothing else to do and all the money in the world can flit from one sacred spot to another, never touching down anywhere else. They go into pure places and defile them. It makes me sick; it all just makes me sick. He's already got the petroglyph, I know he has! And the whole time Sarge is looking at me like I'm a space case. I can't tell you."

"Yes, you can," Jeff said, encouragingly. "You're doing very well."

"I felt like an idiot. I know they shuffled those rocks around."

"The old shell game, huh?"

"He's a master at it, I'm sure. They've been pulling this shit on people for four hundred years. The Vanderveers."

"It's my guess the Sonja witch is in on the whole thing," said

Audrey. "She's probably the ringleader."

"Did you show them the original petroglyph in the wall of the house? The one Stan told you about?" asked Jeff.

"Of course. That was my ace in the hole. On the way back I demanded that we go look at it so I could show them the lichen on it."

"And?"

"The petroglyph was there, but the lichen was gone."

"Whew. Pretty slick," said Jeff.

"Do you think they've got the actual figurine and they're hiding it?" Audrey asked.

"Maybe. Couldn't tell. Ernst is the kind of person that you think maybe you could read. At first I thought he was nice, but I believe he's just extremely smart and extremely devious. Led me right into the trap."

"So did you tell Sarge that you thought they'd done a switcharoo?"

"He certainly knows what I *think* happened. I couldn't exactly make that kind of accusation–not in so many words."

"I don't see why not."

"But unless some evidence turns up, Sarge told me on the way home, he's got no grounds to go back in there and tell them we just don't believe the BLM report. 'I'm sorry about your petroglyph,' he said, 'but there's not a thing more I can do.' Then he left me in the parking lot at the marina. So now they're going to level the island and put a concrete top on the whole thing." LeeAnn was feeling pretty distraught.

"Maybe," Audrey said. "But no point throwing in the towel yet, not if we can delay things. You know how complicated final permits are for a thing like this. I can go to bat on eco-impact–Phil Wilson maybe could help me. He owes me. His company's got some major clout at the EPA. We can snoop around a little, see about the geothermal output, waste disposal, and everything else. Putting five hundred people on that island–I don't care if half of them *are* kezillionaires, as far as we know, they still have to go to the bathroom."

"They've probably been super-careful about all the environmental impact stuff."

"I'll call Peter," Audrey went on. "There's got to be some way to hold off construction. Throw a flag down. If we can slow things down a little bit . . . By the way, when do you think you'll hear back from Vince?"

"How do I know? A month on the Eastern Shore. Who knows when he'll call in for messages."

Jeff said, "What's the name of the people who did the archaeological survey?"

"Danielson & Harkins, out of Idaho. Boise, I think. I asked Sarge more about the process on the way back. Usually the BLM picks the contractor, but sometimes the buyer does, especially if they're in a hurry."

"Or if they have money."

"Isn't that putting the fox in charge of the chickens?"

"It's assuming the firm has integrity, and apparently this one does. Sarge said they were highly regarded by several of the tribes." LeeAnn sighed, then sat down finally on the big, gray silk ottoman that she'd made when they first moved in. "I don't know what we have, really, with the petroglyph gone. I came on really strong to get Sarge involved–just like I did David. Do you know it's the *second* time in two days I've taken a perfectly nice cop type and made him look stupid? I don't know what it is with me."

"Just a frigging ball-breaker," Audrey contributed gratuitously.

Jeffrey had gotten up to make a phone call. "Hi, it's me. I'm with Audrey and L.A. Can I put you on speaker?" he said, hitting the switch.

"Hi there, guys," said Kevin in Bostonese.

"Okay, here's the situation . . . ," Jeff started.

"Hi Kevin," the two women said together. "Thanks for getting all that information," LeeAnn told him. "You were great. Now we want some more."

"Here's what's happened today," Jeff said, giving his partner a quick summary. "We need to see what you can find out about an archaeological consulting firm in Boise. *Danielson & Harkins.*"

LeeAnn interrupted. "And also anything on a Paul Trautman. He's the caretaker for Tree Island."

"He works for VHRI?" In Kevin's accent, the word "work" had no "r" in it.

"I think so. I imagine he's on their payroll or the contractor's."

"You want credit caahds, police record, phone bills, employment . . . ?"

"And military record if any. I'm almost certain there is."

"You got it. Anything else?"

"Pull up the EPA reports on Tree Island," said Audrey. "See if anything catches your eye."

"And Vanderveer," said Jeff. "Deep background stuff."

"Like is he mean to his polo ponies?" Audrey threw in. "We're just

285

groping around in the dark. There's got to be some good dirt somewhere."

"I suspect there is. Well, let me get going on this."

"You sure you have time?" LeeAnn asked.

"For you darlings, no prob. B.D. and I will get right on it."

"Oh, hi, Blackdog!" Audrey called. "Is he right there?"

"He's listening."

"How's he doing with his new responsibilities?" Jeff and Kevin had taken Blackdog on vacation to a wild horse ranch in Utah, where he'd romanced and won a wild dog named Ayla who'd been about to be shot by a neighboring rancher. She'd come back to New York with him, and was expecting.

"He's fine. He wants to know if you'd like to adopt a puppy."

"I'm not sure. Just one more thing." LeeAnn's conscience was troubled. "How illegal is this? This procuring of confidential data?"

"Hey, if you knew what these companies do on an everyday basis, *mild* by comparison."

"Am I going to get you in any trouble?"

"No."

An hour later, horizontal on the living room rug, an exhausted LeeAnn had drifted off to sleep. She was awakened by the hum of Jeff's tiny portable printer. He'd brought his Mac in from the summerhouse, plugged into the phone line, and now was printing out a fax from Kevin.

"What've you got?"

"Rap sheet. Wait a second." He pulled it out and handed it to her.

"Paul Trautman" it said at the top. She looked down the page.

"This is amazing. Look at how much is here, and how easy it was to get. Unbelievable!"

"The information age," said Jeff, "is giving way to the espionage age. Everybody's doing it."

LeeAnn was quiet while she absorbed the information. "He's been around Klamath for awhile. Looks like about three months, from the charge cards." *This is strange, examining somebody's life like this.*

"Klamath Falls. What's he been doing here?" Audrey wanted to know.

"Well, he's put some serious time in at the Red Dirt Tavern for one thing. Got quite a tab there."

"That's a biker hangout."

"Fascist skinhead type?"

"Ehhh, not quite that bad."

Audrey couldn't resist any longer. She grabbed the paper away from LeeAnn. "Here, let me read it to you. Okay, he was born in California, raised by his mother. It says his dad did time in the state pen."

"What for?"

"It doesn't say. Discharged from the Marines after two years and four months. Apparently picked up by VHRI Mexico, that's the first time they show up as an employer, heavy equipment operator. His next job for them was security. Immediate superior, Sonja Al Amin. Ah-hah, look at this, Kevin even got his prescriptions. Prozac?"

"Is that what it says?" LeeAnn grabbed the paper back; she was used to this with Audrey. "Boy, they get everything, don't they? I didn't see that." She read on. "He subscribes to *Soldier of Fortune, Guns, Martial Arts*, etc. He's got a cellular. Looks like there's a number he calls a lot in California."

"Maybe it's his mom," said Audrey.

"Where did he stay in Klamath?"

"Doesn't say. It shows a motel for a couple days. Then nothing."

"Do you think he's been staying out on the island?"

Jeffrey was collecting another page out of the printer. "Danielson & Harkins in Boise looks clean at this point," he reported. "And that's all Kevin has right now."

"Are you thinking that Trautman has the petroglyph?"

"I wish we had some way of getting close to him."

"Oh, I know! I have an idea," said Jeff.

"You know *what*?" He said, getting up, "I think I may have an evening of drink ahead of me."

"Isn't this *sudden*?" said Audrey.

"I thought I'd go check out that tavern where Trautman hangs out."

"Oh, Jeff."

"It's the one place he goes. Chances are he'll come in at some point and I can find out something about him. He doesn't know me. So I get to play private eye."

"Are you sure?" LeeAnn's expressive eyes went through Jeff, questioning him. "*Are you sure you want to do that?*"

"How many times in my life, L.A., do you suppose I'll have the opportunity to play a *straight skinhead*?" He was going into his giddy mode now. "I hardly *ever* get to act any more–this'll be fun."

"You know you'll have to be careful."

"Yes, Mother."

"Jeff, these people at the Red Dirt are blue-collar, anti-New York, anti-black, anti-gay."

"LeeAnn, do I look gay?" And of course he didn't. He picked up his Mac and his printer and started out of the room. "I have to go and create myself a persona."

"Other than a nerdy epidemiologist," Audrey said.

"Do they have pool tables at the Red Dirt?" Jeff was pointedly ignoring Audrey's teasing, getting into his role already. His speech was taking on a western twang.

"Every tavern in Klamath has pool tables, I think."

"Ah, good." Then he was out, the old wooden screen door banging behind him.

Fifteen minutes later he came back in a grungy outfit that looked just a bit too deliberate. "Excuse me, Officer," from Audrey, who was sprawled on the sofa, "but do you have the time?" They all laughed. It was one of the ways Audrey used to regularly humiliate the undercover cops who hung out at Broadway and Ninety-Sixth.

"Am I that obvious?"

"Frankly, yes."

"Well, how's this?" He pulled out a tacky business card he'd made up on his computer. "New and Nearly New Billiard Tables and Supplies," it said. "I thought I looked pretty good," Jeff said, surveying himself in the gold-framed mirror over the couch and stroking his beard. "We're lucky it's not just liberals who are hairy these days. What's missing? A baseball cap. That's what I really need to complete this outfit."

"And a couple of broken teeth." Audrey was trying to be helpful.

"You want a baseball cap?" LeeAnn asked.

"Yeah. Like one of the boys."

"Well, David's are out in the hall closet." She headed into the hall, opened the closet door and started rummaging. There was David's windsurfing cap that said *Big Air*. No good. And an FBI hat his uncle had sent him. *That will never do.* A welding shop, Heaton Steel on Spring Street. *Ah, that's perfect,* she thought. She took it back and offered it to Jeff.

Still regarding his image in the glass, Jeff reached out and set it on his head without examining it first. "Hmmm. Not bad. What do you think?"

The green hat with faded lettering did look good with the soft cloud of fine dark hair, and the beard. Jeff looked like a skinny mountain man. "You'll blend right in," Audrey said. "Maybe they won't even notice the Nikes. You really ought to have construction boots."

"I'm sure David's wouldn't fit me."

"Unless we stuff toilet paper in the toes." LeeAnn started to laugh. And somehow it struck them all as terribly funny, thinking of skinny Jeffrey Longhair Levine striding around a red-neck tavern with balled-up toilet paper in the front of his boots.

It was that scene of hilarity that David must have heard. For he walked in from the kitchen just as the two women, laughing, were adding finishing touches to Jeff. "Not the earring. No, take your earring out."

"But I have a hole there."

"Well then, plug it." Said Audrey. "Tell them you used to play the guitar. Then just beat the shit out of them at pool. That'll impress them." That Jeff could do, no problem. His after-school job, when he wasn't doing commercials, had been working at the Broadway billiard parlor.

"I'm counting on my game to endear me. Just a few sharp moves, enough to let them think they're discovering a talent, and the rest of the night I'll fumble."

"Hi." The words fell like a dead weight. David was standing in the dining room in front of the fish tank, looking at the spectacle in front of him–this visitor from Gotham that he didn't much care for, being dressed up by LeeAnn and Audrey. And wearing *his* favorite baseball cap.

"He's still going to be obvious as shit," Audrey said. "Don't you think so, David? Does this guy look like a redneck to you?" LeeAnn winced. This was not exactly how she wanted to bring David up to speed on the events of the day.

David's eyes went to LeeAnn. "What happened to *you?*" he said, staring at her muddy panty hose and her wrinkled skirt. So the cat was not only out of the bag but beginning to yowl rather ominously–she hadn't given up on Tree Island. In the next few minutes as LeeAnn tried to explain, it seemed to her as if she was telling the whole story not only backwards, but badly. Starting with Ernst's island tour, then the brush-off at VHRI and the trip to the state police. Then the facts on Paul's rap sheet that Kevin had dug up. Too much had happened to tell it logically.

David didn't seem happy.

"Last night you were going to leave it alone."

"How could I?"

"Okay, you reported it to Russo. That's all you needed to do. They'll find the pieces of the petroglyph tomorrow. You probably just didn't know where it was."

"David, they've hidden them!" *Do you believe me or not?"* It was getting out of hand. LeeAnn and David never argued, and particularly not in front of other people.

"I don't know what you're doing going into other people's TRW's, LeeAnn. I don't see it. I really don't see it at all. All you're going to do is get hurt."

"I think we know what we're doing."

"Do you realize that pulling credit reports like that is a five-thousand-dollar fine and three years of not being able to use the system?"

"Kevin can use the system," Jeff announced evenly. "That's his business." The other side of Jeff, the harder side, was starting to come out, the New York city-streets-Jeff that LeeAnn hadn't seen in years. "You got any problem with my borrowing the hat, David?" The two men looked at each other for a moment.

"No. Help yourself," David said and marched out of the room.

"He made his point," Audrey said. "But what are we going to do?"

"Maybe I shouldn't use this business card," Jeff said. "Maybe that's fraudulent, not necessary."

"Oh, go ahead. Don't let David rain on your parade."

Jeff looked at LeeAnn. "I'm sorry, L.A. This is not helping your relationship, is it?"

"David will get over it," LeeAnn said, but she wasn't so sure. "I'll talk to him."

"You still going to go?" Audrey asked Jeff.

He looked at LeeAnn, but she didn't know what to say. "I think I will. What can it hurt? David's pissed off already. Maybe I can get to be buddies with Trautman."

"Yeah, right," Audrey snorted.

"Wish me luck."

"Come here and let me get some lipstick on you." Audrey gave him a sticky kiss on the cheek, which he wiped off, and LeeAnn hugged him. Then Jeff was out the door. LeeAnn and Audrey sank down on the couch and looked at each other.

"I need to go talk to David," LeeAnn said, but she didn't make a move to get up. Why was she talking about it with the woman who might take him away? It was all very confusing.

"Are you sure it's a good idea? Personally, I'd let sleeping dogs lie."

"I have to do it."

"Well at least take a bath first and change your clothes. You're not going to get anywhere with a guy if you're looking like shit. I'm going upstairs." She left.

LeeAnn went into the bathroom, turned on the shower, and got out of her ruined suit. It would take a miracle of dry cleaning to fix what she'd done to it today. She had one foot in the tub when the phone rang. She went into the bedroom to get it. It was Kevin.

"LeeAnn, there's something interesting that's come up, I thought you'd want to know about it right away. It's about Trautman."

"What about him?"

"Well, I think we already assume from the previous stuff that he's not exactly a sweetheart, but . . ."

"What did you find out, Kev?"

"I just got something through Interpol. It seems that he may have been involved in a death in Mexico."

"*What!?*"

"Water rights was one of the issues with the VHRI project there. It seems they were diverting the water from the villagers, forcing them to sell their land. There were some protests and somebody died. An old man named Espinoza. "

"Violently?"

"Allegedly cardiac arrest after getting roughed up pretty badly. That's what I get from Greenpeace. Anyway, it got hushed up. Trautman was investigated but never formally charged with anything."

"Oh Kevin, now I'm worried."

"He was also slapped on the wrist for some stolen artifacts, but VHRI bailed him out."

"Wow. You're sure?"

"Looks like he was exporting Mayan artifacts . . ."

"Kevin, you don't know what I just did. God, I'm sorry."

"What did you do?"

"I let Jeff go off to the Red Dirt Tavern on a spy mission to go snoop on Trautman, play pool with him. Now I'm scared."

Kevin was silent for a minute. "Don't worry, LeeAnn," he said at last.

"Do you think I should call over there?"

"No, absolutely not, you'll blow his cover. Jeff knows how to take care of himself. I'll give him a call later." Then he hung up. She had to try to believe him. Kevin knew all about worrying. When his mom died, he had ended up raising five younger brothers and sisters that were a pretty wild bunch. *If he says not to worry about Jeff, then I shouldn't,* LeeAnn told herself under the shower. But she didn't believe herself.

She dressed in some clean shorts and her old, much-laundered panda bear sweatshirt that she had cut the sleeves out of. The sweatshirt was a little warm, but it was her favorite garment because it made her feel brave. It was a Saturday kind of garment, and even though it wasn't Saturday, it seemed appropriate.

Halfway out on the path to the cabin to talk to David, LeeAnn stopped abruptly. Was this a dumb thing to do? There were two schools of thought in a situation like this: let him cool off, or nip it in the bud. LeeAnn looked up in the sky, wondering if the stars would give her an answer. But it was one of the few hot, humid nights of the year in Klamath and it was overcast. No stars. She'd have to decide for herself.

Finally concluding that doing nothing was worse than doing something, she continued on to the cabin door and knocked. David came and opened it. "Yes," he said, standing in the doorway. "What's up?" She didn't answer.

"Come in," he said. So she went in and sat down gingerly. The cabin didn't feel friendly and off-duty any more. It looked the same as it had the night of the harness lesson, but it didn't *feel* the same. And the lump in her throat was back. It was the absolutely worst time to talk, but she knew they finally would, anyway.

CHAPTER FIFTEEN

Artifacts

One of LeeAnn's tears fell onto the small cube of gray rock that she held in her right hand. In her left was an old, bent, formerly silver-plated nut-pick that had belonged to Maggie's mother. Sitting at the table in the breakfast/weight room, she was carving a circle on one side of the cube, making a wind-rock for David, and thinking about all that they'd said to each other last night. She was trying to be careful. Born klutzy like her dad, she was aware she might injure herself at any moment. She remembered vividly the time that Cliff stabbed himself in the hand with a wood chisel, trying to fix a leg on the dining room table. With a towel wrapped around the wound, he'd gone around to the elderly Irish doctor in a brownstone on ninety-fourth, who had asked if he wanted a shot before it was stitched up. When Cliff said yes, the guy had hauled out a bottle of whiskey. *Which sounds pretty good right now*, LeeAnn thought, *I could use a shot. Of course it always sounds good until you drink it.*

After the scene with David, she thought she'd be awake all night. But probably because of her exhaustion from the day before–and the day before that–she'd slept like a log, once she knew Jeff had made it home from the Red Dirt Tavern. She had crept out to the summerhouse around 2:00 a.m. when the dew was on the grass to find him safely asleep, his bicycle hanging on the wall, his Mac beside him and his cellular, his link to Kevin and the world.

It was after 11:00 now and she was waiting for him to get up so she could find out what he'd found out about Paul Trautman and artifacts. Audrey had risen early and was already off picking the brain of an ecologist over the hill in Medford.

LeeAnn sighed. The rock that she was crying on at the moment was an almost perfect cube shape, granite, about an inch and a half square. She had taken an ordinary square-ish rock from the garden, imagining it had been there all these thousands of years, which it probably had. It was a rock that the native peoples had kicked, or used, or seen, or at least walked over.

She had been working on it for more than an hour, all the while thinking it might help with her confusion to use her hands–and it did seem to be good therapy. She could almost remember having done this before–only her ancestors probably hadn't used a nut-pick and a Swiss Army knife.

With an authentic hammer-stone a friend had given her, she had smoothed and shaped the rock until it was pretty uniform; then, using her knife and the nut-pick, she had carefully carved four circles, one on each side, leaving the top and bottom blank.

Now she was placing dots in the center of each circle, four round mouths blowing wind. Another of her tears dropped on one of them now, darkening the middle of the circle where it fell. *Bull's-eye.* The thought that caused her tears was that this wind-rock might end up being a farewell gift.

As she worked, LeeAnn had been castigating herself for all the things she believed she'd done wrong that had finally caused the relationship to fail. *And they all came out of fear. She was always "too busy, too worried, too scared."* David's exact words last night, she recalled.

Live the magic, not the fear. Live the love. That message was so clear. In different ways it had been clear many times in her life, but she'd always retreated, was always afraid of not pleasing someone. Now it was the fear that she would be destroyed by breaking up with David and wouldn't be able to do right by the Summer Project. That her dream would fall apart because of her own weakness and ineptitude.

Of course, I always think I can do anything when I start out. And worse than that I imagine it won't interfere with anything else I'm doing. Deepak Chopra says we really can *do anything if we set our minds to it, that it's just a matter of our attention and our belief. So I suppose, taken to the nth degree, we could concentrate our minds by rubbing on a wind-rock and cause the wind to blow. The ancient people believed that they could affect the physical world with their thoughts, and it looks like that's what we're coming back around to,* LeeAnn thought. Chopra talked a lot about the nature of matter and our ability to influence it.

Maybe he can help me make some sense out of this, she mused. She got up and went over to the hall closet, got a Chopra tape out, and laid it on the shelf by the back door. She would listen to it in the car when she went up to Chiloquin later. Today was the day she had an appointment with a tribal leader.

She paused to hang on the chinning bar for a minute or two. Did five pull-ups, which was about all she could manage. Her leg muscles were still hurting, but her arms were almost okay. She was getting a lot better at pull-ups from the windsurfing.

Back to her carving. LeeAnn considered whether she was taking a chance just giving this to David, whether in itself it might trigger the ending. Men often question the significance of a gift from a woman, as though it was intended to bind them. *Of course, I suppose it is,* LeeAnn thought, *but is that bad?* The idea was to bond, not bind. There, the wind-rock was done. She set it aside gently.

It was 11:30. She checked the buttons on her Dick Tracy watch. She didn't want it going off again. Jeff was still sleeping, apparently, so LeeAnn picked up her new "Power Deck" by Lynn Andrews and shuffled it. The cards had arrived this morning from Maggie, with a note that said to pick a card every day and read it. Bless her heart. She always had such good ideas. Although she didn't have many answers for herself, Maggie Spencer was always a good guide for the next traveler down a given road. For she had known all of the false beginnings, and had hit most of the dead ends.

LeeAnn fanned the cards out in front of her. There were beautiful images on the back of each. The directions suggested that you pick out one to reflect on each day, *which is kind of the same idea as the Year in Parentheses,* she reflected. *Concentrate your thought focus on one thing at a time.* She closed her eyes, moved her hand over the cards, picked one, then opened her eyes.

"Grief," it said. *Oh, no.* She felt a stir of terror in her heart, then admonished herself. *It's about David and me, the message is only about grieving for the loss of the comfortable, sheltered relationship we've had. That's all it is. It's not about the death of someone I love.*

"Grief deepens you," she read. ***"It allows you to explore the***

perimeters of your soul . . . The pain of grief is not the only teacher in this life, but looked at properly, with awareness and an open heart, is one of the greatest teachers of all . . . What is lost can only come back to us again in higher ways . . ."

Just then the cordless phone she could never remember to keep with her rang. She ran in to retrieve it from the living room couch where they'd left it last night. Maggie, it had to be, and it was. "I was just thinking about you," LeeAnn said, and then promptly burst into tears.

"What is it?" Maggie asked.

"Everything," her daughter answered.

"Okay, let's take it one crisis at a time."

So she told Maggie about the VHRI trip, about getting Sarge involved, and about the shell game on Tree Island with Ernst Vanderveer. Then the scene last night with Jeff dressing up in David's baseball hat, and how David had stalked out to the cabin. And about all of this having happened *after* she'd promised him not to get involved. "So we had to talk, at least I thought we did. When I went out there, he said, 'What's up?' which is always such a hostile phrase and we went downhill from there. At one point he told me he's serious about Audrey."

"Seriously?"

"That's right."

"Oh. Did he say why?"

"She's fun, she's beautiful, and she doesn't worry." LeeAnn was sniffling. "And I'm always too busy, too worried, and too scared." Then she had to laugh in spite of herself. "Hard to argue with that."

Maggie was silent.

"He told me I lose sleep over every little sparrow that's ever been born in the world."

"You do."

"I told him she's just as hyper as I am, just as involved in the Summer Project. 'Yeah,' he goes, 'but she's also having fun, she's living. When do you plan to start living?' he asked me." LeeAnn took a deep breath to hold back her sobs. "It's crazy, Mom, because they'd be about as good for each other as . . . I can't think of anything."

"Oil and water. It's just a crush."

"Well, maybe, but . . . I thought if we could just sit down . . . I wanted us to understand each other, but it was awful, because that was when

I ended up asking him point blank what he felt for Audrey. 'Do you really want to know?' he said to me."

"Not a particularly encouraging response."

"He said, 'When I see her, I just get this feeling . . . ,' and he touched his throat, 'it's like right here. I've never had that feeling before.'"

"Oh, sweetie, I'm sorry."

"And I found myself empathizing, even feeling good for him. I couldn't help but celebrate for a friend . . .'" Her voice cracked, comically, ". . . and I *am* his friend, but oh God, it hurts. For awhile there when we were talking about it honestly, I thought I knew what it would be like to be without envy or fear. And then it hit me. All I could feel was that I was losing him." LeeAnn heard a click on the phone. Call-waiting. "And I told him so."

"Which may or may not have been a good idea," Maggie said. "Wait a sec, I'll be right back, let me get this call."

While LeeAnn waited, she felt the panic rising again, as it had last night. "Everything we've built together is going to be shit," she'd cried in David's arms, thinking about the woodwork they'd scraped in the living room and the greenhouse they were going to build.

"I'm still here, I love you," he said, trying to comfort her. "I'm not going anywhere." She hugged him tightly. "Not right now."

"So what does *that* mean?" she'd said, instantly angry. "Next week? Next month? If it's going to happen, I'd lots rather it happen now," she had told David, gasping between sobs . . . anoxia again. Oxygen deprivation. And you can't live without oxygen . . .

"Okay, I'm back," said Maggie. "That was your brother."

"At this hour?" LeeAnn said. "Is he on his way up here?"

"He didn't say. I told him I'd call him back."

"I hope he's leaving now." It was almost noon, so Peter was either just going to bed or just getting up. When he drove up from Berkeley he was usually late getting ready and didn't arrive until the wee hours, when she and David were asleep. "What's going to happen to us, Mom?" Usually she called her mother Maggie; today was an exception. "What's going to happen?"

"Hey, you can't push fast-forward and find out–life isn't a video-tape."

"The awful thing is that I brought her here. Home delivery of about the nicest little package on the East Coast."

The conversation was all over the place, but that didn't matter with Maggie. LeeAnn could say things to her that she couldn't say to anybody else. Of course, Maggie wasn't one who knew much about successful relationships; she hadn't had one in years. She saw a lot of men, probably had the most active dating schedule of anyone LeeAnn knew, but never seemed to find the right one.

"It looks like Jeff's up," LeeAnn said as she saw the barn-like door of the summerhouse open. "So, my life is in a state of total chaos. Kind of like the world. David and I have reached the all-or-nothing phase. Everything we do from now on is critical. Either he's headed out the door and gone or he's going to do a one-eighty and be right back."

"Would that be okay with you?"

"I don't know. Even if Audrey were to be gone right now, I think it's taken the bloom off the rose." She thought of the yellow roses outside the coffee shop across the street from the fairgrounds. "I don't know if we'll ever feel the same way about each other again."

"I wouldn't be so sure. Try to flow with it. But keep your head above water."

"Easier said than done," LeeAnn said with a laugh, "when I'm drowning in my own tears." *Cliché city.* She held the phone against her shoulder then, picked up the wind-rock and the nut-pick again, and started going around and around the circles, making them deeper.

Remembering that she also needed to nurture her mother, LeeAnn switched the topic. "So how's your life?"

"Well, my algae just arrived. The UPS guy's getting to be a real friend. Big box this time. It's sitting right next to me on the dining room table. So I feel connected to Klamath again. And I just went to a training that was really good." Maggie began to talk about her algae business.

LeeAnn's mom would be sitting by the phone at the window, where she could look straight out and down eleven stories to the Hudson River. Maggie lived in a very peculiar building. The entrance was weird; it had a natural wind-tunnel effect, no matter what the weather was. That had always fascinated Peter when he was little and they used to go to their pediatrician in that building. Winter or summer, fair weather or foul, Maggie always had to struggle to keep the door from slamming shut on one of her children. Their mother had to protect their very *lives* when they went through that door to the doctor's office. That had impressed Peter; he always found the experience exhilarating. She had moved into the building right after the divorce because she got a good deal on an apartment there. At that point in time, she'd been planning to go to medical school. But then she decided massage therapy was better for people. Massage and algae. "So how was the exam?" LeeAnn asked. It was an anatomy test in her exercise physiology class. "Oh, listen to me. Latissimus dorsi, infraspenallis, rhomboid, supinator . . ." She stopped and sighed. "I have no idea how I did." Maggie was both a procrastinator and a perfectionist, not a good combination. School wasn't easy for her.

"I'm sure you aced it," said LeeAnn.

"Oh, I hope so, we'll find out soon enough. Anyhow, I'll let you go," she said. "You'll be wanting to talk to Jeff. Give him my love, and David, too, *and* Audrey."

"I will. We'll be having an official 22nd Century Group meeting tonight when Peter gets in, to talk about the finances." "Then tomorrow we're going to have what was billed as the Celebration dinner, though I expect with most of the invitations gone and my partnership in the pits, I may have a little trouble celebrating."

"You'll do fine. Let me know what happens. Oops, there's another call again." LeeAnn hung up, realizing she'd forgotten to thank her mother for the cards she'd sent.

Jeff was out in the yard, she saw, checking on the pole beans and discussing things with Sillvester, who was raising his backside up high at the end of each pat, which he usually didn't do. Jeff went back into the summerhouse momentarily and returned with a printout from his computer. He was reading avidly as LeeAnn headed out the back door to meet him. Whatever he was studying on that piece of paper he'd received seemed important.

"Good morning," she said.

"Hi." She saw the excitement in his eyes. *He does have some news.* The spring in his step was at about a level four, but then he started to move more slowly, like a battery running down.

LeeAnn was puzzled. "Find out something?"

"Yeah, I did. The bad news is I'm hung over."

"You weren't going to drink."

"Yeah, but what are you going to do? I had four hours to hang around, act un-bored, eat corn nuts, and order drinks."

"You were going to do O'Doul's."

"I did for a while. Which didn't go over big at all, so I had to switch to the leaded stuff. Those guys don't trust anybody who isn't half snockered. 'Have a real beer,' they kept saying."

"You obliged."

"LeeAnn, I had to or they'd have suspected me."

"How ridiculous."

"Anyway, I had too many."

"How many too many?"

"About six. I think I'm dying."

"You dummy," she said affectionately. "You were supposed to eat algae if you were going to drink so you wouldn't feel this bad. Let's walk, get your blood going." They started touring the garden.

"So, you still haven't told me the good news. What's on that piece of paper you're hiding from me?"

"Why don't I finish briefing you about last night first?" He was being a fellow detective reporting in.

"*Oh*-kay."

"Sarge told you there's a lot of skulls on the market, right? They're coming from somewhere. So I wanted to find out if anybody around the tavern had been talking about artifacts."

"Especially Paul." Jeff nodded.

"Did it work?"

"Yes and no. I realized I didn't have a prop, so I took that replica of a rabbit trap that David was making from the yard."

Oh, great, thought LeeAnn.

"I hope he doesn't get upset–I told those guys I found it when I was out pissing in the woods."

"Then they wanted to know where."

"Of course. I told them I had more stuff I wanted to sell, or I might even be interested in buying some."

"Wasn't that a little too obvious?"

"Then Rambo Trautman came in about 10:30. I tried to talk to him. Didn't get very far. He's a wary individual, that one." They were investigating the cherry tomatoes. Jeff selected one and popped it in his mouth.

"He didn't suspect . . . ?"

"No, of course not. Don't you have any confidence in me? And then

I beat the crap out of him at pool."

"What'd you do that for?"

"Partly for the fun of it and partly to see how he acts under pressure."

"And?"

"Poor loser. It's a wonder he didn't go out to his truck and get one of those guns."

"Oh, Jeff," LeeAnn sighed.

Now both Jeff and LeeAnn started grazing on the tomatoes. "Okay, Jeff, it's been long enough. What do you have there that you want to show me?" LeeAnn said, looking at the paper in Jeff's hand.

"Some bank records from First Idaho Federal."

"And?"

"Well, it might not mean anything, but you're always saying to speculate wildly," Jeff said. "Right?"

LeeAnn nodded. "So may I?"

"Go ahead."

"This guy Harkins is an archaeological consultant, right?"

"Right."

"So we gotta figure he pulls down, what fifty, sixty, a hundred grand a year?"

"Knowing what archaeologists get paid, probably no more than fifty, which is more than I've ever made."

"Anyhow, stay with me here. So about the time his report on Tree Island would have been filed with the BLM, he takes out a loan."

"Which at least means he wasn't bribed."

"LeeAnn, the loan was to buy a four-hundred-thousand-dollar house!"

LeeAnn whistled. "Where'd the down payment come from?"

Jeff looked at her. "Exactly. Before that, his mortgage payment had been three hundred and eighty-one dollars a month including taxes."

"So maybe his uncle died and left him some money."

"Maybe. We don't know, but it's a peculiar coincidence."

"Audrey says there's no such thing."

"Audrey *constantly* says that."

They were quiet then, giving LeeAnn time to think about VHRI tactics. "So in this case, it looks like VHRI used the carrot technique as opposed to the big stick they used in Mexico."

"Maybe both. Since this guy was pretty straight-arrow in the past, who knows what it took to get him to cave in?"

LeeAnn nodded.

"Other than the mortgage, he looks clean. Kevin's trying to check into VHRI records, see if there was a payment to John Harkins above and beyond the consulting fee."

In spite of herself, LeeAnn realized, she was feeling better. Her battered heart had stopped bleeding temporarily as she got involved in trying to figure things out.

"There's more. Kevin says the other thing that's interesting here is some payments made to a laboratory for carbon dating. Different from the lab he usually used. See?" Jeff showed her on the paper.

"Right when he took the loan for the house." She glanced up at Jeff. "*Wildly* circumstantial."

"Mmmhmm. How would the survey have been conducted, L.A? With a whole team of archaeologists?"

"Probably not, just one, plus a couple of assistants. He must have had an assistant."

"He might have found a lot of artifacts on that initial survey."

"Maybe even burial grounds, and so VHRI had to hush it up."

"Ergo the big payoff to Harkins," said Jeff.

"Ergo? Really, Jeff."

"And that would also explain why Trautman was sent on ahead, probably to camp out on the island. To dig up the stuff, hide it, and then get rid of it. Maybe that's why he told me he might be able to fix me up with a collector."

"You asked him that?"

"Why not? He said he'd give me the phone number of the guy, but then I asked him to write it down. Maybe he had second thoughts at that point, because he got the number wrong. On purpose or by mistake. There is no such number."

"Clever."

Just then Sillvester, who had been rolling in the dirt, took off like a shot through the garden. "Somebody's here," LeeAnn explained to Jeff. "Silly is our doorbell."

Sure enough, pretty soon the little white terrier Melanie came barreling around the house, toenails skittering on a rock as she raced after Sillvester. "Good." LeeAnn said. "It's Stan. We may be able to find out something from him. But let me do it." Jeff nodded as Stan, dressed in coveralls, came ambling around the back of the house, preceded by that nice round Santa Claus belly.

"Stan, this is my other friend from forever, Jeff Levine."

"Well, very pleased to meet you. This is Melanie. You from New York, too?" LeeAnn watched as the two men shook hands, Stan's arm-and-hammer arm, and Jeff's slim one in a sleeveless T-shirt.

"Jeff and Peter went to Mandel Music School together when they were seven."

"Oh, what did you play?" Stan wanted to know.

"French horn."

"Well, I used to play cornet. A couple of brass players," he said to LeeAnn. He beamed at Jeff.

After chatting for a few minutes, they all went over to look at the hot tub Peter and David had put in the previous year. Peter had improvised some pretty wild piping and it had rebelled finally, and quit; the tub had lain there silent and unusable now for months.

Stan explained at some length what was wrong with the piping and Jeff nodded sagely at regular intervals, though of course LeeAnn knew he couldn't care less about half-inch nipples or plumbers tape. "Oh, I know about Peter and his salvage techniques," he said to Stan. "I built a house with him once when we were teenagers. Cheap is what we call it."

"You're just as bad," LeeAnn threw at him.

"No, Peter's cheap, I'm resourceful."

"Well," Stan finally summed up. "We're going to have to redo this whole thing in PVC; I don't know if you want to bother with it."

"Oh, I think so," said LeeAnn, though she wasn't sure she really wanted it to work. "Peter would be disappointed."

"You ask me," said Stan, "you do better to take your bath in the house. These useless things. All the knickknacks down in the Bay Area have got them."

"All the what?"

"The knickknacks, the homos." Jeff and LeeAnn looked at each other, then Jeff burst out laughing.

"I never heard it put quite that way. Is that a Klamath expression?"

"My dad used to call 'em that. He was a merchant seaman. He told me whenever they'd find one onboard ship, they'd just toss him over." Stan, of course, was delighted he'd been able to amuse his new friend. Jeff looked away so Stan couldn't see his expression. "So, *Ms.*

Spencer," Stan said. "What'll it be?"

LeeAnn's mouth was still hanging open. "What do you think it will cost?" she said finally. "The plumbing."

"Aaaah. Not too bad. Don't worry about it. Well," Stan said, reading her silence as yes, "Let's get this water drained out. I think I probably got most of what I need in the truck." He pulled out a measuring tape. "So, did you stop on Tree Island like I told you to?" he asked LeeAnn. "Did you get to see that petroglyph in the wall of the geezers' house?"

There it was. The subject had been broached, and Stan had been the one to bring it up. LeeAnn glanced significantly at Jeff. "Yes, I did see the petroglyph," she said, "and it's quite a story." She began filling Stan in, wondering how much she should tell him, and then hearing herself spill *all* the beans, because she could never help it.

"I know Russo," Stan said when she got to the part about Sarge. "Good man."

"Yeah, but his hands are tied. Even if he believed me, which I'm not sure he does anymore, I've got no proof. Nothing for him to go on. I've got to do something. The figures on that rock may represent the icons of a very ancient faith," she said, and then immediately worried how this devout Christian would feel about an earlier religion. "Or if not a faith, then at least a cultural system."

Stan was silent for quite awhile, which was unusual for him, as he went about measuring for the new pipes. Finally, he said, "That's pretty crummy if VHRI destroyed the petroglyph or hid it. You don't dare show disrespect for anybody's religion. '*For all people will walk every one in the name of* his *god . . .*'" LeeAnn and Jeff exchanged a look. "That would be like taking a crucifix and smashing it."

Jeff nodded almost imperceptibly. *Go ahead and ask him, LeeAnn,* his nod was saying.

Stan was still talking. "I think I told you how I felt about that Paul fellow. He's not exactly on the up-and-up."

"Oh, I agree," said Jeff, who then went ahead and told Stan about his foray to the tavern, and his run-in with Paul Trautman. "Tough guy; he thinks he's still in the military. The quiet type, you know, time bomb. Likely to wipe out a bunch of people with an AK-47 one of these days."

"That's about how he comes across to me," Stan agreed. "I gotta say it's pretty ballsy of you to go to the Red Dirt. It's a rough place."

"Not as rough as the Broadway Billiard Parlor." Jeff smiled.

"The problem is, Stan," said LeeAnn, "I can't go back to that island and Jeff can't go there either. But we need to find out what they did with the petroglyph."

"Or if there's other stuff they're hiding. Bones or . . ."

Stan caught on. "You mean you need somebody to go out there and check on it for you? That's easy. I could do that."

"You'd do that, Stan?"

"I don't see any . . ."

"Wait," Jeff interrupted. "Before you answer, before you join our little crew, I think you ought to know you'll be working with a knickknack."

"Who?" Stan looked bewildered. "Paul?"

"No, me. I'm one of those. So's my partner."

"Oh. Oh, well. Thoughtless of me . . . my comment. I, ah, I'm sorry." The anguish was apparent on Stan's face.

"So I don't know if that's going to be okay with you."

"Not for me to tell people how to live." Stan was looking Jeff directly in the eye. "I'm . . . glad to know a homosexual." And then he stuck his hand out once more. Jeff took it and then the moment was done.

"So, Stan," LeeAnn started firing questions. "How many people do they have working out there? When are they going to pour the foundation? How much time do we have?"

"Which question do you want me to answer first, LeeAnn?"

"The time frame."

"I think I can help you on that. They've got it laid out in stages. I've got a site drawing out in the truck. Let me go get it, then we'll take a look-see." They walked toward the house together, at which point Jeff's cellular went off. He took the phone out of his shorts pocket and unfolded it.

"Hi, yeah. Yeah, I got it. Where are you going to be? I'll give you a call back." He folded the phone up again. "That was Kevin, just wanting to talk."

"Uh-huh."

"His partner," she explained to Stan as they went into the kitchen. "The other knickknack."

Can I get you guys something cold–iced tea? Smoothie?" Jeff asked.

"Sure. Sounds good to me–whatever you're having," said Stan, who was embracing everything at this point. Next thing you knew,

LeeAnn thought, he'd be in the hot tub.

"Be right back." He disappeared out the other door to the driveway where his truck was parked. LeeAnn began clearing away the wind-rock tools and the old *New York Timeses* that she'd spread out on the table when she was carving.

"So," she said to Jeff who was rummaging in the refrigerator. "It wasn't enough I got Sergeant Russo involved, and David. Now we're dragging Stan Porter into it, too."

"Pretty willingly, I'd say," Jeff commented as he started cutting up fruit.

"Yeah, but as far as David's concerned . . ."

Stan was back then, unrolling a drawing and showing them where the initial construction would take place. "They're going to be leveling this whole part of the island, using the fill to extend out over here." He indicated the south and southeast edges where hundreds of tumbled boulders made up the shoreline. "That'll be done in Stage I."

"And that's exactly where I was thinking there might be something, if there is anything on the island."

"If you look at it geologically, that's where there might be lava tubes." Stan said nodding.

"Caves? Stan, do *you* think there might be caves on the island?"

"Well, there's plenty of them over here," he indicated on the map, "west of the lake, on the ridge . . ."

"Really? So there might be caves on the island?"

"There might."

"Do you know when they're going to start the earth-moving?" Jeff asked, as his Vita-mix began to roar.

"Well, it's only been a couple days since they took title but they've already got an air compressor out there at Squaw Point, getting ready to drill for the blasting. I'd say they're moving pretty fast."

"Of course," LeeAnn said, wincing. "They would be blasting."

"Most of that'll be here," Stan showed her, "and over here."

"Then they'll pour concrete over it," LeeAnn said, "and all hope for finding anything will be gone. When do you think they'll start blasting?"

"They'll let us know a couple days ahead. 'Cause they have to put up warning signs and all. So not before next week, I think. That's when Paul told me the barge'll be here and they can start moving the heavy equipment."

"So we've got till Monday, is that what you're saying?" This was Thursday.

"I think that's a safe bet."

"Well, good. What we need to do is see if there's any trace of that petroglyph anywhere on the island."

"You know where I'd put it?" asked Stan. "The lake . . ."

"And ruin the lichen growth," LeeAnn interrupted. "Oh, don't say that!"

". . . where they know where it is," he went on, "and nobody else does. Wouldn't find it in a million years."

LeeAnn sighed. "You're probably right."

"But what I was thinking, if I had stuff to stash, like a lot of artifacts . . . ," Stan went on.

"Or bones," Jeff interrupted.

". . . and I didn't want to attract a lot of attention moving them . . . I'd lock them up in the geezers' trailer. It's completely boarded up, got a new padlock on the door. And new tires."

"It has new tires on it? It didn't when we were out there," said LeeAnn. *So they must be getting ready to move it.*

"VHRI's had a bunch of surveyors out there in the last month." Stan paused, deep in thought. "I guess it's possible they could have been collecting and hiding stuff."

"Do you know what they keep in the trailer?" LeeAnn inquired. "Is it ever open?"

"I haven't seen it open. I could check around, though, see if I can tell what's inside."

"Well, be careful."

"Oh, I will."

LeeAnn watched as Jeff poured out three glasses of a greenish smoothie and brought them over to the table. Stan looked slightly concerned at the color. "Algae delight," Jeff said proudly, which may have been a mistake, LeeAnn thought; locals tended to be suspicious of the algae, but Stan looked at it, hard, then took a big drink right away.

LeeAnn sniffed at her glass. "Wonderful bouquet," she said, before she drank.

"This is very good," said Stan. "Thank you. You know I never had any of this before."

Jeff had a question, "Here's what I'm wondering. Why would a

company as big as VHRI be careless enough to stash potentially dam-
aging evidence in an old trailer? They'd get it off the island at night,
wouldn't they?"

LeeAnn said, "Unless they went with the rule that you don't do anything unusual. The path of least risk is often the one where you deliberately *don't* take any special precautions. Particularly when you're dealing with a small town where everyone's actions are instantly noted–and
communicated. Klamath is the kind of place where it is not easy to keep
a secret."

"Or Paul might be hiding stuff for himself. The enforcer traditionally has a scam of his own that he's operating, regardless of his loyalty
to the boss. He feels it's his entitlement." They all thought about that for
a moment.

"Let me ask you this, Stan," LeeAnn went on. "Has the trailer been
moved, do you know?"

"Always been right in that spot as far as I remember. Why do you ask?"

"Because that's a common ploy. When there's surreptitious digging, sometimes they use a trailer with the floor cut out and just move
it around on the site."

"Clever."

"You know, Stan, I hope we're not endangering your job with
VHRI."

"Don't worry about it."

"I know it's a conflict of interest, in a way, but . . ."

"There's no conflict here. I'm still doing the job they hired me for,
but that doesn't make what they're doing right. Just because they
bought Tree Island doesn't give them the right to mess with history or
people's religions."

"Well, I better get going," LeeAnn said, finishing up her smoothie.
"I have an appointment to see someone at the tribe." While Jeff and
Stan continued to talk and Jeff washed out the blender, LeeAnn went to
her room and quickly changed into a sundress. Shorts wouldn't be
appropriate to go see the tribe. She ran a brush through her hair and then
headed out the door. Stan was standing at the back of his pickup, opening and closing little drawers and compartments.

"Hope I didn't offend your friend," he said. "Like I said, that was
thoughtless of me."

"Minor, Stan. Jeff's been through it all."

"Well, of course I . . . I don't have any prejudice toward those people. Actually I do, or I did. And I hope he likes me . . . I didn't mean . . . uh . . ."

"Don't flatter yourself," LeeAnn laughed.

Stan caught on that he was being ribbed, started with his spell-able, "Heh, heh, heh," and then went on into a regular guffaw. "Don't flatter myself, huh?"

"I'm sure he likes you, Stan." LeeAnn patted him on the back. "But he's already got somebody." She got into the Jeep and turned the key. It caught, but just barely.

"Doesn't sound too good," said Stan.

"We need a new battery," LeeAnn told him. Then she turned her headlights on, because everyone was supposed to use them all the time on Highway 97; it was a dangerous road.

Approaching the old, long-closed industrial complex where the tribe had its offices, LeeAnn pulled into a large parking lot that was nearly empty. Just a few trucks; this was pickup country. At one of them, an old man with long braids and sinewy muscles was intent on something under the hood of his fairly new Toyota extra-cab. He didn't look up as LeeAnn climbed out of the Jeep and went into the office at the front of the building.

Inside, two women sat tending things; LeeAnn's appointment turned out to be basically with both of them. The women were middle-aged and heavy-set mainstays of community life among the tribe; they were organizers, fundraisers, caregivers, and workhorses for their people. LeeAnn knew both by sight but not by name and she didn't ask now; it would have seemed awkward. She took an office chair and they sat down and talked. The older of the two was babysitting a grandchild who slept in a plywood cradle-board propped on a chair.

Neither woman knew much about the Tree Island transaction; one said the tribe had been called in late on it, and the whole thing had been hurried. "The way I remember, somebody went over and got taken around on a tour, but didn't see anything significant. Course you know the lake was never in our reservation. Just up to the shore of it."

"Do you think there's a chance the island could have been a burial ground, or a sacred area a long time ago?"

"Sacred area, yes, burial ground, no," said the grandmother.

"Why?"

"Because our people did not bury," she said.

"Not till the white man came and told us cremation was wrong," the other woman added.

"Of course, now it's very popular among the whites," said the first woman, looking at LeeAnn.

"So there's no chance of a burial ground on Tree Island, you think?"

"The Piute buried," said the older woman.

"Oh. That's interesting." LeeAnn felt bad she was not telling them all that she knew. But she couldn't share the discovery of the petroglyph, particularly since she couldn't produce it. It might have raised all sorts of questions. And tribal politics were complicated. LeeAnn decided it would be best to disclose the whole picture only to the cultural affairs specialist. After all, he'd been appointed to that job. Also, LeeAnn had no idea where the women stood in the official structure of the tribe.

As though they had read her mind, the older, keener of the two women, the one who wore wire-rimmed glasses said, "You should be getting all this from Gordon. I'm sorry he's not here, but he hadn't taken a vacation in years."

"I know." *The month of August.* "I'll just have to wait for him to get back." LeeAnn said something then about how much she admired the man.

"Did you know he's got some of his writings in a book now?" the grandmother asked.

"No, I didn't. Really? What's the name of it? Can I buy a copy?"

"Oh, yes. Shaw's Stationery ought to have it." She wrote down the name. *The Stories We Tell.* "It's real good."

"I'll buy it."

"He's got a story in there written in the old style."

"They'll have it at the museum or at Shaw's."

LeeAnn was thinking about that book when she finished chatting with the women about twenty minutes later. She said goodbye to the baby then who was awake now, playing with a painted gourd on a stick. She went back outside, climbed into the Jeep, and turned the key. Click. "Shit."

Then the old man was beside her Jeep. He'd appeared silently and stood there waiting for her to speak to him.

"Dead battery," LeeAnn said. "I left my lights on. My battery's old."

"I have cables."

"Can you give me a jump? Oh, great!"

He was already headed for his truck. LeeAnn watched as he drove it over, positioned it opposite her Jeep, and then got out and started to hook the cables onto his battery. She could have climbed out and raised the hood on the Jeep for him, but she discerned that he preferred it this way. So she just waited till he had everything set. He went back and sat in his big Toyota and gunned it while she turned the Jeep engine over. The old V-8 caught instantly. They grinned at each other; LeeAnn got out to thank him. Pay obviously wouldn't be part of this.

"Would you like to have a drink of water?" he asked.

"Oh, yes, I would." He poured her some from a container in the back of his truck and LeeAnn took it. "That's right from the spring," he said.

"*Rivers of Light* water it would be if it's from around here."

"Is that what they call it now?" They chatted for a while. His name was Andy and he was one of the amazingly healthy old people of the Fort Klamath area. *Eighty-nine years old*, he told her, and his smile showed he had a full set of teeth. Whatever it was, the rugged climate, the mineral soil, or the algae in the water that fertilized the gardens, old people were wonderfully alive here.

Andy seemed to enjoy reminiscing. "I remember," he said, "when my father took me into town the first time and I touched the walls of houses that weren't soft. I was amazed. Later," he said, "when I was in my teens, and went into town on the weekends, you just expected at some point to be hauled out of the truck and beaten up by the whites, just for the fun of it." He seemed to hold no bitterness.

"I haven't told many people this," LeeAnn said, "but I'm actually a tiny part Klamath or Shasta myself."

"That's very good," said Andy.

"I used to live in New York and when I found out, I moved out here."

He told her that people who were only part Klamath and moved away often came back here to die. This is the place we believe humans began, you know. It's a good place to be buried."

LeeAnn was sure it was. "I don't know much about the beliefs of the tribe," she said then, wanting to get off the subject of death; she was still thinking about the card she had drawn this morning.

"I'll tell you something then," he said. "The number five is important. We have five fingers on each hand," he held up his hand, "five toes, then we have two arms, two legs, and a head. That's five, too," he said indicating with his hand. "The west is important," he gestured toward the west. "It's where our future lies. The east is our past." He nodded his head toward the east. "The Klamath way," he said finally, "is to forgive the whole house." Then he was silent; evidently he was through talking.

LeeAnn thanked him again, climbed back in the Jeep, and, hoping to heaven she would remember not to turn off the engine before the battery had a chance to recharge, she headed back down Highway 97, thinking about tribal heritage, and the fact that for the first time, with Andy, she'd felt included. Nice man.

CHAPTER SIXTEEN

Threatened

When LeeAnn got back into Klamath Falls she drove to the county museum, which was housed in the old armory. She parked and went into the cool, quiet. She spoke with a woman in the gift shop whom she knew slightly and bought a copy of *The Stories We Tell*.

After paying for the book, she stuck two dollars in the contribution box and went on into the exhibit area. *I just want to connect for a minute with it,* she told herself as she almost ran over to the place where the eleven-thousand-year-old sandal made of sagebrush bark was displayed. *My very favorite thing in this museum.* Not only was the artistry, the eye for beauty apparent, but also the imprint in the sole where the owner's heel had rested seemed to have much of the person's life energy still in it. Was it a woman, a man? Who was this person who had walked the earth eleven thousand years ago? What had that person thought? What did she–or he–believe in? LeeAnn had no idea, of course, but it seemed to help just to look at the shoe.

Then she went back out to the Jeep, which started right up. She gazed at the old train cars, the log cabin, the sheepherders' wagon on the lawn of the museum, then drove off. Several blocks down Main, she slipped into a parking space in front of U.S. Bank, where she planned to get some cash for a celebration–or consolation–dinner with Peter and the group tomorrow night.

Still caught up in her own thoughts and not wanting to go into the bank just yet, LeeAnn opened the book she'd just bought, checked the table of contents and turned to page 294. Her eyes skimmed quickly over the words on the page.

"Once, euksikkni, The People of the Lake, were beset by very hard

times. Indeed! The elders would cry, 'How pitiful we live now, not like our ancestors, even those who passed on not a little while before us!' A new race of people had come to make easier the way of life but brought troubles with them. Disease, warfare, and doubt troubled the People of the Lake. . . . The language of the Tribe and the ways of the land became distant to most of the people. Sweet things to eat and the rapid ways of moving replaced the way that the elders used to enjoy teaching. . . . Bones became weak, muscles became a part of the body that began to work against the body! . . . Now, mighty eyes in the sky rummaged throughout the surface of the world. There were no secrets among the Tribe. . . . The new people, resting in their rich lodges, became large chiefs, not caring for all, just themselves. . . . Soon, they ran out of wood for the fires and had made many untrusting slaves. They became aware, finally, that they would soon have no air to breathe and no water to drink. . . . Now, I say to you! We still live in the time of legends! Heed, listen! Every voice you hear, you may hear for the last time!"

LeeAnn stared at the pages for quite some time, trying to let them fill her with the courage and integrity of the ancient culture. Then, remembering where she was, raised her head, and with a start realized she was looking at the bumper of a maroon Jaguar with the letters VHRI on the license plate.

Was that here when I pulled in? She hadn't noticed, but then she seldom did. So Ernst Vanderveer had to be in the bank, unless his driver was doing his errands for him. Her first impulse was to park farther down the street and wait for him to leave. *But how cowardly can I get? Am I going to let this window of opportunity slam down on my fingers?*

She climbed out of the Jeep, and with her heart beating a little faster, pushed open the door of the bank and walked in. She felt suddenly confused about what she was going to say to this man. What leverage could she possibly bring to bear to get him to admit what he'd done and return the petroglyph? *Why should he, when he's already won the fight? And he knows it.*

There were never any lines at banks in Klamath Falls, but today was an exception. There was Vanderveer, standing at the back of a line that was four deep. Interesting to see him looking like a normal citizen, LeeAnn thought. There were three tellers working with other customers, so it shouldn't take long. LeeAnn took her place behind Ernst just as the line moved up one. Looking at the customers ahead of him and guessing at their business, she estimated that her turn would come up with Linda, the lady with the unfailing smile.

But the line didn't move any more for awhile. LeeAnn waved at Gloria, the bank president, who had worked with her on the Winter Olympics movement. Her pal. Then her attention went back to the man in front of her whose enormous power she wanted to redirect. *Should I tap him on the shoulder? What do I say? Where do I start?* He would have to notice her eventually.

He probably had no idea she was staring at his back. His shoulder blades, sticking out under the light-blue raw-silk shirt, made him look a little vulnerable. *He really is quite a lean machine.* The back of his ears seemed another vulnerable place, they were sunburned, probably from the site visit. She also noticed that Ernst's approximately three-week-old, conservative haircut was beginning to grow out at the back of his neck. He'd been too long away from his barber. It seemed a peculiarly intimate thing to be noticing.

Why, LeeAnn wondered, as she continued to stand there indecisively, *would a man who is the CEO, not only of VHRI but of its parent company, come to the bank himself when he has multitudes to do it for him? Maybe because that's the one sacred act–coming to the holy temple of money.*

Is he by himself? she wondered, looking around and seeing the huge Polynesian bodyguard sitting on the couch, pretending to read *U.S. News and World Report.* I guess he couldn't very well stand in line with Ernst; it would look dumb. *And he must not know who I am or he'd be alerting him,* LeeAnn thought. *Unless they have some hidden set of signals I can't see.*

The three people at the tellers' windows seemed to be reorganizing their entire financial lives. Still, LeeAnn waited. For what, she didn't know. She was hoping for something outside of herself to set things in motion.

The woman ahead of Ernst was called to a teller. So it was certainly time to tap him on the shoulder if she was going to do it. Nervously, she rehearsed options for an opening line.

"Well, hi there, LeeAnn!" Linda called over to her then. "Glad to see you back; how was Russia?" Ernst turned immediately. She'd been so close behind him that he was immediately right in her face. He smiled broadly, as though it were a huge joke to encounter her.

"What an unexpected pleasure," he said.

LeeAnn stepped back. "I was just noticing you could use a trim," she said impulsively. Though it was actually a very good thing to say, because from his expression she could see that it totally threw him.

For a moment Ernst stood there, nonplussed, as two tellers became available at once. "May I help you, Mr. Vanderveer?" Linda called to him. Everyone in town knew who he was.

LeeAnn maneuvered around him with a smile and went to the teller who had beckoned her. *What has gotten into me? Criticizing the man's haircut. Well, whatever it is, flow with it, like Maggie said, and keep your head up,* she told herself.

Distracted, LeeAnn searched vainly in her pack for her checkbook. "What can I do for you today?" the teller wanted to know.

"Well, first I wanted to get my balance."

"Do you know your account number?"

"Of course not." LeeAnn laughed and the woman joined her. "Can you look it up?"

"Sure thing. Spencer, isn't it?" she said as she turned to her computer. She had a good memory. LeeAnn looked over to see how far along Ernst was in his transaction, hoping he wouldn't leave before she got through, and wondering what she'd do if he did. Just run over, probably, and grab him; they absolutely had to talk.

The teller passed over a slip of paper with numbers on it. $342.15.

"Thanks. Oh, *here's* my checkbook," she said as it turned up suddenly and miraculously at the bottom of her pack, where she could swear it hadn't been a moment ago. "Sorry." LeeAnn scribbled a check for $100 cash, trying to calculate if any big checks were getting ready to clear.

Ernst had finished now. So where was his wheelbarrow to carry his money away? He walked over to his bodyguard and stood there, glancing back to let LeeAnn know he was waiting for her. She was relieved; at least she wouldn't have to chase him down the street. She collected her cash, took a deep breath, and made her way toward the one-percenter.

"I seem to be getting conflicting opinions on my haircut," he said. "My driver thinks it's just fine."

LeeAnn simply looked at him, and he laughed. "Of course, I'm paying him to say things like that. You look like you need a cold drink. Will you join me?"

She was caught by his direct gaze. "Where?"

"Well, how about on my plane? My home in Klamath."

"You're staying on your airplane?"

"Can you think of any place better?"

"No, I suppose our local motels just might not make it for you," she said in an uncharacteristically acid tone.

By this time, LeeAnn noticed, they were out on the sidewalk, beside the Jag. She did not feel as if she was in control. "I *do* want to talk to you," she said. "But not on your airplane." She glanced around. "I think *Old Town Pizza* will do just fine." It was right next to the bank. This time of day, late afternoon, it would be pretty deserted, which was probably a good idea.

"I'm going to be a little while, Jerry," Ernst said to his bodyguard, who had materialized behind them. The huge man stood stock still on the sidewalk, looking like a statue from Easter Island as he cast a stony look in LeeAnn's direction.

She led the way into Old Town, choosing the third booth on the left and setting her pack down. It was cool, like the museum. "They only have counter service here," she explained to Ernst as he was about to slide in on the other side of the booth. "We have to go up there to get something," she added in case he didn't understand the concept of self service.

"I'll do it," he said.

She sat down. *Let him.*

"What would you like?"

"Iced tea." He walked over to the counter. Waiting for the teenager to fill up their glasses, he turned to study LeeAnn so carefully and so frankly that she felt uncomfortable. She had the idea that he was planning his strategies. *What's he about to offer? A carrot or a stick? A bribe to buy me off like that Harkins guy in Boise? A date? A threat? People like him can be pretty ruthless.* Ernst. Even the name was indicative. The letters that would make him "Ernest" were missing. She had a sick feeling in the pit of her stomach.

For no reason in particular, LeeAnn remembered the afternoon with David in the coffee shop with the yellow roses–a very different kind of meeting. On this occasion the noticeable feature was the red banquettes. The reason so many restaurants are decorated in red, she'd seen in an article once, is because we need to look at blood to digest well, like hyenas at the kill.

LeeAnn, she said to herself, watching him watch her as he waited for his change, *you have to admit this is a little bit titillating. That you're just the teeniest bit attracted to this guy. Or is it that you're attracted to his power? Of course there is something sexy about power. Partnership women have had to learn to find raw power attractive in a dominator age. To learn to get excited about the dark and kinky side of love.* She thought of the large-boned males found in early dominator era gravesites, buried with sacrificed wives and all of their paraphernalia of power.

Ernst came back to the booth now with two old-fashioned ice-cream-soda glasses filled to the brim and served her iced tea standing up as though he were a waiter. He had Pepsi. *He probably owns Pepsi Asia,* she thought, as he looked around the pizza parlor. LeeAnn wondered again if he'd ever gotten that invitation and the algae articles she sent him. *Did I send it just because I wanted to get his attention?* That might be a difficult question to answer.

"I still think you might have enjoyed the atmosphere on the plane."

"I'm not here to play social games," LeeAnn said, rather unconvincingly, she thought, because again he looked slightly amused. "All I want to know is where the petroglyph is. We don't have to be on an umpteen-million-dollar airplane to talk about that! Have you *found* it yet?"

"No, nothing's turned up," he said easily, as though he were as mystified as she. "I had a team go through the rubble this morning."

Then she blew up. "You deliberately, *deliberately* tricked me yesterday."

"Is that what you think?" Again, smooth.

"Isn't that what happened? I know what I found and I know it disappeared. I just hope you're taking care of it. I understand you don't want your construction delayed but you have no right . . ."

"Ms . . . ah . . . is it Spencer really, or is it Kimball?" It hit her like a bucket of cold water. Her married name. The carrot had just been replaced with a stick. Most people didn't know she'd never changed her name back legally after she and Bo were divorced. Why did it feel so uncomfortable that he probably now knew everything about her life down to what brand of toothpaste she used, or what kind of birth control? What right had he to pry? But that's what they were doing by looking into Paul Trautman's background. *We're using dominator tactics too, so I guess I deserve this. Everybody trying to get something on somebody else.* She felt her courage coming back, so she turned it right back on him.

"I've done some research, too. Do you want to discuss why you got thrown out of Costa Rica and what happened in Mexico? Let's talk about Mr. Espinoza."

"I'm afraid I don't know . . ."

"That's exactly my point. You know somebody died in a protest over water rights–it was a man named Espinoza–in the Jalisco province when you were starting to acquire the property there."

"It was Nayarit, actually."

"Whatever." She was furious. "What you pretend not to know is that your dirty-work guys illegally cut off the water to about thirty small farmers to get their hands on the land."

"Yes, I did know that," he said with evident regret.

"Do you think in Klamath we're more stupid, that we're going to let you run rampant over us?" LeeAnn was surprised at her own courage. Suddenly she wasn't afraid of anything–Ernst Vanderveer or VHRI or even the malevolent Paul Trautman. She was just spitting mad, and it felt so free. So she didn't let him answer, just went on.

"Do you have any idea how much traffic, how much gasoline, water, how it's going to impact the ecosystem here, above and beyond what your people have told you? Do you know there's a precious resource here? Did you get the envelope I mailed you?"

"I haven't seen anything."

Oh shit, she thought. The only invitation to the Global Celebration to go out and it didn't get to him. *Just as I thought.* A hot/cold wave passed over her and her heart sank. *Is the whole idea crazy?* She went on.

"Do you know how important this lake is to the future of the planet? Why don't you spend some of your money researching how to feed all the people in the world instead of building another showplace for half a billion dollars!? Why do you need another hotel, anyway?"

"I don't have complete control over VHRI, you know. LeeAnn, you're very smart. You're very attractive. I make no secret of the fact that I'd like to know you better. But you don't have all the information. When big companies move into rural areas they're traditionally attacked for exploiting the land, as much as they're lauded for boosting the economy. It's a turkey shoot, as you call it. That incident in Mexico was fully explained. Total accident."

"What do you mean 'fully explained'? She looked at him, incredulous. "How much do you really know about what the people who work for you do? Maybe you keep yourself personally faultless, but isn't that the problem in this world? As long as we don't know the people we're hurting, we just put numbers on them and it doesn't matter. Isn't that why you put Ms. Al Amin in charge, so you don't have to know what your people are doing, whose lives you're ruining?"

Grabbing a pencil out of her pack, she started drawing on a napkin. Then she turned the napkin toward him. "Which group would you rather belong to? Here's you," she pointed to three stick figures she had drawn. One was sitting on the head of another who was sitting on the head of the third. "This is what the dominator system looks like. *Ruler, enforcer, and ruled.*" She drew a crown on the guy on top. "Here's you. Here's your enforcers," she pointed to the figure in the middle, "like Sonja or what's-his-name Trautman." She pointed to the bottom figure. "And here's the poor people you victimize. It's the way your society runs and you're ruining the earth while you do it. Nobody's happy. The guy on the top is scared he's going to fall off, the guy on the bottom is getting squashed, and the guy in the middle is getting it from both ends, violence, pushing, shoving, bloodshed, a constant power struggle. It's sick."

"Now here's the way society used to be, and *could* be again." She pointed to the other set of stick figures she'd drawn, three people standing side by side, holding hands like paper dolls. "These people's energy is aligned. They play the role of *scientists* or *artists* or *caregivers*, alternately or interchangeably. People lead at what they do best, the roles are blended. That's what the figure of the Lovers on the petroglyph represents." She sketched it quickly. "A horizontal instead of a vertical society. Do you see? People who are equal."

Poker-faced, Ernst reached over, picked up the napkin, folded it twice, and stuck it into his breast pocket. She couldn't tell if he was still just amused with her. "That is all very well, LeeAnn, but without shepherds, the sheep go off the cliff. We need leaders in this world . . ."

"Partnership is not against leadership," she interjected.

". . . People *want* to be ruled," Ernst finished.

"Isn't that just your colonial heritage speaking? And, of course, your family's been reaping the benefits of rampant colonialization for the last four hundred years," LeeAnn snapped, realizing she'd just said "rampant" a minute before. "The Dutch East India Company was one of the most notorious. Aren't you the ones who burned Jakarta down back in the sixteen hundreds to consolidate your control? Strong-arm tactics to take over the whole of Asia."

"My family is not so *terrible!*" She seemed to be getting to him at last. "You can sneer at colonialism if you like, but look at the good it's done. Sure, there were casualties initially, but in the long run, we've actually cut down on death, wars, poverty, and so on." Ernst stopped and took a drink from his Pepsi. "You know, before we got to those primitive islands, they were divided up into different rajdoms and kingdoms, and were constantly at war with each other. We brought sanitation, we brought trade, we brought the blessings of Christianity. We stopped the Hindus from killing the Balinese, we stopped the Muslims from killing the Hindus. Of course, that's resulted in overpopulation," he conceded, "only because we saved so many lives."

"But you enslaved people."

"Their people had enslaved them anyway. It wasn't as if they were having a wonderful time before we got there."

"So, they're not competent to govern themselves, is that what you're saying?"

"I'm saying that some people govern better than others. For whatever reason. Let me tell you a little story." LeeAnn suppressed a groan. "When I was a student traveling in India, I caught a ride with a professor from Bombay. We were going along on a horrible road, the only highway between the two cities, and of course he was complaining about the way the British were so terrible and so forth. I said, 'Well, wait a minute, the British have been gone for years. Why don't you people have a decent road here? These are two of your three biggest cities.'"

Ernst caught LeeAnn's wandering gaze and held it. She felt self-conscious again. "He looked at me like I was crazy and said, `Well, the British didn't *build* one.' So I said, `But you know you're celebrating your 25th anniversary of independence. It seems to me that by this time you could get together and build yourselves a highway.' And then he looked at me as if I was a *total* buffoon and he said, 'But the British didn't even leave us the plans to build one.'

"Nothing is India's fault. Either the British didn't do it or the CIA is doing it. According to the average Indian, there's at least a million CIA at work in that country. If the newspaper comes out late, it's the CIA . . ." Ernst stopped and looked at LeeAnn for her reaction.

"Don't you see, you perpetuate that attitude with your patriarchal way of keeping people in their place. But it won't work anymore; what you guys are doing with your crazy game of Monopoly just can't continue." How could she get it across? "Let me ask you this. Do you own a yacht?"

"Mmmhmm, yes I do."

"And do you have a helicopter on that yacht?"

"Mmhmm."

"Don't you think that's enough? Don't you think there's some point where you ought to stop accumulating *stuff*? I've always felt that having a boat with its own helipad is kind of a division point in the scale of personal belongings. Beyond that, you really don't need a whole lot more."

His expression was noncommittal.

"Okay, last question. Suppose you knew for a certainty that if you personally continued to amass all this wealth and use up all these resources, that the world as we know it was going to be destroyed? Say on December 31st of this year–that's four months away–that if you don't change your ways, all the people on the earth will perish on New Year's Eve–including you and your children." She stopped. "Do you have children?"

"Yes, two. I'm divorced," he added, as though that had some significance.

"If you knew they were going to be destroyed, would you be willing to fold up the Monopoly board, put the pieces back, and start the game all over again? If you knew *for sure?*"

"It would be very difficult to prove that anything *I* might do . . . ," Ernst began.

"No, let's stay with what we're talking about. Suppose that were *proven* and you knew your *own family* was about to get incinerated? But you could stop that destruction, or at least put it off by changing your ways. Would you?"

"Of course, only a fool would not do that."

"Fine, then all I have to do is convince you it's going to happen. Would you agree to try to find the envelope I sent you in the vast bureaucracy of VHRI? Would you at least read it?"

"What is it?"

"It's an article about the algae in the lake and . . . ," she paused, looking directly into his eyes, "an invitation to a party." They looked at

each other across the table as he seemed to weigh the possible significance of her remark. She didn't let her eyes show any more than they
already did.

"I'll see if I can locate it," he promised.

"And if your people have thrown it out, call me up, and I'll try to
send you another one. It just won't be in color." She handed him a card,
the last and most rumpled of her 22nd Century Group cards. He
smoothed it out and put it into his pocket with the paper napkin.

"I have sympathy for your point of view," Ernst said then, choosing his words carefully, "and admiration for your level of concern. I
will read what you've sent me, but I need to warn you that it's much too
late to change things insofar as Tree Island is concerned. Even if I wanted to." The expression on his face changed, becoming quite grim. "I've
seen nothing to convince me that you're not just obfuscating, trying to
pretend there's a petroglyph."

"I beg your pardon . . ."

"You cannot meddle in our Tree Island project. If you persist in
what you're doing, you need to know I could become the best enemy
you ever had. Believe me, there's far too much money invested for
anyone to be worrying about petroglyphs or archaeology now. So I'm
telling you this very frankly, LeeAnn, *do not interfere.* You're out of
your league."

"Is that a threat?"

"If you think it's a threat, then that's what it is," he said, with a
flash of anger that simply ignited LeeAnn. She stood up, threw a dollar
bill down on the table for a tip, and stormed out.

A few moments later she was driving down Main Street, past Bell's
Hardware, past the Chamber of Commerce, past Wong's, remembering
how it had all ended. She turned the corner and put the Jeep into second as she started up the hill. *What did he mean by 'I could be the best
enemy you ever had'? How much money does he have personally at
stake?* she wondered. *A hundred million dollars? Probably a hundred
million dollars he's borrowing from someone else. What level of threat
does that get me? Don't be silly, you're not going to get found at the
bottom of the lake.* But then again there was that Silkwood thing. She'd
seen the movie and she felt a chill. How evil was Ernst? *Was* he evil?
When you talk to them face to face, it's hard to believe that *any* human
is evil.

She drove up the hill, passing under the huge old maples that lined the street, past historical houses on the left. She turned at the top and started up into her driveway.

Then there was that welcome sight. Peter's car. His wonderful old metallic-green '81 Honda Civic station wagon with a new ding in the back where it had been forcibly wrenched open with a crowbar. LeeAnn parked the Jeep and climbed out.

Peter came out the back door then, his blond hair loose on his shoulders and a grin on his face. Her little brother. She walked up to him and they stood there, just looking into each other's faces, connecting. Peter didn't like to hug right away. Though he loved to celebrate, he was opposed to all set rituals, except for *Aga-dagas*, a Spencerian ritual for success in math tests, blind dates, and violin concerts, in which participants walked around on their hands and knees mindlessly chanting, *Aga-daga, aga-daga.* The only other tradition Peter honored was the family grace before meals, *"Rub a dub dub, thanks for the grub. Yay . . . GOD!"*

"Hey sis," Peter said at length.

"Hi bro," and then they both laughed. "Good drive?" LeeAnn said, asking a ritualistic question, which Peter would not appreciate; she wished she could call the words back. But he responded amiably enough.

"Not bad."

"We didn't expect you till later."

"Sometimes I get up," he said, grinning impishly.

They went into the weight room where Peter promptly hung upside down on the monkey bars. That was probably where he'd been when she drove up. His face was turning red and his hair was streaming down.

"So, what have you guys been doing?" LeeAnn asked.

"Oh, David and I have been out looking at different ideas for the dormer."

"For the greenhouse?" She was surprised, couldn't believe it, actually. *David was still thinking greenhouse?* "Where's David now?"

"He went for beer."

Peter turned right side up again and she brought him up to date on what was happening, which seemed to be all she was doing these days, she thought–recapping. She could become a professional recapper. She told him about the meeting with Ernst, stressing his words at the end.

"I wouldn't think that was a physical threat," Peter said as David came in with the beer and kissed her hello. It seemed as if things were normal between them. But she didn't trust it.

Audrey walked in about two minutes later from her visit with the ecologists in Medford. "These guys have really covered their ass with every damn permit and study–most of it done quietly before the project was ever announced," she said. "How did *you* do?" she asked LeeAnn then. So LeeAnn had to tell the story of her day all over again. The tribe and the bank and then the major encounter with Ernst at Old Town Pizza. Audrey listened attentively and started plying LeeAnn with questions, till Peter interrupted.

"So why don't you go out and roust Jeff and let's get this business meeting over with," he said.

Jeff had gone for a nap, but Audrey fetched him and he came in soon, looking sleepy. They all sat down and had their dreaded financial meeting. Despite Pamela's contribution, the 22nd Century Group was in debt and sinking fast. Peter already had the color seps in process again; the new printing order would be placed soon. Everybody wrote checks to cover the deficit, refusing to let Peter absorb the loss. They adjourned and went outside.

Peter, in one of his giddy moods now, organized a celery-eating contest out in the garden to see who could munch a still-growing stalk right down to the ground the fastest, hands behind their backs. It was kind of funny, particularly when Jeff fell on his face. Then they played frisbee for awhile and even David got into it.

Afterward, they sat around on the kitchen counters and talked about the old days at Joan of Arc Junior High. "Remember the time that file cabinet came flying out of the second-story window at recess?" Audrey asked. And they all did. A corner of it had hit their friend Tyrone on the head and caused massive head injuries.

"I saw Tyrone a couple months ago," Jeff said.

"How was he doing?"

"He's working at the Pioneer market now."

"Is he okay?" LeeAnn asked.

"Ehhh . . . He'll never be okay." They were quiet for a minute.

"I was thinking about the time we climbed down in the subway."

"And jumped over the third rail."

"Where?"

"Seventy-Ninth Street."

"I never knew you did that." LeeAnn was always alarmed by what young males will do. Embarrassing the undercover cops on Broadway was about as daring as LeeAnn had ever been. Audrey, of course, had stolen checks and heisted cars. She was a real tomboy.

"It's a wonder any of you ever lived to grow up." And then she had a sudden fear about even saying that. It was a sobering moment. They got to talking about the city then and what its future might be.

"What's it going to cost to retrofit New York City," Peter was asking a few minutes later, "when its infrastructure falls apart? In twenty or thirty years, it's probably not going to be fixable any more. With all those cables and pipes down there. They'll have to abandon it." LeeAnn imagined ten million people just moving out, transferring the whole population to a bunch of those futuristic biomorphic skyscrapers shaped like seashells, in the Pine Barrens of New Jersey.

What will it be like in the future? What will happen? Why don't more people talk about it? It's probably because we're afraid to know. Subconsciously we realize that we don't spend enough time thinking about it and planning for it. Audrey is right when she says we're in a spaceship going about a zillion miles an hour with nobody at the controls. Is what's happening in this crazy house actually capable of helping that situation? How can we get people together when all we're doing is getting driven apart? Except for tonight. Tonight feels good, actually.

A little later in the evening, Peter got his violin out and started playing Vivaldi. It felt like the old days back at the apartment where his music was one of the most familiar sounds in her life. If LeeAnn shut her eyes, she could imagine they were back there, still kids. He started on *The Four Seasons*, the winter part, and then the spring. Both she and Audrey got misty eyed.

"Five is an important number," her new friend Andy had told her. LeeAnn remembered the words. There were five of them here tonight. She wondered about the significance of that. And, of course, she thought about the card she'd drawn that morning about grief.

As the evening wore on, she tried to watch what was going on with Audrey and David. Nothing seemingly. They weren't even looking at each other. *Is it over, then? Or is this the calm before the storm?* She looked out the window at the hot tub that Stan had fixed. Tomorrow they'd fill it up for their celebration.

CHAPTER SEVENTEEN

The Celestine Dinner

A crazy foolishness seemed the order of the day as the 22nd Century Group piled en masse into Vanna for an expedition to Fred Meyer's, the Northwest's all-in-one shopping chain, about three the next afternoon to buy ingredients for their "celebration" dinner.

With David at the wheel, they pulled out of the bump, bumpety-bump driveway, which was getting to be quite a radical grade what with all the in-and-out traffic lately–they'd have to get another load of gravel–and started down the hill toward town.

Wedged between Peter and Jeff on the mattress in the back of the van, Audrey was reading from a well-worn copy of Maggie's paella recipe clipped from *The New York Times* sometime in the 70's. "I hope they have some decent shrimp in this town," she said.

"That they have," said David. "People splurge on good shrimp when they have the chance no matter where they live."

"And mussels, do you think they'll have mussels?"

"Aaah, not so likely," LeeAnn answered. "Sometimes."

"*Real* saffron?"

"I already have some left over from the last time. In one of those little glass vials that make it look illegal."

"Do you have enough?"

"Yes, Audrey, I have enough."

"We may as well get some anyway. Knowing you, we may not be able to find it."

"No chorizo," said Jeff emphatically.

"No chicken either," said Peter. They were all trying to give up meat. "But definitely clams."

"At least we have peas in the garden. Remember the time we tried to use canned peas? *Yuck.*"

The traditional celebratory dinner for the Spencers had long been paella and it still was. "But there's always a horribleness," Peter had said, "cleaning up. Why do we always pick paella? It costs the most and it makes the biggest mess."

"Yeah, but it's festive as hell."

They headed out past the quaint downtown toward the standardized strip of franchised businesses that made up South Sixth Street–and was taking over most of America.

LeeAnn's watch started chirping and she hit the stop button. "I need to get this watch to stop going off," she said, fiddling with it and thinking about the last time it had chirped on Tree Island, to Ernst's amusement.

"Here, I'll fix it; give it to me," offered Audrey.

"Oh yeah, right, a lot of good you'll do. Just like the last time you fixed it." But she found herself taking it off and handing it over anyway.

They pulled into the parking lot at Freddie's just as Audrey completed all of her expert digital adjustments. "Here, that ought to do it."

"You know you can keep that thing for all I care," said David, getting out. "It looks good on you."

"Wait a minute," LeeAnn said, as David headed to the rear of the van to open the doors. "Don't let these guys out yet. We gotta have a plan here." David looked quizzical; he was ready to go into the store and buy the food. That's the way his mind worked. In a straight line. "We're going to have to split up," she announced.

"What for?" asked Peter.

"I can't be seen with Jeff. What if Paul Whoozie sees us together?"

"Trautman. He's not likely to be here," said Jeff.

"Everybody in this town is likely to be everywhere–and everybody shops at Freddie's at one time or another. It would be just our luck. So," she looked at Jeff. "You and I don't know each other, okay?"

"Okay."

Before they got out of the van, she tore the bottom half of the shopping list off and handed it to Jeff. Thus it was that David and LeeAnn entered the store together, pushing their cart before them, a well-mannered, socially acceptable couple, while the three rowdies, two carts among them, lagged behind about a hundred feet, deliberately bumping their carts into each other.

LeeAnn thought she saw Stan Porter disappearing down the frozen-food aisle. But it was someone else, a stranger–another Klamath good old boy.

Next time LeeAnn looked around for her houseguests, she saw Audrey scrunched up in a shopping cart into her Superball shape, arms tight around her knees, careening down one of the aisles, propelled by Peter and shrieking softly. "Boy, I'm glad we don't know *them*," LeeAnn said to David.

"You do the same thing."

"Only late at night."

As the two groups stood near each other in adjacent check-out lines, LeeAnn noticed Jeff staring openmouthed at what appeared at first glance to be a gay couple in Klamath. "Don't even think it," Audrey whispered to him. "It's just a mirage."

As they loaded a dozen bags of groceries into the van, LeeAnn realized that Paul Trautman could drive past at any moment. But he didn't, and on the way home she let herself relax as they did the obligatory Main Street *Klamath Kruise*, with Audrey pointing out the restaurants she'd sampled and giving unsolicited critiques.

Once they were home unpacking groceries, discussions began on preparation procedures. "So, we peel the shrimp and *then* cook it?" Jeff wanted to know.

But Peter the purist said, "No, never. All the seafood goes in with its clothes on." They were already dividing themselves into factions, LeeAnn noticed. Peter teaming up with David, both being practical, straight-arrow types who applied themselves to any job methodically. Jeff, on the other hand, tended to be wildly creative, leaping about and going in ten directions at once.

"It really depends on the size of the shrimp," Jeff persisted. "Doesn't it? These are pretty small, so maybe . . ."

Then Peter interrupted Jeff with a boisterous, "No *way!*" LeeAnn, seeing an opportunity to flee before the fireworks began, decided to go out in the garden to pick peas. She grabbed a basket and, taking the long way around, went out on the front porch and down the steps to check the mail.

Another phone company was feverishly desirous of her long-distance business, and there were some bills. Headed back around the house, she saw Audrey out by the garden in her bikini, reclining in their only lawn chair, sucking on ice cubes and working on her tan. Perusing *The Celestine Prophecy,* she had a salt shaker and a tray of cubes beside her, just like she used to when they were kids. The salt made interesting little holes in the ice that Audrey seemed to enjoy.

"Move your bod," LeeAnn said as she sat down on the foot of the chair.

"Hi." Audrey said, putting down her book. She was boning up for tonight's celebration, which she had re-billed as the Celestine Dinner. Tonight, Audrey had told them, she was going to get everybody to think about what the implications of James Redfield's book could be for the future of the world. She would share all nine insights, whether they wanted to hear them or not. LeeAnn was the only one of the group who still hadn't read the book, David having just finished it on Audrey's recommendation.

"What are you doing, reading it again?"

"I just want to be sure I have all the insights right." Audrey picked up her bottle of suntan lotion and started to re-oil her body. The essence of Coppertone brought back so many other summers for LeeAnn. She listened to the male voices coming from the kitchen, and the salsa music from the stereo–Audrey always put the radio on salsa–and she sensed that this suspended moment in time would later identify this particular summer. *There are always those moments, those snapshots; this is one I'll definitely have in my album*–Audrey Garcia tanning herself in a white bikini on the green chaise lounge, and the promise of a food fight in the kitchen.

Audrey's little body was still quite perfect, LeeAnn noticed, from her economical breasts right down to those manicured toes. You'd think a real woman would have a little patch of unsightly fuzz *somewhere* on her legs that she'd missed shaving. "You want to help me pick peas?" she asked.

"Do you need me to?"

"No, I guess not. I'll do it." She started to walk away, and thought, *No, I can't keep avoiding this.* She turned. "Okay," LeeAnn said in a no-nonsense tone, sitting down again. Audrey immediately snapped to attention. LeeAnn took a deep breath. "I just wanted to say, *do whatever you need to do.* You and David have your own lives and I'm not going to play policeman. But don't think for a minute it's not going to hurt me, because it will."

"LeeAnn, what are you saying?"

"That maybe you guys just need to do it and get it over with. I don't know."

"Lee*Ann!*"

"Later!" Then she walked off across the yard, leaving Audrey open-mouthed on the chaise. There, she'd done it, she'd done *something.*

Picking peas, LeeAnn could hear a still-lively discussion coming from the kitchen. Then David came outside to check on the hot tub he was filling. When her pea-picking was completed, she decided it was time, so she came across the yard toward him in her halter top and cut-offs, feeling self-conscious. She was about to tell him something profound, but he spoke first.

"If you're going in the house, let's lose the salsa music, don't you think? Put it back on channel twenty-three."

"I will." Standing there with the basket of peas, LeeAnn, in a surge of bravery turned to David. "David?" She got his attention with her tone of voice.

"Yes?"

"David, I've been thinking. Whatever you want to do with Audrey is okay with me. Please don't hold back, get it over with–okay?" Not waiting for his reaction, LeeAnn hurried into the house. She turned the salsa off and reinstated the New Age channel David preferred. Then she went over to the stove and checked the rice, which was her job. She was feeling proud of herself that she had spoken her mind to both Audrey and David; it was off her chest now, only time would tell the outcome.

Rice. She found herself still staring into the wok, the steam rising in the air. Time to grab a beer, take a shower, and get ready for their evening. The *Celestine Dinner*, indeed. David came past the stove then. "We have to talk," he said.

"Tomorrow."

He looked at her, then headed out to the cabin.

LeeAnn dressed carefully, spending more time than she normally did on her appearance. She chose a revealing blue-green leotard top that packaged her cleavage in a most delectable way, and a full-length gauze skirt over it, done in greens and browns and yellows. She wore the pendant David had made for her, a replica of the bone figure she'd found in Yugoslavia. It was beautifully showcased by her graceful bosom and the low-necked leotard. She swept her hair up, clipped it in place, snapped a wide, gold metal belt around her waist and went bare-foot to the dining room.

Selecting one of the big linen tablecloths Maggie had given her, she spread it out, thinking about the fact that it would soon be spotted with dribbles of butter and sangria, and small puddles of grey clam juice. From the china cabinet she took down the gorgeous blue-green goblets that had been a gift from a friend, then lifted down a Wedgewood platter from the plate rail for the shells. It was dusty so she headed for the kitchen to wash it and barely heard the click of the answering machine as she went by. It was just loud enough to make her look down and realize a message was coming in.

"Damn, who didn't turn the ringer back on?" she said, but nobody paid attention. LeeAnn had checked for messages when they got home, and there hadn't been any. She picked up the phone now, but it was too late; someone was just hanging up. She hit Replay.

It was Stan's voice, sounding strained. "I'll be getting back late, but I need to talk to you tonight. I'll stop by." Then he clicked off. No unnecessary words. *Oh God.* She'd expected to hear from him, but he sounded so stark. Now she wouldn't be able to think about anything else till he arrived.

Audrey made a grand entrance from the attic then. She had changed into a powder-blue mini, a dressy affair, with matching bangles on her sculpted upper arms. A fire goddess in celestial garb. She helped LeeAnn finish setting the table. Then everybody gathered around.

"Heads up. Here it comes," said Jeff as he paraded out from the kitchen with their culinary treasure.

"Finally." The paella was always a colorful dish, but this was spectacular. A huge, dark-red Maine lobster graced the top of the pan, below it the saffron-yellow rice, the pimento, the fresh green peas, and clams; Jeff's presentation tonight was superb. David, pouring sangria, watched warily as though the chef might drop their dinner. He still didn't trust Jeff.

"Oh, wait, I have to get something," Peter said. "Don't start without me." He bolted out and came back a minute later from his car with a warm case of Coors.

"You thought I'd forgotten, didn't you? Jeff, this is for all the hard work you did, suppressing your natural verbosity and taking first place, with *sixteen* characters, in the *Mighty Maxims Contest.*"

Jeff led the applause for himself and took several bows as Peter dumped the case in his arms. "Here, *Honor your body*–drink the whole thing." They all laughed. Jeff carried it out to the kitchen to put it in the refrigerator, then came back to sit down.

"Circle?" LeeAnn asked softly, holding her hands out to Jeff on one side of her and Peter on the other. David, at the other end of the table gave her a warm look, a concerned look, a look as if he wanted to talk to her, as he grasped Audrey and Jeff's hands. They were all quiet for about thirty seconds, then Peter, for whom circles were difficult, dropped Audrey's and Jeff's hands to pick up his knife and fork. He began banging them in rhythm on the table. The rest of them picked up their cutlery, too, and followed suit.

"Rub-a-dub-dub," they yelled, "thanks for the grub, Yea-aaayyy *God!*" Then they began their series of toasts, Jeff had three. "To the 22nd Century Group. To August. To the tallest sunflower in the garden." It was over twelve feet tall.

Then Audrey proposed another toast. "To Peter's girlfriend, what's her name, who couldn't be here tonight. And who can't get her head out of her butt long enough to see what a prize she's got."

"Well, that's quite a statement," said Jeff. Peter seemed to take it all in stride. All Peter's girlfriends seemed to piss Audrey off, although they were always small and dark like herself.

"And let me propose a toast to VHRI," Jeff said. "May they decide to do something a little more worthwhile with their billion bucks."

"I'll drink to that." And then they all dug in, and it was heavenly. Even the lump in her throat couldn't keep LeeAnn from enjoying the dinner or enjoying having the rest of them around her. She was paying little attention to the dinner dialogue, listening mostly to the hum of it as it went on in its usual way.

"Well, LeeAnn?" Peter was saying. "Hey, Reverie Girl, what's happening?" He seemed to want a reply. *To what*, she wondered.

"I'm sorry."

"Where *are* you, girl?" Jeff asked. They'd all noticed she wasn't paying attention.

"So," Audrey said briskly, helping LeeAnn catch up. "Here's what we're talking about. To put a limit on the doom-and-gloom stuff, we're going to start this evening with a little *Washington Week in Review*. Each of us come up with our version of the worst possible scenario in our area of expertise and let that end the negativity for the evening."

"Then Audrey can do her Celestine thing and we can stay on the positive side," Jeff added.

"So," Peter said. "Let's start with you, LeeAnn. Your gloomiest prognostication on human relationships?"

She looked at David, then at Audrey and tried to focus her mind.

"Worst-case scenario, one sentence," said Peter.

LeeAnn took a moment to compose it. "An unhealthy, malnourished, illiterate generation, raised on violence and video games grows up and obliterates us all."

"Or maybe they won't wait till they grow up," said Audrey. "Jeff? Next?"

"No, you first."

"Environment. Ahhh, okay, first we lose our ozone in a series of massive UV storms and then we cook in a CO_2 soup."

"Peter? Your gloomiest view on the world of commerce?"

"Somebody will win all the money and all the property, including Boardwalk, and the game will be over."

Jeff nodded. "'Power corrupts and absolute power corrupts absolutely.'"

"David?" Jeff said, carefully including David.

"We will continue to breed like rabbits till we have wall-to-wall people . . ."

"Seven-eighths of whom," Jeff interjected, "will be mercifully wiped out by some killer virus."

"Or some latter day Attila the Hun," LeeAnn added.

"Okay," Audrey said brightly. "Now we know how bad things can get, which brings us to our topic of the evening. Let's use the Celestine framework to see what we can do about it." Audrey, who was always sitting down lower than the rest of them, kneeled up in her chair in order to take the floor. "This is a condensation of the insights from *Body, Mind and Spirit Magazine*," she said, holding up the magazine. "Let's pay attention to how each insight can help us do what we're trying to do. I think we can really use this, given the lousy luck we've been having lately on the Summer Project. Ready?"

"Ready," LeeAnn said, resolving she would suspend her skepticism, and allow the ideas the author presented full weight in her mind.

"Okay. The first insight is noticing that our lives are full of meaningful coincidences that seem 'destined' and that we are guided by an unexplained force."

So that would mean it was no coincidence David and I found the petroglyph, LeeAnn reflected.

"The second insight is becoming aware of history."

How well I know that, LeeAnn thought. It's my job. So far, so good.

"The third," Audrey read, "involves acknowledging and learning to perceive the presence of a primal, enlivening energy that is affected by human expectations."

Is Redfield talking about a God who answers prayers? LeeAnn wondered. *Or is he saying that the energy of the earth is sensitive to human spirituality? We keep wanting God to affect our lives, but we don't often think about how God may be affected by* our *actions.*

"The fourth insight shows us how people compete for energy," Audrey was saying, "and attempt to 'steal' it from each other . . ."

Hierarchy, LeeAnn thought. The dominator system is such a perfect breeding ground for that sort of thing. ". . . because they aren't yet aware of how to draw it from the Source."

From the Love within, LeeAnn thought. Could that love within be DNA memory? Of course, everybody else was undoubtedly coming up with their own interpretations for each of these; she wondered what Audrey thought of as the Source. They'd never seriously talked about religion.

"The fifth insight explains that the universe will provide all the energy we need if we open ourselves up to it; we do this by appreciating and seeing the beauty in all things."

Starting with the beauty of the life force itself, and the fact that all five of us are sitting here alive and well right this minute. What more could we ask for? LeeAnn thought about how much she always worried and how ultimately the universe always seemed to provide. *Perhaps I should let it. I'm going to have to read this book. In spite of Audrey.*

"The sixth insight instructs us to come to grips with the way we attempt to manipulate and control others, and rid ourselves of these behaviors."

If we can learn that, LeeAnn thought, we will all have become partnership people and we will have a peaceful world. She found herself thinking about Ernst Vanderveer and his dominator attitude.

"The seventh insight tells us that the coincidences in our lives happen to guide us; we must pay attention to them, to our seemingly random thoughts, and to our dreams."

Do daydreams count? Like the image of the orange, and the earth, and the people holding hands. The people she loved were here together tonight in Klamath Falls because she'd had that image of the orange a year ago. She had goose bumps as she looked around the table and saw that the others seemed similarly affected, thinking about their own *dreams* and *coincidences* and the effects of them on their lives.

"The eighth insight warns against becoming addicted to another person, and advises us to balance our yin and yang sides."

That's pretty clear. It's what I've got to do in my own life. I need to give up codependency as a lifestyle. Though that's the insight I least want to hear about.

"The ninth insight explains what will happen when everyone–or at least a critical mass–learns and practices the insights." They all looked at each other.

"Global Celebration!" Jeff said aloud, echoing what they were all thinking. So Audrey's idea to bring James Redfield to this table had been a good one.

LeeAnn and David were carrying plates out into the kitchen when she saw Silly take off out of his house like a shot; her heart jumped up into her throat. She was out the back door and almost at the gate by the time Stan reached it. When she opened it for him, he walked right past her. "I'm here," was all he said by way of greeting, and he looked sort of like a man who'd just seen a fairly scary UFO and couldn't wait to tell somebody. The two of them entered the dining room together.

"Hi, Stan," said David, looking bewildered that he had come to visit so late in the evening. "Here, have a seat." LeeAnn hadn't said anything to the others about his coming. She could see them all experiencing that slight jolt which comes when someone new is added to a group that has just shared a close moment.

"How about a decaf espresso, Stan?" David had brought his latte machine over from the cabin for the occasion and was preparing to fire it up.

"No, thanks."

"Have you eaten?" LeeAnn asked.

"Don't go to any trouble." Stan's way of saying *I'm starving.*

"It's no trouble, dinner's already made. Look, it's right here. I'll get you a plate." LeeAnn came back with one.

"Looks pretty fancy." Stan sat down; all six chairs at the table were occupied now.

LeeAnn was on tenterhooks, but Stan didn't say anything right away about what had happened or what he'd seen. First he ate a couple of plates of paella, and complimented the chef. Then just as he seemed about to begin his story, LeeAnn decided she'd better say something. "David, I asked Stan to look around on Tree Island and see if he could find any trace of our petroglyph."

"I see," was David's chilly reply.

Totally missing David's disapproval, Stan launched into his tale. "See, the first problem I had was finding a time to get up to the trailer without it looking funny." *Why doesn't he start at the result, and then tell the story,* LeeAnn fretted. "I was going to go up there in the morning when I first got there, but then some of the other subs arrived, so I had to wait. Finally got a chance in the afternoon when the guys were on break, to mosey on up there. It wasn't really too hard to get up on top of the roof, what with that boulder that it's parked up against. So once I got up there, I looked down through the vent and . . . uh . . . ," he paused, as though gathering his thoughts.

"And?"

"Well, there's a lot of boxes, that's number one." LeeAnn didn't dare look at David.

"What kind of boxes?" asked Jeff.

"Those ammo boxes. No telling what's in 'em. Must be something because they're all stacked in the corner. And a lot of artifacts, on the floor, on the table, in crates."

"I *knew* it. What kind of artifacts?"

"Mortars. Whole pile of 'em. Big ones. Pestles too, anchor stones, couple of tons of stone, I'd say."

"And that's all legal," LeeAnn said, disappointed. "VHRI has a perfect right to collect all the artifacts they want. They own them, unless they're sacred or burial objects. Was there anything else?"

"Yeah, there was a box of beads, and something else in that box. Like a . . . a human figure."

"Like the drawing I showed you of the petroglyph?" LeeAnn was excited now, she felt her heart thump.

"No, this was just a single figure. More like what you're wearing."

"Like *this*?" She held David's replica of the Yugoslav figurine in her hand.

"Yeah," Stan looked at it. "Just a woman's torso, only in black glass."

"Glass?"

"Glass?" Audrey echoed.

"Glass or obsidian, guess it could have been obsidian, but it was polished."

"Now wait a minute." LeeAnn wanted him to describe it again.

"It couldn't be very old if it's made out of glass," said David.

"But if it's obsidian, it might be *very* old. We can find out exactly how old it is."

"How?" asked Audrey.

"Obsidian can be easily dated," LeeAnn said. "You can tell when a piece was made." Her heart pounded louder and louder as she thought about it.

"LeeAnn." David, looking at her intently, seemed to want to head off her speculations before they got too far out. "None of the Northwest peoples carved obsidian. They chipped. They were flint-knappers, they had no capability . . ."

"How do you *know* that?" she snapped, for suddenly LeeAnn knew for a certainty that the figure was ancient. "You've never *seen* carvings like that from this region. Maybe nobody has, but who's to say there couldn't be one? I mean look at that crystal skull in South America, so precisely and perfectly formed. How do you suppose someone made *that*? Different people in a society do different things."

She was getting very excited. Maybe too excited. "How do you know that one of them, or a bunch of them in all those thousands of years didn't perfect individual techniques? I mean, suppose somebody had a *really good* reason to make something very beautiful? Isn't that what inspires people to do art? Never say never." She turned back to Stan. "Tell me *exactly* what it looked like. *Exactly*."

So Stan tried. "Okay, it was lying in the top of the box of beads that was directly under the vent, so I could see it pretty well. About yay big," he indicated around three or four inches tall. "It had . . . uh . . . just the bosom, and . . . the start of the legs . . ." Stan was clearly suffering when it came to describing the female anatomy.

"What color was it?"

"I told you, black."

obody is going to take it away before you get a chance to see the doll."

"Oh, no."

"But I wouldn't worry about that yet, LeeAnn," Stan put his big callused hand on her arm. "It's going to be there till Monday for sure."

"How do you know?"

"Because that's when they're bringing the barges in. They got no way to take it off till then."

LeeAnn got up. "Well, I'm going to call Sarge."

"LeeAnn," David started, but LeeAnn ignored him.

"You didn't see anything else at all that could be a sacred object?"

"That was it. 'Cept for those beads. The box of olivellas."

"Were they burned? Charred?"

"LeeAnn, I couldn't tell that."

Audrey had been quiet till now. "You know, LeeAnn, you oughtta be careful. You can't base a whole . . ."

"I know what I'm doing, all right? I'm going to call Sarge right now." LeeAnn got up and shut the swinging door to the kitchen so she could be alone as she dialed police headquarters. Sarge wasn't expected in till tomorrow about noon, so she left a message. "Please tell him

339

it's just vitally important for him to contact LeeAnn Spencer." Hanging up, she went back to join the others, who had apparently conferred while she was gone and were all convinced it was their duty to keep her from being disappointed.

"Well, I'm sorry if I've caused any rift here . . . ," Stan began.

"Oh, Stan," and she and David both denied it, the way you always have to when somebody thinks they've caused a quarrel. Then to prove it, LeeAnn and David both walked Stan to his truck, where Melanie was waiting in the cab, and David said goodnight to him.

"Sorry you had to get involved," David finished and headed for the basement. "I'm going to collect some towels for the hot tub, LeeAnn," he said. "Are you sure you won't join us, Stan?"

"Not tonight. We're late getting home as it is. Melanie needs her beauty sleep." LeeAnn doubted that he'd ever been in a hot tub. David disappeared down the basement steps followed by Sillvester.

"Try not to get yourself too upset," Stan said. *Now he was doing it, too.*

LeeAnn sighed. "I just want to go out there and get it. Can you understand? *I want to see it.*"

"Course I do. But you just can't get yourself in over your head. David is probably right, it's a piece of glass. Didn't look like any artifact I ever saw, and I've seen a lot." He started to get in the truck. "By the way, there's something else I didn't mention in there." He jerked his head toward the house. "I, ah . . . You know that padlock on the trailer door that you talked about?"

"Yes."

"You said it was new, and that's what I figured too when I saw it. After I'd spotted that little doll through the vent, I wanted to take a closer look at it myself. I was curious, and so, uh, when Trautman was off working with the heavy equipment operators, I thought, Well, if I had the key . . ."

"Stan?"

"Now you know when you buy a new padlock . . ." *Where is this leading?* LeeAnn wondered with some trepidation, "what do you do with the extra key?"

David came out of the basement now and went around the house and in the back door with a pile of towels from the dryer. He must have noted that she was still standing there talking to Stan, but didn't say anything. They suspended the conversation until he'd gone in the house.

"Now tell me, what would you do with that extra key?"

Exasperated, LeeAnn said, "I don't know, throw it in my junk drawer, I guess."

"Exactly." He was pleased with her answer. "So don't you suppose that's what Trautman did, too? You get a new lock at the hardware store. They give you two keys on that little wire ring. You put one on your key chain and you throw the other one in a little tray or a drawer with the worn-out batteries and the grocery receipts and the paper clips and rubber bands. That's what I figured, so I just took a little peek–and there were three new keys in his desk drawer. All the same brand. *SureLocke.*" He took them out of his pocket and handed them to LeeAnn, she felt as if they were going to burn a hole straight through her palm.

"You took these out of *Paul's desk drawer?*" She was incredulous.

"I thought I might get a chance to go take a look at the figure and then I . . . well, I just didn't do it." He must have decided it was wrong, LeeAnn thought. "And then I got to thinking it would be pretty hard to put them back."

"So you're giving them to *me?*"

"I know it isn't a very easy moral decision, what to do here. But I thought you might be able to answer it better than me."

"Why?"

For once Stan seemed to be at a loss for words. "I trust you'll know what's right. What they're doing is wrong." And he went around to get in his truck.

After he drove away, LeeAnn stood there holding the keys that he'd pressed into her hand. *This is crazy,* she thought. *Like some ancient allegory that's now starting to feel Kafka-esque. Standing here holding these purloined keys and I'm on my way to sit in a fish tote hot tub with a fire goddess. Oh dear, oh dear, oh dear . . . Are these the keys to salvation or self-destruction?*

LeeAnn walked back to the house, feeling confused and alone, alienated from all of them now. In her room, she dropped the keys into her waist pack. *What are the rules,* she wondered, *what are society's rules? And, more important, what are mine? The big question, one more time, is it fair to use dominator tactics to achieve partnership*

tree island

aims? She pondered that, as she took off her skirt and leotard, pulled David's old robe around her, and wandered out to the kitchen.

Audrey came down the attic stairs in another mini-bikini. This time it was black, an unusual color for Audrey, but that wasn't what surprised LeeAnn. What surprised her was that in all the years they'd known each other none of them had ever worn a bathing suit in a hot tub. LeeAnn was kind of grateful, although Audrey would be the only one to wear one. If LeeAnn put on a suit too, it would seem really strange; it would become an issue.

The five of them fit easily into the five-foot-square fiberglass tub (LeeAnn expected to hear a hiss as the fire goddess sank into the cauldron), and the water was good and hot. Everyone pronounced Peter's creation a success, and Jeff started passing the chilled Coors around. "No, thanks," said LeeAnn. One glass of sangria had been enough for her tonight.

"I never knew I could eat that much," said Jeff.

"You almost kept up with Peter," Audrey told him. Then they got onto Summer Project business.

"There's no way we can have the new invitations till after the first?" Jeff looked over Audrey's head at Peter.

"Believe me, I've tried everything," said Peter. "Hal's got a city directory to do, and he won't take that off the presses for anything. I wouldn't either."

"So, we just deal with it," Audrey said. "It may be better, coming after Labor Day when people are starting to pay attention again."

Once again, LeeAnn was noticeably not contributing to the conversation, as her latest secret weighed on her. She didn't feel part of the group at all anymore, especially since they doubted her professional instinct. And yet there wasn't a thing she could do to counter their opinion–unless she could get her hands on that figure. She still had a lump in her throat.

"I think I'm going to go put the second load in the dishwasher," she said, climbing out after only about fifteen minutes in the tub. It was enough.

"I can come help you," said David.

"That's okay. I don't want to face it in the morning and I'd just as soon be alone." Without drying off, she wrapped herself in David's robe and went into the house where she put on a cotton nightshirt and then went to tackle the mess. About ten minutes later, Peter and Jeff got out and went to the summerhouse where they'd no doubt be up all night on the Internet. It was a favorite nocturnal activity for both of them.

That left David and Audrey alone in the tub. Of course, they could see LeeAnn inside the house. She continued to try to look busy, slamming pots and pans around, deliberately not looking out, except for sneaking a glance every once in a while. Fifteen minutes later they were still talking in an animated way.

After LeeAnn had made a cup of tea and drunk it, after she filled the dishwasher, turned it on, and cleaned the counter, they were still at it. Of course, you can't tell much from body language when people are in the water up to their necks. *What are they doing?* They were sitting in opposite corners but this was not a big hot tub. From what LeeAnn could figure out anatomically, there couldn't be a great deal going on. Of course, remembering the gymnastic maneuvers she and David had occasionally pulled off in there . . . She breathed deeply. She told herself she had every reason in the world to go back out and climb in next to David, which would automatically cause him to put his arm around her. The dishwasher sighed dramatically just then in sympathy.

Standing at the sink, her hands in hot water, LeeAnn tried to concentrate on letting go of David and everything this house represented. *It's not going to be an instant process,* she thought. *But it's going to happen. I'm going to make myself let go and build myself another life. I've got to stop clutching. David never made any guarantees this would last forever, and now, if it's over, it's over. Whatever's going to happen out there tonight is going to happen. I can't feel responsible for results anymore, or for what other people do.*

Leaving all the dishes out for David to put away (no sense being a *total* martyr), LeeAnn went to her lonely bedroom, taking some small solace in the fact that she had a book waiting for her. She'd stuck her current Sue Grafton novel under the mattress so she wouldn't be tempted to pick it up at odd moments during the day.

Now she snuggled down under the quilt; thankful it was cool again tonight, the hot spell over. Lots of stars outside. Reaching under the mattress, she pulled out *A for Alibi. I can't believe I still haven't finished this book,* she thought. But with all that was happening, she seemed to be reading four or five pages a night and then conking out.

Tonight she began reading page 147. Unfortunately, the scene was all about one of Kinsey Millhone's infrequent sexual encounters. She couldn't breathe, it said. She felt "like a glass rod being rubbed on silk." Wow. *This book is definitely not for tonight,* LeeAnn decided. She closed it, put it on the bedside table, and reached for the cards Maggie had sent her. *I have to do something to keep from going mad,* she thought as she shuffled them. Once again, she drew at random, and was grateful it wasn't *"Grief"* this time. It was . . . **"Magic."**

"If you do not believe in magic, your life will not be magical. . . . Magic, like the power of Stonehenge, is part of the unknowable–that which you cannot describe, but which exists and makes your life extraordinary. It is part of the goodness of your spirit. Magic is what we are all looking for, but if you try to hold it and name it and describe it, you will lose it . . . Out of the mists of dawn, and the mysteries of creation, comes the magic that we call life."

Well, I'm still alive at least. LeeAnn sighed. *And I guess I still believe in magic.* She turned out the light and rolled onto her stomach. She put a pillow over her head and tried to go to sleep. It wouldn't be easy tonight. So she worked especially hard to concentrate on visual images. All her life, when LeeAnn went to bed, it had taken awhile to get away from the worries of the day–sometimes quite awhile, given all that she worried about. Then, finally, she would feel herself slipping happily into that visual space where hundreds of images, faces, geometric patterns flipped through her head, as if she were spinning through a Rolodex. Whenever her Rolodex started, she knew that sleep would eventually come.

At last it started to happen. Hundreds and hundreds of images that she didn't have to *do* anything to; she was just an audience and that felt so good. The last thing she imagined she saw was Stan's little glass doll, and then she was asleep . . .

In her dream, LeeAnn felt the ground shaking, gently at first, then harder. She heard a rumbling then. She was running, running, trying to get away. Falling, then caught. She was underwater. It was dark and she couldn't breathe . . .

When she woke with a start, she was wet with perspiration, and her heart was thudding in her chest. She lay there, trying to remember more of the dream. Part of it was the image she had seen when Sarge told her about the man caught in the pumice layer, one knee up as though running, caught like the people at Vesuvius. Part of it was seeing that man in his death throes, struggling, and then still. She remembered crying; her grief was terrible.

She turned on the light. *Should I pay attention to this nightmare I just had? Like* The Celestine Prophecy *says, my dreams are there to help me. Is there something this one is trying to tell me? Does it have anything to do with Stan's glass doll that everybody says couldn't possibly be old?* She lay there then, trying to picture in her mind how someone in ancient times would shape and polish obsidian; if they were teaching themselves how to do it.

The pumice. Of course, that was how you would polish obsidian. You'd wet a piece of pumice and then scrub with it. Living in a place where there was an endless supply of it, of course that's what you would do. When David polished his obsidian work, he used a series of six or eight grits to obtain that high gloss. But could you do it with just one? If she had some pumice she could try it and see.

I do have pumice. Under the sink in the bathroom. Pumice she'd bought at Bell's Hardware, encased in cellophane like a slim grey popsicle, that she kept for scrubbing porcelain. And there was plenty of obsidian in the basement rock room, so she had everything she needed. She sat up. "Why not?" she said out loud as she swung her legs out of bed and stood up. She thought she heard a noise coming from the basement, but of course she *would* hear something as soon as she was planning on going down there. The old house was rife with noises at night. And LeeAnn's imagination was as strong as her ability to worry.

As LeeAnn padded around the house looking vainly for the flashlight that she'd bought in Russia, and rummaging in the cupboard under the sink to be sure the pumice was there, she couldn't shake the residual fright from her dream. The central emotion was fear. *But there's no reason not to go down to one's own basement in the middle of the night, no matter what the state of one's mind. Bogeymen? They don't exist.* So she resolved to do it. There was nothing in the world to be afraid of . . . Unless, of course, Stan had been seen snooping around the trailer and Trautman had followed him to the house. In that case, there could be a whole squad of VHRI hit men hiding down there at this moment, waiting to get her because they knew she had the stolen trailer keys.

Which is about as far-fetched as it gets, LeeAnn, she told herself. *Of course, I am pretty isolated, with David out in the cabin, Audrey up in the attic with the AC going and Jeff and Peter way out in the sum-*

merhouse. If anything happened, nobody could possibly hear me.
But I need to know, she told herself. *I need to know what to do tomorrow. Do I go to the law? To the press?* She wished Vince would call her back. *He'd know what to do.* Should she hire somebody to go break into the trailer and check the figure? Or was she wrong about the whole thing? Maybe the glass doll was something one of the geezer brothers had made in his spare time. Maybe he polished it with a bar of pumice from Bell's Hardware. But when she talked to Sarge tomorrow, it would all hinge on knowing that the piece could conceivably be authentic, so she knew she had to do it.

She went into the closet and started descending the ladder that David had built, down into the black hole that led to their basement; it was dark enough to be a cave or a mine. When she got to the bottom, in the pitch black, she felt her way to the rock room, reaching through several spider webs for the light string. As she jerked the string, there was an instant of bright light, before–POP–the bulb blew out. Immediately after that, there was a horrendous crashing noise from David's studio.

LeeAnn screamed, then froze in place and waited. She felt absolute terror–that hot/cold prickly sensation that takes over your body. She was numb. Another noise, a smaller one this time. She crouched down and stayed still for a very long time. But nothing else happened.

I have to find out what that is, she thought. Finally she shook off her fear and began groping her way along the wall.

Fumbling in the dark, she felt the switch for the fluorescent fixture over the washing machine. She held her breath, then flicked it on and stared straight into the eyes of a panic-stricken Sillvester. LeeAnn started laughing and couldn't stop for a long time, which only upset Sillvester more.

"Hey, you're more scared than I am," she said, wiping away tears. "Come here." Silly's eyes were still a little wild. "I'll bet you sneaked in when David came down for the towels. Looking for mice in the furnace room again." She caught him in her arms and took him with her to the rock room to calm him down, while she searched for the most manageable piece of obsidian she could find, hoping it was not one that David was planning to make into something. Silly was meowing, but she couldn't let him down, because then he'd be trapped in the basement all night.

Grasping a stiff cat and a piece of obsidian in one arm, she used the other to pull herself laboriously up the ladder. Finally she yanked herself up onto her closet floor and collapsed. She lay there for a minute and then she couldn't believe what she heard, for all of a sudden Sillvester had started *purring!*

"What's gotten into you?; You've never *purred in your life.*" Then, as he started digging his needle claws into her breast and nuzzling, she realized, *Oh my gosh, he wants to nurse. He just realized I'm female.* "Yes, I'm a mommy. Poor kitty, that's what's the matter with you, you were probably never weaned." If his claws weren't hurting her so much, LeeAnn would have laughed. Instead, petting him, she said, "You're just lucky I don't have silicone. You'd pop my balloons."

LeeAnn stood up, closed the trap door, pulled Sillvester's claws from her person, and admonished him to stay out of the basement. He immediately jumped onto her bed and looked at her as if to say, "David may be allergic, but he's not here. Let me stay. Please." Then he kneaded the quilt, demonstrating what he would do to LeeAnn's chest if he had the opportunity. *So all is not lost, at least Silly loves me*, she thought. She left him lounging luxuriously on her bed and took the chunk of obsidian into the bathroom.

If anybody saw me right now, they would think I'd really lost it, she told herself as she carefully lined the washbowl with washcloths and filled the sink up partway. *Okay, now we'll see if with a hammer-stone and a piece of pumice you can make something.*

First, LeeAnn knocked a spawl off the rock, causing a concoidal fracture at the waist of it, then she struck another on the opposite side to simulate an hourglass shape. After that she began rubbing, first with the hammer-stone and then the pumice. Fifteen minutes later she examined her work under the light, and saw a tiny, satin-smooth patch where she'd been rubbing. *It works! All it takes is patience. An ancient person could have done this.*

LeeAnn put the rock down, drained the sink, then headed for bed.

CHAPTER EIGHTEEN

Spying on Paul

It was almost noon on Friday, the morning after the Celestine Dinner, and LeeAnn was at Wong's on Main Street, toying with her fried rice for breakfast. Sometimes if she was feeling vegetarian, which she was right now, she would pick out the miniscule shreds of meat that even the veggie rice invariably came with.

After a surprisingly untroubled sleep, LeeAnn, up before the rest of them, had padded around the house gathering an assortment of clothes. With an uncertain agenda–she might be gone all day or she might be gone for several–she'd finally settled on a bikini top with bicycle shorts, her Lee stretch jeans, and a black T-shirt that said New York over the pocket. That way the layers could be peeled as the day warmed up.

Aware she was being a little dramatic, she'd written David a note to go with the completed wind-rock. It was almost a goodbye note, a may-the-wind-be-at-your-back note, ending by saying she was taking the van and would be gone for awhile.

She had loaded up on algae as she always did when she needed a boost, and then left, convinced that if she tried to talk to either Audrey or David, she would screw up her relationship with both of them forever. *What happened last night?* She wished she knew. Or maybe she didn't. What did they do, if anything?

It had been a truly mind-bending experience deciding where to go for breakfast. Whenever LeeAnn found herself confused or frightened, she tended to retreat to the comforting minutiae of life that is always so ready to occupy our minds with small decisions rather than large. Having deliberated over the finer points of at least half a dozen restaurants, she had ended up at perhaps the least likely of all, eating vegetable fried rice for breakfast. Wong's with its black booths and foil wallpaper, with red velvet fuzz over it in generic fleur-de-lis, and its gum ball machine, was usually a pleasant place to hunker down and feel small town, but this morning it was not feeling as comfortable. Still worrying about David and Audrey, LeeAnn drained her teacup. Best to think about other things

She picked up her chopsticks once again. Her Franklin planner lay open on the table next to her rice bowl, reminding her that it's how we schedule our time that precipitates most of the events in our lives. But the choices LeeAnn faced today threatened to sweep her into total paralysis; she could feel it coming. And the three cryptic fortunes she'd found baked by mistake into one cookie hadn't helped a bit.

Today's page in her organizer entitled Prioritized Daily Tasks was still blank except for a sketch of a female torso, Stan's little glass doll. LeeAnn looked at her elbow watch. Back home, the rest of them were probably still sleeping. She thought of David in his bed in the cabin loft, under the green-and-white-striped sheets, his tanned arm outside the covers. Then she thought of Audrey in her lace teddy and deliberately tried to see her curled up alone in her bed in the attic. Her mind went to the Lovers in the petroglyph, which she had thought of as herself and David, inviolate and eternal.

Her mind went to the glass torso again, which could be the key to it all. If she could prove that it was an object of cultural patrimony and that its discovery was being concealed by VHRI, that fact, all by itself, could save the island. LeeAnn added some highlights to the sketch in her planner. Stan had said it was probably three inches long. She imagined holding it in her hand. She sighed. She knew exactly what it would feel like.

So what to do, what not to do? What I don't *do today,* she thought, *is probably as important as what I do do. Doo-do . . . which is what my life is right now.* She thought of them back at the house, sleeping. *Please Audrey, don't be the one he wants to live with for the rest of his life.* She wanted to cry, but of course she didn't–she was at Wong's.

Impatient with herself, LeeAnn poured one last tiny cup of tea, slammed it like it was a shot, and stood up. She took the little wire-handled carton of leftover rice the waitress boxed up for her, went up to the counter, and stood waiting to pay.

"That's $3.95," the waitress said as she punched it up on the cash register. She took LeeAnn's crumpled four one-dollar bills and drew out a nickel which she handed to LeeAnn. As she looked down to put the coin into the change pocket of her waist pack, LeeAnn thought she caught a flash of a fancy white car passing by on Main Street.

She hurried through two sets of doors designed for winter blizzards and out onto the sidewalk, but it was too late to see if it had been Sonja Al Amin's Mercedes. Vanna was parked just a few steps away; LeeAnn headed toward it. *Okay, choices,* she thought, and she paused in the middle of the sidewalk. *Go out to Tree Island, grab, snatch, steal the glass figurine, and get yourself shot. Not. Go find Ernst and confront him, wheedle, plead, convince, overpower, manipulate. Maybe.*

First you have to get to him. Of course, there's not that many places he could be, if he's even in town. The bank, VHRI, his airplane, or Tree Island. Or maybe she should go out to the State Police and snag Sarge. Tell him what Stan saw in the trailer. But the little voice inside her chimed, *Hearsay, hearsay! And you can't tell him it was Stan who saw it. Stan knows him, for god-sakes.* Or she could forget the whole thing, go home, climb into bed with David, provided he was alone in bed, and fuck his brains out. "Which is maybe what I should have done last night," she said aloud.

She pulled out her car keys but still lingered. *Well,* she finally told herself, *I can't stand here all day. They'll get me for loitering.* So having decided absolutely nothing, she stepped off the curb and went around to the driver's side of the van. She let herself in and climbed up onto the seat, which helped a bit–high seats in cars tended to make her feel as if she were on top of things. She fastened her seatbelt; then, in fair imitation of somebody going somewhere, put her key into the ignition and started the engine. *Which way?* Perhaps Vanna knew. LeeAnn shifted into gear, her thick, honey-colored hair swinging as she turned and checked for cars behind her.

Then she pulled out onto the quiet street and started driving down Main, passing the turn to go home without even looking, as she continued toward the bypass. *So, Vanna, where are you taking me? Nowhere actually,* she realized as she looked at the gas gauge that read empty. Normally LeeAnn was oblivious to gas gauges, and usually fortune protected her, but today, searching for detail to attend to, she just happened to notice. So she pulled in at the Texaco station on Biehn Street and made a couple of pleasant remarks to the attendant. In Oregon you still get to sit in the car while they fill the tank–another thing that addicted her to the state and would make her sorry if she decided to go back to New York.

More and more she was feeling she had to try to talk to Ernst one more time, but still stalling, she pulled into the drive-through at Renaldo's and got a latte.

Sipping her fix, LeeAnn at last drove slowly past the resort offices where a number of vehicles were parked. "Trained Guard Dogs," it said on the side of one of them. *Great, trained to maim and kill probably.* She pictured great sniveling pit-bulls with ropy saliva dangling from their jaws. There was also a utilities truck and a bunch of cars, including Sonja's white Mercedes, so maybe she *had* seen it go by. But Ernst's Jag was not there; maybe he wasn't in yet, so she swung past.

She drove aimlessly after that; she was on Eldorado at one point, then Pacific Terrace (in the toney part of town), trying not to notice the real estate signs here sprouting up everywhere. She pulled to a stop sign; the house on the corner had a Coldwell Banker sign planted in freshly mowed grass. *That's who we'd use,* she thought, *if David and I split.* She thought about all the polite and angry dividing up of stuff that goes on in separations. Divorces are so sad, even the kind where you're not really married. Would it actually come to that?

When she passed a pay phone by the side of the road, LeeAnn decided to try Sarge. With him, she figured, it might be easier on the phone than in person. She was intending to be brave and forceful, but found herself dialing her voice mail first, to warm up. "You have three new messages. Please enter your pass-code." She did.

"New message: This is Dr. Hall's office. You had an appointment this morning at 10:30 to have your teeth cleaned." *Oh, boy.* "Where were you?" said the female voice, sounding amused. "Please call to reschedule." They were always so nice about it, and it only made her feel more guilty.

"New message," only there wasn't; just the empty sound of an open line. *Who was that? One more chance.*

"New message:" Vince's voice, so dear it still caused her heart to skip a beat. "It certainly sounds like you might have got yourself the big one with that petroglyph. Naturally I have serious reservations about any possible Danube connection, but stranger things have happened. If, as you say, it looks *that* much like The Gulmelnita Lovers, who knows?

Or the whole thing could be an elaborate fake." *Conceivably*, LeeAnn thought; she hadn't thought of that. *But the lichen? A skillfully aged carving with the lichen glued on?* "Anyhow, let's talk. Our neighbors down the road here have a phone." He gave the number and LeeAnn scribbled it. "Unfortunately, or fortunately, we'll be on an overnight fishing trip today and back in the morning. Any time after that, give a call to Burt and Louise and I'll try to be standing by." *Burt and Louise?* LeeAnn thought to herself, writing it down. "Oh, and also I'll get my office to fax me the drawings you sent. Have a great life!" That was the way Vince always signed off.

LeeAnn dialed Burt and Louise and got an inane message about Sunfish and Funfish or something. Louise sounded like a heavy smoker. "Please tell Vince Taurini that LeeAnn has . . . further developments to report," she said, deciding she couldn't go into a whole thing about obsidian torsos that were either ancient or else from Woolworth's. "I'm not sure where I'll be, I'm kind of on the road, but I'll keep calling." Okay, that was done.

Now Sarge. She paused for a long minute with her hand on the phone, rehearsing what she was going to say. She dialed and heard the phone ring. Then, of course, it all flew out of her head–the whole rap she'd worked up–it all seemed so lame. A secondhand report that there *might* be some sort of cultural patrimony object that had been glimpsed through a ventilator duct. A figure *maybe* made out of obsidian–about a million to one chance–and of unknown age and origin. She couldn't even say who'd seen it there. So when "Sergeant Russo here" came on the line, LeeAnn began to bungle it from the start. ". . . but we know for a fact there are artifacts being loaded into that trailer," she heard herself saying in an argumentative tone.

"Just *how* do we know that?" Sarge sounded as if he was trying very hard to be patient.

"I can't say. Someone reported it to me." She felt a hot flash of recognized failure. All she could think about was what she was trying not to say. "*They* reported that to me," she repeated uselessly, deliberately using an indeterminate pronoun. She was looking out of the phone booth, feeling like an idiot. Sarge, meanwhile, was telling her a little impatiently that he would need concrete evidence in order to do anything at all. He hinted with his tone that this preoccupation with VHRI on her part was getting close to harassment.

"If you're against the project, you know, that's one thing," he told her. "However, the fact *is*, VHRI has complied with every regulation in the book. You can't argue with that."

LeeAnn nodded as though he could see her. "Yes, I know," she finally said.

"We're checking on the fax you sent, all *right*?" What fax? He must have said "facts," she decided, though that would be peculiar usage. He was silent then, waiting for her to say "thank you" and "goodbye." She reflected on how she must be coming across–just one more community nut.

"Okay?" he said with a definite sharp note in his voice that she hadn't heard before.

"I guess it will have to be," she said. "The only thing is . . . ," and then she was off on another tack, trying hopelessly to come up with something that would convince him of the urgency of it all.

A few minutes later, ashamed of her stumbling performance and glad nobody else had heard, LeeAnn walked back to the van, her cheeks burning as she replayed the end of their conversation in her mind. "With what we've got right now," Sarge had said, "I can't possibly ask for a new inspection."

"It's a felony to disturb a grave site, isn't that what you told me?" She couldn't prove that either. Then she tried another angle. "I also have reason to believe the contractor, Danielson and Harkins, may not have been forthcoming."

Sarge interrupted. "Look, I'm checking on your facts." Fax–facts, there was that word again. "I told you that. So . . ." Then he stopped, but the unspoken words seemed to shout at her–*Don't you realize my superiors are going to get on my ass if I start harassing the people who are bringing jobs to this town? Will you please back* off!

LeeAnn sighed as she climbed back in the van. The other day on the way back in the boat, even *after* the fiasco on the island, he'd still been nice to her. "You were right to bring this to me," he'd said, "the law is the law no matter how big they are." Now he was no longer singing that tune; clearly she'd worn out her welcome.

After chastising herself the next several blocks for her general stupidity, LeeAnn pulled up at Moore Park and turned the engine off. The silence was comforting. She sat there looking out at the water. From the foot of the lake she could see sixty miles to the north, all the way to the ragged edge of the caldera of Mount Mazama, up against the sky. The lake was like glass, so that let out windsurfing. One more option for the day checked off. But she *could* go for a run. Actually a run might help. A run nearly always helped.

Quickly stripping off her T-shirt and jeans, which left her in her bathing-suit top and bicycle shorts, she got out of the van, locked it up, put the key in her shoe pocket, and started off down the road before she could change her mind again. She felt a little catch in her right side; a heaviness that she sometimes felt when she was ovulating and the swollen ovary made her abdomen sore. She rubbed the tender place and the pain went away after a couple of minutes.

Jogging along Lakeshore Drive, LeeAnn tried to avoid thinking, and concentrated on her breathing. But it didn't work. She thought about the black glass doll, wishing she could see it, wishing she could hold it. Wished that probably as much as anything she'd ever wished. Paul, or whoever had found the figure, couldn't possibly have understood its significance if they just set it down in a box of beads. Or maybe it had no significance. *Maybe there's a price tag on the bottom that says Pier 1 Imports.*

Traffic was fairly heavy on Lakeshore Drive today. It was getting hot, the sun-baked asphalt was unpleasantly pungent. Several empty gravel trucks passed her on their way back to the quarry. Lots of activity, which made her nervous. Especially when she noted the VHRI contractor's name on a couple of the trucks. Douglas Santini, the balloon. *They must be doing a lot of work at Squaw Point today,* she thought.

When she got to where Lakeshore Drive joined the road to Medford, LeeAnn turned around, careful not to stop running for even a moment. By the time she started back up the hill on her return trip, her movements had finally become automatic. She had become a machine, a running machine. It felt so good not to have any responsibility other than regularly putting one foot ahead of the other. And sweating. She built her pace till she was running about as hard as she could. By the time she got back to Moore Park twenty minutes later, her bathing suit top and bike shorts were dripping, soaked through as though she'd been swimming. But she felt better. *At least I proved I can still do something. At least I broke out of my stasis.*

Outside the van, she hopped on one foot while she pulled Vanna's key out of her shoe pocket, opened the door, put her running shoes inside, and walked down to the water. She waded in up to her chest, feeling that characteristically silky, loamy touch of the bottom of Klamath Lake on her feet. It was delicious. She swam a few strokes, flipped over on her back, and looked up at the perfect blue sky. A thought was beginning to germinate in her mind, and she moved slowly so as not to disturb it. A resolve of some kind, or maybe more than one; she wasn't sure quite what it was yet.

After she'd dried off with a towel, she climbed into the back of the van where she stripped off the wet garments, put on a bra and underpants, light-blue and lacey, that she'd saved, new, all the time in Siberia for her return home to David. Dressing in her jeans and the black T-shirt again, she went up to the driver's seat and looked around, taking inventory. She had her laptop with her, her VISA card, her fried rice, most of her latte, and three days of her hometown paper, *The New York Times*. (She subscribed by mail and it invariably arrived in batches like Fifth-Avenue busses, three or four at a time, so she had to read them in batches, too).

She also had her water bottle, her Swiss army knife, her day planner, and a supply of field rations that David always kept in the back of the van. Dried soup, dried apple, an immersion heater, five gallons of water. She even had her windsurfing gear–Eff-tu was tied on top. David's board she had left at home. It all seemed so self-contained. She had the sudden sense that she could go anywhere, do anything. She felt free and independent–codependent no more.

Maybe I should head up to the Gorge, look up that beautiful Adam, go sailing, see if I can get myself hit by a barge. Not a bad plan. I think, LeeAnn finally acknowledged to herself, *what's happening is that I am feeling compelled to go up to Squaw Point and see what's really happening on Tree Island.* Yes!

Okay, here we go. Driving a little faster than she usually did, LeeAnn started retracing the route she'd just taken on her run. As she rounded a turn, she held her breath. A little flash of white up there under the tree let her know the trailer was still there.

It was still safe. The poor, ugly old thing, now heavily laden with all those mysterious boxes inside, and mortars and pestles, and what had to be the only obsidian hanowas ever found. *I know that's what it is*, she insisted to herself. *I* know *it's very old. I* know *it is.* In all her years in the field, when her intuition was this strong, she'd never been wrong.

As she drew close to the new road leading out to the point, LeeAnn could see there was an enormous amount of activity going on–a whole *bunch* of trucks parked at the landing, as well as what looked to be a colossal pontoon barge just being unloaded in sections from a flatbed. She pulled over to the side of the road momentarily. *They* are *in a hurry.* Stan had said the barge wouldn't be there till Monday at the earliest. *I'm glad I came,* she thought.

LeeAnn was still a mile from Squaw Point, so it was hard to see exactly what was going on. *I'll have to find a place to watch from,* she thought, *that's closer to the landing, because I may very well have to take off in a hurry and follow that trailer out of here today.* Although how she would follow in a large white van without being noticed was a problem she hadn't worked out.

She pulled out again, scouting the shoreline ahead, looking for a spot where she could park unseen and get a better view. *Do they know my vehicle?* she wondered as she drove the intervening mile. *Is there anybody watching me right now?* She thought not.

At last she found exactly the right place to spy from. Almost directly across the road from the landing, it was one of those little drive-in, around-and-out-again places that are there for no apparent reason. She was sorry that Vanna was so tall and hard to hide. But fortunately, LeeAnn found a large clump of manzanita that was high enough to conceal her presence from anyone passing on the road.

She had to just about high-center the vehicle to get it situated right– which she did with a silent apology to David who, after all, was half owner; both their names were on the titles of both vehicles. As she shifted the van into Park, she realized it might be tough to leave in a hurry, but for now she settled in. Through a fortuitous space between some aspen trees across the road, LeeAnn found she could see virtually everything that was going on both at Squaw Point and on the near side of Tree island.

She took out the new Nikons, which she hadn't realized till now were in the van–one more item in her survival kit. Then she moved over to the passenger side because it was closest, opened the window, and rested her elbows on the door.

LeeAnn trained the binoculars on the dock area, focused them perfectly (since there was no one around to make her self-conscious), and began to scan Tree Island foot by foot in an organized way. There were two boats, the Boston Whaler Paul used, and a spiffy-looking speed-boat. Cigarette boats, they used to be called. This new addition to the VHRI fleet was even more thrumpy than the police boat she'd come over in the other day. Big, fast, and rich. Ernst's style. The kind of boat you'd use as a tender, in the Mediterranean, for the yacht that had your helicopter on it.

"Danger, Men Blasting" signs were everywhere on the island. *It should say people blasting.* She also saw a machine that she recognized as the air compressor that Stan had talked about, sitting on its own set of wheels by the dock. They must have taken it over in the Whaler.

Over the next fifteen minutes, LeeAnn watched as several men worked to assemble the barge. It was quite a deal putting one of those things together; it looked like it would take awhile. So she pulled out her laptop and opened it up. Might as well be keeping a log. Of course, when the old Microsoft Word program she liked too much to upgrade came up, it seemed like a good idea to reread the note she had written David this morning. *Escape, transfer, load, file name. WINDROCK.* She pressed Enter and the fateful letter came up on the screen.

Dearly, it began. That was the way she always started her letters to him, not wanting to say the *beloved* part, but wanting him to hear the word unspoken.

Dearly,

I imagine you're still sleeping so we won't get to talk today like we thought we would. I'm feeling like I need to get away, so I'm taking the van–hope that's okay. I left your board because I might be gone for a night or two. (I just can't stand to sit around and witness the death of this relationship, she had written and then deleted.) Tears started to well up in her eyes so it was hard to see what was written on the screen of the Toshiba.

This is a special magic rock that I'm leaving for you. I made it after reading in Carrol Howe's book about the wind-rocks the ancient people used. I was glad to know about the ancient custom and I wanted you to have one.

The directions are simple, no moving parts. When you want the wind to blow from the north, just rub on the north side. For the south, rub on the south, and so on. And don't laugh. It just might work. Days you want calm weather, just gently rub the top. I hope it works for you. But remember you can't ever know *it's going to work. You can only hope.*

Wind is a funny thing. It lets us know that nothing in life is predictable and that forces stronger than ourselves are always at work. Wind has blown us together on our journey through the past few years and it's been a beautiful trip. But now the wind is blowing us apart. Maybe we're leaving each other forever, until another life someday. Oh, I love you so. Your wind-sister, LeeAnn.

She paused and looked out the window as the tears started to come. Her mind played the picture of herself and David back at the old apartment building, walking hand in hand toward the Jeep. Then they were backpacking in the mountains, sleeping in their green-and-white tent in the middle of the forest. She saw the forest now in her mind all around them, and the stars and the sky. Tears rolled down her face as she saw them lying together on their sailboards in the algae that day, holding hands, sharing the joys of their journey. And that night in Hood River, walking under the highway and past all the closed windsurfing shops, joined arm around or hand in hand, all these years. Always touching.

LeeAnn broke down and sobbed for a long time. She tried to stop but couldn't. Then she tried again. *But how can I spy through these high-tech binoculars when I'm crying my eyes out?* she rebuked herself. *You're supposed to be in Kinsey Millhone mode, L.A., not Weepy Woman mode.*

Suddenly impatient at her tearful state and the sentimentality of the note she had written, LeeAnn began to think of all the things she *hadn't* said. As she did, she felt a new strength coming and, surprisingly, an anger growing. Damn it, why hadn't she said the rest of it? Why had she neglected the part of the message that maybe wasn't so sweet?

LeeAnn looked over at the landing. From the way work was preceding on the barge, she guessed she'd be sitting here for awhile. *I'll fax this when I get to a motel tonight*, she thought. And she began to type.

Dear David,

This is a P.S. This actually is a very important P.S. to my note this morning. All of the above is true and from my heart. However, as I reread it now, I find myself wanting you to know about some other things I'm feeling. First, I've decided not to come home for a few days. I have some clothes and some food. I'll be fine. It's sad that you and I aren't talking better after all these years; in spite of how close we've been, there's still that wall. But in a way, I'm starting to feel stronger than I have–this is the first day that I've actually felt like I can handle whatever happens to us.

Maybe that's because I have something important to do–something I'm sure you'd disapprove of. But that brings me to what you need to know.

If you want the truth, I think you're a jerk, a real doo-doo head for making me feel so rotten when I got excited first about the petroglyph and then the glass figurine. What the hell *do you know about hanowas anyway? That's one area where I* know *that I know more than you do.*

I don't want your silent disapproval anymore because I don't deserve it and it's bullshit. I try not to disapprove of you and what you do and think in your life.

LeeAnn stopped and considered that last statement. Of course, the truth was that she disapproved *plenty*; she just did it in a more manipulative way, by sulking or crying and carrying on instead of saying it straight out. It was time to stop being indirect. Suddenly the resolution that had started to germinate in her mind that morning when she was floating in the lake became clear. Her fingers were lightening fast and the words flowed out.

I'm sick and tired of apologizing to you for not being an enlightened person, and I've decided I'm going to stand up for who I am. That has nothing to do with not being enlightened. I believe in the romance of a monogamous relationship, and I believe that two people can be together forever. I don't apologize to you for not being able to handle the idea of an open relationship. I love you too much. Every woman I know would understand when I say I believe in romantic love. One man and one woman forever together is what I want. That's the dream. You make a decision to love, you make a commitment, and then you do it. It's too easy to think, oh, I'll have some of this, I want vanilla today and tomorrow I'm gonna have strawberry. Bullshit. You have to be tough to stay together with a person. You have to want *to make it work. Maybe it wasn't so hard ten thousand years ago, but it's just as important now as it was then. Maybe the* most *important thing we can do with our lives is to forge a strong partnership and then live for it. Part of the reason kids are so screwed up today is because their parents get married three or four times. What that is is an ego thing, I think. Sure, everybody feels attraction–that's fine, that's normal, that's even fun–but you don't have to act on it. It's very self indulgent to act on it.*

*So here's my bottom line. **Polyfidelity**? No, I'm not into it. No, don't bring it up. If you want to go out there and find something else, then fine,* it's *over. Expecting me to feel differently is not going to work. Monogamy and fidelity are where it's at. I guess I'm ranting about family values; which probably is the un-sexiest phrase anyone has ever come up with for what* should be *the* sexiest *thing there is. It's our basis; partnership between mates is the basis of our lives, and it's very sexy.*

The only thing I got wrong was I thought I was half a person and you were half a person, and together we made a whole. I see now that it's far, far stronger if I can be a whole person and you can be, too, to start with. I think that's what you've been trying to teach me, that we can be two strong people joined. Because then our joining makes a unit that's indivisible. If we believe that we are on the planet for more than just a random reason, then it's that we're supposed to learn from the partner we have. I've learned a lot from you. We choose a partner because they're supposed to teach us something, and the point is how can we ever learn if we continue to take the easy way out?

You say our relationship has been 99% perfect. Well, it's never going to get any better. And it's definitely not going to get any better if you screw around, dishonoring what we have. If you're going to be single, be single. If you're going to be in partnership, be in partnership. Boom, end of sentence. That's it. This gift of sexual union that's been given to us is something we must have reverence for. We have to take care of it. Honor our bodies. *I've been denying what I really felt about you and Audrey. Like saying to myself, I don't really love you enough if I have those feelings. Well, that's ridiculous. I thought I was limiting you by not wanting to open the relationship. But what I had was just a normal reaction. And that's okay. Which is why I'm telling you now, it's basically either all or nothing with us from now on. If you want it, tell me now. If you don't, hasta luego. I'm strong enough to do without you.*

Looking up now, LeeAnn scanned the landing area at Squaw Point, then she looked down again and reread her letter. It was rough and unconstructed, probably repetitive, but she didn't change a single word. Just then another tractor-trailer pulled into the landing, noisily huffing as it idled in the parking lot with a load of port-a-potties aboard. Then LeeAnn noticed that while she'd been writing to David, a ritzy looking silver motor home bristling with antennae had arrived on the scene. Another VHRI toy. A fancy air-conditioned office, no doubt. Communications Central.

It looked as if they were getting ready to load the motor home onto the barge for the first trip across. In truth, it looked like they were getting ready for an invasion; the only thing missing were the humvees. *Boy, if you've got enough bucks, it's amazing how much you can make happen in a short time.* Through the binoculars, she saw that it said "Champion" on the side of the motor home.

It *had* helped to get her thoughts out. She'd been banging on the Toshiba's keyboard for ten minutes now. She realized the battery would run down pretty soon and start beeping at her. She got the adapter out of the glove compartment, plugged it into the cigarette lighter, and prepared to write some more. This could be an important day of enforced reflection. *Maybe I'll even understand life better after today,* she thought.

But then LeeAnn realized another basic truth–she needed to go find a place to pee. So she opened the door of the van, got out, and started prowling around, finally deciding to water a small, friendly looking bush down in the hollow. When she was through, she walked over to the edge of her blind and peered around toward the landing. It looked as if they had finished putting the barge together.

She hurried back to the van, grabbed the binoculars, and trained them on the barge, which sank down lower in the water as they drove the motor home onto it. *Almost certainly,* she thought, *they will be bringing the trailer back on the return trip. Champion in, Nomad out.* How symbolic. Dominators in, partnership out.

She kept the Nikons on that streamlined silver-bullet shape as it floated across in the bright sunshine to Tree Island. The boat driver maneuvered the barge right up to the beach in front of the stone house, and in a matter of minutes a ramp was in place. The motor home was driven off the barge and parked alongside the dock. LeeAnn watched as several architect types immediately went inside. To bask in the air-conditioning, no doubt, she thought.

LeeAnn went into the back of the van, scavenged up some dried apples and some crackers, then returned to the passenger seat where she sat with the computer on her lap, its cord stretched up to the dash.

"3:15 p.m., Squaw Point," she wrote, then summarized what she'd

observed since she'd arrived, up to the point of their moving the motor home across the channel. *"The Nomad trailer still appears to be in the same position. Nobody's gone up anywhere near the tree that I can see . . ."*

About fifteen minutes later LeeAnn noticed workmen, about a dozen in all, beginning to gather down at the dock. VHRI was still using the World War II Jeep; LeeAnn had seen it being driven away over the hill a little while before. Now it came back with four men in it, and they headed for the dock area as well. *I wonder what's going on. Maybe it's break time*, she thought.

Then KABOOM!! She saw the earth erupt, a huge flash over on the far side of the island. An immense cloud of dust began to rise, sparkling in the sunshine. The earth shook. LeeAnn saw in her mind the Lovers being blasted into a million pieces. *No, I won't give that thought energy. Please don't let that be,* she prayed.

When she could finally tear her eyes away from Tree Island, she looked back down, and started typing again. *"3:48 p.m. The worst possible thing has happened. They're starting the blasting. I didn't get to stop it after all. You wouldn't believe what it was like, David."* Suddenly she was writing to David instead of just writing a log. *"The birds went nuts. The ground shook. The lake shivered. Every animal for miles around had its hair turn grey, I'm sure. Mazama must have been like this, only so many thousands of times worse. I really wish you were here, because I know if you could see what's happening you'd get angry too. I felt so . . .* together *with you those two hours working on that rock pile. Never more so. I'll keep that memory.*

"4:08 p.m. There was another explosion a few minutes ago, exactly twenty minutes after the first, as some more of Tree Island got airlifted out. Same routine. The guys get in the Jeep, drive over the hill, probably to set the fuses, then pretty soon they drive back. Everyone hangs around down by the dock area, cheering when it goes off, and afterwards they're looking so jaunty and proud, like each of them is personally responsible. Then they get back in the Jeep and roar back over there to look at what they've done and gloat over it.

"The second time there was a huge landslide around by the south side, where I really can't see. That's the area I'm most concerned about. I'm not giving up yet. I'm just not."

She sat and stared out again for a little while and then began writing again. *"4:30 p.m. I wonder if there is anything worse than feeling absolutely helpless? What hurts so badly is that eventually it numbs us and makes us not feel anymore. The third explosion wasn't as bad as the first. I'm already becoming resigned. When you can't do anything, you begin to think, why feel, why bother trying anymore?"*

In the quiet of the explosion's aftermath, LeeAnn felt as if she were re-experiencing the death of all the people who had lived and died on Tree Island, all the way back in time. Each blast had wounded her. Each time it had felt like part of herself was being ripped apart, along with the relative serenity that had been maintained all these years on the island–if you didn't count the time it was being maintained by a couple of guys with a shotgun. Still, during that time, the souls that rested there had probably been at peace. *It's as though they were sleeping even through the shotgun blasts but now they've been jolted awake.* Her anger built; it had seemed to be building all day on this day of slaying dragons.

LeeAnn's arm had been getting tired of holding the binoculars, and her eyes squinty from looking through them for so long, but now she was instantly alert again as she saw that the Nomad trailer, which hadn't been anywhere in thirty years, was about to be moved. *Little doubt about it.* Somebody had driven the old Jeep up and was positioning it just in front of the trailer under the tree. It looked like Trautman.

She turned the fine focus on the Nikons slightly. It was most definitely Paul; she could tell from the fatigues. Rambo and one of the other men were starting to hook up the hitch. *So I'm glad I waited,* she thought. *It looks like I* am *going on a trip tonight. She started thinking about credit cards and motels and the full tank of gas she'd just got. The prospect of a motel was a pleasant one.*

The second fellow gave a wave now and started walking back down the hill. LeeAnn watched as Paul climbed into the Jeep; she saw the trailer move forward just a bit, then stop. It started to move again, then it lurched and came to a sudden halt. One wheel of the Nomad was down. It sat there now at a kind of crazy tilted angle as Paul jumped out of the Jeep and started kicking it violently.

"Hallelujah!" LeeAnn said out loud. She had to laugh as the image of a hairy hand stuck in a cookie jar came to mind. *He tried to take too much–greed and haste.* Paul looked like a figure on a video game, kicking at the trailer as though he could persuade it to get up and move.

Rage looks so stupid, especially from a distance when you can't hear the sound effects, she thought. Eventually, he gave up kicking and walked back down the hill toward the others.

It seemed the day was finally winding down. It was 7:00 p.m.–kind of late for a construction workday. The architect types exited the motor home, drawings under their arms, and headed toward the cigarette boat. The construction crew went to the Whaler. Segregation by class.

Once ashore on the landing, the men climbed into a variety of vehicles. Paul loaded several white collars into a new tan Suburban that said VHRI in rainbow script on the side. And other supervisory personnel climbed into a Santini Construction van. Then they all drove away and the island was returned to its normal state of serene quiet. LeeAnn could almost see it relax. It lay there wounded, resting.

When the last car disappeared from sight, she got out of the van and stretched. Her stiffness from the windsurfing trip was almost gone. She walked across the road closer to where she could have a clearer view of the whole island. At the landing she looked around at the port-a-potties and big, yellow Caterpillars lined up in a row.

Paul had taken the men back to town, probably to the Comfort Inn or the Olympic out on South Sixth, so he'd be gone for awhile. LeeAnn figured she had forty-five minutes that were absolutely safe, so she sat down by the shore. It felt good to be close to the water. The slight breeze blowing against her cheek was warm, but insistent.

Wind's up, a voice inside of her said. When she failed to listen, it said it again. *Wind's up.* She was tempted by the thought. It was a perfect wind direction for a reach. And her board was on top of the van. She scanned the surface of the water, looking over at the island and the trailer at the top of the hill. Then she walked back to the van and sat inside, even though the forty-five minutes wasn't over.

Restless, she turned on the radio to KSOR, but her mind drifted. ". . . with winds increasing to ten to twenty-five knots," she heard, but she'd missed hearing where they were talking about so it didn't do her any good. Out here you could be in a totally different micro climate just fifty miles away.

She switched the radio off, took the three keys that Stan had given her out of her waist pack, and laid them in the console beside her. Of course, she couldn't do anything now, but if she waited until after Paul went to bed–presuming he stayed on the island at night–she had the means to get across unseen and inside that trailer. Surely one of the keys would fit. How many padlocks had the guy bought lately of the same brand?

Forget it, one voice inside her told the other. *No, I can't forget it. The trailer is right on the edge of the island; it would hardly even be trespassing. I just need to* look *at that figurine.*

And get yourself busted, the other voice chimed.

I don't want to take anything.

Nonsense. If you find the figurine, and if it looks old to you, you know *you'd take it with you. And that's* stealing, *LeeAnn.*

Maybe. But if it's what I think it is, I'll do anything I have to do to try to save it. Even get busted, if that's what it takes. In fact, maybe that's the way to go. Get some publicity; file a class-action suit through the Tribes. That ought to get some attention.

Sure, LeeAnn. And you can direct the whole operation from jail.

"Why did Stanley Porter have to do this to me?" she asked out loud. *Why did he provide me with this temptation that I've been moving closer to all day? Who does he think he is, handing me these choices? It* is *all at stake, all the time.*

She fingered her bone necklace, remembering again the day she found it. *Indecision could destroy me,* she thought. *If something was ever meant to be, this is it. I'm equipped to do it. I'll wait till he's asleep, cruise over, open the trailer, get the figurine. I know right where it is. If it's not what I think, I leave it. I can decide then. I can always take it straight to Sarge and throw myself on his mercy. Tell him they hid the petroglyph and they were going to do the same with this. So I may get busted, which gives me major claustrophobia. But what am I alive for? I'll do it.*

LeeAnn was watching when Paul Trautman returned to the Squaw Point landing, just before 9:00 p.m. He'd been gone an hour and forty minutes. He got into the Whaler, started it up on the third try, and drove the boat across to the island. She heard him kill the motor as he glided up to the dock, watched him climb out and tie up the boat. Then he disappeared into the stone house.

At 9:15 lights came on, and not just inside the house—a flood illuminated the front yard as well. LeeAnn watched with the binoculars. She waited. Paul came outside with a McDonald's bag in one hand and a beer in the other. *No wonder his mind doesn't work right, when he eats all that garbage. I wonder what time he goes to bed?* Moments later he was back inside again for another beer. Definitely a beer, the way he put his head back and guzzled. *Go ahead, Paul, have another beer.* It would be better for her, she thought, if he got a little tipsy.

CHAPTER NINETEEN

Chased

She had promised herself she would wait until it was dark before she got her board down from the top of the van. But as soon as the light had faded sufficiently on the eastern side of the lake, she untied Eff-tu and laid her down in the grass in a small, flat clearing out of the wind. Then she turned on her bright little penlight from Russia that was in the van's console, so she could see as she opened the PVC case David had made to keep her mast in. She put the two parts of it together, laid them out on the ground, then went back for her sail. A moment's hesitation. Which size to rig? Four point eight; better safe than sorry. Too big a sail can literally blow you away; she could miss the island entirely.

Why don't I just swim over? she asked herself. *Because it's pretty far and the current would likely carry me past the island before I got across.* Klamath Lake was almost like a river, so much water always flowing swiftly south. No, it made more sense to sail, she decided. She took her sail out of its bag, threaded it onto the mast, and slid the boom down over it to the height she'd marked with nail polish. Then she adjusted the lines on the boom clamp, snapped it shut, and yanked at it to make sure it was tight.

David had seen to it that they bought all the best little pulleys and hooks so LeeAnn could out-haul, down-haul, and up-haul without help. But it took some strength to pull that sail absolutely tight. So far, she was doing fine. She blessed David, as she tightened the battens, for the lessons he'd given her. Finally she had mast, boom, and sail all together, so all she'd have to do when it was time to go was snap the Chinook into the universal after she got it down to the water. Her rig was set.

Back in the van, she waited for Paul's light to go out. Finally about

12:30, he came outside and stood in silhouette for a long minute, maybe a minute and a half, LeeAnn thought, peeing. The characteristic stance of a man urinating was hard to miss. He went inside and his light went out.

Time to get ready. First, LeeAnn took off her gold chain with the Yugoslav figurine and laid it in the console. She couldn't stand to lose the talisman of their love. Then she put the three padlock keys on one small ring along with her key to the van and stuck them in her shoe pocket. She had decided to keep her shoes on for this trip, for use on the island and for gripping the board better. Since she'd forgotten her booties.

Now what's the best thing to wear? LeeAnn went around to the back door of the van and rummaged through the locker. *Same old, same old, nothing much there.* So she'd keep on her dark jeans and black T-shirt. Both were light in weight, dark in color, good for concealment.

She stepped into her harness with the blue-and-white checkerboard pattern on the butt, pulled it up, snugged the leg straps, and began adjusting the rest of it, buckling all the buckles. Just putting it on somehow made her feel stronger, more armored. The straps under the legs lent a parachutist/jet pilot/astronaut sort of feeling.

It had been twenty minutes since Paul's light went out. *Even if he gets up to take another leak, I'm safe for an hour, maybe more. Maybe all night. If he wakes up and looks out, he won't be able to see me,* she thought. The night was dark. LeeAnn put her small flashlight into a plastic baggie she found in the back of the van.

She rolled the baggie up as best she could, stuck it in her *New York City* T-shirt pocket, and fastened it in place with a small safety pin from the accumulated junk in the console. With luck, she would wade in, wade out, and not get wet at all. But you never can tell. She put her Swiss army knife in her right jeans pocket.

The thirty minutes LeeAnn had allotted herself to wait after Paul's lights went out were finally over. As she got out of the van, she hid her Toshiba under the seat, double-checked everything one last time, then locked up. Heading for the water, she picked up her board. In almost total darkness, with great care, she carried it across the road, then headed down through the trees on the other side.

It wasn't as easy as she thought. She tripped, and then she banged the board against a tree trunk in the dark. It didn't seem quite prudent to use the flashlight to find her way. *Since I'd have to be holding it in my teeth anyway.* The thought made her giggle. *God, I'm nervous,* she thought. *Take a deep breath, LeeAnn. Relax, you'll feel better.* She stumbled down the steep bank, laid the board on some rocks, and headed back for the sail, looking both ways before she crossed the road.

The wind was pretty strong now. It had even tried to tug at her board as she carried it across the road, which meant that the sail could easily get away from her; she'd have to be careful. She wondered if David would be worried yet, but of course, he'd have no reason to since she said she might be gone for a couple of days. *No one will miss me.*

She made her way back to the little hollow where the van was parked with the sail laid out beside it. The wind was starting to howl. She could hear it more clearly from this sheltered spot. She picked her sail up, remembering to put the leading edge into the wind like David did, lifted it over her head, and started out. It was even harder to deal with than the board, tough to maneuver so that a tree branch wouldn't poke a hole in it.

Just as she crossed the road, a gust got it for a second. But she recovered, staggering down to the shore where she managed, just barely, to hook it into the receptacle on the board before it could take off on its own.

So far it had gone pretty smoothly. LeeAnn could see the island better now that her eyes had adjusted. She pushed the board into the water and flipped it upside down to protect the fin till she could get it into deeper water.

Wait a minute, she thought. *What fin? Where's the damn fin?* Of course, David always took it off so the two boards could nest on top of the van. *My fin is back in the equipment drawer. Shit! How stupid. I hope it's there anyway.*

Feeling panicky, LeeAnn dropped her board on the shore and hurried back across the road. Standing by the van, she hopped on one foot, got her keys out of the shoe pocket, opened the back of the van and turned on the overhead light, retrieved the fin, then spent the next ten minutes looking for the fin screw to put it on with.

She remembered that David had pulled her fin screw out of his pocket the day they rigged at Rocky Point. *So is that where it is? In David's pocket? Or on his dresser where he always laid thing out so neatly at night?* For an instant she was filled with rage, feeling scared, dependent, ashamed, foolish, stupid. Simply not competent for this kind of undertaking, or for most kinds of undertakings–like going through life alone. *I'm missing a fin screw just as my greatest adventure is about to materialize. I cannot sail without a fin, which means I'm still dependent on a man. Just an ordinary screw with a Phillips head is about to stop me,* she thought, as she rummaged through the storage areas. It was an old board, and had a peculiar way of attaching the fin.

Another ten minutes later LeeAnn still had not found the fin screw or any other screw even remotely resembling it. But she wouldn't give up. Was this a sign she shouldn't go? A coincidence of warning?

I can tie *the fin on,* she thought. *If I had a piece of wire or some thin nylon line I could thread it through the place where the screw goes and tie it on just fine.*

She tried a shoelace from her running shoe, but it wouldn't go through the hole. And there was no wire. Doubled-up dental floss might do it, but she didn't have any. Then it struck her. Triumphantly she went around to the console and picked up the gold chain that held the Venus figure. She pulled the figure off and examined the chain. It looked strong. She could drop it through the hole, then double it back and tie it. As good as wire. She locked the van and replaced the key in her shoe pocket.

Back at the shore, her hands shook as she tied the fin in place and tested it to see that the knot would hold.

Okay, Eff-tu, let's see you do your stuff, she whispered. *This is a perfectly easy reach; just take it slow.*

She positioned the boom over the bow of the board, holding the mast with one hand, the boom with the other, stumbling a bit on the rocky bottom as she waded out. *I'll be back here in fifteen minutes,* she told herself, feeling a small rush as her feet got wet. The water was *cold.* Now the trick of taking off dry. *Raise your sail too early or don't transfer your weight right, and you get dunked.* This time, however, it seemed easy. She stepped aboard and was on her way.

What a peculiar thing this was, sailing in almost total darkness. An eerie feeling because she suddenly realized she couldn't read the water, couldn't see ahead. But it also felt pleasantly wicked, because no one in the entire *world* knew what she was doing right now. As long as Paul stayed asleep, or even if he stumbled outside, as long as he stayed away from the trailer–she'd be very quiet–no one would ever need to know.

The wind let up a bit, and then was suddenly stronger. It was impossible to make out these wind patterns on the water. *Just be ready for anything. The main thing is not to sail it right up on the beach, but to get off in time. You don't want to get too close to shore with this rickety fin.*

She felt a few drops of rain, or was it spray? It was clear that a genuine windstorm was starting. *Best to get this over with while it's still manageable.* LeeAnn was better than halfway across when she realized that if she decided to liberate the figurine, she hadn't brought anything along to put it in. *Will it fit in my jeans pocket? How dumb. Don't let it get to you, LeeAnn,* she told herself. *Don't beat yourself up over mistakes you've already made. At least you didn't try to sail without a fin.*

She could make out the dim shape of the island ahead now and the little cove that she'd be coming into in a few minutes. The stone house on the left where the rock piles were, and the path up to the promontory on the right where the tree and the trailer were.

The moon began to peek out from behind a cloud. It was pretty dim, but she could see a little better. She wouldn't take the path to the jeep road because it led past the house. It was safer to climb up from further down near the shore where David and she had come down the other day. That way she wouldn't come anywhere near the house. And there were plenty of places to stash the board around the corner, where Paul couldn't see it, even if he woke up and started prowling.

The shore was coming up fast. LeeAnn hopped off and promptly went in up to her chin before one foot found the bottom. When she got to shore, she stopped, pulled her flashlight out, unwrapped it from its baggie and wiped it dry. She turned it on. It was still going. But there was water under the glass. *How long will it last,* she wondered.

She hid Eff-tu behind the rise of land that led up to the trailer. Then in the pale moonlight, she began to climb. It was about two hundred feet up, but not dangerously steep. When she got to the top, she looked around to make certain she was alone. And she was, except for the ancient tree. It seemed like she could feel its comforting presence. She walked around to the back door of the trailer and pulled her key ring out of her shoe.

Hoping there was no alarm, she grasped the padlock and inserted the first key. *But it won't be the first one,* she predicted, *it never is.* And it wasn't. Nor was it the second. The third key turned and the lock clicked open.

She looked around, removed the padlock, then opened the trailer door very, very carefully. Nothing seemed to go off. She put the padlock back on the hasp so she wouldn't misplace it, and so the door wouldn't slam shut completely behind her. She switched on her flashlight and with its dim and dimming light, she looked inside.

The floor was crooked. Everything in there was at a crazy angle. The first thing that struck her eye, by the door on the right, was a pile of huge old mortars of immense weight. Just like Stan had said. *That's undoubtedly what tipped the trailer.* Most of them were lava rock, the shape of a hard-boiled egg with the top cut off and the yolk removed.

They were piled carelessly, or maybe they'd fallen when the trailer was moved. The largest of them was one with the bottom broken out; a huge mortar, and the pestle with it was broken as well, making LeeAnn imagine that perhaps a husband had broken it to set his wife's spirit free, and had become broken himself in the process. The male broken to free the female.

LeeAnn stepped inside, and her weight made the trailer rock ever so slightly. The biggest mortar rocked and the broken pestle inside moved as well. It was as though they were acknowledging her. She watched as the rocking slowed and then stopped.

LeeAnn shone the weak light around the room. There were shelves and cupboards all around the trailer, and a table bolted to the floor at one end. There were several dozen shallow wooden boxes stacked against the opposite wall.

She selected one, feeling slightly sick to her stomach because she thought she knew what was inside. She tried to open it, but it was nailed shut, so she took out her Swiss army knife and pried off the top.

Bones! Just as she thought. Packed in old newspaper. She unwrapped part of a tibia. Then a small fibula, a child's. She had handled lots of human bones, but the people who'd owned these bones and used them and walked around with them felt extremely close to her right now. She found herself thinking of the man Sarge had told her about–the one whose skeleton was found in the volcanic ash. She saw him in life for the flash of an instant; the image was strong.

The flashlight was flickering, so every second was precious. Glancing up at the vent above that Stan had looked down through, LeeAnn checked from his line of sight to where the figurine would be. The table below the vent was littered with what looked like a hundred objects.

Now the bulb of her penlight was definitely flickering and its light growing orangey. *What am I going to do when it goes out?* she wondered. *It will be pitch black in here. I'll have to crawl over every surface, climb around this whole place, feeling everything, to find the glass doll. Let me find the figure now, at least let me see it.* And then she did. It was packed in cotton in an open pasteboard box that was lying in a carton of olivella shells. She held the light close to it, but didn't touch. A female torso–made of a grey-black shiny stone that was *surely* obsidian–breasts and shoulders, a long waist, the tops of the legs just disappearing into a squared-off base.

In the dim light the figure sparkled. And then her flashlight went out. LeeAnn reached for the figure in the dark. When she picked it up, it was as though she'd held it many times before. She felt its energy, and her hand seemed to remember every curve.

She took a moment with her fingertips to trace the contours, understanding for the first time what it would be like to be blind, yet able to perceive beauty and integrity of artistry by touch. David had that sensitivity of touch.

A woman's hand had fashioned this, she knew that. It had the spirit of woman. Over the wind she thought she heard a noise; her mind went to the guard-dog truck she'd seen at VHRI. She imagined a dog's jaw clamped on her ankle. *It was time to get out of here. Time to decide.* The decision took no time at all. *Okay,* she said silently to the figurine which she now knew, more compellingly than she'd ever known anything, was *very* real and very old, *you're coming with me. Right now.*

How to stow it safely? LeeAnn had her running shoes on but no socks; they'd gotten sweaty when she went for her run so she hadn't put them back on. Otherwise she could have tied the figure in a sock and then tied the sock to her clothing. Maybe she could carry it in her bra. She tried that, but the bra was flimsy and old; its elastic had pretty much given out so there was a good chance she'd lose it that way. LeeAnn saw the glass doll in her mind's eye at the bottom of the lake, silt drifting over it.

Finally, she settled on her front jeans pocket where there was some slight danger that if she scrunched over too far, conceivably she could break it. The jeans were fairly tight. She tried bending and scrunching. It seemed okay. She nestled the figure sideways in the bottom of the pocket, under the harness. It would be secure there, she thought. Then she thought about carrying one of the bones with her as additional proof. She tried to see where the box was that she had opened. She would take the child's bone.

If there was only some light, she thought, so she could see what she was doing. And then suddenly there was, as someone switched on the overhead light and it flooded the room. There was Paul Trautman, with a lantern in one hand and a gun in the other, standing at the door, blocking out her entire future. LeeAnn stood there like a doe caught in the headlights.

Bare feet, baggy grey sweatpants, washboard stomach, with tattoos, no shirt, and that cold, expressionless face. Paul Trautman. Battery lantern in one hand, handgun in the other. His arm, his hand, his gun; her eyes could not help but be drawn to the black hole at the end of it. Paralysis was taking over. Fear does one of two things, it either propels or paralyzes. All of her life, it had paralyzed LeeAnn.

"Don't move," he said. She couldn't, anyway. "How did you get here?" he demanded. "Is there more than one of you?" His eyes took in her sopping T-shirt, her dripping hair. "Got wet, did you?" She was standing behind the table that was bolted to the floor. Trautman moved his head so he could see around the boxes piled on top. Then he pointed his lantern at the reactor bar on her harness, smack in the middle of her stomach. He laughed. "Are you in the habit of sailing at night? In over your head, it looks like," he added.

They stared at each other. *So this is what stark terror feels like,* she thought. *And the funny thing is, some part of me doesn't care, as though this is just the end of an episode I'm watching. I've always wondered what it would be like, going to my death.*

She tried to stare at him as though she were simply surprised, not afraid. As he shone the lantern over every part of her body, it felt as though he were touching her, molesting her with the light. A wave of nausea followed the beam, a prickly sensation on her skin, as though she could feel the heat of the bulb.

"Get over here," he said.

"Why do you want me over there?" she asked, in a funny, high-sounding voice.

"Good question." He put the lantern down on a shelf. Keeping his gun on LeeAnn, he pulled a small cellular phone out of his sweatpants pocket and dialed with his thumb. He looked up at her. "For the time

being, stay right where you are. And don't give me any of your shit."
She could see his expression change as someone answered.

"Yeah, it's Paul. Get her on the phone. Then wake her up!" He
waited. "Good morning." The tone was unmistakably intimate. "About
0100. Listen, I think I know the answer to this question, but I wanted to
check with you. The motion detector in the Nomad went off a little
while ago . . ." *God, how stupid I was*, LeeAnn thought. "And I have
a . . . uh, delicate situation on my hands. The line's secure. No. Inside
the trailer. Exactly. No, she appears to be alone." He looked up at
LeeAnn, then focused on her wet jeans and the little puddle of water on
the floor.

"So, the question is, how would you like me to handle this?" He listened, nodding. LeeAnn could hear the sound of Sonja's voice, but not
her words. He smiled slightly. "That's what I thought. You know me,"
he said softly. Then he folded the phone and put it back in his pocket.

What did that *mean?* LeeAnn tried to hear what was going on in
Paul's head, but the little room was so crowded, with him in the doorway, and the spirits of the people whose bones were in the boxes all
around. So many of them. It felt like so many of them were there.

"You need to do *exactly* what I say," Paul said carefully. "I don't
want to have to shoot you." For a moment it sounded as though he
meant that in a kindly way. But he didn't, she realized. *He doesn't want
to shoot me because he would rather* drown *me so it will look like an
accident.*

She imagined it happening, could feel him yanking her by her hair,
pulling her into the lake, then holding her under. She could feel the
water closing in on her head. She tried not to think that too loudly so he
wouldn't hear the thought. And tried to make her eyes into one-way
glass so he could not read it. But she realized he was thinking *exactly*
what she was thinking; she could see it in his face.

His eyes now followed the beam of light on her body, the running
shoes, the wet jeans, the harness with the straps going under the crotch.
He was in no hurry; in fact, he was enjoying this.

That gave her just the edge she needed to start thinking rationally,
or at least thinking. LeeAnn had a sudden vision of running at Paul,
pushing him away, somehow fleeing. But it was impossible. Wasn't it?

"Put your hands up on top of your head."

She had to stop thinking about the figurine in her pocket because he would pick up on that and know it was there. But she wanted to touch it for courage. Then she thought, *dummy. It's already touching you; you've got it touching your leg. It can give you courage from there.*

"Hands up."

She put them up, and as she did, she seemed to see herself from above. As though a part of her, the part with the sense of humor, hovered at the ceiling, watching dispassionately as the ghostly scene unfolded. This LeeAnn was entirely separate from the one who still stood behind the table, terror in every cell.

Paul beckoned now with his head, a backward jerk like gangsters do in the movies. *He had a couple of beers before bedtime, you know,* the ceiling-LeeAnn commented calmly then; *he's bound to be a little slow in his reactions.*

He looks pretty damned alert to me, replied the other LeeAnn who was standing trembling on the floor.

As long as you keep eye contact, you have some control, the ceiling-LeeAnn advised. *Look at where he's standing, and what's right beside him. Study your surroundings, but don't glance away. If you do, you'll lose. It's your power against his power. Stand in your power, woman.* Was this voice coming from the ceiling-LeeAnn or from the ancestors around her? She couldn't tell anymore. *Keep his eyes on yours, or at least on your body.*

She saw it then. Saw what she had to do. She saw the huge mortar lying on its side.

"Do I have to come and drag you over here?" Trautman asked with quiet rage in his voice. She'd seen him kick the trailer; she knew what that rage turned against her could do. "Get over here. Now Git!"

She started toward him then, keeping his gaze on her face by force of will. Then just before she got to the door, LeeAnn suddenly lunged with her whole body, swiping her hip and her elbow against the huge fallen mortar, tipping it off the shelf, then jumping out of the way just as it fell heavily onto Paul's foot with the sickening thud of a smashed melon.

Paul doubled over in his agony and LeeAnn tripped over him, tangling arms and legs. He writhed in pain and she crawled off of him in haste, hitting her head on the doorjamb, then stumbling to her feet and racing out the door, running for the bushes and starting down the hill. Then in her memory she heard what she hadn't heard when it happened . . . the clatter of Paul's gun as it fell to the floor.

I could have picked it up, she thought. *Damn it. Should I go back and try to get the gun?*

But she didn't dare. He'd recover himself in a minute and come after her. He hadn't yet, though. So she kept on running, slipping and sliding down the hill.

There was no sound from the trailer for long seconds, then Paul's "Awwwwieeee," high and raspy like a vacuum cleaner sounds just before you smell the burning rubber and it self-destructs.

The moon had moved behind a cloud and it was dark, blessedly dark. LeeAnn seemed to be guided as she moved. *All I have to do is jump on my board and sail back, run to the van . . .* Then she heard him coming, a wounded animal crashing through the brush pretty far behind her. She expected a bullet in her back at any moment.

At last she got to where her board was hidden behind the rocks. She started to push it out into the water, but then she thought, *Shit! He's got a boat. This is stupid.* She let go of the rig and was racing, literally *running*, through waist-deep water to get to his boat before he did. As in a bad dream, she couldn't make her legs run fast enough so she had to swim. Finally she was at the boat. She pulled herself up at the helm and looked inside. No keys. Panic threatened to overtake her. *I won't let it,* she vowed. She reached up to the dock and pulled the bow line off its cleat, then swam around and did the same at the stern. She towed the boat out as far as she could in the few precious seconds she had.

LeeAnn dove under and half swam, half ran back toward her board. Looking over her shoulder, she saw to her horror that the Whaler was drifting slowly back to the dock. Paul still hadn't appeared. She leapt up onto her board, up-hauling in one motion as she did. The board started moving forward slowly in the dark. Did he see her? The moon was starting to emerge now. Then POP! Was it her cam snapping or a gunshot? She didn't know.

In the new moonlight, almost bright as day, she could see Paul, gun in hand, limping badly, then stumbling as he started to step into the boat. Crash. He half-fell and was caught between the boat and the dock. "Goddamn it!" he yelled, and again, across the water, she heard that same clatter. *The gun.*

Oh, please let it fall in the lake, she prayed.

"FUCKING CUNT!"

LeeAnn kept on going. Then she heard the motor try to start, aaaaaaaa, aaaaaaaa. Then it stopped. *Thank God.* The wind was beginning to pick up as she moved out of the cove. Soon she'd be out in the channel and gone. Aaaaaaaa, aaaaaaaa again.

By that time LeeAnn was really moving. She'd gotten a gust and was starting to plane. She could hear him yelling again, "You Fucking Cunt!"

My Indian name, LeeAnn thought. *Fucking Cunt* and *Bad Foot,* the voice inside her was giggling. She felt giddy; she finally had wind and was getting away.

Then the boat engine burst into life and he was after her, closing the distance between them in no time. How foolish her hope had been. The Whaler was light and fast. *This isn't going to work.*

He was coming up on her starboard side and she jumped from the board, but too late. He grabbed her shirt, and then her arm. Crazily, she held tight to the boom; she wasn't going to let go.

He wrestled her around, bringing her elbows together at her back and pulling her roughly into the boat, scraping her back and her legs, wrenching her hands off the boom.

He tossed her facedown on the deck. She could hear her bones thud as they hit. She wondered if the bruises would show up on the autopsy. He kicked her and it was horrible pain.

"Don't you know to stay out of other people's business?" She tried to turn on one side. If she could just get to the Swiss army knife in her pocket. "Why the *fuck* did you have to interfere?" He was about to kick her again. She lay there with her eyes squeezed shut.

"Goddamn cunt," he repeated accusingly, as though he wanted her to acknowledge that's what she was. Then he didn't say anything else.

LeeAnn's head was down near the bilge in the stern; she could smell the fuel. *Why didn't I cut his gas line when I had the chance back at the dock?* she thought. *If I could only distract him, I could reach over there and do it.* She tried to move into a fetal position so she could pull her knife out of her pocket. She dared to raise her head a little, just a little, to see if he was watching.

Paul was kneeling on the seat, leaning over the side of the boat, trying to grab onto her board. There was no gun visible. LeeAnn watched him as he took hold of her boom and tied it to the stern line, glancing back as he did so to be sure she hadn't moved.

Then he reached into a compartment in the console, pulled out a rag, and began wiping off her rig, erasing all trace of his fingerprints. *Great, all I've done by trying to escape is make it more convenient for him to kill me out here in the middle, away from the island.*

LeeAnn's right arm was underneath her. She tried to move it very, very slowly toward the pocket where her knife was. There. She felt the hard surface at last as she got her fingers on it. Very, very gradually she was able to extract it from her pocket. Then with her fingernail she found the place to open the big blade.

Trying to arch her body slightly to give her hands space to maneuver, she forced open the blade. But a wave rocked the boat just then, she fell back, and the blade promptly closed on her hand, the weight of her body forcing it into her flesh. She felt warm blood pour all over her fingers and she wondered if the knife was going to cut her fingers off. It hurt so much! If only she could use her other hand, but she couldn't. It seemed forever before she could at last open the blade again and then it hurt even worse. She clenched her fist, trying to slow the bleeding. *My God, my fingers.* Meanwhile, Paul was still busy getting ready to stage her death.

He put the rag he'd wiped the fingerprints with back in the console of the boat. Then he turned toward LeeAnn just as a sudden gust caught her sail and flipped it up against the gunwale, where it slapped hard at Trautman, momentarily concealing LeeAnn and startling the hell out of him.

In one instant, she was gone. She didn't even remember slipping over the side. She swam under the boat, surfacing at the stern. Leaning over the port side, Paul was still battling the sail, which responded by flipping up in his face every time he tried to push it back on the water, flapping noisily as though it were alive.

It was amazing how easy it was to slice the rubber hose, unnoticed. The gas spurted and stung her hurt hand horribly. Paul turned. *"Hey,"* he yelled, as she quickly cut her board free and pushed off from the boat with her feet.

She held the knife in her teeth then and did a video-caliber water-start, up in about two seconds and moving away from him. *I'd better assume he can fix that line or switch tanks,* she thought, *so I better haul ass out of here. But this time I'm going to try to use my brain and not try to outrun him.*

Her best hope now was to go where he couldn't. Tipping her sail forward, LeeAnn turned sharply downwind and headed straight for the mudflat to the south of Tree Island, sailing with one hand, the one that wasn't wounded, as she folded and pocketed the knife.

As she approached the mudflat, LeeAnn remembered how solid it had seemed when she and David had looked out at it from the island. Just in time, she thought, to kick up her daggerboard. She touched mud, then felt the fin sliding through. She hoped the chain would hold. Would that she had spent a little more, like the clerk wanted her to, and bought a heavier chain.

Why was his boat already trying to start up again? What had he done? He must have taped the line together. He must have had duct tape. Because a moment later his engine did start and then he was behind her, less than a hundred yards away and gaining fast again.

Oh please, oh please, oh please.

Then that blessed sound, *Yes!* His engine cavitated as the prop struck mud.

Wowowowowowowaoh!" Then it struck again, "wowowoowo wowowaohaaa!" It stopped dead and there was silence, except for the wind. The lake now held him fast. It had sucked his gun down too, she knew that now for certain or he would have been shooting it at her now.

Now in the lee of Tree Island, LeeAnn had lost the wind; she glided to a near stop. Drifting slowly, she was fascinated with the situation in which she found herself. Her enemy had been stopped, but so had she. *LeeAnn in the lee.*

Then on cue, the moon came out from behind a cloud and lit the scene. Paul had gotten an oar out and was trying vainly to push himself off. He stared over at her. "You think you're so goddamn smart, don't you? DON'T YOU!" he yelled. They were only about seventy-five yards apart, but he couldn't touch her. He couldn't hurt her. He probably couldn't swim, or he'd have been in the water already.

He was yelling; he was howling. It was hard to make out the words. "Answer me, Bitch!"

Captive audience to his tirade, yet detached from it, she did a very slow jibe, thinking about the night, and the strangeness of it. *A girl-woman on a butterfly and a boy-man with his broken toy. His mechanical things that had seemed to make him strong had all failed him.* It was a lesson on the lake with only two people to witness it.

He was trying to start his motor again but to no avail. *He spins, he goes around in circles while I slice through and keep moving,* she thought. She could feel the yielding, spongy sediment beneath her as she moved slowly forward. Her fin held. Then just when she thought he couldn't hurt her, couldn't touch her, he did. "I know who you are, LeeAnn Spencer," he yelled. "And I know who your boyfriend is." His words cut through her as none of the others had. "Now you're *both* gonna eat it, you're both gonna die!" But it didn't affect her. *No I don't believe you. I won't let that happen!*

As LeeAnn pumped her way back toward open water, she knew there was a change coming over her. Each slice of air she took with her sail was filling her spirit with new strength. The moonlight showed a glowing path down the lake, a lake so huge that it gave her some comfort. Even if he got himself out of the mud, he'd still have a job finding her. *And, with any luck, he may have burned his engine out.*

For the next few minutes, as she headed out toward the main body of the lake in increasing but still manageable winds, she thought about what Paul Trautman was capable of doing. *Would he try to kill David? Was he that crazy?* Too bad the lake wouldn't hold him long enough for him to start thinking about how stupid it is to be a dominator. She was amazed that in her fear she could think about that.

Then the wind was hers and it began to carry her down the lake. Her hand hardly hurt at all. She realized there was no hope of getting back to Squaw Point on the western shore now. To try to beat upwind, all the way across, against both current and wind, and with a tricky fin would be impossible–it would just take her back to Paul. So downwind it would have to be, all the way to Klamath.

Paul's shouting had become just faint white sound. LeeAnn quite coolly began blocking it out as she set about doing what she had to do to maneuver in these winds. She had been shielded by the island; there was no way she could have known how fierce it was becoming out here.

The danger was not over. She had escaped from Paul, but now she was facing the elements, and there were several of them. *Wind, water,* and *cold.* The whole thing felt like a fairy tale, an allegory. *First this challenge, then another and another–is it never going to end? Don't worry about it,* she thought. *Don't borrow trouble.*

The real problem at the moment was her hands, which were getting extremely cold, especially the wounded one. She didn't know how badly it was cut, would not have imagined she could still use it, but she could. She was hanging on for dear life. She began to shiver. Her black T-shirt was so wet, so cold, taking all her body heat, wicking it away from her. And the waves were splashing her, keeping her soaked with spray.

The farther down the lake she got, the bigger the waves became. Her attention was on negotiating the next wave coming at her, so when the *gust* happened it was like getting hit by a freight train. Or like somebody grabbing you by the belt and jerking you straight UP as hard as they could.

Like a human pinwheel, she felt herself spinning, feet first, up, up, up, and then in a swift and savage arc, straight back down toward the board, head first. She was still holding on and hooked in as the boom drove itself into the front of the board. That must have been when she hit her forehead. LeeAnn sank into the water as the wind took her sail and slapped it back over on top of her, trapping her underneath.

First, dazed, she did nothing but float. Then, recovering a bit, she tried to push the sail up, but the wind held it flat. Then she tried to swim out from under, but the plastic boom strap was stretched tight and she couldn't get it free. She *had* to breathe. She had to, but she couldn't. Water in her throat. Coughing. Choking.

She lay helpless, face up tight against the sail under the water. She was dying. She thought about her parents and Peter and the glass doll that would be lost forever now. Then the image of Adam came back to her, kneeling in the windsurf shop, tapping her on the hip. "This is your quick release," the man with the Jesus look had told her.

LeeAnn reached back but her wounded hand was so cold she couldn't make it work. She tugged, struggling frantically. Her lungs were about to burst. In a last desperate effort, she reached back with both hands and tugged at both buckles at once. Both released at the same time; she swam out from under and her reactor bar sank into the water just as her head popped up.

She was choking, waves were going over her, and she was hyperventilating, so LeeAnn was only vaguely aware of her board floating away. She coughed and choked and finally got air in her lungs. *My board!*

She began to swim for it, but her shoes were pulling her down. The board was getting further downwind all the time. A couple of times she lost sight of it momentarily in the waves. She was sure she would never catch up with it with her shoes on. But they wouldn't kick off, so she had to go underwater and pull them off one at a time with her hands. Which was hard to do.

There goes the van key, she thought, as the left shoe, the one with the pocket in it, dropped toward the bottom. *And the padlock keys.*

With a stronger stroke then, she caught up with the board. She clung to it for a few minutes, grateful to be reunited. *Good old Eff-tu,* she thought. Then she felt for the figurine in her pocket. It was still there and it seemed to be in one piece.

She and the glass doll and Eff-tu drifted down the middle of the storm-tossed lake, close to a mile from either shore. It was a shoreline so barren she knew there would be no place to hide even if she could get to it. No place to get out of the wind or out of sight of Paul if he came looking.

With the reactor bar gone to the bottom of the lake, LeeAnn's harness was useless. Now she'd be depending on the strength of hands and arms that were already so numb she could hardly feel what they touched. She couldn't see her fingers but knew she had chilblains, like those she had as a kid. And that her fingers were stark white from knuckles forward. None of her fingers worked very well, and the ache from the blow on her head was pounding at her. Pounding. But she had to get up and sail.

She put her foot on the board, trying to steer it around and get up. She tried again and again. It was as though she'd forgotten how. She started to cry. She was so cold. Then she lost the rig and had to swim after it again. Her cut opened and her hand began to throb. She wondered about blood loss. It was so dark, and the waves kept breaking over her. Finally she got her back to the wind, in the right position, and her heel up on the board. Eff-tu pulled her up gently and they were away. She knew she would have to hang on all the way to the yacht club if she was going to survive.

CHAPTER TWENTY

Hanging On

LeeAnn was barely making it. Shivering terribly from the cold, she didn't know which was worse, being up on the board in the icy, buffeting winds–or down in the choppy water struggling to swing her board into position for taking off again.

Rig recovery, they called it. Most of the last fifteen minutes had been spent doing that, or drifting, flying the sail and body-dragging through the water because she was just too tired to get up. But she couldn't keep doing that–it was too slow and would take the heat from her body faster than anything. How many times had she fallen? She didn't know. It also wasn't clear whether her jaw was chattering with the cold or whether she was sobbing.

The wind was beginning to change direction. It was still coming from the north, sweeping down the lake, but starting to gust from the west as well. The moon no longer lit her path. There had been some lightning earlier, but no rain.

LeeAnn had been watching for lights on the shore against a dark night sky, and she could see some now. She estimated Klamath Falls was not more than two miles away. Safety, warmth, David. *And all I have to do is get there.* She was studying those lights, thinking of the warmth of her bed and of David's welcoming arms–surely he would welcome her–when her board encountered an object in the water. She wasn't going that fast, so it happened as though in slow motion. She was just slowed by *things* all around her, brushing against her legs. Reeds! She'd been blown into a marsh. *The Henke Marsh probably.*

"Now what am I going to do?" she wailed aloud. She was so tired, so cold. Such an uneven battle, the wind was so strong, and she was

384

caught by the blowing reeds. She was sobbing with frustration now, as she jumped off into the water. Her fingers were aching so with the cold that she almost couldn't grasp the boom anymore. She tried to pull the rig free, but failed.

Every time she attempted to up-haul, she seemed to get blown further into the marsh. She tried to pull herself along on the reeds with her hands, but the frigid wind was totally against her, buffeting her further inside. The end of the mast kept getting caught, and each time it did, she had to get in the water and free it. Her mast, her sail, her fin–everything was becoming twisted in the interlacing tangle of dead and dying reed beneath her. She would be next. It was a claustrophobic nightmare, and she began to panic. She suddenly *hated* the wind that was holding her captive, pinning her down, keeping her in this prison with ropes that bound her and bars that thrashed their prisoner.

Too exhausted to attempt to free herself any longer, LeeAnn tried to prop the sail to provide a little shelter, but it kept blowing around and slamming down again. In her sopping-wet jeans and T-shirt, barefoot now, her hair plastered across her face and no strength to push it back, she hunkered down, defeated. The figurine in her pocket, underneath the harness, didn't seem to be giving her much courage anymore. So she just crouched there on the board waiting for the wind to die, trying not to die herself before it did.

There's no use trying to move, she thought. Her rig was a tired butterfly trapped in the wet and the dark, she upon it, crumpled and cold, curled up, and almost beyond caring. She was just trying to think about *something, anything*, to stay awake till the wind died down or she found the strength to move on. It was imperative not to sleep. It was impossible not to.

First, she thought about the warmth of her bed–and David. David and Audrey. That didn't help. Then she thought about Paul Trautman. She wondered if he got his boat out, if he was still alive. Did he walk to shore? Did he struggle through that muddy goop with his terribly damaged foot, or did he lie down and pull himself along in the mud? She pictured him trying to crawl, sinking down till his face was in the muddy water and he was breathing it.

Maybe he pushed himself off with an oar and got the Whaler started again. She'd been listening for boats. If he made it to shore, what would he do next in that terrible rage? Would he find her van and tear it apart? Would he go to the house and hunt down David and kill him? He was just crazy enough. Then she thought about the image of the orange, and all the people holding hands, and she felt tears rolling down her face as she realized she probably wouldn't be at the party after all. The human family reunion.

She began to try to move her arms and legs to generate some heat. Now all she could see in her mind were the rapidly changing pictures and images of her mental Rolodex, which meant she was starting to fall asleep. All she wanted to do was to curl up in as small a ball as possible and close her eyes. But then she seemed to hear Audrey's voice, the good drill sergeant that she was, barking in that gravelly little voice of hers, *"Okay, so let's think about something to keep your mind moving. How about hypothermia–that's relevant. LeeAnn Spencer. What do you know about hypothermia?"*

Let's see. LeeAnn thought back to the refresher course in First Aid she and David had taken before their backpacking trip two summers ago. And she conjured up the textbook in her mind. The colder she got, the easier she found it was to see things. She could even picture the typestyle on the page of the book–Times New Roman, it looked like. Keeping her eyes closed, she read the quiz.

"**Hypothermia can be caused by:** ❑ **conduction,** ❑ **convection,** ❑ **wind chill or radiation,** ❑ **all of the above.**"

All of the above. Yes, Ms. Spencer, you get that right, she thought ruefully. Also exacerbated by exhaustion and hunger. She thought with vague desire of her carton of fried rice and thermos of lukewarm latté back in the van. She had intended to wolf it all down on her return from the island.

"**As the patient's temperature drops, shivering stops**"–she saw the words in type moving across her field of vision. "**Indications of hypothermia: lethargy, clumsiness, mental confusion.**" *Maybe not yet.* "**Irritability.**" *Those damn reeds.* "**Hallucinations.**"

She rubbed her eyes but it didn't seem to help. Tried to look around, but it was dark as pitch. She thought of the explosions today and she remembered that column of earth rising, billions of particles from the island sparkling in the summer air; she'd breathed its dust.

She remembered the Chopra tape she'd listened to on the way up to tribal headquarters. Saying it was all just atoms, the whole thing, all

386

mixed up. We are part and parcel with the universe. Every time we breathe, we breathe out billions of atoms that used to be part of ourselves and then other people breathe them in. She thought about the millions of atoms in her body that had once been in the body of Buddha or Genghis Khan. So many people. We are all one. Breathing in the chilly air now, she could feel herself becoming a part of the cosmos, becoming mingled . . . To be mingled again was good.

It was lighter in the sky. The wind was beginning to die, and the waves rolling past the marsh were lessening in height. But waves of sleep came over her now and began sweeping her away to a warmer place. For just an instant, the spirit of her lost daughter embraced her and she felt strongly the circle of life that was unending and unendable. The rattling of the reeds and the sigh of the dying wind echoed through her head and she began to slip away. Then it was sweet, she was slipping back in time, slipping down, down, down . . .

But then that sense of time eternal was interrupted by the insistent "chirp, chirp" of a cricket. And that small sound brought her to awareness again. Aware enough to lie there listening to the quality of it, the space of the intervals between it. *A tiny cricket out here that's as cold as I am.*

It sounded like David playing games. Was it David? No. *His watch! That silly watch.* Automatically, she hit the button at her elbow and it stopped, replaced by silence. Then she wished it were still going. She missed the sound already.

She lay there, replaying the sound in her mind to keep from falling asleep again. *It's close to dawn,* she thought, opening her eyes. There was just the faintest hint of light in the east and she found herself roused and strengthened by the thought of a new dawn. Rubbing her arms and legs she began to feel life coming back into her body. And as she breathed, she smelled the algae, fresh and green. It helped wake her up. Maybe she could think logically again.

Clearly, her best chance of survival lay with getting warm. Maybe she could use the sail to help. *I could de-rig and wrap it around me,* she thought. But if she did that, the decision would be permanent. There would be no way she could re-rig. *I will have to paddle out of the marsh. With the wind gone, there's no possible way to get home now anyhow, except to paddle.* This was a deserted part of a little-used lake, so the chances of being rescued by an early morning boat seemed slim.

Except for Paul. She had that nagging sense that he was hunting for her, and as dawn came, she realized she could be seen from the lake. *What time is it?* she wondered. She looked down at David's watch, which was glowing in the dark. It was always 3:21 when the alarm went off. But at the moment what it showed was 4206. Her mind worked slowly; that *was . . . altitude.*

It was lighter now so she could see how tightly the reeds were holding her mast. It was a terrible tangle. First, she began working to release the out-haul, then the down-haul. She unthreaded the sail from the beautiful carbon mast, pushed the mast down into the mud, then slipped the boom over it so that possibly she could find it later. In the back of her mind there was just the slightest thought that *maybe, just maybe, I'll come out of this alive and want to sail again.* Fog had begun to rise from the lake and roll slowly toward her.

The mylar sail was crackly and not too cooperative as she pulled it around herself. She thought about taking the battens out so it wouldn't be so stiff, but it didn't seem worth the effort.

She managed to wrap the sail around her body and tuck some under both knees so it wouldn't slip off. It wasn't much help though. Maybe her body heat would warm it. *What body heat?* She attempted to paddle out, but almost immediately the fin caught on some reeds. She turned and reached down to free it, and as she did, the sail unwrapped itself from her body and fell into the water.

Trying to paddle after it, she reached underneath her board with one hand and ripped savagely at the tangle of reeds holding her fin, forgetting about the gold chain. She felt it break and then she was holding the fin in her hand. She let it drop to the bottom. After that, the board moved freely but with a scratching sound on the bottom as it passed over the vegetation just below. She retrieved her sail and knelt on it.

LeeAnn dug her hands into the muddy sediment and pulled herself along until she emerged into the open water. Without a fin, the board started to turn in lazy circles, so she dropped one leg in the water to use as a rudder. Her arms, hands, and legs all were numb now, but somehow they still functioned, with a delay.

It all felt quite mystical as she moved through the fog, with clouds rising all around her in an otherworldly way. The faint light in the east was a tease, just a hint that there was something warmer above, that the sun still existed.

LeeAnn stopped once to kneel back and look up at the coming light. Then as she started to paddle again, it was as though a soft voice were speaking to her. *Try to endure as you travel,* it said. *Have the courage to believe.* Then LeeAnn understood courage. *Courage is to believe.* It's one and the same thing. She realized that *courage* is *faith.* Soon the sky was entirely shut out by the fog. There were no reference points left at all. She concentrated on trying to stay straight, watching the ripples that would indicate current she could follow to head south.

Then she heard the faint beginning of a mosquitoey sound, far, far away. It sounded like an outboard motor, but she wasn't sure. She wished she could tell one kind of motor from another. Then it was definite, a boat was coming through.

It grew louder for awhile and then seemed to be moving further away. Of course, it might be an early morning fisherman. Though the boat seemed to be going too fast to be trolling. Yet it had a pattern. It got louder and then softer, louder, then softer again, evidently crisscrossing the lake, moving from shore to shore. *A super-thorough fisherman. Or Paul!* The sound had gone further away now; it would be two or three minutes before it came close again.

She thought about the letter she'd left for David on the computer. *Sonja's people will find the van,* she thought, *they'll probably think to look at my laptop and erase the file. That's going to be my last message and David will never read it. After I finally got honest with him.*

The sound was getting louder again, nearer. The fog was thinning, pea soup no longer. *Who ever decided that fog looks like pea soup?* she thought irrationally. *It doesn't at all.* Because of the fog, she still couldn't see the boat, but she could tell it was propelling itself in her direction. *She puzzled over why, when she was down to her last moments, there was such calm. I've got no strength,* she thought. *No more strategies. There comes a point when you don't run any more, when you surrender.*

The boat was quite close now, moving rapidly from the north; she tried quickly to calculate the odds that it could be anyone else. Then she saw the beam of a light shining around on the water toward her. Paul's lantern! Some last survival instinct made her slip off the board into the freezing water and hide under the crumpled sail. Then she heard the boat idling beside her. She felt him grab the sail and pull it away from her. Then his hand grasped the back of her T-shirt to pull her into the boat. "Jesus, God, LeeAnn!"

With instant fusion in her soul she realized it was David! She sobbed. He lifted her into the boat. She had the sensation of being laid down gently with the sail over her. Soaking wet, freezing. "Got to get you warm, quickly," she heard, before she passed out.

In her next moments of consciousness, LeeAnn found herself lying in the front seat of a car, facing unfamiliar upholstery. Was it Peter's car? Audrey's? Someone got in and slammed the door. Then he pulled her over so her head was cradled on his precious leg, the steering wheel above her. "Can you talk to me, LeeAnn?" David's voice.

"I thought you were Paul," she whispered. She saw David's face above her in one small bright flash of consciousness. When she came to again, she heard herself saying, "In my pocket. I found it! Take care of her. She's very old."

"LeeAnn, talk to me."

You're trying to see how my mind is working, aren't you David? she thought. *See if I can think, right? You know from that course we took that I'll be okay if I can think.* "See if the patient is lucid." *Years of being a cop; he knows what to do.*

"I don't want to take you to the hospital if I don't have to," he was saying very carefully.

No, don't, please don't. She felt terror at the idea. *Paul might come and find me there,* she thought, but she was too tired to say it. "Home. I want to go home. I'm all right."

He nodded and then started the engine. She could feel his thigh muscle tighten under her cold jaw as he moved his foot from brake to accelerator. *Riding home again on David's leg.* That wonderful right leg that got more loving than the other. LeeAnn felt very sleepy, but off and on she tried to listen to his voice.

"I don't know if you can hear me, LeeAnn. But I love you. I read what you wrote and I . . . I understand. You never once told me not to be myself and I've been telling you for a long time not to be yourself." He was silent for a time. "I'm ashamed of myself for that. I do respect you for standing up for what you believe in. I thought I'd lost you."

He couldn't see the tears on her face; when they hit his bare leg, he probably thought it was water from the lake. LeeAnn started shivering. "I don't want anybody else. I really love you, I really, really do. LeeAnn.

Do you still love me?" His right hand was rubbing her shoulders.

Then they were home; she knew by the bump bumpety-bump up into the driveway. It was quiet and she was alone in the car for a time. David came back and gathered her up in his arms. She could hear Sillvester yelling. Then she was conscious of being laid down on a bed. "Put your arms up, LeeAnn," she heard from a great distance. She felt her clothes being pulled off. Warm blankets rubbing her naked body. Moments of drifting.

She could hear water running. Opening her eyes, she saw that steam was billowing out of the tiny bathroom in the cabin. Like the fog rising from the lake. Then David came toward her, scooped her up, and held her in his arms again, wrapping her in their big grey bath sheet. She looked at all of the colors of the room–suddenly saw colors again as he carried her into the bathroom. The world was so beautiful.

Holding her, he stepped into the shower stall with his clothes still on. He rocked her gently. She'd never felt so secure. Her face buried into his shoulder, she smiled, breathed in the thick warm air and gradually let herself come to consciousness again.

Hold me, hold me, hold me. Will I ever be warm?

The water was raining down on them, as they stood in embrace like the wooden figure of lovers on their mantle. She turned her face up into the spraying water and was conscious of it spilling down her body. There seemed no way to become warm without burrowing into him. Finally he turned off the water. She was starting to wake up.

David toweled her off in the closed space of the bathroom, a serious look on his face as he patted her skin dry. She felt as though she were being formed again under his touch. Then he wrapped her again in the towel and carried her to the sofa bed which he'd opened out sometime–she didn't know when–and piled high with quilts and blankets. He took off his own wet shirt and jeans then and quickly slipped into the cocoon with her. She was enveloped by the warmth of his body.

For the next ten or fifteen minutes, or who knows how long, all LeeAnn thought about, all she felt, was the rising and falling of his chest, his breath. Breathing in his breath, his pheromones, as the warmth of him spread through her skin and into the very center of her being. He began to stroke her back ever so gently and softly, and their bodies responded to the touching.

"Please make love to me," she whispered after a little while.

"Do you want to? Are you sure?"

"Yes," she said. "But I have to get up first."

"No you don't," he said.

"I'm ovulating."

"That's okay."

"Whaaat?"

He kissed her. "That's even good."

Then he was over her, kneeling. She saw the power and the gentleness in him. He was every man and she was every woman. Looking into her eyes he said, "I love you, LeeAnn. I'll *always* love you." As he moved above her, she saw the strobe light again, sunlight and shadow, as it had been on the pebble beach at Tree Island. Their souls joined as his beautiful silhouette moved at a faster and faster pace in the rapidly blinking light.

"Oh, David . . . David . . . David!" And then it all exploded and there were atoms flying out into the universe and making light.

Later she realized she felt the new spirit enter her at that instant. For one crystal moment, she had the knowledge of it all, of life . . . of death . . . and the beginning of new life again. She *knew* it.

Afterward, they lay perfectly still together for a long time, mingling their thoughts, and silently celebrating the thoughts and feelings, sensations, and textures of the past five minutes of their lives.

LeeAnn drifted off and then drifted back. When she opened her eyes, David was sitting on the edge of the bed, watching her.

"Here, drink this." He handed her a hot glass mug.

She sat up and took it, "What is it?"

"Cognac, honey, hot water, lemon. It's going to do you good." She smiled a little. It was their perennial cold remedy that they took with Vitamin C and algae.

"Don't bother with the algae," she said as she took a small sip.

"I didn't. I figured you probably already swallowed half the algae in the lake."

They were both starting to laugh when there was a knock at the door. David looked up, but neither of them said anything. Audrey opened the door. "I saw the car was back," she started, then, "*LeeAnn!* Oh, I'm *so glad* to see you!" She grinned as she lunged toward her friend. "I'm so *glad* you're all right!" The two women hugged.

Clutching LeeAnn to her, Audrey turned to David, "What on earth happened? I woke up and saw your note in the kitchen." Then to LeeAnn, "He left a note saying that he was going out to look for you. So what *did* happen to you?"

LeeAnn briefly told both of them the story of the day—just the high points. "You tell me that's from Pier 1." She pointed toward David's dresser. Audrey jumped up and looked at the figurine without touching it for a long time. Without saying a word, she came back, sat on the bed, and looked at LeeAnn solemnly.

"Yes. It is wonderful. And a miracle you're safe. A bloody miracle you're alive."

"I'm only alive because of this watch that woke me up in time," LeeAnn said, holding up her arm. "And her—she kept me company." She didn't know if the figure itself was magic, but surely the energy someone had put into it was.

David spoke to Audrey then, "How about staying with LeeAnn for a few minutes? I'm going to go get Peter and Jeffrey. We've got stuff to talk about." He left.

"So," Audrey said, quiet for once. "You did have courage. You got tested and you came through. You were always wondering about that."

LeeAnn thought about it. *Yeah. Once I figured out what courage is about. That it's about belief.* Aloud, she said, "You know, it's not really that hard letting go."

"What did it feel like?" Audrey asked.

"I think the defining moment for me was—maybe I didn't have an actual out-of-body experience, but it was when I realized that my little girl may not be with me anymore, but she's not dead. My baby is not gone, do you know what I mean?" Audrey nodded.

Then they cried together and held each other. "Life doesn't stop; we don't stop. I don't think I'm going to feel hopeless anymore when I think about death or losing somebody."

Audrey nodded.

"You know," LeeAnn told her, "you really ought to have that baby if you want to. I'm not trying to give you advice."

"Of course you are." Audrey was trying to blot her tears carefully as if she had mascara on, though for once she didn't.

LeeAnn took another sip of the hot toddy and felt that much better. "Well . . . ," she sighed. They both smiled again.

"I'm supposed to leave today. I'll be riding back to Berkeley with

Peter this afternoon," Audrey said.

"You will? I'm sorry I walked out on you guys yesterday. Nothing personal."

Audrey replied, "Hey, sometimes you have to go think things out. That's what we were doing night before last, too, David and I in the hot tub. Talking about you."

"Somehow I didn't think you were talking about me."

"But we were. We talked a *lot* about you." She thought Audrey was just about to tell her what they'd said about her when the door opened, and Peter, followed by Jeff and David, burst into the cabin. Peter was not the least bit averse to hugging his sister now. He and Jeff both grabbed onto her at the same time–a LeeAnn sandwich, she thought.

"Hey, take it easy, I'm beat up enough as it is. See this? Look at this over here." She said, pointing out her bruises.

"That's one hell of a bump on your forehead," said Peter. You're going to have a major black eye."

"I am? I guess I am. Look at these on my shins," she said, showing off more injuries. "And does anybody want to stitch up my hand?" She showed them her hand. "I did that to myself."

Jeff looked at it. "You could use a topical antibiotic and a butterfly bandage. I think I've got one in the car," he said, going to get it.

How appropriate, LeeAnn thought. *A butterfly.*

"And you *definitely* need something to eat," said Audrey. "Madam Omelet to the rescue!"

"In a minute," David said. She came back and sat down. "I figure we only have time to go over this once. We have some decisions to make. Let's start by going over what we know for sure." LeeAnn felt the mood in the room changing; quite suddenly the cabin felt like Fort Apache. But maybe that was just from the cop sound in David's voice.

"I'm going to tell you everything that I know and then ask LeeAnn to pick it up from there. Let's quickly go back over everything that's happened since last night and then decide what we're going to do next."

David started by saying how, despite LeeAnn's note saying she might be gone a couple of days, he'd begun worrying about 11:30 last night. "I decided I'd go out and check the all-night restaurants. LeeAnn tends to sit in restaurants when she's in crisis. But there were only a few open, Vallier's, Mollie's, and Denny's; she wasn't at any of them."

"I knew she wouldn't sit in a bar, and there wasn't anywhere else

to go. And really, after I thought about it, all roads led to Squaw Point."
He smiled at LeeAnn. "I knew you would have been drawn up there; I
know how your mind works. So I rode around until I found the van,
parked in a really quite excellent hiding place."

"Thank you," she said.

"When I saw the Yugoslav figure in the console, I thought you'd
taken it off to get rid of me." LeeAnn silently shook her head.

"How did you find the van?" Jeff wanted to know.

"Just drove around looking for fresh tire tracks leading off into the
bushes. It was about 1:30 when I found it and turned on the laptop. I
couldn't read it all, so I just skimmed your log." He looked at LeeAnn.
"It's absolutely amazing how you talk yourself into things. Then when
I saw your board was gone, I knew you'd done it, you'd sailed out to
the island. Dumb shit, it was *howling* out there." He smiled happily and
then continued.

"I thought about swimming across but I wasn't sure I'd make it.
The current was strong and the wind was gnarly, both going the same
way. I would have stolen the cigarette boat if I could have but it was
locked up tight. There were no lights by the dock over on Tree Island
so I couldn't be sure, but I figured that's where you must be, so I had
to get a boat.

"I realized that it wouldn't help to call the police, because I knew
from experience they weren't going to act on a missing person right
away–especially if it's a boyfriend looking for his girlfriend. Plus, I
didn't want to blow the whistle on you if you'd done what I suspected
you had.

"So I drove . . . I don't want to tell you how fast, to the yacht club
to borrow Stan's boat. The damned fence was locked and brilliantly lit,
so I had to . . . you know . . ."

He didn't finish the sentence, but LeeAnn could just see him climbing over and hating every moment of breaking the law. "I know how
you must have felt," LeeAnn said and David looked at her with a grin.

"I've put enough people in jail," he said. "I don't ever want to go
there. So I took Stan's boat, which fortunately had some gas in it."

"What did you do, hot wire it?" asked Jeff.

"No, I know where he keeps the keys. I headed up and circled the
island. No lights, no one around, and no boat docked."

"What time?" LeeAnn wanted to know.

"Had to be close to three. So I headed off, just started looking, combing the lake, back and forth."

Sillvester, who'd been standing in the kitchen of the cabin, trying not to be noticed, now came over to the bed. David scooped him up and handed him to LeeAnn. He nestled in her arms, nuzzled her chest, and began to purr.

"I was looking either for your board or Paul's boat. I was scared. And then I spotted the Whaler out on the mudflat but it was empty. And that was worse. There was blood in the bottom. Could have been fish blood."

"That was my blood," said LeeAnn. "What's happened to Paul? *That's* the major question."

"He probably climbed out and made it back to the island." David sounded confident that he had.

LeeAnn said, "Yes, but he could have just as easily tried to walk back, fainted from the pain, and drowned in a foot of water."

"Not necessarily, LeeAnn. Most likely is that he's okay," Audrey said. LeeAnn thought they were both being optimistic for her sake.

"Well, either way, alive or dead, he's trouble," Jeffrey said as he picked up the phone and started dialing. "Let's see if we can find out. Yes, I'd like the number for the hospital."

"It's Merle West Medical Center," David prompted him. "And don't tell them who is calling."

"Merle West," Jeff said to the operator. LeeAnn tensed. Sillvester purred.

CHAPTER TWENTY ONE

Hunkered Down

LeeAnn watched Jeff closely as he stood there using the cabin tele-phone. All she could see was his back, so she waited for a change in his posture to indicate what he was being told on the other end of the line. Preparing herself for the worst.

"Ummm, okay. Thank you very much." He put the receiver down and turned around. "He's not at Merle West as a patient, at least not under his right name." LeeAnn forced eye contact. "And if he was a DOA, they would have said something, LeeAnn."

"Like, 'You need to speak with the Bad News Department. I'm going to connect you now,'" Audrey mimicked and LeeAnn shuddered.

"You guys are assuming he had ID on him," Peter interjected.

"What do we do–call up and ask if they have any dead people who look like ex-Marines?"

"I think it's a good sign he hasn't been admitted. That leaves the ER, which is the most likely place he'll go," said David.

"How are you going to call there without letting on somebody's interested?" LeeAnn asked. "I mean this town is *small*, Jeff. They'd probably hand him the telephone."

"Give me a little credit, will you LeeAnn? Where's that number?" Jeff looked down the page in the phone book and then dialed.

"Jeff?"

"Trust me."

Peter was standing over by the dresser, examining the figure of the obsidian woman. He was holding it in the light, running his finger along the surface of the stone to feel the texture.

"Hi," Jeff said into the phone, "I'm over at X-ray? And I've got a patient record here but no patient?" The rising inflection made him sound like somebody new on the job. "Trautman? Paul Trautman. I don't know either. Oops, my mistake, I figured it out. Sorry." He hung up.

"No Paul Trautman," said Peter.

"He could have seen a private doctor," Audrey said. "That Sonja woman would have summoned one."

"Or they may not have found him yet," LeeAnn added. "He may be dead."

"He's not dead, LeeAnn. *Stop saying that!*" Audrey scolded. "Stop giving it energy. Even if he is, it's not your fault."

"I wonder if we should call the police anonymously," Peter said. "And tell them that somebody in a boat may be in trouble?"

"I already did that," said David. "Stopped at a pay phone right after I found his boat. What I think we need to do . . ."

"Wait a minute, wait'll I get through checking, will you?" Jeff said. "How many urgent care centers are there here?" he asked, looking in the phone book.

"Two, I think," LeeAnn said. "Or three."

"Urgent Care." He looked at his watch. "Not open yet. "And Basin Immediate Care." He picked up the phone, started to dial.

"Basin Immediate?" repeated Audrey. "You've got to be kidding. How does it go . . . Hasten, Jason, bring the basin . . ."

"Quit it, Audrey! It's a very good place. It's the best."

Jeff was hanging up the phone. "They don't open till nine, according to the message." He was back at the phone book. "Here's one more." Jeff dialed again. "Hi there, do you have a patient named Paul Trautman?" Suddenly he was a middle-aged, chatty, Klamath Falls version of Mrs. Doubtfire. There was a pause, then his arm went up in an extravagant YES! gesture.

"Oh, you *do!*" he pumped it twice. "Well this is . . . um . . . pharmacy, the . . ." He waved his arm wildly.

LeeAnn hissed, "Safeway."

"Safeway . . ." Jeff was loping around the room, trying to think. "Well, when did he leave your office is what I want to know." Mrs. Doubtfire began to recover herself. "About what time did you release him? I mean, we're concerned about . . . ," his arm waved again, ". . . when his last pain medication was administered. I know you understand," Mrs. Doubtfire chuckled. "We just didn't want him doubling up on the dosage and maybe hurting himself." Though Jeff was still high-stepping around the room, his voice remained completely well-modulated.

"Well, we just wondered. You know, the patient–Paul, that's his name, isn't it? He looked a little . . . I don't like to make a judgment, just a little *out there* with those tattoos . . . You never know, do you? So do you mind telling me what *did* happen to him? Mmm. Mmmhmm."

There was a pause while the person on the other end went on, and on. Jeff held the phone away from him. The woman's voice continued. "So, that was pretty lucky," he said at last. "Oh, my. Well, at least he'll be able to walk." A long pause. Jeff looked at LeeAnn steadily while he listened intently. He smiled. "My goodness, they can fix that, too? Isn't that wonderful. Well, thanks ever so much. Tah-tah." He hung up.

"*Tah-tah?* Jeffrey Levine, Geez!" Audrey rolled her eyes.

"I couldn't resist."

LeeAnn took a deep breath and let it out. She *hadn't killed anybody*; hadn't been responsible for anybody suffocating in the mud. Relief flooded her veins.

"You were really sweating that, weren't you?" Peter said.

"I don't know what I would have done."

"What did they say, Jeff?" Peter asked. "A quick digest."

"Trautman came in a little after six this morning. Brought in by a couple in their nineties from Fort Klamath. He evidently flagged them down on the road. Told them that his car broke down, he was trying to push it, and it rolled over on his foot."

"You found out a lot."

Jeff shrugged. "I think she liked me. They put a temporary cast on him–he's going to need some surgery. But he claimed he didn't have time right now; otherwise, she said they would have sent him right over to Merle West. Then according to Beverly–that's my friend's name–some rich lady with a foreign accent picked him up in a white Mercedes."

"And we know who that is."

Jeff came over and sat down on the edge of the bed. "So, it looks like he's going to be okay."

LeeAnn nodded.

"And his foot will, too." Jeff would understand how much she hadn't wanted to hurt someone.

"Good," she said. "Even if he's just exercising in a prison yard, I don't want him limping because of me."

"So we know that Paul got picked up at the clinic by Sonja, but how long ago?" asked Peter.

"About an hour."

"Where does she live?"

"Up by Loma Linda is what she told me."

"She would," said LeeAnn.

"So the two of them are probably holed up somewhere, figuring out their next move," said Jeff.

"I think you can bet on it," David agreed.

"The first thing they're going to do," said LeeAnn, "is move the trailer off the island."

"One of us needs to get up there right away and make sure they don't take off with the evidence," said Jeff.

"Well, wait a minute. Tell me a little more about this Sonja person," Peter said. "Somebody clue me in."

"She's part owner of the company, a major shareholder, Project Chief."

"And ruthless as hell, from what we can gather went on in Mexico," Jeff said. "The stuff Kevin unearthed. It looks like Paul reports to her."

Jeff turned to look at LeeAnn. "I'll get up there and make sure the trailer doesn't disappear."

"Or if it does, follow it," said Audrey.

"I can do that."

"What if Paul sees you?" L.A. asked. She was suddenly worried about Jeff.

"I don't think Paul's going to be seeing anybody today. Not with all the Percodan they've given him," said Jeff. "Besides, Audrey and Peter have got to leave. And you need David with you."

"Jeff, whatever you do, please don't put yourself in danger." LeeAnn pleaded. There's something I haven't told you guys yet." They all looked at her. "It's maybe the reason this whole thing is getting so heavy. What they're hiding up there is a burial ground. Those ammunition boxes are *filled* with human bones."

Audrey gasped audibly and David frowned. "How do you know?"

"Because I opened one. They're nailed shut, but I pried one open."

"Which means they'll stop at nothing to get the concrete poured to cover up the whole thing," Jeff said. "I'd better get my ass up there. But first, let me go get my camcorder. I figure I can get some footage of anything that's happening on the island. I have a great zoom."

He came back a couple of minutes later with the camera. While David and Jeff examined it and inspected the state of its batteries, LeeAnn picked up the phone. She got their attention when she asked for Sergeant Russo.

"You're calling the police?" whispered Peter.

"I'm just trying to reach Sarge. I promised myself if I got back I'd give myself up," she whispered back.

"Uh, uh. No!" Audrey said, with a throat-slashing motion.

"Ah–okay, when will he be in? No, no message. Thank you." She hung up. "He's on personal leave. They said he'll be back Sunday morning."

"They probably have caller ID," said Peter. "LeeAnn, before you make any more phone calls, and Jeff, before you go anywhere, let's think about something." He waited till he had their attention. "Okay, so we know Paul's alive, but do they know *you* are?" He looked at LeeAnn. "Do we *want* them to know you are?" Everybody looked at everybody. "*Do* they know you're alive?"

"Not necessarily," she said. "Vanna's still up there." *It would be strange to have someone think you're dead,* she thought.

"So her board is missing and she hasn't come back to her van."

"LeeAnn's board is down in the basement," David said, "I unloaded it from the station wagon when I came to get you guys."

"So unless anyone saw you at the yacht club or bringing her home . . ."

David shook his head. "No, it was absolutely deserted. There was zero traffic on the way home."

"I was totally out of it." LeeAnn was remembering the smooth, silent ride, David's knee lifting each time he'd come to a stop sign. "Almost there," he had told her softly, "almost home."

"So, David," Jeff asked, "how come you didn't bring the van home? You've got a lot of stuff in there." There was a moment's hesitation on David's part.

"So as not to disturb things in case it was a crime scene." David meant in case she was dead or hurt. "But I brought you something, LeeAnn." He went into the kitchenette for a second, then handed

LeeAnn her waist pack with its planner in it.

"Oh, thank you!" It felt good to get it back. Just having her planner made the future palpable again. She laid it down beside her in the bed.

"*And* your laptop." He picked that up from under the hide-a-bed and deposited it beside her.

"Oh. So you *did* disturb the crime scene!"

"Carefully," David grinned at her.

Peter went on. "The minute they know LeeAnn is safe, we've lost some advantage–knowledge is valuable. So it's better if both sides are guessing than just one. *They* don't know if you're still alive and *we* don't know how far they'll go to save their half of a billion-dollar project."

"Quite far, I suspect," said Audrey.

"Well, what do you think, do you think they're making plans right now to come and get me?" asked LeeAnn.

"No. Nonsense," Audrey said, contradicting herself. "So what does Paul know for sure?" she asked. "Did he see which way you went?"

"There was only one way to go–downwind."

"Could he have seen you go under and the rig float away?" David asked.

"Probably, the moon was out at that point."

"Could he have seen you get up after that?"

"Probably not. I drifted a *long* way first."

"So maybe they do think you're dead."

Now Peter had a question again. She could see that data was scrolling to his printer. "If you were Paul, LeeAnn, what would you have told Sonja about what you did? What did Sonja *want* him to do? What instructions did she give him?"

"Kill me."

"Are you sure?"

"Virtually. That's sure what it sounded like. And looked like. Remember he was looking into my eyes the whole time she was talking."

"What would Sonja have told Vanderveer? And what will Vanderveer do now?"

"I don't know."

"Do they know you took anything?" Audrey asked.

"I can't see how. Unless they check the trailer now–if they even know the figurine's important. Possibly Paul's the only one who even knows about the glass doll."

"And we don't know how much he knows about artifacts. Does he think he shot you?" David asked. "*Did* he shoot at you?"

"I still don't know. I thought I heard something, but then I've never been shot at before." They all fell silent for a few moments.

"Well, I'm out of here," Jeff said. "For every minute we waste, I could already be there . . ."

"It's going to take awhile to get it loaded on the barge and across to shore," said Audrey. "The trailer."

"Yeah, but they've got heavy equipment in there now that can move anything."

"Hopefully," said LeeAnn, "the broken axle will slow them down a little."

"I doubt it," said Peter.

"What do you think the chances are that they reported LeeAnn's B&E?"

"*Please* don't call it that, Audrey."

"I don't think they'd go to the police with it. Because then they'd have to produce the trailer." Peter sounded sure.

Jeff was opening the door to leave just as David came back in with a funny look on his face. He was carrying LeeAnn's rolled up pink-and-green sail. "I needed to check. You've got a nine millimeter hole in your sail." He started to unroll it.

Audrey inhaled audibly. "Omigod."

"See? Very neat. In the mylar." He put his finger on it. "Clean."

It was so harmless looking. LeeAnn stared at it. She knew that scratched-up place; it was right in her line of vision when she stood up on her board. Right exactly where her head was.

"Could anybody prove that was a bullet hole?" she wanted to know.

"Probably not."

"Nice aim, for a guy who's hurt and at night, in the middle of a windstorm." David's expression was grim. "He's somebody to contend with." Jeff was starting out the door.

"Hey, Jeff?"

"Yeah?"

"If anybody sees you poking around up there, tell them you're looking for your friend. Your friend's girlfriend. A windsurfer. But don't tell them that right away. Tell them as though you're kind of embarrassed to be looking for her. And act stupid, not too swift."

"That shouldn't be too tough," said Audrey.

"Check on the van if you can, you may be able to see it through the trees. I doubt very much they'd mess with it." Jeff nodded. "The trailer's the main thing. Then give us a call. There's a place called the Odessa store. People could listen in on your cellular."

Jeff paused, thinking. "I tell you what. I'll go ahead and use the cellular. Let them listen," he said. "If the trailer's gone, I'll tell you that I haven't found LeeAnn. If you don't hear from me, then that means it's still there and I'm watching it."

"Okay," said David. "Sounds great."

Jeff came back to embrace LeeAnn. Audrey stood up and gave him a big hug. "Will you get out of here, you faggot!" she said affectionately. "And for godsakes, be careful." And then he was gone.

They all sat down again. Five had become four.

"What I'm wondering about," Peter said, "is are they watching us right now? Would they put a tap on the phone? Just how far outside the law do these companies operate?"

David shrugged. "There's enough spy shit on the market, they could be listening to our conversation from a couple of blocks away right now. But we can't focus on that because if we do, we'll just get paranoid."

"I doubt they're actively in the crime business. What do we know for sure? That they're concealing artifacts."

"And maybe that they bribed an archaeologist," Audrey interrupted.

"And that Paul pointed a gun at you. Which he had every right to do, given that you were trespassing. But he never actually tried to drown you."

"No, but he wiped his fingerprints off my boom. And he shot at me."

"If we can prove it. Apart from that, there's no actual crime committed."

"Look, let's try to cut through some of this, shall we?" Peter was an excellent monitor. "Bottom line, what's their aim?"

"To proceed as quickly as possible. Get the concrete poured, get everything covered up," his sister said.

Peter went over to the figurine again and picked it up. His blonde hair was down today, long and loose on his shoulders. "This looks absolutely timeless–how do you date it?" he asked his sister.

"You measure the amount of moisture that's been lost since the artifact was made. Obsidian contains a certain amount of moisture and it dissipates at a given rate, so we can tell when it was chipped."

"Not how old the obsidian is, but when it was chipped or carved?"

"Right."

"And how long does that take to do?" he asked.

"Usually weeks before it comes back. I don't know where we could get it done in a hurry. I think we might need some archaeological clout."

"And once you turn this over to the police," Peter commented, "it's all according to their time schedule and out of our control."

Audrey looked at LeeAnn. "So, you can't give it to the police."

David turned to LeeAnn, "How much time does the actual lab work take?"

"Only a few hours if they would do it right away. But what'll happen, David, if we go through police channels?" David was starting to pace, a difficult undertaking in the miniscule cabin.

"If you report what you've done and turn it in, then it becomes evidence. It could take weeks, months."

Then Audrey said, "Couldn't Vince Taurini help, LeeAnn? Did you ever get hold of him?"

"No but he called back." LeeAnn started looking through her planner for Burt and Louise's number that she'd jotted down on whatever page she'd opened to randomly at the phone booth.

"What day is this?" she asked. "I got a message from him yesterday. If I can just find the number . . . You know," she said to no one in particular, as she leafed through, "it's totally illegal to send out stolen work. It's what Harkins or whatever their name is did. To send stolen artifacts to a lab. I could be drummed out of the corps."

"Hey, it's also totally illegal to steal artifacts," Audrey pointed out. "So you're already in trouble." LeeAnn finally found Burt and Louise's number back in a space allocated for the fourteenth of last July. She dialed.

"Well, who's calling?" the whiskey-cigarette female voice inquired in a Southern drawl.

"Hi, Louise?" she said. "This is LeeAnn Spencer, calling from Oregon."

"Hello darlin'."

"Vince gave me this number; he said you could get hold of him for me. Oh, thanks." She put her hand over the phone. "She said she'll go get him," LeeAnn said to the rest of them. "She said it's just across the yard."

Nobody sitting in the cabin said anything for the next three and a half minutes, as LeeAnn formed her own picture of what Burt and Louise's place looked like and how far Vince had to come from his. Then finally Vince's voice came on.

"I was wondering when I was going to hear from you," he said. "What's happening?"

LeeAnn gave him a very abbreviated version of her adventure and David's eyes were on her as she did, plainly appreciating her precision in the professional area, and her understatement of the drama.

"Carved obsidian? And you think it's authentic?" Vince was spilling over with excitement. "Boy, you come up with them one after another, don't you?" LeeAnn was a little proud. After all, he'd been her mentor. "And that's also on Tree Island, huh? I wish I could get on a plane right this minute." LeeAnn wondered if anyone else could hear their conversation.

"So what we've got here is a big dilemma," LeeAnn told him. "They may do this, they may do that. They might have a tap on our phone at this very moment. Let's assume they don't."

"So you need a lab that can hydra-date on a weekend, within a couple hundred miles. You got an airport there? And where is Klamath in relation to Portland? Oh, I know, there's a guy in Eugene. Let me put you on hold."

"Okay," she turned to her audience of three. "He's checking. How far are we from Eugene?"

"Three hours," said David.

Vince came back on the line three or four minutes later. "Sorry it took me so long. What I was checking on was whether this guy . . ." Call-waiting beeped on the line.

"Do you want to get that?" he asked LeeAnn.

"Well . . . No, that's okay."

"I'll be right back. I'm just going to give this guy a call on Burt and Louise's other line, if that's all right."

"Oh, by all means." There was silence. She heard the second click on the call-waiting, wondered again if she should get it. Then, after that, was the call-waiting disconnect. *Too late now.*

Vince came back. "He'll do it tonight, if you can get it over there by two."

"That's great! We can do that." They all nodded.

"I've still got him on the line. Let me get the address so you can write it down."

"No." Sudden intuition told her that wouldn't be wise. "How about if you tell him we'll have it there by two, hang up, and fax me the address? You have my fax number."

Vince understood. "You got it, kid. He'll clear his decks and give you a rough date sometime this evening. So we'll at least have a ballpark idea."

"Is he going to need payment up front?" LeeAnn asked, thinking of her abused VISA.

"No, he trusts me, so he trusts you."

"Well, thanks. I hope your life's going okay."

"It is. Keep me up to date, will you? And if you ever need bail . . ."

"Thanks a lot, Vince."

"Or a full-page 'Free LeeAnn Spencer' ad in the *Times*, signed by all sorts of academic types. You're pretty sure about this one, aren't you?"

"I'm positive. My love to the family." LeeAnn hung up the phone.

Peter said, "It's all settled. Audrey and I are going to drop it for you, then take the long way around to Berkeley."

"Well, let's get your obsidian lady packed up." Audrey started bustling around, giving orders. "David, can you take care of that? We don't want to see anything happening to her at this point."

Then the phone rang again. LeeAnn reached for it, thinking it was Vince calling back, but Audrey pushed her away, then grabbed up the receiver and said, "LeeAnn!?" in a breathy, excited voice. "Oh," she said then in a dull, hollow tone. "No. I'm sorry, I just thought . . . I'm terribly sorry, I thought it was my friend. Who's calling, please?" Audrey hit the speakerphone in time for them to hear, in a thick French accent:

"This is Perrine Thibault. I am a freelance writer." Audrey mouthed the word, "Sonja." "And I am trying to reach Ms. Spencer." Audrey clicked the speakerphone off just as quickly as she'd turned it on.

"Oh, you have the right number, all right, but we haven't seen LeeAnn since yesterday," Audrey listened. "Oh, I hope soon. Could I get your number? Well, I can't really tell what's a good time to call back. I apologize for the way I greeted you, it's just that, well, she and her partner had a little disagreement. No, we're not too worried. As soon as she shows up. Thanks so much." Audrey exhaled and hung up.

"Quick thinking, Aud," said Peter.

"Do you know how close I came to answering that call?" L.A. said.

"Did she think we couldn't tell who she was?" said Audrey. "The witch." She went over to the bed. "LeeAnn, I don't know if I should leave or not."

"Go. You can take care of Peter. As soon as we get the date from the lab, I'm turning myself in to Sarge."

"Promise me you guys'll get out of town tomorrow if this thing isn't resolved. If you think there's any danger at all . . ." Audrey looked as if she meant business.

"We will," LeeAnn promised.

Peter said, "So Audrey, go get your stuff, will you? Your clothes, your hair dryer, and all your goop."

Miraculously, a few minutes later, Audrey was packed and ready to go. Peter, with the faxed address from Vince in his hand, came in to say goodbye. LeeAnn's brother was looking worried and tense as he took the box from David, who had packaged the figurine in his usual expert way. You could probably have dropped it out of an airplane without hurting it.

"I've marked the map to Eugene," David told Peter.

"Thanks, dude."

LeeAnn got out of bed to hug her brother and her still-best female friend. It was hard to see them go. She walked to the door with them.

"I won't go out to the car with you," she said. "In case anybody's lurking around."

"Say goodbye to Jeff for us," said Peter. "Tell him I'll see him in the city." Then they were out the door, with David accompanying them to Peter's car.

"Be careful! Please be careful!" In her mind's eye she could see a truck veer into their path on I-5.

She heard the car door slam (Audrey, no doubt) then Peter telling David, "We'll leave you a message later on my machine at home. So call me from a pay phone. My access number is 111."

"Isn't everybody's?" said Audrey. "You ought to be able to remember that. Well, so long–you take care of that girl, David."

LeeAnn heard Peter's car drive off then. David came back in and the two of them were alone. She didn't know why, but LeeAnn suddenly felt panicky and claustrophobic in the cabin. "Are we going to spend the whole day out here?" she asked a few minutes later.

"Probably be a good idea." Then the telephone rang again.

"We can't even tell who's calling, with the answering machine in the house." David nodded noncommittally, as the phone continued to ring and they made no move to answer it. "I'm hungry, David," she said.

"I can go fix you something."

She looked at him. *But I don't want to be here alone,* she thought without saying it.

"What do you want to do, LeeAnn?"

"I don't know."

He sighed. "Well, let me go in and see who called. Then we can talk about it."

LeeAnn waited. She didn't know why she was being so weird. For some reason, she just didn't want to be in the cabin. *If I'm having to hide,* she thought, *at least I want to be in a larger fortress.*

"Whoever it was didn't leave a message," David said when he came back.

"What do you think are the odds that they already have somebody watching us?"

"Who knows? Probably pretty remote."

"Then let's chance a quick dash to the house. David, why don't you go outside and see where we can be seen from? Just walk around the yard."

"I don't need to. I already know. They'd have to be inside one of the houses above us. Or have a high-powered telescope from KAGO hill." That was where the radio station was.

"So. What do you think?"

"I think if you're going to do it, sooner's better than later. We may be watched later. Up to you."

"I want to do it."

So they hurried across, feeling like pedestrians in Sarajevo, and a little bit foolish at the same time.

"These are not the kind of people who take potshots at people's homes," David said after they made it to the house.

"I don't think we can expect a drive-by," she agreed.

"I doubt it," David said from the refrigerator, where he was pulling out a bunch of items for the breakfast that Madam Omelet didn't get a chance to fix. "But if we're keeping you hidden, then we need to do it right. You need to duck under this window here, go in the living room, and lie down on the couch. Meanwhile, I'll try to give a good imitation of a guy spending the day alone, pining for his lady love."

LeeAnn got down on her hands and knees and crawled across the kitchen floor. "So maybe what you ought to do later is call John and Eva and ask them if they know where I am. If I'm hanging with them."

"Good idea."

"And Julianne. And Kate Rander."

LeeAnn was giving these orders over her shoulder as she made her way on her hands and knees, favoring the cut fingers Jeff had so neatly bandaged. Through the living room she went, past the fish tank and the hutch, over the blue Chinese rug to the white brocade sofa, where she climbed up and lay down.

Ah, this is better, she thought. She wanted to sit up and look into the gold-framed mirror over the couch to check her damaged face, but perhaps she could be seen if she raised up that high. "How does my eye look?" she asked David.

"You don't want to know." He came over and covered her with her great-grandmother's quilt from the sea chest. "You're beautiful," he said. He kissed her.

"Am I?"

"Very, very beautiful. Just take it easy." She lay there for a few more minutes, enjoying the feeling of being pampered. Then she didn't know what to do; it was strange not to be doing *something.* She spent some time examining David's watch, which had survived and had probably saved her. Water resistant to three hundred feet it said. *Which is silly,* thought LeeAnn. *Like speedometers that say you can go 150 miles an hour.* LeeAnn pushed the buttons that took it from altitude to stop watch to time. It said it was 10:07 a.m., Saturday.

"Ooh, ooh. David. David!"

"What? Can I get you something?" He came to the door of the dining room, looking concerned.

"It's just that it's ten o'clock, *Car Talk* is on NPR." *Car Talk* was the only entertainment LeeAnn interrupted her life for; she was a public radio nut. David grinned in relief and obliged her by turning on the radio.

The next hour was an exercise in bliss. LeeAnn forgot all about Paul and Ernst and VHRI as she enjoyed the very best of everything. Her home, her loving, attentive partner, and a splendid breakfast. While she ate, Click and Clack doled out doses of their wacky automotive philosophy that was really a metaphor for everything. She laughed uproariously, and Jeff was nice enough to wait till the show was over before he called in to report.

David brought the phone over to LeeAnn so she could eavesdrop.

"I'm sorry, David," said Jeff. "I haven't seen a trace of LeeAnn. I just can't find her."

LeeAnn's heart sank, that was the code for *no trailer*. It was gone. Thank heaven they had the Obsidian Woman at least, since the human bones were rattling off down some highway somewhere.

"I think she's really gone this time," Jeff was saying. "I've looked all the places she hangs out."

"Well. It was worth a try. I can't think of anywhere else. But thanks, buddy."

"She'll show up. You know, David . . ."

"What?"

"You must really have *pissed* her off, man." Jeff couldn't resist.

"Hey," David said in an annoyed-sounding voice, "all I did was ask you to look for her, *man*. I don't want . . ."

"Okay, I'm sorry, all right?"

"Sure, I'm upset, that's all. So, you want to get together later, watch some videos?"

"Sounds good to me, dude," said Jeff. "You seen *Superman* lately?"

"No. And maybe a comedy."

"Sure. Anything. Whoopi Goldberg maybe."

David was looking out the dining room window as he talked; suddenly LeeAnn saw his body tense. She wanted to raise up and see what he was looking at, but she didn't dare. He moved away from the window. "Ahh, okay, yeah, that'll be good." He sounded distracted. "Coors or Weinhard, if you can, but it doesn't really matter. Later, man." He hung up.

"What is it, David?"

"There's a guy from the phone company up the pole in the alley. Could be coincidence but . . ."

"Is that how they would do a tap?"

"It's one way. If they can't get in this house or the switching station downtown, it's another option."

"Can I look?"

"No."

"Could this be a VHRI guy?"

"It could be a bribed phone-company employee, it could be somebody who works for VHRI. Who the hell knows? Maybe I should go out there . . ."

"Absolutely *not*. At least that's one good thing—we can surmise they haven't heard our conversations up to now." David went to the back door and LeeAnn sat worrying.

About five minutes later, David reported that the guy climbed down from the pole and walked back down the alley. David went to the back door to check. "He's just disappeared around the corner," David said. "If he had a truck parked there, I couldn't see it. I don't like the way this is going, L.A."

"So what do we do? Do you want to call the police and see if we can get some protection?"

"That'll do a lot of good."

"You don't think they'd help us?" she asked.

"Sure, they'd drive their car around the block a couple times and alert VHRI that we were onto them. Cops can't watch over everybody who thinks they're in danger. Especially after we explain you're playing possum. No way."

An hour later, David came up the ladder from the cellar and out LeeAnn's bedroom. He had been down in his shop, drilling a little hole in his wind-rock so he could attach it to the silver windsurfer key chain he had just gotten from his grandmother. He came over and showed it to her now.

"So I'll always have it with me."

"That's good. You know," she said to David as he sat down on the edge of the couch where she lay, "I was thinking about pumice. I didn't even know what pumice *was* when Maggie and I scoured the sea chest with it."

"This chest?"

"This one. Mom and I spent *hours* on it. I was about ten. But before I moved out west, I never even thought about where pumice comes from."

David shifted his long frame to get comfortable. She was conscious of the place where his hip touched her leg.

"Did you hear they've closed the pumice mine at Shasta? It's where they get the pumice they use for stone-washing jeans, but it got too hot inside; the magma is too close. They're thinking the mountain might erupt."

"Shasta? That would be something. That would put Klamath on the map."

"Or take it off. No, actually, the ash would go the other way and blanket California." He idly rubbed her leg, careful to avoid the bruises.

"You know, the other night when I got really upset with you guys? I went down to the basement at three in the morning to get some obsidian so I could prove my point about polishing it."

"Did it work?"

"You're darned right. Go look on my dresser."

He did. Open-minded now. LeeAnn looked at her grandmother clock. *They should have dropped it off at the lab by now.* She thought of Peter's station wagon on the road on the other side of Eugene, headed south. Safe. If she pictured it that way, it would be. She willed it so.

David came back, inspecting the tiny spot on the obsidian that she had polished. "It looks as good as I could get it with four or five grits," he said. "Definitely could get a high polish that way. I'm going to play with it a little while myself if you don't mind." He went into the bathroom and got a towel, the pumice bar, and a bowl of water to dip it in, then sat at the dining room table and started polishing obsidian, just to make it clear that he was nervous, too.

Finally, Jeff came in about 4:30, with Henry Weinhard's Special Reserve, *Superman,* and *Nunsense.* LeeAnn breathed a sigh of relief. He and David popped a beer, and staged a conversation in the kitchen, in case David was being watched. LeeAnn made her way on knees and elbows–her hand was hurting quite a lot–back to the kitchen doorway, where she lay down on the blue Chinese rug.

"And I want to tell you, they had one hell of a time grading that road to get the equipment up on the plateau. They didn't quit till almost four."

"Did they finish?"

"Apparently. They got their grader up, a steam shovel, a crane, and a Caterpillar. Looks like they're ready to go. I've got a bunch of video if you want to look at it. A lot of activity. It was Grand Central Station for awhile there, with Sonja showing up in her designer site-visit outfit and Paul limping around with his cast."

"*Paul* was there?"

"How did he look?" asked David.

"A little woozy. Mostly he sat down. And then Stan showed up in his boat."

"You're kidding!" LeeAnn was astounded. "What was he doing there? He doesn't work on the weekend. What happened?"

"I don't know. I can show you on the tape. He had an argument with Sonja, it looked like.

"Oh, no."

"Do you think we dare pull the shades so I can show you guys the video?" asked Jeff. "You can see the whole thing for yourselves."

"I think we better wait till it gets dark," said David. "It would look kind of strange."

While they waited, they watched part of both movies and then David walked down to the Blue Ox, where he could use a pay phone without being seen, hopefully, to find out if there was any report yet from Audrey and Peter. Jeff set up his Mac on the living room floor so he and LeeAnn could browse the Internet.

For about forty-five minutes they diverted themselves by looking up the twenty-four time zones and printing them out in a map of the world that looked like twenty-four surfboards lined up in a row. Then they got into examining the personality of each one.

"Where would you most like to be on the eve of the millenium, Jeff?" she asked. "If you had your choice."

"New York, no doubt about it. Home."

"Me, too, though Rome wouldn't be bad either. Where the Roman calendar started. Last night I was afraid I'd have to send my regrets."

"You'd never miss a party, LeeAnn," Jeff told her, "especially your own."

"It *is* going to happen, isn't it, Jeff?" she asked. "A real family reunion."

"Hey, you were the one who convinced the rest of us. Now all you have to do is talk another five billion people into it."

"David's back." She heard his footsteps. When he came into the room, characteristically, his face didn't show whether he had any news or not.

"Did they call?" LeeAnn asked him.

"There was a message from Peter on his home phone." LeeAnn breathed her relief. "Just that they made the delivery successfully, were headed south on I-5, and that they expect the lab report to come in about 11:00 tonight. They'll call us. Peter said they'll figure out some kind of code."

"Oh, good."

"And he said Audrey especially wanted you to know she's taking very good care of your brother, not to worry."

LeeAnn laughed. "I wonder what that means."

"So, David, did you see anybody while you were out there?" Jeff wanted to know.

"I saw a guy sitting in a car across the street a block and a half down."

"Could he see the house from there?"

"Yeah. But who knows, he could also have just been waiting for his girlfriend or something. He was parked out in front of one of those rental units."

At dusk, David pulled the shades, and at last LeeAnn could move around. The three of them sat around the big TV in the living room. Jeff put the tape in the VCR and switched it on.

They were looking at Tree Island from what looked like about a quarter mile away, but the quality of the footage was pretty good. "Where'd you take this from?" David wanted to know.

"Right on shore, not too far from where your van is parked. I left Audrey's car and hiked in. By the way, there were footprints leading to and from the van."

"I hope those were mine," said David.

"Not unless you made eight or nine trips."

"Which at least proves somebody's not being very professional. These are not people, I think, except for Paul, who regularly indulge in crime."

They watched the video as one of the huge yellow Caterpillars was being transported over on the barge. "What do you think those things weigh?"

"God, I don't know." David still didn't like them; you could tell that.

"Now," Jeff said. "Watch, there's Sonja's Mercedes pulling into the landing at Squaw Point." The time and date showed up on the screen; LeeAnn could imagine the tape being shown in a court trial.

"I wonder where Ernst was," she said. "Did he ever show up out there?"

"Nope. You said he doesn't deal with day-to-day operations."

"Do you think he knows everything that's going on?"

"Maybe not," said Jeff.

He knows, LeeAnn thought. *He has to know.* "Look," LeeAnn pointed to the screen. "There's Paul." They saw Paul talking with one of the workmen. He had on a grey shirt and the new jeans he'd worn at the airport, one leg rolled up, and a big white cast on his foot. The telephoto lens zoomed in close, but you couldn't tell what anybody was saying.

"I always thought I ought to learn how to lip-read."

Now the camera was panning the area below the plateau on the south end of the island, where most of the construction work would be done. "That's where I think the burial ground is," LeeAnn said. "Can you freeze frame?" Jeffrey did. LeeAnn went over and pointed on the screen to a flat spot just above a point where masses of boulders sloped down steeply to the water's edge.

"Why would the burial ground be there?"

"Because it's level. Also because you'd want to be able to see to the east and to the west from that spot, sunrise and sunset. That's kind of standard for a lot of cultures. Underneath that, below the burial ground, and behind these tumbled boulders somewhere is where any caves would be." LeeAnn pointed to the place on the screen.

"You know, David," she said, "that day we found the petroglyph I had the crazy idea that . . . I want to show you guys. Would you go get the sketches that we made of the petroglyph? Do you mind? My next-to-the-top drawer. I'm sorry, I'd do it myself but the window shades are still up in there."

"LeeAnn, enjoy being waited on while you can." David went into their bedroom and brought back her drawings of all the symbols and marks on the seven pieces of the petroglyph that they'd found.

"Call me crazy, but this has been nagging at me for awhile. I was fooling around with these the other day. Putting them in different arrangements . . ."

"What are you getting at, LeeAnn?" asked Jeff.

"Well, you see all these other symbols that were once part of the petroglyph? I was thinking they might conceivably be a map to a cave where the figurine was located."

"A *map*?"

"Well, my theory is that the stone lovers on the rock are–that it's a *drawing* of a statue that actually exists–or existed at one time."

"It wouldn't be a map," David said unequivocally.

"Why not?"

"Because why would anybody make a map so that anybody else who came along could find their most precious possession?"

"David," she said gently. "You're applying the wrong mindset. Back in partnership times people didn't steal, so nobody had to hide anything," she paused. "These symbols obviously *mean* something–history, journey, or location. *Something*. I'm going to guess it's *location* because that's the only theory that can do us any good right now."

Both men nodded.

"See here? "There was a double arch over the figure. "This could indicate that the figure is inside a chamber. That's what it looks like anyway. Now if this symbol had been over *here* in the original . . . but we can't tell how they were grouped because we don't know how the pieces of rock fit together."

"You know, maybe a computer would help," Jeff said. "I see what you mean, though. I can scan this in on the Mac and then we can put it in all kinds of different arrangements."

"Terrific!"

"But let me show you the rest of the footage first. The part where Stan arrives." He unfreeze-framed the view of the south side of the island, then fast-forwarded to a shot of the staging area between the dock and the old stone house.

LeeAnn watched Sonja emerge from the shiny motorhome office with the contractor, Douglas Santini, behind her. They stood there, conferring. Then the camera darted suddenly over to the dock to catch Stan climbing out of his fishing skiff. He walked up the path, over to Sonja, and started talking and gesturing.

"What's he saying?" Stan was pointing toward the promontory at one point, and Sonja gazed up at it, then glared at Stan.

"Look what happens now." There were a few more words, then Stan strode off, fuming. Sonja stared after him for a moment before resuming her conversation with Santini.

"I just hope he didn't screw things up for us, or for himself." LeeAnn watched Sonja giving orders to her men.

"I wish we could call Stan and find out what happened."

"Probably not a good idea," said David. "If there's a tap."

A half hour later, Jeff was busy clicking his mouse, moving all the hieroglyphics around. "That one. No, move *that* one," LeeAnn said. "The one that looks like the golden arches."

More time went by but they still weren't any closer to solving the puzzle, even though David and Jeff had gotten into some esoteric stuff, figuring out how many zillion possibilities there were for arranging the seven pieces. "But it's especially tough since we don't know how many pieces of rock are still missing."

LeeAnn couldn't help but see how well the two men were getting along. She detected none of the abrasiveness that had marked the earlier days. She also noticed they were settling into her hypothesis, adopting the map theory as their own.

Then LeeAnn was aware of a dog yapping, and immediately after that, a rapping at the back door. "It's Stan."

"I'll get it," said David. He was gone for several minutes. LeeAnn could hear low voices, then Stan and Melanie followed him into the living room, the dog's toenails clicking on the polished wood floor.

"Well, there you are. Dave told me about your adventure. You okay?" she nodded. "That's a real good shiner you got there." He sat down. "Well, I'll tell you. They're up to no good. You were right. I told that Ms. Al Amin off."

"Stan, what did you *do?*"

"We had quite a little talk."

"What happened?"

"I was out in my boat, fishing, this afternoon. I went by Tree Island and saw the trailer wasn't there any more. It all makes sense now."

"What makes sense?"

"All that scurrying around, hurrying up the construction because they're worried about what they've got in there."

"David told you about the bones I found?"

"Yes, he did. Gives you the willies."

"So what did you say to Sonja?"

"I just pulled up at the dock–she was standing around all dressed up

giving orders–and I went over and asked her where the trailer was."
LeeAnn blanched. "She told me it was none of my business so I told
her, 'Lady, everything on this lake's been my business for fifty years.
And I don't like what you're doing one bit.' So she fired me."

"Oh, I'm sorry." LeeAnn and David exchanged a look and she
thought about the possibility he'd been followed to their house. Could
they be getting themselves in deeper every minute?

"That's okay. I don't want to work for them." Then he didn't seem
to want to talk about it anymore. "So what is it that you're doing?"

Jeff explained. He showed Stan the video footage and then the
computer-enhanced diagrams of the petroglyph pieces. "So we're trying to decipher it, trying to figure out if it's a map."

"Let me see that last shot on the video again," Stan said, sitting on
one of the dining room chairs that David had pulled over to the television for him. "Yeah, see there? See that shape? It could be an elevation–like an architect's drawing. And if it is, then this shape here, this
symbol–doesn't it look a little like those two boulders down at the south
end?" Jeff brought up a view of the south side of the island on the video
then. Sure enough, there were two huge boulders, but they didn't look
to LeeAnn much like the symbol on the petroglyph.

"Well, I mean if that one hadn't fallen over," said Stan.

"Stan! You're right! That's exactly what it looks like. We've been
puzzling over this for hours. What an eye!"

"Well! That's what I do all day, you know." Stan said modestly.
"Look at the shape of rocks."

"You're a genius, Stan," said David. "It's unmistakable, now that we
can see it." Jeff rewound and freeze-framed on the shot of the boulders.

"Look at that–see the M-shape? If that one were standing up," said
LeeAnn. "That's it. Okay, now let's see where the figure would be–if
those are the right boulders and if there's a cave under there. Look,
down below the boulders. See, there's like a huge bulge in the rocks.
I'll bet you if there is anything, it would be right under that bulge in the
middle of the boulders."

David looked at Jeff.

"So there's still a chance we could find something before they fill
it all in with concrete," LeeAnn added. She knew she was taking a big
step with her words. Both men looked at her.

"Somewhere down under these rocks right here," Jeff said, nodding. "That's do-able. That's something we could probably scout out in a couple of hours."

"And if we found any signs of a structure or a cave under there, we could call the media and do a sit-in. We could go out there tonight," she said.

"In the dark? You think we could mess around out there and not get caught?" Jeff wanted to know.

"It's way around on the other side of the island from where Paul is," LeeAnn said. "I don't think they'd be expecting anybody to check out those boulders. Would you have people guarding the whole island?" she asked David then.

"Probably not. It's pretty big," he said. LeeAnn wondered if that was a correct assumption, but she knew even if it wasn't, that wouldn't be likely to stop them at this point.

"How would we know what to look for?"

"Good question," LeeAnn said. "It kind of depends on how much time there was when the ancient people had to seal up the cave–presuming there was a cave and presuming it was sealed up. If they were in a hurry, they might have piled bunches of rock over the entrance, in which case we'll never find it in the time we've got. Or there might have been five hundred years when people were starting to become divided and suspicious about other people's beliefs. So people who believed in partnership had to become secretive–but didn't have to hurry too much. In that case I'd look for a capstone."

"And what would a capstone look like?" David asked. "What would we look for?"

"It would be a worked rock or rocks," she answered, "that had been shaped to fit into an opening. Of course, they didn't have metal–they would've been breaking rock with rock, so it would still have a rough look. It's not going to be easy to spot, that's for sure."

"I've got a question, LeeAnn," Jeff said. "How many rocks down would we have to go when we check?"

"Just the top one."

"And if we don't see anything?"

"We wouldn't have time to do anything more than that. If we see an obvious capstone, we pull it out, and go down. Otherwise, we just check any holes that lead down under the boulders."

Then Jeff said, "I've got an idea how we could check for caves pret-

ty easily with my videocam. *If* we decide to go out there," he added.
"Let's wait for the lab report before we decide. We ought to get a call from Peter any time now."

But the call didn't come and about thirty minutes later, when she checked on them, the three men were standing in LeeAnn's closet where the hole for the ladder went down, rigging some sort of nylon cords onto Jeff's video cam. They were trussing it up like a marionette, so by manipulating the strings, they could turn the camera any which way. Now they were testing to see how they would lower it between boulders to look for a cave. Jeff pulled the makeshift robot up and turned it off.

"Okay, roll that back," said David. "Let's see what we got."

"Oh, nice!" Jeff said, looking through the viewer as he ran the tape backwards. "This'll definitely work."

"Do you have any hair ribbon, LeeAnn?" Stan turned to ask her.

"Yes, why?"

"Cause we need to mark the line at one-foot intervals so we can tell how far down the camera's going–see how deep the chambers are."

LeeAnn thought it wasn't necessary but she went to her top dresser drawer. Under the box for David's watch she found several satin ribbons: yellow, green, blue, and orange and took them back to Stan. She left the three boys in her closet then, happily tying ribbons at intervals to the nylon line.

Everybody took a break a little later to eat leftover tamale pie that LeeAnn found in the freezer and heated up. They were just beginning to despair of ever hearing from Peter or Audrey when the phone rang. David picked it up.

"No, she hasn't shown up yet." He mouthed *Audrey* to LeeAnn. "They're home, Jeff," he said aloud, "and she wishes they'd stayed in a motel. A lot of driving. Do you mind if I put you on speaker, Audrey? I'm trying to cook myself something."

Audrey's voice came on. "So, did LeeAnn ever show up?"

"Not yet."

"Tell that ding-dong, when you see her, that I had a wonderful time–the whole experience of Klamath Falls was just absolutely . . . different." LeeAnn smiled. "Oh, and Peter wants to talk to you, too." Then Peter's voice came into the room. LeeAnn was so glad to hear it.

"Hey, David."

"Hey, man."

"Thanks for the hospitality."

"Any time."

"I just wanted to let my sister know, I've got the report from the hospital on our Mom. This may be one of the things that got her worried–why she took off. So when she shows up, be sure to let LeeAnn know that Maggie is *okay. Really* okay. Blood pressure *100* over *77.*"

"Oh?"

"Which, given her advanced age, is pretty darn *exceptional.*"

"A 100 over 77?"

"That's right. So there was nothing to worry about at all."

"Okay, I'll tell her." David hung up. "Did you hear that?" The excitement on his face made him look incredibly beautiful. "LeeAnn, you were right. *Seventy-seven hundred years.*"

"Mount Mazama!" LeeAnn exclaimed. Bingo.

"That's what he meant, isn't it?"

"Of course it is! It would have been carved right about the time Mazama erupted."

"That little glass doll–seventy-seven hundred years? Well Gol-ly!" said Stan.

"Which means the petroglyph is maybe that old, as well." said David.

"Or older."

"So the question is, do we go out to Tree Island now or not? We have the proof now."

"And in the morning we can get an injunction."

"Maybe, but probably too late for whatever's there. Which we now know could be not only profoundly old, but profoundly important."

"What time is it?"

"11:45. Tomorrow's Sunday; I'll bet they'll be working as soon as it's light."

"So let's do it!" said David.

"We'll need to take my boat," said Stan.

"I'm afraid I used up most of your gas last night looking for LeeAnn, " said David. "Sorry."

"No problem," said Stan. "I'll just go get my gas cans out of the boat and take them down to the all-night Texaco."

"I've got a fuel can that I use for the snow blower," David said. "I'll go get it, save you a trip."

LeeAnn was painfully aware, as the men fiddled with gas cans and as she dressed in her black New York T-shirt and dark jeans–her skullduggery outfit again–that they were doing all this based on *her* hunch and the shape of two boulders. And that there would be danger for these people she loved.

"David," Stan asked. "Do you have a gun?" David shook his head; he hadn't had a gun in the house for years, once he'd stopped being a cop. *Guns attract guns,* was his theory. "Well, I guess it will be okay, I don't like them much myself."

They piled into Stan's truck, David, Stan, and LeeAnn up front, Jeff and Melanie in the back, and drove to the Texaco station on South Sixth to fill up the gas can from the snow blower. It didn't look as if they were being followed. There were almost no cars on the street this late at night in Klamath Falls.

"David, let me out for a minute," LeeAnn said when they pulled up at the gas station.

"What are you going to do?"

"I know it's after midnight, but I think we need to let somebody know what we're going to do." He gave her a look. "Trust me." She thought about Silkwood again, as she headed for the telephone. Stan was paying the guy for the gas as she looked in the phone book.

"Stan?" she called. "Do you know where Sergeant Russo lives?"

"Out on Homedale somewhere, I think." There it was, *D. Russo.* Blessing a town where a cop could list himself in the phone book, LeeAnn picked up the phone, put a quarter in, and dialed. "They told me he was on personal leave," she told Stan while she waited, "but it occurred to me he might've been home the whole time, painting his house or something." The phone rang three times, then a woman picked up.

"I'm awfully sorry to wake you. This is LeeAnn Spencer. Is this Adriana Russo?" She was glad she remembered her name. "I know your husband won't be at work until tomorrow but I was wondering if he might be there? This is really important."

"No, he's not. But he is on his way home." Adriana Russo was apparently used to being awakened in the middle of the night; her voice was low and pleasant, with a rich Neapolitan accent. "He may telephone me from Winnemucca."

"Oh good. Would you give him a message then, please? Just let him know that they're going to start bulldozing out at Tree Island early tomorrow morning. And tell him that we've located bones and other artifacts that have proven to be very old and that he should come out to the island just as quickly as he can when he gets back. Whether to arrest me for trespassing or to arrest them for bulldozing. Because that's where it'll be happening."

"And you are LeeAnn Spencer?" Obviously, her husband must have mentioned her. "Yes, I am."

"I'll be very happy to deliver your message. Let me get a pencil."

Winnemucca, Winne-mucca, went through LeeAnn's head in a singsong. He would be calling from Winnemucca, where, in a cut-rate motel she and David had once written an entirely unsolicited ad campaign for the Nevada town, laughing hysterically as they did. "Come to Winnemucca and win a mucca."

"What's a mucca?"

"Come win-a-mucca and find out." It was pretty dumb really, but it had amused them. Then Adriana came back on the line.

"All right. S-P-E-N-S-E-R," she spelled laboriously in her strong accent. "Is that correct?"

"Close enough, and thank you so much. I saw your picture; you have a lovely family," said LeeAnn, and hung up.

She got back into Stan's truck and they roared off into the night.

CHAPTER TWENTY TWO

Pink Lady IV

Piloting Pink Lady IV, Stan hugged the western shore of Klamath Lake, deliberately overshooting Tree Island by about a quarter mile. Then he cut the engine and they began to drift back, LeeAnn in the front of the boat with Stan, Jeff and David in the back. The moon had set, giving all the glory to the stars. It was a magnificent sky, and LeeAnn pitied the poor city people who never saw stars like these.

The night was silent, except for the lapping of the water against the rocks and as they approached the island, the faint sound of some insects. She smiled at David and he chirped briefly. Then she looked at the crickety watch he had loaned her; 2:22 a.m. Sunday, it said. Last night while they were waiting for the phone call from Peter, David and Jeff had taken the watch on as a project and finally got it working right, although its chirping in the marsh the other night could hardly be considered a mistake; it had saved her life. She was almost sad they'd fixed it.

She looked around; it was all so very different from when she'd been here just twenty-four hours ago. The wind and water so wild then, so quiet now. And she'd been alone then. That was the biggest difference. She felt safe and confident now, surrounded by her friends. And she imagined they were going to succeed in their mission; she just felt that way.

Ten quiet minutes after Stan cut the engine, they drifted close to the steeply sloping south shore of boulders on Tree Island that was their goal. Stan had gauged it well. The current was swift, the lake almost like a broad river thirty miles long. He began maneuvering them into a tiny cove where they couldn't possibly be seen from the water. With the end of his paddle, he fended them off from a large flat boulder on the shore.

"This is a cool little hideout in here," Jeff whispered. "How'd you know about it?"

Stan shrugged. "I've fished here all my life." Then he held the boat steady as David and LeeAnn stepped up onto the boulder that was about waist-high, and Jeff began handing off the equipment to them. It was a convenient landing spot, reminding her of Plymouth Rock.

The assembled gear included Jeff's camcorder in its case, the home-made harness and marionette sticks for it, some extra nylon cord, a couple of climbing ropes, David's headlamp (which he promptly put on), a rubber mallet, crowbar, tire iron, and hammer, all stashed in a purple nylon windsurfing gear bag. Plus some food and water LeeAnn had thrown into a day pack. She never went anywhere without provisions. As they left the house, she had grabbed a jar of peanut butter, and one of sweet pickles, a loaf of frozen whole-wheat bread she'd made six months before, a box of raisins, and some raspberry BG Bites.

"I think I got another pry bar in here that might help," Stan said, reaching around in the seat to open a toolbox. He'd elected to stay with the boat and keep a weather eye out while the others did their search.

"Are you going to be okay?" David asked.

"Ah, here it is," he said at last. "I'll be fine."

"Thanks." David took it, opened the purple gear bag, and added Stan's pry bar to the tool collection inside. It clunked as he put it in. He slung the bag, heavy with iron tools, over his shoulder, and LeeAnn picked up the heavy daypack with her injured hand, wincing as she did. She kept forgetting. She switched to the other hand.

Then she looked up, way up. The slope was daunting in its size, this pile of boulders that looked as if it had been so casually poured from God's hand. Back at the house when they had scientifically surveyed the situation on the video, the project had seemed doable. But now, standing at the bottom of the hill, it did not look so easy. Everything out here was on a much bigger scale than in the east, LeeAnn remembered.

They started to climb. The rock was still warm to the touch from the day before. Up they went, like lizards, feeling very small. It was the kind of slope LeeAnn felt fairly comfortable climbing *up*. Coming *down* would be another story. It was her hope they wouldn't have to do that in the dark in a hurry; she had never been a good climber. "Klutz of the world" was what Audrey used to call her.

Behind her, Jeff must have loosened a fair-sized rock; it started rolling thunderously down for what seemed like ages before finally plopping into the lake. It was a heavy sound, like the dull thud of the mortar on Paul's foot, which didn't help with LeeAnn's state of mind.

"Everything all right up there?" Stan called softly.

"We're fine," said Jeff. "Just clumsy me."

LeeAnn tried to watch her footing carefully after that. She held her rejuvenated Russian flashlight in her hand. But for the most part, the stars gave them enough light to climb by. David turned his headlamp on and off quickly a few times. "There's bedrock under here," he said at one point after he waited for her to catch up. "See?" He shone the light on it to show her. "Could be a lava tube in there. Or maybe not." She nodded.

Most of the time they couldn't see the bedrock. The boulders that overlaid it were two to three feet in diameter, precariously balanced, with a lot of smaller ones scattered in between.

Surely they were high enough now, LeeAnn thought, several minutes into the climb. It was a good place to start looking, right in the middle of the bulge. But David kept leading them upward. "David," she whispered softly, but he shook his head and pointed, so she continued to follow. She wondered if she had gotten pregnant last night. She wondered if the three of them died tonight, if Peter and Audrey would continue the Summer Project. *One thing at a time, LeeAnn.*

That sky was something. The Pleiades were right above her, she noticed–the seven daughters of Atlas put up there by the gods to save them from the pursuit of Orion. They looked like candles in the heavens.

At last they were at the top. David, Jeff, and LeeAnn crouched under the lip of the fallen-away boulder as a light, misty rain began to fall. But the stars were still shining, so it was a starlight rain, LeeAnn thought. The rock below glistened in the dim glow reflected from the still surface of the lake. They could see the shape of rocks better when they were wet, but of course it was also going to make them more slippery.

David turned to LeeAnn. "The reason we want to work from the top of the pile down is so we can visually check the stability of the rock better that way before we move any. So hopefully we don't start an avalanche that will bring them all down on us."

"Or bring VHRI running," Jeff said. "Good idea."

"Can you see?" David asked, indicating the area below.

"Yeah, I can see," said Jeff.

"Sort of," LeeAnn told him, though the horribly swollen black eye made it a little difficult.

"Well, here's what I thought. We start from here and fan out about . . . yay much." He spread his arms out to delineate a fan-shaped section of the hill of rock below them. "Do the width of the boulders behind us here, and then down, say a hundred feet, to a hundred and fifty feet wide at the bottom. That'll take in the whole bulge."

LeeAnn looked at the bulge. She felt as if she could see right through the rock down into the cavern that she so hoped would be there, *knew* was there.

"We have two hours," said Jeff.

David said, "What you can do, LeeAnn, is mark the rocks you want us to check. I brought some chalk." He handed her one of those big fat pieces they give kids for writing on sidewalks. It was yellow and as thick as a cigar.

"And when we get something real," Jeff said, "we'll lower the camera down. If we find anything more than a couple feet deep."

"Okay, let's do it."

"Just tap on the rock with your flashlight if you think you've got something," said David.

"Isn't that sound going to carry as much as our voices?"

David was quiet for a second. "We really can't worry about it too much," he said. "We're doing this job or we're not. And I think the chances of their coming . . . ," he paused. "If they've got people watching this side of the island, then we're toast, anyway. Of course, they don't think we're too interested in artifacts right now. They think we're looking for you."

The first few rocks LeeAnn chose for Jeff and David to move were heavy, but they didn't reveal anything hidden underneath. LeeAnn worried about David lifting rocks; he still had problems with his back from the time they'd gone prospecting for gold down by Susanville and he'd single-handedly tried to reroute the Yuba River. He'd ended up flat on his back in the van, and LeeAnn had to drive him miles and miles on twisting mountain roads to the emergency room for morphine.

They started moving down over the top of the bulge. Finally, Jeff found a cavity probably almost five feet deep and about as wide, from what they could see–the opening at the top was quite narrow. LeeAnn watched tensely as Jeff lowered the camera. "Okay, now turn it on,

Jeff." Jeff turned on the intense light of the camera and lowered it into the hole.

"Okay. Yeah, it's deep enough, all right." You could see the glow of the light through cracks between the surrounding rocks. It showed how fragile the whole structure was.

"It's okay," David said to LeeAnn, reading her mind.

"This could all settle at any moment."

"Yeah, but it won't." *Suddenly David is an optimist?* she thought.

Jeff turned the camera harness in a slow circle, manipulating the sticks up and down to aim in all directions. "What's that?" Jeff said. And LeeAnn heard what sounded very much like the faint barking of dogs. "Listen."

"Do you think that's on shore?" she asked David, who was standing beside her looking down into the hole as Jeff fished it.

"No. Nobody living within miles that I know of."

"Could they be coyotes?"

He looked at her as though he were undecided about answering. "No, they're not coyotes." *So they are guard dogs, hired canine thugs,* she thought. LeeAnn immediately had that creepy feeling at the back of her ankles that you get when a dog's chasing you and you're waiting for their teeth to sink in. David always told her to turn around and give them a kick, but she didn't know if she could. She listened intently but the sound didn't seem to come closer, and pretty soon it died away. *So we know they have dogs now, but that doesn't mean they're going to let them loose,* she thought.

Jeff was pulling the camera back up now. Blue, green, yellow, blue, yellow, red. Six feet. "Here, let me rewind." Jeff began running the tape back.

"There. That's enough. *Hit Play,*" David said.

"I can always fast-forward." They were all getting nervous. Pretty soon, if they didn't watch it, they'd start to bicker.

"We've only got about another hour," David reminded Jeff a few minutes later.

"If you've got anything," he told him, "we can excavate this thing further. But let's decide."

"I don't know," Jeff said, rewinding again for LeeAnn. "Here, LeeAnn." He handed her the camera and she looked through the viewer. It had been swinging some when Jeff shot the footage, which made for a dizzying scene.

"No, I don't think so. I don't see anything obviously human-made."

"Do you think I ought to go down?" David asked her.

"Not this time."

LeeAnn began to doubt herself as she worked her way slowly down the hill, playing her light over every rock. *I don't know nearly enough about Native American culture, for one thing. Those lines above the figures that I thought meant a cave could just as well have represented a rainbow or an aura.*

She kept on marking likely rocks with the chalk and helping Jeff and David move them. When they'd been at it for two hours, LeeAnn straightened up; she was tired. Bone tired. She sighed, and just then David came over and started rubbing her back. "Oh, thank you. Your back must be hurting too," she said. It was probably why he had thought to rub hers.

"It's okay." He put his arms around her waist and they looked at the sky together. "It may not happen, you know," he said.

"I know."

The stars were fading. It would be another hour before official daybreak, but already they could see their surroundings better. LeeAnn turned and looked up at the shadowy form of the big bulldozer perched above them, its yellow color almost beginning to be evident. *They think they can alter the earth to suit themselves,* she thought. David must have felt her start to tense up again. "Hey, shoulders down."

She tried, but hope was dying. So many boulders–a couple of acres of them. A field of rock that would normally take a team *weeks* to explore. And that's if they had a crane to lift the heavy pieces out of the way. Actually there was a crane right above them; it just wasn't theirs to use. She could feel the discouragement settling over her, that familiar lump beginning to form again in her throat. Only a few times had they found a cavity large enough to make it worthwhile to put the camera down. And only once promising enough for David to go down inside.

She looked back up at the fallen-away boulder and its mate. They'd been landmarks on the lake for how long, she wondered. And by tomorrow, they would be covered with tons of earth and rock. LeeAnn sighed and then went back to the rock she was currently inspecting. Perhaps it was her imagination, but this one seemed as though it had been deliberately fitted into the space created by six adjoining boulders. *This one's worth trying.*

She marked the flat top of it with a star; X's seemed so negative. The rock was hexagonal and just about flush with the others on all sides. She tapped on the top of it and David immediately made his way over from where he'd been working with Jeff.

"You want us to do this one next?"

"If you don't mind." LeeAnn studied the rock again, shining her light into the tiny crevices between it and the surrounding rocks. Of course this could be just the result of settling over the years and finding the best fit, the way the change in her pocket settled down after she'd been running a bit. It was probably nothing.

As the men moved their tools over for what would have to be the last try of the night, a vague shape for what to do next began to form in LeeAnn's mind. *If we don't find anything here,* she told herself, *at six I'm driving out to the airport and waking up Ernst . . . Somehow I have* got *to get to him. And I will. We have to stop him.* She clung to that belief, so she wouldn't feel too much disappointment if this last excavation failed to produce anything.

Jeff moved a small rock to get at the hexagonal stone better, then he jumped back; a grass snake was sleeping there. David picked it up gently and moved it out of the way. It lay still for a moment, then seemed to realize something unusual had happened and wriggled off.

If I can find some way to persuade Ernst to hold up the bulldozers just for this morning . . . Then when Sarge gets back from Winnemucca . . . Her attention came back to watching David trying unsuccessfully to get the stone out. "This is *really* tight," he said. And it was; the rock was quite firmly stuck. "You know what I need?" David sat back on his haunches. "I need something that will fit in here, another really narrow blade. All this stuff's too big."

LeeAnn offered her Swiss army knife but it was adjudged too puny. "How about a big screwdriver?" she asked. "There was one in Stan's toolbox."

David started to stand up. "I'll go get it."

"No, you keep working. I'll get it."

He considered. "You don't want to climb all the way back down, L.A."

"No problem. I wouldn't be able to do what you're doing." She threw him a kiss, thinking how it often feels a little scary to part with someone you love, even for a little while. "I'll be right back."

David bent to his work and LeeAnn started down the hill, traveling mostly on her butt. But at least she was getting there, she thought. Below, in the slowly gathering light, the lake was quite beautiful, but she didn't dare look at it; she was concentrating on the next rock down. She slipped once on an especially slick spot, but caught herself in time. *Above all else,* she thought, *what I can't do right now is fall.* She remembered that the tread on her running shoes was basically gone.

She thought she heard a dog bark again, but the sound was faint. Finally down onto that huge flat landing rock, she walked the length of it as Stan watched from the boat, waiting for her to say something. "Do we need to go?" he asked anxiously.

"Not quite yet." She sat down on the edge of the landing rock, dangling her feet down toward the boat. "David needs . . . ," she pointed to the toolbox. "I thought I saw a great big screwdriver in there. Could you get it for me?"

"Sure thing." He opened the box. "So how's it going?"

"Nothing so far. We're working on one fair possibility now, but how can you tell? I just know the rock fits in there really tight, on six sides."

"That's a good sign." Rummaging among the tools, Stan pulled out one of those big screwdrivers with the clear lemon-yellow handle. It was about eighteen inches long, an honest old-fashioned tool. "This okay?"

"Just right. This'll do it."

"We'll probably want to take off at six," she said. He handed it to her. As she began to stand up on the landing rock, LeeAnn felt a slight depression under her feet and hands that was familiar to her from so many archaeological sites–on stairs and sidewalks and roads where foot traffic had worn a depression in the surface. Her heart thumped.

"Would you shine that light over here, Stan, just for a minute," she said with suppressed excitement. "Look, look at that. Isn't that a path worn in the rock?"

After a bit, Stan said, *"Yes, it is."* He sounded awestruck. "You're right, LeeAnn. That's exactly what it is. And you know the wildlife didn't do that. Not with a twenty-minute swim and a whole island to land on. It had to be humans." As he shone the light ahead, they could see a clear path in the grey rock, a place where obviously thousands of feet had trod.

pink lady iv

"I'd better get back. Let me go tell David."

"You take care," Stan called after her softly. She started climbing back up over the boulders with considerably more energy than when she climbed down. It renewed her spirit to think about all the people who had passed this way–maybe five hundred generations worth. Her mind quickly did the arithmetic that Jeff would have volunteered. *Suppose three people walked across this rock every day, that's a thousand trips across it a year. For ten thousand years? A thousand times ten is . . . Take ten thousand and add three zeros, that's ten million footsteps.*

She thought about all those people coming to Tree Island, perhaps to visit partnership figures, or perhaps for other reasons–a long, stable, peaceful civilization, *that maybe could tell us how to live better. And we're about to wipe out every trace of it here.* She thought about Ernst Vanderveer and her anger grew again. *He's insulated himself from it all; he doesn't know about the enormity of the legacy he's messing with when he comes into a place like this and starts building these awful things.*

It was absolutely silent now in this hour before dawn, and the air smelled good with the dampness from the rain and the algae in the lake. When she got back to the place where Jeff and David were still trying vainly to pry the rock out, she handed Stan's screwdriver to David.

"Perfect," he said, inspecting it. He inserted it in a place he'd chipped away in one of the rocks that abutted the hexagonal one. Then he reached in with the pry bar in his right hand, the screwdriver in his left. Jeff was helping with a crowbar that he'd gotten a good grip with. While they worked, LeeAnn planned to tell them about the path worn in the landing rock, but she didn't get a chance for Jeff and David started to lift the boulder then. It looked to be roughly the same shape and a little bigger than the box a basketball comes in.

"It's coming!" Jeff said suddenly. And it was. With it, suddenly, came the unmistakable dry, dusty smell of ancient air mingling with the scent of the algae.

LeeAnn started trembling. "Careful, careful." They were breathing air that hadn't been breathed for thousands of years, she knew.

"I think you found the big one, LeeAnn!" David said, his voice sounding tight and tense, after they removed the capstone and the rock next to it, and were looking down inside with their lights. It seemed to be a constructed shelter. The floor of the cave was at least fifteen feet down, maybe a little more. Jeff put the camera into the harness.

"I'm shaking," he said.

"I am too," LeeAnn said. They all laughed.

"I can't get it right." Jeff was fiddling with the camera.

"Here, let me help. We've only got about thirty minutes to sunrise, if that. We can't waste time."

"You know something?" David said. "Forget the camera. I'm going down."

"David, it's a long way down."

"I can let myself down on a rope, then you can hand me the camera. I'll be able to see a lot better than from up here." He and Jeff started to rig one up. They thought they had it secured, but they must have been nervous because as David let himself down, it slipped and he fell the last few feet. A gasp of pain, then total silence.

"David. Are you hurt?"

"Just tweaked my back. I'm okay." More silence. LeeAnn was not convinced. "Okay, give me the camera." Jeff handed it down with its light on; it illuminated David's face, and LeeAnn could tell he was in a lot of pain. Then he moved away from the entrance and LeeAnn and Jeff looked at each other. There wasn't a single sound from David. She looked at her watch. He was making them wait till he could be sure. *That was just like David*, she thought.

Finally, he came back and looked up at them. "There's a bunch of fresh rockfall down here, probably from yesterday's blasting; let's hope it's stable. I'm not absolutely sure of what I'm seeing, LeeAnn," he said, his voice sounding extremely excited. "But I think you ought to come down here."

She sat down on the edge and prepared to lower herself down the rope that Jeff had reattached to a different rock. But her cut and swollen fingers just couldn't grasp it right and she was conscious of feeling awkward and scared. The bottom seemed so far down. "Here, I've got you." Bracing himself, Jeff grasped her wrists from above and lowered her down, down, down, as far as he could.

"And I've got you now," said David, as he reached way up over his head and grasped her ankles. "You're going to have to just let go and sit down on my shoulders," David said. She felt top-heavy as Jeff let go. She tried to scrunch her body so she could grab onto David's head before she fell backwards on the rock floor. And she managed to do it, clutching onto his ponytail as David steadied her. Then, trying not to hurt his back anymore, she slid down his tall frame till she was standing facing him.

Still holding her in his arms, he turned her around. Then he picked up the camcorder again; its bright light filled the space. LeeAnn glanced up at the domed ceiling above; it reminded her of the restored mammoth-bone house she'd worked on that summer–only it was rock instead of bone–but she saw the same careful workmanship. The chamber was about twelve by twelve. It was cool and dry down here and there was the scent of antiquity, like autumn leaves when they turn to dust, only much, much richer. It was a blend of about a hundred different scents. "I want you to look at this," he said.

Her heart was pounding as he guided her with his arm around her shoulder to a waist-high crack about eight inches wide in the new-fallen rock. They could see through to the part of the chamber that was against the hill–where the opening to an ancient lava tube would be, if there were one.

David played the light on some debris that was resting on what looked like a rude altar. She saw part of a basket and small piles of grain. There were beads beside that, on a rotted necklace of rawhide. "Look at that, is that amber?" Where would amber come from? she wondered. *A long way off.* And there was some turquoise too. Big, beautiful pieces. She thought of the goddess Artemis and the gifts on her altar in Greece that had come from all over the earth.

When LeeAnn finally spotted the figure lying in the dust, she didn't recognize it at first. Then she gasped. "It's there. *It is!* It's The Lovers. But it's broken."

The statue was like the petroglyph they'd found. And very like the Gumelnita Lovers from Europe too. But it was in two pieces, one of them propped up on the shelf–the female–the other lying on its back beside it. Thick layers of dust covered them both.

"You did it," said David. "You found your Lovers." It seemed to LeeAnn as if everything around her was pulsating. The energy of the earth felt so strong. Like the day on the pebble beach. *I need to touch them,* LeeAnn thought, *I need to get to them.* But there was no way. The fallen rock was blocking the access.

"Let me have the camcorder," she said, because she could bring the view closer using the zoom. She looked through the eyepiece and focused. "Oh! Look at the edges where they used to be joined, David,

tree island

look. You can see they've been apart for a long time."

And it was true, the edges on both figures were very worn. LeeAnn wondered how many people had carried them how far, through barren land and hard times, caring enough to keep them together. They'd evidently found a home on Tree Island and then, when times became unsafe for symbols of male-female equality, they had been hidden safely in this cavern by others who loved them.

Unbidden tears started rolling down LeeAnn's face, interfering with her view; she handed the camera to David and he gazed through the lens.

LeeAnn and David stood there quietly for quite a long moment, in this place of reverence for the physical expression of spiritual union. It was powerful. Both had felt the energy of the love that surrounded them. *This time I* know *we're feeling the same thing,* LeeAnn thought.

"It looks like they're carved out of basalt," LeeAnn said, more to herself than to David.

"I would guess that's right."

"Okay, how can we get them?"

"We can't," David said. "And we have to get moving." He looked back at the entrance above. "But we'll come back. Take some video now; it's the best we can do."

"Maybe I could get through . . ."

"That space is ten inches tall and eight inches wide. Let's feel lucky we've got some pictures."

"We have to *at least* reach one of them. Look, if that one rock weren't there, I could go under and get them. I would fit." *It was a tiny space, true,* she thought*, but then thin people fit through very tiny spaces.* She would just have to deal with her claustrophobia.

"Honey, the whole thing could give at any moment." It was the first time he'd ever called her Honey, she noted.

"We could shore it up." "

"It's not worth your life, LeeAnn."

No? she thought, but did not say.

"Just take some more footage, then even if this collapses . . ."

"I've *got* to *get* it so we can have it *tested.*"

"Tested? Can you date basalt?"

"It's been done, it's not very easy. But we can probably tell from the stone's chemical signature where it's from. Or at least eliminate places that it's not from."

Jeff poked his head down then. "You guys had better get going."

"We'll be right up," David said. "We have a major discovery down here. Everything okay?"

"Nothing's happening. There's not a soul in sight," Jeff said.

David turned back to LeeAnn. "You're saying you could tell if it came from Beringia?" he said. "Or Siberia? Or Europe?"

"You might be able to. That's why I need to get it, David, before more rocks fall. I've *got* to know."

"But . . ."

"It's worth it to me." He took a long, level look at her, then at the tumbled rock. "It'll only take a few minutes."

"Okay. All right, let's see if Jeff wants to help. Jeff, you want to come down?" He was down in a flash, even though he turned his ankle badly as he landed. He sat down and held it.

"Aaaoh." Gritting his teeth, he tried to grin.

"You okay?" They were all wounded now. *Good,* LeeAnn thought, *now nothing worse will happen to us.*

When he'd recovered a little bit, LeeAnn led him over by the opening on the other side of the chamber, through the new-fallen rock. She shone the camera light for him. "Look, right by the remains of that basket. Propped up. That's the female. And the male is lying over there."

"It's hard to believe," Jeff said in a hushed voice. "It's our parents. Everybody's parents."

David glanced up at the opening at the top where they could see from the growing light that dawn was almost upon them. "Okay, Jeff, let me explain what we've got here." David had become very matter-of-fact. "We need to move this rock, this one, and this one, so they'll support these others. Then when we pull this one out, LeeAnn goes through, picks up one of the figures so we can test where it's from and we're out of here. Five minutes. There's some risk." He pointed to the collapsed part of the ceiling. "Or we get out of here now. We would need your help so it's up to you."

Jeff nodded slowly. "Of course we're going to do it," he said then. "No problem with that decision."

So they started to work. LeeAnn set the camcorder down on a rock in the "on" position.

"I'll just let it run so I can record audio," LeeAnn said. The idea, though she didn't say so, was that in case something happened and they didn't make it off Tree Island safely, and the figures didn't either, maybe the camera and the videotape would, someday. She began to dictate a description of the find.

She could see David struggling with his back pain as he and Jeff lifted rocks–Jeff had to take much of the strain–and over and over she wanted to say, "Let's go, it's not worth it," but she couldn't bring herself to. Five minutes, ten minutes went by before David was finally satisfied. "Okay, I think that'll hold it. Let's hope," he said, looking at LeeAnn with enormous love and more than a little worry.

He and Jeff grasped the rock that they needed to move to enlarge the opening and pulled. LeeAnn watched, holding her breath. But the rest of the wall held.

"Okay, LeeAnn. Go for it." Leaving the camera rolling, LeeAnn got down on her hands and knees. David patted her on the fanny as though she were climbing into the back of Vanna. This, however, was more like crawling into an MRI. She started through, pulling herself forward on rough rocks. *Hurry and get in there and get out,* she told herself. But terrible dread seized her then. She thought she couldn't move, and she almost couldn't.

Wedging her head and shoulders into the opening, she reached and reached and reached. Then finally, "I'm touching it," she announced. Straining, stretching, she could just barely touch the male figure with her fingertips, but her hips held her from going any further inside. "I'm getting it." With the middle finger on her bandaged hand, she tried to nudge the figure closer to herself; she didn't want to push it further away.

Then at last! "I've got it, I've got the male," she said as she grasped it in her hand and pulled it toward herself. A small stone came down, rattling as it fell and rolled. Had she disturbed something, she wondered as, without warning, there was a terrible roar. The earth above them began to shake alarmingly and a white fire of fear arced through LeeAnn's body.

Stones started hitting her back, hurting her. *My God. It's going to fall in on us! Is Shasta erupting?* She felt David trying to shield her body.

"It's that damned Cat!" he yelled. "We've got to get out!" She could hear its engine above them then and realized they'd all be entombed. Herself, David, Jeff, and The Lovers on their sweet altar. She imagined a boulder pulverizing the figures and crushing her own torso. She heard Jeff cry out and that made her scream. Her anger was worse than her fear. As stones and earth continued to rain down on her back and legs, bruising her, punishing her, she cried out, "Stop it, stop it, stop *killing* us!"

Then all of a sudden it stopped and the earth wasn't shaking any more. A couple of stones fell, and some gravel. And then nothing. Just sudden, inexplicable peace. *How did it stop?* She wondered. *Nobody could hear us from down here. It can't be that I* willed *it to stop. Can it?*

"David?"

"We're okay. Can you get out?"

"Yes." She shone her light at the female figure then, wishing she could get it too. "Wait," she said. "I think I can get the woman too." She struggled then, managing to force her body through the opening, hoping she didn't disturb the whole thing and cause it to come crashing down on her.

Then she was inside that womb-like place. She lunged forward and clutched the female. Holding both figures, she turned and wriggled back through, feet first. It was a tough squeeze. She stood up as David and then Jeff hugged her.

"We've got nothing to carry them in," LeeAnn said. Nobody had big pockets. So she pulled her shirt out of her jeans, tied it tight around her midriff, put both figures in her bosom, and buttoned it up. She wondered how long it had been since the male and female had touched each other.

She was never really sure how they managed to get out, crippled as they all were. Sheer adrenaline. She could still hear an engine outside, but it wasn't shaking the earth. First Jeff shinnied up the rope. Then David made a foothold for LeeAnn with his clasped hands and she reached as far up on the rope as she could. She had never in her life successfully shinnied up a rope.

"LeeAnn, come on! Hurry!" Jeff said. "You've got to see what's out here. Come on." She managed to climb the rope just far enough for Jeff to grasp her wrists and pull her up the rest of the way.

The first thing she saw was the bright ribbon of light on the horizon in the east that illuminated the scene. She blinked in the light of a new day that somehow surprised her that it had dawned without them. She spotted Stan, puffing up the boulders in a great hurry, putting his hand on his knee to lift himself each new step. Behind him, a boat was speeding up the lake. It was the thrumpy police boat, she realized.

Then she turned around and saw what Jeff was excited about. There, on the golden grass of the old graveyard was a rainbow-colored helicopter, its rotors still turning. As she watched, a man jumped out of it and started running toward a second Caterpillar that was rumbling toward them from a distance. It was *Ernst Vanderveer,* waving his arms, motioning to the operator with all of the "Cut!" "Stop!" hand signals anybody's ever invented. At last the driver must have recognized his boss, for he brought the big earth-moving machine to a halt.

Amazement overcame LeeAnn. It was Ernst Vanderveer who had stopped the destruction. Ernst who had saved their lives and the Lovers. She was incredulous. He was supposed to be the evil one.

It was about an hour later, a time when Klamath Falls people would just be waking up, getting ready to go to church or clean out the basement or whatever. David had been given a shot of morphine for his back; he was drifting in and out of sleep while they waited for transport to get him off the island. They were lucky there were first-aid supplies on the helicopter. Jeff had limped over and got them, and then administered David's shot.

Lying beside David on a blanket on the long golden grass, LeeAnn was writing up her notes in her Franklin planner. She'd filled up all the pages for several weeks ahead, and was now somewhere in the middle of September, recording her observations of the find.

With an Ace bandage on his ankle, Jeff had hobbled down to the boat to get Stan's beat-up Styrofoam cooler, which everyone agreed would be the safest thing to pack the figures in. Meantime, LeeAnn was still cradling them like newborns next to her on the blanket. She abandoned her notes for a moment to curl up on her side and study them. She carefully traced the smile on the woman's face, five dots in a broad semicircle, and wondered about the artist who first decided to express a smile that way.

She hadn't had a chance to thank Ernst yet; he was down at the police boat, which was docked beside Pink Lady IV. Evidently he was seeing to Paul and Sonja. They had driven up over the hill in the old army Jeep just about the same time the helicopter landed–and had been politely apprehended by Sarge. LeeAnn had watched as they were taken down over the path on the Landing Rock to the police boat. The whole thing had been handled very nicely.

She thought about Ernst again. How could she have been so wrong about someone? From the very beginning she had misread his every signal. She had jumped to the conclusion that he was a self-obsessed power-hungry dominator and that's all he was. She had put him in the role and kept him there. How often, she wondered, do people end up just acting the role we assign them? How often in the past had she indulged that inverse snobbery of hers that caused her to look down on anybody who had a lot of material goods? As though they weren't worthy of her usually open minded attitude. Just because his enforcers used less than ethical methods didn't mean Ernst was bad. Only that perhaps he wasn't as careful as he ought to be. Maybe he just had too much territory to supervise.

Jeff came back up over the rocks now with the battered two-dollar cooler that was all soiled and scruffy looking. He knelt down on the blanket to take one more look at the figures and soon Stan came over, too. "What are you going to wrap those in, LeeAnn?" Stan asked her.

"I don't know."

"How about letting me donate my shirt," said Jeff and he pulled it off his skinny chest. "It's pretty soft." It was his Westchester 1979 Bike Race T-shirt, from the year he'd won second place. He loved that shirt, which was probably why he especially loved loaning it now.

Not to be outdone, Stan offered his shirt as well. On behalf of The Lovers, LeeAnn graciously accepted both shirts, but she was reluctant to pack the figures up just yet. Partly because she wanted to study them some more, but also because she'd have to wrap them separately, and they'd been so long apart.

She had the foolish thought that maybe all we needed was to get them back together. Maybe that's all the magic that had to happen, and we'd all be okay again.

LeeAnn wondered if it would turn out that the figures had been physically brought from a great distance, or if it was just the idea of partnership that had been brought. It didn't matter, she reflected, whether the love was flashed by mind or carried by hundreds of generations. *It's the equal love of these two that's important.* She was so glad she'd found them. Remembering her fear going into the chamber, she realized it had taught her something about rebirth. To be reborn you first have to crawl back into the womb. That's the hard part, the contraction before expansion again.

"Say, Sarge, you mind if I get a couple of shots of you?" said Stan, who had begun snapping pictures with the throwaway camera that was in his boat. "They might want to use them for the paper."

Sergeant Russo was making his way back up from the rock shelter, where he'd gone to see about getting some supports in to shore it up.

"I'm not sure you want any pictures of this ugly mug," said Sarge in ritual Klamath self-effacement. But he paused for a moment to let Stan snap a couple, then came over and squatted down beside the blanket where David and LeeAnn lay.

"I think it's not going to be a problem to get some timbers in there, LeeAnn, to preserve all those artifacts for you."

"Good."

"But for now we're going to leave them in situ. I'm sure VHRI's got some two-by-fours around here somewhere."

"Say, Sarge," said Stan, "I was wondering how you ever managed to talk Vanderveer into that rescue mission. The guy's smart; I would have thought he would just as soon have seen it all covered up."

"That's kind of the way I felt too, Stan. So I ah . . . after I talked to my wife, and found out from her what was happening–the message from LeeAnn here–I knew there wouldn't be time to get a warrant. So as soon as I got back in town I just hustled over to the airport and appealed to Vanderveer's better nature."

"Did you wake him up?"

"Guess I did. I told him, look, you don't have to do a thing unless you choose to." I had no other authority, realistically, no proof, no leverage, and no time, so what did I have to lose? I thought he might appreciate my being frank." Stan nodded sagely.

"I told him if he did nothing, in a couple hours it would be too late. 'So you decide what you want to do,' I told him. I said they'd probably be covering up one of the oldest sites in North America, but that if it wasn't covered up, depending on what we did discover, his entire project might be halted."

"You just gave it to him straight, huh?" said Stan, admiringly.

"Couldn't do much else."

"So what did he say?"

"He said, 'We're wasting time. Let's go.' Then he rousted his pilot up and the two of us flew the helicopter over here." *Flight of the Kiwanians,* LeeAnn thought.

"Then on the way I told him what I'd turned up on the BLM contractor when I was in Idaho. Nothing definitive, but . . ."

"Sarge, you were in *Idaho?*" LeeAnn asked, surprised.

He nodded. "After I got that fax from you, I decided I better check it out. And it was easier to do it on personal leave than try to get . . ."

"I didn't send you a . . ." She caught Jeff's look then.

"You realize it was something I wasn't going to ignore, LeeAnn," Sarge said. "I hope you realized that."

"No, I didn't."

"I didn't have a lot to go on except for your fax . . ."

"Right, right. My fax," she said slowly, looking at Jeff, who had the grace to shrug guiltily before saying, "I sent it for you–after Kevin turned up all that info. I thought it couldn't hurt," he added.

"Right."

"And afterwards, when I thought it hadn't done any good, why mention it?" Jeff told her.

"Well I'll be eternally grateful you sent it, Jeff. And that you arrived in time, Sarge. Kinsey Millhone I'm not. I guess you've noticed."

"Oh, do you read those books? My wife and I are reading one."

Then Stan started asking more questions again, about exactly what time he and Ernst had taken off from the airport, and what they'd been able to see from the air. Paul and Sonja arriving on the island, Sarge said. Then he told Sarge what it meant to him when he saw that chopper coming in. "I'd been worried to death about these kids . . ."

Calmed by the gentle hum of their conversation, LeeAnn took a deep breath and looked out at the lake. Neither she nor David was very injured but they were being pampered like invalids. And with all these other people running around taking care of things, it felt as if she and David were part of a larger human community that was actually working. She had the sense that more and more people were starting to network love and logic around the world–the exchange between Sarge and Ernst being a good case in point. Once again she saw the vision of the orange and the earth and the people holding hands.

LeeAnn re-propped the daypack that she was using as a pillow, leaned back against it, and breathed a deep sigh of relief. She could feel the hard outline of a cylindrical object against her back. *A jar of peanut butter.* "Hey, any of you guys hungry?" It turned out they were.

"See if you can find your hard-boiled egg in there," David said, his tongue thick with painkiller. "I found one in the fridge and stuck it in there for LeeAnn."

"Oh!" LeeAnn said as she found it. "How sweet."

"Hey, maintenance morphine for you, dude. Have you noticed how much more *pleasant* he is?" Jeff said.

David smiled weakly. "Get you later."

LeeAnn started to dole out food now, slicing the bread and spreading the Laura Scudder thickly with her Swiss army knife. Jeff followed up by sprinkling raisins on each sandwich. "Pickle? Who wants a pickle? Would you like to have the egg, Jeff? I can . . ."

"No, you eat it, L.A. I know how you feel about them."

So they began to eat. LeeAnn saw that the police boat with Paul and Sonja aboard was getting ready to leave. She watched, thinking about them and criminals in general and hoping nothing too terrible would happen to them. Of course, Paul had tried to kill her. But even people who kill people don't usually want to, she mused. They just get themselves boxed into a corner–and there's a lot of tight corners in a dominator society.

Ernst started back up over the boulders. He was climbing a whole lot better than she had, LeeAnn noticed. She thought about him again for a minute. Maybe the whole order of things doesn't *have* to be disturbed. If these one-percenters will just go in the right direction, there'd be nothing wrong with letting them lead. *They definitely have the resources.* She hadn't dreamed Ernst would willingly forego a billion dollar project. And yet he had. Would wonders never cease.

He paused by his helicopter to talk to his pilot briefly, then came over to join the others. LeeAnn thanked him for all he'd done, including saving their lives. Then she uncovered The Lovers who were lying together on the blanket in their nest of donated shirts. Like everyone else who had seen them, Ernst was rendered speechless for a time.

"I love the smile on her face," he said at last, looking at LeeAnn.

"So do I," LeeAnn agreed. "The connect-the-dots smile. But you know what I didn't see till we got them out? Something else about them that's exactly like the Gumelnita Lovers." She turned the figures over and fitted them together. "See?"

Everyone smiled then. For the male figure's arm was around the female. "You know what that reminds me of?" Jeff said. "Remember the famous three-million-year-old footprints of prehuman figures, a man and a woman walking side by side, and they figured out from the way their weight was distributed, that the man had to have had his arm around the woman?"

"I remember," LeeAnn said. "They did a reconstruction of those people that was so dear. That's exactly what this looks like."

"Kind of timeless, isn't it," said Ernst, looking at LeeAnn. Once again she noticed that keyhole iris in his grey-blue eyes that was so distinctive.

She covered the figures again. Then she asked Ernst what the extent of his losses might be as a result of his actions this morning. "What does this do to your plans?"

First he grinned that John Lindsay grin, then he answered her question seriously. "I'll go back to the office and start figuring it out. The Board of Directors will be pretty upset, and my father will be livid, but we'll figure something out. Who knows, there's a lot of land around Klamath that . . . well, let me just say there are some other options."

He's already repositioning, thought LeeAnn. *An incurable entrepreneur.*

"We're not going to give up on the possibility of VHRI somewhere in Klamath." Sarge looked relieved to hear that.

"Can we offer you a sandwich, Ernst?" Jeff said then. "We made a couple extra. Peanut butter."

"Goodt." The slight Dutch accent.

"Raisins on it?"

"Wonderful."

Jeff handed him a sandwich. Looking at the food, Ernst seemed to be thinking. Then he reached into his pocket and pulled out a key chain, only there wasn't a wind-rock attached. Instead there was a little plastic box, which he flipped open. Inside were little green capsules with algae from the lake. LeeAnn couldn't suppress a smile. He'd evidently read the literature on algae she'd sent. "Care for a little offering from the lake?"

She, Jeff, and David each took one, and Stan, after a moment or two of indecision, accepted one as well. Then, in silence, they ate their meal.

The rotors on the helicopter were starting to turn now, and David stirred at the sound. Ernst looked over. "Let me go see about getting you aboard, Dave. My pilot said he could take a couple of seats out, fix up a berth so you can stretch out."

"Thanks," said a sleepy David.

Ernst got up and started toward the chopper. Then he stopped and turned back.

"By the way, LeeAnn. I'd really like to help with your party. I think we can make it happen." Then he continued across the golden grass toward the helicopter.

LeeAnn glanced over at David and he looked back, proud of her. "Fribben," he said.

PART THREE

Future Dreams

My Dream 2000

I Dream . . .
That on 1 January 2000
The whole world will stand still
In prayer, awe and gratitude
For our beautiful, heavenly Earth
And for the miracle of human life.

I Dream . . .
That young and old, rich and poor,
Black and white,
People from North and South,
From all beliefs and cultures
Will join hands, minds and hearts
In an unprecedented, universal
Bimillennial Celebration of Life . . .

I Dream . . .
That in the year 2000
Innumerable celebrations and events
Will take place all over the globe
To gauge the long hard road covered
by humanity
To study our mistakes
And to plan the feats
Still to be accomplished
For the full flowering of the human race
In peace, justice and happiness.

I Dream . . .
That the few remaining years
To the Bimillennium
Be devoted by all humans, nations
and institutions
To unparalleled thinking, action,
Inspiration, elevation,
Determination and love
To solve our remaining problems
And to achieve
A peaceful, united human family on earth.

I Dream . . .
That the third Millennium
Will be declared
And made
Humanity's First Millennium of Peace.

By Robert Muller (written for Earth Day 1977)

448

CHAPTER TWENTY THREE

Where Are We Going?

Riding along in the passenger seat of her retrofitted 1997 silver Subaru station wagon with "SAIL TO LIVE" on a bumper sticker on the front and "LIVE TO SAIL" on the back, LeeAnn experimented with the voice controls on her new organizer. A wide silver bracelet of graceful design, it looked like something you might pick up in Santa Fe or Taos; she was delighted with it. The screen that scrolled the words she was hearing or dictating was quite small, but that didn't matter because it projected a larger hologram. Almost all commands were verbal, which was good, given LeeAnn's proclivity for punching the wrong buttons.

She spoke the word "update" and a list of half a dozen communications came up. Literally billions of computer-generated messages were sent daily in the U.S. alone. Computers nowadays performed all sorts of routine duties: paying bills, booking transportation, making appointments, confirming deals, shopping for the best price, and a host of other tasks. After synthesizing the results of its inquiries, a person's organizer–LeeAnn had named hers Maia–would generate a friendly memo, telling her basically all she needed to know.

Peter had been particularly delighted with the recent developments in bullshit reduction; he had been such a prisoner to pro forma detail. *Maybe in a few years,* LeeAnn mused, *all communications among humans will be the meaningful kind; machines can deal with the rest. Won't that be wonderful.*

She pulled up her schedule. *Yes!* The airline reservation had come through. Six a.m. on January 3, 2011, out of Klamath Falls to Maui. Five days of windsurfing. *That will be good,* she thought, *no matter what happens tonight.* LeeAnn allowed herself to fantasize for a few moments; she was pretty good on her board by now. She even did some moderate wave-sailing, catching air from time to time with modest leaps out of the water. No loops though. Probably never.

They were passing through a young forest of mixed pine now. This area around Chemult, north of Klamath Falls, had been a desolate and depressing site of beetle-killed trees only a few years before, miles and miles of them just dead and awful. Now the land was all replanted, and not just with one type of tree, but with a mix simulating the forest that had been there hundreds of years before. It was the same computer-driven technique they were using to repropagate rain forests.

Yawning and stretching, Shalise, daughter of Jeff and Kevin's Blackdog, that golden puppy from long ago, got up from where she'd been lying in the back, looking up at the clouds, and wandered up to sit behind the steering wheel. On this road you seldom saw anybody but a small child or a pet at the wheel. As a German Shepherd in an old Corvette sailed by in the express lane, Shalise gave him a passing glance, which he acknowledged with some interest.

LeeAnn focused again on her organizer. A map on today's schedule showed she'd been cleared to the first shopping hub on Autoway 97, where she would be automatically routed off. Meanwhile, travel on this experimental road was magnetically controlled, so you could sit there doing nothing if you wanted to. LeeAnn would reach her destination in fifty-five minutes, the organizer told her, traveling at eighty-five miles an hour. (Some people, LeeAnn among them, still refused to give up miles for kilometers.)

Her organizer quietly chirped four o'clock, and LeeAnn felt her body tense as the Public Audio news began. There would of course be only *one* major news story today. "Tonight," intoned a voice that reminded her vividly of Cory Flintoff from the old National Public Radio, "as we complete ten years of survival into the new millennium, people will gather in places all over the world to hear the First-Decade Report. It's estimated 4.5 billion people will be present and participating. Following the broadcast, we will begin the first twenty-four-hour holiday since 2001." *Time to celebrate the planet's survival,* LeeAnn thought, *or ponder its demise, depending on what they have to tell us.*

The newscaster began naming scientists from the twelve Partnership Solutions Centers around the world who would be reporting for their colleagues on the four critical areas: *health, commerce, relationships,* and *environment*–which, of course, was the way Peter had divided up the areas of human behavior so many years ago. Fortunately, as with many ideas whose time has come, it was no longer clear who'd thought it up in the first place. Though her name had been on some of the earliest RSVPs, most people had no idea LeeAnn Spencer was any more real than Betty Crocker, which suited LeeAnn just fine. That way she had her life.

All in all, the first globally monitored decade had been surprisingly successful. But in the area of environment, there was one major problem. Tonight everyone would be awaiting the latest figures on damage to sea life from deadly UV ray storms that had been bombarding the earth through a thinned–and still thinning–ozone layer. All the experts had expected the situation would soon be turned around, but recently, before that could happen, several species of phytoplankton had unexpectedly begun dying off in alarming and ever-increasing numbers, contradicting all of the computer models. Whether the species would be wiped out entirely, possibly within months, was not yet clear.

Nor was it clear whether their loss would result in an unbreachable gap in the food chain that could end all life on the planet in a rather precipitous way. *It takes only one hole in the dyke; one tiny gap in the food chain could cause the whole system to go kerklunk.* The latest sea-death analyses would be released tonight.

Wouldn't it be awful, LeeAnn thought, *if we were to make it in all the other areas, if we were actually on the way to conquering hate and greed and sloth and violence and then we die anyway, loving one another and being sorry?*

Stop it. Negativity attracts. LeeAnn tried to hold back the rush of adrenaline that always struck her when the image that had been haunting her for days surfaced once more. The image of the lambs–thousands of dying lambs in Australia, blinded by the UV rays, panicking in their darkness. The story had been on the Seg24 news about two years ago. It always made LeeAnn picture humans stumbling in the same way, blind and sick, their bodies failing them, step by step.

The dying of the human race was what she saw in her mind's eye these days, just as she used to see the orange and the earth, and the people all around, holding hands. She dreamed of it. Had nightmares of it. *What if it should happen to us? What if I should live to see it happen to the people I love?* She fought to blot out all the images that were flooding into her mind.

Then the sound of something coming up from behind startled her. *Oh!* It was only the train from the coast, moving rapidly past LeeAnn's line of vision. She glanced over at the Cardio Car where people were pedaling, tread-milling, or stair-climbing their way along. Audrey especially liked the practical innovation. Passengers traveling Cardio got a slightly reduced fare based on the fact that they were contributing marginally to the train's power source, and with double-decker cars, the contribution would soon become more substantial, which made people feel good. Plus, Cardio Cars had great sound systems. So on most lines, it wasn't surprising that there was a waiting list to escape what had been aptly renamed Sedentary Seating. Practically nobody wanted to be grouped that way any more.

Right after the train passed, the Subaru's path diverged from the highway, as LeeAnn and Shalise were shunted off the system. They came to a halt at a small combination shopping center and rest stop. As LeeAnn got out of the car, she took a moment to stop and feel the sun on her face. It had rained earlier and there was still that clean, fresh smell of wetness in the air. She opened the rear door and Shalise, wagging her great feathery tail, leapt off the tailgate onto the sidewalk, then waited responsibly for LeeAnn to activate the electronic lead. It was never necessary for Shalise, but it was the law.

LeeAnn had named Blackdog and Ayla's golden puppy for the chalice in Riane Eisler's book, *The Chalice and the Blade*, and then spelled it differently so people would pronounce it the French way, which sounded better to her. Not too many dogs were named for books, but it always pleased people who were familiar with Eisler's work. And it suited Shalise. The dog, who was now thirteen years old, sniffed the ground, pleased at their destination, then pranced along as they headed toward the entrance of the Friends of People, the storefront with the poster in the window that said, "It takes a whole village to raise a pet."

All the pet brokers were busy today, with the holiday coming tomorrow. This franchise business had gained enormous popularity in recent years, spreading all over the hemisphere, as it became clear that fewer household pets would be a good idea and that they could easily be shared. People were traveling so much these days, and what was the point of your animal doing time in a kennel when it could be going out to other people who needed a friend? *Pimps for Pets* is what Audrey had initially dubbed the service, but it worked.

"Hey, Shalise," said the woman behind the counter. "You just got another booking–Tracy and Ken." They were a couple who liked to spend weekends running on the beach with a dog.

A slightly more vigorous wagging of tail confirmed that Shalise recognized the syllables. She worked probably three or four times a month, usually repeat business. She was paid human minimum wage, which was currently $10 an hour, and was always free to refuse an assignment. She seldom did. Her wages averaged about $15,000 a year, which was good, although her father made a good deal more. Blackdog, in New York, had been working almost constantly, visiting seriously ill children in hospitals for an outfit called The Animal Connection, ever since his wife Ayla had died. It beat sleeping eighteen hours a day.

"Well," LeeAnn said when they were through registering, cupping Shalise's face with her hands. "You go have a great time, I'm going to go have lunch."

The dog seemed to be asking a question.

"Oh, yes. Of course," LeeAnn responded. "Up." Shallie stood on her hind legs, placed her paws delicately at either side of LeeAnn's waist, and hugged her. It was a greeting Blackdog had taught his daughter. They looked into each other's eyes for a moment, then Shalise dropped down and trotted around behind the counter.

LeeAnn exited the shop and made her way across the parking lot to one of her favorite restaurants. She passed under the familiar golden arches where the sign read, "Fifteen trillion gallons of water saved." She walked through the decorative "in-house greenhouse" where all the trimmings were grown hydroponically in a solution rich in algae and mineral dust. She picked up her Big Mac, hold-the-cheese-please, and iced herbal tea, carried it back to a booth and happily chomped down on lunch, as the juice from a thick slice of beefsteak tomato ran down her chin.

LeeAnn had always been a real snob about fast-food places, but now you could get a very healthy meal at most of them. It was McDonald's that had been instrumental in getting the animal flesh out of hamburgers, and that's what won LeeAnn's fervent loyalty. Back when the Ogallala Aquifer, which supplied the water for eight states, became unusable, EarthSave had come up with its 20% Program–getting people to pledge they would eat only 20% of the meat they formerly ate.

McDonald's ran a promo for their new TexPro burger patty. "Free Big Mac if you can guess whether you're eating beef or veggie," they advertised. It turned out almost *nobody* could. The howlingly funny video vérité commercials that came out of that triggered a major mainstream culture shift as all the other fast-food giants followed suit. The question, "Where's the beef?" had finally been answered. The answer was that nobody particularly cared. And grasslands all over the world were beginning to be restored as a result.

Back in the Subaru, and now having to operate the car herself, LeeAnn found herself stuck in a nasty traffic jam. They still didn't have the Autoway extended all the way in to the Partnership Center yet; the control strips were still being installed, so the road was torn up. Of course, the First-Decade Report tonight was also causing some of the congestion. A lot of key people in the sciences would be videoconferencing from their offices, then watching the report at the Partnership Center's dome with their families.

Spread over a thousand acres bordering a wilderness area, the Center for Partnership Solutions was one of twelve around the earth, one for every two time zones. Normally, fifteen hundred people worked here, mostly on internships, engaged in unprecedented network connection and collaboration across all fields of science. Since computers handled most routine matters, nearly everyone had a creative role. There were no drones, no secretaries, no paper pushers, which made for a lively, egalitarian group that was fun to be around. It had a kind of Walden II atmosphere about it.

Sometimes LeeAnn wished that she worked among these people. Instead, for a number of years she had worked mostly on the Tree Island archaeological site. She spent a lot of time alone, both on the island and in her lab, discovering and sharing the incredibly useful insights into ancient times that Tree Island was providing. Human habitation in the Klamath Basin had turned out to have happened eons earlier than originally estimated, with a relatively small but stable population extending over many thousands of years.

It had never been proven that the Tree Island Lovers had been carried across the land bridge from Europe and Asia to the Americas. Or from the Americas going the other way, as the Klamath people believed. So the mystery of the uncanny resemblance between the Danube figures and the Tree Island Lovers remained unsolved. LeeAnn was almost glad of that. For what her discovery may have proved instead, she thought, was that *ideas* travel. *And love travels.* That it is in the air, like radio waves, all around us all the time, and all we have to do is tune into it.

LeeAnn noticed a lot of traffic starting to come from the other direction—people from the Center just getting off work. Most people nowadays worked the increasingly popular "five-to-five" twelve-hour shifts, with three and a half days on, three and a half off. That spread the work force around the clock and around the calendar, maximizing use of facilities and increasing twenty-four-hour availability of nearly all goods and services. And it meant you could count on always having the same days off.

With the new freedom to choose day or night hours, a surprising number of night people like Jeff and Peter had emerged. In fact, when all was said and done, almost half turned out to prefer nights. One of the best things about their shift, said the new "night-bird" converts, was that you could catch every single sunrise on earth.

Mandated holidays were fewer than they'd been in the 20th century. But you could elect up to ten personal-belief-system holidays, be they political or religious or simply bacchanal. By being able to customize their schedules, people felt like they had a little more control over their lives.

Finally, traffic thinned. Approaching the Partnership Center, LeeAnn drove the Subaru onto an elevator platform at the new parking enclave, where two halves of a plastic bubble were waiting to enclose it like the prize in a gumball machine. She got out of the car and watched as she always did, till the big capsule clicked together and disappeared underground, where it would be shot by pneumatic tube into a holding pod where it would stay until retrieval by a signal from her organizer later. The mental image of cars zooming around all by themselves under the ground pleased her greatly. Capsule parking ensured that no one would scratch your BMW or mess with your luggage in the back seat. In fact, there were no humans involved in the operation at all.

Slinging her day pack over her shoulder, LeeAnn headed toward the entrance to the Center a few hundred yards away, where everyone passed under the FountainGate, a high and dramatic archway of water.

They didn't get wet, just refreshed by all the negative ions. Every time she went through the gate, she felt her mind clear. That was the purpose of it, after all.

The highlights in LeeAnn's dark blonde hair sparkled in the afternoon sun as she strode along. In the years that had passed since the Tree Island discovery, LeeAnn had changed very little, her body not at all, and her face only in a very nice way. A few tiny new learning lines had been added and there was a different set to her expression. It was a little more open, as though she saw more, perhaps understood more and feared less. LeeAnn still had bangs, still wore her dark-honey-colored hair straight. It was just past shoulder length and still luxuriantly thick.

She was wearing her newest spansuit today, her favorite to date. Made from a close-up photograph of a wave, it was dark blue, juxtaposed with the lovely aqua color of sea-foam and the white of a life-size cresting wave. The close-fitting, one-piece body suits, made of a breathable material that dried in sixty seconds flat under a special light, had originally been developed for ultraviolet protection. But now they had become a major fashion statement.

Amazingly realistic, quite stunning representations of art and nature had recently become possible, with new screening techniques that produced superb photo transfers of animal plumage, nature scenes, or abstract design. A person could become a forest, or a birthday cake, or almost anything they wanted to be, quite inexpensively. That was because the new spansuit industry, like a growing number of other industries, prided itself on a pricing policy that reflected the true cost of manufacturing, rather than what the public might conceivably pay.

Spansuits revealed every curve and so were definitely for people who felt good about their bodies. Which included more and more of the population these days. The epidemic of obesity that had hit developed countries in the late 20th century had just about been licked. So the spansuit craze had simply exploded, with a rapidly growing accessory market that added all kinds of finishing touches–sarongs, vests, hats, scarves, belts, capes, matching covers for briefcases and day packs.

As the important influence of color and form on our psyches was becoming more and more apparent, the language of clothing was taking a giant step forward, as everybody, especially kids, indulged their wildest fantasies in dress. You could buy dark skin or light, you could even buy suits with freckles. LeeAnn noticed a guy going by just now all wrapped in a balance sheet, with just a touch of red ink here and there. The human race seemed to be getting its sense of humor again, as the primitive T-shirt utterances of the 20th century visibly matured.

LeeAnn guessed that probably eighty percent of the people she passed were wearing the new suits. Of course, people who worked at the Partnership Solutions Center tended to be in the advance guard. At the word "guard," she caught herself in mid-thought; she was working diligently to delete all dominator phrases from her vocabulary. *Advance what? Advance cadre,* LeeAnn decided and murmured the words "cadre, definition" into her organizer. "Cadre," Maia replied in a pleasant New England voice, "a nucleus of trained personnel capable of assuming control and training others." That said it pretty well.

As she got closer to the FountainGate–words ending in "gate" were *still* being coined–LeeAnn felt the faint mist being carried gently in the breeze. It reminded her of the feeling she'd had at Bridal Veil Falls in Yosemite. Taking a deep breath, she stopped for a moment to check out the scene. In the last few weeks, since the extent of the death of the phytoplankton had become known, the spirit of most everyone seemed reminiscent of the Battle of Britain, when the sense of purpose and connection had tended to drive away fear.

Everybody she saw right now walking past her knew about the sea deaths, and they all seemed to be handling it. She did not see great fear in the faces of those in this crowd. There was a sense almost of exhilaration. She felt closer to others because of the crisis and she knew they felt the same. She wondered if people need crises to feel linked, and that's why we create them.

Once inside the Center, LeeAnn approached the sign that said *Bikes and Blades,* which were the two chief means of transportation here. Some people were standing in line, others were pulling blades out of their bags or briefcases, and sliding them into the grooves on their athletic shoes. Then off they went. Blading was great for some, but there was no way LeeAnn was ever going to try it. Unlike windsurfing, all it took was one slight lapse in grace to do major damage.

She stepped up to the bike dispenser, and it released a standard model in robin's-egg blue, which was good, since the next one was a yucky lime green. Then she was pedaling down the cobbled pathway toward the area where her brother worked. Peter wasn't growing buildings by biomorphic replication yet, but his work at the Center was the next best thing. It was part of a global study to coordinate building-material requirements of a growing population with their food, fuel, water, and oxygen needs, so humanity could reliably calculate how much space each person would need to live comfortably on the planet in the 22nd century without depleting anything.

She rode on past small study fields and greenhouses where varieties of hemp, bamboo, banana, and kudzu were growing. In another section of the garden, plant materials were being compacted into building blocks. Peter's group was also studying the quality and characteristics of the various organic mixtures: the cost, structural strength, weight, acoustics, even their scent. A lot of people still thought he was nuts, but Peter was working on an edible building block–a great way to store food against famine. Just saw off a little piece and boil it up for cereal.

With several patents pending, Peter had prospered as much as any-one in the family–except for Maggie, of course. Several years back, she had managed to sign up the New York City public school system on algae and thus gotten the superfood into the small bodies of millions of inner-city children. It seemed to have helped. Joan of Arc Junior High wasn't nearly as dangerous these days.

When she got to Human Habitat, Peter's section of the grounds, LeeAnn stopped the bike and stood straddling it as she looked for her brother up and down the twisting, turning paths of blue blacktop. It wasn't blacktop actually, but some composite material that utilized waste oil and came out in a spectacular shade of peacock that looked so good with the growing plants.

Of course, her brother had had something to say about the way all this was designed. He'd gone before the CPS board with his early pro-posals, and later worked with Ernst Vanderveer on implementation. Ernst and Peter had made a pretty good pair actually, when it came to spending the billion dollars that had originally been allocated for the one-percenters' retreat at Tree Island. After construction on the resort had been halted, VHRI had switched its emphasis and funds to design and construct the physical plant for the Partnership Center, which actu-ally had turned out to be more profitable for them.

Here came Peter on his blades now, moving with a wonderful rhythm. LeeAnn could practically feel the sway as he leaned out in a leisurely way, crossing his feet like a pianist crosses hands, exquisite in his timing. *Blading,* LeeAnn thought, *must surely be the most graceful motion on land that there is. Land surfing.*

As he spotted LeeAnn, he skated on one foot, his arms outstretched, his other leg behind him like a Cypress Gardens water-skier, and she burst out laughing. Back on both feet, he leapt over a small bush and then came to a swooping, swirling stop before her.

"Why do you have to be so good at that?" she said.

He grinned. Peter, who was almost fifty, still had his ponytail, and he was wearing a spansuit of remarkably subtle abstract design. Today's outfit, clearly musical in origin, depicted tonal patterns through shades of color. Peter's suits, which he designed himself, were always revealing of his state of mind. If he felt he needed centering, he might choose one whose lines, patterns, and colors all gathered at the heart chakra. Other days, the message was more diffuse. But whatever Peter wore evoked definite feelings of strength and harmony in both wearer and viewer.

LeeAnn's brother still didn't like to hug on cue when he greeted people, so LeeAnn didn't force the issue. "Audrey told me to come on by and get the lunch," she said, "so you won't have to carry it over." Their great-grandmother's picnic basket would be a little unwieldy to rollerblade with.

"Oh, okay."

"You look disappointed. You weren't about to break into it, were you?" LeeAnn teased.

"Who, me?" He shrugged. "Come on."

She followed him on the bike along the bluetop path. At the rose trellis outside his studio, Peter touched a wall for support as he slipped the blades off his shoes and stuck them in his waist pack. Then they entered the large glass-walled, plant-filled space where ten-year-old Jordan, Peter and Audrey's son, was hanging from monkey bars while he waited for a drawing to print out. People still used paper for architectural drawings, which pleased LeeAnn–rolled-up plans always seem to have so much promise. The monkey bars were a family tradition; in LeeAnn or Peter's offices, you could always come for a visit and literally hang out.

"Hey, L.A.," said Jordan. Blond and rangy, Jordie had his father's blue eyes but the pointed chin, full lips, and olive skin came from his mother.

"Hi, how you guys doing?" L.A.'s greeting took in not only her nephew but also his best friend Tyrone, who was lying on the floor conducting business on his cellular. Tyrone was smaller than Jordie and quite black. He wore glasses that gave him a deceptively subdued look. At twelve, Ty already had his own successful software company that he'd started the year before. Eleven was young to begin a business, but not unheard of anymore–for the enormous capabilities of teens and preteens had finally again been recognized. The useless years of hanging out in malls learning Materialism 101 were gone.

Under NewEd, which was essentially a whole new system of education, kids went to classes four hours in the morning, then attended neighborhood science labs, art studios, or care centers for the rest of the day–except two hours of compulsory RecTime, which could be spent in a number of different ways. It seemed to work. With the expanded opportunity for early experimentation, few kids reached puberty without knowing what they wanted to do with their lives, which was good. How much harder it was, LeeAnn thought, to figure things out after the hormones kicked in.

Jordan had about decided he would go into interspecies communication when he grew up. That came from working with his mother at the Marine Mammals station. He liked architecture, too, so maybe what he'd do, he thought, was create hospitable environments in which interspecies communication could take place. "Like a welcome center for aliens, something like that," he said.

College, fortunately, was no longer a thing to be paid for; it was something you worked your way through, doing whatever was needed to prepare for your chosen vocation. Which made student loans a thing of the past. The new programs had added greatly to the productive work force, and it didn't seem to have taken anything from childhood. Except that the games young people played were more closely tied to, and had more effect on, the real world. And the games adults played, less so.

The only downside to NewEd LeeAnn could see was that the ability to spell or do even simple arithmetic without a computer seemed irrevocably lost. Balancing that shortfall, there was a growing awareness among kids about the twenty-four segments of the earth; almost every child was a whiz at geography.

The study of history had been vastly simplified, as the past five to ten thousand years of nearly unrelenting blood and guts were now being taught in context–and in proportion–to the far more peaceful times that stretched back half a million years ago. So, it was no longer obligatory to memorize the dates of battles, which LeeAnn had always thought an idiotic exercise anyway. Instead, *History of Marriage* was an important core course, and parenting (or *mentoring*) courses were mandatory from first grade on.

"This is the new idea that we're getting ready to file on," Peter said, laying out the latest drawing from the printer.

"It's pretty simple actually," Jordan said, with his mouth full of popcorn. He had his father's appetite and drove Peter nuts by constantly chomping in his ear.

"The idea is to create an essentially indestructible block that can be utilized over and over in tropical climates. It's got to be light and mold-resistant, easy to ship . . ."

"Affordable," Tyrone added.

" . . . and in this example, the blocks would interlock."

"Like Legos for the real world," LeeAnn remarked. "And edible, huh?"

A faint, silvery bell tone caused her to glance at her organizer bracelet. "I better get going. Where's the lunch? Audrey told me I'd better come take it to keep you guys from getting into it."

"Mom outdid herself," said Jordan. "She was still cooking at one o'clock this morning."

"It's in the cooler," Peter told her, indicating a large glass-walled, built-in cooler in the wall of the office. She lifted the heavy basket down and took a peek in at all the bright little thermal dishes that really did keep food hot or cold–the 22nd Century Group's picnic menus had become more and more elaborate over the years. Then she closed the basket, and Peter helped her bungee it onto the back of the bike.

"I think that'll do it," Peter said, testing his work. Bungee cords and duct tape, thank goodness, were still mainstays of daily living in the 21st century. Then he looked at his planner, which had beeped at him. "Audrey's saying she still might make it in time."

"Well, let's hope so." LeeAnn's sister-in-law was the only one in the family who had a daily commute. The train that left Coos Bay on the coast at 4:15 p.m. would normally get her here by 5:55, which would be in time for the First-Decade Report broadcast. But tonight every nonessential service on earth would stop for an hour, and that would include Audrey's commuter train if it were late. So if she were still on board when the broadcast started, she'd have to participate from there.

"See you at the Dome," LeeAnn called to Peter and the boys as she pedaled off. Retracing her route through the Habitat gardens, she thought about her brother and her best friend and the really rather excellent partnership they had eventually forged together. True, it had been kind of a long shot, Peter and Audrey actually making it as life partners. It took awhile before Audrey's bossy ways began to melt away. Peter simply hadn't responded to them and that had helped. But it took some powerful adjusting for both.

The plus side was that they shared several important qualities. Both were as silly as could be; when you went to visit, you could be sure to spend most of the time laughing. Both Peter and Audrey loved to eat. And both were strongly sexual beings. Peter had always dug small brunettes, and Audrey at last revealed that she had always dug Peter. Even though, as she said, "I managed to successfully sublimate for years."

"Sublimate?" Jeff had guffawed when she came up with that one. "Sublimate? Is that what you call that wanton lifestyle you lived?" Then, of course, he insisted on showing her the definition in his dictionary. "'Sublimate, to direct the expression of desires toward more socially or culturally acceptable ends.' Sure. Right."

"Yeah, but look at what you didn't read." She snatched the dictionary. "Alternate definition. 'Sublimate. To cause to pass from a solid to a vapor state by the action of heat, and then condense to a solid form.' Now if that isn't a perfect description." And it was.

Bonded to Peter, Audrey Garcia-Spencer was in about as solid a state these days as anyone could be. Their child, their lifestyle, the kind of love that Peter found he was capable of giving had all changed her; traumas from childhood she'd never been able to shake were now pretty well put away. To LeeAnn's profound relief, her best friend no longer sucked salted ice cubes.

LeeAnn took a shortcut through a residential section, and then the Clinton Science of Commerce Department grounds where circular dome-shaped buildings with sod roofs sat unobtrusively among the trees, reminding her of the wooded U.C. Santa Cruz campus. It was good to see more circles and curves, fewer rectangles in architecture. Circles, she'd noticed, were becoming more important again in society. The sacred circle, the community circle. Interlocking circles. LeeAnn had always imagined circles as having permeable edges; they seemed to be able to slip into one another or gently bounce off of each other at will. She thought of the old dominator society as being made up of rigid triangles or quadrangles with sharp corners that constantly gouged and poked.

There it was. The *God Is Love* sculpture was visible now through the trees. She gazed at it as she rode the rest of the way to a viewing area. Fifty feet high, it was a statue of a woman and a man in prayer or meditation together. Sitting cross-legged facing each other, holding both hands, the couple looked into each other's eyes with enormous hope and courage. The sculpture had been commissioned to commemorate the spontaneous ecumenical movement born out of the heartbreak of the African orphan crisis. Similar sculptures with the theme of love were being placed at other Partnership Solutions Centers around the world.

The alloy that the statue was made of had all the best qualities of plastic and metal. It was amazingly light and easy to work with and it looked exactly like bronze. Just gorgeous. And it could be recycled easily if they ever got tired of it. In time, ideas might change and icons with them. This one LeeAnn loved, however. This one she hoped would stay till the end of time.

Squinting in the bright sunlight, LeeAnn looked up at the scaffold where several artists were working. Molded on-site, the figures was being finished now by a team that to his–and LeeAnn's–great joy, included her husband, David. Like the rest of the 22nd Century Group charter members, he had benefited greatly from being in on the ground floor of the partnership movement. He'd been involved as one of the collaborating artists from the start.

Right now they were working on buffing the space-age material to create a luminous look, as David put it. Trying to achieve that look of ultimate connection.

LeeAnn heard a cricket sound and smiled. Pretty soon she saw David step off the platform and heard the whir of his PowerPak as he descended, scaring her as he always did, by fooling around, zooming back up and then down again. It shouldn't have frightened her. The PowerPak was quite a conservative device actually, utilizing tiny, almost noiseless jets of supercompressed air that provided just enough power for the small ascents and descents they were making.

Now, floating just above her, he turned his body sideways so he could kiss her while still hovering, reminding LeeAnn of dragonflies in the distant past. She laughed as he made the delicate adjustments necessary to get his pursed lips close to hers. He grinned at her, she grinned at him, and several onlookers grinned along with them.

It was a smoldering kiss when they finally got it together. Just their lips touching. The pheromones were still dizzying. Finally, David put both feet on the ground, turned off his Pak, and took LeeAnn in his arms for a strong embrace. Then she pulled back to look at him. His chiseled face showed great satisfaction these days. At nearly sixty, he still had the wonder of a child at the unexpected power of his talent. And, finally, he was working on pieces of a large enough scale to engage him thoroughly. David's only real problem in the 21st century had been the bad back that he'd reinjured on Tree Island. But he'd finally windsurfed and worked his way into enough muscles so even that didn't bother him anymore.

"Where's Marina?" LeeAnn asked, after a minute.

"Three guesses," David grinned, then pointed toward their daughter, who had just gotten back from visiting Maggie in New York and auditioning for Juilliard. She was standing across the courtyard talking to two boys. Marina spotted her mother then and ran toward her, flinging herself into LeeAnn's arms for a long hug, then pulled back to look at her. "Fribben," Marina said.

"Fribben," said LeeAnn.

At thirteen, just slightly smaller than LeeAnn, Marina showed promise of looking almost exactly like her mother someday. The same high-breasted, long-waisted figure, long legs, and a round little butt. Her hair was darker, and slightly curly, but her face and figure were so like LeeAnn's that people passing them on the street would often point and smile.

"You ready to come?" LeeAnn asked David.

"Not quite yet. I'll be over in a few. Got to clean up first." He headed for the Geo-showers, where he could scrub down in his Spansuit, then dry off in sixty seconds, one of the great conveniences of the new form of dress.

"Should I grab a bike, Mom?" Marina asked as LeeAnn started to get back on hers. There were several sitting nearby with their out-of-use indicator showing. The bikes were provided free to visitors. "You'd rather run, wouldn't you?"

"Actually, I would," said LeeAnn.

"Then I'll ride the bike." Marina inspected it, then got on. "This is actually a pretty decent machine," she announced, as they started moving along at a fair clip. "You know, for standard issue," she added. Cyclists would probably always be snobs about their bikes, LeeAnn thought, and Marina was already an avid bike person. She and her class had already crossed the U.S. on the new cycleway and were contemplating the one to Central America.

They were under the Walkways now, the Center's system of covered passageways with bells in the ceiling that rang in series every hour. Thousands of the small bells that had been rung at the start of the millennium had later been donated and installed in the Walkway ceilings with a mechanism that rang them in relays, so that their music traveled all the way through the complex. It made a soft, tinkly sound, as though some spirit were passing through.

Bells had become the big thing in that Celebration year. The newspaper hats that LeeAnn and her friends had envisioned everyone could share had never really caught on. Maybe they looked too military, or maybe it was just too hard to remember how to make them. Instead, in the weeks just before the big party, it had seemed like everyone on the planet was trying to make a bell, find a bell, test a bell, or ring a bell. And most everyone did. It was estimated that two billion bells were rung that night.

Bell choirs, understandably, were popular for a time afterward; different faiths could ring bells together, even when they couldn't agree on words. And there was always a pealing of bells or chimes at almost every event, even on television commercials, for the first year or so. Then *celestial rock* had evolved from that, the all-percussion dance music that made you feel like you'd died and gone to heaven. It was great fun to dance to; David and LeeAnn often went out dancing.

"So did they ever get that dome installed in Times Square?" LeeAnn asked her daughter.

"I don't know. Not as of this morning when I left. It was still in the river."

"We can check it on the news when we get to the Dome." LeeAnn was talking about the tricky business of installing a clear plastic dome over the Times Square Plaza in time for this First-Decade New Year's celebration. Everyone seemed fascinated with these engineering feats. Due to the difficulties of working in the congested Forty-Second Street area, they had molded the dome on a platform in the Hudson River and then had been waiting to lift it into place with helicopters at a time when there was absolutely no wind.

"So how was Maggie? How was your visit?"

"She was great."

"I'm glad to hear it," LeeAnn said. "Anything else?"

"And the audition went great, too, if that's what you were wondering, Mom." Marina grinned. Like her father, she always held back both good news and bad. "Especially the pas de deux. I'm pretty sure I made it."

LeeAnn ran alongside the bike, listening while Marina told her all about it. Marina was a dancer and planned to be a choreographer. LeeAnn delighted to see the joy her daughter took in that expressive body of hers as she blossomed with all the grace LeeAnn hadn't had, and the beauty, both inner and outer, that she did have but had never acknowledged in herself. It was okay, however, to celebrate it in Marina.

These days, hundreds and sometimes thousands of dancers commonly participated in globally broadcast performances, weaving complex patterns and deeply dimensioned forms, which Marina executed in spectacular pen-and-ink drawings. Like David, Marina could draw splendidly, just as LeeAnn could not. *Aren't genes wonderful things?* LeeAnn thought.

Then, "Mom?" It was one of Marina's more serious *Mom*'s.

"Yup? What is it, Honey?"

"How worried are you about tonight?" She was riding closer to her mother now.

LeeAnn took awhile to consider her words before answering. "It doesn't do any good to worry." *Boy, it took me a lot of years to learn that,* she thought. *Now if I could just practice it.*

"There's a pretty good chance we're all going to fry, isn't there?" Marina went on in a deliberately light tone.

"I wish you wouldn't put it that way. Don't say 'fry.'" Again the images of the blinded lambs. "And I don't think that's what the prognosis will be."

"But if it is, if it looks like it's really going to happen, do you think they'll tell us the truth?"

"Maybe. Maybe not." LeeAnn sighed. "They may not know. It's not that exact a science, so I think they'd have to cloak it in 'if's.' I doubt anybody's going to come right out and say, 'Hey, we're all doomed. Kiss yourself goodbye.' Not tonight anyway."

"But what if we *did* get a doomsday report," Marina persisted. "What if they *do* say we're on our way out?"

Well, first there's denial, she thought, *which may be what we're in the process of right now.*

"What will people do? Will they panic?"

"I don't know; I doubt it." Somehow she couldn't picture that. "We've had quite awhile to get used to the idea. And we're all in it together. That helps."

"What do *you* really think is going to happen?" Marina asked her mother. "Give me your most honest assessment."

LeeAnn, of course, would try to comply; she and David never pulled punches with their daughter. She thought back to reading *On the Beach* years ago, with the couple in it who had to make the decision to euthanize their baby after nuclear war had poisoned the planet.

Then she remembered the TV movie, *The Day After*, another drama about cataclysm for the human race. Was that the kind of fate we were headed for? "Well, I think . . ." She tried to envision the future but couldn't see it clearly. Fear had blurred her vision. All her life, till now, she'd felt like the future was easy to transport herself to, to move around in and imagine. To invent things for. After all, her birth sign was Aquarius. Now it was so much harder to see. Finally, she said, "I think it'll be a fast dance for awhile . . ." Her "however" was unspoken, but Marina pounced on it.

"You think we *are* going to make it then?"

"Yes, I believe I do." And in that moment, at least, LeeAnn believed herself. "And you, what do you think? Give me *your* most honest assessment."

"That's about what I think too. But either way . . ." She glanced over, regarding her mother solemnly. "I'm not sorry you brought me into this world." Marina's eyes looked shiny from the tears she wouldn't allow, and LeeAnn's were damp as well. "I wanted you to know that," she said in a formal kind of way.

"Thank you." LeeAnn fought to keep the tears back.

Then LeeAnn's daughter took a deep breath. "So, since we've established we're not going to fry right away, how many years do you think it will be before we do? Five years? Ten years? Twenty?"

"I don't know. At the worst, five years. Ten. We could speculate, but what's the point?" Then she made a monumental effort to show some confidence. "As my grandmother used to say," LeeAnn smiled, "why borrow trouble?"

"I guess she was right," Marina said. "So let's not." And that ended it. A moment later, Marina had taken off ahead and was doing tight figure eights on the pathway. Then wheelies–in spite of the picnic basket. Marina always did wheelies and did them well. *No way,* vowed LeeAnn to herself, *are we going to let her life be cut short!*

Six o'clock bells now. As the sound started from about a half mile back, moving swiftly, LeeAnn ran faster and faster. Then it approached from behind and passed, rippling through her body with a rush. The sound of hundreds and hundreds of bells. Wow. The Dome was just ahead. She ran up to it with Marina on the bike beside her, then slowed to a walk to get her breath. Marina got off the bike and activated the kick stand. "Thanks, bicycle," she said, flipping up its not-in-use flag. Marina had always spoken to inanimate objects.

"So, are Uncle Jeff and Kevin already inside? Do you want to check?"

"Jeff and Kevin location," LeeAnn spoke into her organizer.

"Seg21," Maia's sweet voice replied. Groups of people were approaching the huge transparent structure now, mostly those who planned to picnic and settle in early for the broadcast. Tonight, the Dome would be filled to capacity, as would domes all over the world.

The dome-shaped plastic structures, which screened UV waves out, and were fabricated on-site using inflatable molds, had been developed for the Millennium broadcasts in 1999 and 2000, but had since been adapted to many uses. There were domes for dancing, with music coming from every inch of the ceiling above, for trick rollerblading, for skateboarding, for cinema, of course, and for special events, like this First-Decade Report.

Made from a clear but reflective material distantly related to acrylic, the Dome's interior surface provided a high-quality screen for visual images that were just slightly and pleasantly curved toward the viewer. Anyone could lean up against one of the portable backrests that were provided and look up in perfect comfort at the program of their choice. Watching the screen was like watching a sky show. Sometimes a half dozen films would be showing in the same dome simultaneously, with audio and video beamed exclusively to different sections of the dome.

where are we going?

The light and airy-looking structure that was the Partnership Center Dome enclosed a meadow about the size of a large city block. Twenty-four climate-controlled arched entrances were spaced evenly around the perimeter of the Dome, with large blue mosaic numbers from one to twenty-four inlaid in the sidewalk like the hours on a twenty-four-hour clock. Outside the Dome, a graceful pavilion of wrought-iron grillwork dispensed showers of geothermal water spraying from all sorts of interesting places. Some came from the ground, some from above.

"Wait a sec," said LeeAnn. Taking off her shoes and pack, she stepped under the flow of water, which bathed her with just a trace of a vitamin-based natural detergent and then rinsed her. After she dried off and put her shoes and pack back on, she and Marina went into the ladies room. When they came out of the stalls, they washed their hands and brushed their hair. None of the groups of women coming in and out was saying much. LeeAnn could feel a growing tension in the air. This was no ordinary night.

Marina, who was wearing a scarlet macaw spansuit with a cute little sarong mimicking tail-feathers, took matching feather earrings out of her pack and put them on. More jungle motif. LeeAnn pulled an ocean-wave, floor-length wraparound out of her day pack and slipped it on; just a little dress-up for evening. Then they went out to join the small crowd that was milling about outside.

Holding the picnic basket between them, LeeAnn and Marina made their way up toward the entrance to the Dome. Just inside, people were viewing the evening news as they moved slowly from one segment to the next. At a standard community dome, of which this was one, the global news was always playing around the inside perimeter.

On the wall between each of the twenty-four entrance archways was a number over a wonderfully sculpted relief map of that segment of the earth, done in the same new alloy as the God is Love sculpture. The maps, about ten feet high, were like tall, narrow surfboard-shaped slices of the earth. Every mountain range was shown, and the water was so blue and beautiful you wanted to touch it. Cities and towns were depicted with tiny lights, their number indicating the size of the population.

Next to the map of each segment was a screen continuously showing news from that area. So you could walk slowly around the world watching live news from each of the segments, understanding, as you did, exactly where it was happening. There was no question in anyone's mind where anything was anymore. Zambia had the favorite singer in all the world, and all kids over the age of three knew exactly where he made his home. Watching the news had become a self-orienting experience.

Most people who worked at the Center had gotten into the habit of stopping by the Dome daily, either before or after their shift to catch up on what was happening in the world. Feeding face or guzzling cocktails was no longer top priority. Then, after the news, you could move around the inner areas of the Dome and find the film you'd like to watch or the interactive games you'd like to play, in that way generally meeting up with people who had interests similar to your own.

Of course, that was the very best thing about domes–that they provided an ideal place to meet new friends or hang out with old ones. There were no economic or age divisions, no high restaurant tabs, no alcohol, no muggings, no date rape, and usually no big commute to get to a dome. Most communities had at least one, for they were now recognized as a major means of rehumanizing relationships. Usually they were limited to a city block in size, because research had shown that people feel most comfortable in a village-sized group of people. Admission to domes in most places was free, paid for from the money saved by reduced crime.

Peter had always stressed that architecture was a vital element to social connection, and, as he pointed out, with the advent of domes, the whole phenomenon of electronic entertainment had become proactive. Instead of lying in a recliner isolated from the world, punching your channel changer, you were walking *through* that world with friends, changing channels by *physically moving* to a new one. It seemed a better way of enjoying simulated travel and adventure.

There were also smaller domes for houses, *home-domes*, that were starting to be manufactured. A family or neighborhood group could lie around the yard together and watch several events, interactive or not, without the slightest interference with one another's enjoyment. Yet they'd still be together. The Monday night football controversy was becoming ancient history.

Kids lucky enough to have domes at their school could wander about till they found their areas of interest. The old theory that children left alone would eat the food that was best for them had turned out to be true with nourishment for the intellect as well. From preschool on, daily viewing choices were automatically tracked and the data collected helped to guide the children in later career decisions.

What LeeAnn liked best was *Radiotime*. From 11:00 p.m. to 6:00 a.m. at the Partnership Center Dome, it was all radio, from 1940s comedies to contemporary live broadcasts from every part of the world. (English continued to be the language of choice for international communication, but it was rapidly being enriched with additions from a hundred other languages.)

During Radiotime, lights were turned down low inside the Dome and you could see the stars above, or if it was raining, watch the drops rolling down the outside surface, while you stayed toasty dry inside. When they were little, Marina and Jordan used to beg to be allowed to stay up to listen to the new signals that had started coming in from outer space in '03 and '04. Eventually, Jordan would fall asleep but claim later he could understand more when he was in the alpha state between sleeping and waking.

Finally, LeeAnn and Marina made their way into the Dome, where a green lawn in earthflower design made a pleasant setting for shrubs and flowers, and even a small stream with a footbridge where teens tended to hang out. In the center of the Dome, there was a fireplace, a small but necessary component for human gatherings, it seemed. Any time of the day or night you could find people sitting around the tribal hearth, staring into the firelight, reflecting on things, or maybe reconnecting with ancestral memories.

As LeeAnn and Marina threaded their way through family groups and groups of friends, crossing the paths that separated segments, Marina made sure they passed close to the footbridge, catching the eye of one of the boys she'd been talking to earlier. "This is what Sheep's Meadow was like in its very best days, Marina," LeeAnn said. She still remembered the seventies in New York fondly.

When they got to Seg18, they stood watching live shots of preparations for the New Year's Eve celebration not just in New York, but in Hudson Bay, Haiti, Venezuela, Brazil, Chile, and Peru. There was just a brief glimpse of the installation of the dome at Times Square, but it was enough to satisfy LeeAnn.

They moved on to check out the news in Seg19 and 20, on their way to Seg21 where Jeff and Kevin were. It was always surprising to LeeAnn how much of the news had to do with oceanographic developments. Now that people identified with segments, they seemed to feel stewardship over their particular part of the ocean. It was kind of like adopting highways for cleanup, only on a much larger scale. Of course, since the sea deaths had started, there was even more avid attention to the oceans.

Finally, over in the home zone (Seg21 contained the part of Oregon that Klamath Falls was in) at a spot where they'd picnicked several times before, LeeAnn spotted Jeff. He was just greeting Peter and Jordan, who'd beaten LeeAnn and Marina there. *Beaten*–another dominator word she'd have to get rid of. *Preceded might be better,* she thought, though it sounded kind of stiff.

Jeff was just back from Africa, where Doctors Without Borders was completing an inoculation program for all HIV-related viruses. Soon they would destroy the last of the laboratory-stored organisms that caused the disease, just as smallpox had once been systematically destroyed.

Jeff and Kevin were still living in the apartment in New York. Their dream of buying a brownstone had evolved over the years into a dream of owning the apartment where the idea for the Millennium party had been born, though no one outside their 22nd Century Group really knew that. Because it would have raised the value of the apartment beyond what they could afford.

Now the building had finally gone co-op and they owned their own home. No roommates anymore, except for the aging Blackdog. They had gotten some slightly better recycled furniture for the living room and modernized the kitchen–Kevin had been going to culinary school lately–otherwise it looked just about the same.

Situated in a little hollow, the spot Jeff and Kevin had chosen for the extended family to gather in tonight resembled a sand trap on a golf course, with grass and fine sand and some excellent places to sit. Jeff, sitting with a small high-speed computer clamped on his knee and an intent look on his face, was checking something or other on that tiny DNA-based device of his that could crunch more data than a late-nineties mainframe. Kevin, by contrast, was sitting slowly pouring sand from one hand to the other, contemplating the fluid stream and looking quite absorbed in what he was doing. That was another nice thing about the Dome; you could always find something to do with your hands and feet.

Kevin was wearing a spansuit that was a photograph of himself in running shorts and T-shirt and his own fair skin, down to the freckles. Jeff was attired in part of the solution to a three-hundred-year-old math puzzle; if somebody recognized it, he knew he'd found a friend. LeeAnn saw now that David, who'd bladed over, was just making his way down on the other side. He stopped to talk with someone. Stubborn about ultraviolet exposure despite LeeAnn's constant chiding, David was wearing shorts.

As she and Marina approached, LeeAnn could hear Jordan and Kevin already heavy into decoding talk. Lively discussion was the only kind of male posturing Jordan knew. "What it really comes down to is frame of reference," Kevin was saying. "Like the Rosetta stone."

"Yeah, that makes sense–you get the frame of reference a species is coming from, then you get it all," said Jordan. "That's the thing. Boy, I wish I could get a job with you guys," he said. Kevin still worked as an encrypting consultant, but had some marginal contact with those who were working to decode the continuing radio signals from space. Jordan was green with envy.

LeeAnn settled in on the grass with the basket beside her and listened to them talk. After a 20th century in which people seemed to be all talking at once, listening was a growing phenomenon in the 21st. She thought about the amount of energy the people she was closest to put into it. Peter listened to plants, Audrey to whales, Marina to music, Jordan to the laws of the universe and the voices of other species. Already such a rich life, and her nephew was only twelve. Jeff listened to the vagaries of viruses, Kevin to mind-expanding sounds from outer space. David listened to the artistic muse within himself, and LeeAnn to ancestral voices.

What thrilling and frightening times, she thought. *If someone had been asleep for all these years and then woke up like Rip Van Winkle, what a strange and wonderful world (well, mostly wonderful) it would seem.* A much more *alive* world than she'd grown up in. And a *clearer* world–if only because most everyone now knew how much they didn't know–and were curious to learn.

David sidled in and sat behind LeeAnn, providing the most luxurious, most delicious backrest on the planet. She leaned up against him, and he put his arms around her waist. She shed her shoes and buried her feet in the sand; Jordan started pouring little mounds on top to bury

them deeper. LeeAnn took a moment to bask in the knowledge that her loved ones were all still safe. "Well, I guess we'd better do our picnic, hadn't we?" she said. *First the gathering and then the feast.*
"Without Audrey?" Jeff wanted to know.
Peter looked at his watch. "I don't think she's going to make it. We better eat."
LeeAnn set the elaborate old wicker picnic basket in front of her, opened up both sides, and took out her great-grandmother's silverware. Then she laid out the tablecloths, the linen napkins, the chopsticks, the lemonade, and the Russian rye bread that Audrey and Jordan had made together. Also the brown rice, black beans, at least four kinds of salad, and several desserts.
A quick search at the bottom of the basket revealed two hard-boiled eggs just for LeeAnn, and lots of spawned salmon, which looked quite beautiful. It was the only kind of meat LeeAnn ate anymore. Salmon had come back in huge, almost infinite numbers in recent years; the Northwest tribes were flourishing as a result. And maybe the salmon didn't mind too much. *If you're going to eat another creature,* LeeAnn thought, *then why not at least wait until it's finished its life mission.* "Did the pig mind?" LeeAnn remembered Peter asking that question when he was a little boy contemplating a pork chop.
They ate for awhile with gusto, and Jordan was right, Audrey *had* outdone herself. Audrey used a lot of cumin and coriander in her cooking, and that was just fine by LeeAnn.
Peter took out his pocket organizer, which had evidently just signaled him. "Audrey?" he spoke into it. "Oh, good." Then he smiled as his screen blinked a return message.
"What'd she say?"
"'Eat already . . .'"
"Tell her we already did."
". . . and happy anniversary to you two clowns."
David grinned. "You guys remembered." It was their thirteenth wedding anniversary today. LeeAnn and David had been married under the ancient tree on Tree Island, after it had become very apparent that Marina was on the way. LeeAnn hadn't mentioned it because David didn't usually like to make a fuss. She lay with her head in David's lap and thought back to those days. Jeff and Kevin would be having their twenty-fifth pretty soon, she realized. How time hurries by.

"Kevin and I have a little surprise for you," Jeff announced then.

"Who, us?" asked David.

"That's right. The anniversary couple. You're going to go on a VR trip together. Fifteen minutes. Tonight. Right after the broadcast."

"You're *kidding!*" said David, clearly tickled at the idea.

"Oh, you guys, that's so nice," LeeAnn told them. "You guys!" was a recent Audrey-ism, and they'd all caught it. "How'd you ever manage that? Especially for tonight."

"By reserving a year ago."

Virtual reality trips, alone or in groups, had become the most sought-after activity on the planet, and rapidly improving simulators couldn't even begin to keep up with ever-increasing demand. Hospice patients had *first* right to fulfill their wildest fantasies, and people in suicidal depression were next. VR was the preferred treatment for many emotional and physical ills, as well as for balance and dexterity training, for learning courage, and for developing all sorts of other skills.

"And you reserved it a year ago?" said Jordan. He was amazed anyone would plan so far in advance.

"Hey, your mom and LeeAnn had a date for the millennium that they made twenty-five years ahead," Jeff told him. "When they were eleven."

"That the rest of you then muscled in on," LeeAnn pointed out.

"Along with a couple billion of our friends."

"That's true, we did," said Jeff. "So we thought we ought to make it up to you now."

"Where are we going to go?" asked LeeAnn.

"Well, you're always talking about Southeast Asia."

"Great!"

"And you've got a choice, historical sites, jungle trail, oceanic algae ponds, . . ."

"The algae ponds." David was fascinated by the oceanic algae ponds there. "Okay by you?" he asked LeeAnn.

"Fine by me," she said. "I'll be delighted to go *anywhere* with you for fifteen minutes."

"I'll let them know," said Jeff. He typed some words into his computer. "Okay, now the last question is, how would you like to get down?"

"What do you mean?" asked LeeAnn.

"You can just beam down, or they can land you by parachute. You can sky dive . . ."

"Sky dive?"

"Sky dive!" said Marina. "You've got to."

LeeAnn shuddered.

"Oh, come on, it's not real, mother; you can't get hurt," Marina said.

"Yeah, but I could get sick. Or scared." She thought about the sensation of dropping through the sky and then dangling from a parachute. It made her dizzy even to contemplate it.

"You won't even get scared," Marina said.

"I'll be with you," David said. "Can we go tandem, Jeff?"

"I'll ask."

"Thank you both," LeeAnn said to Jeff and Kevin as she lay back down, with her head in David's lap. Though she wasn't quite sure if she meant it.

LeeAnn noticed they'd started running images on the ceiling of the Dome now, very faintly, almost subliminally, reminding her of the personal Rolodex that she always flipped through when she was falling asleep. There were flashes of dozens of images from the New Year's Eve celebrations in 1999 and 2000, images of unity and love and celebration worldwide that were familiar to nearly everyone now, after ten years of frequent replay. Still, every time she saw them, LeeAnn relived that transcendental moment when it was finally January 1, 2001, for *everyone* *when* the *last* segment, *Seg24, finally* came aboard, into the new millennium, and there was the sense that humanity was all snug in the same spaceship together, hurtling through time, joined as One People.

The tears LeeAnn could never help shedding when she was reminded of that night started to come now. For someone whom David always claimed cried at supermarket openings, any reminder of the event that had made her wildest fantasy a global reality was a surefire weeper. Two billion bells all going off at the same time and about four billion people yelling themselves hoarse–who wouldn't weep?

A teardrop at the corner of LeeAnn's eye was threatening to fall into her ear, where it would undoubtedly tickle. Before that could happen, however, David came to the rescue and kissed it away.

CHAPTER TWENTY FOUR

Ringing Bells

The images on the ceiling of the Dome became brighter now. The lights began to dim and the music came up as voices of people from each of the twenty-four segments of the world began coming in, one at a time, from the twenty-four segments around the Dome.

"I am Per Olaf from Norway."

"I am Yoshi Nagamo from Japan. We are the 22nd Century Group, *'Making sure we get there.'*" The map of each segment of the Dome lit up as the voice from that area spoke.

A male voice familiar to billions came in now, then the counterpart female voice synchronized with it, weaving in and out. To LeeAnn, his expressed all the hope and optimism–all the outer-directed attention to the world and to others–that was part and parcel of his personality. Hers, vibrant on many levels, was the voice of a humanist, a wise woman, with the quality of wild child mixed in there too. They were the world's favorite news anchors these days, R&G, Reeve and Goldberg, male and female. They came out onto the podium as the words,

WHERE WE STAND
WHERE WE MUST GO
HOW WE GET THERE

scrolled across the ceiling of the Dome. "Good morning. Good day. Good afternoon. Good evening," Reeve said, turning in each of the four directions, north, east, south, and west.

"Are you all out there?" yelled Goldberg with a big grin, and there was an enormous roar of response as interactive television allowed the sound to travel back from most of the sites where people were gathered.

The roar of several billion people, each of whom knew his or her voice would be heard by all the others, was a very large sound. But in a way, it was also almost soft, for it was all the voices speaking together.

"We have survived our first ten years in the new millennium," said Reeve. "How do you feel about that?" A moment's pause for translations, then another tumultuous shout around the earth, before Reeve and Goldberg could resume speaking. LeeAnn was wrestling to get her emotions under control, so she didn't hear what they were saying right away, but the impression was of humor and warmth. The white-haired Goldberg was making a tribute to human courage, "And *animal* courage, too," she added with a grin. *"It takes a lot of guts to share this planet with us."*

The world of humans laughed—another lovely sound. Then rippling images of some of the myriad other living beings who share our space flashed across the screen.

"With life comes courage," Goldberg said.

"With the gift of life comes the gift of courage," said Reeve and Goldberg together. *"It is born in us, the gift of our ability to endure, and to hope."* Bells rang now with a mournful sound as cameras panned slowly over the Great Nuclear Desolation Area. Nearly everyone in this Dome knew someone who had lived and died there.

"In their memory," said Goldberg.

"For their spirits," said Reeve. *"Spirits that are still on the journey with us."* Voices from all segments began to sing,

Ancestors,
Sky people,
All here today,
Hear my heart song.

The verse was repeated by the people in the Dome.

Hear my respect,
Hear my love,
Hear my grateful tears fall.
I am truly blessed.
I am truly blessed.

Voices reverberated through the Dome, then there was silence. The bells in the Walkways outside the Dome rang then, their sound on the evening breeze incredibly sweet. LeeAnn went totally to pieces; she was sobbing in David's arms. Fortunately, he had brought several clean, white handkerchiefs.

"Where were you *on the night of December 31, 1999, as the world prepared to enter the third millennium?"* Goldberg asked everyone now. *"What were you thinking and feeling? What were you doing that night?"* Sounds from the celebration at the beginning of the Year in Parentheses echoed through the Dome then as, on-screen, explorer Martyn Williams and the teams of world youth that carried the messages of millions of their fellow humans were reunited at the South Pole.

Of all the images from the '99-to-2000 Celebration, this was the one most often repeated. The scene shifted to catch moments of jubilation around the globe as those millions of human vows were sealed in ice. Cameras caught the faces of children everywhere, watching, children of many colors. LeeAnn could see through her tears so many sweet young faces in the crowds, sharing their feelings of utter joy with one another, just as they had in LeeAnn's original imagining of the orange, and the earth, and the people holding hands.

"These children ten years ago were entering a new space," said Goldberg, "both in time and in quality of life, and you could tell they knew it. One way they knew was that for the first time in a long time, through a massive airlift program, *all were fed*. Virtually everyone had enough to eat. Tribes in the farthest corners of the earth, understanding that a festival was to be held, accepted the gifts of food for their people.

"And after they'd been fed, these children watched cousins of their color–and every other color–trekking across the globe, from pole to pole, risking, suffering, and overcoming–for their sake. The impressions made on their minds and hearts during that unforgettable dawn, the scenes of unity and joy and thanksgiving all around the earth, were almost too rich to behold, as both givers and receivers rejoiced." The awesome sound of humanity celebrating swelled to a crescendo.

Then stillness. And on the screen, a lake in Africa, at dawn, quiet. A skinny man in a boat, poling.

"What did the celebrations and the Year in Parentheses do for us?" Reeve asked. "Really, ten years later? Let's look back and see. Did it end hardship and pain?"

"No." Goldberg replied. "Major meanness still exists around this planet. But we're a little nicer to each other than before, and it's getting better all the time."

"We decided during the Year in Parentheses that we wanted to teach ourselves to get along better," Reeve said.

"To share more," Goldberg said.

"To heal ourselves," said Reeve.

"And to heal our earth. How have we done?" asked Goldberg as cameras ranged over the earth, moving from treetop to satellite view, then swooping down again, showing forests and cities and oceans. What's the score on our developing humanity?"

"Well, for one thing," Reeve said, "we don't fight as much as we used to. In the 1990s there were dozens of wars going on in the world; today there are six. They are small–except to the people in them–and we hope they will soon be ended."

"And what is it we used to fight about so much?" Goldberg asked him. "I forget."

"Religion. Food, water, land, money," Reeve replied. "And sex."

"Ah, yes. In the ancient battle between the sexes, there's good news," Goldberg said. "All over our world, women are taking their place in equal partnership with men. New status for women and for children has been the single biggest change in our society in this decade–the way that male and female partners relate and the respect that we give our children. We have a long way to go, but we've begun."

Reeve spoke now. "Remineralization of our soil is another enormous change taking place." The screen showed fields of growing grain in Ukraine, in New Zealand, and in South Africa. "That, along with new and effective uses of our enormous algal resources are helping to reduce conflict over food." Scenes of harvest around the globe were shown. "That hunger has plagued the human race now seems absurd. It will soon be a thing of the past." There was loud and sustained cheering at that.

"A third change," said Goldberg. "The tremendous reduction of grazing animals all over our earth is reducing territorial disputes, environmental depletion, and competition for water and land. With profound changes in human diet, fresh water is becoming far more abundant." The screen showed waterfalls, streams running, and children swimming in a clean, clear lake.

480

"As a result of all these things, humans are feeling less competitive, less territorial. Less warlike."

"But strangely," said Reeve, "it was one of the greatest tragedies ever to take place on earth–shortly after the Millennial Celebration–that has made perhaps the greatest positive difference in the way we humans regard one another." Now the powerful images again, beginning with the famous still-photo of a two-year-old African child sitting beside her dead mother, as fat tears rolled down her cheeks.

"This child's mother," said Goldberg, "died from the AIDS-X virus that swept Africa, killing, within weeks, three million HIV-infected adults, most of them parents of young children."

Reeve spoke now. "The horror is that *they did not need to die!* Their lives were lost because they lacked access to the new, inexpensive combination of drugs that was successfully reversing the disease in more prosperous populations.

"It took this tragedy–the loss of cousins we were just getting to know," as scenes of adults dying and the haunted eyes of orphaned children filled the screen, "to wake us up to the truth that *it is not right for some to have it all, and some to have nothing. It will be on our collective conscience forever that once again . . . ,*" he paused as a collage of human suffering from hunger, disease, war, and holocaust was projected on the screen, *"once again in a shameful recent history, humans have committed genocide by neglect, and by greed.* And once again it has been the children we have hurt the most."

"The only thing we can do now," Goldberg interjected, "is to try to make it up to them." The screen showed ragged, frightened, grieving children, many carrying babies, crowding into emergency refugee centers.

"Kind-hearted people have always rallied to others in times of tragedy," Reeve continued, "but perhaps never in such overwhelming numbers as they did during the orphan crisis, readying schools and dormitories, nurseries, hospitals, sending food and money, letters, and love. More than half a million families immediately and voluntarily moved to Africa to take up permanent residence and help." The screen showed scenes of families adapting to primitive conditions. "Their actions have become the model for the global family."

"Never again will we selectively neglect our family members," said Goldberg, "gauging the amount of help we give by how closely their skin color or their philosophy matches our own. Humans are

humans and we're all one family. The word orphan no longer exists."

The poignant images of children on the ceiling of the Dome were causing even David to mist up now, LeeAnn noticed. She turned to kiss him, then smiled at Marina, who was smiling back through tears of her own. Marina wanted to be a mother someday.

Reeve went on, "When the tragedy struck and we jointly became guardians of so many innocent souls all at once, decisions on how to raise them had to be made quickly. It was vital that the adults not seem to be in conflict, especially in matters of faith."

"Emergency ecumenical councils were called," said Goldberg, as the screen showed a formal procession of clergy in Addis Ababa, carrying banners identifying themselves as Christian, Islamic, Buddhist, Unitarian, Bahai, Catholic, Jewish, Eastern Orthodox, and more. "Their task was to come up with text describing humanity's basic *shared* belief in God–belief they could impart to the new culture that would soon emerge from the ancient continent where humanity began. It was a chance to make a fresh start at linking for the whole human race; everyone seemed to realize that."

"After weeks of deliberation," said Reeve, "the unanimously agreed-upon words were read from the pulpit by a ten-year-old child." The screen showed a small Ethiopian boy, a large pulpit, and a huge, hushed gathering. He cleared his throat, looked around at all the wise leaders, and then began to speak. "God is Love," he declared in ringing tones. "And family is sacred . . ."

It still sent shivers up her spine. *Surely*, LeeAnn thought, *there is nothing more important on this earth than family.* She remembered the night she'd sat in the van at Squaw Point so many years ago, pounding away on her laptop. "I don't *believe* in polyfidelity or fooling around and all this other stuff," she had typed furiously. "I believe in commitment and working at it and being a family." *What if I hadn't written that letter to him that night?* she thought, looking at Marina and Jordan. *What then? These two might never have been born, and how much poorer our lives would have been.*

"As it looks now, the ten-thousand-year detour that humanity has traveled may be ending," Goldberg was saying. "We're headed back to the main road. The question tonight is, will we find that road still passable?"

"Treacherous times lie ahead," said Reeve. "The next ninety years will be the most dangerous humanity has ever faced. But *if we can make it through this century to the 22nd,"* he went on in that characteristically and contagiously optimistic tone, *"we will have built the foundation that will create a lasting future for our race."*

He walked back to the podium. "After intermission, we will focus on the very vital specifics. Where we are–have we met our minimum goals for the first decade of the 21st century? And if not, how do we catch up? *Can* we catch up? I will say now," he was speaking very carefully, "that *some of the figures are not very hopeful.*"

LeeAnn felt a wave of emotion pass through the audience.

"But they are not hopeless, either. It's going to be up to all of *us,* together, to extend the window of opportunity for our survival."

As he finished, it was almost as if everyone on earth could hear everyone else breathing. Then the screen faded, leaving the words, "The following fifteen minutes of silence are brought to you by Microsoft."

As the lights came up slowly, a lot of people began hugging one another. Some in the audience, eyes closed, held up one hand, palm out, in the Christian way of silent connection with their god. Others began to write in their electronic journals. Over by the footbridge, LeeAnn saw teenagers engaged in passionate discussion, while in Seg22 next to them, someone began playing a flute softly. It had a comforting sound.

Then LeeAnn spotted Audrey striding her way across the Dome from Seg18. *Oh, good!* She always came through what she called the New York entrance, overlooking the fact that Seg18 was also the home of a lot of other cities and towns, from Quebec to Argentina.

I'm so glad she got here, LeeAnn thought, as she watched her old friend approach. Ever since she'd been a small child, it had been the impossible goal of LeeAnn's life to get all the people she loved in one place and then keep them there. Now she savored one more small victory in that direction.

Audrey stopped to greet a friend effusively, and then another whole group of people, gesturing with her hands in a language Peter called *Big Apple 'Sign.'* Aud-ball Garcia-Spencer didn't philander, and she wasn't into her looks as much anymore, but she could still make entrances–and did.

Wearing a spansuit emblazoned with the solar disk of the goddess Isis, Audrey, at fifty, looked *good*. Fresher, happier, healthier than at forty or thirty–or ten for that matter. Her face looked a bit older; the laugh lines around her nose had deepened. Her curly hair was longer and turning grey. She usually wore it piled up on top of her head because she spent so much time in the water at her work. And these days, wonder of wonders, her face was scrubbed clean of cosmetics.

"I'm almost glad I'm late," she said after she greeted everybody and settled into the group. "It's wild what's happening out there."

"What's happening?"

"Nothing. That's just it. Nothing but this incredible level of *expectancy*. I had to walk from the train station, and nothing's moving; there's no sound. Nobody's even talking; everybody I passed was just listening to their 'com' units. So it feels like the whole world is in a state of suspended animation, even the cats and dogs. But at least we're all together." LeeAnn didn't know if she meant the eight of them or the whole world. "So, you ate already? How was it?"

Audrey basked in the praise of the others as she made quick work of the food they'd saved for her. She still had the tiniest waist, the most perfect small body. "I know the broadcast started already," she said then, looking a little tentatively at Peter, "but I was too busy getting here to listen." More likely, LeeAnn thought, she didn't want to hear bad news when she was away from Peter and the rest of them. "What did I miss?"

LeeAnn started to fill her in.

"All the good stuff first, huh?" Audrey said. "I think it's kind of pathetic, media up to their old tricks," she said. "Keeping us in suspense till the bitter end."

"I don't think that's what they're doing," Jeff told her. "I think they designed the show the way people like it. First we want the chance to count up everything good we've done. Positive reinforcement. We did this and we did this so maybe we can also do *this*. Celebrate first so we can face whatever it turns out to be. *The celebration sandwich, remember?* Celebrate, accomplish, and celebrate again, like we did in the Year in Parentheses."

Kevin nodded. "And maybe it will give us a sense of calm knowing that we've done everything we possibly could."

Except for starting sooner, the voice inside LeeAnn wanted to shout, as the tears began to come again. And then she couldn't help herself. **"Except for starting sooner!"** she blurted out, sobbing, and looking at all of them with hurt, self-accusing eyes. *"Oh, why didn't we?"*

"Nothing to do about that now," said Peter gently. As tears rolled down LeeAnn's face, she gazed at her brother, her beautiful blue-eyed brother, so much freer and more fulfilled these days. *What if he were to die? What if I were to watch him die?* She felt David's warmth against her back as she nestled in his arms. *What if we're back in this dome in six months or six years, gathered with our families, saying a global farewell and trying to be brave about it? How could I ever watch another daughter die?* "Oh, David, David, David."

"Shhh," he said, stroking her hair.

The stories *On the Beach* and *The Day After* came swimming back again and made LeeAnn feel sick to her stomach. Fear began to take over her body, the old fear that used to make her want to beat her way out of the night and into the light where she could breathe. Nightmares as a child were always like that. Always suffocation and darkness. How many children had those nightmares, and for how many of them, would they come true?

Again she saw in her mind the footage of UV-blinded baby lambs stumbling around, trapped in blackness; she knew what they must feel like. She *felt* it. Panic. Absolute panic. She'd been reading up on the ways in which human life on the planet might end–all the different scenarios–reading them in fascinated horror, as though knowing all about it might keep it from happening. Now she fought to keep from conjuring up the gruesome images in her mind. At the same time, so as not to embarrass her family, she was trying hard not to hyperventilate and lose control completely in the middle of this dome full of people.

Of course, David could feel what was happening to her anyway, but he just held her steady and said nothing. She thought about how brave *he* was being. How brave Marina had been when they'd talked earlier. *She went off and did wheelies to make me laugh. That was for me. It's like everybody is trying to be brave for everybody else, because if even one of us falls apart then we might all go ballistic. So I'd better quit it,* LeeAnn told herself. And to her own surprise, somehow she did. She dried her eyes and sat up. The rest of them had just been letting her handle it by herself.

"Yeah, but so what did Mary say back?" LeeAnn heard Jordan say then. He was asking his mother about one of the orcas she worked with. "What do you *think* she was thinking? What were the *rest* of them thinking?"

"Yeah, I was wondering that too, Audrey," Kevin said. "Are the marine mammals aware of what's going on, do you think?"

"They know we've got a problem," Audrey told him. "They've seen a decline in their own food supply, and I think they understand we're working on it; we've tried to communicate that. Whether they know we're responsible for *causing* it, that's another question."

"They know," said Jordan. "At least *I* think they do. They're not stupid."

"You know what I think?" Marina started, but the lights were going down. Intermission was over. "I think . . ."

"Shhh," said Jordan. "Let's listen."

"What are they going to do first?" asked Kevin.

"Health," said Jeff.

The words, ***"Honor Your Body: The State of Human Health,"*** lit up the screen in enormous letters, and Audrey nudged Jeff. "There's your blurb, Mr. Taciturnity."

"Well, it's still the shortest," he said with a modest shrug. Jeff had lost no opportunity over the years to remind Audrey that her maxim was four whole characters longer than his.

"You already got a case of Coors for it," Audrey reflected. "What else do you want?"

"Yeah, Coors," Jeff reminisced. He looked like he could use a beer right now.

Goldberg's voice came over the speaker system. "Overall, in the first decade of the new millennium, human health has improved radically." A montage of healthy people engaged in strenuous activities came up on the screen. Humans were becoming quicker at following rapidly changing images, so literally hundreds of pictures of brimming health were absorbed by several billion minds in moments. Just seeing them made LeeAnn feel stronger in her own body.

"Soil revitalization has restored elements that had been scarce in cultivated foods for hundreds or even thousands of years–and particularly lacking in the second half of the 20th century. As a result, we're seeing a sharp decline in degenerative diseases of all kinds. Arthritis, heart disease, cancer, stroke.

"The end of osteoporosis means we have eighty-and ninety-year-olds on roller blades. Nerve regeneration has meant reversal of paralysis in many people," said Reeve with a smile. "And advanced treatment for radiation sickness has helped to restore health to twenty million survivors evacuated from the Desolation Area. Reduction in the stress of daily life has also contributed to reducing illness.

"Although the health picture is generally bright," he continued, "there *is* a dark side. Skin cancer, particularly melanoma–in epidemic form–still remains to be contained. Spansuits will help with that. Global vaccination is nearly complete for HIV and the flesh-eating bacterial infections. But tuberculosis has been harder to lick than we thought, and we don't know what other diseases may be out there ready to strike those of us whose immune systems have been compromised."

"It's not pretty to think about," said Goldberg. "Okay, those are the pluses and the minuses on human health. Now for some figures–the good news and the bad.

"Based on the estimates of a hundred global teams from ten scientific disciplines, a child growing up in the 21st century with an optimal diet and lifestyle, having a quality relationship with a life partner, and *living in a stable or improving environment*, in a world free from war or epidemic disease–that child could expect to live in good health to between one hundred thirty and one hundred fifty years of age." There was a murmur throughout the Dome; the figure was unexpectedly high.

"However, if any of those factors are absent, death is likely to occur a great deal earlier. In some of the worst-case scenarios, life expectancy for 21st century children could be reduced, very quickly, to as little as ten to twenty years of age." There was no audible reaction to this news. *What could anybody say?*

"Now, here are the figures for the rest of us," Goldberg said. LeeAnn's eyes scanned the rapidly scrolling table of birth-dates and survival estimates. It said that under a best-case scenario, she might live to be a hundred and twenty, David, to a hundred and ten. *What will the world be like then?* she began to wonder. Then the section on health was over.

As LeeAnn watched, the words, **"Partner With Nature: The State of the Human Environment,"** appeared on the screen. Audrey's section.

"Three of the four areas of human behavior, those having to do with *Health, Relationships, and Commerce,* are uniquely related to–and largely controlled by–us, the human race," said Goldberg. "We can *do* something about them."

"*Environment* takes in all the rest," said Reeve. "The entire nonhuman universe." A chart on the screen showing the various phyla seemed to LeeAnn to emphasize how tiny and insignificant humans were in the general scheme of things. "We share this earth with more than *thirty million* other species."

"This is the world where, like it or not, some things are beyond our control," said Goldberg.

"Many of the changes that humans have set in motion in our environment cannot instantly or perhaps ever be recalled," said Reeve. "We need to remember that."

"Here's one life form," he pointed to the phylum of algae, "that counts dearly to all of us. This ancestor of all life on the planet that has given so much to others. Blue-green algae was the first organism to photosynthesize, to use the energy of the sun for life, and all other life sprang from that.

"For eons, all of the phyla acted in relative harmony with one another. But over the last several hundred years, *as human population has proliferated out of control,*" LeeAnn saw David nodding in vigorous agreement, "we have changed the very face of the planet." A globe showed the slow darkening of the continents with its burgeoning human population. "We expect overpopulation will eventually be brought under control as more and more couples pledge to try not to have children during the first five to ten years of marriage–if at all. This simple step should be enough."

"But meanwhile, the epidemic expansion of human population has already damaged our earth. And in the process, this important life force called algae," Reeve again pointed to the algal phylum, "has been misunderstood, ignored, and grossly underutilized. We're changing that. Billions of tons of algae are now being used for the nourishment of humans and friends of humans." There were shots of algae being used in food production and algae being plowed into the soil.

"Algae is helping with virtually every ecological battle in which we're engaged," said Goldberg. "CO_2 levels, for example, are improving; that is partly due to the accelerated production of algae, which produces life-giving oxygen many times more rapidly than do trees. New computer-aided techniques for repropagating rain forests will also help enormously in this effort."

"During the Year in Parentheses, we learned that if we were to succeed in reducing carbon dioxide to manageable levels by the year 2100, then this was where we needed to be by 2010," Goldberg said, pointing to a chart. "And we've made it. Unprecedented cooperation from developing nations–and the international auto industry–has been an enormous aid. This is one battle we're winning."

"As we all know, the picture is not that rosy in the area of ozone," Reeve said then, and LeeAnn could feel the tension in the Dome rise sharply. She watched Audrey's and Peter's eyes meet. Then Kevin put his hand on Jeff's shoulder. David's arms tightened around LeeAnn, while Jordan and Marina, sitting side-by-side, continued to stare fixedly at the screen.

"Here's the problem," Reeve said, pointing to a graph. "By the end of the year 2010, we needed to be *here* to turn around losses in our ozone layer in time. We're not there. At the moment, we have a failing grade in this area. But that's not our greatest worry; it could be made up later. What is alarming is the unexpected and quite catastrophic recent loss of phytoplankton in the sea. This is an occurrence that was not foreseen. The reason for it has not been explained, and we do not yet know what to do about it beyond continuing to work on reversing ozone loss as rapidly as possible, while we study the situation and seek remedies."

"If ozone levels continue to fall," said Goldberg, "there is little chance the phytoplankton can survive." Again the screen showed the phylum chart, highlighting the endangered species. "Without them–well, if you take a look at the food chain without these vital links, you can see that massive breakdown will inevitably occur. The first stage of this is already happening. The next link to go will likely be this one, then this, then this." The attention of everyone in the audience was riveted on the chart.

"We do not yet have the answer to this most critical global problem that humanity has ever faced. Let's make that clear. But many hypotheses are being tested as rapidly as possible and more are being developed every day. *That is where our hope must lie.*"

"Today there are more than six billion intelligent humans on earth," said Reeve. "Among us, there must be one or two, or a hundred, or a hundred million women and men who together can solve our planet's plight. Are you one of them?"

"Don't think we can't do it," Goldberg interjected. "Remember when we wondered how we would ever get food to all of our fellow humans in time for the Millennial Celebration? But we did it. By believing, by working hard, by cooperating. *By spending money!*" There was a ripple of laughter. "And by *innovating*. If we believe, we can manage this, too. Humans have immense capability for invention. That above all, perhaps. It is our greatest curse, and our greatest blessing."

"One hundred thousand grants, beginning at a million dollars each, will be awarded for ideas our global teams think are worthy of development. If you have a theory, work it up. Study, learn, consult with others; form your own team, then get your ideas and theories to our teams." Web addresses and instructions began coming up on the screen. A few people around LeeAnn were copying them down; she noticed both Jordan and Marina were among them.

"And while we wait for the miracle solution," said Reeve, "let's also divide the job up and attack this problem on a daily basis, segment by segment. We must immediately cease the production of ozone-damaging chemicals in every segment of our earth. Volunteers in each segment will be asked to help monitor ozone conservation efforts. In carrying out this job, it's important to point out that national sovereignty will not be affected, as all nations have now signed the Johannesburg Accord."

"There may be no alternative to humans wearing full-body clothing for the remainder of this century," said Goldberg. A variety of spansuits were shown. "And we may also need to find ways to shield and protect some of Earth's other inhabitants." Shots of animals and fish, marine mammals with UV scars and burns on their skin. "Some species may not make it–probably quite a few."

"But since we don't yet have the technology to move to another home," said Reeve, "we have no choice but to face this battle and pour our sweat, toil, and tears into fighting it." The world's favorite male news anchor didn't look like Winston Churchill, but for a moment he sure sounded like him. The two anchors walked back to the podium and stood together. He had his arm around her.

Then the words, *"Link With Others: The State of Our Relationships,"* came up on the screen.

"I still think that's the best one going, L.A.," Jordan whispered to his aunt.

"DNA evidence has confirmed," said Reeve, "that 51st cousin is the most distant relationship there is among humans. We're all related, we're all connected; we're all *at least* 51st cousins. So it's how we cousins get along, one-on-one and a billion-on-a-billion, that's the subject of this section."

"Over the past ten years—and really over the last fifty—armed conflict has ceased being so central to our lives. Violence and killing have been losing their fascination as, led by our media, we begin to shift from a death-oriented society to a life-oriented one. Today we are five times *less* likely to be killed by our fellow humans than we were just twenty years ago."

"An important cause of this," Goldberg said, "is that today we focus nearly as much on positive news as we do on negative. Preparing for the Millennial Celebration gave us a good start in that direction. In the two years preceding it, our journalists and videographers brought us images of the preparations, and the more positive future-view these images tended to promote. And that helped us turn our expectations around.

"Then authors and creators of film and television shows also began to concentrate on happier stories. The immense influence of storytellers, the people who shape our society—and perhaps our fate as well--is becoming more clearly evident every day, as their stories teach us once again that there is something more exciting and emotionally gratifying than death. *And that is life.*

"*Kindness,* we are learning, is more fascinating than cruelty," Goldberg continued, "and *love* has more appeal than hate. The media have also helped us to learn about our natural world. And in loving our planet and our fellow beings, we are relearning to love ourselves. That's important!" She paused.

"In our examination of human relationships tonight, let's start by looking at the status of family, *the model from which the rest of society always takes its lead.* In the last half of the 20th century, the family unit seemed to be falling apart. In many cases that failure caused the product of the family—its children—to fail as well." The screen lit up with graphs showing the percentage of children raised in broken homes and the correlation to later achievement, or lack of it. C H I L D R E N W H O K I L L was the title on one of the charts.

"We're beginning to turn all that around," said Reeve, "with a strengthening of the family. Marriage is up, divorce and infidelity are down. Here's a figure for you. Ninety-two percent of marital partners worldwide are faithful to their spouse these days. Or their spouses, in cultures where there is more than one. With increasing equality between wives and husbands, marital partners are enjoying sexual relations with each other more frequently, and that's good. Why? Here's why."

"The joy and celebration of birth is almost universally felt. But often it's not very lasting," said Goldberg, "because that pleasure is *designed* to diminish over the years. And in some humans it becomes quite faint, very early on." Scenes of parental neglect were shown. "Social scientists are learning that continuing, committed *physical* love between parents may be nearly as vital to the quality of their children's lives as the original act of procreation, because it keeps the family together. We're also learning that many people probably don't need to have children. They're not suited to it, and shouldn't feel obligated to do so."

"Physical love," said Reeve, "is what forms a family in the first place. Physical celebration can also keep that family healthy, just as group celebration keeps a society healthy. As we learn to respect and to love our partners, as we learn to respect and encourage our children's competence and intelligence, we once again honor and revere the family connection. Family continuity. *Family values.* It's *family* that makes life possible–*family,* whether biological or elective, that gives life meaning. For God is Love and Family is Sacred."

"So the family is doing better these days," said Goldberg, as the letters for C O M M U N I T Y came up behind her. "And that goes for the community as well. Following the lead of the emerging partnership family model, on the community level, we're also seeing that what was formerly mainly a vertical society is quite rapidly becoming a more horizontal one. Overall, there's more linking and less ranking among more groups. People are feeling more willing to just pitch in and get things done." Scenes of community projects in villages, towns, and cities were shown.

"With fewer unmet needs in our society, and fewer things to disagree about these days, it's not surprising that we have less government," said Goldberg. "Remember how it used to be? All that bureaucracy. And all those enormous expenditures on defense while kids went hungry." There were pictures of all the weapons of carnage, then shots of a vast military fleet in mothballs.

"At the end of the first decade, government budgets are down, government debt is down. There has also been a turnaround in the runaway government growth industry of the 1990s," Reeve continued. "Prison construction is down, and rehabilitation is becoming more effective.

"Under *managed confinement*, there is strong incentive for detainees to learn and practice work skills." Shots of the National Detainee Job Center showed accountants, seamstresses, factory workers, and computer operators being separated by skills and tested.

"Detention wages are divided between the families of the victim and the detainee. The faster a debt to society is paid, the sooner the person is allowed to rejoin that society." Then the screen showed elaborate quilts being completed by young gang-types.

"Procedures for minor offenses have also taken on a pragmatic approach as more and more community service and recycling centers are being combined." Shots of detainees retrofitting cars, composting, and sorting cans and bottles. "The central idea here, of course, is to make that which society has trashed into something useful again. Even serial killers, when they elect, can serve as living laboratories that will benefit humanity through unrelenting study of their minds.

"While government is shrinking, *citizen participation* in government is up. Following the lead of New Zealand, the U.S and a number of other countries finally got it right by giving financial reward to the voter instead of to the politician. First they offered a tax credit for voting. But perhaps more important, based on the theory that if you don't participate you shouldn't benefit, the rule was made that no tax refunds would be paid to people who were qualified but chose not to vote. When that happened in the U.S., voter rolls immediately returned to postsuffrage levels. And as they began voting, more people suddenly started to get interested in the issues again.

"One of the first acts of the newly enlarged and empowered electorate was to pass massive campaign finance reform, thus effectively eliminating the simplistic, patronizing, and almost universally despised campaign commercials that had *caused* a lot of the voter apathy, and *antipathy,* replacing them with more substantive forums that were free. Politics quickly became less interesting to opportunists, and government began to attract a new breed of servant-leader. Term limits were no longer necessary."

"We're proud to say," announced Goldberg, "that legislatures worldwide are now 32% female. And not only is politics losing its gender bias, political parties are also losing their labels. *Conservative,*" said Reeve, "again means saving things, as in 'conservation.' And *Liberal* has once more become a word that simply means 'generous,' as in, 'He gave her a liberal helping.'"

"At the end of the day," said Reeve, "it all comes back to family. When the human family is based on love, then human community is based on love, and even government becomes vulnerable to love. Through family love, a message of love can circle our earth. And even reach out beyond."

It seemed as if everybody in the Dome took a deep breath. LeeAnn certainly did. The closing shot on *Relationships* showed again, as she had hoped it would, the Pole-to-Pole teams, planting humanity's flag in the snow. She thought about all the buried messages. *If we should perish after all,* she thought, *and someone finds traces of us some day, maybe at least they'll know we tried.*

Then it was Peter's turn, as **"Share the Abundance: The State of Human Commerce,"** scrolled across the giant screen of the Dome. Reeve's tall form appeared against a backdrop of stock exchanges around the world.

"Economic benefits from the Year in Parentheses began even before *it* did, as the Celebration itself brought stimulus to nearly every village and town on earth." The screen showed all sorts of new businesses in the most remote and primitive areas as the world prepared for its party. "It made entrepreneurs out of a lot of folks and helped to start spreading prosperity around."

Goldberg picked up the narrative. "In the year 1995, 1% of the people in the world owned better than half of humanity's assets." Opulent estates flashed on the screen. "Today, 1% of the people in the world own 30% of the assets, which is still enormous wealth.

"The biggest factor for change here has been the unprecedented voluntary sharing of personal assets with public institutions," (massive art collections were shown) "and enormous personal gifts from private individuals to their cousins at large, inspired by people like Ted Turner and George Soros.

"Also important in the redistribution of wealth has been the proliferation, worldwide, of the system of network marketing, sometimes called *re-union marketing*. It has contributed both to the strength of the economy and to the quality of family life, enabling parents to work and take care of their children at the same time, the way humanity has almost always done." There were scenes of people engaged in various home occupations, their children alongside them. "Commuting to work is decreasing in volume and frequency. It's also becoming more pleasant." A Cardio Car was shown.

"As this process of rehumanizing business has helped to make families more secure, commerce more stable, more fair, and more humane, ultimately this leveling-out process has also helped people at the upper levels feel more comfortable about themselves. In this first decade of the 21st century, excessive wealth has begun to feel foolish to many well-to-do people. As somebody said a few years ago, 'If you have a helicopter on your yacht, maybe that's enough toys.'"

That's me who said that, thought LeeAnn. She was generally modest, but that was one thing she was proud of. Early on, she'd made a couple of speeches acknowledging praise for her ideas. But it was funny, only that one statement had stuck.

"The rule today," Goldberg said, "honored both in the observance and the breach, is to create for yourself enough affluence for major enjoyment and no more. With so much money being freed from stagnant capital pools and pouring back into the economy, infrastructure is once again becoming state-of-the-art." There was a visual of European and Asian Autoways, similar to the short stretch of experimental road that Oregon had just put in. (The U.S. was still a little behind in that area.)

"Business competition, of course, is as exciting as it's always been," she continued. "Perhaps even more so, since somebody–nobody knows who–got the bright idea that if it's a game, then let's treat it like one. With that inspiration, the Business Olympics, or Global Games, were born. The Games, which had their genesis in crude computer software . . . ," (visuals of the early games were shown) "have in only a few years become the most ultra-sophisticated contests on earth." Visuals of the advanced Games were shown.

"Many of the same financial giants," (Donald Trump's face came on screen) "are continuing to trade with one another, buying and selling the goods of the world with their customary boldness and greed. None of that has changed--the only difference is that for the first time in history, some of the heaviest hitters aren't using the earth's resources as their gambling chips anymore. So we're not as nervous as we used to be about watching; in fact, we can even cheer them on." Scenes of crowded domes; spectators going wild.

"And though it's only a game, the purse is very real, with a hundred million dollar first prize every year, as well as thousands of runners-up awards." The screen showed the first grand-prize winner, wearing a power suit reminiscent of LeeAnn's, running down the aisle of a dome, and then having to be lifted onto the stage in her high heels and skirt.

"Global debt is down." The camera followed Reeve as he walked into a giant graph and pointed to a column that towered over his head. "There used to be this much debt in the world." Then he put his foot on a column next to it that was about the size of a tree stump. "Now there's this much."

"We're learning the vast difference between lending and investing. With investment, you invest part of yourself, you have risk *with* other human beings, not just leverage *over* them." The screen showed a small family sweating out a mortgage payment. "We're learning that debt puts a strain on relationships and should not be an overwhelming element in our society."

"And here's perhaps the most significant figure in the world of economics," said Goldberg. "Forcible commerce, where services or goods are taken without payment . . ." There were shots of child labor, of prostitutes, of tenant farmers, ". . . or people or animals perform services they don't want to perform, used to constitute a majority of the world's business. That's changing. Forcible commerce is estimated now at less than 40% and falling."

Reeve said, "To sum up, there has been a fundamental alteration in the way humans interact in the exchange of the goods and services of this world." The graphs faded away and Peter took a deep breath; his section was over.

"That's our First-Decade Report," said Goldberg. "Facts, statistics, projections, and just plain guesses by a global team of specialists, more than *one hundred thousand* in number. We thank them."

"Now," Reeve said, "it's time to rejoice. For just five minutes from now, the first segment of our earth, Seg1, is about to enter a new year and a new decade." The screen focused on that section of ocean and earth–mostly ocean, very little earth–out in the middle of the Pacific Ocean that was Seg1. It included much of New Zealand, Fiji, a little bit of Siberia, and some Antarctica, too. Views of all the cities flashed across the screen, the forests, the jungles, the tundra, and people in all their variety.

"You are our cousins, our brothers and our sisters, our family," he said, "and we want you to know we are with you. You lead the way tonight, and we shall follow. As humanity moves into a new and unknown chapter in our lives, let us all say a prayer for the safety and survival of ourselves and our children for thousands of years to come."

"If another person is near you right now," Goldberg said, her words addressed to virtually everyone in the world, "take that person's hand." As everyone in the Spencer extended family reached out to take hands, Jordan solemnly placed his right hand down on the grass and looked expectantly at Marina, who understood exactly what he meant. She put her hand over Jordan's. Then LeeAnn put hers on top of that, and David his over hers, then Jeff, Kevin, Audrey, and finally Peter. At that point Jordan pulled his small hand out from the bottom and laid it on top of his dad's. They were all blinking through their tears as familiar music began to swell, and a chorus of humans everywhere sang,

> From all that dwell below the skies
> Let songs of faith and hope arise
> Let peace, good will on earth be sung,
> Through every land by every tongue.

"Let us be grateful for the good news," said Reeve, "and strong enough to change the rest." The world watched then and waited as numbers on the face of the old-fashioned clock ticked away the last seconds of the year twenty-ten. Or *two-oh-one-oh*, as Jeff insisted on calling it. Like the school clock in Jeffrey's kitchen, its big hand, that now extended in shadow form all the way across the ceiling on the Dome, moved slightly back before moving forward, counting out each second like the precious commodity it was. *Time. The most important thing there is,* LeeAnn thought, *and the least.*

Everyone was listening to the ticking of the clock, as the big hand headed in its hesitating way for the top of the dial.

Five,

four,

three,

two,

one,

"Happy New Year, Segment One!" Reeve and Goldberg shouted, and a roar of congratulations went up from the entire world, as scenes of celebration in Seg1 burst upon the screen. It was several minutes before things quieted down.

"For the next twenty-four hours," said Goldberg, "the Earth's people are on hiatus. Let us take this time to make common cause with one another and with the living creatures around us." Reeve and Goldberg, holding hands, walked to the center of the podium, as the camera started to pull back.

"Now we wish you good night, good morning, good afternoon, and good evening." They turned in each of the four directions, as the deck of the ship on which they were standing was revealed. Reeve and Goldberg were out in the middle of Seg24, in the Pacific Ocean, which would be the last place in the world to begin the new year. They would be reporting hourly until then.

Then it was over, and in this Dome as, LeeAnn imagined, in thousands of domes around the world, for a few moments there was silence, as the lights went off and the heavens lit up the Dome. It was a starry, starry night. Most of the people continued to gaze up at the sky for a bit. You could sense an enormous amount of thinking going on. Then slowly they began to gather their belongings and get up to leave.

"Hey, you guys," Peter said at last. "Let's get these two over to Virtual Reality. Get them to start the New Year right." David gathered up the picnic things and they followed the crowd as it slowly made its way through the arched exits of the Dome with the numbers of the global clock, 1 through 24, written in blue-green mosaic outside. It was a mild, mellow night for January. A misty rain had begun to fall, but the stars were still brilliant. It was a starlight rain; LeeAnn liked that.

The Partnership Center's virtual reality building was only a few blocks away so they walked. Inside was an old-fashioned staircase, a bit of whimsy complete with stone lions that reminded LeeAnn of the entrance to the main library in Manhattan. They zoomed up the stairs, everyone taking them two at a time, Jeff and Jordan way ahead. Putting the problem of global survival on hold for the evening, LeeAnn followed the others down the hall and into the trip room reserved for David and LeeAnn for the next fifteen minutes, on the occasion of their thirteenth anniversary. She was determined to enjoy herself.

"Hi!" The name-tag on the VR tech, a startlingly handsome blond man with a dark beard, said his name was Adam. LeeAnn's mind went whirling back to another time and another man named Adam. She'd never quite forgotten the clerk in the windsurf shop in Hood River. This one looked much the way she remembered him, the same beautiful open visage and dazzling smile. Now he was helping her with all the various straps and buckles. How strangely reminiscent this all was.

"When you get to your destination," said Adam, "remember, that part is not programmed. Bear in mind we have real cameras at the algae ponds. These people are expecting you; they'll see you as holograms, so you can behave just as if you were there."

"When you move or speak," he said, "the hologram they see will move and speak as well, and the computer will translate your spoken words. If you choose the *cultural translation* option, it will give you, and the person you're talking to, an in-depth translation, including how an expression originated, what it means in their society, when it came into use."

"How great!" said Jeff, as he began to engage in a discussion about semantics with anyone who would listen.

"Will you be quiet, Jeff," said Audrey.

Adam was starting to give instructions on the sky diving, and LeeAnn decided she'd better pay rapt attention. "Remember, you can always abort," he said. "At any moment. Just press this button and you'll be back here in the studio." *But then I wouldn't be with David*, LeeAnn thought, *or he'd have to come back with me.*

"Okay. You all set?" Adam asked.

In their seats, side by side, strapped in, hooked up, and wearing all kinds of sensors, LeeAnn and David both nodded. So Adam put the goggles over her eyes and it was dark. "Here you go."

Then LeeAnn could feel the vibration of the engine of the old plane that she was suddenly riding in. And she could see the endless sky outside, beyond the cargo door that was open wide. David was behind her.

"You ready for this, babe?"

She looked down. Way, way below her were green fields, blue ocean, and tiny little matchstick huts. "Oh my gosh. I don't believe I ever said I'd do this."

"Well, you promised, so let's go."

"Are you going to push me out?" The wind was whistling around them.

"No," he said, "I'm going to hold you. And I'll wait till you say 'when.'"

So then it was up to her. *Am I going to do this thing?* "Okayyyy, . . . '*When,*'" she said at last.

"Now," David whispered in her ear, the word delivering a jolt to her body as he took LeeAnn in his arms, stepped off, and they fell free.

Oh, the feeling! Turning upside down, twisting. The green earth below so beautiful. David holding her as they fell in tandem, linked. Dropping like a rock. The air rushing up against her body in her ocean-wave spansuit. She started to giggle. *Lois Lane at last.* "It's neat. I *love* it!"

"David, LeeAnn," said Adam's voice. "I think it's time to pull your ripcord. It would normally be automatic, but since you can't really mess up, we thought you'd enjoy doing it yourselves." David and LeeAnn were smiling at each other.

"Ready, shall we?" David said. "Okay. 1-2-3, Pull!" And then they were suddenly yanked up by their harnesses, and it was as if they were dangling from a hook in the sky. *Harnesses again*, following her through life. She looked up at the glorious colors above her; their parachute was yellow and orange, and the sky was bluer than she'd ever seen. Then she looked at the earth below. They were floating down softly. There were green fields and blue algae ponds, and ocean beyond. The music of *Akuna Matata* came over the sound system then, turned up loud, and LeeAnn laughed. The song from *Lion King*. Jeff had to have arranged that. A message about not worrying.

Then just as she was relaxing and feeling delighted with the whole experience, the ground started suddenly to come up terrifyingly fast. LeeAnn clutched onto David. Faster and faster. Rice fields coming up. Then, WHOOSH, her feet went into the soft mud up to her knees, just as they had in the sediment of Klamath Lake when she jumped off her sailboard. The spongy, clean mud of algae residue. And it didn't even hurt.

In the next thirteen minutes they saw it all. Greeted by Li and Xuan and their kids, they were taken on a tour. The family, showed them where water was diverted from the river, just a small stream of it. And where it flowed through the family's algae ponds and back into the mouth of the river. Other ponds were situated on a sheltered section of beach, for saltwater varieties of algae.

The family explained which varieties were used for food, which for fertilizer, and which performed the task of wastewater cleanup. LeeAnn asked questions, and David learned, as usual, just by looking. They watched some harvesting going on, and they smelled lunch cooking, but they couldn't taste it—the technology for virtual eating had yet to be developed.

Then, too soon, she and David were walking along the path to the place where Adam had instructed them they would be picked up.

"Can this be real, David?"

"It's virtual reality," he answered.

"No, I mean the whole thing—this life we're living, the Dome, Marina, Jordan, the world the way it is now, all of this?" She indicated the miles and miles of algae ponds before them.

"Why wouldn't it be? Why do you question it?"

"Because it seems kind of idealized in a way, except for the ozone, and that's going to be fixable; I know it is."

"So? Why *can't* something *ideal* be *real*, LeeAnn?" he said. "Isn't this the way we're supposed to be? Happy, healthy, *connected*?"

Strangely, then, behind David's words, LeeAnn heard the sound of a fax machine, the warbly, wonderful, sexy sound as it sought to connect with another of its species. She puzzled over it for a moment, then began to have an inkling about why it was happening. *This is only* virtual *virtual reality*, she thought. *This whole thing is a dream.* But she was still in it, so she decided to take advantage as long as she could.

"Okay, guys," Adam's voice was coming to them from everywhere as they stood at the edge of the rice paddy where they'd landed thirteen minutes before. "You guys ready for your orbiter experience? We're going to hitch you a ride home."

"Beam us up, Scotty," David said, and instantly they were in an

501

orbiting space station, whizzing around at an accelerated speed. From the porthole you could see the blue earth, veiled in wispy clouds, breathtaking in its beauty as it seemed to turn below them. There was Bangkok, where Stan, with Habitat for Humanity, was doing masonry work for God. Was he really, or was that just part of the dream? Knowing Stan, it was probably real; it was what he'd always wanted to do.

Was it a moment later or was it a long time? LeeAnn lost track for a bit. "Look, LeeAnn," David said, "There's North America coming up. New York, there's the Mississippi River, the Rockies. And there's the Cascade Mountains . . . and . . ."

But then she heard the beep of a completed, satisfied fax. So it was over. *No, she told herself. First I need to see what's happened to Tree Island. I need to get home before I wake up,* she vowed to herself. So she kept her eyes shut and, thinking of Dorothy and Toto, willed herself to conjure up a view of home. Of Oregon.

Re-entering her dream, she managed to put herself in David's arms, flying through the sky. *"Look, there's the lake,"* he said. She looked and there it was. Mount Shasta to the south, and the Crater Lake caldera to the north. Between them, Klamath Lake, like a huge star sapphire in its setting.

As they drew closer, there was Tree Island, resplendent with golden grass in the sunshine, blue water all around. And one gnarled and wise ancient tree on top. Peace still reigned in this most precious part of LeeAnn's world. Nothing bad had happened to her island. *Oh, I'm so glad.*

Then suddenly they were headed down toward the surface of the lake at such a terrific speed it took LeeAnn's breath away. First she thought it was a hang-glider out of control they were descending on, but then a windsurf boom magically appeared in her hands–the new Neil Pryde boom she'd been saving up for. She and David were flying in tandem behind a sail that was iridescent, like dragonfly wings. As they touched down on the water, they must have been doing thirty knots. Pure thrilling speed on a nice, big, stable board, with a satisfying staccato chop. A dream ride.

LeeAnn looked around. There was Rocky Point, and Eagle Ridge. The lake seemed the same, except over on the shore at Squaw Point, there was a small white cottage that hadn't been there before. Tied up at its dock was a boat that looked familiar. The Whaler. And outside, relaxing on lawn chairs, were Paul and Sonja, caretakers, gatekeepers for Tree Island. *I wonder if they're happy?* LeeAnn asked herself. *But how could they live here and not be? Tree Island teaches people how to be happy.*

She was about to wave to them when the fax sound came in again and another machine answered. The two connected. This time there was no way to stop herself from waking up. One last moment of sailing on the lake. Skimming over the water, free as a bird. Dancing on a blue-green planet. Then slowly she came to consciousness and felt David's arms still around her.

When she opened her eyes, there were bright colors, light streaming through the bedroom window, shining on her maple dresser and David's tall, skinny chiffonier, which was back in their room now. The two pieces of furniture looked good rubbing up against each other. Almost like the Tree Island Lovers. Her short, stocky dresser seemed to be smiling and the taller David dresser leaned slightly toward its mate.

On the other side of the room, she saw her wonderful beat-up, secondhand carbon mast and boom. David and Stan had gone out in Pink Lady IV searching the marsh several times in the last two weeks and had finally come back with them, triumphant, last night. She'd kissed them both and cooked them dinner.

As she lay there in the stillness of the September morning, LeeAnn thought about her three favorite activities: making love, giving birth, and dancing on a blue-green planet. *And all of them are now in my future*, she thought. *Even another child. Marina. We must teach our daughter about the past,* she thought. *For the past is prologue.*

She walked back through her dream then, flew through it actually, reliving each little part she could still remember, lying absolutely still so the images wouldn't be jarred away. But her memory of it was fading fast.

Did my mind actually make all of that up? I guess so, which means a lot of it may not be technically accurate. After all, LeeAnn had no scientific knowledge of futuristic pneumatic parking devices, or magnetically controlled traffic, or economics. And she didn't even know a whole lot about ozone. *But that doesn't mean all that stuff wasn't right,* she thought. *Deepak Chopra says we can pick up all knowledge from the cosmos, that it's all out there, available to us.*

She looked over at David, but he seemed to be fast asleep, so she went back to thinking about her dream. *The parking thing is doable,* she thought, *and the Domes, the Friends of People; nothing too odd about that. The road, with magnetically controlled traffic, I don't know. Cardio Cars, sure. And hey, I invented spansuits! I always wanted one; I guess that's why. Wish I could buy one.*

I wonder if we really could do a virtual reality trip like that. I wonder if the ozone situation really is going to threaten our lives. I wonder if humanity will find some way to deal with it.

So, after all, it was just a dream, perhaps, something my brain recycled from bits and pieces input in the past? Or was it a forevision of the future? Or is a forevision only a forevision if we make it so?

If you believe it, you'll see it, she heard in her mind. Wayne Dyer said that. *If we have the power to imagine something, then it's already virtually real. In my dream I asked David if it could be too good to be true. But is that the measure? For if this wonderful life that I'm living right now, in this room, in this house, with this man is real, then* that future life–people getting along better–can be, too. Maybe not everything will happen just the way I made it up, but enough of it can to make the world a little better place these next thousand years.

I hope Marina will live to see the 22nd century, she thought, putting her hand on her still-flat stomach to say good morning to her little girl. It was six weeks since she'd flown home from Russia. Three weeks since they found the Lovers. A week since they'd done the first pregnancy test. Then they didn't believe it, so they'd done another. So much had happened in so little time.

The fax machine had finished receiving. It went click, and began printing out the product of its brief union, which, LeeAnn mused, judging from the rich sound of the warble, was probably quite an extraordinary message. It was *long,* at least.

She was beginning to wonder who was sending it, but at that moment, David opened his eyes and smiled, and the fax message faded in importance.

"Do you believe in dreams?" she asked him.

"I do." He hoisted himself up on his pillow and stretched, looking around, blinking. He tousled LeeAnn's hair as he almost always did when he woke up.

"Do you think that physical events can be influenced by our

thoughts?"

"A lot of questions this morning. Yes, I do." He kissed her, then gently pulled the white nightgown away from her breast. "Let's look at those nipples again." He took his time examining them. There was a faint pink ring all the way around the aureole, slightly swollen. "Mmm, looks pretty promising to me."

His touching felt so good. LeeAnn began to want David. She was floating, there were pheromones all over the place as he looked into her eyes with that sweet, serious look on his face.

"Are you sure a baby is what you want, David? Why? What changed you?"

He looked up at the ceiling and paused for a long moment. Then laughed suddenly. "I guess the best way to describe it is, ever since *your* near-death experience, *I* haven't been the same." They laughed. "Of course, we still don't know for sure that it's going to happen."

"Oh, yes we do," LeeAnn said. "We had a girl."

"We did?"

"Trust me."

"Oh, okay."

He started to caress her then. Every inch of her skin. His mouth kissing first the palm of her hand, then moving up her arm, ever so slowly, to her shoulder. Then he bent to kiss her midriff, her waist, her hip. As his lips and fingertips moved over her body, every one of her twenty-seven trillion cells had goosebumps.

"Oh yes, oh yes, please." But then there was the harsh intrusive sound of the phone ringing.

"Oh, dear, oh dear." It rang again. They had slowed, in fact nearly stopped what they were doing by the time the answering machine came on.

"Hello? LeeAnn, David?" It was Sarge's voice. "Are you there? Dominick Russo here."

David looked at LeeAnn.

"I think we better answer," she said. "They were going to have divers at the site this morning."

David gave her a look and picked up the phone. "Sarge, hi there. Yeah, good to hear from you. LeeAnn's right here. So, you got a report?"

"Put him on speaker," LeeAnn said to David. So he did and they both lay back down.

"Yeah, I just got back in with the Dive Service guys," Sarge said. "We were out at the island at five o'clock this morning."

"Did you find anything?"

"We sure did. I didn't want to disturb you any earlier, but let me have you talk to the diver. Here he is."

"Hi there," LeeAnn said, "Who's this?"

"I'm Jamie. Over/Under Dive Services."

"And what did you find?"

"Well, the handgun—we got that right away, about where you said it would be, by the dock off the stone house, stuck down in the mud in four feet of water. Couple of shots fired, Sarge said. And then we located the petroglyph, too."

"You did? Thank heaven!"

"In ten feet of water, right off the shore of the island, where Ms. Al Amin said it would be. She drew a map for us, so it wasn't too tough."

"Was the lichen still on it?"

"Yes, it was. On the main piece, at least. But I didn't raise it; I didn't want to hurt anything. I thought if you'd like to go down with us–Sarge says you're a diver."

"A reluctant one."

"That way you could supervise getting the pieces up."

"Oh, all right."

LeeAnn made a date to dive with Jamie later that afternoon to bring the petroglyph up, and then Sarge came back on the phone.

"Maybe after that you can come in and sign your complaint." He was talking about her criminal complaint against Paul and Sonja, something she'd been putting off. Probably because she'd remembered more than once something her friend Andy from the Klamath tribe had said. He had told her that the Klamath way was to forgive the whole house.

"I think they're going to be rehabbed, those two, I really do," LeeAnn said. Of course, she didn't tell Sarge about the dream.

"Well, you may be right about that. As I understand it, Stan Porter's been out to the jail to see them a couple of times. And they've asked to see him regularly."

"Then it's a done deal," David decided. "That pair's already on their way to being saved." He leaned over and started nibbling on the back of LeeAnn's neck. She felt impelled to abandon the phone call then and there but of course that would be rude. Her skin was responding in waves, delicious waves. But then he sat up, squeezed her toes through the covers as he got out of bed and pantomimed lifting a cup to his lips.

"Oh, don't go," she mouthed, reaching for him, but it was too late. He was gone, his lovely naked-as-a-jaybird butt disappearing around the corner. "Any word on the origin of the Lovers?" Sarge was asking.

"Only that the rock might match some in Siberia."

"That's pretty interesting."

"Nothing proven. And I doubt that it will be," she added, remembering the way it had turned out in her dream.

Sarge talked about where the Nomad trailer had eventually been found, in a parking lot next to a dumpster over in White City–and the lab tests on the bones, which were still inconclusive.

"Oh, and on the thing with Harkins, the archaeologist. It seems Trautman went to Idaho in the spring a couple of times and threatened the guy as well as bribed him." *A combination carrot and stick,* LeeAnn thought.

Finally she was off the phone. She thought about following David out to the kitchen and woman-handling him there. *No,* she thought, *I'll wait.* So she lay back on the soft down pillow, luxuriating in the feeling of sleeping in. It was Saturday, her favorite day of the week. She took several long, deep breaths.

Then because she wasn't used to doing *nothing at all,* LeeAnn began to think about the fax that had wakened her. *I wonder what it could be about? It sounded so delicious, maybe I better check who it's from.* The decision made, she bounded up out of bed, the skirt of her long white nightgown trailing after her.

She looked beautiful. All the injuries sustained in rescuing the obsidian lady and the lovers had healed. Even her black eye, which was a whopper, had faded to the point where it was the color of violet eye makeup. When she remembered to touch up the other eye, they matched.

Barefoot, she padded across the carpet, grabbed the fax–a two-page letter written on VHRI stationary–and flopped down again on the bed to read it.

September 15

Dear LeeAnn and David,

Thanks so much for dinner. Since our talk, I've been investigating costs for the global party invitations, including translation into every language and dialect we can find, plus braille. I'm figuring in the cost of hand-delivery where there are no post offices, as well as later pick-up of the RSVPs. We're talking to UPS, FedEx, and some of the other carriers.

Bottom line, I'm finding this is not nearly as daunting a project as we originally imagined. After all, consider how many letters your American "Publishers Clearinghouse" sends out every week. (LeeAnn could hear his little Dutch accent in the written words.) *And it has to be done. I am more convinced than ever that what we need right now on this earth is a Celebration that will bring the world together.*

I've been doing a bit of what you'd call networking and I think there's no doubt we'll have access to all the funds we need. In fact, we may have to limit contributions from governments, multinationals, and religious institutions, so that nobody gets too much credit.

Here is why I think we will be inundated with support. I made exactly ten phone calls to strategically placed friends, and each of those people made ten calls. That's one hundred and ten people contacted; ninety-eight have said "Sure," and all we have done is talk to them. They've seen nothing in writing. I also talked to Martyn Williams, and I agree he's a very impressive fellow.

The following is a list of mostly public figures who would like to get involved immediately. (The list read like a Who's Who of science, entertainment, government, business, and the arts. LeeAnn realized this fax was her deliverance. What could be more delicious than for the dream to happen and for her to still have a life? Peter was right. There's no need to be a martyr to a cause.)

Thank you, LeeAnn, for sharing your notes on the Tree Island Lovers. I find it hard to overestimate the importance of this find. It occurred to me that if you don't as yet have any kind of logo or symbol for the Global Celebration, why not use a simple outline drawing of the (rejoined) Lovers, similar to the one you used in your notes?

Why not? LeeAnn thought. *Good idea.* She began to imagine people all over the world looking at pictures of the Tree Island Lovers, a Tree Island logo . . .

"Good news?" David, still nude, came in with two gorgeous lattés, sprinkled with cinnamon on top just the way she liked it. He must have finally brought his espresso machine back from the cabin. He sat down on the bed and they clicked cups as the phone began to ring again.

He sighed; she stood up. "Do you know," LeeAnn asked, "what I consider to be one of the finest inventions of the 20th century?"

"No, what?"

"This little button right here," she said, picking up the phone and switching the ringer off. "And then there's this, too," she said as she turned the volume all the way down on the answering machine, and switched the sound off on the fax. She started back to bed, then paused to look around for any other potential disturbers of the peace. She spotted the message machine that would still emit troublesome humms and clicks if anybody called. She was still staring at it, wondering what to do, when David handed her several soft down pillows. She stuffed them around all the machines. Pillows were another nice invention.

Climbing onto the bed, she sat cross-legged, and picked up her latte from the table. "Gotta give this up," she said looking at the sinful beverage before her, before raising her cup to David.

"It's organic decaf."

"Yeah, but the milk."

"Rice Dream."

"Oh."

"So, enjoy."

"Salut." They sipped.

"You know what Ernst said in the fax he just sent us?" she grinned. "He said they're thinking about sending the invitations out in lots of five hundred million."

"You're kidding."

What would five hundred million envelopes all in one place look like? She remembered thinking about a thousand lost invitations blowing in the wind. Now she saw them by the billions, wafting around the globe. "Imagine five hundred million people opening their mail at the same time," she said, handing David the fax. "Here, read this."

He scanned the letter, his gaze quickly scrolling down both pages. "This is unbelievable, what Ernst is doing." he said as he looked at the names on the list. "No, actually, it's believable," he said at last, offering it back to LeeAnn. "These are all the people that we knew would come along from the beginning."

"What you mean, *we, Kimosabe*?" LeeAnn laughed.

"At least we *hoped* they would."

"You *did—all* along?"

"Of course I did. I just wasn't *quite* as hopeful as you were."

She took the fax from David and laid it face down on the table. "This frees me," she said to him. "Do you know how much?"

"I think I do." They looked at each other, and desire hit them both at the same time. A slow smile started on the faces of both.

"Do you know what's going to happen now?" she asked him.

"I have a pretty good idea."

"Well, you're wrong. I'm not *entirely* predictable, you know. First, it's *Power Deck* time!"

"Oh." They'd played several times during the last few weeks with the cards Maggie had sent. LeeAnn picked up her deck from the bedside table, shuffled it, fanned the cards, and held them out to him.

"You first," he said.

"No, let's share–you pick one for both of us."

David took a long time deciding. LeeAnn fanned the cards again, a little better, then laid them on the table. He looked at them awhile, but that didn't seem to work either. "I need to hold them," he said. So she gave them to him. He closed his eyes and thought, then fingered one that apparently felt good to him and pulled it.

"What does it say?"

"Ecstasy."

LeeAnn clapped with delight. "*Yes!* Of course, that's *exactly* the one I was hoping we'd get. I *willed* it that we'd get that one. And I didn't even have to stack the deck."

"Shall I read it?"

"Please."

"'Within your instinctual nature,'" David began in that wonderful airline pilot, partnership-cop voice of his, ***"'are the seeds of ecstasy.'"***

"Oh, yes." She started now to play with his body, trying to kiss every hair on his chest separately; there actually weren't that many, so it was theoretically possible.

"'We tend to live in our minds, in our emotions. Occasionally in

spirit and almost never in our instinctual depths.'" His voice resonat-ed as she kissed his chest and it tingled her lips. "Oooohh, yes," David said to her. "Right on. Do that some more. That's divine."

"Divine," she smiled. "I like your choice of words."

"'We are born . . .'" then he stopped, obviously distracted by what she was doing.

"Go ahead," LeeAnn dared him.

He tried to continue, but it was pretty clear desire was getting in the way of concentration. He looked into her eyes, took a deep, deep breath and then another before finally returning his attention to the card. *"'We're born as wild as mountain lions but live most of our lives like sheep, forgetting and denying whole parts of ourselves.'"*

"I know, I know, let's not forget *any* part of ourselves," LeeAnn said, and she didn't. There was a brief recess as she made certain with her lips that no part of David was either denied *or* forgotten.

At last, David tried again to read. "You need to listen to this, LeeAnn. This part's pretty apt."

She lay back and listened.

"'Sit on the earth, with your back up against a tree.'"

"You're making that up. Really, is that what it says?"

"Really. That's what it says. Then he repeated it. *"'Sit on the earth with your back up against a tree and get in touch with your roots, which move deep into Middle Earth. This will restore your joyousness and balance.'"*

David looked up then and gazed at LeeAnn as he spoke the words he had just seen on the card. *"'Ecstasy,'"* he concluded, *"'is like a windhorse waiting to be ridden. Take courage and live your passion in ecstasy.'"*

"Oh, I will."

"'It is the last wild ride before your passage into enlightenment.'"

David held out his arms and LeeAnn moved into them.

*It was a ceremony of greeting. **A ceremony of hello.** Bells were ringing.*

The End

PART FOUR

Fiction To Reality

(Journal of a Novel)

Decide to Network

Use every letter you write
Every conversation you have
Every meeting you attend
To express your fundamental beliefs
and dreams
Affirm to others the vision
of the world you want
Network through thought
Network through action
Network through love
Network through spirit
You are the center of a network
You are the center of the world
You are a free, immensely powerful
source of life
Affirm it
Spread it
Radiate it
Think day and night about it
And you will see a miracle happen:
the Greatness of your own life.
In a world not of big powers,
media and monopolies,
But of five billion individuals.
Networking is the new freedom,
the new democracy
A new form of happiness.

By Dr. Robert Muller
Chancellor of the University
for Peace in Costa Rica

A Story About Networking, Serendipity, and Building Coalition

Cleaning house one day in 1989, I happened to hear a public radio interview with author Riane Eisler that helped me understand, in twenty minutes, why humans are so unkind to one another and what we could do to change that. For the first time, I understood how our history could relate to our future.

I wrote, she phoned, we met, and I began this long project to try to express the meaning of partnership in a work of fiction. In 1990, I put together what I'd learned from Riane, and from archaeologist Marija Gimbutas, and had written half a cave-diving novel about LeeAnn Spencer and her friends, set in Crete, when economic reality intervened and I had to take a job writing a television show in Los Angeles.

The day I finally got back to Klamath Falls in 1992, I attended a talk by John Robbins at the August Celebration, the annual celebration of the algae. I came away from Robbins' talk with a new understanding about how we can help restore health to our planet by making small changes in our diet. That day I also had my first contact with a group of about 12,000 algae networkers from across North America who had a global vision and whose leader believed that *everything we do should start and end with celebration.*

Initially doubtful about the usefulness of the algae but fascinated by the celebration concept, in 1993 I left my heroine LeeAnn in her cave in Crete and proceeded to research and write *August Celebration: A Molecule of Hope for a Changing World.* Afterward, in '94 and '95, as the networking group grew to 300,000, as I traveled to promote the book or filled my house to the rafters with August Celebration visitors, I began to understand the group's maxim. *That the greatest of all human needs is the need for connection.* I felt connected.

Talking to my new friends about Riane Eisler and partnership–and talking to Riane about celebration–I began to conceive the idea of a LeeAnn Spencer story in the area between Mount Shasta and Crater Lake that I had begun to appreciate as a place of great power. I went to the Rivers of Light ranch in Fort Klamath to work out the plot. My plan was for a little adventure novel that would mix *celebration theory* with *partnership theory.* But as soon as those two got together, the whole thing started to grow.

During one of the phases of drafting the book, I hid away in Kauai, where I happened in on the annual gathering–from the mainland and Pacific islands–of people whose life is the sea. Surfers and scientists, divers and sailors, swimmers, bodysurfers, and windsurfers, all united in a group called Save Our Seas. Through my daughter, I also came to know the women and men who maintain the ancient outrigger canoe and sailing canoe traditions. We all started talking about celebrating the millennium, and a tiny network began to form between people who believe in celebration and people who celebrate our seas. It eventually resulted in hundreds of windsurfers from Cape Hatteras to New Caledonia to Kauai sailing for global unity on April 6, 1997, a thousand days before the millennial year begins.

If there's one thing I've learned from the experience of writing *Tree Island*, it's that everything LeeAnn has been dreaming about is already happening. All over the world, coalitions like ours are quietly forming.

In the process of preparing for the Day-1000 windsurfing event, I met, on the Internet, Dr. Robert Muller, former Assistant Secretary General of the United Nations, Bob Silverstein, founder of the CountUP 2000 movement, and, through the August Celebration network, Martyn Williams, leader of the Pole to Pole 2000 expedition. Muller, Silverstein, and Williams are already networking with groups that represent hundreds of millions of people. And we've all begun to work together as a group.

I guess the thing I want to get across to you most of all is that this global party business is not an idea dreamed up to promote a book. *Tree Island is a book written to promote an idea.* That's why in good conscience I can urge you to urge everyone *you* know to read it, or at least to learn about the ideas of many people that it contains.

With this 22nd Century Group Founders' Edition, I want to appeal particularly to members of the August Celebration network who have the numbers, the energy, and the global contacts to help turn the fiction of global celebration to reality. At this writing, we have just over two years to get ready. So, let's get started.

P.S. On the following pages you will find a few of the resources, people, and organizations doing good things that I've encountered in the process of writing this book. I urge you to explore them.

PARTNERSHIP

Riane Eisler, author of *The Chalice and the Blade* and other books. Her multidisciplinary work in evolutionary studies, human rights, and peace, feminist, and environmental issues is internationally recognized. She is a cultural historian, lecturer, and co-director of the Center for Partnership Studies in Pacific Grove, California.

The Chalice and the Blade: Our History, Our Future and *Sacred Pleasure: Sex, Myth, and the Politics of the Body* by Riane Eisler are published by Harper San Francisco and are available through all bookstores. (*Chalice*, $16.00; *Sacred Pleasure*, $15.00). *The Chalice and the Blade* is also available in 16 foreign editions, including German, French, Italian, Norwegian, Finnish, Greek, Czech, Spanish, Portuguese, Russian, Japanese, and Chinese.

The Chalice and the Blade: Our History, Our Future, two audio cassettes. Riane Eisler reads a condensed version of the book. Published by New World Library, 14 Pamaron Way, Novato, CA 94949. $17.95.

The Center for Partnership Studies. Founded in 1987 by Riane Eisler and David Loye, launched in the wake of rapid global interest in Eisler's cultural transformation theory and partnership model thinking sparked by *The Chalice and the Blade*, this is the research center for the Partnership movement. The address is PO Box 51936, Pacific Grove, CA 93950. Website: www.partnershipway.org

The International Partnership Network (IPN). This is the membership organization for the Partnership movement. Headquartered in Tucson, Arizona, under the leadership of Del Jones. The address is International Partnership Network, PO Box 323, Tucson, AZ 85702.

OUR LAND

John Robbins, considered by many to be the most eloquent and powerful spokesman in the country for a sane and sustainable future.

Among his books are *Diet for a New America* and *May All Be Fed: Diet for a New World*. "By consciously making our choices as to how and what to eat, this intimate and fundamental part of our lives can be an effective expression of our desire to create a healthy life for ourselves and contribute to the health of others." Published by William Morrow and Company, Inc., 1350 Avenue of the Americas, New York, NY 10019.

EarthSave. For membership or to purchase educational materials, call 800-362-3648. For information about EarthSave and John Robbins, call 502-589-7676 or write to EarthSave, PO Box 68, Santa Cruz, CA 95063.

OUR HEALTH

The Cell Tech Solution. Since 1992, Cell Tech, a blue-green algae company, has made algae from each harvest available to "people who have the greatest need and the fewest resources." Here are some of the Cell Tech Solution projects around the world that are providing unique and much-needed assistance to the areas they serve:

Guatemala Project: A Bridge Across Nations. Donations can be sent directly to The Guatemala Project, c/o Michael Linden and Anna Ineson, PO Box 614, Waldoboro, ME 04572, or call Erik Ireland at 800-927-2527, ext. 04991.

Chernobyl Project. Contact Carlos Richardson at 619-571-8949 or at e-mail:

Nicaragua: Healing the Wounds of War and Poverty. Contact Spirale at 418-688-1133, fax: 418-688-7545, e-mail: ixchel@sympatico.ca

Kenya Kids. Contact Karen Memrick at 800-919-9054.

Indigenous Peoples Project (Navajo Reservations, Big Mountain, Arizona). Contact Karen Ferreira at 800-927-2527, ext. 3825; e-mail: gaiasoph@cdsnet.net

Compassion in the Himalayas. Contact Sherri Winkelman at 800-927-2527, ext. 00653.

Ghana Project. Anyone wishing to volunteer in Ghana should contact Martyn and Martina Williams at 800-927-2527, ext. 07121.

OUR HERITAGE

The Klamath Tribes McLeod-Rutenic Basket Committee. At Fort Klamath in the mid-1800s, an aged chief told a soldier the 7,000-year-old story of the eruption of Mount Mazama that had been passed down for hundreds of generations. Yet today, only 150 years later, in one of the oldest continuous cultures on earth, few tribal members speak the language that preserved that story. And a priceless basket collection is about to be lost to the Tribes because they can't afford the sum needed to repurchase it. These are the people *Tree Island*'s author hopes to honor in the story of the mother of Starlight Rain and her life-sustaining water-basket. Tax-deductible donations should be made to Klamath Tribes, Basket/Artifact Fund, c/o Gordon Bettles, PO Box 436, Chiloquin, OR 97624. For further information, contact The Klamath Tribes, 800-524-9787.

OUR SEAS

Save Our Seas (SOS). A Hawaii-based international nonprofit organization dedicated to preserving, protecting, and restoring the world's oceans for future generations and all life forms on the planet. SOS sponsored the first ocean recycling project and ocean pollution survey in conjunction with the 1993 Trans Pacific Yacht Race; initiated the annual celebration of International Oceans Day throughout the U.S.; conducts the middle school coral reef monitoring program, Ocean Pulse; organizes the annual Oceans Conference in Hawaii; and publishes a quarterly newsletter. Contact Terry Tico or Carl Stepath, 808-826-2525, fax: 808-826-7770, e-mail: sos@aloha.net. Also see their award-winning website: planet-hawaii.com/sos

OUR FELLOW CREATURES

UCLA's People Animal Connection. A small group of volunteers who are demonstrating how much we need to connect with our fellow creatures in a far deeper way than we have recently. If we access more of the love that other species have to offer, it will surely help us to think and act in a better way. The People Animal Connection (PAC) is an Animal Assisted Therapy Program using UCLA Volunteers and their tree island

dogs to provide a more humane environment in medical treatment facilities for patients, family, and staff. For more information on how to start
a People Animal Connection Program in your community or to help the
group at UCLA, call 310-206-2127.

OUR FUN

U.S. Windsurfing Association. Phone: 541-386-8708; fax: 541-386-
2108; write to: PO Box 978, Hood River, OR 97031.

American Windsurfing Industries Association. Phone: 509-493-
9463; fax: 509-493-9464; write to: 1099 Snowden Road, White
Salmon, WA 98672; e-mail: awia@gorge.net; website: www.awia.org

American Windsurfer **magazine.** Phone: 603-293-2721; fax: 603-293-
2723; write to: Bayview Business Park, #10, Gilford, NH 03246.

WindSurfing **magazine.** Phone: 407-628-4802; fax: 407-628-7061;
write to: PO Box 2456, Winter Park, FL 32790.

WindTracks **magazine.** Phone: 541-247-4153 or 541-247-2310; fax:
541-247-3463; write to: PO Box 6062, Pistol River, OR 97444.

Wind Sport **magazine.** Phone: 416-406-2400; fax: 416-406-0656; write
to: 2255B Queen Street East, #3266, Toronto, Ontario M4E163,
Canada.

New England Windsurfing Journal. Phone: 203-876-2001; fax: 203-
876-2868; write to: 26 Fenway Street North, Milford, CN 06460.

OUR GLOBAL CONNECTIONS

The Harijan Foundation. This organization promotes the principles of
truth and nonviolence in all spheres of human activity. The 50th
Anniversary Commemoration of Mahatma Gandhi will be on Saturday,
September 12, 1998, the eve of the date when Gandhi, in 1933,
announced a "fast until death" to eliminate untouchability. For details,
contact Christian Drapeau or Martha Hopewell, PO Box 1665, Klamath

Falls, OR 97601; 888-573-2427; e-mail: mhope@taconic.net

Gandhi & King, A Season for Nonviolence: In Commemoration of the 50th and 30th Memorial Anniversaries of M. K. Gandhi and Martin Luther King, Jr. (January 30, 1998—April 4, 1998). Task force teams have been set up in 30 cities, and nearly 200 cosponsoring organizations are participating. Contact Bob Alan Silverstein, New Jersey, New York & International Advisory Committee, People for Peace Project, PO Box 570, Roosevelt, NJ 08555; 609-443-5786; fax: 609-443-4307; e-mail: PforPeace@aol.com. Website: www.GandhiKing.com

Dr. Robert Muller was born in Belgium and knew the horrors of World War II, of being a refugee, of Nazi occupation and imprisonment. After the war he devoted the next 40 years of his life behind the scenes at the United Nations focusing his energies on world peace. He rose through the ranks at the UN to the official position of Assistant Secretary-General. Known as the father of global education, he also has been called the *Philosopher* and the *Prophet of Hope* of the United Nations. Now in active "retirement," Dr. Muller is Chancellor of the University for Peace created by the United Nations in demilitarized Costa Rica. He is the author of 14 books, including the *World Core Curriculum in the Robert Muller Schools.*

World Core Curriculum. This magazine aids and chronicles the implementation of the World Core Curriculum as it proliferates. For more information, contact The Robert Muller School International Coordinating Center, 6005 Royal Oak Drive, Arlington, TX 76016; fax: 817-654-1028; e-mail: rmswcc@airmail.net

Ideas & Dreams for a Better World: The First Five Hundred Ideas, by Dr. Robert Muller, Best-Seller Books, 7456 Evergreen Drive, Santa Barbara, CA 93117; fax: 805-968-5747. For other books by Robert Muller, contact the United Nations Bookstore, Room GA 32B, United Nations, NY 10017; 212-963-7680 or 800-553-3210. (Twenty-six of Dr. Muller's first 500 ideas already have been implemented.)

Bob Alan Silverstein, a coordinator of the **One Day In Peace, January 1, 2000**, campaign that is spreading around the world, with endorsements from many world leaders, celebrities, institutions, and organizations, as a symbol of celebration and hope for a new beginning for humanity. These are two of the supporting groups:

One Day in Peace Network. The One Day in Peace Network is a network of groups and individuals promoting a day of peace on January 1, 2000, as a symbol of a new beginning for humanity. Contact One Day in Peace Network, PO Box 90352, Santa Barbara, CA 93190; 805-569-3361; e-mail: info@oneday.net. Website: www.oneday.net

CountUP 2000. CountUP 2000 is an empowering change in perception. Through the Power of Celebration, the Year 2000 can be a new beginning for humanity, and we can make each day COUNT from Now until Then and Beyond. Contact CountUP 2000, Box 570, Roosevelt, NJ 08555; 609-443-5786; fax: 609-443-4307; e-mail: info@countup2000.com. Website: www.countup2000.com

Pole to Pole 2000. An international team of twelve young people trek from the North Pole to Antarctica on a quest for global harmony. Martyn Williams is one of the foremost guides, expedition leaders, and adventure business managers in the world. He is the first person in the world to lead successful expeditions to the three extremes, the North Pole, South Pole, and Mount Everest. To support the expedition, contact Martyn Williams, 1704-B Llano Street, Suite 317, Santa Fe, NM 87505; 505-466-8220; fax: 505-466-3523; e-mail: martyn@trail.com

PLEASE SEND POSSIBLE ENTRIES FOR FUTURE EDITIONS: *LET'S NETWORK!*

Dedication

The story of *Tree Island* is dedicated to all partners everywhere, but especially to the memory of Stanley Grover,

> hero of my first book,
>> father of my children,
>>> and a splendid singer of songs.

Though he was probably best known for the love song, "Younger Than Springtime," it was another Rodgers and Hammerstein classic from *South Pacific*, performed in sixty cities during the racially troubled 1950s, that he was proudest of.

So here, Stanley, in your honor, are those lyrics you so loved.

YOU'VE GOT TO BE CAREFULLY TAUGHT

You've got to be taught to hate and fear.
You've got to be taught from year to year.
It's got to be drummed in your dear little ear.
You've got to be carefully taught.

You've got to be taught to be afraid
Of people whose eyes are oddly made,
And people whose skin is a diff'rent shade,
You've got to be carefully taught.

You've got to be taught before it's too late,
Before you are six or seven or eight,
To hate all the people your relatives hate,
You've got to be carefully taught!
You've got to be carefully taught!

Imagine how our world would be if we weren't taught that any more!

About the Author

The daughter of an inventor and a poet, born in New England and raised in the military, Linda Grover graduated from Las Vegas High School and worked as a secretary for several years. At twenty-one she became Clerk of the House Indian Affairs Subcommittee in the U.S. Congress.

Following her marriage to Broadway singer/actor Stan Grover, she moved to New York City. There she worked with the National Committee for an Effective Congress and the International Rescue Committee before becoming the mother of Cindy, Steven, and Jamie.

Her first book, *The House Keepers*, Harper & Row, serialized in the New York Post, was the humorous account of a seven-year battle with City Hall to save the old West Side apartment building that the Grover family lived in. Her success led to an active role in reform politics.

Grover's second book, *Looking Terrific: The Language of Clothing,* written with Emily Cho, became a New York Times bestseller and Literary Guild Selection. Grover is also the author of *August Celebration,* about the discovery of the wild-grown algae superfood in Klamath Lake. It has sold a half million copies to date.

Linda has served as network television headwriter for NBC (*The Doctors*), CBS (*Search for Tomorrow*) and ABC (*General Hospital*). She also created *Aaron's World* for CBS-EMI and has been a New York City taxicab driver, a cook at a retreat center, a water-ski instructor, a Manhattan restaurant reviewer (with the nom de plume of Meredith Stein) and an actress in "Kick the Habit" anti-cigarette commercials.

These days, Linda makes her home in Oregon with her golden retriever/border collie, Shalise. She plans to spend the rest of her life windsurfing, promoting global partnership, and celebrating.

To purchase *Tree Island* or Linda Grover's other books, check with your local bookstore, or order from Friends of Tree Island by phone, toll free 24 hours a day, 800-900-6202; by fax 541-883-3136; or from our website, www.treeisland.com

LeeAnn has asked me to give you this envelope.